ILLUSION

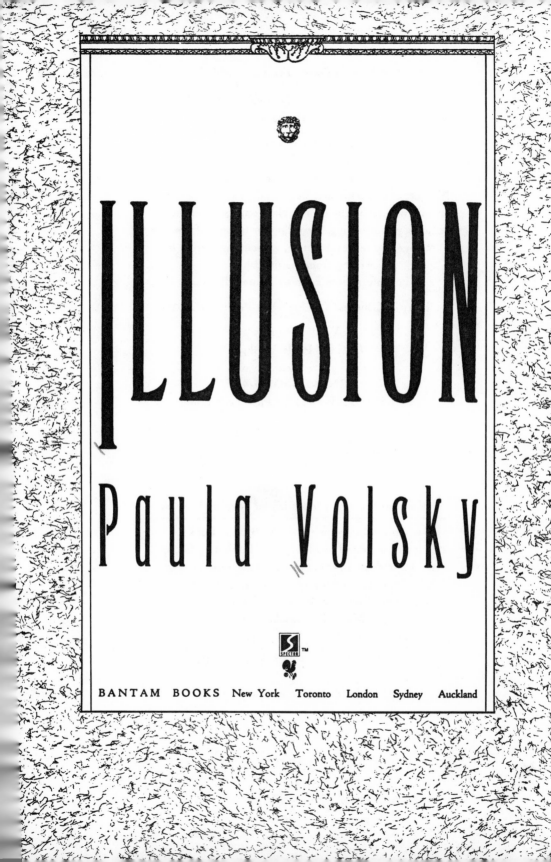

ILLUSION

Paula Volsky

BANTAM BOOKS New York Toronto London Sydney Auckland

ILLUSION

A Bantam Book / February 1992

Published simultaneously in hardcover and
trade paperback.

Library of Congress Cataloging-in-Publication Data

Volsky, Paula.
Illusion / Paula Volsky.
p.   cm.
ISBN 0-553-08145-4
ISBN 0-553-35135-4 (Trade Paperback Edition)
I. Title
PS3543.O634I43   1992
813'.54—dc20   91-21082
CIP

Published simultaneously in the United States and Canada

Bantam Books are published by Bantam Books, a
division of Bantam Doubleday Dell Publishing Group,
Inc. Its trademark, consisting of the words "Bantam
Books" and the portrayal of a rooster, is Registered in
U.S. Patent and Trademark Office and in other
countries. Marca Registrada. Bantam Books,
666 Fifth Avenue, New York, New York 10103.

S. F.

To Donald Maas,
catalytic agent,
with thanks

ILLUSION

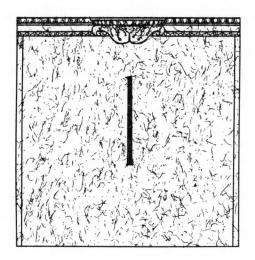

When one of the serfs was caught with a bundle of seditious pamphlets in his pocket, the Marquis vo Derrivalle was understandably infuriated. Bad enough that a serf should be reading at all, for literacy overburdened the menial mind, resulting in mental and moral injury. That the pamphleteer in question should prove none other than the execrable republican Shorvi Nirienne, whose writings the Marquis had specifically proscribed, was doubly offensive; and it was more than certain that the culprit, a featherheaded young dreamer by the name of Zhen Suboson, was in serious trouble. Even now, Zhen was locked up in the stable, awaiting interrogation and the inevitable punishment. If he escaped with less than a dozen stripes, he'd be lucky. Before sunset, the lad's fate would be decided. In the meantime, crazed speculation ran rife among the field workers and house servants.

The Marquis vo Derrivalle's daughter Eliste might never have troubled her head over such a matter, had it not been for the extraordinary attitude of her maidservant Stelli Zeenosgirl. Sullen and lackadaisical, with an expressionless nonchalance sometimes skirting the edge of insolence, Stelli at the best of times was no prize; and now, since the news of Zhen's arrest reached the chateau, she'd waxed utterly incompetent. Within the space of two hours she had broken a vial of perfume, overturned a jar of powder on the vanity, torn the lace on a morning negligee, and botched her mistress's coiffure so abominably that Eliste, in despair, was forced to liberate the glinting mass of fair curls, which now hung loose and unfettered as a child's. It was really too tiresome. And yet Eliste, regarding herself in the gold-framed vanity mirror, was forced to admit that the juvenile style suited her very well. Her hair was certainly one of her chief beauties, and what better way than this to display its enviable sheen and extravagant length? Moreover, the curly tendrils spilling over a clear white forehead somehow emphasized the changeable luster of the largest pair of thick-lashed gray eyes in the entire province, if not in all the land of Vonahr. At seventeen, passionately loath to play the ingenue, she aimed for sophistication. For all of that, there could be no denying—the effect of that great honey cloud framing her heart-shaped face was delightful. She would let it stay that way, at least for the rest of the day. Perhaps that sulky jade Stelli had done her a good turn, if only by accident.

The mirror reflected most of the sunlit bedchamber, in all its disorder. Open boxes and trunks stood scattered about the floor. The armchairs and window seat were heaped high with gowns, petticoats, fichus, shawls and manteaux, scarves, feathers, and ribbons. Hatboxes stood piled against one wall, silk and woolen stockings dangled from the open bureau drawer, fans and gloves cluttered the escritoire, shoes and boots and chopines lay underfoot, snowdrifts of crumpled tissue paper rose in the corners. It was another week before Eliste was scheduled to depart for the capital city of Sherreen to take her place at court as a Maid of Honor to the Queen, but packing was a protracted affair—one for which Stelli, as usual, displayed neither aptitude nor enthusiasm. Even as Eliste looked on, the maid crushed a thin muslin nightgown into a tiny ball, which she thrust by main force into the depths of a too-full trunk.

Eliste stiffened with an irritation disproportionate to the offense. It would have been different had she not been so certain that the other girl, but a few years her senior, was deliberately destructive. It was one thing to know, quite another to prove it. If taxed, Stelli would doubtless plead inadvertence, in that monosyllabic, elusively impertinent manner of hers. The thing was impossible to verify, and in any case, really beneath notice. Taking a deep breath, the Marquis's daughter addressed her maid with studied composure. "Not there, girl. Take it out, fold it, and put it in another box."

With a barely perceptible shrug, Stelli obeyed. Every movement a wordless insult, she sauntered across the room, treading on scattered garments as she went. An ivory fan cracked beneath her heel.

"Take care, clodhopper!" The exclamation burst from Eliste, and she regretted it immediately, for she, like many of the more progressive among the Exalted class, deemed it cruel to reproach inferiors for the limitations of intellect and ability imposed by Nature.

Stelli, however, appeared unmoved. The thick-skinned, dull insensitivity of her kind armored her against insult, or so it appeared. In which case, what in the world accounted for the maidservant's chronic ill humor? Surely the girl, who owed her present comfortable situation solely to the high esteem in which her brother Dref was held by the vo Derrivalle family, ought to appreciate her own singular good fortune. How could she be so stupidly ungrateful? Occasionally Eliste wondered.

Stelli slouched to the bureau and began to sort through the jumble, tossing hairpins and jewelry around with minimal efficiency and maximal clatter. Presently she dropped the curling iron—perhaps by accident, perhaps not—and the implement hit the floor with a solid thunk.

Eliste started, jaw muscles tightening. Deliberately she relaxed, striving to suppress all annoyance. In that instant she realized that what she felt exceeded mere irritation, amounting to actual dislike, which was clearly inappropriate. One might reprimand a clumsy or incompetent servant—one might express displeasure or dissatisfaction—but one did not stoop to personal animosity. Curiously, the reverse did not hold true. An easy, pleasant condescension marked good breeding. Many of Eliste's friends and family members liked certain individual serfs and servants, sometimes even regarded them with warmth bordering upon real affection. She herself liked Stelli's brother Dref immensely, and always had. She liked him so much, in fact, that she would be sorry—yes, actually sorry—to leave him behind in a week's time. She might even miss him a little. Did that, as she sometimes suspected, carry liking too far, perhaps to the verge of absurdity? No, certainly not. Dref pleased her, but she was equally fond of Hussy, the red satin mare that she rode nearly every morning. She would miss beautiful Hussy. Likewise she was fond of Prince vo Plume, the modishly minute lapdog that she intended to carry with her to Sherreen. There was nothing ridiculous in such affections—they were indicative, in fact, of the tender if wholly artificial sensibility appropriate to marriageable daughters of the Exalted class. The gush of fashionable sentiment, however, remained at all times suitably channeled, dammed as required by standards of behavior precluding so much as an instant's forgetfulness of the vast gulf existing between Exalted and all other mortals. Aristocratic education notwithstanding, Eliste personally disliked her maid. Having consciously recognized that fact at last, the mental response was prompt:

I will not take that sour slattern with me to Sherreen, she thought. I'll get another one and train her. That little wench Kairthe, in the dairy—she looks bright and pleasant, she should do. I hope Dref won't be too disappointed that I don't want his sister. If he is, too bad. The jade has been given every fair chance. Having reached this decision, her mood improved at once.

Stelli was still jangling brooches and bracelets. She had not bothered to pick up the fallen curling iron. Knowledge that the other's blighting presence was but temporary enabled Eliste to speak pleasantly. "Put that aside for now, girl. Come here and brush my hair."

Stelli dropped a handful of jewelry. One of the bracelets rolled off the bureau and onto the floor. She ignored it. In silence she crossed to the vanity, took up the brush and attacked her mistress's hair as if raking burrs from the tail of a plough horse.

Eliste endured the punishment in silence for a time. At last a particularly vicious tug yanked her head backward so violently that a cry of angry pain was wrung from her.

"You stupid, clumsy slut, get out of here before I slap you!" Instantly, Eliste colored to the roots of her hair. Never before had she spoken so to an inferior. She was always kind to animals and serfs, and she entertained great contempt for women who beat their servants without good cause. In yelling and threatening, she violated her own standards of behavior, and was correspondingly ashamed.

Stelli seemed neither frightened nor offended. Rather, her black brows rose slightly, and her lips curled in the satisfaction of confirmed expectation. She laid the hairbrush on the vanity with elaborate care.

Ridiculous, absurd, humiliating, to engage in a contest of wills with an insolent servant, as if she were an equal. Surely the liberality of such so-called enlightened modern philosophers as Rees-Raas Zhumeau and Stai vo Jouvelle, who prated of human fraternity and universal education, was never meant to include recalcitrant menials? The puerile rantings of renegade lawyers and journalists like Karri Del, or the dangerous Shorvi Nirienne, who openly called for the restriction of traditional Exalted privilege—surely these things inspired entertaining debate with houseguests in the quiet hour before dinner. But they were stimulating intellectual exercises, nothing more, and what had they to do with reality? The real world held no place for such impracticality.

Stelli hadn't gone yet. She was still standing there, feet planted firmly, arms akimbo, stance expressing a graceless, dogged determination. Was she deaf as well as disagreeable?

"Didn't you hear me, girl?" Eliste could rarely bring herself to pronounce the other's name. "Get out. Go busy yourself elsewhere. Tell the housekeeper to find you something to do." This was a deliberate insult. A lady's maid was never expected to lower herself to the level of the ordinary household servants. An angry tirade could scarcely have expressed Eliste's disapprobation more forcefully, but as always, Stelli seemed indifferent. Incredibly, she did not move. Still she stood there, staring at her mistress's face in the mirror. Eliste's brows drew together, and her cheeks flushed. Given the provocation, she had proved patient; at this point, however, additional indulgence could only be interpreted as weakness, which ought never be displayed. Serfs were notoriously quick to exploit the weakness of their masters, but they were calmer and actually happier when ruled with a firm hand. Eliste drew a deep breath, but the reprimand died unspoken on her lips as she met her servant's reflected gaze. Stelli's eyes—dark as obsidian and usually about as expressive—now blazed with an odd mixture of defiance and something that almost seemed like fear. The expression was so startling that Eliste forgot her anger. "What is the matter with you?" she asked, kindly enough.

Stelli, fully prepared to withstand verbal assault, was taken unaware by the unusual forbearance. Scowling and uncertain, she folded her arms.

"Come, what is it?" Eliste persisted, curiosity aroused.

Stelli hesitated. The olive-skinned face beneath the frilled mobcap, ordinarily so impassive, now reflected conflicting emotions. Eliste waited expectantly, and at last the maid replied with an effort, "It's Zhen ... Miss." As always, she pronounced the honorific with perceptible reluctance.

"Who?"

"Zhen Suboson. My lord the Marquis has Zhen locked up in the stable. What will happen to him now?"

"Oh, the boy caught with the pamphlets, is that who you mean?"

Stelli nodded.

"Well—" Eliste shrugged, "he'll be punished, no doubt. He certainly deserves it."

"Deserves?"

"He disobeyed my father's orders. What's more, he must have done so quite intentionally. The Marquis can hardly let that pass, can he?"

"What will be done to Zhen?"

"Oh—" Perceiving the other's concern, Eliste responded with easy compassion. "Nothing too dreadful. Perhaps a few stripes, scarcely more. Father is no barbarian. The lad need hardly fear for his limbs." Her reassurance was more than rhetorical. In an earlier, more violent age, erring serfs were commonly subject to mutilation and dismemberment. Times had changed, however, and the current enlightened generation of the Exalted limited corporal punishment to flogging, kicking, and the pillory, except in extreme cases.

Stelli seemed to have trouble translating her feelings to words. At last she replied, with evident difficulty, "Zhen mustn't be beaten."

"It won't be so bad. It will be over quickly, and then his slate will be clean."

"No. He mustn't be beaten."

"What, are you saying he's innocent?"

"Yes. Innocent. That's right."

"Foolery. He was caught carrying Nirienne's scribblings. How do you account for that?"

"It's only paper and ink. He shouldn't be beaten for such a trifle."

"Don't you understand the principle involved? My father has banned Nirienne's writings from this estate. Your friend Zhen willfully disobeyed, and that is why he must be punished. He won't really be hurt, and if this teaches him to behave himself, then everyone will be the better for it. Can't you see that?"

"Zhen's done nothing so bad." Stelli's grasp of principle appeared weak. "He mustn't be beaten. He can't bear it."

"Well, I'm afraid he'll have to. If he's a bright lad, then he'll learn his lesson, and there's an end to the affair. No one will hold a grudge against him."

"You don't understand."

"What do you say to me?" Again, Eliste's astonishment overcame anger at the servant's remarkable impudence.

"You don't understand. Zhen mustn't be beaten, he can't bear it. He isn't strong. He isn't like most of us, he can't endure abuse."

"Abuse? You don't know what you're saying. Really, you are stupid."

"No doubt. Well, you're the smart one here . . . Miss."

A touch of sarcasm? Would she dare? It was unclear, and in any case too trivial to bother about.

"What I'm saying is, Zhen's always been kind of puny," Stelli continued with unwonted expansiveness. "He's skinny, he's got a weak stomach, he can't take the heat in the fields, and he gets these fainting fits."

"The details are unnecessary."

"He's sort of weak, and not meant to take a basting. And I've been thinking—" Clearly it was difficult for Stelli to ask for anything, but the cause overcame her reluctance, and she continued stoically. "I've been thinking that you might ask your father to go easy on Zhen. Will you, Miss?"

"Well, I don't know. It might not be quite so simple as that." Intrigued by the novelty, Eliste swung around in her chair to face her servant. "To begin with, Father's angry, and not all that likely to heed my advice. Beyond that, I'm not quite certain this is right. It might be best in the long run that the boy learn his lesson now—"

"He's learned it, Miss. He's learned it, you may be certain of that."

"You sound very definite. Do you know him so well, then?"

"He is my intended."

"Ah?" Eliste regarded her maid with interest. It would seem that the sullen Stelli was human after all, and the rush of surprised cordiality at the discovery threatened to overwhelm old hostility. "I didn't know you were promised."

"Zhen and I came to terms about eight weeks ago, Miss. Last week the steward handed down his Lordship's permission, and I thought our troubles were over. And now this." Stelli's habitual insolence was expediently diminished. For the moment at least, she looked and sounded almost winsome. "Zhen's got no harm in him, he's just a dreamer. He wants looking after."

"Well. I never guessed." Eliste's sympathies were now fully engaged. "We must see what we can do about this."

"You'll speak up for Zhen, Miss?"

"Gladly." A sunrise smile lighted the servant's face—she looked years younger when she smiled—and Eliste added, "You mustn't rejoice too soon, Stelli. Father's annoyed, and he might not listen to me. But I'll do my best—that much I can promise."

"No one could ask for more, Miss. It's good of you, it truly is." Stelli was unmistakably surprised. "It's very good. With you and my brother both to speak up, Zhen's bound to come out of this healthy."

"Your brother? What's Dref to do with all this?"

"He's promised to talk to the Marquis."

"Oh, that's a bad idea. He'd better not do that."

"Why? Dref's a real good talker."

"Indeed he is—few better—but now isn't the time. You see—the fact is—" It was extraordinary to explain matters to a servant, but somehow seemed appropriate in this case. "My father is now feeling that literacy among you people ought to be discouraged, or perhaps forbidden altogether. It's too late in Dref's case, of course. Dref's been reading almost as long as I have—"

"Longer." Stelli mouthed the word silently, almost unconsciously.

"—But there's no point in reminding the Marquis of that just now—it would only make things worse. Best to keep Dref out of this for the moment. You understand me?"

"Very well, Miss, but I'm afraid it's too late." Eliste's brows arched, and Stelli added, "Dref's set to put his voice in with the Marquis. He's already on his way. He'll be here any moment."

Automatically Eliste rose and stepped toward the window, then stopped as she realized her error. Her bedroom was at the front of the house, its windows affording a view of the manicured lawn and the long, tree-lined drive leading to the grand front entrance reserved for family members and visitors of rank. Dref would go to the back door, of course; his approach invisible from her present vantage point. She turned back, lifting her eyes to Stelli's face. Eliste was moderately tall, but the other girl towered above her by half a head, an unusual circumstance in a land where physical height commonly denoted correspondingly high birth. Moreover, Stelli was strapping and almost majestic: erect of carriage, broad-shouldered, strong, and so heroically proportioned that Eliste's slender form seemed almost insubstantial by comparison. It was vaguely offensive that a servant should look down upon her mistress from such imperial height. It was more than presumptuous, it was somehow threatening, at least in Stelli's case. But

Eliste was not thinking of that now. "Run down to the kitchen door," she directed. "When you see Dref, tell him to go away. No, wait." She changed her mind, before Stelli had taken a step. "You stay here and mend my gown you tore. I'll tell him myself." Without another word, she turned and hurried from the room. After a moment, Stelli quietly followed.

Through her disordered sitting room sped Eliste, ignoring the plaintive yaps of Prince vo Plume; out into the corridor whose ancient wallhangings, remnant of a medieval past, depicted the warlike deeds of the mailed vo Derrivalle ancestors; down the doglegged stairway, with its dark bulbous balustrade heavily carved and fluted in the manner of the past century; through chambers of old-fashioned, agreeably battered size and comfort; along the uncarpeted pass-through to the vast kitchen, unchanged for generations, without regard for the startled stares of the lounging scullions; and thence through the tiny mud closet and out onto the old stone landing upon which the servants were wont to promenade when the rainy season transformed lane and path into rivers of mud. It was not rainy season now. It was early summer, and the hot, dusty air hazed softly over the Derrivalle fields, pastures, and vineyards. For weeks now, the weather had been fine. The roads between chateau and the city of Sherreen were now quite dry, in optimal condition for Eliste's impending journey by coach. And that was as it should be. For surely it was only right and proper that Nature accommodate herself as required to the needs of the Exalted, her own most favored children?

Eliste gazed south across the level green lawn bounded by an undisciplined boxwood hedge. Behind the hedge lay the flower gardens, and beyond the gardens, the fields began, the cultivated rows stretching on as far as the eye could see. To the southeast a stand of Derrivalle timber rose, the tall trunks masking the green-brown fish pond. On the far side of the pond, quite invisible from the house, a cluster of cottages inhabited by the serfs; and then the thickly forested hills, a picturesque and mysterious realm, reputedly the haunt of brigands, ghouls, and renegade magicians, and beyond doubt the site of Uncle Quinz's rustic hermitage. The popular philosopher Rees-Raas Zhumeau claimed that Man in a natural setting manifested his noblest qualities. Such theories appeared vindicated by the existence of Quinz vo Derrivalle, sweetest and most unworldly of Exalted recluses. It was said that Quinz's mastery of the traditional forms of Exalted magic was extraordinary, almost unparalleled. Eliste could not have answered for that, for she never thought about it. But she knew beyond doubt that he was loving and lovable, kind, naive as a child was commonly supposed to be, and sometimes capable of truly entertaining magical tricks.

The southwest view was less inspiring. There could be seen the neat, sturdy outbuildings—stables, carriage house, springhouse, smokehouse, henhouse, dairy, and so forth—the vineyards and winery—and then the long rutted road leading down the slope to the dull little village inhabited by peasants owing their feudal duties to the Marquis vo Derrivalle.

A static scene, save for the soaring birds and the tiny mannequin figures of the serfs laboring in the distant wheat fields. And then through the gap in the hedge broke a tall, lean figure, and Eliste's blood quickened in pleasurable anticipation. Silly—but then, Dref Zeenoson always had that effect upon her, absurd though it was. Well, perhaps not so absurd, after all. Dref was amusing, beyond doubt. A serf possessed of such freakish quickness and cleverness was surely worthy of unusual regard. It was because of that mental agility that he had been her companion since earliest childhood—hers, if not his, as he was the older.

Some fourteen years earlier, just at the time that Eliste's education commenced, the remarkable abilities of the ten-year-old Dref Zeenoson had been directed to the notice of the Marquis vo Derrivalle. Dref, it was noted, could add, subtract, divide, and multiply sickeningly long columns of figures in his head, producing the correct sum within seconds. Never mind the fact that serfs lacked the logic for mathematics—he could do it. When shown a scene, or a collection of objects, he could later describe what he had seen with an accuracy leaving no doubt that he viewed concrete images within his mind. Before he was three he knew his letters, and more important, understood their application. He learned to read, almost upon instinct, it seemed, and he remembered all that he had read. Before he was seven, he had acquired a penknife, and used it to carve out the interlocking parts of little wooden machines powered by wind and water. He could play the flute, the harmonica, the ocarina, the fooge, and the glass organ like a son of the Exalted. He made up tunes, wrote them down according to his own system of notation, then played them upon a variety of instruments. He could sculpt in clay and plaster, paint in watercolor and tempera, ride or shoe a horse, compose a poem, cobble a shoe, catch and clean a fish, set a snare, cook a pheasant to perfection, build a model folly or fortress. In short, there was almost nothing the remarkable boy could not do, and it was commonly supposed that he must carry Exalted blood within his veins, as no other explanation for such unserflike talents appeared to exist.

The Marquis had taken note. It occurred to his Lordship that the young prodigy's abilities—so potentially profitable of use—should be cultivated. Thus Dref Zeenoson had been granted the almost unbelievable privilege of an Exalted education. He had taken his instruction alongside the Marquis's own daughter, questioned her tutors, devoured the contents of the manor library, and then proceeded to secure scores of additional volumes of his own by bartering with the visiting peddlers. He had even gone so far as to assist the bright but inattentive little Eliste with her lessons.

He was seven years older, and infinitely more knowledgeable than she. During the earliest years of her education, Eliste had loved and admired him to the point of idolatry. She had followed him everywhere about the estate, quoted his sayings, nagged him continually to play at Blue Cat with her. A little later on, of course, she had come to recognize his inferior status, and admiration inevitably dwindled. The reproof and ridicule of family members alerted her to the impropriety of her affection. She was, they informed her, growing up; and a young lady, a daughter of vo Derrivalle, did not run wild and barefoot through the woods in the company of serfs. A vo Derrivalle chose her friends among her equals, carried herself with dignity, and above all, never forgot her position. Unless, of course, she *preferred* to live among serfs. If she preferred it, Eliste was certainly quite free to leave the chateau, to march on down the lane to the little smoke-filled sweat-smelling cottages where the serfs dwelt amidst their fleas, and there she might make her home beneath a moldy thatched roof. Quite likely she'd be happy in such a setting, what with her affinity for serfs. They'd teach her how to till the soil, shovel dung, scrub floors, eat offal, and pick lice. She might take her cup and dish when she went, but not the silver spoon engraved with her name and family crest, because it was obvious a mistake had been made. She could not be Eliste vo Derrivalle, daughter to his Lordship. Clearly she must be some lowborn imposter, a peasant's whelp switched at birth with the Marquis's child. Only this could explain her attitude and behavior.

Eventually the little girl's worst tendencies were corrected. Newfound comprehension of her own rank was marked by an increase in self-conscious dignity. Familiarity on the part of inferiors was no longer tolerated. At age eight, Eliste vo Derrivalle was a very haughty young lady indeed, much given to verbal and physical rebuke of servants. It did not last long, of course. Before much more time passed, she had developed the easy confidence, the sense of serene native superiority characteristic of her class. Conspicuous self-assertion gave way to a more relaxed assurance, and she adopted the air of casually authoritative kindness to which most underlings responded so well. Most, but not all—and never Dref. Difficult to assume an air of careless superiority with *him*—he had ways of making her feel ridiculous whenever she tried it. Her assumptions of Exalted dignity were wont to provoke the sarcasm for which, as he well knew, she would not have him punished. Old attachments died hard, and she could not rid herself of her affection for Dref; but it was a mistake to let him know it—he was apt to presume. Really, he was entirely too free in his manner, addressing her without deference as if he imagined himself her equal, or even her intellectual better— more experienced and more knowledgeable than she. In all conscience, she ought not tolerate it. Her weak indulgence only encouraged his insolence.

And there, even at a distance, the insolence proclaimed itself in his upright carriage, in the free swing of his long stride, in the unsuitably proud lift of his dark head. It was difficult to put into words, but something about Dref Zeenoson's very appearance was subtly offensive to Exalted sensibilities. Like his sister, Dref was taller than a serf ought to be. His legs were too long; his figure too attenuated, agile rather than powerful; his features too chiseled; lean, sharp-jawed face too mobile, too expressive, sometimes dangerously so; hands too fine and adroit, too well-tended; no black semicircles under the short nails, no embedded grime. Unlike the typical serf, Dref Zeenoson was fond of bathing. Weather permitting a plunge in the pond, he contrived to keep himself clean, thus obviating the need for costly perfume to which he would in any case have had no access. (But Dref, she reminded herself, would have obtained perfume if he had ever wanted it. If he couldn't get it by barter, he'd have concocted his own, using flowers, herbs, oils and extracts, whatever came most readily to hand. Dref was like that.) The young man's lack of ordinary peasant stench was refreshing but subtly presumptuous. A cart horse should not resemble a racehorse, and a serf's style should not ape that of his betters.

, He had dressed in his best for the occasion, she noted. He had abandoned his patched yellow-gray smock in favor of a shirt of white linen, coarse but clean and decent. Over it he wore a short jacket and a neckerchief. In place of his usual baggy pantaloons he wore knee breeches and a pair of threadbare white stockings. The hideous wooden sabots had given way to hand-me-down leather shoes, with steel buckles carefully cleansed of rust. The scrupulously neat appearance, intended as a mark of respect, was ill-timed. He looked too spruce, too independent, too indefinably . . . uppish. Just now, the Marquis vo Derrivalle would only resent the effrontery.

He looked up, saw her waiting there, and waved. She returned the salute, smiling, and watched without moving as he made his way across the lawn and mounted the old stone steps. An instant later he was bowing low before her—all very well, in theory, but somehow it came off wrong, like so many of his ostensibly servile gestures. Serfs and peasants were wont to bob like arthritic drunkards, shoulders hunched, knees stiff, arms either locked or dangling limply. But Dref, with his spare, loose-jointed frame, could make a leg worthy of a dancing master. Sometimes it seemed as if those faultless courtesies were almost burlesque in their perfection, almost insolent in their fluid grace—or so it looked to Eliste, who knew him. Perhaps no one else had ever noticed. And yes, he was doing it now, bending just a satiric shade lower than propriety demanded. He straightened, and she spoke without thinking. "Why don't you just grow a forelock and tug it? That would suffice, and you wouldn't need to bow."

"But I prefer to bow. It's a splendidly expressive gesture." His voice was pleasantly low and his speech singular. The excellent grammar and literate fluency were incongruously linked with the drawling accent of a northern provincial peasant.

"I know. Too expressive. I'd take care, if I were you."

"Gladly. How shall I achieve perfect discretion?"

"Perfect impertinence is more your style, but you will never achieve it, being wholly imperfect."

"Then my constant imperfection achieves a perfect consistency."

"Thus destroying its own constancy."

"And preserving perfect imperfection."

"Serfs should not aspire to paradox."

"To what shall we aspire, beyond subservience?"

"Oh—" She considered. "Loyalty. Duty. Reliability."

"So much you demand of your horses and dogs. Nothing more?"

"Honesty. Unfailing amiability."

"You ladle out a sorry mess of watered gruel."

"A malcontent might think so. But simple fare is most nutritious, you'll grant."

"Come, your imagination lags. What more?"

"Humility," she suggested helpfully. "Proper respect for your betters."

"How shall I know them? The judgments of nature and society rarely coincide."

"It's hardly your place to make the distinction."

"Burdened as I am with eyes and a brain, how shall I avoid it?"

"Don't be impudent."

"Surely I have not offended?" he inquired with intolerable solicitude.

"Oh, you won't offend *me*—I hardly take you so seriously. But don't try your nonsense on anyone else, or you are looking for trouble."

"It's never necessary to look for trouble. It comes unsought and unwelcome as your father's tax collector in autumn."

"And like my father's tax collector, tarries with the refractory."

"And to prolong the conceit—most abuses those incapable of self-defense."

"The innocent need hardly fear abuse."

"There you reveal your own ignorant innocence, child."

"Ignorance! Innocence! Child! How dare you? Take that back, Dref!" She stamped her foot. "You just take that back!"

"I do. What could I have been thinking of? I am deeply sorry. I will never call you innocent again. Still, I must note certain exceptions to the sterling principles you've cited. Take Zhen Suboson, for example."

"Your sister's intended, the young firebrand."

"Scarcely such a desperate character. Only a harmless idealist with a childish penchant for forbidden political tracts. Unworthy of your father's notice."

"I'm inclined to agree. I gather you are here to speak on this Zhen's behalf." He nodded.

"Don't do it." His brows rose, and she added, "It's the wrong time. As I told your sister a few minutes ago, my father has worked himself into a fine rage over this foolish little affair. Already he regrets his mistake in permitting even occasional literacy among his serfs. Seeing you here now, unsummoned, absent from your work without permission, dressed above your station, assuming airs as you always do, will only add fuel to the fire. You'd best keep out of it, Dref."

"I should like nothing better. Poor Zhen is a particular friend of mine, however, as well as my sister's intended, and he requires assistance. The lad is hardly capable of defending himself."

"Well, I've promised to drop a word in my father's ear."

"Have you? I am relieved." He had abandoned his bantering tone, for once. His eyes—large, brilliant, and black as Stelli's—reflected unwonted concern. "Zhen might hope for no better advocate."

In recent years he had adopted toward her an air of sardonic exaggerated deference, and she had grown used to it. Now, in the face of this unexpected earnestness, reminiscent of the Dref she remembered from childhood, she found herself uneasy, even embarrassed, and she replied hastily, "I've already warned your sister—there's no guarantee I'll succeed."

"I pray that you do, else young Zhen stands to suffer, and he is not strong."

Still disquietingly grave, and she felt a momentary pang, something akin to guilt or shame, quickly dispelled by annoyance. She was a little bored, she decided, and more than a little regretful that she had stooped to involve herself in the trifling concerns of inferiors. Now she shrugged and answered coldly, "Really, I don't see why you and that sister of yours persist in exaggerating the importance of this incident. If Zhen Suboson—or whatever the lout's name is—receives a whipping, is that so dreadful? No doubt his skin is thick; he'll feel little. In any case, he wants discipline. He was deliberately disobedient, and punishment may serve to correct his faults."

"Ah. Would it correct yours, I wonder?" No need now to complain of his gravity. His teeth flashed white against his sun-bronzed face in a smile she found somehow unsettling.

"Mine? What do you mean?"

"Perhaps you have none? But let us assume for the sake of argument that his Lordship's daughter is not without flaw. Would a good hiding, publicly administered and followed by a healthy sojourn in the pillory, improve her character?"

"Very good, buffoon!"

"Perhaps you have presumed to read the wrong book—or you have spoken too freely—or failed to pay your taxes on time—or even ventured beyond the boundaries of the Seigneur's estate without permission. Then surely you want discipline, and punishment is indicated. It is for your own good, after all."

"How absurd you are—truly droll. But what folly to suggest that the restrictions governing the lower orders ought apply to me, or indeed to any member of the Exalted! We are hardly of the same clay."

"Are you quite sure of that? Is the difference among men so very great? In the opinion of certain natural philosophers, the so-called magical powers of the Exalted, which we have been taught to fear, are extinct, or exhausted, or at best aberrant."

"Then your natural philosophers are natural fools. What of my Uncle Quinz? Doesn't he possess magic?"

"Beyond question," Dref admitted. "But is he not extraordinary, almost unique?"

"Oh, I'm sure not," she returned carelessly. "In any case, there you are. There is your living proof of the innate difference between the Exalted and the common sort. As for applying the same laws to each, you might with equal justice demand identical rights for sheep and shepherd."

"Well, little shepherdess, no doubt you'll tend your flock with care, to the greater glory of all who love to feed upon mutton."

"Comedian!" she exclaimed, a little nettled. Then she looked into the black eyes, whose expression she found she could not read, and it occurred to her that her analogy, intended only as a neutral observation of obvious fact, might have offended him—might even have caused him pain. Instantly contrite, she strove to make amends. "But you mustn't think that what I say applies to *you*, Dref. You're different, most unusual, and everyone knows it. You are so clever, so ingenious, you rise entirely above your station. Everyone suspects you of Exalted ancestry. Indeed, but for an accident of birth, you might almost be one of us." There; that should make things right. The highest praise, and every word of it true.

He did not look mollified, however. He was smiling, yes, but she recognized that expression—it meant trouble.

"I must own myself unworthy of such honor. My veins are scarcely graced as you suggest." He spoke slowly, broadening his vowels and slurring his *r*'s in a deliberate exaggeration of his natural peasant drawl, to her annoyance. "I am nothing more than I appear, and thus as worthy of contempt, oppression, and exploitation as every other member of my class."

"Poor Dref. Do you know what your trouble is?" She allowed him no time to answer. He was not going to get the better of her this time. "You cannot accept reality. Nothing is ever good enough for you. You persist in railing against mankind, society, the world, and everything in it. No doubt the sun, moon, and stars likewise fail to meet your standards. Thus you grumble of tyranny, cruelty, oppression, and exploitation. Well, perhaps a few of the Exalted have abused their privileges from time to time. We are not perfect, after all. But where is the remedy? The Exalted, endowed with special qualities, suited by Nature to govern and to guide, merely perform their natural function in the world. Would you do away with the ruling class, thus abolishing government? Would you free the populace to run wild, to the destruction of civilization? Do you prize unbridled license above peace and security, above life itself? There must be leadership, rule and order, to ensure the general good; else chaos overwhelms us all. Is that what you want?" Her eyes were dancing as she concluded. She had him pinned, she was certain.

"I must admire the facility with which you parrot the sounding phrases gleaned at your father's table. Alas that a retentive memory is in itself no substitute for reason." Ignoring her affronted scowl, he continued, "Has it never occurred to you that stable government and Exalted ascendancy aren't necessarily synonymous? Or that the questionable existence of certain peculiar abilities doesn't necessarily mark a 'natural' ruling class? Or that the judicious restriction of Exalted privilege needn't herald the onset of anarchy?"

"Well"—she shrugged—"I'm sorry to disappoint you, but history teaches us differently."

"History was never your strong subject, little Elli," he remarked, and she glanced at him in surprise, for he hadn't presumed to employ that diminutive in years. He must have been more agitated than she'd realized, to let it slip out. "You have forgotten that the nation of Vonahr was not always the absolute monarchy that it is today. In earlier times, the power of king was limited, and the subjugation of the peasant class correspondingly incomplete. The ordinary laborer enjoyed a degree of personal freedom unknown in our day. In fact, it was not until the time of the Dread Scourge epidemic—that is, scarcely two hundred years ago—that laws were passed binding peasant to soil, thus establishing our happy modern condition of serfdom. Needless to say, matters did not end there, and now, in an era that unaccountably prides itself upon its enlightenment, an Exalted landowner is legally free to imprison, chastise, mutilate, or even execute his own serfs without fear of outside intervention."

"Most serfs aren't so badly off. The lazy ones like to complain, that's all." Eliste was growing bored and uncomfortable. Why couldn't he have confined himself to the usual badinage? It was so much more enjoyable.

"There we hear the effects of pernicious training upon the immature mind."

"You are insufferable. Worse, you grow tedious."

"Then I will conclude quickly. It goes without saying that the Exalted master rules all circumstances of his human cattle's lives—from birth, at which time the infant serf is marked with the symbol identifying him as manor property; through childhood, during which the youngster is schooled in servility, while access to formal education is customarily denied; through adolescence, wherein labor or craft is chosen and assigned at the Seigneur's pleasure; through adulthood, wherein seigneurial permission is required to marry, to build a cottage, dig a well, or plant a private vegetable garden; through old age, whose advent is generally accelerated by want, hardship, and hopelessness; and finally unto death itself, at which time the unspeakable Corpse Privilege grants the Seigneur the right to dispose of the serf's mortal remains—to grind them as dog's meat, should he see fit."

"That is offensive and revolting! No one would ever dream of doing such a thing, and you know it!"

"Do I? It must not be supposed," Dref continued dryly, "that seigneurial authority limits itself to the trifles I have touched upon. Throughout the course of an impoverished and generally miserable life, the serf—together with the supposedly free peasant—continually toils, only to see the best fruits of his efforts harvested by the Seigneur. The instrument of despoliation is the tax, of which an impressive assortment exists. There is the well tax, the oven tax, the mill tax, the bottle tax, the right-of-way tax, the seed tax, field tax, vine tax, orchard tax. Old age ushers in infirmity, and the loss-of-labor tax. I could go on at length, but there is no point in naming them all. Suffice it to say, there exists no aspect of the peasant's life untouched and unspoiled by the rapacity of his oppressors. His youth and strength are commodities owned by his lord. He labors from dawn to dusk to pay the price of Exalted luxury, while his own children suffer hunger and cold. He owns no voice in the formation of the laws that chain him, though they govern every breath he draws from birth to death. In the eyes of the law, he is scarcely more than a draft animal. Yet woe to the serf who thinks to better his lot by fleeing the estate of his master. Outlaw and outcast, hunted and despised, friendless and facing starvation, the beaten wretch generally comes crawling on back to his kennel within days. In the unlikely event that he fails to do so, no matter; the mark he bears upon his flesh will betray him, ensuring his swift recapture." Smiling thinly, Dref glanced down at his own right hand, the back of which bore a black tattooed letter *D* identifying him as a Derrivalle serf.

Eliste felt the color flame in her cheeks. For a moment confusion and an odd sense of mortification held her tongue-tied. Almost she moved to clasp the blemished hand, and the foolish impulse added to her discomfort. She felt herself somehow blameworthy, and the sensation was so disagreeable that she sought refuge in anger. How dare he presume to reproach her, how *dare* he? His complaints actually verged on accusation. Unbelievable that a serf should speak thus to her—outrageous, and not to be borne. Lifting her chin, she answered with an affectation of cold boredom, "I assume there is some point to this prolonged, tiresome recital?"

"The point is only this: that the rule of a king and his Exalted is neither a law of Nature, nor yet a historical inevitability. Change is quite possible. This true, the systematic victimization of the populace over the course of centuries builds a debt of blood and pain that may be repaid with interest, one day."

"And what is *that* supposed to mean?"

"Sufficiently goaded, even the meanest of slaves are capable of turning on their masters—at which point the demands for justice and for vengeance become indistinguishable. It is something you and your peers might wish to consider."

For a moment she stared at him, astonished; then trilled an artificial little laugh. "My, how earnest you look—how grim and funny. It's not like you at all. I see now why my father banned the writings of such self-proclaimed sages as your Shorvi Nirienne. He was right to do so, for these rabble-rousers are making a dreary pedant of you."

"Education can do that. Shall I say what yours is making of you?"

"That's enough!" Her precarious coolness broke. "You go too far, and I won't listen to any more! It's stupid and boring, and if you spoke this way to anyone else in my family, they'd order you whipped!"

"Ah, the great panacea. No doubt we'll witness its salutary effects upon Zhen Suboson."

"That again—I'm not interested! The creature can bleed, for all I care! No, I don't mean that, I take it back!" She paused a moment to compose herself. Dref was watching her expressionlessly. For some reason he seemed to delight in baiting her today—he was in an odd humor, certainly—but she wasn't about to give him the satisfaction of seeing her lose her temper. When she spoke again, her manner was carefully careless. "I will speak to my father about your friend, as I promised. Having received the assurance you came for, you've my leave to withdraw. You are not amusing today, and truly I've little interest in continuing so wearisome a conversation." Turning with a disdainful switch of her skirts, Eliste flounced into the house.

Dref stood looking after her until a tiny flash of motion caught his eye and he turned to the great woodpile that bulked beside the doorway. A crouching figure rose, and his sister stepped forth from her hiding place behind the heaped logs.

"Don't look so surprised," Stelli advised. "I've always wanted to hear what goes on between you and Princess Snot."

"Hush, Stelli—you'll only make things worse."

"Don't hush me, you're no better than me. What I want to know is, what are you going to do about my Zhen?"

"If you've been listening, then you already know. Eliste has agreed to intercede with her father on Zhen's behalf."

"And you believe it? That mincing little bitch won't trouble herself on our account, you may be sure. I want you to talk to the Marquis. You're a real good talker, and you promised."

"So I did, but this way is better. Eliste's intervention will be far more effective than mine could ever be. Trust her, she'll do her best."

"Her best's none too good, since she cares for nobody but her own self. If you think she's any friend of *yours*, you're an ass, for all your precious learning. I don't trust her, and I won't trust you either if you don't do what you promised. You've got to speak up. Zhen's your friend, and you owe him. Well?" She folded her arms. "Will you?"

"Zhen's chances are best if I keep out of it."

"Keep out of it! You mean you won't even try to help? What kind of a dirty pig are you?" Stelli exclaimed. Her black eyes were hot as melted pitch, and her aspect perceptibly threatening as she advanced upon her motionless brother. "You owe him! It's because of you he's in this mess. It's your fault!"

"Mine?"

"Yes, yours, and you know it!" She was too close to him, face thrust forward, eyes blazing into his from a distance of inches. "Who was it taught Zhen to read in the first place? You did! Who gave you leave to teach him? Nobody! Then who went filling his head with crazy ideas about politics and laws and things he didn't need to know about? And who got him started reading all that trash that none of us has any business meddling with? You did all of that—you did! You got him thinking that anything you said or did was right. You've been sneaking those pamphlets for years—oho, don't think I didn't know—and you never got caught. Poor Zhen tries it, and lightning strikes. Now he's in trouble all because you led him to it, and you won't stand by him! Fine friend! Pah—you pig, you make me sick!"

Dref, for all his eloquence, was momentarily mute. His silence suggested guilt, real or imagined.

"Cat got your tongue? That's funny, you find plenty to say to Princess Snot. Maybe you're too good now to talk to anyone but the Exalted, you're so learned, so special like she said, and your hands are so clean!"

"This is Zhen's best chance," he answered at last.

"That's funny, that makes me laugh." She did not appear amused. "You already know what any decent person would think. But let me tell you one more thing. If any harm comes to my Zhen because of all this, you're going to be sorry. I'll never forgive you, and I'll make sure you're sorry."

Without awaiting reply, Stelli flung off in the wake of her despised mistress, leaving Dref Zeenoson alone with his comfortless thoughts.

liste did try her best. Directly following her conversation with Dref Zeenoson she sought out her father, locating him in his study—a favorite haunt wherein the Marquis vo Derrivalle pursued his sole hobby: the preservation and study of medical curiosities. There he often sat, surrounded by his treasured collection of misshapen human bones and skulls; two-headed embryos, three-armed fetuses; mummified dwarves and hunchbacks; shrunken heads; abnormal organs, eyes, and brains preserved in chemical baths. Often he would spend hours at his desk composing and polishing some careful description of his latest freakish marvel, and at such times he was almost happy. Not today, however. One glance at her father's face informed Eliste that her cause was all but hopeless. Out of temper and out of sorts, the Marquis had started drinking hours earlier than usual. Now, although it was barely midday, his cheeks were suggestively flushed, his eyes bloodshot and puffy-lidded. A taciturn, handsome man in the prime of life, much resembling his daughter in face, with the same fine features and fair complexion, a little vain of his appearance, the Marquis was customarily fastidious. But now his peruke was out of curl, his cravat was twisted awry, and yesterday's lace hung limp at his wrists. His heavy frown and the compression of his lips communicated choler. Eliste regarded him with little optimism and less affection. Raised by servants and tutors, in accordance with the custom of the time, she'd had little contact with either parent throughout the course of her life. She saw them at mealtimes, at family gatherings and feast days, generally in the midst of kinsmen and servants. Her dealings with her morosely laconic father were uncomfortable and blessedly infrequent. In a case of this sort, she hardly knew how to approach him. It was with much reluctance that she touched upon the matter of Zhen Suboson.

"Insubordinate. Disobedient. A troublemaker," stated the Marquis.

"Oh, surely not, Father. A thoughtless youth, merely."

"Not sufficiently thoughtless. When we have driven all subversive thought from his head, he will be much improved."

"But a whipping." Eliste's nostrils flared in distaste. "It is so disagreeable. This Suboson is my maid's intended. If he is beaten, she'll sulk for days, and I shall be forced to endure her foul humor, so do think of me. Are there no other means of correction?"

"None so effective. We must consider the mental and moral limitations of the culprit. This serf will find a sound thrashing quite comprehensible."

"I suppose so. But really, it's unpleasant to think of such things. I believe you might let him off, and be none the worse for it. What harm in a little leniency, just this once?"

"Great harm. You have not yet learned how to deal with underlings, that is clear. The serfs of our degenerate age are presumptuous and recalcitrant beyond endurance. It is unwise to indulge them."

"Then perhaps an hour or two in the pillory—without the whipping—"

"Insufficient. The serf deliberately flouted the will of his Seigneur, and he must suffer for it. There is no other means whereby discipline will be maintained. Presumably the sight of this Suboson's blood will prove instructive to others contemplating similar disobedience."

"But the fellow's offense was quite trifling, scarce worthy of serious attention. Only consider, Father . . ." Eliste spoke on in vain; her arguments, pleas, and cajolery served only to solidify the Marquis's resistance. His face was hardening even while she watched; the bloodshot gray eyes went steely and the drink-slackened jaw set. Opposition was worse than useless, probably only fueled the other's quiet rage, and in any case, it was a cause for which she had little true feeling. Every word she uttered was worsening things for the miserable victim, and presently she had to give it up. Additional insistence would only have increased the severity of Zhen's punishment, which already stood at twelve strokes of the lash, followed by pillory confinement until sundown.

Even as it was, her intervention bore undesirable consequences. Zealous in defense of his threatened dignity, the Marquis now took it into his head to combine the spectacle of Zhen's chastisement with a long-overdue Purring, or performance of the ritual gestures and exclamations of joy with which serfs traditionally greeted the return of their Seigneur following prolonged absence. The Marquis vo Derrivalle had spent a recent joyless month in Sherreen, transacting business and renewing his acquaintanceships at Court, whose elite members regarded him as a provincial booby. The experience had chafed his spirits, which now required the balm of adulation, spontaneous or otherwise.

Eliste looked on in silent disgust as the appropriate orders were issued to the household steward. No sooner had the servant left the room than she made her feelings known. "To order a whipping in conjunction with the Purring is grotesque," she observed. "Worse than grotesque, it's downright tasteless."

"I do not share your opinion," the Marquis replied expressionlessly.

"You cannot really mean to do such a thing. It's outrageous. Call the steward back and tell him you've changed your mind. Or let me tell him." She reached for the bellpull.

"Leave that alone. You speak your mind rather too freely. It is best you learn that I tolerate disrespect neither from my serfs nor from my family members."

"I meant no disrespect, Father. I was only trying to——"

"In contradicting me, you merely confirm my judgment. I have been lax. It is time you recalled who is master here. The double spectacle of Purring and punishment may serve to jog your memory, and therefore you will view them both."

"I'd rather not."

"Immaterial."

"I'm engaged, I've other plans."

"Cancel them."

"I won't!"

"I will have a couple of the footmen drag you from your chamber by force, if necessary. You will find it uncomfortable and most undignified."

Her complaints were fervent but useless. The Marquis was in no mood to brook opposition; and thus, hours later, in the early evening, when the serfs' labors had ended for the day, Eliste found herself down by the stables, where the pillory and whipping post stood.

The Marquis and his daughter sat in a one-horse open chaise, with the Marquis himself handling the ribbons. Eliste would rather have taken them herself, for her father's competence was momentarily open to question. The Marquis had continued drinking throughout the day. He carried his liquor well; only the glassy sheen of the gray eyes and the tremor of the hand grasping the whip suggested diminished control. In the west the sun blazed fiercely, despite the lateness of the hour. The days were long now, and it would remain light for another two hours or more. A broad straw hat with a veil of rose gauze, and a tilting parasol held in a lace-mitted hand, shaded Eliste's white skin against the punishing rays, but could not banish the intense heat. Beneath the veil, her forehead was damp with sweat, and her light, balloon-sleeved gown of raspberry voile was beginning to stick to her flesh. Unobtrusively she plucked at the dress, tugged at her corset, and wished herself a thousand miles away, or at least back in her own room with a loose cool dressing gown, a chilled verbena tisane, a good poem or play to read, and a decent maid to ply the feather fan. The spectacle before her lacked appeal. She'd never in her life witnessed a Purring that proved anything less than farcical.

All the Derrivalle serfs, house servants and field workers alike, were assembled and ranged in orderly rows. That they were there against their will was evident in the sullen sagging shoulders, the shuffling footsteps, the downcast resentful eyes—resentful, she thought, as never before; but perhaps that was only imagination. All of those faces were familiar to Eliste, but some in particular drew her eyes irresistibly. There was Stelli, strong jaw set, black brows lowering, baleful black eyes beaming defiance. Beside her stood her father Zeeno, bowed head uncovered in the presence of the Seigneur, eyes dutifully downcast—all very proper, but wasn't it perhaps a shade too perfect? Where, after all, had his offspring learned their insolence? But these were ridiculous fancies, quickly dispelled, and her gaze jumped to the little dairymaid Kairthe, whose big round eyes in a small round face promised biddable good nature. *That one, definitely,* thought Eliste. *She'll replace Stelli, the sooner the better.*

Her efforts to focus her attention upon a pleasant prospective acquisition were unsuccessful, and her eyes traveled, against her will, to Dref Zeenoson's face. It had always been upsetting to her, even painful, to watch Dref participate in a Purring. In some manner she could hardly define, she felt shamed, humiliated for his sake, and that was clearly absurd. Dref Zeenoson, a serf born and bred, was only fulfilling the natural obligations of his kind. It was right, proper, and indeed inevitable that he should do so. Probably the ritual imposed no very great hardship on him—despite his peculiar cleverness, he could hardly possess the fine sensitivities of his Exalted masters, and it was a mistake to imagine that he suffered the pangs that she herself would experience if subjected to similar indignity. Nevertheless, she did not like to see him here—and could not seem to forbear looking for him. There he was, only a few yards distant, once again attired in his ordinary working garb—a wise move, in view of the Marquis's present mood. His tanned face was frozen and rigidly expressionless, the eyes unreadable. So he appeared at every Purring—she had seen it often. But today something in his complete stillness seemed somehow wrong, even ominous. For reasons she couldn't explain to herself, Eliste was uneasy.

At a command from the steward, the Purring commenced, and the serfs plodded through the time-honored sequences. First came the harmonious exclamations of gratitude attendant upon the safe return of the Seigneur. Then the traditional obeisances: the bowing, scraping, and dirt-thumping, designed to express both veneration and fear. Then the Kneeling Parade, so difficult for those with aging joints; followed by the formal Suit for Indulgence, droned out in unison by all present. With a gesture, the Marquis vo Derrivalle signaled his assent, whereupon the assembled menials ventured to raise eyes hitherto fixed firmly upon the soil. It was commonly taught that the magical glance of an Exalted possessed the power to kill. Hence, that power must be consciously leashed before inferiors might safely encounter Exalted eyes. In recent years the legend had been widely questioned; still, few dared disregard it altogether. But Dref dared, and so did his sister. Their eyes had remained fixed on the Marquis's face throughout.

The Purring continued, and Eliste fidgeted, prey to discomfort and impatience. The sun was low in the sky, the shadows long, but the heat continued infernal. Her palms were sweating and itchy, her lace mitts damply intolerable. Setting the parasol aside for a moment, she drew the mitts from her hands. If anyone disapproved, so much the worse.

No one noticed. The Marquis did not so much as glance in her direction. He was watching his serfs, who now cut lackluster ceremonial capers. Halfheartedly they spun, hopped, pranced, and cavorted. Their leaps were perfunctory, visibly listless. The Marquis observed it, and frowned. Leaning forward in his seat, he caught the steward's eye, and tapped the butt of his whip upon the carriage floor. Instantly the steward clapped his hands, and the vigor of the serfs' capers increased. But the mandatory enthusiasm was short-lived, and the Marquis's frown deepened.

Eliste's gaze returned to Dref, whose wooden-jointed shuffle conveyed indifference verging on insult. Then, almost as if he felt the pressure of her gaze, he turned and met her eyes. His face was perfectly impassive, deliberately unrevealing; but for some reason the pain shot through her, a rush of misery and shame so acute that it brought tears to her eyes. She did not know the cause—perhaps an attack of the vapors?—and fortunately it did not last long. Dref turned away. Her inexplicable tears dried, and the gauzy veil shielded her momentary lapse.

The capering drew to a close, and the Purring concluded with a Grand Ululation, uttered without élan. As the last quavering cry died away, the Marquis nodded a curt acknowledgment and the kneeling serfs arose, most of them dripping with the sweat of their unwilling exertions, all of them coated with grime. His Lordship's expression remained sour. The spectacle had not fulfilled his expectations. The sweat shed on his behalf was insufficient, the tribute was grudging, and his pique remained unassuaged. It required the sight of sufferings greater than his own to restore his spirits. The Marquis drew forth a lace-edged handkerchief, patted his moist brow, and gestured irritably. It was the signal for Borlo Bunison, the Derrivalle blacksmith and designated dispenser of the

Seigneur's justice, to initiate the second half of the proceedings by fetching Zhen Suboson from his stable-prison. Before Borlo had stirred, Dref Zeenoson stepped out of his place in line. The steward clapped his hands frantically but ineffectually. Dref advanced several paces toward the chaise and paused. The Marquis's brows rose in surprised displeasure.

"Seigneur, may I speak?" Dref inquired in a voice that carried, despite its quietness. He stood straight and tall, somehow achieving a look of consequence, despite his shabby garments.

That unconscious pride subtly galled the Marquis, whose present temper demanded deference. Without troubling to reply, he turned to the steward and snapped his fingers. The flustered steward hurried forward to lay a hand on Dref's shoulder. The young man shook him off easily.

"But one word, Seigneur," Dref persisted. "I entreat you."

The word "entreat" exerted a soothing effect, and the Marquis hesitated.

"Why not?" Eliste murmured, negligent manner masking an acute sense of foreboding.

"Very well," the Marquis conceded. "Be brief."

A wondering mutter arose among the watching serfs. The steward's quick reproof quelled them, but could not still the whispery agitation of their ranks.

"Seigneur, I ask leave to plead on behalf of the serf Zhen Suboson." Dref spoke quickly, clearly cognizant of his master's limited patience. "I beseech your mercy in the commutation of this serf's corporal punishment, on the following grounds. The first—that Suboson is young, ardent, highly impressionable, and too subject to the force of questionable influences. Be patient with him, Seigneur—already he has perceived his errors, and maturity will grant greater wisdom. The second reason—that the serf Suboson is not robust. Since earliest childhood this loyal retainer of your Lordship has suffered fainting fits, palpitations, shortness of breath, and every variety of illness. He is constitutionally unfit to endure physical hardship. Therefore, I pray your Lordship will display the large compassion that is the hallmark of Exalted nobility, in sparing the lash and accepting the contrition of a misguided but truly repentant servant."

It was not a poor effort, but the Marquis reacted badly. To Eliste, the reason was obvious—Dref simply spoke too well; better, in fact, than the Seigneur himself. Those polished, elaborate sentences did not fit the mouth of a serf. That glib eloquence seemed to mock the articulation of his betters. And despite Dref's careful adherence to all the requisite forms of humility—despite the respectfully uncovered head and belatedly downcast eyes—the effect was not convincingly reverent. The young man had not mastered the finer points of servility, probably never would. His speech, his appearance, his manner were indefinably vexing, and the Marquis's hackles rose. His bloodshot eyes gleamed, but he replied with apparent composure, "Back to your place."

Dref did not move. "Seigneur, hear me," he persevered, and behind him another startled murmuring arose. "You are eminent, great, and fortunate. You possess wealth, rank, and influence. Much has been given to you—nearly everything, in fact, that the world holds valuable. Such ease and plenty must surely foster generosity to those less favored than yourself. I ask you to display that generosity now, in extending mercy to Zhen Suboson, and to all others whose lives chance has entrusted to your power."

Worse and worse. He should never have equated Exalted power with the careless gifts of Fortune. The reference suggested a possible impermanence unpalatable to his Lordship. And there was still that damnable articulateness.

Flushing angrily, the Marquis snapped a single command. "Back."

Dref reddened in turn, but still he did not move. "Seigneur, an act of charity costing you nothing purchases the gratitude and loyalty of your subordinates—"

"Purchase? They are mine by right," the Marquis observed. Turning to Borlo Bunison, he commanded, "Fetch." Borlo made for the stables.

"Seigneur, if you will but consider—" Dref attempted, but this time he had overshot his mark.

"Enough." The Marquis's hand clenched on the butt of the whip. "Back, or we shall witness a double thrashing." He did not raise his voice, but his sweat-dewed face had darkened ominously. Eliste regarded him with mingled nervousness and distaste.

Dref hesitated a dangerous moment. The serfs watched in rapt silence. Once more the steward approached to lay a hand on his arm, and this time Dref suffered himself to be drawn away. Eliste drew a relieved breath, and then grew angry. What business had he causing difficulties and frightening her so? If he'd gotten himself in trouble, it would have served him right.

Borlo Bunison emerged from the stable, a horse whip tucked beneath his arm. With him came the wretched Zhen Suboson, composed but waxen-pale. Eliste recognized him at once. She had seen him often enough about the estate but never before known the name of this quiet, fragile, big-eyed boy of about nineteen, with the mop of dust-colored hair, the large head tapering from broad brow to pointed chin, the long neck and outsize Adam's apple, set atop a short and skinny body. His smock had been removed in the stable, exposing a small hairless chest and narrow, bony shoulders. It was hard to imagine what the strapping Stelli saw in such a runt. But Zhen's white face was intelligent and sensitive; perhaps that explained it.

Borlo led his captive to the post, which Zhen was required to embrace. Tossing his whip aside for the moment, the blacksmith drew a length of cord from his pocket, bound the other's wrists securely, and fastened the cord to an iron ring sunk into the oak some six feet above the ground. Zhen offered no resistance. He had been schooled in submission since infancy. In any case, the huge and iron-muscled blacksmith could easily have broken him in two. Resting his forehead against the post, Zhen quietly awaited the worst.

Borlo stepped back, retrieved the whip, and cast an inquiring glance at his master. The Marquis inclined his head. Borlo half turned, lifted his arm, and sent the lash singing through the air to meet the victim's exposed flesh with a sickening slap. Eliste started at the sound. Zhen stiffened, his hands clenched, and he pressed his face hard against the post. No sound escaped him. Three more evenly timed blows followed, and Zhen maintained silence. Angry red welts marked his back, but the thin skin had not been broken. It was clear that Borlo Bunison was by no means putting forth his best efforts. This might not have mattered had Zhen but produced the whimpers, moans, and squirming contortions the Marquis's frustrations demanded; but the victim refused to oblige. Two more cracking strokes, and Zhen remained stubbornly silent. His eyes were squeezed shut, his lips drawn back in a pained grimace, and he was quivering all over, but still he did not cry out. His resistance verged on open defiance, and as such his master regarded it. The Marquis caught the blacksmith's eye, gestured with the crook of a single finger. Borlo's heavy shoulders sketched a shrug, and the force of his blows increased. The whip descended on Zhen's shoulders with a wicked snap, and this time a tracery of blood welled in its wake. Eliste shuddered and turned her face away. The scene before her, perhaps combined with the breathless heat and the tightness of her stays, was exerting its effect, and she was growing a little light-headed. It was neither the time nor the place to indulge in a ladylike faint. Lifting her veil, she breathed deeply; but the hot, heavy air brought no relief. Thrice more she heard the thud of the lash on naked flesh, but not a sound from Zhen. Then an excited murmur arose among the watching serfs, and Eliste turned back to look.

Her eye fell on Borlo Bunison, who stood motionless, head cocked a little, horse whip dangling limp at his side; then traveled to Zhen Suboson, whose back was now marked with the blood of four long, crisscrossing cuts. But that was not the worst of it. Something was wrong with Zhen, something that went beyond the predictable reaction to an ordinary flogging. The boy's sweat-soaked face had gone a dreadful shade of gray. His head was flung back, eyes and mouth wide open. For some reason, he seemed to be drowning on dry land. His chest heaved, he gasped desperately, and inexplicable spasms racked his small frame. Some moments later, his knees buckled and he slumped within his bonds, whose tension was now all that held him upright.

Borlo looked to his master. The Marquis crooked a finger. The blacksmith shrugged and lifted his arm.

"Stop it!" Eliste exclaimed, much to her own surprise. Several of the serfs stared at her, but the Marquis appeared deaf. "Father, that boy is sick."

"Shamming," replied his Lordship, without turning his head.

"Surely not. Call it off, Father. Please."

"You are easily hoodwinked." With a snap of the fingers in Borlo's direction, the Marquis commanded, "Proceed."

The lash whistled, and blood welled from a new cut. It was unclear whether Zhen Suboson felt it. His body was jerking oddly, but he appeared unconscious, or nearly so. One more stroke, the twelfth and last. The lash bit deep, but this time there was no reaction. Having maintained perfect silence throughout the ordeal, Zhen now hung motionless and insensible.

Tossing his whip aside, Borlo trudged to the post and loosed the captive's wrists. Zhen tumbled full length to the ground. Once again the blacksmith hesitated.

"Proceed," the Marquis repeated.

Grasping his victim under the armpits, Borlo dragged the recumbent body toward the pillory. As Eliste looked on in dismay, Zhen's body bounced over rock and sod. She had the feeling that she ought to do or say something, but she didn't know what. How, after all, could she dispute his Lordship's direct orders?

As it happened, she didn't need to. Before Borlo reached his destination, the Marquis's personal barber and leech, Guielle Ezoir, had broken out of line to approach his fallen compeer. Kneeling, Guielle listened for a heartbeat, searched throat and wrist for a pulse. Finding none, he lifted his head to proclaim, "Seigneur, he's dead."

Total silence greeted this announcement. The assembled serfs stood staring. After a moment Eliste's eyes jumped without volition to Stelli Zeenosgirl, who appeared frozen, perhaps momentarily uncomprehending; then turned to the Marquis, whose expression had not altered in the slightest.

"What is the cause of death?" inquired his Lordship calmly.

"Seigneur, it's hard to say," replied Guielle Ezoir.

"He has not bled to death, I presume?"

"No, Seigneur. Poor Zhen was always sickly, though."

"Ah. He was congenitally defective," observed the Marquis, interest quickening.

"That's one way of putting it, Seigneur. Zhen's had these attacks ever since he was a child."

"Attacks of what nature?"

"I can't be sure, Seigneur. It may be he had an excess of the melancholy humor that made for inner rebellions."

"I see. An internal flaw, possibly of unusual nature. In that case, you will perform a dissection in order to determine the precise nature of this serf's imperfection. Assuming success on your part, I shall observe the abnormal organs, and perhaps if warranted, submit a monograph on the subject to the Royal Academy."

A general intake of breath, a collective stirring of shock or revulsion fluttered the ranks of the serfs. Eliste stared, astonished and disgusted. Guielle Ezoir looked helplessly thunderstruck. Almost, for an instant, he seemed to contemplate remonstrance, then thought the better of it and dipped his head in mute acquiescence.

"As the carcass is bound to corrupt swiftly in this weather, I cannot countenance delay. You will perform your task this very evening," the Marquis informed his leech.

Guielle, though clearly troubled, bowed in silence shared by all of his fellows—all but one. For the second time that evening, Dref Zeenoson presumed to address his master without leave. Dref was white beneath his tan, and his face was set like a death mask. Certainly there was something peculiar, even unnerving, in his aspect; something suggestive of violent currents swirling beneath an ice-skimmed surface. Advancing to stand almost as if protectively before the corpse, he observed much too calmly, "Your Lordship's decision no doubt inadvertently imposes additional suffering upon the family and friends of Zhen Suboson. I trust this is far from your Lordship's intent, and therefore I request the Seigneur to grant his serf the ordinary decency of conventional burial."

The Marquis appeared to debate the necessity of reply. At last he chose to answer, "Following surgical investigation, the remains—those that have not been set aside for chemical preservation and future study—may be collected, reassembled, buried or otherwise disposed of, the sooner the better. I consent to this."

"Seigneur—" Dref's hands were tightly clasped behind his back, and still he spoke with rigid self-restraint, "Zhen Suboson is not a laboratory specimen, nor is he a domestic beast bred for consumption. He is a human being like yourself, entitled both in life and in death to a certain basic measure of human dignity. No man possesses the right to defile his remains."

"That is incorrect. I shall indulge your impertinence in view of the singular circumstances that apparently cloud your judgment, and thus condescend to remind you that the Corpse Privilege numbers among the hereditary seigneurial rights."

"It is not a right, but rather, a power," Dref returned very deliberately. "And the tyrant choosing to exercise that power is altogether vile."

Eliste's breath caught and her eyes widened in pure disbelief. He had gone mad; no other explanation was possible. Grief or sunstroke had curdled that fine mind, and now he was totally mad. More than one of the listening serfs gasped audibly.

"What did you say?" the Marquis inquired incredulously.

"I said that the Corpse Privilege is an abomination, one of the very worst of the myriad outrages inflicted upon the populace by a privileged and useless minority. Did you hear me that time? I wish to be certain that you do."

No answer from the astonished Marquis. Eyes fixed on Dref's face, Eliste shook her head urgently.

Ignoring the signal, Dref resumed, "The inequities of our laws are immoral, and the resulting ruthlessness of the Exalted is demonic. Nothing could illustrate the truth of this more vividly than the events of this day, which commence with the discovery of a young serf's transgression. The nature of the crime? Zhen Suboson was caught reading the forbidden essays of Shorvi Nirienne. And why, at the outset, has the Seigneur found it necessary to proscribe Nirienne's works? Clearly because his Lordship fears the ideas contained therein—perceives the concepts as perhaps threatening to his Lordship's parasitical way of life. Finding it easier to suppress such ideas than to confront them, the Seigneur issued his prohibition; which Zhen Suboson, cursed with an active and inquisitive mind, disregarded. Disobedience discovered, the boy is locked up in the stable for hours without water, on one of the hottest days of the year—treatment that would not be meted out to the worst of the horses for which that stable was constructed. At the end of the day, he is removed from the stable, tied to a post, and publicly whipped to death; at which time the Seigneur, no doubt resolved to mitigate his loss of property, consigns the corpse to the dissection table. And there, within one day, is epitomized the relation of Exalted to serf, oppressor to victim, predator to prey. In his acts of cowardice, tyranny, cruelty, and homicide, the Marquis vo Derrivalle proves himself a fit representative of his class; one whose deeds inspire a disgust ultimately reducing to simple—contempt." Dref had not once raised his voice. His restraint added immeasurably to the force of his denunciation.

Awful silence. The spectators seemed paralyzed. Face purpling, the Marquis struggled for reply, but his fury was too great to express itself in words; and in any case, he was no verbal match for the serf. Temporarily deprived of speech, he sought outlet in action. Abandoning the chaise, the Seigneur advanced a few unsteady paces, halted several feet from his motionless accuser, and plied his whip. The strokes descended upon Dref's shoulders, sides, and upraised arm. The young man's reaction was purely instinctive. Ducking beneath the flying lash, he sprang forward, wrested the whip from the Marquis's grasp, and flung the weapon aside. The Marquis slapped his serf's face hard, and the blow cracked like a pistol shot. Without thought or hesitation, almost reflexively, Dref doubled his fist and struck back, to send his master sprawling.

For a moment the Marquis lay where he had fallen, then sat up slowly, one hand pressed to his face. His nose was bleeding. A thin red stream trickled down his face to drip off the side of his chin. The sight might easily have provoked laughter; just now, no one exhibited the slightest amusement. The watching serfs were elated but badly frightened; and Eliste, certain of her father's reaction, was terrified. Dref himself seemed somewhat at a loss. As he stood absently rubbing his knuckles, his expression reflected bemusement.

The Marquis rose. His face was blank. A display of emotion could only have demeaned him further. Turning to Borlo Bunison, he commanded simply, "Attack."

Borlo was glum but obedient. Striding forward, he made a grab for the younger and lighter man, who easily eluded him. Borlo threw a punch, which Dref dodged. A second swing was equally ineffectual. This time Dref sprang in, drove his fist into the blacksmith's midsection, and slid out of reach again. Despite the speed and force of the blow, Borlo appeared to feel nothing. His adversary might just as well have struck a brick wall—an increasingly angry brick wall. Borlo's heavy brows were lowering, and a scowl creased his forehead as he lumbered in pursuit of his annoyingly nimble opponent. The next time he struck, it was with sufficient force to stun a bull, had the blow landed. Once again Dref dodged, hit, and danced away. A slight grunt escaped Borlo Bunison as the other's fist thudded home; beyond that, he appeared impervious.

Catching his steward's eye, the Marquis held up two fingers; whereupon the steward issued commands to two of the largest and sturdiest young plowmen in his immediate vicinity. The plowmen jumped into the fight. Aware too late, Dref spun to meet them, and a whizzing fist took him full in the face, striking him to the ground. Before he had stirred to raise himself, both plowmen flung themselves upon him, their combined weight pinning him down. Borlo Bunison approached without haste, gazed impassively down into his adversary's eyes, then drew back his foot and kicked hard. Dref's face contorted as the toe of Borlo's hobnailed boot slammed into his ribs. Several more kicks followed in quick succession. Eventually this diversion palled, and Borlo ceased; whereupon the plowmen hauled Dref to his feet and held him upright. Borlo considered briefly, then threw a series of sharp, jabbing punches into the prisoner's face and body, concluding with a straight right to the point of the chin. Dref's head snapped backward. An instant later he sagged unconscious between his two captors. They released him, and he slumped to the ground.

Nausea threatened to overwhelm Eliste. Never in her life had she witnessed such brutality, and scarcely would she have credited its existence upon the Derrivalle estate. That the victim of violence should be Dref, *her* Dref, rendered the scene doubly nightmarish. Now she sat struggling for breath as her eyes traveled from the corpse of Zhen Suboson, to Dref Zeenoson's motionless form, and back again. Poor Zhen was far beyond help. But Dref still lived, now the object of his master's particular hatred, and in danger of the direst punishment, if she knew her father. Eliste glanced sidelong at the Marquis. He stood a few paces distant, red-splotched handkerchief still pressed to his face, although the bleeding had ceased. His eyes were fixed upon the combatants, his face quite expressionless. Now was the time to address him, before worse punishment for Dref was decreed. When she spoke, her air of unconcern was tolerably convincing. "Why, the wretch is either delirious or else quite mad. Surely he hadn't the least idea what he said or did, and must not be held accountable."

"Mad," the Marquis repeated meditatively. "What structural anomalies might not distinguish the brain of a lunatic? Surely the matter is worthy of investigation."

Eliste froze momentarily, all too aware of her error, then replied with indifference, "Perhaps he is only drunk. Probably that is the explanation. In any event, it seems very tedious to me, very absurd, all this furor over a single unruly serf. I should think it beneath your notice, Father—or is it perhaps the current fashion in Sherreen, this preoccupation with menials?"

The Marquis turned to glance at her sharply; encountered a faint but perceptibly patronizing smile. He frowned. As she had intended, her reference to the capital city stirred unpleasant recollections of his recent sojourn therein, during which he had so often been made to feel the clumsy provincial. He had a morbid fear of his peers' ridicule, although he would never have admitted it. Perhaps he *was* lowering himself, perhaps his concern was excessive, but it was not too late to rescue his threatened dignity. "Scarcely a preoccupation," his Lordship replied coldly. "And yet I can hardly overlook his offense. Seigneurial duty includes the magisterial function."

"Well"—Eliste carefully adjusted the brim of her hat—"the fellow has been punished. In the meantime, the heat is oppressive, the spectacle unappetizing, and I am perishing of discomfort. I wish to return to my chamber, at once."

"Punished? No," the Marquis informed his daughter. "A minor drubbing does not begin to expiate so great a crime. More is required, but not this instant. The hour is late, we are all fatigued, and the culprit is insensible. I shall order him confined under Bunison's guard until morning. When he is awake and fit to profit by the lesson, he shall receive punishment commensurate with his offense."

Eliste watched in well-concealed dread as the Marquis crooked a summoning finger. The steward immediately advanced to receive his master's low-voiced commands, which were in turn relayed to Borlo Bunison and a clutch of his cohorts. Two of the plowmen lifted Dref from the ground and carried him off to the stable, while the corpse of Zhen Suboson was borne toward the icehouse. The

Seigneur returned to the chaise, mounted, and took up the reins. He had wiped all the blood from his face; his movements were calm and deliberate. But his nose was inflamed and swollen, his face mottled red and white, and the blazing bloodshot eyes belied the artificial composure.

"Commensurate with his offense?" Eliste prompted.

"Exactly so." The Marquis purposefully raised his voice to a volume audible to the assembled serfs. "The tongue that reviled the Seigneur shall be cut out. The hand raised against the Seigneur shall be cut off. Nothing more is required, and nothing less. This is perfect and unquestionable justice."

Eliste stared at him speechlessly. The serfs were similarly mute. Fortunately, the Marquis vo Derrivalle neither expected nor desired reply. Shaking the reins, he clucked at the horses, and the chaise rattled off toward the great house. As they went, Eliste could not forbear casting one look back over her shoulder; and immediately she regretted it, for the last image she carried from that place was the face of Stelli Zeenosgirl, with its look of frozen horror and hatred.

pon her return from Zhen Suboson's accidental execution, Eliste sought her own chamber, there immuring herself in miserable solitude. And there she remained, ceaselessly pacing the floor, quick footsteps matching the tempo of her mental activity, as the hot evening deepened to equally breathless night, the lamps and candles were lit all over the house, and a veiled orange moon rose in the starless sky. Time passed. Her mind continued to race, and gradually her mood changed, initial despair giving way to gloomy conjecture, culminating in the startled realization that Dref Zeenoson's situation was not entirely hopeless. The power of the Marquis vo Derrivalle, far from absolute, might perhaps be circumvented. Dref might yet escape what amounted to destruction, provided he received assistance. It would not be easy, and she herself could not save him, but there was another who might; someone she would have to seek out this very night, as soon as she could safely get away.

So Eliste's thoughts ran as she paced her chamber alone. Only once was her solitude broken, when she permitted brief admittance to a servant bearing a cold meal on a covered tray. Hours had passed since then, but the tray still sat untouched on the table where the servant had left it. Her mind filled with horrific visions of Dref Zeenoson's impending mutilation, Eliste could not have eaten to save her life. Dref himself, on the other hand, locked up in the stables and unaware of the fate that awaited him, would probably welcome the nourishment. Assuming that he had regained consciousness, he was by this time probably both parched and ravenous. Eliste paused in her pacing, walked to the table, and lifted the lid from the tray to discover a plate of cold meat, cheese, fruit, biscuit, and fresh butter. Alongside the plate stood a stoppered carafe of cold mint-scented tea. Wine would have been better, but certainly Dref would appreciate anything he received. That he *would* receive it, she did not for a moment doubt, for she had laid her plans with care. Throughout the long hours she had plotted, and now at last, in the dead of night, while all the household slumbered, it was finally time to move.

Breath now quickening, Eliste hurried to the huge old clothespress, threw open the door, knelt to rummage within, and dragged forth a dusty valise. Thrusting her hand back into the press, she felt blindly about the floor and soon located a key. It was not easy to open the valise. The lock, untouched for the past four years or more, was stiff and a little rusty. Feverish determination prevailed, the key turned reluctantly, and the lid creaked back on its hoarse old hinges. Within the valise lay her secret possessions—the garments and all the rest of the hidden gear—just as she had left them so long ago; long unthought-of, but perfectly familiar. Last remnants of a hoydenish childhood whose recollection faintly embarrassed her, she had never thought to look on them again. Yet somehow she had never quite been able to throw them away, and there was no denying the thrill of illicit excitement that swept through her at sight of her former treasures. Old memories stirred, and the past was suddenly quite immediate.

Eliste gazed only a moment, then stood and began to pull off her clothes. The wilted voile dress went first, followed by layered petticoats, kid slippers, stockings, and garters. Off came rings and bracelet. The corset, with its tight lacing, presented certain difficulties, but eventually she freed herself, and her rib cage swelled in gratitude. Clad only in a short chemise of lawn, she stooped, grabbed garments from the valise, and with a speed born of much experience, donned bloused linen shirt, loose drawstring breeches, knitted socks, and flat, sturdy walking shoes; items unobtrusively purchased at fairs or from peddlers by the adventurous child she had once been. The shoes still fit, even after all this time. The tight, pointed little slippers she'd worn in recent years had apparently kept her feet from growing much. Eliste took a few experimental steps, unconsciously smiling. She'd almost forgotten how comfortable such clothing could be. Her right hand dived, seemingly of its own volition, into her breeches pocket, to bring forth a narrow grosgrain ribbon with which she bound her hair at the nape of her neck. At the bottom of the valise still lay the belted tunic, lined coat of masculine cut, gloves, hat, and boots. In view of the sultry weather, she needed none of them tonight. The lantern and the canvas satchel were essential, however. She scooped up both articles. After a moment's hesitation, she also grabbed the old clasp knife, and dropped it into the satchel. Its blade was short and dull, but perhaps Dref would find a use for it.

Crossing to the table, Eliste transferred the cold food from plate to napkin, tied the corners, and dropped the bundle into the satchel. Alongside the food she placed the carafe of tea. She began to draw the bag shut, but stopped as another thought struck her. Money. Dref would surely need money, and she had plenty. Her netted silk purse lay in the bureau's top drawer. Quickly she fetched the purse, tossed it into the satchel, closed the bag, and slung its strap over her shoulder. The lantern sat on the table where she had left it. The candle inside was almost untouched. Using a taper from one of the wall sconces, she lit the lantern, replaced the taper, and then she was ready to go.

Eliste passed from bedchamber to sitting room and then, almost to her own surprise, paused at the corridor door. She had forgotten that she'd always used to stop there to listen for the sound of footsteps in the hall, but it seemed that her feet remembered. There was no sound now. Softly she eased the door open a trifle, applied her eye to the gap; saw nothing; opened further, stuck her head out, glanced swiftly left and right. The corridor was dark and deserted. Quietly she slipped from her sitting room, closing the door behind her, and turned left to slink like a feral kitten down the hall as far as the steep and narrow servants' staircase, which she descended in expert silence. Halfway to the bottom, she hesitated a moment, then set her back to the wall and edged sideways down the next several steps. Once again, her feet had remembered—this section of the staircase creaked.

Moments later she emerged into the kitchen, where a few banked embers glowing on the hearth added their heat to the already stifling atmosphere. A couple of scullery maids slumbered on their pallets in the corner near the open window. Perhaps the light of the lantern disturbed them, for one tossed and muttered restlessly in her sleep. Eliste froze. Only when the maid had sunk back into quiescence did she resume her careful progress. Through the mud closet she crept, out onto the landing for her first sweet breath of comparatively fresh night air. Her pulses leaped then, and all the old, nearly forgotten sense of forbidden delight came flooding back as she regarded the misted moon, the black sky, the dim expanse of empty lawn and garden. It was a good thing she had brought the lantern. She would need it tonight.

Without troubling to use the steps, she sprang from the landing, came down lightly on the balls of her feet, and set off across the lawn at a trot. A slower pace would have conserved energy, but she had a considerable distance to travel, and dangerously limited time. Through the gap in the hedge she passed, through the rose-perfumed flower gardens, under the arbor, and into the fields. Just once she glanced southwest toward the stable wherein Dref lay imprisoned, then firmly turned her eyes southeast, toward the forested hills, whose darkened bulk she could just barely distinguish by moonlight.

It was a good twenty minutes' trot across the fields to the stand of Derrivalle timber. Despite the long hiatus in nocturnal ramblings, Eliste was scarcely breathing hard by the time she arrived. It would seem that her fondness for riding had kept her in reasonably good condition. Around her towered the tall, straight trunks. Above her spread a canopy of branches, their foliage masking the moon. The weak jouncing light of her lantern provided the sole illumination. Nevertheless, she did not slacken her pace, and soon emerged from the shadows to find herself on the shore of the fish pond, beyond which stood the cottages of the serfs. Ordinarily, those hovels were darkened from sundown to cockcrow. Now rushlights burned in the windows of two of them; it was not difficult to guess whose.

Skirting both pond and cottages, Eliste trotted on. Soon the ground angled sharply upward, and the swift pace became a little difficult to maintain. She had reached the first of the hills, and she was back amidst the trees again, traveling a small but well-remembered path, now choked with brush and weed that braked her progress. When she came to a bend in the trail, where the big moss-covered rock had so often served as her bench, almost she halted at the familiar resting place, but tonight resisted the impulse. On she climbed, the way much steeper now, and her trot slowed to a walk. Over the crest of the first sharp rise, pleasant relief on the downward slope, then up again, along a stone-strewn dried watercourse as far as a small, flat clearing, where further progress was apparently blocked by a sheer cliff of naked featureless rock that rose for a hundred feet or more. Apparently blocked. Eliste knew better. Confidently she moved left along the base of the cliff, until she came to a fungus-bracketed tree stump, among the exposed roots of which lay a flat stone. Eliste pushed the stone aside to reveal a small tile-lined compartment housing a lever of bronze. She pulled the lever once, almost roughly; then back again, very gently; then twice more, back and forth quickly. Replacing the stone, she settled herself on the ground to wait.

She did not have to wait long. Not ten minutes had passed before a small area some fifteen feet up from the base of the cliff began to shimmer with faint phosphorescence that would have been invisible in daylight. Eliste fixed her eyes on the spot, and as she watched, the glow sank slowly to ground level, and the rock itself appeared to simmer like lava. The simmer intensified to a boil, the glow increased, and a figure appeared to step from the stone; whereupon the ghostly light vanished.

Rising, Eliste greeted the apparition with a smile. "Uncle Quinz," she said.

"My dear little girl." His answering smile beamed genuine affection. "It has been too long." He had materialized like a ghost or demon of the night, but it was impossible to imagine him inspiring fear. Quinz vo Derrivalle was slight of build, frail, and short—a little shorter than Eliste herself. He had the pallid bleached skin and the hugely protuberant, colorless eyes of the nocturnal creature that he was. In the low light of the single lantern, he looked pale and fragile as a moth. The monochromatic effect was enhanced by shapeless, loose-hanging garments of twilight gray, and by the nimbus of long, baby-fine, cloud-white hair floating about the narrow face. His brow was high, bulging, and almost unlined; nose long and drolly upturned; beardless chin fine-pointed and delicate; great eyes magnified by thick-lensed, wire-framed spectacles. His outsize ears stuck out sharply, protruding through the weightless mist of white hair, and he possessed the fascinating ability to wiggle either or both at will. His hands were deft and adroit, yet most of his gestures were tentative, even timid. His expression was mild, benign, often a little confused. His age was almost impossible to guess, but one thing was certain—he was older than he looked. "Uncle" Quinz was in fact a younger brother of Eliste's long-deceased paternal great-grandfather.

Throwing both arms around her kinsman, Eliste hugged and kissed him so fervently that Quinz staggered beneath the onslaught. Regaining his balance, he returned the hug with a pleased if bewildered air, then took her hand and began to lead her straight toward the cliff.

"Come, child," Quinz invited. "We shall go back to my cottage, where it is cool and pleasant. We shall drink sweet cider, chat to our hearts' content, and perhaps you may persuade me to play a game of Blue Cat with you."

"Uncle Quinz, I haven't played Blue Cat in years!" Eliste tossed her head. "I'm not a *child*, you know!"

"What, no more Blue Cat? A pity, it is one of my favorites. What about Ring-a-Greebie, then? Ring-a-Greebie is nearly as delightful as Blue Cat."

"Certainly not!"

"Hide the Owl? Blind Boatmen? Gavoozio?"

"Uncle, I am *seventeen years old*!"

"That is gratifying, my dear, but what has it to do with Blue Cat?"

"I can't play baby games anymore. I'm an adult now."

"You are? You are?" Pausing at the very foot of the cliff, Uncle Quinz surveyed her anxiously. "When did that happen? You look much the same to me."

"That's only because I'm not wearing my good clothes. If you saw me in my aquamarine sarcenet, then you'd know I'm all grown up."

"And therefore you cannot play? But how very sad. I am sorry." An alarming thought struck Uncle Quinz. "Does this mean that I, too, am barred from Blue Cat? I do not think that is at all fair."

"No, no, Uncle. You may do as you please, of course."

"Ah, I am relieved. In that case, my dear, let us return, and you shall instruct me in the finer points of the game. To teach is not to play, and therefore you need not suffer the pangs of conscience. . . ." As he spoke, Uncle Quinz extended his left arm, which appeared to sink shoulder-deep into the granite face of the cliff.

Eliste started a little. "I'll never get used to that, no matter how often I see you do it." She pressed her own hand flat to the rock, felt the rough, unyielding contours beneath her palm. "I could swear it's real, it seems so solid. How do you make it feel so hard?"

"Illusion, my child, pure illusion, designed to protect my privacy. I am glad my poor shadows entertain you. But come, close your eyes, and your Uncle Quinz will lead you through safely."

"No, Uncle, not tonight. I didn't come for a visit. I'm here because I need your help."

"My dear little girl, you look quite unhappy. What can I do to restore your pretty smile?"

"Uncle Quinz, a friend of mine—no, not actually a proper friend, just one of the serfs—he's in trouble. More than trouble—real danger. Do you remember a serf named Dref Zeenoson?"

"That clever, so talented lad? Yes, indeed. A remarkable boy, quite astonishing. He is ill?"

"Worse, much worse. Oh, Uncle, Dref's gotten himself into such a mess, his life is over if you don't help him. I mean truly over; he'll be destroyed forever. He hit my father—he must have been mad to do such a thing—he hit the Seigneur, knocked him flat and bloodied his nose. I thought my father would have Dref whipped to death for that. He didn't, but only because he was able to think of something even worse. Dref's to lose his—his tongue, and his right hand."

Quinz's great eyes enlarged, and he made a brushing gesture, as if to repel a prospect too gruesome to contemplate. "Surely not. Surely it cannot be. Was it not but an empty threat, intended to teach the lad a lesson?"

"No, it's real. It's to be done tomorrow morning. Father meant every word. It's unjust, horrible, and so dreadfully"—she groped for the right word, but the one she settled on was simple—"cruel."

"Ah. This makes me sad." Uncle Quinz shook his head, white hair wafting. "My nephew Ubair's son—that is to say, your father—inherited his grandfather's callous heart. When he was a boy, deliberately breeding abnormal mice to produce a race of tiny two-headed monsters, I worried about him. I'd hoped that age might serve to mellow his nature, and yet—alas . . ."

"Uncle Quinz, I came here tonight hoping that you'd help Dref escape. He's locked up in the stable now, with a huge hulk of a blacksmith guarding the door. Alone, there's nothing I can do for him. But you, with your magic, could surely find a way, if you will. Please, Uncle, say you will! Otherwise, tomorrow morning,

Dref's tongue—and—his hand, his *right* hand—will be—he'll be—" She was trying hard to speak calmly, but she was losing the fight. Her throat had closed up like a dirt-clogged rainspout, and the words could barely emerge. Her face crumpled, her eyes burned, and the tears gushed forth.

"Oh, please don't cry, child," Uncle Quinz begged. He patted her shoulder, stroked her hair clumsily, and fidgeted. "Please don't. We'll help the boy, the two of us. He'll not be harmed, I promise. I'll deal with the blacksmith, and we'll have your young friend out of that stable this very night. Please believe that, my poor little dear, and don't be sad anymore, or I'll start crying, too." The huge eyes behind the thick lenses were indeed starting to fill.

Her muted sobs subsided to sniffles. She wiped her eyes on the sleeve of her shirt, swallowed hard, and managed to whisper, "Thank you. Bless you, Uncle Quinz."

His face reddened, and he answered hastily, "Pooh, child, no need to thank me before I've done anything. And if we're to do anything tonight, then we had best begin, had we not? It is a long walk to that stable, and I am no longer spry as I once was. Come, my dear, there is no time to lose. Let us be off. And try to smile, please do—all will be well, and we are having an adventure!" There was only enough time to snatch up the lantern before he reclaimed her hand and hurried her off down the path.

"Couldn't you just use your magic to fly us there or something?" Eliste inquired as they stumbled down the steep stony trail.

"How delightful that would be! But I am sorry to confess that your old uncle is not nearly so clever. I can but produce illusions—or sometimes, if it is there, detect and cultivate the buried consciousness in creatures and objects. But, child, no one can break the law of Nature that prohibits Man from flying."

"If it's a law, then what about those new balloons?"

"Those what?"

"Balloons, Uncle Quinz. Big, brightly colored ones filled with hot air. If the balloon is big enough, it can lift a basket carrying people, and then—it flies."

"You don't mean it!" He stared at her, entranced. "Now, *that* is magical! I am overwhelmed! But how exciting, how wonderful, how truly extraordinary! My dear, it is hard to believe. Balloons! Are you *sure*?"

"Yes, I've spoken to people who have seen them."

"Oh, how I wish I could see one too! Brightly colored, you say? How lovely. What a glorious spectacle it must be! And to think I never knew! Alas, isolated as I am, I miss a great deal. Truly, the world has passed me by."

"Oh, Uncle, if that's the way you feel, then why don't you come visit us more often? Or better yet, why don't you come down to Derrivalle and live with us? Everyone would love to have you there."

Smiling, he shook his head. "Dear little girl, I could not do that. How should I study, how should I practice my art at Derrivalle? The distractions would destroy my concentration. The noise, the bustle, the comings and goings—no, I could not work there. It is only in solitude, in a quiet rustic retreat, alone and undisturbed, that I may hope to achieve the serenity that my work demands. I must be alone and at peace."

"It doesn't sound very lively. Aren't you lonely?"

"Sometimes," he admitted. "Sometimes. But it is the only way."

"Have you always lived like this?"

"Oh, not always, child. A very long time ago, when I was a lad, I lived in the Derrivalle manor, as you do now. There was companionship, affection, pleasure, and luxury—I still remember. But I discovered at an early age that I possessed certain mental abilities peculiar to some Exalted. I discovered, too, that the development of those abilities meant more to me than anything else in the world. And I also learned that incessant practice, combined with a life of self-denial, are required to develop them. Therefore, when I was seven years old, I was sent to Bozhenille Commune, in the Aussadie, where a band of Exalted masters had founded a settlement in the hills. There they had gathered to practice, to learn, and to pass on their knowledge to children of proven ability. It was not an easy life there," Uncle Quinz remembered. "The work was demanding, and the masters— oh, some of them were quite terrifying. I had to sleep on the floor, when I was used to a feather bed, and eat nothing but brown bread and vegetables, when I longed for chicken and cream cakes. The dormitories were unheated, and there was no hot water. I had to rise at four in the morning, work in the kitchen or gardens until ten, eat, and then take lessons until suppertime. In the evening, a couple of hours were set aside for study, and then it was bedtime. Anyone caught talking during study hours was locked in the woodshed all night long, and anyone caught with a light after curfew was whipped. It happened to me once, when they found me reading in the privy at midnight, and once was enough to teach me my lesson. Master vo Nilaiste thrashed me so soundly, I wasn't able to sit down for a week. And I never dared break those rules again."

"Uncle Quinz, it sounds perfectly odious! Didn't you hate it there? Weren't you homesick?"

"Very much so, in the beginning. For the first four months, I cried myself to sleep every night."

"Oh, and you were so young! How could they treat little children that way? Why did the parents allow it?"

"The parents had consented to grant the masters free hand. In any case, those harsh practices were designed to teach the discipline and self-denial essential to the art. Indeed, they were intentionally difficult lessons, meant to weed out all but the most dedicated of scholars, and in this they were effective. Fully a third of the students returned to their homes before the end of the first quarter."

"Well, I should think so. *I* would never have submitted to a beating—never. I'd have burned the house down first. And if they tried to lock me up, I'd have run away."

"I thought of running away, many times. Once I even went so far as to pack my belongings in a sack. But each time I was tempted, I thought of the art I was learning—the abilities I was developing, the illusions and sentient Inanimates, and all the rest—all the knowledge that I'd be giving up if I fled that place. For mind you, there was nowhere else I could have learned so much. I'd think of that, and the urge to run would fade away. In the end, I chose to stay. And do you know, once I'd really decided that, the harshness and privation somehow became much easier to bear. I stayed at Bozhenille for fifteen years."

"And never came home in all that time?"

"Well, once a year for a two-week holiday. But after the first few years, I didn't enjoy the visits. I no longer had anything in common with parents or siblings, who, for reasons I cannot fathom to this day, regarded me as an oddity. Conversation was difficult, and I could not feel that Derrivalle was truly my home. It was always with mixed sadness and relief that I would return to the Commune. At the end of fifteen years," Uncle Quinz continued, "I had learned everything the masters of Bozhenille had to teach. At that point I might have remained at the Commune as a master myself; or I might have taken my place in the world as an Exalted vo Derrivalle. Instead, I chose to renounce the society of men for the sake of my art. Perhaps it was a wickedly selfish act, but then again, perhaps not. There are so few these days willing to accept the restrictions that our discipline demands—so few left to guard and to build upon the old knowledge. I should like to believe that my discoveries possess value. In any event, wicked or no, I have never regretted my choice."

"Why, Uncle, I think it was a noble choice," Eliste told him.

"Do you truly, my dear?" He seemed reassured.

"Of course. But how is it that you never told me this interesting story before, and you're telling me now? Oh, I see what you're up to. You're trying to keep my mind off my worries."

"Ah, clever child, you are far too sharp for your uncle."

"That will be the day. I'm glad you're contented, Uncle Quinz. All the same," Eliste decided, "it doesn't sound like much fun to *me,* and I'm glad that I never had any magic."

"Actually, you cannot be certain you have none. It is present in our family, and you might, in fact, discover a certain hidden talent, should you ever care to search for it. Think, my dear, how like a treasure hunt! I would be happy to assist."

"Oh, no! No, thank you, I want none of it. I'm finished with lessons, and study, and all such dreary stuff. I want excitement, I want something new, I want some fun."

"Ah, to me Blue Cat is fun. But what is fun for you?"

"Sherreen will be, I know it! I'm going next week, you remember. I'm to be a Maid of Honor to the Queen. Think of it—only another few days, and then I'll be at Court!"

"I have never seen the Court," Uncle Quinz observed mildly. "What will you find there, my dear?"

"Everything in the whole world, Uncle. There'll be famous people from the great families, music and dancing, plays and puppet shows, games and hunting, parties and picnics, suppers, masquerades, the most wonderful clothes and jewelry, no end of things to see and do. It's where everyone alive wants to be."

"Everyone?"

"Well, everyone who can, of course. Everyone who wants to be at the center of things."

"What things?"

"New things, exciting things, all the best in life."

"You make it sound very splendid, my dear. I hope it fulfills all your expectations. But I shall miss you."

"I'll miss you too, Uncle. But don't be unhappy—it isn't as if I'm off to Bozhenille Commune for fifteen years. When the weather's good, Sherreen is only six days from here by coach. I'll be back to Derrivalle several times a year, and I'll visit you often."

"I must console myself with that, then. In the meantime, my dear, you might tell me more of your impending journey."

Eliste obliged, treating her kinsman to an exhaustive description of her plans, her hopes, her doubts, and the wardrobe she intended to carry to Sherreen. The subject was absorbing, and she spoke at length, with enthusiasm, all fear for Dref Zeenoson momentarily dismissed from her mind. As far as Eliste was concerned, Dref's escape was all but accomplished, his safety assured from the moment that Uncle Quinz had agreed to help. Innocent and absentminded though he seemed, Uncle Quinz somehow managed to get things done, and his intervention was invariably effective. Never, throughout her entire life, had she known Quinz vo Derrivalle to make a promise he couldn't keep; and he had promised now. Thus she was still burbling on about Sherreen when they broke from the cover of the trees to emerge onto level ground; chattering still as they made their way around the fish pond and through the trees; and still as they struck off across the fields, heading west toward the vineyards and outbuildings. Uncle Quinz listened with every appearance of wondering interest. It was not until they neared the carriage house, behind which lay the stables, that he lifted a cautionary finger to his lips. Her conversation cut off at once. In silence they edged along the south face of the building, pausing at the corner to peer warily around the wall.

The moon was now low in the sky, but the obscuring veils of mist had thinned. A stone's throw distant loomed the dark rectangular mass of the stables. Borlo Bunison sat there on the ground, back propped against the closed door, heavy staff lying across his knees, head sunk on his breast. He was asleep, his large body blocking the sole entrance.

"The blacksmith," Uncle Quinz observed in the smallest of whispers. "A healthy specimen, to be sure. What admirable muscular development!"

"The brute's enormous. How shall we get past him?"

"I shall cast a glamor. You must not be alarmed. Promise?" Eliste nodded, and Uncle Quinz touched her cheek approvingly. "My brave girl." Folding his arms, he bowed his head and stood motionless.

Eliste watched with curiosity. Uncle Quinz's tricks were wonderfully entertaining. Which would it be this time? The Singing Cloud he'd done for her birthday last year? Fire Flowers? The Phantom Giraffe? Interest sharpened to uneasiness as the seconds passed and he did not move. Usually the magic was prompt. Was Uncle Quinz experiencing difficulty—perhaps even losing his knack, just now, when it was most needed? She was on the verge of asking when he began to speak: a low, muttering, repetitive chant, all of it gibberish, as far as she could tell. His voice was peculiar—deeper and more authoritative than she had ever heard it. His breathing was deep and controlled, his expression so remote, so uncharacteristic, that for a moment it almost seemed a stern-faced stranger standing there. Eliste stared at him, perplexed; and as she stared, she thought that his aspect altered. Or perhaps it was the air about him that was changing, thickening and swirling, teasing her vision. Squinting, she rubbed her eyes, but her sight failed to clear. Or rather, her mind failed to clear; for she was vaguely aware that it was her perceptions and her understanding that Uncle Quinz's magic had truly mischiefed. Her eyes were irrelevant; he had somehow infiltrated her consciousness. Love and trust him though she did, her instinct was to resist; instinct notwithstanding, she had no notion of mental self-defense. And even as she watched her kinsman, his familiar short figure faded from view. Eliste gasped, and the lantern dropped from her hand. Her uncle was gone, and in his place stood a gigantic wolf, far larger than any natural wolf that ever lived. The creature's luxuriant fur was twilight gray, the long guard hairs on ruff and chest tipped with white, muzzle and prick ears beautifully penciled with darker markings. The pale eyes were huge and greenly phosphorescent.

It's Uncle Quinz, Eliste inwardly insisted. She was breathing hard, heart sprinting, every muscle tensed and ready to run. *Only Uncle Quinz. He told me not to be frightened, and I promised.* Given a little time, she would have succeeded in calming herself. But there was no time, for more alarming transformations were in progress. Eliste felt herself changing. Her body bent, legs curving impossibly, arms lengthening, jaw expanding, teeth and fingernails thrusting. Her insides convulsed momentarily. She sensed the painless distortion of bone, joints, and muscle; the shift of contour, expansion of ear and coccyx, wavelike spread of thick honey fur. And then her point of view dropped, and the ground was close. The claws of her four feet dug into the soil, and she felt the balanced weight of a long furry tail, the quiver of sensitive nostrils, the cooling play of air upon a long lolling tongue. Terrified, she felt her ears flatten, her lips wrinkle, and her back arch, hair bristling along the spine. Her cry of alarm was translated to a keening lupine whine.

"Calm yourself, my poor little girl." Somehow Uncle Quinz's voice issued from the gray wolf's mouth. "There is nothing to fear, child."

"What has happened to me?" She heard wolfish whimpers and her own voice, simultaneously. The sound was bewildering as it was fearful, and her tail clamped down hard between her hind legs.

"Nothing, my dear. You are absolutely unchanged, and so am I. It is not real."

"It is so! Change me back!"

"Child, there is nothing to change. Trust your uncle, and do not fear illusions. Now come, take up your lantern and let us proceed."

His confidence quelled her rising panic. Without thought she responded to the authority in his voice, automatically stretching forth her right front paw as if it were still a hand with which she might grasp the fallen lantern. Her confusion deepened as she felt her fingers close upon the cord-wrapped ring. At the moment of contact, she beheld a ghostly image of her own hand, superimposed upon the wolf's paw. The image faded, and only the paw remained. Thoroughly confounded, she extended her muzzle to take the ring in her mouth.

A series of muffled yelps escaped the gray wolf. "Forgive my laughter, child, but you are a rather comical sight," said Uncle Quinz. "Wouldn't you prefer to carry the lantern in your hand, my dear?"

Her muzzle heated, and she knew she must be blushing. Hastily she transferred the burden back to her right front paw.

"There, that is better, is it not? Now come, follow me, do exactly as I do, and we shall soon be rid of the blacksmith fellow. Is it not thrilling? What an exciting excursion this is!"

Lips spread and tongue protruding slightly in the lupine equivalent of a smile, Uncle Quinz loped off across the stable yard, with Eliste trotting close at his side. Unconscious of their approach, Borlo Bunison slept on. Uncle and niece halted some ten feet from the blacksmith. For a few seconds they stood watching him, their heads cocked at identical angles, ears canted forward, greenish eyes alight. Then Uncle Quinz commanded sharply, "Wake up, fellow! Borlo Bunison, away with you this instant!" Eliste could distinguish the words without difficulty, despite the overlay of wolfish growls.

Borlo Bunison's lids lifted. He beheld the two giant wolves, and at once he was fully awake. His eyes bulged, and his hands tightened on his sole weapon, the staff. For a few moments he sat paralyzed and staring. Then, very softly, he rose to his feet, and without turning his head, began to fumble at the iron latch on the door behind him.

"Stop that," Uncle Quinz commanded. *"Leave it alone!"*

Borlo heard only a blood-curdling snarl, which froze him where he stood. Uncle Quinz's head was down, his hackles up. His lips writhed back to expose yellowish fangs. The breathless moments passed, while man and illusory beasts stood motionless. And then, unobtrusively, Borlo's fingers crept once more across the latch.

"Don't touch it!" Eliste exclaimed. "I'll bite you, Borlo!" She was startled, almost alarmed by the ferocity of her own growls. "Go away—get out of here now, you unspeakable pig! *GO!*" As she howled the last syllable, flecks of foam sprayed her contorted muzzle.

"Good, child!" Uncle Quinz muttered. "First-rate!"

Borlo could not have understood the words, but the sentiments communicated themselves. His shaking hand dropped from the latch, and the snarls ceased at once. Sinking back on their haunches, the two creatures regarded him expectantly. For a time Borlo stayed where he was, long staff defensively poised. Nothing happened, and at last, very gradually he began to sidle away. The wolves sat watching him go. Borlo's pace increased. Reaching the corner of the building, he ducked around the wall, turned tail, and and fled for his life.

"Ha!" yipped Eliste. "Look at him run!"

"Very gratifying, my dear, but he will probably be back soon with reinforcements. We've little time to spare."

"Oh—you're right, let's hurry." Bounding forward, Eliste pawed and scratched at the stable door, without result. She nosed the latch, then gnawed uselessly, whining her frustration.

"Child, you are perhaps a trifle confused." Stretching forth his right forepaw, Uncle Quinz effortlessly unfastened the latch and pulled the big door open. Once again, Eliste thought to glimpse a shadowy, transparent human hand briefly superimposed upon the lupine appendage. "In you go."

"Wait." She turned to face him. "Change us both back, Uncle Quinz. Otherwise, we'll scare the life out of Dref, not to mention the horses."

"Ah, very considerate. Although the horses would not be deceived." Eyes narrowed to almost-sleepy slits, the gray wolf spoke softly. The long hackles smoothed themselves, the ears twitched, and the twilight fur seemed to soften to fog, before the animal faded completely from view. And there was Uncle Quinz again, mild and amiable as ever. At the same time, Eliste felt herself changing, inside and out. Her true physical being reasserted itself abruptly as air rushing in to fill a vacuum, and she found herself once more human, whole and healthy, the lighted lantern still clasped in one hand.

"Oh," said Eliste. "Oh."

"Come, child, no time to lose."

They slipped into the stable, closing the door behind them, and instantly Eliste was enveloped in the rich odors of horse, hay, sweat, dung, leather, and saddle soap that always filled the place. Before her stretched the long cobbled aisle lined with stalls housing the Marquis vo Derrivalle's prized horseflesh. Many of the animals had awakened at the opening of the door, and a number of shapely heads now poked inquiringly out into the aisle. Eliste's gaze jumped to the stall of her own pet mare Hussy, but no starred chestnut face was visible now. Hussy still slept, her unseen presence betrayed by the occasional snuffling exhalation. Eliste had never been in the stable at night before. The silence, the shadows, and the weak orange light of the single lantern glancing off wide equine eyes lent mystery to an otherwise familiar scene. Even Uncle Quinz seemed somewhat affected, for his voice was bemused as he inquired, "And where have they hidden the lad, my dear?"

"Softly," Eliste admonished in a whisper. "Some of the grooms sleep in the haymow above. This way, I think." Tiptoeing with exaggerated stealth, she led her uncle to the back of the building, whose rear wall was faced with storage bins, racks, and one stout windowless tack closet, firmly shut. Pulling the heavy bolt, she opened the closet, and lantern light spilled in to illuminate the reclining occupant. A dismayed gasp escaped her.

Dref looked ghastly. His face, a dreadful mass of cuts and purple bruises, was streaked with sweat and dried blood. Both eyes had been blacked, and one was swollen nearly shut. Also swollen were his lips—puffed, split, and dark with caked blood. His nose had providentially escaped breakage, but it was unlikely that all his bones had fared so well. As he raised himself to a sitting position, he moved with evident pain. Bracing himself against the wall, he pressed one hand to his side. The other went up to shield his eyes against the orange dazzle of lamplight.

"Already?" he muttered.

"Dref, don't you know us?" Eliste whispered, terrified.

"Eliste?" He squinted against the light. "Master Quinz?"

"Quite right, lad," replied Uncle Quinz. "We have come to deliver you. Such an adventure!"

"The Seigneur—?"

"Dref, don't try to speak," Eliste directed, breathing an inward sigh of relief. He was neither blind nor altogether dazed, as she had initially feared.

"Here, drink this." She proffered the carafe of tea. He gulped it down, almost desperately. When the vessel was empty, she told him the worst. "My father has ordered your mutilation in the morning."

"Typical."

"Be quiet. We are going to take you out of here right now, but we must hurry. The blacksmith and his louts may be back any moment. Can you stand? Anything broken?"

"Borlo has cracked my rib, I believe."

"Lean on me." He obeyed, and she helped him to his feet. He rose with a hiss of sharply indrawn breath, to stand swaying and dizzy. Uncle Quinz offered a supportive shoulder and the three of them proceeded haltingly along the aisle, under the inquisitive eyes of the horses, back to the exit and out, latching the stable door behind them.

Once out of doors, Dref's head cleared. He breathed deeply of the fresh night air, and his step steadied. They increased their pace then, bundling the fugitive around the carriage house and out across the fields within seconds. Eliste cast a quick glance back over her shoulder. She saw no lights and heard no voices as yet, but surely Dref's escape would be discovered long before morning. And what then? No doubt the affronted Marquis vo Derrivalle would order the erring Borlo Bunison soundly whipped. So much the better. And what would happen, it occurred to her for the first time to wonder, if the complicity of the Seigneur's only daughter were to be discovered? Of course, she would be protected; her unworthy, irresponsible disobedience would be carefully concealed, in order to preserve her matrimonial marketability. But the Marquis would be furious, and she would surely feel the weight of his wrath. Would he go so far as to cancel her impending trip to Sherreen, even to his own ultimate disadvantage? He might indeed be that angry. Beyond question, she would be severely punished, if the Marquis vo Derrivalle found her out. He must never find out. She fought the urge to break into a run.

Eliste glanced briefly at her companions. Uncle Quinz was a little winded and breathing hard; judging by his exhilarated expression, excitement seemed the likeliest cause. Dref's shortened strides were uneven. He was limping slightly, and one hand remained pressed to his ribs. Facial bruises and swelling completely masked his expression, if any.

Around them stretched the cultivated fields, plowed soil soft underfoot, vegetation neat and low—a broad moonlit expanse whose open sweep left them perilously exposed. But straight ahead rose the timber stand, its dense shadow offering temporary cover. They hastened across those last few yards at a pace approaching a run. Only when they had reached the inadequate shelter of the trees did they dare to pause.

"Where shall we put him, Uncle Quinz?" Eliste inquired, as if weighing the fate of a stray dog. "Your house? For tonight, at least?"

"Certainly the lad is welcome," replied Uncle Quinz. "He may stay as long as necessary."

"Oh, that is perfect. They'll never find him there, not if they search for months." She turned to the fugitive. "Did you hear that, Dref? Right now we're taking you to——"

"No," said Dref. "I will leave Derrivalle tonight."

"Don't be absurd. You can't leave, you can barely walk. Tonight you'll go to Uncle Quinz's cottage, rest and recover there. While you are mending, I'll persuade my father to pardon you, or at the very least, to reduce your sentence, and then you'll return. If by chance I should fail with the Seigneur, we'll consider your departure at some future date. Don't worry, I've money for you in this bag, should you actually need to go. There's food in there, too. But tonight you shall not consider——"

"Eliste. Stop," Dref advised. His swollen lips formed words with some difficulty. It was obviously painful for him to speak, but his manner was equable, even a little amused. "In the first place, I am quite capable of walking, or running, as required. In the second, your chances of persuading his Lordship to reduce my sentence are virtually nil. If I'm to survive unmaimed, I must leave at once. I know that, and you know it, too. Otherwise, why would you have brought me food and money tonight? For which, by the way, I thank you." Removing his hand from his ribs with reluctance, Dref reached out and slid the strap from her shoulder, taking possession of the canvas satchel.

"I gave you no leave to take that!"

"I beg your pardon, Miss. I thought you had brought it for me. Shall I return it?"

"That impudent tongue got you into this pickle. If you were one-tenth as clever as you think you are, you'd have learned when to hold it. You madman, why did you speak that way to my father? What made you do it?"

Dref considered. "Pure spleen," he decided.

"Idiot! Be serious for once. You cannot go. It is a foolish thought, impractical and—and illegal. You are a serf, legally bound to the Derrivalle soil. That's the law, and there are sound reasons for it."

"Sound indeed, from the Exalted viewpoint, but let us descend to more mundane considerations," Dref suggested. "By morning, the Seigneur will raise all the countryside against me. My description will be posted in every tavern and market square in the district, and I'll never dare show my face. But if I run at once—tonight—the way is still comparatively clear, and will continue so for some hours. It's the best chance I'm like to have. As I don't fancy vivisection, I plan to take it."

"But where would you go, what would you do?"

"Go? Anywhere I please. There's an entire world waiting," Dref replied, and now his listeners caught the leashed excitement vibrating beneath the cool exterior. "Do? Again, exactly as I please. I am not without talent, and I'll find a way of putting it to good use at last. They say the New Reasoning has heated Sherreen to the boil these days. Perhaps I'll see that for myself. If I cut straight across the hills and walk all night, I might pick up the morning stage on the King's Highway."

"Lunacy!" opined Eliste, startled as if a supposedly broken-winged hawk had suddenly taken to the air. "What about your cracked rib?"

"I'll have it taped when I can."

"That is not satisfactory! You shall not go, because—because—"

"Because—?"

"Because *I do not wish it!*"

"Little Elli." His battered smile expressed amused affection. "I'll miss you."

"Miss me—?" For the first time she realized that he was truly going, and when he went, she would never see him again. The thought was remarkably disturbing, almost shocking. She could barely keep from grabbing his arm. "No, wait. This is impossible. I order you to stay. You will resent my decision, but it is for your own good."

He started to laugh, then winced and ceased abruptly, hand pressed tight to his ribs. "Perhaps you shouldn't have unlocked that stable door. But your innate decency got the better of you this time."

" 'This time'? And what is *that* supposed to mean?"

"That I'm grateful for what you've done tonight." Dref turned to Uncle Quinz. "And I thank you, sir. The two of you have truly given me my life."

"Ah, it has been a delightful excursion, lad. Would you care to take the lantern with you?"

"No, sir, I'm better without. And now, I'm off. Eliste, good-bye. I'll not forget you. Come, don't scowl like that. Will you shake hands?"

Shake hands with a serf? So taken by surprise was she that his unbelievable presumption went unreproved. Without thinking, she extended her hand, which he took in his own and pressed once.

"Thank you, little Elli. Good-bye." He released her hand, which she now regarded with an air of amazement. Swiveling on his heel, he hurried away without a backward glance.

"Good luck, Dref," she called after him. She could not tell whether he heard.

For a couple of minutes she watched as he made his way around the moonlit fish pond, circling wide to avoid the cottages on the far side. The dim light barely served to inform her that his strides were uneven but swift, and his limp minimal. A moment later, he rounded the angle of the nearest cottage, and his tall form vanished from sight. Eliste turned to her uncle. "He's—gone," she observed stupidly.

"Indeed, dear child, our mission is accomplished! Are you not happy?"

"I suppose so." In reality, she was feeling tremendously let down, almost desolate. When she had made her plans, hours earlier, she had anticipated the triumph of Dref's release from the stable. Her imagination, however, had not carried her on to the inevitable sequel—his permanent departure from Derrivalle and from her life. "Do you think he'll be all right?"

"He's a resourceful lad. We may hope for the best."

"Yes. Well. I guess—that's that."

"Excellent. And in celebration of our success, my dear, may I not prevail upon you to come back to my cottage for a glass of cider and a game of Blue Cat?"

"Not tonight, Uncle Quinz. It's very late, I'm awfully tired, and I'd better return to my room before I'm missed. Another time, I promise."

"Whatever you think best, my dear. You *do* look tired, and rather sad. You're not ill?"

"No. I'll be fine. Uncle, I'd like to thank you for all your help tonight. You were wonderful."

"It was truly my pleasure, child. So thrilling it has been! Should you ever require assistance in your future illicit ventures, do not hesitate to call on your Uncle Quinz!"

ref's disappearance caused a sensation. No serf had ever successfully fled the Derrivalle estate. No fugitive had ever remained at liberty for longer than a week. Generally they returned of their own accord—defeated, chastened, and justly terrified of the Seigneur's wrath. The more stubborn cases were delivered by wagon like trussed-up parcels—the lucky ones. Less fortunate offenders ran behind their captors' horses, or else they were dragged. Four years earlier, the Marquis had purchased a brace of hounds whose near-supernatural tracking ability inspired a healthy terror. Since then, no one had dared attempt flight—until now. Dref Zeenoson's incentive was considerable, and his resourcefulness proverbial; no doubt he'd give the hounds a good run. The more enterprising among the house servants were already taking odds on the sortie's duration. The most enthusiastic partisans gave Dref a full week of freedom; but such was the esteem in which the escapee was held that no one bet on anything less than three days.

The odds changed abruptly when it became known that the dogs had followed a cold trail as far as the King's Highway, where they lost the scent once and for all. The most likely explanation involved the fugitive's use of wheeled transportation; but the means whereby he had procured such remained mysterious. No farm wagon would have carried him out of the district; no private carriage would have paused for a shabby pedestrian; and the Sherreen stage would not have taken him on unless he could pay. Fresh from his stable-prison, Dref surely carried no money, and would have had access to none; in which case, his apparent discorporation at the side of the road partook of the miraculous. The admiration of the serfs rose accordingly. As the days passed and the fugitive remained at large, new hope was born, and whispered conversation centered upon the previously unthinkable: that Dref Zeenoson would evade capture altogether—that Dref Zeenoson was free. It was the stuff of which legends were made.

The Marquis vo Derrivalle failed to share in the burgeoning enthusiasm. Thwarted and flouted, the Seigneur turned his anger upon the nearest and most obvious culprit—Borlo Bunison, whose job it had been to guard the prisoner Zeenoson throughout the night. Borlo was sent for and questioned, whereupon the wretched smith recounted a ridiculous tale. It seemed that giant wolves with fiery eyes had chased him from his sentry post. He had only just managed to escape with his life. Never mind the fact that wolves commonly held to the high ground, seldom venturing from the hills save in winters of direst famine. Never mind the fact that no wolf of any description, much less giant, had been seen upon Derrivalle land in years; or that wolves were retiring beasts, ordinarily disinclined to confront human beings. Never mind all of that—Borlo clung doggedly to his silly story, thus casting much doubt upon his own veracity, sobriety, and sanity. For it became clear, in the face of rigorous interrogation, that he genuinely believed in his tale's truth. Following his flight from the stable, he had roused the coachman, sleeping in the carriage house, with demands for assistance. The coachman, compliant enough, had of course seen nothing; but the incident itself seemed to verify the strength of the smith's convictions, if nothing more. A swift search of the area had revealed no wolves, and Borlo, armed with the coachman's borrowed pistol, had returned to his abandoned post. Never intellectually inclined, the smith did not think to check on the prisoner, and Dref Zeenoson's flight was not discovered until the next morning.

Liar, lunatic, or simple drunkard, the bungler was going to pay. Punishment was promptly administered by the Seigneur himself, and for once Borlo Bunison stood on the wrong side of the whip. The smith endured half a dozen quick strokes of a handy riding crop before he was permitted to depart in disgrace. Borlo's debt had been paid, but the Marquis was far from appeased. For days, his search parties combed the district. Notices and descriptions were posted in every village for miles around, and a small reward was offered for the return of the runaway serf. All to no avail. No one had so much as glimpsed the fugitive in passing. Dref Zeenoson had vanished into thin air.

And along with Dref vanished his sister, or so it initially appeared. The morning following Zhen Suboson's death and Dref's escape, Eliste awoke to find her rooms silent and untended. The music box whose notes ordinarily roused her from slumber had not been wound. The requisite goblet of chilled fruit juice was absent from its usual place on the stand beside her bed. Her clothes had not been laid out, and Prince vo Plume had not been fed. It really would not do. Frowning, she rose, stalked to the closet housing Stelli's pallet, and rapped imperiously. No response from within, and she kicked open the door. The closet was empty. Stelli's meager possessions were gone. Seriously annoyed now, Eliste yanked the bellpull hard. Minutes later, one of the housemaids answered the summons, to furnish the assistance her young mistress required in dressing. Eliste asked after Stelli, and learned that the maid had been seen leaving the manor house, sack upon her back, at the break of dawn.

Had the girl followed in Dref's footsteps? Reluctant to draw the matter to the Marquis's attention, Eliste made discreet inquiries among the house servants. Hours later she discovered that Stelli Zeenosgirl had been spotted entering her father Zeeno's cottage early in the morning. So the stupid, irresponsible wench had simply cleared off, without notice, without permission, and without the slightest consideration of her masters' needs. She would rather sulk in a hovel than serve in the manor house as a lady's maid? Very well, good riddance. It would be easy enough to drag her back, but best let her stay where she was. She might grub in the fields until her hands were raw and her stiff-spined back was breaking, if that's what she wanted, and it would serve her right. She didn't know when she was well off, she was an ungrateful fool, and she'd always been a wretched maid. Moreover, her voluntary departure simplified matters—there would be no awkwardness involved in finding a replacement.

For some days past, Eliste had had her eye on little Kairthe, the dairymaid, and now she summoned the child for a brief interview. Well, perhaps not quite a child—Kairthe was all of fifteen, healthy and well-grown—but her round freckled face, tiny snub nose, and wide blue eyes lent her an infantile air. She was medium-size and slender—useful in that she might easily stand in for her new mistress during dress fittings—and her braided hair, pinned into a neat coronet, was a shade of honey not unlike Eliste's own. Best of all, the girl was nothing like Stelli. Her manner was respectful but vivacious. She moved lightly, her voice was soft, and her blue eyes rested on the Marquis's daughter with an expression of undisguised, uncomplicated admiration. It was so agreeable that Eliste engaged her upon the spot.

She soon discovered that she had stumbled upon a treasure. Dazzled by the glory of her sudden ascent from dairy to manor house, Kairthe seemed to have made some secret vow to be the best maidservant the world had ever seen—and it was likely she'd succeed, before long. True, she was inexperienced, unaccustomed to dealing with the complexity of ruffles and ruchings, ignorant of lace-mending techniques, sometimes a little confused between morning and afternoon dress. But she was hardworking, sunny-natured, quick to learn, and more important, eager to learn. She had a clever eye for color and form, very useful in coordinating accessories; she possessed a natural, magical ability to coax her new mistress's long tresses into the most flattering puffs and curls; and she knew how to beguile the temperamental Prince vo Plume.

There was still a lot of packing left, and not much time. Kairthe threw herself into the task, accomplishing more in three days than Stelli had managed in the preceding three weeks. Never had packing been managed so deftly. Kairthe handled Eliste's possessions with care amounting to reverence, wrapping each article in tissue paper prior to careful storage. Before the week was out, the heaped garments had disappeared from armchairs and window seat. Mending and cleaning were perfectly completed. The boxes and trunks scattered about the bedchamber were filled with meticulously wrapped packages, each coded with colored string, according to Kairthe's own system, with scented sachets embedded between the layers. Jewelry was polished and packed away in quilted satin rolls. Flagons of perfume, stoppered crystal vials, powder jars, hand mirrors, and similar breakables nested safe in their own straw-lined crate. It was done beautifully, and Kairthe finished it all with time to spare. So excellent was her work, and so pleasant her company, that Eliste soon forgot that the hostile, defiant presence known as Stelli Zeenosgirl had ever existed to trouble her.

During that time, Eliste remained alert to all mention of Dref Zeenoson's name. At first she expected to hear of his recapture; but the hours passed, then the days, and no such news reached her. Gradually, her uneasiness began to subside. Fortunately, no one thought to connect Borlo Bunison's idiot tale of wolves with the magical illusions of which Uncle Quinz was a known master. Quinz vo Derrivalle was so retiring, his demeanor so mildly innocent, his visits to the estate so infrequent, that even his family members tended to overlook his existence. In any event, what possible reason might Quinz vo Derrivalle have to interfere with the Marquis's administration of justice? Fortunately again—very fortunately— Eliste's involvement in the affair went unproved, if not altogether unsuspected. Her father interrogated her only once, but at some length. For the space of an endless hour and a half, she sat as if nailed to a chair in his study, while he plied her with question after question. She responded blandly and fluently, inwardly praying that her schooled composure masked the sickening uneasiness that roiled at the pit of her stomach. She sensed that he did not quite believe her; but he extracted no confession, and no shred of evidence existed to implicate her. At last the Marquis professed his grudging satisfaction, and Eliste was permitted to depart. Thankfully, she fled the study. She was safe.

The week galloped by, and then it was time to go. Eliste's departure was a fairly great occasion, with parents, visiting cousins, a couple of maiden aunts, and assorted servants assembled at the great front entrance to see her off at dawn. There on the white-graveled drive that circled before the broad stone stairway waited the second-best carriage, which was to carry her all the way to Sherreen. Second best or no, the big berlin was imposing, with shining, freshly varnished sides, scarlet trim, polished brass studs, and the Derrivalle arms blazoned on the door. The rack on the roof was piled high with her baggage, neatly strapped and buckled. The coachman sat on the double perch, scarlet reins and whip in hand. The four matched grays, eager to be off, stamped and fretted. Long before the journey was over, their eagerness would wane. Beside the coachman sat one of the stoutest of the footmen, attired in the midnight-green Derrivalle livery, and conspicuously armed.

Adieux were formal and scarcely heartfelt. Eliste cared little for her vaporing, self-absorbed mother, and vice versa. The aunts and cousins were almost strangers. The servants were for the most part pleasant, self-effacing nonentities—which was all that they were permitted to be. She had already bid a fond farewell to the one family member she cared about, Uncle Quinz; and the only other person who mattered was gone for good. There remained her father, whose sense of propriety now dictated a display of moderate paternal devotion. Following a tedious but mercifully brief spate of advice and instructions, the Marquis handed his daughter down the broad stone stairway, led her to the carriage, bent his head to kiss her lightly, once on each cheek. The unwelcome contact chilled her. Into her mind, quite unexpectedly, popped the vivid image of her own prettily buffed pink fingernails raking across the Marquis's fair, indifferent face to draw blood. Now, where had that come from, and why? A rush of revulsion followed. To save her life, Eliste could not have returned those empty kisses. Arranging her features into a dutiful smile, she swept her father a low curtsey and quickly entered the carriage. Behind her came Kairthe, carrying Prince vo Plume under her right arm. In her left hand the maid bore a hamper containing food, drink, games, puzzles, lap desk with writing and sketching supplies, embroidery hoop and silks, books, poems, and anything else likely to ease the tedium of a long journey.

One of the footmen folded up the stair and closed the door behind Kairthe. It shut with a final-sounding snap. A last chorus of farewells, a flutter of waving handkerchiefs, a crack of the coachman's whip, creaks and rattles, and they were off at a trot. With a yap of ecstasy, Prince vo Plume exploded from Kairthe's grasp to fling himself crazily from seat to seat, fast and unpredictable as furry shrapnel; then, initial hysteria subsiding, he jumped into his mistress's lap, reared up, and thrust his silky white head out the window. Eliste followed suit. Behind her, a knot of relatives and retainers stood waving. Her parents, she noted, had already disappeared. She waved once, then withdrew and did not look back again.

At first it seemed a great thing, to be traveling to Sherreen, all grown up and on her own for the first time. Here she was, mistress of the family's second-best conveyance for the duration of the journey, with money of her own to spend as she pleased, a maid instead of a governess to attend her, and no one in sight to tell her what to do. The new freedom was exciting, and she chose to taste of it immediately by doing what she would never have dared do in the presence of parents or teachers—making herself comfortable. It was going to be another hot day. Early morning though it was, the air was already warm and glue-heavy. Before the carriage reached the big, lion-headed stone pillars at the end of the drive, she had stripped the white lace gloves from her hands and the blossomy hat from her head. Off came the cropped, tight-fitting broadcloth jacket of her blue-gray traveling costume, off came the high, white lawn fichu swathing her throat, off came the earrings, heavy bracelets, and pointed gray kid slippers. For many hours, until they stopped for the midday meal at some inn, probably in the town of Grammantes, she would be seen by nobody other than Kairthe, who was scarcely apt to disapprove. Kairthe herself, in her loose, yoked blouse, drawstring skirt, and scuffed sandals, was the picture of comfort.

The carriage rumbled along the steep dirt lane that led down to the village of Derrivalle. The way was familiar and the scene humdrum; but Eliste, in departing, viewed her surroundings with new interest, and thus could not help but note the dreary squalor of her father's domain. The mean little houses were rickety and tumbledown. Fences were broken and thatching black with rot. Garbage and ordure lay everywhere, rats ranged openly, and a number of the grimy toddlers already playing beside the road were large-eyed and pinch-faced with hunger. *Can't these animals even bother to bury their own filth?* she wondered, and then the thought came unbidden, *What good would it do them even to try, in such a foul sty as this? A proper Seigneur would finance repairs.* But that was a tiresome matter with which she did not care to concern herself; and in any event, no business of hers.

Derrivalle was so small, the carriage passed straight through in a matter of minutes, rattling on along the narrow tributary road that would shortly merge with the King's Highway. Eliste surveyed with appreciation the rolling countryside for which her home province of Fabeque was renowned. The hills were steep but rounded, still green despite the hot weather. No other region in all Vonahr possessed meadows so intensely green, or soil so richly black; and nowhere else, certainly, were such huge and fragrant orchards to be found. The orchards stretched on for miles, and the tart spicy fruit they yielded was the source of the famous Fabequais cider, and the even more famous Fabequais apple brandy. Her eyes cut across to Kairthe, who was staring out the window, entranced. The scenery was lovely, but surely not *that* extraordinary. Then Eliste smiled as she recalled that this was the first time Kairthe had ever ventured beyond the village of Derrivalle. If the child thought *this* remarkable, just wait until she saw Sherreen!

Within the hour they reached the King's Highway, a broad, rutted, well-traveled way curving south through Fabeque like a slow dusty river, through the villages and hamlets, through ancient, sleepy towns such as Grammantes, Fleuvine, and Beronde, before crossing the Niay Rise into Sevagne Province, a great lush expanse of lake-riddled farmland, at whose southernmost point the capital city of Sherreen straddled the water of River Vir like a colossus. And a colossus she was—the largest, most vital, most exciting city in all of Vonahr, perhaps in all the world; center and source of jeweled dreams.

The hours passed, and the novelty of the excursion began to pall. Prince vo Plume, quickly losing interest in the great green world that he so rarely glimpsed, curled up on the tufted leather seat and went to sleep. Eliste took up a book of poetry and began to read, undeterred by the jolting motion of the carriage. Only Kairthe remained glued to the window, fascinated by the endlessly changing panorama of hills, meadows, farmland, and village. Twice during the morning they stopped to rest and water the horses, the second time in a tiny village whose name, if it had one, Eliste did not know. Kairthe got out of the carriage to walk Prince vo Plume, and returned a short time later bubbling over with excitement at her discovery of a village well that differed significantly in construction from the well at Derrivalle. Eliste did not trouble to leave her seat. She was, she decided, growing bored.

Her boredom subsided in the early afternoon when they rolled into the town of Grammantes, with its intact medieval city wall, its cobbled streets, quaintly gabled and timbered houses, and its ancient guildhalls of rose-flecked Fabequais granite. Kairthe was almost overwhelmed at the sight, and even Eliste perked up. There were several shops scattered along the length of the main thoroughfare, and the market square contained a moss-covered fountain flanked by old stone benches. Just off the square stood the Smiling Sergeant, an inn of good reputation. Through the gate and into the courtyard the carriage clattered. It stopped before the entrance, and Eliste hastily readjusted her appearance before alighting for her midday meal.

She was quite aware of the stir she created with her fine carriage and horses, her smart clothes, and her little retinue of maid, lapdog, coachman, and footman. When she swept into the Smiling Sergeant, she knew that every curious eye in the room was fixed on her. Never before had she felt so adult; more than adult— downright worldly. The wide-eyed wonder of little Kairthe added agreeably to her sense of sophistication. Eliste was enjoying every moment.

Enjoyment resulted in a leisurely lunch. She lingered indolently at the table, while the coachman and footman tended to the horses outside. A couple of hours passed before she paid her reckoning and left.

Off again, and now the time passed slowly. Kairthe remained fascinated by the changing scenery, but Eliste was bored, and already tired of sitting. She was tired of the jolting motion that rattled her teeth despite the cushioned seat. Above all she was tired of the dust: billowing clouds of fine, dark grit from the road that stung her eyes, chafed her nostrils, clung to her flesh, her hair and clothing.

Another six hours of dusty progress, and they came to the Black Sheep Inn on the outskirts of Fleuvine, where fresh novelty renewed Eliste's flagging interest. For the first time ever, she was to engage a room of her own in a public inn. She took the best and costliest the Black Sheep could offer: a big chamber filled with massive, old-fashioned oaken furniture, with a separate sleeping closet for Kairthe, and a velvet-curtained alcove wherein a wealthy, retiring customer might dine in seclusion if she chose. All the privacy, comfort, and solid respectability in the world, however, could not dispel Eliste's sense of low adventure. The chamber in which she would spend the night was, after all, *public*. There was no telling who might have used it before her, but the possibilities were exciting. The bed she would sleep on had been used by strangers, many of them perhaps not even Exalted. The lavender-scented sheets that would actually touch her body had between washings encountered unknown and probably common flesh. The sense of intimacy with a faceless populace was piquant, diverting.

She dined downstairs that evening, liking the inquisitive attention of the Black Sheep patrons, liking the bustle, liking the naive excitement of Kairthe, who stood behind her chair to serve her throughout the meal. Afterward, however, she found herself at a loss. She could not very well sit up late into the night drinking ale in the common room, and there was little else to do. Somewhat deflated, she repaired to her chamber, and found herself obliged for once to resort to reading for recreation. Kairthe, who was illiterate, chose a book with a handsome black and red cover for her. It turned out to be *Todaytomorrow*, Shorvi Nirienne's famous attack upon the traditional privileges of the Exalted class. Eliste accepted the offering with a sigh, for she was neither historically aware, nor politically inclined. The volume itself she had acquired by surreptitious means, purely for the satisfaction of circumventing her father's proscription. To her, the machinery of government was dry stuff, scarcely worthy of notice, much less contemplation. Apathy notwithstanding, she began to read, and soon, to her own surprise, discovered herself caught by Nirienne's eloquence and idealism.

> It will be noted that the period termed the Golden Age of the populace came to an end at the time of the Jurlian/Zenki Wars, when an attack by a league of our foreign foes necessitated centralization of power, apparently justifying the assumption of absolute authority by Dunulas the Great. It was this era that witnessed the true rise of the Exalted, whose unusual ability to shape illusion rendered them invaluable in time of war. The support of these talented Exalted having

become essential to the security of the Vonahrish monarch, Dunulas and his successors courted the favor of their most treasured subjects. Thus the Exalted were granted extraordinary privileges, not the least of which lay in total exemption from personal taxation. This exemption inevitably shifted the burden of national expenditure from the Exalted, in whose hands by far the greatest share of wealth was already concentrated, entirely onto the shoulders of those least qualified to bear it—the peasant farmers, whose prosperity correspondingly declined. Once begun, the Exalted degradation of the peasant class proceeded apace, the process facilitated by a series of wars, droughts, famines, plagues, and abortive rebellions.

Thus he described the origin of the present "inequity," as he presumed to term it, and then went on to explain just what he thought should be done to correct it. . . .

The man was unbalanced, no doubt of that. His dreams of justice and equality demanded nothing less than complete reformation of the entire social structure—a mad, impractical, unrealistic ambition, yet Nirienne's fiery rhetoric kindled powerful emotions. No wonder this renegade lawyer's writings were called inflammatory, no wonder his enemies sought to ban his books, to silence him at any cost. Shorvi Nirienne was a visionary of the most dangerous sort.

Eliste read for two hours, almost a record for her, then snapped the book shut. "He'll end upon the gibbet," she muttered, and tossed *Todaytomorrow* aside. Nirienne's theories were not so easily dismissed, however, and a little later that night, when she lay abed in the dark chamber, his words still rang in her mind.

The journey resumed at dawn, and the second day of travel was almost identical to the first, with the same jouncing progress interrupted by rest stops for the horses, a midday meal taken at some undistinguished village inn, then the long, dull stretch before dinner and sleep in the mill town of Beronde. The view from the carriage window eventually palled, even for Kairthe. Eliste and her maid spent endless hours playing at cards and dice for wooden counters, playing at guessing games, at rhyming games, at any games they could remember or invent, with Prince vo Plume curled up in a silken heap on the seat between them.

Late in the morning of the third day they crossed from Fabeque into the Sevagne, but the difference was not noticeable, at least not at first. By the middle of the fourth day, however, when they stopped for lunch at the Green Cockade in Penaude, the menu was distinctly exotic, offering such Sevagnie specialties as duck with frolloberry sauce, Boulenc sausage, turnip salad, and stuffed pears. The kitchen boy who served up the food spoke with the quick, clipped Sevagnie accent, and he wore a carved bone earring, something never seen on any man north of Beronde. To Kairthe, it was a revelation. She gazed with wonder at the kitchen boy, whose headlong conversation was all but unintelligible to her. Her round eyes grew rounder yet as they shifted from the earring to the unfamiliar dishes, to the distinctively crook-necked bottle of local wine on the table. Eliste was similarly impressed, but unwilling to admit it. Mostly for Kairthe's benefit, she assumed an air of nonchalance, but could not repress a smile of surprised pleasure as she took her first bite of Penaude Tart, with its glazed apricots and cherries, toasted almonds, and liqueur-laced custard.

The scenery was gradually changing. The steep hills of Fabeque had given way to gentler terrain, the roads were smoother, the fields flatter and filled with chestnut cattle of the Sevagnie Red strain. The villages were closer together, and the stretches of open countryside were shrinking. A broad silver river appeared to the left of the road. It was the River Vir, and the King's Highway now curved and recurved to follow the water's glinting course. A succession of two-faced villages had sprouted along the river's edge—one face, spotted with inns and taverns, turned to the highway; the other, wharf-nosing out into the river that served as a second highway. The Derrivalle carriage no longer traveled alone on the road. There were other vehicles large and small, many individual riders, and an assortment of pedestrians. Time passed, and a faint smudge marking their destination appeared upon the horizon. The air of Sherreen was notoriously foul with smoke.

It was farther away than it looked. Their fifth night was spent at yet another inn. Rising at dawn, they made an early start, traveling alongside the river in the muted, soft-edged cool of the morning. With the sun rose the density of traffic both on land and water. Boats and barges plied the Vir, while the number of vehicles kicking up dust on the King's Highway was extraordinary by Derrivalle standards. Around midmorning they reached Trouniere, where they paused briefly. Once an isolated country village, encroached upon and eventually all but engulfed by the growing city of Sherreen, Trouniere now unofficially existed as an outermost district of the capital. Eliste, gazing out at the crowded town square, could sense a new vitality in the air. The people here walked quickly, purposefully. Their gestures were emphatic and animated to the point of exaggeration. Their faces seemed astonishingly mobile—jaws wagging, mouths quirking and pursing, eyebrows jumping, eyes darting; compared to the relatively impassive Fabequais, they resembled mimes. And their conversation—so swift, so loud, so incessant! Listening to the laughter and chatter from the safety of the Derrivalle berlin, Eliste could feel her own excitement rise.

On rolled the carriage, and the King's Highway narrowed to the width of a city street, while the buildings grew taller and closer. The traffic, crowds, and noise increased—never had Eliste heard such noise, or seen such mobs of noisy, pushy, busy people. The carriages, carts, barrows, sedan chairs, and pedestrians were literally clogging the street, and progress slowed to a crawl. Beggars and hawkers were swarming around, screaming for attention. A few of the more insistent and hideous of the mendicants were actually pawing at the carriage door. Kairthe shrank back from the window. The coachman's whip snapped angrily, and the beggars retreated. A moment later, and they were back again. Alarmed, Eliste tossed a handful of copper biquins into the street, and wretched humanity began to converge from every point of the compass. Then the unseen obstruction cleared, and they began to move again, forward into a square that marked the intersection of five separate streets, and now there could be no doubt that they were truly in Sherreen itself.

The rough, bumping motion of the carriage suddenly worsened. The great varnished body shook, creaked, and groaned in pain. They had come to the first of paved city streets, and the clatter of their wheels over irregular granite cobbles was deafening. Up ahead loomed the old city wall, with its northern gate thrown wide open. The coach passed on through, and Eliste caught her first sight of something she had often heard of but never actually witnessed—a Stupefaction, one of the vast, mysterious mechanical devices created by the magic of early Exalted. Endowed with dull awareness, and designed to perform a variety of functions, these devices had once been dubbed the Sentient by their ingenious inventors. With the decline of Exalted discipline, however, the Sentient had fallen into disuse. Disuse had resulted in boredom, followed by apathy, depression, and eventual loss of consciousness. Perhaps the Sentient had truly died; but many believed they only slumbered, awaiting an Exalted summons to rouse them from their long sleep. The modern term "Stupefaction" doubly described the machines' condition and their astonishing appearance. Such a one still stood at the North Gate. Created to serve as a watchdog, guarding the city against invasion, the Stupefaction actually somewhat resembled a crude mechanical dog, with a huge steel barrel of a body set upon four columnar legs; a long segmented neck that must once have been flexible; an outsize head equipped with hinged jaws; immense bulbous eyes concealed behind closed steel lids; and round dished ears of steel gridwork.

Eliste gazed marveling after the bizarre contraption until it passed from view. Thereafter she could maintain no further pretense of sophisticated indifference, and did not try. Unashamedly she gaped out the window at the shops, houses, taverns and cafés, statues, monuments, fountains, and passing Sherreenians—this last perhaps the most interesting spectacle of all. The variety among the pedestrians was remarkable. Within the space of minutes, she glimpsed beggars, peasant laborers, tradesmen and shopkeepers, marketwomen and grisettes, students, liveried servants and footmen, assorted soberly clad bourgeois, sailors, uniformed gendarmes, Royal Guardsmen, and shabbily bedizened females who could only have been prostitutes, mingling freely in the streets. Ladies and gentlemen, of course—the quality, the Exalted—were less visible, for such folk traveled in carriages and curtained sedan chairs. That fellow Exalteds were out and about the city, however, could not be doubted, for even as Eliste watched, a footman in black and lemon came running down the street shouting, "Make way!" and behind him came gleaming a brand-new yellow carriage with black trim, drawn by four matched black horses. So brilliant was the finish on the yellow carriage, so sleek and graceful its lines, that the heavy Derrivalle equipage appeared ungainly by comparison. As the carriage passed, Eliste strained her eyes for the occupant and caught a flashing glimpse of a portly figure, a pale full-moon face.

"Who, Miss Eliste?" Overcome with admiration, Kairthe had once again forgotten to maintain silence until directly addressed. Her enthusiasms sometimes overcame her training, but fortunately her new mistress did not mind—in fact, found the spontaneity endearing. "Who?"

Eliste had noted the arms blazoned on the yellow carriage, and now she cudgeled her memory. "Vo Lieux-v'Olliard, I think," she decided. "Very old name, famous in the east, a great fortune."

"How grand, Miss! Will you see him at Court, when you go?"

"Quite likely," Eliste replied with studied unconcern, but could not resist adding for the sake of effect, "I shall see them all, including the King himself, no doubt. And you shall see them too, child."

"Kill me dead! Are we going now, Miss? To the King's palace?"

"Now? Of course not."

"But aren't you to be Maid of Honor to the Queen?"

"Yes, but not today."

"Oh. Very good, then. Maybe you could tell me, Miss Eliste—what *is* the Maid of Honor, anyway?"

"Well, in the first place, you mustn't say 'the' Maid of Honor, as if I were to be the only one. There are twelve Maids, young ladies of good family, chosen to wait upon the Queen."

"Wait upon her how, Miss?"

"Attend her at all times, provide companionship, help her to dress, to undress, to bathe, carry her messages, run her errands, perform her bidding, smooth her path—"

"Oh, you mean you're to be in service as lady's maid to the Queen like I am to you, Miss?"

"In service as lady's maid?" Disliking the sound of it, Eliste tossed her head. "Certainly not! We are speaking of the Queen, remember. Attending her is a great honor, a *privilege* reserved for the fortunate. It's nothing like servitude."

"But you're to do just the same things for her that I do for you, it sounds like, Miss."

"It may *sound* that way, but I assure you there's all the difference in the world. Don't be such an infant, Kairthe!"

"Yes, Miss."

The carriage was rolling along a narrow littered street lined with indifferently prosperous wineshops, cookshops, pawnshops, and tenements. Quite suddenly, it emerged from the shadows into a sunlit circle of handsome old houses, with a little round fenced park at the center, where children played under the supervision of their starched, frilled nurses. The contrast was startling, and the words burst from Eliste: "I love Sherreen!"

"Me too, Miss," said Kairthe. "Will we go by the King's palace, d'you suppose?"

"I've no idea. It's a good thing Coachman knows his way around this place, for to me it seems a great maze. I'm afraid I'll never learn it."

"And why should you need to bother, Miss, when there'll always be carriages to carry you anywhere you want to go?"

"Yes, that's true."

The carriage clattered on past the circular park, up the street and through an enormous open area whose white marble monument and columns surmounted by eagles marked the famous Dunulas Square; then on into a region of large and classically beautiful town houses built of cream-colored stone. Again forgetful of propriety, Kairthe once more initiated conversation. "If we're not to go to the King's palace today, Miss, then where are we going?"

"To my Grandmother Zeralenn—my mother's mother. We're to stay with her, for now."

"Your granny—well, that's nice, Miss, that's very nice. Fond of her, are you?"

"I've never met her, she never visited Derrivalle. I hope we'll get on."

"Oh, most likely you will, Miss. Grannies are generally decent sorts of people. I remember my own gran—she'd lost her teeth, and she was so ugly her face looked like a cow stepped on it, and she smoked and sucked on a dirty old clay pipe so her breath stunk something fierce, but a nicer, sweeter, pleasanter old thing you'd never find—"

"Well, I don't think *my* grandmother will be anything like that," Eliste interrupted. "She's a great lady, a countess in her own right, famous once, and said to be the greatest beauty of her day. She must have been, because she was mistress to the King's father, and before that, to his grandfather. The mistress-in-title to two kings! Not simultaneously, I don't think."

"The what, Miss?"

"The mistress-in-title, the acknowledged mistress." Kairthe's eyes remained blank, and Eliste added, "That is to say, she was more or less the King's wife, in all but name. She was not the Queen, but she enjoyed the King's highest regard and affection, shared his life to the greatest extent that circumstance allowed, wielded great influence over him, and was therefore herself important. . . ."

"With the King's father, and before that, his grandfather, Miss?" Kairthe still appeared confused.

"Yes, and over fifty years ago she bore Dunulas XI a son, who would have been a duke if he'd lived."

Comprehension dawned at last. "You mean to say," Kairthe stammered, red-faced, "that your old granny's a *harlot*?"

"No, of course not! Hold your tongue!" Eliste was similarly red-faced. "She served the King, and that is a great honor—as well as a *duty*, don't you understand that? It's not what you said—I assure you, there's all the difference in the world. Really, you are such an infant!"

"I guess I just don't understand, Miss Eliste, but I'm trying. Maybe it will all make sense when I see your gran."

"That will be any moment. I think we've arrived."

The carriage had stopped on an immaculate tree-lined avenue, before a great cream stone town house of dauntingly perfect proportions. Eliste wondered if its owner would prove equally daunting and perfect.

tand. Walk away from me, turn, and come back slowly. No, leave the pastries where they are. And do not walk too swiftly. I wish to observe you at leisure." Zeralenn vo Rouvignac's manner inspired instant obedience.

"Yes, Grandmother." Setting her plate aside, Eliste dutifully rose. Down the length of the private sitting room she paced with all the grace she could muster, spun with a practiced swirl of gauzy skirts, and returned. As she walked, she covertly studied the grandmother who openly studied her. Zeralenn must have been in her mid-seventies at least, but somehow she had cheated time. At even a slight distance her face appeared almost unlined; and a beautiful face it still was, with its intact oval shape, classically regular features, and long hazel eyes. The beauty was somewhat diminished, in Eliste's opinion, by an unnecessary layer of paint and a sprinkling of heart-shaped black taffeta patches. Zeralenn's hair, heavy with pomade and gray powder, towered in the old massive style. If she felt its weight, she showed no sign, but sat fiercely upright in her great armchair, spine never touching the cushions. Perhaps early training accounted in part for the perfection of her posture, and certainly her underwear had something to do with it, for she was encased from breast to hip in an old-fashioned, rigidly boned corset. Obsolescence notwithstanding, the style suited her; her waist was still small, and the flesh that swelled above the low, square-cut neck of the archaic panniered gown was white and smooth as a girl's. Age betrayed itself, however, in her hands, which were veined and lightly spotted, despite recourse to countless creams and lemon-scented rinses. In one of them she clasped a carved, beribboned ivory stick.

Zeralenn's personality impressed itself upon her surroundings. Eliste had noted the combination of traditional elegance, luxury, and originality the moment she walked into the house. She had felt her grandmother's presence in the formal yet comfortable bedchamber to which she and Kairthe had been escorted upon arrival; and again in the dining room, where she had shared the table with a band of visiting kinsmen, including a number of interchangeably boisterous children. Zeralenn vo Rouvignac herself, however, did not appear. It was not until the meal was concluded that Eliste had received a note summoning her to the mistress's suite. There she had finally encountered her fabled grandmother, and found herself subjected to the most rigorous inspection of her life.

"Curtsy," Zeralenn commanded. "Again, and lower. Rise and spread your fan. Now snap it shut, with an air of finality. There, that will suffice. You may resume your seat."

Eliste complied.

Zeralenn eyed her granddaughter in speculative silence for a time. Eliste grew uneasy and resentful under the prolonged scrutiny. She could feel the angry color mounting to her cheeks. Etiquette precluded verbal complaint, but there were other ways to make her displeasure known. Lifting her chin, she returned her grandmother's regard with a cool composure verging upon insolence. It was a trick she had picked up from Stelli Zeenosgirl, an acknowledged expert.

Noting the expression, Zeralenn smiled, somehow contriving to bend her lips without crinkling the skin around her eyes, which had remained almost unlined. "Good," she decided. "You've a dash of impudence, some hint of spirit. You are nothing like your mother, for which we must be thankful. There is much of your father in you, but that cannot be helped—perhaps, if we are fortunate, the resemblance is purely superficial. In certain gestures and attitudes, I see something of myself as I was—a most promising sign. All in all, I believe there is hope for you."

"Hope, Grandmother?"

"Do not address me by that title. I find it depressing, as you yourself will no doubt find it one day. Upon that fateful occasion, remember me if you can, for I shall not be present to witness our mutual discomfort. If 'Grandmother' is offensive now, all the more abhorrent must 'Great-Grandmother' inevitably prove. No, I shall never suffer it. In the meantime, you will address me as 'Madame.' That is acceptable."

"Hope of what, Madame?" Eliste fought an urge to giggle.

"Success, acclaim, power, and fortune. Had you never thought of that, girl? Why indeed have you come to Sherreen?"

"Because it is fine, exciting, gay, and grand here."

"Quite correct. There *is* no other place. Do you imagine, however, that your tiresome dolt of a father, with his mummified midgets and his pickled gallbladders—do you imagine such a man would finance your presentation at Court in pure paternal generosity? It is a costly undertaking, you realize—the clothes, the jewels, the glittering necessities. Has he assumed such expense in order to satisfy your youthful hunger for excitement and novelty?"

"Well, certainly he hopes for a good marriage. That goes without saying." Eliste shrugged.

"You must dispense with that gesture. It is considered gauche."

"It's natural, and I don't see anything wrong with it."

"Nothing wrong with Nature? Let me inform you, Granddaughter—" Zeralenn tapped her ivory stick upon the floor for emphasis. "Nature is a capricious force, whose malevolent manifestations we must oppose with all the force and vigor at our command. Spare me your puling self-proclaimed philosophers, your Rees-Raas Zhumeau and all his sorry ilk, with their maundering celebration of the pastoral fantasy. They weave fables of a world that never was and never could be, a feeble exercise for childish minds. The reality of Nature is nasty and brutish, more often than not. Art and Will together joined may conquer Nature, or at least dress her to advantage. Under my tutelage, Granddaughter, you will acquire such art."

"You don't think I dress to advantage?" Eliste inquired, cutting to the heart of matters.

"Certainly not, but you exhibit signs of good instinct. Rest assured, I do not hold you to blame for your failings. Trapped in the wilderness of Fabeque throughout your life, deprived of civilization's amenities, how should you know aught of elegance? The wonder is that you have somehow managed to escape the worst taint of provincialism. Truly, saving a few small errors, you are not instantly recognizable as a bumpkin. This unschooled grace stems in the main from your store of inherited abilities, of which I am doubtless the source. In the time yet remaining before your scheduled presentation at Court, we shall develop those abilities, camouflage your faults and emphasize your advantages, polish and refine you until you are fit to compete."

"Compete, Madame?"

"Do you not hope for a brilliant marriage or liaison? Do you not long for wealth, ease, eminence, independence—all the inestimable benefits attendant upon such a match?"

"Surely, but—"

"The eldest scions of the noblest Exalted houses are few," Zeralenn pointed out. "It is only the eldest, mind you, worthy of consideration; for they stand to inherit. The daughters of the Exalted, on the other hand, are numerous, and their ambitions are drearily consistent. Each of them, regardless of age, rank, and beauty or lack thereof, deems herself fit consort to a future lord, and selects her target accordingly. I have always considered mathematics a distasteful and irrelevant discipline, but occasionally it has its uses. Do you understand me, Granddaughter?"

"Perfectly, Madame." Eliste suppressed a snicker.

"You do not appear greatly concerned."

"Not greatly." Eliste just barely prevented herself from shrugging again. Saving her contact with Dref Zeenoson, who didn't count, her experience of young men was limited. Nonetheless, she had met sons of the Exalted at fairs, at parties and balls about the district, and under her father's own roof. For the most part, they were a poor lot—weedy, awkward, self-conscious, visibly uneasy as she was uneasy inside. There wasn't one of them with a tenth of Dref Zeenoson's wit and vitality. Exalted heirs, one and all—but completely outclassed by a serf. It was really too absurd. Her observations had strengthened Eliste's assurance, with predictable results; the young men had flocked around her at every social gathering of the past two years or so, and she had little doubt of her own power. Of course, they were *provincial* young men. Could things be different in Sherreen?

"You must not imagine the young Exalted beau of Sherreen as a creature similar in many respects to the Fabequais louts of whom you may possess some knowledge," Zeralenn advised, as if reading her mind. "You will find him a different specimen indeed—relatively sophisticated, discerning, experienced, perhaps even jaded. It is no small matter to engage the attention, much less the affections, of the most eligible."

"Perhaps it is they who should worry about engaging *my* attention." Eliste tossed her head.

"Ah, not bad." Zeralenn laughed outright, but still without wrinkling the skin around her eyes. "Not bad at all. It is often just such cool effrontery that triumphs. It is an attitude that you might do well to cultivate, once you are fit to carry it off properly. Just now, such a pose could only expose you to ridicule."

"Ridicule?" Eliste's chin came up.

"Do not poke your chin, Granddaughter." Zeralenn tapped her stick sharply. "And do not shrug at me; I have already prohibited that gesture. I trust your memory is not defective."

"My memory is excellent." Eliste scowled. "And I will not be spoken to that way. I am seventeen years old, no longer a child, and I will not be treated like one by you. As for the rest, I will poke and shrug to my heart's content."

"Ah, that willful temper marks you as my granddaughter indeed, and as such you will certainly please yourself. If you must play the ruffled country mouse come to Court, I'll not interfere."

Unsettled by her grandmother's air of acid amusement, her vanity threatened,

Eliste hesitated, chewing her lip, and then inquired grudgingly, "Very well, Madame. What are these glaring defects of mine to which you insist on calling attention?"

"They call attention to themselves, Granddaughter. My effort in that respect is redundant. I would not, however, deny your urgent curiosity, and therefore I will tell you. The freedom of your movements, your gestures, your naive manipulation of the fan; the style of your hair, your lack of paint, your turn of phrase— although, thank Fortune, the accent of Fabeque does not pollute your tongue— the transparency of your emotions—all these things reveal your ignorance of the Sherreenian style."

"Then it would seem I am a hopeless case—in *your* opinion, at least."

"You angle for praise. Well, then, you may have it, such as it is. You possess certain natural advantages. You are by no means ungraceful. Your figure is well-proportioned, if a trifle meager. Your hands, arms, neck, and feet are more than adequate. You are well-favored. Your lips are not so tiny as the mode demands, and a slight upward tilt bars your nose from perfection. Your eyes and complexion, however, could not be improved upon. Your hair is luxuriant, of good length and sheen, but an unfortunate color. Blondes are passé, I am told. This year, the Court sighs over the raven locks of Madame v'Aucluse. Perhaps we shall alter your color."

"No!"

"Be that as it may. In short, you offer up a fine collection of raw materials much in need of refining prior to public display. This refining I myself will perform."

"Why, Madame?" Eliste was torn between appreciation and annoyance. She was not yet fully convinced that she required improvement. "Why should you trouble yourself?"

"As I molded myself so many years ago, so now I will undertake the task once more, with you. Upon the day that you secure the most desirable masculine prize at Court, thus ensuring your own greatness, I shall know that I have repeated my early triumph. This will afford me both satisfaction and diversion, by which you would do well to profit. Now, Granddaughter—do you accept my assistance, and will you be absolutely ruled by me? It is a considerable offer, you realize, which you would be mad to refuse. Well?"

Eliste hesitated.

"Speak up, girl!"

"I accept your offer with thanks, Madame. But I don't promise to be absolutely ruled by anyone." It came out before she had known what she was going to say.

"Impertinent little hussy. You are my granddaughter beyond question. I see it more clearly with every passing moment. We shall make do, no doubt. We shall begin by examining your wardrobe, little of which is apt to prove salvageable."

"**Oh,** you're wrong, Madame!" Eliste assured her. "The gowns I've brought with me are new, most of them made for this trip."

"New and equally impossible, no doubt. Your costume, while fetching, shrieks rusticity. We do not wish you mistaken for a runaway shepherdess."

"Mistress Zoliay was the best seamstress in Grammantes!"

"Grammantes—pish!" opined Zeralenn, with a contemptuous flourish of the stick. "Heed me, Granddaughter. My judgment in these matters is irreproachable."

Almost without volition, Eliste's eyes traveled over the bows and flounces of her grandmother's antiquated gown.

Noting the look, Zeralenn smiled dryly. "Do not be deceived by the obsolescence of my own attire. Do not imagine it chosen in ignorance, sentiment, or senility. I am perfectly versed in the current mode, yet affect the costume of my youth because it suits me, it pleases me, and sets me at my ease. Owing to my age and eminence, I am revered as a stately eccentric—it is one of the very few advantages of age. The same toleration, however, would scarcely be extended to you, were you to appear at Court garbed as you are now. You shall have new gowns, I will bear the expense, and there is an end to the matter."

"Madame, your generosity—"

"Is prompted by self-interest alone. Do not imagine otherwise. This project arouses my interest, and I am willing to finance my diversions. As for your bucolic fripperies, throw them away. Or better yet, give them to your woman."

"Give all those new clothes to Kairthe? She's a Derrivalle *serf!*"

"I glimpsed her below as your berlin arrived. She resembles a milkmaid."

"She was one."

"We shall endeavor to conceal her base origins. Your woman must walk spruce and trim, Granddaughter, else she does you little credit. Soon you will perceive— Ah, but look, here is an example before our eyes." Zeralenn rose from her chair to stand very erect. She was at least an inch shorter than her granddaughter, but somehow managed to create the illusion of superior height. Back poker-straight, she made her way to the nearest window. She moved without a trace of a limp; the ivory stick was purely decorative in function. Eliste followed.

"There." Zeralenn pointed. "There across the street is Madame vo Bellesandre, come to call upon her aunt. Behind the Bellesandre walks her woman. Do you see, Granddaughter?"

Eliste followed the pointing finger to behold a tall, broad-shouldered, strikingly handsome brunette attired in summer's white lawn descending from a chaise. The attending maid was sleek, plump and self-satisfied in a sashed periwinkle gown of obvious quality.

"There, Granddaughter. That is the way your woman should look. As for the other, that is the way *you* should look. Do you note the fluid simplicity of her attire? Her modiste relied entirely upon the cut of the fabric to achieve that effect. Little ornamentation was required."

"I see. Yes, I see that." Eliste pressed her nose to the glass. Suddenly her own ruffled afternoon gown seemed clumsy, juvenile, embarrassing. She could feel the telltale heat in her cheeks, and to disguise her discomfort, inquired inconsequentially, "She is very pretty, isn't she—the dark lady?"

"Perhaps, if you admire that amazonian type. Myself, I perceive a certain lack of delicacy there. Fortunately for the Bellesandre, Feronte does not share my opinion."

"Feronte?" Eliste's eyes opened wide. The Duke of Feronte was King Dunulas's younger brother.

"Madame vo Bellesandre is his Grace's current mistress."

"His mistress!" Eliste gazed in fascination after the Duke's favorite, now vanishing through the door of her aunt's town house. Mistress to royalty was an honorable and enviable position, yet still carried an aura of faintly scandalous glamor. "Oh, she must be extraordinary!"

"As a matter of fact, she is decidedly dull. Her beauty is almost masculine in style, her conversation is insipid, her mind second-rate, and it is said that she managed to attract the Duke solely by reason of her ability to recite pornographic doggerel while performing acrobatics. I own this an impressive accomplishment, yet not in itself sufficient, I think, to hold Feronte indefinitely. Greater variety is required for more lasting success. No, the Bellesandre's days are numbered, and the Duke will soon seek a replacement. A newcomer at Court, provided she is clever, daring, and well-sponsored, might at so critical a juncture exploit her advantage of novelty to the fullest."

Eliste swiveled sharply to face her grandmother. "Madame, do you suggest that *I*—"

"I suggest that you examine all possibilities with care."

"I've never even considered—"

"Consider now. But come, be at ease, Granddaughter—no one is demanding so momentous a decision of you this instant." Zeralenn permitted herself another unwrinkled smile. "As of now, the possibility I have touched upon does not yet exist for you—and will not until we have achieved the requisite polish. We shall commence tomorrow, at which time you will visit Mistress Nimais, one of the few contemporary modistes truly comprehending her own profession. You will be measured and fitted for new gowns. Sketches will be rendered, fabric samples chosen and delivered to a milliner of ability—Mistress Zelure would be best for you, I think. Time permitting, we shall also carry you to the shops of the New Arcade, where suitable fans, gloves, ribbons, laces, and sundries may be selected.

Upon our return, your lessons in deportment will commence. It will be a full and strenuous day; but not, I believe, unduly burdensome. Until then, you are free to amuse yourself as you see fit. Good day, Granddaughter. I will see you tomorrow morning."

The next day, Eliste woke early in the unfamiliar bedroom. Kairthe was already up and at work. A goblet of fruit juice and a plate of sweet rolls waited on the stand beside the bed. Eliste ate quickly, rose, and with her maid's assistance donned a new white muslin gown whose violet lace ruffles now seemed painfully provincial. Her hair was caught up in a careless, almost disheveled knot—a style that Kairthe had already spotted upon several soignée Sherreenian heads, and which she was able to duplicate with surprising facility. The girls descended to find Madame vo Rouvignac in the foyer. Kairthe eyed Zeralenn with awe. It was the first time she had met her mistress's grandmother face-to-face, and all at once she went clumsy and fidgety. Zeralenn bestowed a glance of pity upon the red-faced maid. Charitably she refrained from comment. Together the three of them exited the town house.

Outside awaited the Rouvignac landau, cloud-gray with silver trim and surprising flame-colored reins, the coachman liveried in black and silver. A black-and-silver footman assisted their entrance, whereupon they discovered the carriage already occupied. A young girl of about fourteen sat waiting for them. She was chubby and lacy as a lavender sachet, with a poreless pink skin, quick little brown eyes, turned-up nose and rounded chin, a varnished crown of ash-brown curls, fingernails lacquered in two colors, and a precocious plump bosom too exposed by an unsuitably décolleté summer dress. One of the crowd of youthful kinsmen gathered about the dinner table the previous evening, one of the vo Rouvignac cousins. The face was familiar, but Eliste could not remember the name.

"Good morning, Great-Aunt. I am quite ready to go," the girl announced. Without awaiting reply, she turned to Eliste. "Good morning, Cousin. Is this young person with you your woman? What is her name? She is very rusticated, but not repellently so. If you but give her a new gown, and command her to dress her hair anew, I think it not unlikely she will catch the eye of Great-Aunt's new footman, who is a very pretty youth, let me assure you. The undercook is equally pretty, but something coarse, to my mind. Being rusticated, however, perhaps your woman's tastes are not overnice. Me, I do not yet have my own woman, for they tell me quite untruly that I am too young. My birthday is but months away, however, and time flies. I am much abused, to my mind. Perhaps, Cousin, I might borrow your woman to wait on me when I walk abroad?"

Kairthe's round eyes grew rounder. Before Eliste could reply, Zeralenn spoke. "Child Aurelie, you are here uninvited, and your presence is superfluous. How did you discover our plans? Were the servants loose-tongued, or did you listen at the keyhole?"

"But Grauntie—!" the girl protested.

"I have instructed you not to address me by that revolting title."

"But you are surely my great-aunt, and it seems to me—"

"Child Aurelie, you are forward, shrewd, and presumptuous. Leave the carriage. You will return to your chamber."

"But, Madame, do you not visit the modiste and the milliner? I wish to inspect these people. Perhaps they will serve my own purposes when I am presented at Court months hence—"

"Years hence, Child Aurelie."

"Pah, I am fit now. Will you wait until my bloom is past?"

"In intellect, you have as yet scarcely budded."

"And today I must visit the New Arcade for antique gold lacing and rosettes of the color True Love's Lament—"

"Enough." Zeralenn turned to Eliste. "We will overlook the unwitting outrages of this half-savage infant, whose offenses are rooted in simple ignorance. Forgive her if you can." Her voice sharpened, but still she did not frown. Her forehead remained almost unlined. "Child Aurelie, leave us."

"But *Madame*! That's not fair! That's not—"

"Oh, let her come with us," Eliste suggested. "I'd enjoy the company, and where's the harm?"

Zeralenn wavered, ivory stick poised indecisively.

"Please, Graun—Madame. *Please!*" Aurelie's expression was piteous.

Zeralenn struck her stick sharply against the roof. The coachman plied his whip, and the carriage began to move. Aurelie settled back in her seat with a sigh of satisfaction. Down the tree-lined street the landau creaked, past rows of immaculate cream town houses, gardens and fountains, and at last beneath the marble archway marking the boundary of the Exalted section known as the Parabeau, wherein Zeralenn vo Rouvignac resided. Beyond the Parabeau, the way grew less elegant but more interesting. They passed through a prosperous bourgeois neighborhood, where the newly rich merchants bedizened their dwellings with frilled and gilded cupolas, silvered wrought-iron lacework, and hideous painted statuary. Farther on, beyond a green park, the streets narrowed, the buildings were old and tumbledown, the pedestrians threadbare and gray-faced. Hooting urchins flung clods and insults at the passing landau, despite the coachman's nimble whip. Vagrants huddled in the doorways, and the reek of unwashed humanity weighted the air. And then they were out on the old

Boulevard Crown Prince, rumbling by the Havillac Gardens, site of numberless duels; then on through bohemian Rat Town, with its famous wineshops, coffee-houses, cafés, and beggar musicians. Beyond Rat Town crouched the wretched slums of the Eighth District, which impinged upon the ancient prison known as the Sepulchre, wherein victims of royal or Exalted wrath were interred along with the worst of criminals.

Eliste regarded the Sepulchre with morbid curiosity. The place was a historic hellhole, famed for its antiquity and its celebrated inmates; notorious for its damp stinking cells, lethal air, and periodic epidemics. Worse even than the known reality were the rumors of torture and atrocity inflicted upon political prisoners. It was widely believed that suspected enemies of the Vonahrish monarch were subjected to the grisliest of magical torments. That these rumors were unverifiable neither diminished their fascination nor prevented their general acceptance; and as the years passed, the old prison's reputation waxed in sinister luster. Initially constructed as a medieval fortress guarding a narrow bend in the River Vir, the Sepulchre was square in outline, with a high castellated tower at each corner, massive inner and outer walls, a ponderous keep with skinny grudging windows; the whole conveying a sense of infinite solidity, overwhelming weight and mass. Later on, when the fortress had become a prison and additional space was required, a warren of subterranean corridors and dungeons had been excavated. And it was there below ground, in those infamous torture chambers, that the legend of the Sepulchre was born in blood.

Past the Sepulchre sped the landau, on across the old Bridge Vinculum that spanned the Vir; through the jungle-vital Waterfront Market; beneath the projecting gables of ancient timbered structures housing jewelers, goldsmiths, moneylenders; then on through the dignified Circle of the Grand Monarch and into Riquenoir Street, where the greatest of modistes invented and decreed the fashion.

Throughout the journey, Aurelie never stopped talking. Her discourse centered chiefly upon her own desire to serve as a Maid of Honor. The Maids, it seemed, enjoying high visibility and popularity, were perfectly situated to attract the attention of the great beaux of the Court. Moreover, the favored girls flaunted the most glorious gowns, displayed to great advantage when they were carried in dashing little open phaetons around the Girdle at Havillac Gardens. Surely there could be no better life! And Eliste, who had actually won the coveted position, was doubtless the luckiest of women.

"Your good fortune is remarkable, Cousin," Aurelie remarked. "For the honor is prodigious, the rivalry to secure it keen, and it must not be forgotten that provincial Exalted—Fabequais, Vaurvais, Jerundie, and the like—are held in little esteem. Mind you, *I* am guilty of no such injustice. *I* do not regard our country kinsmen as oafs, boors, boobies, and blundering bores, at least not all of them. I do not doubt there are exceptions, and let me make it quite clear, Cousin, I perceive much hope for *you*. With your great eyes, and *such* lashes, I cannot doubt the impact of your charms. Indeed, that fragile look is never truly out of style, and no doubt but you will find your admirers, among whom you must choose wisely. I am informed that the handsomest gallant at Court is the Count Rouveel-Nezoir vo Lillevant, who composes poetry and is exceedingly well-made. The famous duelist, the Cavalier vo Furnaux, is likewise a pretty fellow, said to be of an amorous disposition, conqueror of countless women—"

"Child Aurelie, you will cease this inane prattle," commanded Zeralenn, much to Eliste's frustration.

"But, Grauntie—"

"You will cease," Zeralenn insisted, "for I will not have you parading your own folly. In any event, we have arrived."

The carriage halted before a spotless stone shopfront whose tiny brass plaque announced the establishment of Mistress Nimais. The passengers alighted and entered the shop, to find themselves in a foyer resembling the salon of a well-appointed town house. The furnishings were quietly opulent, the atmosphere formal. By no sign other than the bell over the door that rang at their entrance was the commercial nature of the establishment apparent. A gray-clad shopgirl appeared to greet them, to seat the three ladies, to fetch them biscuits and ratafia. Kairthe remained standing behind Eliste's chair. When Eliste passed the maid a handful of biscuits, Zeralenn's brows rose, while Aurelie's eyes rounded.

Presently Mistress Nimais herself appeared. The modiste was a slight, desiccated woman of indeterminate age. She wore a plain black gown with a white collar, a white cap with lappets completely concealing her hair, and no jewelry. She greeted her Exalted customers courteously but without deference, almost as if she imagined herself their equal. Mistress Nimais was known as the Queen's favorite dressmaker. In light of royal patronage, the woman had acquired unbecoming delusions of grandeur, which were generally tolerated for the sake of her genuine talent. Her fees were exorbitant and her manner too consequential, but her creations were worth any price and her services desperately in demand. Presumably, it was Zeralenn vo Rouvignac's famous name that had purchased so prompt an audience.

Now Mistress Nimais led them from the foyer back into the huge workroom, where two dozen little seamstresses labored in dedicated silence. Wood and plaster mannequins—lifelike down to the last anatomical detail—stood scattered disconcertingly about the room. The walls were lined with shelves bearing bolts of the most dazzling fabrics Eliste had ever seen—row upon row of glowing silks, radiant brocades shot with gold and silver, velvets deep enough to sink into, gauze transparent as a sigh, black lace spangled with jet and crystal, iridescent embroideries representing the labor of several lifetimes. The floor and tables were littered with pasteboard cartons, some of them open. Eliste glimpsed silk flowers, rosettes and cockades, laces, scallop-edged ribbons, jeweled buckles and buttons, fringes and silken tassels, feathers and curly plumes in every color. It was nothing like Mistress Zoliay's shop in Grammantes. But there was little time to admire, for the seamstresses with their chalk and tape measures were closing in on her like sharks. They led her into a curtained, mirrored alcove, where they swiftly divested her of gown and chemise, took an embarrassingly complete set of measurements, and then proceeded to cut, pin, and fit a muslin pattern to her body. It seemed to take forever. In reality, they finished the entire job within minutes, and then they dressed her and she emerged from the alcove to find Zeralenn and Mistress Nimais deep in conversation. The modiste held a sketch pad and charcoal. Eliste drew near. The older women took no heed.

"Ivory for the presentation gown," decreed Mistress Nimais. "In the shade Dawn Murmuring. A touch, but a touch only, of gold embroidery about the hem and train. No other color at all, for an effect unusually simple and striking. Narrow, very soft, slim lines, subtly hinting at indiscretion. Thus." Her charcoal flew over the paper, and a figure took shape. Eliste stared, while Aurelie and Kairthe drew near to peep over her shoulder. "She has the height and presence to carry this look. Lowered neckline. No jewelry. Hair drawn back, to cascade in curls; minimal headdress without jewels, ivory plumes full but not long. Thus all parts of the ensemble conspire to guide the eye whither we will, to what we most desire to display—in this particular case, to the face."

"It is a pretty enough gown, but monstrous plain, is it not?" inquired Aurelie. "Would not some ribbons and a double row of netted poufs about the hem improve it? The color Innocence Betrayed is all the rage, and would no doubt suit my cousin. A necklace with matching earrings would be very genteel, as well. To my mind—"

The same doubts had troubled Eliste, but here in this temple of fashion she would scarcely have dared question the high priestess. Now she was glad she had held her tongue, for Zeralenn and Mistress Nimais turned identically freezing, astonished eyes upon the young girl.

"Child Aurelie, you embarrass yourself," observed Zeralenn. "Mistress Nimais composes her ensembles with an artist's eye. If you are unable to appreciate her subtlety and skill, that is your misfortune, which you need hardly advertise by word of mouth."

"La, Grauntie! I protest, I meant no ill; I'll swear it is a very pretty dress. When

I am fitted for my own presentation gown, however, I trust Mistress Nimais will express my personality in terms of more vivid color, glittering jewels and dramatic allure—"

"Enough." Zeralenn's stick rapped the floor. "Foolish child, you are fit only for the nursery."

"The nursery—I! The nursery—oh!" Aurelie lapsed into outraged silence. Zeralenn and Mistress Nimais resumed their interrupted conference, heads bent over sketches and fabric samples. Eliste hovered nearby, interested but superfluous, as the designs for morning, afternoon, dinner, and dancing gowns evolved. Her opinion was not sought, and intimidated by the atmosphere of the place, she did not offer it. In any event, there seemed little need. There was something almost magical in the vision and instincts of Mistress Nimais. Relatively untutored though she was, Eliste could sense genius at work, to her benefit. Passive as one of Nimais's plaster mannequins, she allowed the process to continue uninterrupted.

They finished at last. A pile of sketches lay before Mistress Nimais, and a spread of swatches in richly melting shades of ivory, peach, rose, smoked amethyst, and raspberry. A schedule of fittings was arranged, a viewing and a final adjustment session. Countess vo Rouvignac and Mistress Nimais inclined their respective heads in a manner suggestive of mutual understanding and respect, even something akin to regard. Swatches were collected, and trimmings cut, labeled, and bundled for the benefit of the appointed milliner; whereupon Mistress Nimais surprised them. Caught up in the enterprise and creative impulses fired by the youth, prospects, and prettiness of her client, the modiste declared herself unwilling to relinquish artistic control. No alien hand would design the hats to accompany her gowns—she herself would handle the project.

It was surely an honor; beyond that, it saved hours' or days' worth of time. This last counted heavily, for Eliste was tired and curiously annoyed. She had already discovered that ordering and fitting—two primary occupations of the fashionable woman—palled quickly. As a young, unmarried girl, of course, she lacked authority. She was being treated almost as a child, or even a puppet, her own tastes disregarded by all, and it was galling beyond words. Almost she was tempted to rebel. But self-interest dictated compliance, and she had no legitimate cause for complaint; quite the contrary, in fact—her new wardrobe would be superb. Wisely, she nodded and smiled in silence. More sketches, more trimmings, this time with silk flowers, plumes, and misty pastel clouds of tulle veiling so fanciful and extravagant that Eliste forgot all else for a while, and only the sound of Kairthe's stomach rumbling in hunger alerted her to the passage of time.

It was well into the afternoon when they left Mistress Nimais's shop. Zeralenn suggested lunch at a café of good reputation—another novel experience, for Eliste had never visited a café—and the landau clattered down Riquenoir Street in the direction of the New Arcade. The huge Arcade, housing a collection of shops on two levels beneath a great, glass-paneled roof, was one of the most popular Exalted haunts of Sherreen, where ladies of quality congregated to inspect and purchase exquisite inessentials, to gossip while sipping cordials in the little chocolate houses, to parade their newest fashions, to see and be seen. True, the place was a magnet for tourists, and the shops were always crowded with all manner of provincial simpletons. That did not diminish their appeal, however, and Eliste was curious as any other newcomer. She was pleasantly atingle with anticipation as the carriage neared the bottom of Riquenoir Street.

Between Riquenoir Street and the New Arcade stood the King's Theater, in the midst of a tangle of lanes crammed with coffeehouses, wineshops, taverns, and cookshops. Here it was that beggars voracious as rats assembled to importune the well-heeled patrons of the theater. Here the political-minded often gathered to dissect the latest disasters. And here today, for some reason, the traffic had stopped. The coaches stood motionless in the street, their path blocked by hordes of agitated pedestrians. The landau halted. There was no way forward, and no room to turn. Zeralenn's ivory stick banged the roof in vain.

Eliste stuck her head out one window, Aurelie and Kairthe took the other, while Zeralenn remained motionless, neck and back set in a rigid straight line, staring icily straight before her. The landau was trapped in Breakleg Lane, only a few dozen yards from the theater. A number of gigs and carriages stood like islands in the midst of a restless human sea. Hundreds of citizens, most of them shabby, milled in the street. Eliste looked around her, interested but a little impatient, for she wanted her lunch. Many of the pedestrians were clutching the yellowish paper sheets of a broadside or cheap newspaper, something of the sort. In view of its size, the crowd was surprisingly silent. The customary Sherreenian babble was almost entirely stilled. Then Eliste became aware of a lone speaker's voice, not far away, and she followed the eyes of the crowd to the green-bronze statue of legendary Viomente, greatest of actors, caught and frozen forever in the throes of declamation. Viomente gestured atop a great granite pedestal; right up there beside him declaimed a threadbare youth in the loose pantaloons, open-necked shirt, and soft cap of the university student. The youth held one of the dingy paper sheets, whose printed content he was reading aloud to the largely illiterate audience. It took a few moments of listening before the sense of the matter began to impress itself upon Eliste's unprepared mind. When she understood, her breath caught.

It was an attack upon the Queen Lallazay. Couched in the ugliest of terms, the essay accused the foreign-born Queen of whoredom, venality, and diverse crimes against the people of Vonahr. Despite all brutality, or perhaps because of it, the language possessed a powerful raw vigor that riveted the listeners' attention. Eliste herself was fascinated and repelled. She did not for one moment believe that Queen Lallazay had lain with every officer of the King's Guard; nor did she credit the existence of an infamous Purple Closet, housing a collection of whips, goads, ticklers, chains, and manacles of solid gold, encrusted with diamonds and emeralds. She did not believe Lallazay guilty of incest, nor yet of bestiality; and if such a lover as the Queen's Stallion actually existed, it was doubtful that the sobriquet demanded literal interpretation. She did not believe that the Queen participated in orgies, dallied abed in the afternoons with her friend the young Princess v'Arian, or delighted in corrupting the morals of pubescent boys. Eliste believed none of these things, but could not forbear listening. Kairthe and Aurelie were similarly mesmerized. Kairthe's mouth was hanging open, and Aurelie was literally leaning out the window, straining to catch every word. Only Zeralenn sat inflexibly upright, motionless and apparently deaf.

Atop the pedestal, the student read on, and now a mutter of bitter resentment began to stir the crowd. Indignation intensified as the speaker launched into a denunciation of the Queen's criminal extravagance, larding his diatribe with fanciful descriptions of the royal jewels, furs, and gowns purchased at the price of the commoners' tears and blood. The matter was less colorful than that of Lallazay's alleged concupiscence, but more directly related to the actual grievances of the peasantry, and it drew an immediate response. Shouts of indignation interrupted the student's discourse.

"Who *is* that foulmouthed lunatic?" Eliste wondered aloud. "Why is he permitted to spew such filth in public?"

No one heeded her.

The student read on. Now he spoke of the King, limning the introverted Dunulas XIII as a maundering, weak-willed nonentity, dominated by his grasping harlot-wife; a dunce, an ass, an acquiescent cuckold; a shifty, shuffling, lying fool straight out of the old comic plays. It was a childishly simpleminded attack, instantly comprehensible and thus appealing to the city mob. Shouts of heartfelt execration arose, and Eliste's nostrils flared fastidiously. "Phew, they stink and they bay like dogs," she observed with a disdain calculated to conceal her own uneasiness. Formerly she had imagined hostility to Crown and Exalted confined to a small group of malcontents and fanatics. But the present reaction of the Sherreenian crowd suggested otherwise, and the implications were disagreeable.

The reader neared the end of the essay, and the tempo of the prose picked up. Whoever composed it knew how to build to a crudely powerful finale. The sentences grew shorter, simpler, stronger; the individual words were sharp and harsh in sound, most of them monosyllabic, spitting from the speaker's mouth with the force of a fusillade. In tune with the spirit of his material, the student quickened the pace of his reading. His chest heaved, he brandished a clenched fist, and his voice rose in genuine fury as he spewed forth a final spate of accusations, concluding with a demand for the arrest and trial of King Dunulas and Queen Lallazay for "vile crimes against the Vonahrish people." A pregnant pause followed, broken at last by a single, reckless hurrah that broke the spell of silence. The crowd exploded into delirious cheers.

"That is treason." Eliste was astounded. "That is absolute *treason*. He should be arrested. Why doesn't someone silence him?" Her voice drowned in the roar of the crowd. There was no point in trying to talk. Elbows propped on the window frame, she rested her chin upon her hand and watched. Outside milled and shouted the heated Sherreenians. Copies of the printed sheets were flying from hand to hand. The seditious student still occupied Viomente's pedestal. Now a number of the more athletic citizens clambered up to pump the young man's hand, to clap his shoulder and thump his back. Eliste shook her head, amazed and disgusted. Her attitude did not go unnoticed. A leering, beard-straggled face bobbed up at the carriage window. A fist clutching a crumpled paper thrust forward. Eliste flinched away from it. The paper dropped into her lap. Face and fist disappeared.

Eliste froze, aghast at the alien intrusion. Slowly her eyes dropped to the paper in her lap. After a moment she poked at it with the tip of her fingernail, half fearing contamination or explosion. Nothing happened, and gingerly she unfolded the rough-fibered sheet to expose a cheaply printed newspaper entitled *Neighbor Jumalle's Complaint*. Her eyes hurried down the page. The lead article, called "Whore's Plunder," she had just heard read aloud. Other essays, shorter but equally pungent, denounced the iniquity of Dunulas's reign. All were forceful, shrewd and profane, transparently inflammatory, obvious, and effective. All were clearly the product of one hand, one mind. The writer had created a carping, combative, coarsely jocular peasant persona known as "Neighbor Jumalle." Most likely that "Neighbor" was the rag's sole editor, a person calling himself "Whiss v'Aleur," whose name appeared at the top of the first page and the bottom of the last.

Eliste's lip curled as she took in the pseudo-Exalted form of the name "v'Aleur." No member of her own class could ever have stooped to such infamy. The presumption of the sewer-minded journalist was outrageous. She would have liked to have seen him jailed for his gall no less than for his treasonous libel. The lowest dungeon of the Sepulchre was none too good.

Eliste felt a pressure upon her back and turned her head. Aurelie was reading *Neighbor Jumalle's Complaint* over her shoulder.

"Filthy! Odious! Insufferable!" opined Aurelie.

"Do you speak of the essayist or the reader? Are they one and the same? Did that skinny fellow compose the thing? Is he Whiss v'Aleur?"

"No, it cannot be," returned Aurelie. "He is too young, too soulful, too pretty. His hair is wavy, his complexion lively, his form well-knit and athletic. He is somewhat buck-toothed, but by no means ill-favored. All things considered, it is clear his aims are noble."

"Well, it's not so clear to me," returned Eliste. "No one should be allowed to fling such muck about in public. We shouldn't have to hear it. I think he ought to be locked up."

"You display uncommon good sense, Granddaughter," observed Zeralenn. The noise outside was subsiding, and her remarks were effortlessly audible. She did not deign to glance out the window. "These people block the thoroughfares, impeding our progress, offending our eyes with their ugliness, our nostrils with their stench, and above all our ears with their obscenity. Their verbal effluvia dirties the city air, and it is not to be borne. Where is the law to protect us?"

As if in answer to her query, a half dozen of the city Gendarmerie rounded the corner of the King's Theater to advance upon Viomente's statue. Straight through the crowd the gendarmes cut, and those citizens slow in yielding passage were roughly shouldered or thrust aside. The youth on the pedestal saw them coming. Without an instant's hesitation, he turned and sprang from his perch, straight out into the thick of the mob. Dozens of hands were raised to break his fall. He was set down gently upon his feet. A path opened magically before him, and the young man broke into a run, reaching the edge of the crowd within seconds. Pursued by the cheers of his admirers, he disappeared down a neighboring alleyway, and the path closed behind him. In vain the gendarmes thrust forward. Arms interlocked, a host of jeering, hooting savages opposed their progress. The commanding officer snapped an order. Reversing their weapons, the gendarmes plied their musket butts freely, and the citizens fell back. Jeers and hoots gave way to screams of pain and rage. As the laborious advance resumed, somebody hurled a rock. The missile arced from the heart of the crowd to strike a gendarme squarely between the shoulder blades. A grunt of pain escaped the victim, and the mob howled. A barrage of rocks followed and one of the soldiers fell, blood streaming down his face. The gendarmes raised and leveled their muskets. A single warning shot sped over the heads of the citizens, who seemed not to hear it. Rocks rained down on the soldiers, who responded with a salvo of musket fire. Five shots rang out as one, and five Sherreenians went down, two of them dead upon the spot. For an instant there was a red stillness, and the groans of the wounded were clearly audible. At once the gendarmes set about reloading, and the crowd snarled like a malignant, thousand-headed beast.

The commanding officer of the gendarmes was blessed with presence of mind.

Voice reverberating through Breakleg Lane, the officer exclaimed, "Crowd Queller! The Queller comes!"

Mystified, Eliste shot a questioning glance at her cousin.

"A secret royal appointment," Aurelie explained in an excited whisper. "His Majesty's Queller of Sherreen is an Exalted dignitary whose magic subdues unruly crowds."

"What does he do to them?"

"No one knows, for his full powers are never actually called upon, but his methods are said to be dreadful. Perhaps we shall see for ourselves!" The prospect did not appear unwelcome to Aurelie.

The threat of the Queller was extraordinarily effective. The mounting electric charge of violence faded from the air like aborted lightning. A nervous gabbling arose, and the crowd churned in angry confusion. During that lull, the gendarmes completed reloading, raised and leveled their muskets.

"Return to your homes," the officer commanded with apparent assurance. "In the King's name."

Muttering from the crowd. A few uncertain boos, a couple of defiant oaths. A number of citizens began to melt away down the alleys.

"Retire now, or we open fire."

The trickle of retreating citizens increased to a flow, but the greater part of the crowd lingered undecided. Then came a pounding of hoofbeats, and an armed party of masked horsemen swept into Breakleg Lane. At their front rode a man whose black-robed figure was concealed beneath a voluminous black cloak bearing the royal insignia of Vonahr. A peaked black hood with slits cut for the eyes covered his entire head, and his hands were hidden by taloned gauntlets straight out of some medieval artist's best nightmare. Through the crowd the horsemen cut to the base of Viomente's statue, and there drew rein. The effect of this sinister apparition was immediate. Cries of consternation arose, and those citizens nearest the statue shrank back, many taking flight. The masked horsemen, apparently oblivious, sat like faceless idols. In preternatural silence the black-clad Queller surveyed the scene, featureless gaze slowly sweeping left and right. Unable to sustain that uncanny stare, a crew of citizens fled. Those remaining appeared sullenly irresolute. From beneath his great cloak the Queller produced a long and narrow device, about the length and breadth of a musket. Unlike a musket, however, this mechanism was silvery and shining, bright with glass lenses, burnished wire convolutions, luminous metallic whorls.

"What is that thing?" inquired Eliste, amazed. Somehow the contraption in its outlandish complexity reminded her of the Exalted-crafted Stupefaction at the city gate.

Aurelie's shrug disclaimed knowledge.

The Queller snapped a lever, pulled a bolt, fingered a whorl, and the lens at the end of the device glowed with poison-colored light. Thin shrieks of alarm greeted the sight, and the crowd swiftly dwindled. A sizable band of citizens remained, however; and it was to these stubborn malcontents that one of the Queller's minions addressed himself in ringing metallic tones, for the Queller himself was inscrutably mute. "Rioters and ruffians, in the King's name you are commanded to disperse. Leave this place, else Exalted magic blasts you where you stand. His Majesty's Queller of Sherreen now readies a magical device whose light induces blindness, deafness, and paralysis of all limbs. Those touched by its rays are ruined, and worse than dead. Dogs, you deserve no better, and yet your King in his charity offers mercy. Return to your homes, and no harm befalls you. Disobey, and you are lost. Now go."

Many believed him. Citizens streamed from Breakleg Lane. As they went, they vented their frustration by striking and kicking the carriages trapped in the street, and the Rouvignac landau shook beneath the assault. The entire frame vibrated, and Eliste, rattled like a die in a box, clutched at the window frame and hung on grimly. Her distress deepened as clods, pebbles, and sticks flung by passing peasants came pelting in through the open window. The threat of the coachman's flying whip was not enough to prevent a lantern-jawed slattern from leaning in just long enough to spit into Aurelie's face. A cry of fear and disgust was wrung from the young girl, who shrank back into the corner, rubbing her cheek as if the saliva burned. Eyes wide, Kairthe slid from the seat to crouch in a ball upon the shaking floor. Only Zeralenn appeared unaffected as she sat erect and rock-steady, chin up and face expressionless, gazing straight before her as if unconscious of plebeian impertinence.

Not all were cowed by the Queller's menace. A short distance from the Rouvignac landau, a broad-shouldered, long-limbed man clad in a laborer's smock and bandanna was trying to stem the crowd's retreat. Both arms uplifted, the man cried out that the Queller's magical device was a sham, a fake, a useless Exalted toy. The people must stand their ground. The people held the true power, and now was the time to prove it. Whether this plea might have swayed the crowd was never to be proved. Before the laborer had finished speaking, one of the horsemen drew a pistol, took leisurely aim, and fired. The target fell dead. Completing his adjustments, the Queller hoisted his luminous device to shoulder level and sighted along the barrel. The citizens' retreat became a stampede; in screaming panic they fled the site. Within moments, Breakleg Lane was all but empty. A handful of carriages remained, and a scattering of bloodstained bodies. The Queller and his cohorts did not linger. Turning their horses, they trotted off, leaving the surviving city gendarmes to deal with the wounded and the dead.

Eliste surveyed the scene in white-lipped disbelief. Her shining Sherreen had not delayed in displaying its darker aspect. Beside her, Aurelie sat pop-eyed, both plump little hands pressed to her face. Kairthe huddled miserable and trembling on the floor. Only Zeralenn's steel-spined composure remained perfectly intact. "Grandmother—Madame—"

"One moment." Zeralenn's stick banged the roof. An instant later, the landau began to move. The way was clear, and Viomente's statue soon receded into the distance. "There, that is over, and a disgraceful inconvenience it has proved, delaying our progress and costing so heavily in time that I fear we must forego luncheon if we are to visit the shops of the New Arcade."

"Madame, surely we aren't going on to the shops today!" Eliste exclaimed.

Zeralenn's brows rose. "Such was our original intent. I perceive no reason to alter it."

"But we've just seen people fighting and dying in the streets! After that, how can you think of—of buying ribbons?"

"The rioting and the ribbons are entirely unrelated matters. The sight of the one has no bearing upon desire for the other. Your logic appears faulty, and your memory equally flawed."

"My memory?"

"Yes, for you forget who you are. Granddaughter, you are a vo Derrivalle of the Exalted class. As such, your actions are in no wise influenced by the complaints of the canaille. Such boorish incivilities are altogether beneath your notice, and you demonstrate your quality in ignoring them."

"Be that as it may, I'm in no humor for shopping today." Eliste's chin set.

"You are easily turned from your purpose. You must display stronger character, an undaunted spirit, and a more vigorous resolution, if you are to thrive in the Court."

"And you a gentler sensibility, if you are to thrive out of it," Eliste dared.

"Ah, insolent creature, you are my granddaughter beyond question." Zeralenn turned to her other charge. "And you, Child Aurelie? Do you not wish to visit the New Arcade?"

Aurelie shook her head vehemently, eyes downcast.

A muffled sob escaped Kairthe. Lacking a handkerchief, she wiped her eyes on her sleeve.

"I am disappointed." Zeralenn eyed the drooping girls severely. "Most disappointed. Very well, you will have your way. We shall return home, where Eliste's lessons in deportment commence. With matters of such import to occupy your mind, Granddaughter, I trust you will squander no additional attention upon the inconsequential insolence of a mindless unwashed rabble."

liste had no time to dwell on events in Breakleg Lane. The days that followed
were too busy; filled with dress fittings, shopping expeditions, and lessons in
deportment. Never before had she realized the complexities of courtly etiquette. There were hundreds of rules that seemed to govern every possible
situation, and Eliste was expected to know them all. Many she had absorbed in
the nursery, like any other child of her class. But the details pertaining exclusively
to palace procedure she did not know, and did not particularly care to learn. It
struck her as absurd, this intense preoccupation with form and appearance, with
the minutiae of rituals formalized as slow ballets. Zeralenn, however, explained it
to her: "It is in our outward actions and gestures, Granddaughter, that we express
devotion to our King, our traditions, and our way of life. Those time-honored
rituals confirming the sanctity of his Majesty's person, the stable and ancient
hierarchy of the royal court, symbolize the stability and continuity of society as a
whole."

It was not the sort of talk that a newly appointed Maid of Honor found at all
entertaining, but Zeralenn brooked no recalcitrance, and Eliste found herself
trapped, banished to the study for hours on end with no companion but the Count
vo Bourray's ossified old *Mirror of Courtiers*. For lack of anything better to do, she
read; and gradually the rules, maxims, and precepts burrowed into her unwilling
mind. She learned that a marquise yielded precedence to a lowly viscountess at the
funeral of a member of the royal family, provided the viscountess's husband was
one of the pallbearers and the marquise's was not; she learned that a baron whose

bride's grandfather had sprung from the bourgeoisie lost his eligibility to serve as Master of the Revels upon a Princess Royal's birthday; and other items of similar import.

Much more interesting were the lessons in the effective use of fan and train. Zeralenn, whose skills were unsurpassed, provided demonstration, and Eliste soon discovered that the clever manipulation of a trailing skirt added immeasurably to the grace of her movements; while the tilt, swirl, and flutter of a fan constituted an entire language. Zeralenn called in a dancing master, and Eliste, hitherto familiar only with the old-fashioned gavottes and quadrilles popular in Fabeque, learned the newest steps, the latest music. She learned the names of the currently fashionable composers, poets, playwrights, novelists, and philosophers, although she did not go so far as to read the works of the latter. She learned that boiled beef with carrots was provincial, while ortolan with champagne sauce wasn't. She learned to play Folly, Peril, Kalique, and other such fashionable games of chance. She learned to paint her face, and this last was a revelation.

Secure in her young alabaster complexion, Eliste had always disdained artifice. But her grandmother insisted that a naked face at Court would mark her as provincial, if not downright backward. As usual, Zeralenn's will prevailed, and a woman from Mistress Zelure's soon came with her pots of color in modern muted tones. Eliste submitted grudgingly. She was scowling as they draped a towel about her shoulders, another about her hair. The scowl faded as she witnessed a subtle transformation taking place. The cosmetician possessed a light, sure touch, and the finished product was nothing like Zeralenn's old-fashioned mask of red and white. In low light, the new cosmetics were almost invisible. But somehow her eyes looked twice as large, her lips inviting as never before. A single star-shaped patch on her cheekbone emphasized the white clarity of her skin. Eliste stared into the mirror, enchanted. Behind her, Zeralenn smiled and Aurelie clapped her hands in delight.

Aurelie had from the first displayed a feverish interest in Eliste's education, which she viewed as the pattern of her own. With the exception of the required reading, every facet of the polishing procedure fascinated her. There was no detail, from the selection of perfumed gloves and lace-topped silk stockings, down to the choice of fingernail lacquer, that failed to engage her attention. She trailed her cousin everywhere, from merchant to modiste to cobbler, blithely unconscious of her great-aunt's annoyance, relentless in her enthusiasm. Amused and flattered, Eliste made no objection, and eventually Zeralenn capitulated, resigned to the presence of the adolescent incubus. Thereafter, Aurelie received instruction alongside Eliste, and the effects were immediately apparent. The younger girl started to rouge her cheeks, at the same time developing an obsession with the game Peril, whose octahedral dice and wooden tablets she carried everywhere.

Along with Eliste and Aurelie, Kairthe showed signs of change. Having inherited several of her mistress's discarded Grammantes-crafted gowns, which fit her almost perfectly, Kairthe now altered herself to suit the new garments. The countrified coronet of braids vanished, replaced by a smooth chignon and a lace cap. She took to washing her face and hands regularly. She kept her fingernails clean. No longer did she gawk openmouthed, fidget, point, titter, spit, or pick her teeth in public. Her ready blushes were not so easily banished, but this was a matter beyond her control. Even Zeralenn admitted that the erstwhile milkmaid was now almost fit to attend a lady.

Zeralenn's pleasure in Eliste's progress was undemonstrative but unmistakable. "You have grown tolerably civilized, Granddaughter," she conceded at the end of a busy month. "There remains room for considerable improvement, yet I think it safe to assume you will not disgrace yourself at Court. But a little more effort on your part to master all nuances of the curtsy, and you will be ready."

There was not much time left to master nuances. Only another week remained before Eliste's presentation. One week only to paint and polish herself to perfection, and then she would be judged by the most demanding, unforgiving critics in the world—courtiers only too eager to fault her face and figure, her clothes, her mind and manners. Thereafter, as a Maid of Honor in residence at the Beviaire, their Majesties' vast Sherreenian palace, she would endure the continual scrutiny of the curious, the envious, the malicious. At best, they would carp and gossip behind her back. And at worst—should she impress her Exalted audience as truly inadequate, graceless, and plain—it was even possible that she would lose her place, for there were no ugly Maids of Honor. Why, they might send her packing back home to Fabeque! Eliste shuddered at the thought, and worked all the harder on her curtsies.

The days hurried by too quickly. Riddled with self-doubt she had never known before, Eliste would have slowed the clock if she could. The pretty face and quick mind of which she had always been vain were all very well for the provinces, but were they worthy of Sherreen? Might she not seem awkward and absurd at Court, despite all of Zeralenn's teachings? What if they found her silly and skinny and dull? What if they *laughed* at her as—her grandmother's acid phrase still rankled—"a ruffled country mouse come to Court"? Sometimes she could almost hear it—the cool Exalted amusement, the covert mockery.

I'll crawl into a hole and die, she thought.

Impossible to confess these fears to her grandmother. Zeralenn would only scorn such faintheartedness. Kairthe would not understand, and Aurelie was too featherheaded to serve as a confidante. Eliste kept quiet, put on a brave face, and the hands of the clock whirled around the dial.

All too soon the appointed day arrived—a warm, bright day that augured nothing but good. Immune to the promise of the sunshine, Eliste kept to her chamber, pacing the floor for hours on end. Worn and nerve-chafed by midafternoon, she lay down for a nap, and the hours raced by while she slept. When she woke, the sunlight was already slanting in low through the window, and it was time to prepare for the coming ordeal. Kairthe helped her to dress, tying satin garters, lacing boned corset, fastening corset cover and petticoats, and finally wrapping a light, voluminous dressing gown over all. In came the cosmetician from Mistress Zelure's, to paint Eliste's face with the hand of an artist; and after her came Master Divou, greatest of Sherreenian hairdressers. Master Divou labored with his combs and brushes, his jars of pomade and metallic powder, his pins, clips, and curling irons for the better part of two hours. At the end of that time, Eliste beheld herself metamorphosed. Her hair, glistening with gold powder, was drawn severely back from her face, and sculpted into an elaborate mass of curls, with long strands cascading down her back; the whole surmounted by the delicate, pale-plumed headdress. The hairdresser departed amidst squeals of admiration. Eliste rose, tossed the robe aside, and Kairthe reverently draped her in Madame Nimais's slim, incomparably graceful ivory gown. When the last of the concealed buttons had been fastened, she turned to inspect herself in the cheval glass.

"Miss," breathed Kairthe. "Kill me dead!"

Eliste smiled at an image elegant and sophisticated beyond her best imaginings. She moved toward the glass, paused, and swept a curtsy, masterfully cut skirts rippling and swirling like wind-kissed water.

"Lay me bleeding!" Kairthe exclaimed in rapture.

Eliste's confidence returned with a rush. Artistry and artifice had transformed her, and in them she would place her trust. She would be a success, she was sure of it.

Outside, the sun was setting. Twilight came late at the height of summer, yet there still remained another hour before she was due to set off for the Beviaire. Eliste resumed her pacing, picking her way with care among the boxes and strapped trunks scattered about the room. Her possessions—including Kairthe—were shortly to be conveyed to the Maids' Quarters of the palace, wherein the Queen's select attendants slept within call of her Majesty. When Eliste repaired to the Maids' Suite very much later that night, she would find servant and wardrobe awaiting her. Kairthe regarded the impending transition with a naive, untroubled optimism that her mistress envied.

The gilded clock on the mantel struck the hour of eight. Eliste cast one last look into the mirror, finding some reassurance there.

Nobody's going to call me *a country mouse.*

With Kairthe following in her wake, she exited her room and descended to the foyer, where her chaperone Zeralenn waited, along with a group of inquisitive young kinsmen assembled there to see them off. The youngsters whistled and clapped as she came down the stairs, but Eliste barely noticed, for her attention anchored upon her grandmother. Zeralenn was arrayed in full court dress. The trailing skirts of her midnight-blue gown, spread over vast panniers, were misted with black lace. Her powdered hair, dressed over a wire frame, towered to improbable heights. Black plumes nestled among the rigid curls. Sapphires and black pearls shone darkly at throat, ears, and wrists. She had exchanged her ivory stick for one of ebony and jet. Masked with paint and patches, she looked much as she must have appeared some forty years earlier, when she had reigned as Dunulas XII's favorite.

"You are beautiful, Madame," Eliste remarked, almost in awe.

"Kind words to a relic of a bygone age, Granddaughter. Fortunately for all concerned, my own appearance is a matter of no consequence. The same cannot be said of yours. Turn slowly, let me see you."

Eliste pivoted, gold-embroidered train flaring with calculated grace. As she completed the turn, her questioning gaze sought her grandmother's face.

Zeralenn studied her minutely from every angle, missing nothing. Her remorseless eyes measured, weighed, judged. After what seemed an interminable pause, she declared, "Granddaughter, I believe you will do." This, from Zeralenn, was considerable; but she went even further. "In fact, I will confess—you carry yourself with much distinction. I am proud of you, very proud."

Eliste's eyes stung. For a moment she thought she would cry, disastrous tears that would streak her beautiful rouge. "Thank you, Grandmother," she said softly.

"Never address me by that title," Zeralenn commanded, but she was smiling.

As they crossed the foyer together, the kinsmen crowded close to babble compliments and blow kisses. No one presumed to touch them, however, save Aurelie. Throwing her arms about Eliste, she planted a fervent but careful kiss. "It is your night of triumph, Cousin," the girl observed. "You are fashionable beyond words, and your coiffure is altogether killing. The gallants will die for love of you, and the other women will all be sick with jealousy, as I shall observe for myself when I visit you in the Maids' Suite. I *may* visit you, may I not? And you will conduct me about the Beviaire, introducing me to significant persons, will you not?"

"Child Aurelie—" warned Zeralenn.

"I should desire beyond all things to pay my compliments to her Majesty Lallazay——"

"Foolish infant, enough!"

"But, *Grauntie*——"

Suppressing a grin, Eliste threw her cousin a wink.

The Rouvignac landau—freshly cleaned and polished, flanked by four footmen—waited at the door. The passengers entered and they were off at a trot, clip-clopping smartly along the Avenue Parabeau, between the rows of cream town houses now bright with lanterns. Presently they passed under the old marble archway, over the cobbles and on into Dunulas Square, bounded on its far side by a spear-pointed pale enclosing the Beviaire and its grounds. Past the Dunulas Monument they rolled, past the eagle-topped columns, along the pale to the eastern face of the square, where the barrier was pierced by a lofty gilded wrought-iron gate guarded by uniformed pikemen. Noting the Rouvignac arms on the landau, the sentries offered no challenge, and the vehicle passed into the royal enclave. A white-graveled drive crunched beneath their wheels. Eliste strained her eyes eagerly. The carriage lanterns and the flambeaux in the hands of the footmen illuminated a broad expanse of lawn dotted with trees and shrubbery tortured into geometrically precise cones and spheres. And there, straight ahead, at the crest of a slight rise, stood the Beviaire itself—a massive structure whose central section dated back to the time of Dunulas IX; a vast, formal, intimidating sprawl of sandstone and marble, ablaze with light. Before the great front entrance, carriages came and went, pausing only long enough to disgorge glittering contents. Eliste's mouth was suddenly dry. She played nervously with her gold-spangled fan, and stole a glance at her grandmother's profile.

Beside her, Zeralenn sat upright, impassive and impervious. Of course. *She* had nothing to fear. Unless . . . Eliste remembered then that Zeralenn vo Rouvignac had retired to dwell in relative seclusion upon the death of Dunulas XII, not showing her face at Court for the past— How long had it been? Eighteen years. For reasons best known to herself, though doubtless involving both pride and propriety, she had not returned for eighteen years. And now at last an old woman, though still remarkably handsome, she had come back to serve as sponsor to her granddaughter. How must she feel—she, once celebrated as a great beauty—to display herself again after all these years? She showed not the slightest sign of concern, and yet it could not have been easy for her. Eliste was not the only one with worries.

Up and around the curving drive to halt before the entrance. Dry mouth and moist cold palms.

"Courage, child," Zeralenn admonished. "Only that, and you are sure to triumph."

"You, too, Madame."

"Ah, those wide eyes are sharp. My own granddaughter, beyond doubt."

And then it was all swift confusion as a brace of footmen handed them from the landau and ushered them to the door, where a quartet of white-wigged attendants, clad in the royal livery of purple and gold, bowed and scraped like stiff-jointed marionettes. The Rouvignac servants retired, but Eliste scarcely noted their disappearance as her grandmother shepherded her through the great entry, across the cavernous foyer, and on along polished marble corridors shining with gold and crystal and flame, thronged with silk-and-satin courtiers whose gems seemed to burn with their own dazzling light. Eliste's vision actually blurred for a moment, colors melting, shifting and swirling, picked out with a thousand points of fire. She gazed about her, a little bewildered; but she did not pause, for her grandmother's hand was on her arm, firmly steering her on into the gilded labyrinth. To Zeralenn it was all perfectly familiar; a source of little interest, much less wonder. She scarcely wasted a glance on her surroundings. Only once, she paused to exchange a few gracious words with an ancient footman, a shriveled remnant of the past reign, who alone had recognized the once-famous Zeralenn vo Rouvignac, greeting her with a bow so deep it set his old bones creaking.

Candle flames multiplied in vast mirrors; glowing silks, brocades, plumes, and jewels; gold everywhere, ice-slick marble gleaming underfoot; and then the great Queen's Presence Chamber, with its floor laid out in intricate sunburst patterns of polished tile, its vast chandeliers with star-shaped faceted lusters, and its high, vaulted ceiling, enameled in the darkest blue and inlaid with constellations of gold. The Presence Chamber was crowded with courtiers, and the warm summer air was heavy with the odors of musky perfume, burning wax, and overdressed, trussed, and overheated bodies. Before the night was over, those scents would thicken, augmented by the inevitable fumes of wine and tobacco, smoke, sweat, hair pomade, and wilting flowers; but for now, the atmosphere was bearable. At the far end of the room, a group of musicians attired in matching suits of the royal purple and gold tuned their instruments. Near the center, a blue canopy edged in gold bullion shaded a dais bearing two great gilded armchairs, respectively occupied by Dunulas XIII and his queen Lallazay. Eliste stared in passionate curiosity. King Dunulas was short and stout, with an emptily innocent face. His peruke was perfectly curled, and his embroidered suit of salmon brocade was irreproachable; yet somehow he conveyed a sense of awkwardness, discomfort, and uncertainty. His posture was poor, his gestures curiously limp. He looked good-natured and ineffectual. It seemed likely he was uxorious. Periodically his eyes cut to his wife's face, as if for guidance or reassurance.

And Queen Lallazay? Where was the rapacious, stupidly sly harlot of fable? She looked pretty, soft, and fervent. Her gown of mermaid green-gold set off a rounded petite figure decked in emeralds. Small features, hair luxuriant and naturally fair, complexion hectic, aspect theatrically vivacious. Whispering conferences with her physician and mentor, the Doctor Zirque, periodically interrupted the animated display. Dr. Zirque—pallid of eye, hair, and flesh—was acknowledged ruler of the Queen's caprices. It was he who had moved Lallazay to engineer the Marquis vo Lavaire's fall two years earlier; similarly, he had induced her to persuade the King to banish the Count vo Sobrinne from Court. Some said that the doctor's influence derived from the Queen's dependence upon tranquilizing pills and draughts of his devising; concoctions so soothing to her tight-strung nerves that she often vowed she could not get through the day without them. Others thought him her lover, her lapdog, her evil genius. He was loathed by courtier and commoner alike.

A hesitation at the door, a brief exchange with a liveried attendant, and then the usher's voice rang out:

"Her Ladyship the Countess vo Rouvignac. The Exalted Eliste vo Derrivalle."

All eyes turned to the door, for the name vo Rouvignac still carried weight. The woman who had managed to mesmerize two kings was worth looking at, even in old age. King Dunulas himself looked up, clearly eager for a glimpse of the "Madame Zera" who, in his youth, had once seemed something like a jeweled and fascinating aunt.

Eliste watched her grandmother, who appeared unmoved and imperturbable as ever. The face beneath the immense coiffure was expressionless as Zeralenn advanced upon the throne. Eliste kept pace, careful to maintain the gliding motion in which she had been so rigorously drilled. Through a corridor of courtiers lining the approach to the dais they moved, and Eliste could feel the pressure of eyes. Public attention, initially focused upon the legendary old beauty, was now shifting to her young companion. Eliste could sense curiosity, speculation, and merciless appraisal. She heard a murmuring arise on either side. They were discussing her, she knew, probably finding fault, and she could feel the hot color burn in her cheeks. It would never do; she could not afford to blush and falter like a silly adolescent. Deliberately she concentrated upon her movements—studied and balletic as her most demanding tutor could have wished—and the ploy was successful. She no longer heard or heeded the whispers, and her face cooled. They reached the dais, and both women sank in profound curtsies. Eliste remained kneeling as her appointed sponsor Zeralenn rose to pronounce the formal phrases of presentation. The King extended his hand, which Eliste kissed without daring to lift her eyes. When she kissed Lallazay's hand, however, she risked a quick upward glance, and saw the notoriously clothes-conscious Queen studying her gown and headdress with undisguised feminine interest. Somehow the observation was reassuring.

Eliste stood to behold the King press her grandmother's hand warmly. Without glancing behind them, she and Zeralenn backed expertly from the dais to take their place among the other courtiers, and there they remained as the presentations continued. For a time Eliste saw nothing but the King and Queen; royalty filled her entire vision. She watched in awe as they submitted their hands to a seemingly endless succession of Exalted kisses. Presently, however, her pulses slowed, the sense of breathless enchantment faded, and the world reasserted its existence. Her eyes began to travel about the room, sliding from one glittering figure to the next, even noting a few familiar faces. Not far away stood the portly, moon-faced vo Lieux-v'Olliard, whose yellow and black carriage was the finest in Sherreen, and whose family fortune was unarguably likewise. Just to the left of the royal dais stood Madame vo Bellesandre, dark and striking in her lemon brocade. Beside the Bellesandre, one hand resting upon her waist, stood a man with the powerful, solid build of a wrestler, only just beginning to soften about the middle; and a broad swarthy face like a fire-hardened version of the King's, with a bold jut of nose, ripe lips, and implacable jaw—who could only be the Duke of Feronte, profligate younger brother of the King. Feronte's appetites, said to be matched only by his stamina, were renowned. Decisive and assertive as his brother Dunulas was vacillating and yielding, the Duke was regarded by many as the man who should have been king. So great was his fame, in fact, that a monarch less trusting than Dunulas XIII might well have considered the quiet removal of a potentially threatening rival. Dunulas, however, filled with shy goodwill, and innocently certain of the world's benevolence, took actual pleasure in the popularity of his sibling, and thus the Duke remained to entertain and scandalize the court. Eliste noticed now that Feronte was staring at her, his dark eyes unabashedly appraising. A number of the men did likewise, but none of the others was quite so brazen about it. When he saw that she had become aware of him, Feronte's white carnivore's teeth flashed briefly. Royalty or not, his insolence was insufferable. Eliste's brows contracted. With a lift of her chin, she looked away, but not before noting Madame vo Bellesandre's look of hurt amazement.

Now that lady's going to hate me. Bother.

The presentations ended at last. King Dunulas gave a signal, and the musicians struck up, commencing with a vijouille, one of the fashionable new dances. The music, lilting and delicate, set toes tapping almost uncontrollably, but etiquette demanded royal initiation of festivities. Reluctant but dutiful, King Dunulas handed his queen down from the dais. Never did he seem more awkward and self-conscious than when obliged to dance. No other activity set off his short, ungainly figure to greater disadvantage, and he knew it. Beside him, Lallazay floated graceful as a mermaid in her natural element; but the King shuffled his way through the complicated steps with furrowed brow, eyes squinting in earnest concentration, lips moving as he silently counted time to the music. One such exercise in self-abasement, his duty as king and husband demanded. After that, his obligation fulfilled, he would be free to seek some quiet corner, there to talk comfortably of hunting, hounds, and horse racing with his friends vo Lieux-v'Olliard and vo Brajonard. Dunulas's face brightened visibly as the dance neared its end. Soon the music ceased, and applause rippled through the room. Leading his wife back to her throne, the King bowed gracelessly and retired. The musicians struck up again, this time a quick, light Lanthian drinnado. Almost instantly, the Queen was surrounded, for etiquette and custom now permitted her to favor such partners as she deemed worthy of honor.

In the opinion of the conservative-minded, Lallazay abused her freedom. Bad enough that a wife and queen should consent to dance with multiple partners, but this might have been excused on the basis of royal obligation, had she but limited herself to graying dodderers of irreproachable character and nonexistent appeal. This she did not do, but rather selected as her partners the gayest and most gallant of Exalted beaux—handsome, irreverent young men who flattered, flirted, and joked with her, treating her more like an actress than a queen. Now Lallazay stood in the midst of a chattering, pleading gang of them. Her eyes were sparkling, her face was flushed; she fluttered her fan, tossed her head, and laughed delightedly. To detractors, it seemed undignified at best, perhaps even improper. And this seeming looseness, while probably innocent enough, darkened the Queen's reputation; especially among the bourgeois and peasantry, whose suspicions were lovingly nurtured by diverse enemies of the state, ranging from agents in the pay of foreign powers, to domestic malcontents and professional agitators, right on down to such sewer slime as the rabid journalist Whiss v'Aleur.

As Eliste watched in extreme interest, the Queen teasingly brushed one man's shoulder with her fan. Bowing low, the chosen cavalier proffered his arm, and the pair moved off to join the throng already gliding to the strains of the drinnado. Lallazay's suitors remained where they were. The night was young, the pretty Queen an incorrigible coquette, and it was likely they would all have their chance, in time.

Eliste's attention was tinged with envy. Not a bad thing, by any means, to attract such a swarm of admirers! Of course, Lallazay was queen, even if she didn't act the part, and rank conferred an unfair advantage. Deprived of her royal aura, as an ordinary courtier, would she ever have enjoyed such triumph? More to the point, would the new Maid of Honor? In Fabeque, Eliste vo Derrivalle was accounted a belle, but what did that amount to here at Court, among the *real* gallants, the sophisticates, the people whose opinions mattered?

What if nobody asks me to dance?

Already the floor was full, and here she still stood, unnoticed and unsought.

Was it all a mistake, coming here? Is it too late to go home? What would people think if I did? Maybe I could say I'm sick? Maybe I could pretend to faint? No, Madame would never be deceived. Maybe I could just sneak out when she isn't looking? No doubt I'll have my chance—everyone still admires her, understandably so, and she'll surely be asked to dance before I am.

And even as she thought it, she turned to find a man bending over her grandmother's hand. For a moment she glimpsed the top of a silvery peruke, the sheen of a mulberry brocade coat, and then he straightened and her brows lifted, for she faced the handsomest old man she had ever seen. He was tall—as tall as Dref Zeenoson—lean and long-legged, with the rangy build and upright military bearing of a cavalryman. He must have been about sixty-five or seventy years old—his age betrayed by the network of fine wrinkles surrounding his eyes, the grooves bracketing his mouth, the heavy veins cording his hands, the slightly withered skin of his neck above an impeccable white cravat. Yet the eyes beneath the gray brows were still brilliantly blue against healthily sun-bronzed flesh. His features were straight and sharply chiseled, and what she had thought a silver peruke was in fact his own thick, unpowdered hair, worn long and clubbed at the back of his neck.

Eliste forgot her troubles, for the old gentleman before her was surely worthy of attention. He was staring down into her grandmother's face with the still look of a successful gambler. Zeralenn's expression was masked by the layer of paint. Her hazel eyes were a little wider than usual, and perhaps a little brighter; that was all.

"Countess, you restore my flagging faith in Exalted magic. Your conquest of Time must answer all doubts," observed the stranger.

"Time, sir, may be deceived momentarily, but never conquered. Beauty's great adversary is sometimes negligent, sometimes preoccupied, but ultimately invincible. In the face of that destroying power, neither beauty nor magic endures," replied Zeralenn.

"But glance in the mirror to discover your argument refuted."

"What a gallant liar you still are, Meureille. You have not changed a whit in— How long has it been, this time?"

"Eight years, this time—four spent campaigning in Gidunne, and later in the Low Krenetz. Thereafter, having attained that state of physical decrepitude so wrongly regarded as the outer mark of inner wisdom, I was appointed his Majesty's Ambassador to Strell."

"Ah, cloistered as I am, even I have heard of your heroics in the Pilarian Mutiny."

"Scarcely heroics, Madame. Desperation graced with undeserved good fortune is the truer description."

"Yet you are called 'Savior of Jerencia,' I believe."

"Such colorful sobriquets, like counterfeit jewels, are gained at little expense, worn briefly until their false luster dims, then discarded and forgotten by all."

"You do yourself much injustice, as always. Your present eminence is but a fitting tribute to your accomplishments; less, perhaps, than you deserve, but greatly more than you acknowledge. Happily for all Vonahr, your modesty does not blind the King to your merit. It is said his Majesty has called you home to accept a marshal's baton. May I assume that the honor conveys high office in Sherreen?"

"If it does so, I shall be obliged to decline. The marshal's baton I would accept gladly, if it is offered, but not a post in Sherreen. For reasons that you already know too well, I prefer to live abroad."

"Still so obstinate, after so many years?"

"Always."

"How long do you remain among us, then?"

"Two or three months, perhaps. One purpose in my return has already been accomplished. And you, Countess? Have you tired of your seclusion at last, that you grace the Court with your presence tonight?"

"Seclusion, sir, suits my years and of late my character. Tonight's appearance is but a brief aberration. I am here as sponsor to my young granddaughter, who now takes her place as a Maid of Honor. To my mind, the child shows promise. But allow me to introduce her, and you may judge for yourself." Zeralenn turned to her protégée. "Exalted Eliste vo Derrivalle, may I present his Excellency the Cavalier Faquenz vo Meureille, his Majesty's Envoy to Strell. Cavalier, Miss vo Derrivalle."

"Excellency." Eliste curtsied.

"Exalted Miss." He bent low over her hand. "You carry the mists of early springtime in your eyes. Such youth and grace must gladden the hearts of all beholders."

"Your Excellency is too generous. But youth and grace must strew their blossoms at the feet of Jerencia's hero. His fame, reaching so far as the wilds of my own province Fabeque, may be likened to the noonday sun, overwhelming to the foggy mists of early springtime."

The Cavalier vo Meureille laughed aloud at that. "Exalted Miss, I believe you favor your grandmother, and higher praise than that I cannot bestow. Allow me to be first in paying homage to the Court's newest beauty." He could hardly have been more charming, yet somehow she fancied he grudged every moment that diverted his attention from her grandmother. As if to confirm her judgment, he favored her with another perfectly gallant bow, then turned back to Zeralenn.

"Madame, they play the drinnado—some say invented by Gelaziel when he first beheld you, walking at dawn in the gardens of Palace Meleche. If the story is not true, then it should be. Will you dance once more?" He extended his arm.

"Cavalier, I thank you, but it is fifty years since I walked in the gardens of Meleche, and I am no longer fit for the drinnado."

She was almost certainly lying. What she really meant was that she didn't care to leave her granddaughter standing alone and ignored in the midst of a roomful of strangers. Eliste's face tightened. Zeralenn felt sorry for her, sorry for the country mouse! More and more she was wishing herself home in Fabeque, where people looked up to her. Just when she was on the verge of inventing an attack of the vapors, legitimate excuse to retire, a solid dark figure materialized before her, bowed perfunctorily, and straightened.

"Exalted Miss, honor me," suggested no less than the Duke of Feronte.

The look he had given her but a few minutes earlier she had found offensive, and she had no reason to change her opinion now. His expression was arrogant, even insolent; the tone of his voice, downright peremptory. Her first impulse was to refuse him, royalty or no; but she quickly thought the better of it. Anything was better than continuing a wallflower. With only the briefest of hesitations, she accepted his arm and he led her out. Realizing that the eyes of half the Court were trained upon her, Eliste silently prayed for a demeanor as unrevealing as Zeralenn's. Slanting a sidelong glance at her partner, she saw that he was studying her face and figure with the same unhurried, unconcealed deliberation that had already aroused her hostility, embarrassment, and gratification. She looked away quickly, but not for long, for he swung her brusquely about to face him, and she caught a strong, not unpleasant whiff of brandy and tobacco.

Feronte proved an unexpectedly expert dancer, moving with a buoyancy surprising in a man so durably constructed. He spun her lightly through the steps, and Eliste found herself enjoying the exercise. Despite her aversion to the Duke, she was almost sorry when the drinnado came to an end. As the music finished, she curtsied and extended her hand, expecting him to escort her back to her grandmother. Feronte grasped her wrist firmly, and then he did not move. She threw him a startled glance, which he met blandly.

"Your Grace—?"

"Exalted Miss, I claim the next dance," announced the Duke.

"It is promised elsewhere," she lied.

"Then your designated partner must humor my fancy."

"Impossible. Return me to my chaperone, if you please."

"Not yet."

"I wish it. Must I insist?"

"Not at all. Go if you must."

He bowed, maintaining his hold on her wrist. She jerked her arm, but he did not let go. She could not free herself without an obvious struggle. Was he mad, or drunk? He appeared neither. Despite the inflammable breath, he was rock-steady on his feet, his movements sure and controlled. Eliste's eyes flew in search of Zeralenn, who stood immersed in conversation with the Cavalier vo Meureille, and totally unconscious of her plight. Not so the other courtiers, whose amused and knowing eyes she encountered everywhere. Had she been back at home in Fabeque, she might have quietly ground the sharp high heel of her shoe into the instep of the too-insistent suitor; but here in Sherreen, presumably one did not employ such tactics against his Majesty's own brother.

Eliste's dilemma was resolved when the musicians struck up again, this time an old-fashioned, slow trierge. Feronte captured her free hand. She could feel the heat of his flesh through her glove. For a moment she pulled back, glaring at him, then relaxed and reluctantly followed his lead.

"There, that is better, is it not?"

"Better for whom, your Grace?" She'd got control of her face again, and her expression was mildly disdainful. "Your little jest does not please me."

"I rarely jest."

"That is your misfortune, but not one with which I intend to concern myself."

"Your intentions will alter as you come to know me."

"I do not particularly care to know you."

"So much the better. The majority of women, ambitious of achieving indispensability, insist on plumbing the deeps of a man's character. Thereafter, their self-love is wounded when he fails to return the compliment. It is refreshing to meet one willing to forgo the preliminaries."

"I do not understand his Grace's meaning."

"I had thought to find you more perceptive, but with such a face, it hardly matters."

"His Grace attempts gallantry?" she inquired with the suspicion of a sneer.

"I can't trouble myself with pretty speeches. You'll have to do without them from me."

"Possibly there are other sources."

"You will not seek them."

"His Grace appears confident."

"With reason. When all is said, you are an unknown, a newcomer indifferently connected and of relatively obscure provincial origins, while I am—Feronte. You are young but presumably ambitious, else you would not be here; thus the outcome is not difficult to predict." He shrugged minimally. "There is the reality of it."

"The reality of it is that the Duke's dreary cynicism is equaled only by his coarse presumption." Her grandmother would have shuddered to hear her, but her mouth seemed to have bolted.

The Duke, however, appeared unruffled, remarking only, "My plain speaking offends you, but you must learn to bear it."

"*Must?* Do I hear you correctly?"

"Probably not, in the midst of these chattering monkeys. There is a quiet chamber at the end of the gallery where we shall not be disturbed. We will go there now, and you'll hear me clearly enough. Come."

Her astonished eyes jumped to his face.

"We may finish the trierge first, if you prefer," he offered, evidently misinterpreting the look.

"Your Grace may finish it alone." Freeing herself with a sharp twist of the wrist, Eliste turned and stalked away, indifferent to the avid attention of the surrounding spectators. If he tried to stop her again—if he dared lay a hand on her—she *would* step on his foot, no matter whose brother he was. Feronte, however, made no attempt to detain her. If she had glanced back, she would have seen him gazing after her, unwonted interest stirring in his dark eyes.

It seemed that the Duke's attention had established her acceptability, for now everyone wanted to dance with her. No longer was she the wallflower, dependent upon her chaperone's company; in fact, caught up in a whirl of activity, she quite lost track of Zeralenn's whereabouts. Thereafter, she danced every dance, from gavotte to drinnado, with an assortment of partners that rivaled even Lallazay's. Every young gallant—and some not so young—was determined to inspect the new Maid of Honor at close range. They were so numerous and so varied that Eliste couldn't hope to remember all the names and faces, but a few of them made an impression.

The Marquis vo Lieux-v'Olliard—he of the moon face and stellar fortune—was placid and dull, filled with talk of his country estate, his new and splendid town house, his carriages, horses, yacht, and coin collection. Still, he seemed kindly and harmless; and when he offered to drive her around the Ring at Havillac Gardens in his jewel of an open phaeton, she did not refuse outright.

The Count Rouveel-Nezoir vo Lillevant, whose black hair, translucent blue eyes, and faultless profile had won him the reputation as handsomest man at Court, was dashing and impetuous as vo Lieux-v'Olliard was staid and mundane. A poet of acknowledged talent, author of countless sighing sonnets, poignant pastorals, and languishing lyrics, he seemed the ideal figure of romance, yet suffered one significant disadvantage. Despite the greatness of his title, vo Lillevant was all but penniless, his fine appearance at Court maintained by courtesy of the moneylenders. He was now thousands of rekkoes in debt, more than he could ever hope to repay save by means of a wealthy bride's vast dowry.

The Exalted Vequi v'Isseroi, third son to the Duke of Lesigne, was loquacious, ebullient, and flown with eccentric enthusiasms. Short, slight, endlessly energetic, with tiny black eyes lighting a wide-mouthed, snub-nosed face, his natural ugliness was enhanced by fashionably jeweled teeth. Diamond chips had been set in two incisors, and each canine sported tiny emeralds resembling bits of trapped watercress. Eliste found the teeth unsettling, yet nothing could quell the charm of Vequi's conversation, which swooped dizzily from topic to topic, but always returned like a well-trained falcon to the matter of magic. Vequi fancied himself heir to the magic of his forebears. How true this might be was difficult to judge; as a courtier and amateur jockey, the young man could not have studied the art with anything approaching the dedication of a true master like Uncle Quinz. Noting her skepticism, he promised proof to satisfy her doubts before the night was out. Then, fiendishly skillful in rousing her curiosity to fever pitch, he bowed and left her.

Exalted Stazzi vo Crev, slim and elegant, was the best dancer of them all. The witty Vicount vo Renache, almost as clever as Dref Zeenoson, paid outrageous compliments. Cavalier vo Furnaux, notorious rake and duelist, had the delicate smooth face of a girl, and stammering speech. Redheaded, freckled Baron vo Pleniere-v'Orenne bombarded her with risqué jokes, savoring her reactions with the air of a mischievous urchin.

All were satisfyingly attentive. Perhaps that had more to do with their own private rivalries than with the new Maid's attractions, decorative though she was; but Eliste was not inclined to analyze the pleasure out of her success. As the party expanded from Presence Chamber out onto balconies, down the galleries, into the Swan Chamber where the buffet waited, she moved in a cloud of cavaliers. She drank champagne with vo Lillevant, nibbled ortolan wings with Pleniere-v'Orenne, flirted shamelessly with vo Renache.

Then back to the Presence Chamber for more dancing, with a glorious plethora of partners. The first sight to meet her eyes there was Zeralenn vo Rouvignac out upon the floor, pacing beautifully through the gavotte opposite the Cavalier vo Meureille. At a distance, Zeralenn looked like a girl in antiquated costume, while vo Meureille seemed courtly and perfect as a figure of legend. It was pretty to see them, but Eliste had no time to admire. There was vo Crev to consider, along with vo Furnaux, vo Lieux-v'Olliard, and the others. Her attention was occupied, but not so completely that she failed to note the Duke of Feronte persistently hovering at the edge of her vision. He was always there, off to the side, watching her with his flatly purposeful dark eyes. Twice more he had tried to approach her, and each time she had sought the sanctuary of another partner. After the second attempt he had withdrawn to study her from a distance, and she had managed to dismiss him from her thoughts until she encountered the corrosive stare of Madame vo Bellesandre, whose undisguised animosity reminded her that no Exalted female save the Queen had by word or gesture acknowledged her existence since her entrance. They were deliberately ignoring her.

It was awkward, but Eliste didn't waste much time worrying. There was little she could do; moreover, her grandmother's training had fortified her against self-doubt. Lightly, she danced, knowing that the eyes of all the court followed her, for this one night at least. Prettily, she traded amusing rococo artificialities with her partners, and the hours whirled by. Shortly after midnight there came a brief lull, during which it was announced that Vequi v'Isseroi had consented to favor the company with an exhibition of Exalted magic in the Swan Chamber. Recalling their earlier conversation, Eliste smiled to herself.

Those determined to witness the marvel included the King and Queen, the Duke of Feronte, and a number of the greatest courtiers, all of them intrigued by any novelty. In the Swan Chamber, Vequi v'Isseroi stood beside the buffet table. When the spectators had assembled—when he had spied Eliste standing among them—the young man began to speak. A born showman with a natural flair for drama, Vequi wasted little time on preliminaries. His brief introductory remarks, calculated to rouse the awe of the listeners, were followed by a half minute's still, brow-pleating silence. At last the silence was broken by an incoherent muttering. Vequi's eyes were squeezed shut, his lips quivered with emotion, he gestured sinuously. As his muttering waxed in intensity, the sweat started out on his brow. The pace of his movements built, his breath came in gasps, and a low moan of mystic fulfillment escaped him. At that moment, the light of the chandeliers began to wane. Within seconds, five hundred candle flames dwindled to tiny points of light no brighter than distant stars. Only the candles in the two wall sconces behind the table burned bright, and by that backlight, Vequi was visible in striking silhouette. A murmur of excited admiration arose, in which Eliste did not join. She might have been more impressed, had she not so often watched Uncle Quinz perform similar feats without benefit of theatrics. By comparison, Vequi v'Isseroi seemed a bit of a mountebank.

Staring eyes fixed upon the table, Vequi uttered an unintelligible command. For a moment nothing happened, and then, amidst a sprightly clinking of glass and silver, a host of ornate edible confections came to life. A brace of golden suckling pigs, honey-glazed and wreathed in ivy, stood up on their platter, spitting the apples from their mouths. A roast peacock clothed in full plumage fanned its tail and climbed to its feet. A flock of assorted headless game birds rose up, flapping their naked crispy wings, while the pastry lid of a great pie sprang a fissure, liberating a horde of baked quail. Jellied eels began to wriggle, poached salmon stood on their tails, and a huge boiled lobster rattled its scarlet armor. Imbued with impossible elasticity, a gang of multihued fruits and vegetables bounced about like tennis balls. Above them all, mounted upon a flower-decked pedestal, the great ice sculpture carved in the likeness of a sphinx opened her beautiful predator's eyes and spread her frigid wings. Gravely the edibles bowed to King Dunulas, who smiled, well pleased with the spectacle. Queen Lallazay, obviously enchanted, clapped her hands, and the courtiers oohed in delight.

For a moment longer they seemed to stand there, alive and sentient, before the illusion broke. The air stirred, the solid forms wavered, shifted, and blurred, and the edibles resumed their rightful inanimate state. The lights came up, and all was as it had been. The performance was over, and the courtiers broke into spontaneous, enthusiastic applause. Cries of admiration arose, and the King himself addressed a word or two of praise to the magician. Vequi accepted the tribute with apparent humility, belied by his triumphant eyes.

Eliste smiled and applauded politely, while inwardly wondering, *Is that all?* The spectacle had been charming beyond doubt, but minor; and the abrupt, perfunctory conclusion was distinctly clumsy. Compared to the magic of Quinz vo Derrivalle, Vequi v'Isseroi's antics were downright amateurish. Yet nobody seemed to know it. The faces around her were bright with what looked to be genuine admiration. Were they being polite, or was it possible that they truly didn't know the difference between trifling diversion and real magic? Familiar since earliest childhood with the work of a master, Eliste had always taken her uncle's abilities for granted. He was simply Uncle Quinz, delightful and eccentric; his feats but an ordinary manifestation of natural Exalted talent, nothing more. The rescue of Dref Zeenoson had perhaps begun to open her eyes for the first time to the full wonder of her kinsman's accomplishments. And now she saw the King's courtiers uniformly awed by a little display that would have set Quinz vo Derrivalle yawning.

Beyond doubt, Vequi himself was innocently certain of his own success. Here he came, shouldering his way through the crowd to Eliste's side, his air of gleeful self-satisfaction verging on the unseemly. Eliste congratulated him, complimented him. Her eyes were wide with the admiration that he seemed to expect; artificial admiration, but Vequi didn't guess it—they almost never did. So much her own experience, confirmed by Zeralenn's advice, had already taught her.

Scenting conquest, as he imagined, Vequi now trailed her everywhere. So too did a number of others, most of them subtly and skillfully encouraged, with the exception of Feronte. Conversation ranged widely, jumping from politics to art to sport to the latest gossip of the salons, so swiftly and bewilderingly that Eliste, sometimes confused, found herself relying on her eyes and her smile, which usually served her well enough. The best conversations were those whose topics, if any, were afterward impossible to recall. One piece of intelligence, however, stuck in her mind. Later she could not remember its source. But after the ball, as the powdered footman conducted her through the mirrored corridors of the Beviaire to the Maids' Quarters, wherein her belongings were already waiting, she considered a bit of news that had somehow snagged her imagination. For reasons she could hardly define, it seemed significant that Shorvi Nirienne's latest book, *The Promise,* should have been banned, its author outlawed. Nirienne had asked for it, of course, what with his demands for the abolishment of Exalted privilege, for the reform of the legal system, for a Charter of Human Rights, and for the reestablishment of an old-style elected Century to limit the power of the king. More was involved, of course, than the mere proscription of some renegade lawyer's rantings. Nirienne had already collected a sizable band of devoted followers, the self-styled Niriennistes, whose complaints might go far in influencing popular opinion. It was wise to silence that too-eloquent voice, and therefore it made good sense to order Nirienne's arrest. Eliste was sorry, for the punishment seemed severe. She would not have wished confinement in the Sepulchre upon her worst enemy, but there was obviously no help for it—for the sake of the nation, Shorvi Nirienne had to disappear. It might seem harsh, but public safety sometimes demanded strong measures.

In a modest apartment overlooking University Square in the bohemian section of Sherreen known as Rat Town, a man worked with feverish haste. He was throwing garments, keepsakes, books, and papers into the small trunk that stood open on the sitting-room floor. All too soon the box was full to overflowing, too full to close; and its owner, pale but determined, began pulling clothes out and flinging them away to make room for more of the precious books. Before he had completed this task there came a knocking, and he froze, breathlessly still save for his hunted eyes.

"Shorvi, it's I—Daquel." A hurried whisper, a familiar voice.

Shorvi Nirienne opened the door to admit a hugely tall and broad young man with a round soft face whose boyishness was deliberately offset by the addition of a bristling ginger mustache. Nirienne himself was altogether different. Middle-aged, no more than medium height, with narrow-shouldered, unathletic build, brown hair going to gray, and a mobile, ascetically nondescript face, he was saved from anonymity only by the uncommon brilliance and depth of his intelligent brown eyes.

"It's official," declared Daquel. "They're coming for you. In fact, they're on their way."

"So. I'm almost inclined to stay and greet them."

"Do that and you'll spoil the good work of all your friends, whose efforts deserve better. Come, sir. There's a cart and driver waiting below to carry you to a safe house in the Eighth District. One of our lads will pass the word to Madame your wife. I'll take the box, don't trouble about that, but now's the time to move."

"Who owns this safe house?" Nirienne did not stir.

"One of Oef Fuvay's cousins. A Madame Hiroux, something of the sort."

"And does this Madame Hiroux know the risk involved in harboring a fugitive?"

"Nothing to it if she's not caught, is there?"

"Fine bravado, my friend."

"Come, no need for concern. Doubtless this cousin feels the risk worthwhile, as do we all. But you should know you add to her danger by dawdling here."

"It sticks in my craw, this slinking and skulking. No, you needn't say anything, Daquel. I'm coming. Here, let me give you a hand with that box."

Together they forced down the lid of the trunk, and young Daquel hoisted the heavy burden to his shoulder with disconcerting ease. Shorvi Nirienne touched the pocket of his loose summer coat, verifying for the hundredth time the presence of a rolled sheaf of paper—the unfinished manuscript of his latest treatise. Satisfied, he nodded, and the two men left the apartment for the last time, made their way down four creaky flights of stairs, past the dozing concierge, and out into the street where the cart awaited.

Nirienne stopped short at sight of the driver, who was a stranger. He glimpsed long limbs, a youthful face.

"That's Beq, the new man," Daquel explained. "A very cool hand, I can tell you."

Nirienne nodded without emphasis, as if withholding judgment. Daquel deposited the trunk in back, and they climbed up onto the seat. Beq cracked his whip, and the cart rolled off down Cider Alley. Nirienne cast one uneasy glance back over his shoulder, just as a party of gendarmes rounded the corner at the end of the street. Spying the cart, the gendarmes broke into a run. Nirienne nudged his companion, and Daquel lifted two fingers to his mouth to shrill a piercing whistle. Instantly Cider Alley swarmed with shouting university students, Niriennistes all. The noise, crush, and sudden confusion were astounding, but under the leadership of a young general clouded in false white hair and whiskers, order swiftly emerged. Efficiently, the students ranged themselves across the alley. The gendarmes charged, and the shouting swelled to a roar, but the line held.

Beq whipped his horse to a rattling canter. The cart bounced and jolted over the cobbles, down Cider Alley, then out onto wide University Street, which bypassed two colleges, then carried straight on into the wretched slums of the Eighth District. Many a citizen gaped in surprise after the hurrying vehicle, but no one attempted to interrupt its progress, and apparently no one recognized its celebrated passenger.

Behind them, Cider Alley rang with screams, threats, and curses as assorted denizens of Rat Town came rushing from taverns and tenements to hurl themselves into the fight. Few knew the actual cause of contention, but that didn't matter—enough to see that university men defied the hated Gendarmerie. The unlucky soldiers, faced with overwhelming force, were swiftly chased from the neighborhood, escaping with minor cuts and bruises. Curiously, the defeat of the gendarmes failed to appease the crowd, whose emotions—pent over the space of many lifetimes—seemed suddenly to demand outlet. At the same time that Shorvi Nirienne was being ushered into his garret refuge in the boardinghouse of Madame Hiroux—situated, ironically enough, almost within the shadow of the Sepulchre itself—the mob raged through the streets of Rat Town; smashing, rending, and looting all in its path. Every wineshop along Cider Alley was picked clean, cookshops were raided, windows and glass lanterns were shattered, and bonfires bloomed like orange flowers. Presently the crowd exploded from the alley out into University Square, where the old King's Tower rose behind the Ten Monarchs—life-size marble representations of ten of the present King Dunulas's most illustrious ancestors. For some reason, the sight of the Monarchs seemed to induce hysteria. Shrieks of execration arose, and the mob surged forward to rip the famous statues from their pedestals. The Monarchs fell in quick succession, to shatter upon the cobbles; but this impersonal annihilation brought no satisfaction. Stones appeared in the hands of the rioters, and with these crude instruments the marble fragments were swiftly reduced to white gravel, kicked far and wide by plebeian feet. This done, the mob swirled howling through the square in search of fresh prey; and it was more than likely that the ancient lecture halls of the university would have fallen victim to popular wrath, had not the Crowd Queller of Sherreen, in the company of his minions, arrived upon the scene.

It was nearly dawn. The rioters, for all their rage, were tiring. The young Niriennistes had long since retired, their purpose accomplished. In the absence of strong leadership, the well-established fear of the Queller reasserted itself, and slivers began peeling off of the human mass, to disappear down darkened alleyways. Those remaining were slow to accept defeat. The Queller's masked followers were obliged to shoot no fewer than four before the crowd was persuaded to disperse. The wounded and dead were carried off and the Queller's party withdrew soon after, leaving University Square empty save for a scattering of glass-bladed debris and a spread of white marble wreckage, all that remained of the Ten Monarchs.

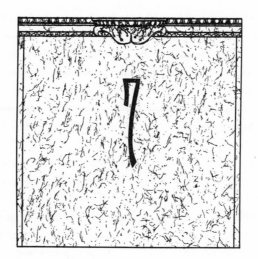

The Maids' Quarters were surprisingly cramped and mean. Anticipating royal splendor, Eliste was dismayed to find herself sharing a plain, drafty chamber with three other girls of her own age. The room contained four narrow beds, one washstand, two chests of drawers, and a single cheval glass. A small adjoining chamber housed four big clothespresses, and four pallets for the maidservants. Two other suites of identical nature opened upon a stuffy communal sitting room. A fourth and far more luxurious suite belonged to the aged but still gimlet-eyed Marquise vo Quivesse, official Mother to the Maids. A short dim corridor connected the sitting room to Queen Lallazay's vast apartment.

The spill of boxes, baskets, hampers, and loose sundries cluttering every horizontal surface bore testimony to the inadequacy of the furnishings. The full extent of that inadequacy did not become fully apparent until the morning, when four girls competed for washstand and mirror. The contest began about dawn, when Quivesse came creaking in to roust her charges from their beds. Eliste opened her eyes reluctantly. She had come from the Queen's Presence Chamber but a scant two hours earlier, flushed with champagne, excitement, and a sense of wicked worldliness. Now she was paying for it. The other girls were already up. Fluttering and chattering, tousle-haired and sleep-rumpled, they jockeyed for space about the washstand. Their maidservants circled the group like solicitous satellites, and the air was alive with giggling insults. No bleary eyes or pasty complexions here, Eliste noted. Her roommates were fresh and well-rested, or at least contrived to appear so. The girl splashing at the basin, for example—the short one with the black curls, spaniel eyes, and golden skin—glowed with an almost un-Exalted vitality. Beside her, exquisitely muted by contrast, stood a slim human lily whose pale oval face and delicate features suggested otherworldly innocence. Behind them both loomed a very tall girl whose snub-nosed, cheerfully unremarkable face was offset by an almost embarrassingly voluptuous form, displayed to advantage in the flimsiest of silken wrappers. All of them were pretty, polished, unnervingly self-assured.

"No malingering, girl." The voice of the old Marquise broke in on Eliste's thoughts. "You are here to serve her Majesty." Without awaiting reply, she stooped and yanked the coverlet to the foot of the bed.

Eliste sat up, hastily adjusting her nightgown. A fresh chorus of giggles arose, and she colored deeply. Throwing vo Quivesse an indignant glance, she jumped from the bed. Kairthe swathed her in a light dressing gown, and she started for the washstand.

"One moment."

Eliste halted, scowled. This last was a mistake.

"Perhaps you imagine, Exalted Miss, that you are here to entertain yourself." Quivesse folded her arms. "Perhaps you think yourself a great chatelaine, or perhaps you think that you are queen. Allow me to inform you otherwise. Your new post as Maid of Honor, no sinecure, carries many obligations. It is to be hoped that your own sense of duty might ensure industry, modesty, decorum, and responsible behavior. If such is not the case, then I am here to safeguard her Majesty's interests. Do not think to evade *my* vigilance, Exalted Miss. I have been here many years, and I have dealt with countless Maids of *Dishonor*! There is no trick I haven't foiled, no crafty stratagem I do not know. There is nothing you can devise that I have not seen and conquered long before you were ever born. Therefore, do not hope to shirk or slack. You will carry your own weight, you will perform your tasks faithfully, you will conduct yourself with dignity and decency, or else you will answer to me. Do I make myself clear?"

Not trusting herself to answer, Eliste turned away.

"This is worth at least one black mark on the list. Perhaps more. You have not started off on the right foot, Exalted Miss. I advise you to take care." So saying, Quivesse withdrew.

Glowering, Eliste stalked to the washstand, splashed her flaming face with tepid water. Her roommates studied her with undisguised interest. Her obvious discomfort evidently awakened their sympathies, for the diminutive brunette remarked consolingly, "Don't mind the Watchdog. She's like that with everyone."

"Watchdog?"

"That's our name for the Quivesse, and she's earned it, with all her snapping and snarling."

"She is very choleric," observed the statuesque one. "Dyspeptic, too. Flatulent—"

"Both in body and mind," interjected the brunette.

"It is her liver, I suppose," continued the statue. "Or else her spleen. Or perhaps she fears that she is universally disliked."

"With good reason," chimed in the lily, whose unexpectedly deep, husky voice contradicted her ethereal appearance. "Watchdog indeed! Meddlesome gray bitch is perishing of jealousy."

"That's exactly right. She can't stand it that we're young, and it drives her mad to see us amusing ourselves. She does everything she can think of to spoil our pleasure."

"Much good it does the shriveled old stick. Could she stop Putsie vo Crev from dining in vo Furnaux's room? Or Frisse v'Enjois from making an ass of herself over what's-his-name with the striped waistcoat? Or Derinne vo Doliet from running off with Rouveel-Nezoir vo Lillevant for a week? There are always ways of getting around the Watchdog."

"Someone *should* have stopped Derinne that time, though. Lillevant went and got her with child. At least she *claimed* it was his."

"I don't blame her. He's so beautiful! I wouldn't mind—"

"Very good, I'll tell him you said so."

"Don't you dare! I'll *demolish* you!"

"But did anyone ever find out for certain if it was really Lillevant's work?"

"Could have been anyone's," opined the lily. "Derinne's reputation already stank like a serf in summer, if you'll recall. Lillevant wasn't about to marry her, and neither was anyone else, after that little escapade."

"Oh, is *that* why she was packed off back to the country so suddenly?"

"Clever girl. Which is more than can be said of the wretched Derinne. If the poor little trollop had possessed the least glimmering of intelligence, she'd have secured one of Dr. Zirque's revolting but effective potions, and so ridded herself of all encumbrance, with no one the wiser."

"You should know!"

"Ah—well!" The lily smiled and shrugged. "But Derinne, sentimentally irresolute in such matters, must sit vacillating until her condition becomes apparent to all. Whereupon the Watchdog goes mad, runs to and fro, foaming at the mouth and crying out that Exalted Miss vo Doliet's transgressions exceed all measurable limits, and she is therefore altogether and forever off *The List*, cast into outer darkness, her vile name utterly and irrevocably *expunged*—it was all very amusing."

"What's this list she speaks of?" Eliste interrupted. "She said I had a black mark."

"We all have black marks."

"I have five."

"And I, six."

"I've racked up a score of fifty-three, so far," announced the lily, "and I'm hoping to hit a hundred before the end of the year."

"But what exactly is this list?"

"Nobody knows."

"No doubt we'll find out one day."

"In breathless anticipation we await the moment of revelation."

Laughing, they introduced themselves. The little brunette was Gizine vo Chaumelle, her family great landowners in the Jerunde. The semidraped statue was Neanne vo Zeurlot-v'Innique from the Sevagne, daughter to his Majesty's Minister of Finance. The deceptively pure-faced lily was Merranotte v'Estais, granddaughter to no less than the Duke of Rivennier. Eight other girls of similar age and rank inhabited the neighboring suites, known respectively as Maidsrose and Maidsblanche. Eliste's arrival, timed to fill the vacancy created by the abrupt departure of the luckless Derinne vo Doliet, brought the total count of Maids up to the requisite dozen.

Chatter continued as the servants began to dress them. As Kairthe laced her into Madame Nimais's weightless peach tiffany morning gown, Eliste acquired more information. She learned that the Maids of Honor subsisted on an average of four hours of sleep a night. She discovered that indefatigable purging maintained a small-waisted figure. She found that gifts from wealthy patrons augmented the contributions of tightfisted provincial fathers. She was informed that the secretions from the musk glands of the vebarine, mixed with olive oil, ground nessumut, and saliva, infallibly blocked conception. She learned that the Cavalier vo Furnaux, catholic in his tastes, preferred very blond boys to indifferently blond girls. She heard that the Queen's incessant coquetry masked an essential coldness, or perhaps an unconscious warmth never awakened by the King's inexpert advances. She discovered that King Dunulas did not visit his queen's apartment more often than once a month, and never stayed longer than half an hour.

The edifying conversation was cut short by the return of the Marquise vo Quivesse, who entered to announce that the Duchess of Feronte, First Lady of the Queen's Bedchamber, required the presence of three or four Maids to assist in the survey of the royal wardrobe. The girls in Eliste's chamber, Maidsmauve, had been selected. They were to report to the Duchess at once and serve her as directed, after which they would be free to amuse themselves until the Queen's levee, scheduled for midmorning. There was no definite time allowance for breakfast. The Maids of Honor, regarded as so many hothouse blossoms, were evidently expected to subsist on candlelight and compliments. In reality, they were forced to scrounge for themselves as best they could.

The girls filed from the room. A sharp clucking sound from the Marquise arrested Eliste.

"One moment. This was delivered for you not fifteen minutes ago. I considered withholding it, but in view of the sender's noble eminence, deemed it only fitting to trust in his chivalry, if not your prudence. Here." Quivesse extended a small package wrapped in wine velvet and black satin ribbon. Attached to the package was a square card bearing an embossed crest, which Eliste studied in momentary incomprehension.

"Feronte!" whooped a voice at her ear. Eliste swiveled to find Merranotte v'Estais just behind her. The human lily appeared unaccountably amused. "There are his arms, in every sense! Feronte commences a new siege. A new fortress, a new campaign! But do his old cannon still fire, or have age and rust done their work? I wonder. Ladies—come see! Look here!"

Eliste reddened as her roommates came trooping back in. Noting the look, Merranotte shrugged. "Come, child, no blushes. You've a new set of sisters, every bit as tiresome and officious as real sisters could be. No point in holding back— you shall have our opinions whether you want them or not. Now, what has he sent you? Let us see!"

Torn between eagerness and embarrassment, Eliste stripped away the ribbons and wrappings, opened a brocade-quilted box to reveal a circlet of fine, translucent jade links, glittered in emeralds and clasped in gold. Following an unsatisfying attempt to drape the chain about her wrist, she observed, frowning, "It must be meant for a giantess."

"Little savage, that is an anklet! Try it on!"

"On my *leg*?"

"Try it, try it!"

Eliste complied. Handing the ornament to Kairthe, she raised her peach-cloud skirts to present a silk-clad, lace-gartered calf. Kairthe fastened the gold clasp, and Eliste rotated her ankle experimentally. The jade links, wonderfully cool, gleamed like deep seawater.

"Ah, it suits her!"

"The color is tremendous!"

"She must wear her skirts short to show it off!"

"Indeed she must, and start a new fashion! Short in the front, with a brief ruffled train run on drawstrings."

"And we shall call the new mode 'Citadel Stormed,'" Merranotte suggested helpfully. "Or perhaps 'Feronte's Conquest'?"

" 'Feronte's Folly' might be more appropriate," Eliste returned. "But let us see what he writes." The color burned in her cheeks, belying her artificial composure. Opening the card, she read, " 'Exalted Miss—I invite you to dine with me this evening. A footman will appear to escort you to my apartment at ten o'clock. I prefer that you do not wear perfume.—Feronte.' " She looked up. "Blunt, isn't he?"

"His Grace minces no words," Neanne agreed. "And after all, why should he?"

"What will you say to him when you meet?" Gizine demanded. "Will you be melting and languishing, or will you be all cool and mysterious?"

"What will you wear?"

"Will you be nervous? *I* should be petrified!"

"I've no reason to be nervous," Eliste informed them, "for the simple reason that I'm not going."

"Are you serious?" Gizine's spaniel eyes rounded.

"We're speaking of his Majesty's own *brother*," Neanne pointed out. "You can't refuse his invitation!"

"I'm not interested in his pedigree, and I'll refuse if I like."

"You're new, and you don't understand—it just isn't done."

"Well, it is now. I'm not going." Eliste's jaw set.

"Why ever *not*?"

"Because—because—I just don't like him, that's why. He's a deal too sure of himself and too peremptory, almost insultingly so. I consider him . . . impudent."

"You loony, you'll ruin your own chances. Don't you know that a duke *can't* be impudent?"

"This one can. As for this summons of his, I'll be glad to tell him what he can do with it." Eliste tore the Duke's card in two and tossed the halves away.

Merranotte v'Estais shouted with laughter. "Oh, the citadel is well-guarded, the gate is firmly barred. Feronte has his work cut out for him. This promises much entertainment. Actually, my dear, I think your strategy not unsound—his Grace will find the challenge piquant, and your resistance will surely awaken his ardor."

"That's not why I'm resisting," Eliste told her. "I don't want his ardor, or anything else of his, for that matter. Kairthe—" She snapped her fingers. "Take that anklet off me, drop it in its box, and carry it back to the Duke of Feronte. Thank his Grace on my behalf, and convey my regrets that I am unable to accept his invitation."

"You want *me* to speak to the Duke, Miss? To the Duke himself?" As she spoke, Kairthe was already stripping the ornament from her mistress's ankle.

"Or to one of his lackeys. It is of little consequence which."

"Kill me dead!" Kairthe exclaimed, and her fellow servants exchanged amazed glances. "How'll I ever find him in all this great anthill of a place, Miss? It goes on for *miles*, don't it?"

Muffled giggles arose among the Maids of Honor. The Marquise vo Quivesse's lips thinned.

"Ask the servants for directions," Eliste advised.

"Can I mark a trail to find my way back?"

"No! Just ask!"

"Can I use the pot before I set off? I'm that nervous!"

"I don't want to hear about it! Really, you are such an infant!"

Suffocating with laughter, Neanne clutched Gizine for support. Quivesse's foot began to tap.

"Well, don't pitch a screamer, Miss! I'm gone!" Box in hand, Kairthe scurried from the room.

"She's an original, that one," Merranotte observed with a smile. "But truly, my dear, I think you do yourself a disservice. Feronte's gift is pretty and becoming. Why refuse it?"

"I do not wish to offer false encouragement."

"Why not? That is an integral part of the game, and by no means the least enjoyable."

"I am not playing a game with the Duke."

"But he is playing one with you, and you may as well return the compliment."

"What he does scarcely dictates *my* actions."

"Gad, what relentless rectitude, what provincial probity, what vinegar-virtue! Or else what uncommon arrogance!"

"I don't want to obligate myself to Feronte."

"There you mistake the matter. In accepting an admirer's gift, you do not obligate yourself in the slightest. Here in Sherreen, the gallant so crass as to regard a lady as his debtor could only be dismissed as a boor. His offerings are merely the rightful tribute to your charms, and as such should be encouraged, even demanded. And that, too, is part of the game."

"She's right, you know!" chimed in Gizine vo Chaumelle. "You should never have given up that gorgeous anklet! *I* never should!"

"How could you bear to let it go?" inquired Neanne. "It was almost as beautiful as Lillevant himself, and *so* much in the mode!"

"Our transplanted wild rose will know better the next time," opined Merranotte. "That there will be a next time, and soon, I do not doubt for a moment."

"That will do, you featherheaded chits!" The Marquise vo Quivesse clapped her hands sharply. "Enough! It is time to earn your keep. The Duchess awaits you—now go."

"Her Grace of Feronte—oh, I'm dying!" exclaimed Gizine.

"What a farce—I can't endure it!" cried Neanne.

Brows lifted, Eliste turned to Merranotte.

"That's right." Merranotte correctly interpreted the questioning look. "Her Grace of Feronte, First Lady of the Queen's Bedchamber, to whom we must now look for direction, is your royal tomcat's oft-betrayed spouse."

"His wife. Delightful. Things couldn't be better. I don't suppose there's much hope that she won't be told of this?"

"Afraid not, child. Too many witnesses. Her Grace will know within minutes, if not already. But what of that? She should be used to such news by now, and in any event, the plaints of an aging, jealous wife are only the stuff of comedy. She might make herself a trifle disagreeable, but you can afford to laugh."

"But it's all so sordid, such a disagreeable way to start out."

"You have brought it on yourself," Quivesse informed her. "You young girls of today have no standards, no pride. If a great noble such as his Grace takes note of you, it is because you have sought his attention. If his duchess scorns and detests you, it is because you have given her cause. Therefore, cease your complaints. Whatever failure and censure you suffer, be assured it is no more than you deserve. Now, go."

The confrontation with the Duchess of Feronte wasn't nearly as bad as Eliste had feared. The Duchess—a horse-faced, large-handed, impassive woman, proud daughter of one of the oldest great families, and some years senior to her straying spouse—greeted the new Maid with detached courtesy and set her to work cataloging Lallazay's numberless gloves. If she knew of the Duke's interest in Exalted Miss vo Derrivalle, she was too well-bred to show any sign of it, but went about her work in dignified composure that revealed nothing. In the absence of overt hostility, Eliste's tension eased. Her three roommates, mischievous scandalmongers all, were no doubt disappointed. But Eliste, considerably relieved, was able to relax and take stock of her surroundings, marveling at the scope of the full-size suite of rooms that housed the Queen's astounding wardrobe. One of the chambers contained a walk-in closet given over entirely to the storage of gloves, which reposed in innumerable wooden boxes, stacked on narrow shelves specially designed to receive them. In the closet sat Eliste, opening each box in turn and entering brief accounts of the contents into a great ledger: "1 pr. glv., wrist-length, lavender suede, white silk embroidery, Strellian cutwork. 1 pr. glv., 3/4 length, dk. blue kid, silver buttons, crystal + silver beading." And so on, interminably. The purpose of the survey was not apparent, but the work was easy, the chance to inspect the Queen of Vonahr's personal belongings novel, and time passed quickly. In the adjoining chambers, Gizine, Neanne, and Merranotte busied themselves with similarly inconsequential tasks.

Long before their respective labors were completed, the Maids of Honor were dismissed. Preparations for the Queen's levee had begun. The four girls repaired to their sitting room, where for the first time Eliste encountered her compeers from Maidsrose and Maidsblanche—a gaggle of pretty, noisy, frivolous young Exalteds, doll-perfect in their pastel silks, similar in type to her own Maidsmauve roommates. In accordance with what appeared to be a well-established custom, food began to appear on the tea table in the middle of the room. Someone had charmed a bagful of chocolate-raspberry cream puffs from the palace pastry chef. There was a basket of late strawberries, a heap of yesterday's petit fours, a pile of bonbons, and amidst shrieks of universal approbation, Merranotte v'Estais brought forth half a dozen bottles of champagne, properly chilled. No one asked where they had come from. Merranotte's flair for unorthodox procurement was proverbial, and it was usually better not to question her methods.

Corks popped, flutes materialized, champagne flowed, and bubbles danced. Eliste regarded her glass with misgiving. Champagne for breakfast seemed so marvelously luxurious, she scarcely dared confess that she would actually have preferred fruit juice at that hour of the morning. But it *was* fruit juice, she reminded herself—the very best kind. And she would look like a straight-laced ninny if she refused to drink it. Still somewhat reluctant, she took a tentative sip. The champagne was sweet, selected to complement a pastry breakfast; light and seemingly innocuous. Forgetting her doubts, she drank freely; and only the winged lift of her spirits, the warm sense of pleasure and assurance that flooded her veins, might have reminded her that she partook of something more potent than ginger punch. All around her, the Maids were giggling and nibbling, sipping and gossiping like so many flowers imbued with human appetites. They spoke of fashion, food, and flirtation; and the atmosphere of giddy gaiety waxed hilarious when Gizine vo Chaumelle informed the company that the newest addition to their sisterhood was the latest object of Feronte's imperious attentions. Frisse v'Enjois proposed a toast to "the Feronte Enterprise." Screaming with laughter, they clinked glasses, and Eliste felt herself accepted.

As the carouse continued and the champagne did its work, the talk grew racier and the anecdotes more outrageous. At first Eliste only listened, scandalized and delighted. Presently her bubble-bolstered confidence mounted, and she was chattering and giggling along with the rest of them. All the provisions were consumed, down to the last crumb of frangipane-filled petit four. The last bottle was drained, and it was time to move on to the Queen's levee. Eliste stood up, a little uncertainly. A curious sense of mild paralysis stiffened her joints, and by some trick of vision, the room and everything in it seemed to have receded. So much for champagne in the morning; although, she noticed hazily, none of her companions seemed at all impaired. Suddenly dizzy, she swayed, and might have fallen had not a slim white hand reached out to steady her.

"Careful, child," Merranotte v'Estais advised. "Here—chew one of these." She offered a small white pastille.

"What is it?" Eliste's tongue felt thick and slow.

"These excellent tablets come from the ingenious Dr. Zirque. Just one of them will keep you awake and alert for hours. Thus it becomes possible to drink champagne to your heart's content; to dance or game until dawn; to diminish those dreary intervals of sleep, or to dispense with sleep altogether, if you choose; and still remain fresh as spring rain, or at least appear so."

"Truly? How do they do that?"

"I could hardly say how. Dr. Zirque, plebeian that he is, and little more than a glorified mechanical, may perhaps concern himself with such matters, but I do not. Enough to know that they are effective, always useful, and not infrequently essential. Chew it slowly, my dear, else we shall have you flying about the Queen's bedchamber like a great peach-colored bird."

Eliste chewed and swallowed obediently. A moment later a rush of new vitality swept the sluggishness from her mind and body. Suddenly she was alert and charged with energy—enough to sustain her for days, weeks, years; assured, optimistic, even joyful; and alive, she was certain, as never before. Exhilarated, she laughed aloud.

"Hush, a little discretion," Merranotte advised.

"I feel wonderful!"

"Did I not promise?"

"Wonderful! Could I get some of these?"

"Assuredly. They are easily procured, and almost indispensable. Another few days here, and you will not understand how you ever existed without them."

Vigor more than restored, Eliste followed her sister Maids through the short corridor back into Queen Lallazay's apartment, this time proceeding directly to her Majesty's immoderately feminine bedchamber. In the middle of the room rose a great, carved and gilded four-poster boasting an arched canopy draped in pink flowered silk; pink silk hangings lined in gold; priceless lace coverlet; and a mountain of ruffled, frilled, and embroidered white pillows. Propped up in bed as if newly awakened sat her Majesty—face freshly painted, hair glistening with pomade and sculpted into clusters of curls, each ruffle and ribbon upon her lingerie bedjacket faultlessly ironed. The Queen had, as was her wont, submitted herself to the ministrations of waiting women and hairdresser for the space of two hours before climbing back into bed to receive her callers. The morning light filtering through the pink-swathed windows was cunningly muted, and in that flattering soft glow Lallazay looked young as her own Maids of Honor. Now she sat sipping chocolate and whispering earnestly up at Dr. Zirque, who bent over her with an air of dedication. Often she gestured, expressive hand fluttering distressfully from her brow, to her throat, to her heart, while the doctor nodded in understanding and grave compassion. Deployed about the room were the Queen's closest personal attendants, ranging in age and kind from Lallazay's own choice of the youthful and charming Princess v'Arian, to a grim knot of prune-faced duchesses whose rank entitled them to royal proximity.

The Maids advanced in single file to kiss their mistress's hand. Lallazay greeted them kindly but inconsistently—beaming upon her particular favorites, bestowing vague, puzzled smiles upon those whose names she did not remember. The line moved quickly, and then Eliste was pressing her lips to the neroli-scented, nervous little hand whose nails, she noted for the first time, were bitten to the quick. Lallazay produced the obligatory smile. Her eyes fastened attentively upon Madame Nimais's inspired creation; she seemed hardly to note the wearer. Eliste straightened; nodded with a certain distant civility to Dr. Zirque, whose social status was ambiguous; and backed neatly away. In the face of familiarity, her awe of royalty was fading fast. Around her tittered and snickered the incorrigibly light-minded Maids. Frisse v'Enjois poked an elbow into her ribs and pointed. Eliste followed the pointing finger to behold Neanne vo Zeurot-v'Innique— attired in a morning gown cut low to exploit her natural advantages, cut to the extreme limit of propriety or perhaps beyond—bending and swelling over the Queen's hand. Dr. Zirque's watery eyes were fixed upon Neanne's décolletage. His narrow face was noticeably flushed and moist. Eliste's merriment rose almost unquenchably. She clapped a hand across her mouth and studied the carpet. A couple of sputters escaped her, and she bit a knuckle. She must be cool and Exalted and self-possessed. Yes, she must. She stole a glance at Frisse, beet-red and tremulous. Her eyes jumped back to Neanne, unconsciously indecent; her self-control slipped, and the giggles quivered on the verge of escape. Almost she considered dashing from the room. She might have done so, had the Queen's callers not begun to arrive at that time. First and foremost among them were the Duke and Duchess of Feronte. The Duchess was cool, impeccable, impenetrable; Feronte equally so.

He didn't appear to see her. As he fetched chocolate and biscuits from the sideboard for his wife, he seemed not to know Eliste was there. If she had not refused his gift, he might have thought it worthwhile to acknowledge her presence. As it was, she did not exist. Only once the Duchess of Feronte's eyes shifted to the new Maid's face, to rest there for a levelly appraising moment, and in that brief moment the Duchess's awareness revealed itself. Eliste's amusement died a quick death. All of a sudden she felt cold and shabby, guiltless but inappropriately ashamed.

She did not have to endure the Duchess's scrutiny for long. Having paid their respects to the Queen, the Maids of Honor retired to the sidelines, there to fulfill their customary ornamental function. The four Maidsmauve roommates took possession of a pink brocade love seat and a couple of gilt chairs in one corner. Disposing their wide skirts prettily, they sat watching and whispering behind their fans as the most Exalted of visitors came striding, marching, gliding, or mincing into the Queen's bedchamber. Presently the room was filled with patched and powdered courtiers—a rainbow swarm of them, the majority clustered about the Queen. Lallazay, still sitting up in bed, was chattering and gesturing with girlish, exaggerated animation. Teasing, bridling, tossing her head and laughing continually, her clear, high-pitched tones were easily audible above the hum of respectfully muted Exalted conversation. The greetings continued, and the guests began to diffuse throughout the room. Chairs, settees, window seats, and even footstools were quickly occupied. Clumps of conversationalists stood scattered here and there, with a high concentration of activity centering about the sideboard with its urns of chocolate and plates of biscuits. Seating herself at the little white and gold spinet, the Princess v'Arian began to pick out a tune, the sugared notes softly underscoring the well-modulated babble of Exalted voices.

Eliste gazed about her, spying many familiar faces, a number of them belonging to her dancing partners of the previous night. Even as she watched, the Exalted Vequi v'Isseroi appeared upon the threshold—a little disheveled, visibly out of breath, and quite shamefully late. An amused buzz greeted his conspicuous arrival. Rushing to the Queen's side, Vequi bent to kiss her hand, muttering contritely. Smiling, Lallazay slapped his wrist lightly, evidently pardoning him without reservation; whereupon the scene lost its interest, and Eliste resumed her survey of prospective suitors. Noting her absorbed expression, Merranotte remarked, "They will be over here as promptly as etiquette allows."

"Who will?"

"The gentlemen."

"Which gentlemen? I did not observe," Eliste lied.

"Oh, did you not?" Merranotte laughed, so infectiously that Eliste could not resist echoing her. "They'll be upon us like hungry wolves, probably within moments."

"Well, I should hope so," interjected Gizine. "Otherwise, Putsie vo Crev and her Maidsblanche gang will never let us hear the end of it. They'll gloat."

"*I* should not care to be ignored!" Neanne remarked.

"Given the depth of your décolletage, my dear, there is little fear of that."

"*I* should loathe sitting here alone, forsaken and forgotten and *ignored*! I should abominate it! If it happens, I shall certainly die!"

"Cheer up, you're saved. Here comes Furnaux."

"Aha! That will put Putsie's nose out of joint, and properly!"

To them came the Cavalier vo Furnaux, armed with a plateful of walnut biscuits, a mouthful of compliments, and a misleadingly guileless smile. Biscuits and compliments were accepted with equal enthusiasm. Shortly thereafter, Putsie's elegant brother Stazzi vo Crev joined them, to be followed in quick succession by Vequi v'Isseroi, by Gizine's wealthy admirer Nelille vo Denz, and last the Marquis vo Lieux-v'Olliard, a little old and staid for that heedless young group, but quietly determined to stay. The gallantries and witticisms flew; banter was quick and often barbed. But Eliste, used to dueling with Dref Zeenoson, was easily able to hold her own. Moreover, it seemed to her that Merranotte's pastille had imbued her mind with an almost supernatural sharpness, and she was correspondingly self-assured. Riveting Vequi with a coquettish slanting glance, she challenged, "And must we assume that last night's magical exertions drained the vitality of the Exalted Vequi? How else shall we account for an entrance so dramatically delayed?"

Vequi's jewel-flecked teeth flashed in a multihued smile. "Happy the man whose failings warrant censure of the radiant Miss vo Derrivalle. Her very reproofs impart distinction, and her approbation—nothing less than immortality."

"Very pretty, sir, but you evade the issue."

"Bear with your humble servant, Exalted Miss. I do not evade the issue, I merely approach it in gradually diminishing circles, like any good hunter. Slowly, moving with infinite care and discretion, I draw near. I pause, I wait, I weigh, I consider. Eventually I pounce, by which time the original issue has inevitably been forgotten."

"Vequi, is there no end to your nonsense?" Gizine inquired severely.

"None, Exalted Miss, in which infinite capacity surely lies my greatest social asset."

"Your greatest social asset will lie in your absence, if you won't satisfy our curiosity," Merranotte warned him.

"Ah, the Poison Lily! Very well, Exalted Miss, I would not risk *your* displeasure. Then know, ladies, that last night's exertions failed to drain my vitality. My vitality is equal to all occasions, and I ask nothing more of life than the fair vo Derrivalle's consent to prove it. Alas, no similar élan fires the veins of my coachman—a sorry rogue if ever there was, whose faint heart occasioned this morning's mishap. When he encounters difficulty, do you suppose it arouses his valor, his warlike spirit? It does not. No, the slightest setback utterly unnerves him. The very first obstacle and he is overcome, and I along with him. It is almost enough to drive a man pedestrian. But I have given the matter much sober consideration—"

"Sober—surely not!" Neanne tossed her head.

"And I believe I have hit upon the only sane and reasonable solution to the problem. I have decided that we must start breeding coachmen," Vequi informed them. "We breed horses for speed, dogs for cleverness, and cattle for size, not without success. It is only reasonable to assume that the same principles, judiciously applied to our serfs, may eventually produce the ideal coachman—sharp-eyed, steady-handed, resolute and courageous, impervious to weather, with an excellent sense of direction and an innate understanding of horses. In time, assuming the line flourishes, we whip breeders, as we shall be known, may perfect the type to such an extent that we shall become suppliers of purebred coachmen to the monarchs and nobility of all civilized nations. And having accomplished this, we may turn our efforts to the creation of the perfect, true-breeding valet, the perfect gardener, and above all, the perfect cook. But first things first. In order to commence, we require the services of a coachman nonpareil, together with a fertile female of notably equine demeanor. Might not her Grace of Feronte volunteer?"

Gales of malicious laughter greeted this sally, and the red-faced Gizine managed to choke, "Vequi, what a frippery you are!"

Vequi bowed, and Eliste, still laughing, inquired, "And what was this terrific obstacle that routed your coachman?"

"Streets full of riotous peasants, that's what. Between the Beviaire and the Girdle at Havillac, the streets are almost unnavigable. Everywhere the beggars, the laborers, the little shopkeepers, and such rabble swarm and howl, clapping their hands, hurling rocks and clods. What they think to gain, I cannot pretend to guess. It is all very noisy, very foolish, very annoying. They clog the streets, impeding progress, and worse, they frighten the horses."

"That's true." The Marquis vo Lieux-v'Olliard nodded his white-wigged head gravely. "On my way back from the New Arcade, the din in the streets threw my blacks off stride, and some fool put a scratch on the side of my cabriolet. A bad business. Disgraceful."

"But what is all this din about?" Eliste persisted. "What's happening?"

"You are behind the times, Exalted Miss. You've not yet heard last night's news," Vequi told her. "You must have known that the chatterbox Nirienne was earmarked for the Sepulchre, charged with treason, sedition, and writing bad verse, or whatever."

"I'd heard that."

"Well, when the gendarmes called at his lodgings last night, they discovered an empty nest. Nirienne had very sensibly withdrawn, but the wretched slum was riddled with his clownish partisans, who seized the opportunity to rampage through Rat Town. Up and down the streets they cavorted like third-rate mummers in search of an audience. Presently they emerged into University Square, where the destruction of the Ten Monarchs provided momentary amusement. Half of them were screaming for liberty, half of them were screaming for blood, and all of them were stinking of garlic. Presently some zany of a self-styled demagogue got up to harangue the crowd, which responded with heartfelt grunts and hoots, hot blasts of fury laced with an infinity of garlic——"

"How do you know all this, Vequi?" inquired Merranotte.

"Perhaps by my Exalted magic." Vequi was clearly enjoying himself. "Have I not proved my power? You must have faith, my lily, faith! In any event, you may rest assured that the destruction of all University Square was averted only by the arrival of the Crowd Queller and his men, who stampeded the human herd in time to preserve the lecture halls. Peace, or a good facsimile thereof, was restored——"

"Temporarily," suggested Nelille vo Denz.

"Just so. The uproar recommenced about dawn, continued long enough to delay my attendance upon her Majesty, and presumably has not subsided yet."

"To my mind," Furnaux offered, "they are welcome to bellow, grimace, prance, and loot wineshops to their hearts' content, provided they confine their idiotic impertinences to Rat Town, the Eighth District, and other such inconsequential pesthouses. Amidst such squalor, the flame that consumes must be viewed as a purifying agent."

"They've not confined their idiotic impertinences," Vequi told him. "That is all the trouble. They're racketing all over Sherreen."

"But why?" Eliste demanded. "If Nirienne escaped—and I can't be altogether sorry that he did——"

"Ah, the sentimentalist—the young romantic!" Stazzi chaffed.

"He is a cut above Master Whiss v'Aleur, you'll grant," Merranotte suggested.

"V'Aleur—come, does a rabid mongrel deserve notice?"

"If Nirienne escaped," Eliste persisted gamely, "then what are they shouting about? What do they want? What would it take to make them give over and go home?"

"The Crowd Queller is what it would take, and we may hope that the King will soon see fit to dispatch him," said Vequi.

"Beyond that, there is no solution," Furnaux agreed. "I'm told they scream for bread and justice. Alas, there is not enough bread for all, and never will be—that is only the way of the world. As for justice, they are not intellectually equipped to encompass the concept. Such abstractions are best left to those capable of understanding."

Eliste nodded in reluctant agreement.

"They shout for a brief time," observed vo Crev, "and then they are silent. What else is left to them? When all is said and done, they cannot know what they want, for in that they require guidance, as children do."

Somehow Eliste found herself thinking of Dref Zeenoson. He had not been at all a child, despite his youth, but it did not seem the time to say so. Her confusion deepened when a liveried footman materialized at her side to hand her a folded note. For a moment she stared at the paper square in incomprehension, wondering where it had come from. Then, impelled by instinct, she raised her eyes to encounter the gaze of his Grace of Feronte, who stood alone on the far side of the room. The Duchess was nowhere in evidence. Presumably she had faded away at some point or other, her exit unnoted by all save her interested spouse.

Following their companion's glance, the Maids traded significant smiles.

Eliste considered returning the note unopened, but curiosity got the better of her. Unfolding the paper, she read silently:

Exalted Miss—

Inasmuch as my offering failed to please you, you are encouraged to select an alternate more to your liking. Please convey notice of your choice at the earliest opportunity, at which time you may specify the date and hour of our next meeting.

—*Feronte*

The unmitigated boor!

The furious color burned in her cheeks. The undisguised amusement of her companions added fuel to the fire. Almost she considered passing the note around the room, to the delectation of all, but concluded that such an act would reflect more discreditably upon herself than the Duke. There were better ways. She shredded the note thoroughly, and then, eyes locked with Feronte's, tossed the fragments into the air to loose a tiny, momentary blizzard.

The quiet snickers all around her gave way to open laughter. Gizine and Neanne clutched one another. Merranotte's lips turned down at the corners. Even Lallazay was watching, astonished and not altogether pleased with her new Maid's bid for attention. Feronte himself did not change expression. Dark eyes impenetrable, he regarded her. Then, bidding brusque farewell to his satellites, he wheeled and made for the exit, where the appearance of a brace of frozen footmen discreetly signaled the close of the Queen's levee.

Eliste scarcely noted what happened thereafter. The levee ended, and she was back in the Maids' Quarters with her roommates. The Queen had no further need of their services throughout the day. The other girls vanished, all of them sought after. Eliste herself, she recalled almost as an afterthought, had made a number of assignations: Stazzi vo Crev for the midday meal, vo Lieux-v'Olliard for a stroll about the Beviaire Gardens, Vequi v'Isseroi for a hand of Antislez, vo Renache for a cup of punch at Madame vo Feuraillon's night-fest. All of these she scrupulously if indifferently honored, carried along on a rush of energy born of Dr. Zirque's white pastille. The effect lasted for many hours, far into the night. Later, much later, she returned to the Maidsmauve chamber, tired to death but wide awake, depressed and dry-mouthed, desert-eyed, shaky-limbed, jumpy, and prey to the jerk-muscled jitters. She didn't know what was wrong; but when someone offered her another pastille, this one veal-pink and guaranteed to bring quick repose, something impelled her to refuse.

Sleep was impossible. Condemned to consciousness, she occupied herself as best she could with Merranotte's surreptitious copy, obtained no one knew where, of the latest *Neighbor Jumalle's Complaint*. The ooze-minded editor, the self-styled "Whiss v'Aleur," was foul and abusive as ever. This week, this issue, he accused the young, widowed Princess v'Arian of poisoning her husband, in order to remove all obstacles standing between herself and total domination over her unnatural lover, the Queen Lallazay. As time passed and the candles burned low, Eliste read on—half amused, half horrified, wholly revolted. In her disgust, she quite dismissed the public significance of the muckraking journalist. He was a madman, an asinine liar, an ugly joke—but surely no cause for concern. For who outside a public hospital could be so misguided as to believe in Whiss v'Aleur?

The meeting had been publicized by word of mouth alone, yet it was well attended. The old vacant warehouse at Number 17 Pump Street in the Eighth District was crowded with members and would-be members of the People's Reparation Party, as the disciples of Whiss v'Aleur had taken to calling themselves. Lured by the prospect of viewing their elusive champion in the flesh, the faithful together with the merely inquisitive had turned out in force. The crowd was heterogeneous, its components varied in age, occupation, and station; ranging in kind from large-handed laborer, to lank-haired marketwoman, to shopkeeper, student, idler, random malcontent. Dotted here and there throughout the room, a few liveried retainers fidgeted in fear of recognition. Far more prevalent were the beggars, whose orchestrated pleas suggested intelligent organization. The plaints, entreaties, and veiled accusations issuing from dozens of throats exerted their inevitable effect, arousing guilt as well as resentment, pity as well as contempt, the whole resulting in reluctant charity, exploited to the ultimate degree. A grudging rain of small coins pattered into a host of outstretched unwashed palms. Consciences assuaged, the spectators were free to turn their righteous wrath upon the true source of their woes, the privileged class. The obligation of this class to redress all social and economic wrongs was not questioned for a moment by the zealots of the People's Reparation Party. Such obligation, after all, lay at the heart of the faction's very title.

The level of excitement among the spectators was high. All of them without exception were familiar with the style and content of v'Aleur's rancid *Neighbor*

Jumalle's Complaint. All admired and revered the splenetic daring of "Neighbor J," as they affectionately dubbed the editor, but few had actually encountered him. Whiss v'Aleur, so outrageously outspoken in print, had hitherto proved retiring in person. His public appearances were infrequent, relatively unheralded, and with good reason. Unabashedly seditious in his sentiments, radical and subversive in his ambitions, Whiss v'Aleur was doubtless destined for the gibbet, should he fall into the hands of the Gendarmerie. A rendezvous with Master Sherreen, as the city executioner was known, would shortly follow his capture; and this prospect had until now fostered a certain public discretion. Those so fortunate as to hear him in the taverns and backrooms that were his haunts described v'Aleur as dynamic, a spellbinder, magically persuasive, an inspired and inspiring orator; but such witnesses were rare. Now, for the first time, "Neighbor J" had consented to address a sizable gathering of his followers—a decision presumably reflecting the burgeoning power of the People's Reparation Party and the mounting confidence of its leader. It was a considerable occasion, perhaps a historic event. All present sensed as much. Restless, impatient, hungry for direction, and disposed to unbridled enthusiasm, the Reparationists awaited the revelations of the master.

Restlessness was not confined to the audience. In a tiny corner office originally intended for the use of a clerk-accountant, and walled off from the rest of the warehouse by a couple of flimsy partitions, waited three men. One of them, seated at the desk, was elderly, gray-haired, drably clad, drooping and physically frail, irresolute, and indefinably unworldly of aspect. A second—decades younger, massive, ungainly, uncouth, with a flat, broad, impassive face—occupied a second chair. His hands were extraordinarily large, almost freakishly so—heavily boned, fat with muscle, and never still. He held a collection of interlocking wheels, cogs, gears, and springs; and with these mechanical parts he toyed continually. The third man, nearly forty years old and hovering on the brink of middle age, was somewhat below middle height, slight and meager in build, plainly but scrupulously dressed. His thinning black hair was drawn severely off a tall brow; his narrow, sharp-jawed, thin-lipped and sallow face was marked with the traces of boyhood smallpox and dominated by a pair of prominent, hugely translucent green eyes, so pale as to appear quite colorless in low light. Evidently possessed of excess nervous energy finding outlet in constant activity, he paced tirelessly about the office, pausing every two or three minutes to consult his pocket watch.

Although the differences among the three men were very great, they did not preclude a certain subtle similarity. Perhaps it lay in the shape of the eyelids, the curve and depth of the skull, the bony angularity of the wrists; or most probably in the combination of the countless nearly invisible shared characteristics that marked them as members of one family.

The green-eyed man paused to check his watch for the hundredth time. The babble of conversation on the other side of the partition intensified, and then a call—half pleading, half imperative—rang out: "Whiss!" The audience took it up; an emphatic, monotonous chant like the hiss of monster bellows.

Whiss v'Aleur started at the sound, and his hands jerked. He wheeled sharply to face the old man seated at the desk. "Come, Father—no more delay," he urged. His voice was rather high-pitched; penetrating, and effortlessly compelling.

"I am uncertain." The old man shook his head. "I do not know that it is necessary—or wise—or right."

"We have been through all of that, more than once, and there's no time left to argue. The thing is settled. You know this. Moreover, you wouldn't have troubled yourself to travel all the way from Neuss, had you not intended to lend your assistance."

"But do you truly require my assistance? It is never wise to employ arcane power unnecessarily, and I question the present need. Whiss, you are eloquent beyond all measure, and so you have always been, without benefit of magical illusion. Therein lies your greatest strength and talent. What need to enlarge upon the gifts of Nature?"

"Ah, Nature." Whiss's lips twisted. "Easy enough for her cherished sons to laud her bounty. Yet her generosity is scarcely consistent, and we are not all of us similarly blessed."

A note of subtle accusation sharpened his voice. The older man heard it and sighed. Another might have supposed that Whiss spoke of the inequities existing between Exalted and peasant, but his father knew better. Whiss, born entirely devoid of magical ability into a bourgeois family whose members were frequently gifted, had sensed himself underprivileged, outcast, and despised from the very start. His physical shortcomings—the short, skinny frame that precluded athletic prowess all but requisite to youthful popularity, the pockmarked visage and decay-prone yellowish teeth that further set him apart, the squeaky voice suggesting effeminacy—all these had aggravated a galling sense of insignificance. His own very real advantages of energy, persistence, iron determination, and persuasive eloquence, he had always counted as inadequate compensation.

Investigation into the source of the plebeian Valeur family's unlikely recurrent magical aptitude resulted in the predictable verification of an Exalted ancestor's indiscretion. Such mésalliances were illicit, illegal, and of course inevitable; but the young Whiss had not accepted the discovery in a spirit of philosophical resignation. Viewing his ancestors' peccadilloes as an outrage, his closest relatives' abilities as a personal affront, and his own varied deprivations as a clear manifestation of cosmic injustice, he had sought success, admiration and self-validation in academic achievement.

His intellect was sound but not remarkable. His willpower and persistence, however, went far beyond the ordinary. By dint of wide reading, much memorization, and indefatigable application, he succeeded in amassing a store of knowledge that many, including Whiss himself, mistook for brilliance. The cultivation of his mind inspired him to the cultivation of his talents, most notably his persuasive powers. And there he displayed extraordinary ability.

Hardly out of school, he was already producing countless essays, tracts, and pamphlets; discovering therein a flair for creative vituperation that won praise, censure, and above all, recognition. In secret he practiced and perfected the arts of oratory, through infinite labor transforming his liability of a voice into an instrument of power, range, and expressiveness. His manner in debate became assured, challenging, intimidating. Frequently he enlivened his addresses with shouting outbursts of seemingly spontaneous rage, stimulating to his audiences and terrifying to his opponents. And he began to be noticed, his name known in Neuss, sleepy capital of Vaurve Province; his pamphlets quoted; his aggressive, bullying style imitated.

His success among the political clubs and debating societies of Neuss fostered the young man's erroneous vision of himself as an original social philosopher. In truth, his concepts encompassed little beyond intense hatred of absolute monarchy, a longing for revolution, and the subsequent establishment of a just, profoundly moral society. Nothing new; yet the manner in which young "v'Aleur" (as Chorl Valeur's son now styled himself) propounded his views was electrifying, and provincial listeners not overly discriminating. Whiss v'Aleur had succeeded in arousing considerable local turmoil, and felt himself a personage of some distinction by the time his activities caught the professional attention of his Majesty's Lieutenant of Vaurve. And all the cherished magical power of Chorl Valeur might not have sufficed to save his son's neck, had Whiss not wisely chosen that moment to depart Neuss. He had fled under cover of darkness, drifted about the provinces for a year or so, eventually making his way to Sherreen, where he was all but swallowed alive.

The provincial firebrand found it no easy matter to make his mark in the capital. The eloquence deemed astonishing in Neuss went almost unnoticed in Sherreen. For years Whiss v'Aleur eked out a pinched, precarious living— sometimes hack writer for beggarly hire, sometimes journalist, editor, printer's assistant, tutor, or scrivener—forever struggling, forever obscure.

They knew him well, however, at the political clubs—he had hung around the Green Star League for months, until the extremism of his views was criticized and he had quit in disgust; but not before loudly condemning the entire membership as dolts and weaklings. He had fared better for a while at the Barracier Club, until the year he stood as candidate for Secretary Treasurer. Losing the election, he had furiously denounced the Balloting Committee as corrupt, and withdrawn forever. Similar spectacular incidents—and spectacular they truly were, for Whiss in a rage was like a demon beside himself—had marked his departure from several of the smaller clubs, but he had not faded altogether from view. He was still to be glimpsed in the most politically oriented of the cheap taverns, nursing a frugal glass of wine for hours on end, debating and haranguing far into the night. He often turned up at the gatherings and rallies, always attired in the same threadbare but meticulously clean black suit—and alone, always alone, for the rhetoric that often won admirers and followers never bought personal friends, and he had never been glimpsed by human eyes in the company of a woman. Sometimes he could be found on the street corners, handing out copies of his latest tract to all who would accept them—an eccentric, vaguely risible figure, hungry for something or other, one of the familiar cranks of Rat Town.

And so matters might have continued indefinitely, had not a bewildering variety of social, political, and economic circumstances begun at that time to exert their influence in strange concert, the effect of one somehow disproportionately reinforcing the effect of another, and another, to set up chaotic vibrations rocking the old Vonahrish class structure to its foundations. These circumstances— ranging from the near-total depletion of the state treasury by the wars of the last king's reign, and consequent crushing increases in taxation; to restrictive trade regulations designed to protect the profits of the Exalted at the expense of the petite bourgeoisie; to three years' drought resulting in widespread crop failure and hunger; to the invention of the astonishing Griffe's Loom, the near-simultaneous invention of the Caux Furnace, and the resulting construction of new mills and factories about the largest towns, followed by a massive migration of free peasants from farm to city, and the creation of festering slums; to the increase in literacy, so conducive to the spread of the fresh and comparatively liberal concepts arising at home and abroad, product of many minds from the Lanthian Rion Vassarion to the homegrown Shorvi Nirienne, and grouped roughly together under the title of the "New Reasoning"; to the weak, well-intentioned indecisiveness of the present king, and the unpopularity of his queen; to the increasingly widespread suspicion regarding the decline of the old Exalted magic, ancient basis of Exalted privilege—all of these forces and more, acting in inexplicable interrelation, transformed the Vonahrish population, creating an angry, turbulent audience, eager to embrace a "Neighbor Jumalle."

Whiss v'Aleur's time had come at last. The very first issue of his *Neighbor Jumalle's Complaint* caused a sensation by reason of its novelty. Seditious pamphlets, broadsides, tracts, and journals had flooded the city for years, but never before had there appeared a persona more fit to express the prevailing mood than that contentious, fearless, foulmouthed democrat, "Neighbor J." A sizable segment of the populace had taken the Neighbor to heart at once. Instinct and insight taught Whiss v'Aleur the double source of his creation's appeal, which lay rooted in fantasy and greed. The Neighbor's untrammeled virulence, his freedom to defy and defame the great with apparent impunity expressed the deepest longing of every wretched, angry peasant huddling in the slums of Sherreen. In their minds and hearts, they identified themselves with Jumalle, vicariously assuming the mantle of his power, his audacity and independence. He spoke for them in their own crude language, yet imbued his words with a defiant eloquence that they themselves could never achieve. Moreover, his oft-repeated conviction that Crown and Exalteds owed the people material indemnification for the accumulated wrongs of centuries—indemnification to be paid in money, property, chattel, or even in blood—struck wildly responsive chords of righteous avarice in the hearts of a multitude.

Cognizant of his own greatest strengths, Whiss had labored to augment them. Subsequent issues of *Neighbor Jumalle's Complaint* waxed in scurrility, obscenity, and verbal violence, and the journal's popularity had soared. The editor acquired a coterie of worshipful followers, and the People's Reparation Party was born, its burgeoning strength finally reflected in this evening's first more or less public meeting. "Neighbor J" was at last emerging into the light—muted lantern light only, perhaps, but it was a start.

But could he hold an audience? Would his eloquence move and rule them, as it must, were he to succeed? It was all very well to rant in taverns and on street corners, where his verbal pyrotechnics were viewed as so much free entertainment. But before a *real* audience—favorably disposed, to be sure, yet at the same time demanding, critical, temperamental—what reception might he expect? Should he inadvertently offend them, confuse or simply bore them, they might shout him from the rostrum. One miscalculated word, at so critical a juncture, and he stood to lose all that he had fought so hard for, all that was rightfully his due—recognition, fame, influence, consequence, significance—all.

Impossible now for Whiss v'Aleur, confidence undermined by years of dreary anonymity, to regain the assurance of his early provincial days. As time raced on and the night of the meeting drew near, the doubts and questions buzzed ceaselessly in his brain, fraying his nerves and haunting his dreams. At last, mere days before the event, he had posted an urgent summons to his father—his first contact with Chorl Valeur since the night he had departed Neuss. And Chorl, perennial prey to conscience in the matter of his unlovable and endlessly unfulfilled son, had answered the call, traveling all the way from Vaurve Province to reach the Eighth District of Sherreen a mere two days prior to Neighbor J's address. With him, to serve as porter and bodyguard, had come his gigantic and inarticulate young nephew, Bierce Valeur, who now sat observing the scene in characteristic silence. It was Whiss's intention that Chorl should use his quasi-Exalted magical powers to cast a glamor, altering the perceptions of the spectators; rendering them super-susceptible to the influence of the speaker, suggestible and prone to adoration. Such intervention would surely guarantee success; yet it was nonetheless galling, after years of effort, to find himself relying once more upon the arcane abilities of a father who had passed his talent on to a daughter, to younger sons, but never to the oldest son, who should by right have received it in full, never to the oldest son, whose genius and ambition could have made best use of it, never to Whiss. And now, to add insult to injury, at this last moment Chorl was unexpectedly recalcitrant. Chorl Valeur, who owed his deprived son every possible reparation, just as surely as Crown and Exalted owed reparation to the deprived commons—Chorl now demurred and hesitated, reluctant to lend his magical aid, stingy as he had always been.

Nerves stretched to breaking, only just able to hold his frustration in check, Whiss paused in his pacing, drummed his fingers upon the desk, and remarked tautly, "I require your assistance less for myself than for those waiting out there to hear me—the miserable, the oppressed."

On the other side of the partition, the chant continued:

Whiss. Whiss. Whiss.

"Will you fail us all? Do you owe nothing?"

The note of accusation was more pronounced than ever. Chorl shifted unhappily in his seat.

"Do you owe nothing?" Whiss repeated, perceiving his advantage. "To me, or to those out there I seek to aid? Do you care for no one, for nothing save your studies? Do you take all and give nothing?"

With his usual sure instincts, he had managed to touch a nerve. Chorl, who had neglected and all but ignored his family for the sake of magical self-development, was easily moved to guilt, and correspondingly manipulable. The old man bent his troubled gaze to the floor.

"Come, look at me." Whiss's trained voice lashed without warning, and his father glanced up, startled. "You've duties, obligations to others—think of that, for once. You favor the cause I serve—Vonahrish liberty and justice—do you not?"

Chorl nodded uncertainly.

"Now you must prove it. Give me the help you led me to believe I might expect from you. I demand it."

"That's right, Uncle Chorl. You near promised to help Whiss." The third man, the hulking Bierce, spoke up for the first time. Although he addressed his uncle, his little eyes remained fixed devotedly upon his cousin's face. Dazzled by the fame, dominant personality, and above all by the mesmeric fluency of

"Neighbor J"—captivated by the odd magnetism of the kinsman possessing all the qualities that he himself lacked—Bierce had fallen promptly and thoroughly under his cousin's spell. Within forty-eight hours of his arrival, his loyalty was fixed, his ambitions established. He desired nothing beyond Whiss's approval, Whiss's esteem, and perhaps a measure of Whiss's reflected glory. To these goals he was committed now and forever.

"Son Whiss, and Nephew Bierce," Chorl returned in earnest innocence, "I'm not sure you've considered the implications of this thing you're asking of me. To influence the perceptions of others by artificial means is an act that raises many ethical issues. To be sure, the Exalted have used their powers of illusion selfishly and irresponsibly throughout the ages. For this they surely deserve censure. But if those among us who possess their ability without their privilege repeat their offenses, then surely we are no better than—"

"You near promised to help Whiss," Bierce repeated, as if he simply did not hear the other's words. "Now you have to." Setting his wheels and gears aside, he rose and took a few steps around the desk to pause before his uncle. Staring down from his great height, he added, "Whiss needs you."

Chorl Valeur gazed up into the expressionless face looming so far above him. His eyes traveled down his nephew's massive frame to the big hands hanging loosely clasped and very near him. His eyes widened a little, and he paled.

Whiss v'Aleur observed the reaction, mentally filed it away for future reference, but he appeared to notice nothing. His voice was gently grave, manner earnest and ingenuous as Chorl's own, as he observed, "It is for the best possible cause. Father, why have you spent a lifetime perfecting your magical art, if not to use it in this great endeavor—the liberation of your own kind? As a man of the people owning the magical ability of an Exalted, your position is unusual and your potential value almost incalculable. It lies within your power to ensure the triumph of right and justice. Will you not use that power? You will be known to history as a hero and patriot. Come, Father—will you not join us in the fight?"

He had offered the old man a face-saving means of acquiescence, and Chorl seized upon it at once. "Very well," he conceded. "I will do my best." Only his wrinkled oatmeal pallor and the rigid tension of his clasped hands revealed his lingering reluctance. Bierce returned to his wheels and gears. Chorl expelled his breath in a faint sigh, while Whiss permitted himself a smile of gratified idealism.

Outside the office, the chant grew louder:

Whiss. Whiss. Whiss.

"Let's go, then." The fear seemed all at once to have drained from Chorl into Whiss, who now stood white, tense, and crazily resolved. For one moment, time slipped and Chorl Valeur was back thirty years in the past, looking down at a puny, intense, and unappealing boy determined to excel; and that recollection made it easy.

Speaking with a conviction that almost made his compliance seem voluntary, Chorl told his son, "You're wrong in thinking you require magical aid. Your own natural eloquence might carry you anywhere. Since you won't trust in that, I'll do what I can, and you may be certain your audience will perceive you as their hope and savior."

Whiss threw him a glance half skeptical, half astonished. Then, tight-lipped and glass-eyed, he squared his shoulders and abruptly exited the office through a gap in the partitions. The audience was chanting his name. As he appeared, the chant swelled to a roar. A few swift strides took him to the makeshift podium. He mounted and turned to confront a sea of faces. For a moment they merged and blurred before his eyes. He did not pause to look behind him, and thus he did not see his father, head bowed and arms folded, murmuring studiously to himself. Whiss hesitated a moment, then threw wide his arms in an expansive gesture of greeting and acknowledgment. The roar of the crowd built to a crescendo, and then, as he stood there perfectly motionless, died to an expectant hush. When the room was silent, Whiss allowed his arms to sink to his sides and spoke at last, in a conversational, almost casual tone; inconsistent with the flamboyance of his initial gesture, yet suitable in style to the tastes of Neighbor Jumalle's admirers:

"So. This is good. I see there are still men and women among us not to be scared off by the blood-drinking demons. What demons? You don't really need to ask that, do you? You already know, better than anyone should have to know. We all know about the demon Want—the demon that tells us that hunger and cold are all that we can expect, all that we deserve. We know about the demon Injustice, who tells us that other men are better than we are, that other men's children are better than our children. When the lackeys of the Exalted kick us around like dogs, and we tell ourselves it's the way of the world and we've just got to swallow it—well, that's when we shake hands with the demon Injustice, isn't it? All of us know him. And then, of course, there's the demon Fear—he's one of our closest comrades, the one we can rely on. Why, all of us are close to him as lovers. When we daren't speak what we think—when we don't care to show our faces in a public place for thought of the trouble it means—well, that's when we're snug between the sheets with Fear, isn't it? Like it there in bed with Fear, my friends? Having a good time there? Like getting buggered floor to rafters and back again, every day of your lives? No? Want to pay him back as good as he gives? I see. So *that's* why you came here tonight!"

A gale of laughter greeted this sally, and Whiss's confidence returned. He found he could sense the mood of the crowd; instinctively he knew its fears, its hungers, hostilities, and needs. And sensing these things, he recognized his own power. He could influence these people. He could read their minds and hearts. Their emotions lay open and accessible, like the keys of a harpsichord upon which he might play music of his own composition. In that moment, his doubts vanished. He had nothing to fear from his listeners. He could do with them as he pleased.

They were still laughing. He had intended to wait until the laughter subsided of its own accord, but now he knew he did not need to wait, for he was master here. He lifted his hand, wordlessly enjoining silence, and sure enough, the noise died away.

"You can get even with the demons, my friends," Whiss resumed. "You can have satisfaction for everything they've ever done to you and yours. And how do you pay them back? I'll tell you how. You do it by making them pay *you* back. Did you hear that? You make them pay you back. With interest."

Affirmative cries from the audience.

"That's right. But how do you get payment out of a demon?" Whiss inquired. "How do you put the squeeze on Want or Injustice? How do you corner our old comrade Fear? There's only one way I can think of, and I've got a hunch that everyone in this room already knows what it is." A pregnant pause to advertise the significance of what was to follow. "You do it by proxy. You go after the demons' representatives here among us. You take what's due you from those who do the demons' work—from the demons' human spawn, as it were. And you know who that is, don't you? Don't we *all* know who that is?"

Angry voices answered him:

"The Exalted!"

"The King of Fools and his Whore Queen!"

"All the Privileged and their little toadies!"

"You're right!" Whiss told them. "You're dead right, my friends!" The shouting rose in volume, and he allowed it to continue for a time, for the noise stirred their blood and their passions, which suited his purpose. And as he stood there waiting, something happened. It seemed to Whiss that the air rippled. Faces, bodies, lighted lanterns—everything about him wavered momentarily. He feared a fainting fit then, bane of his sickly boyhood. But the qualm soon passed, his vision cleared, and all was as before—almost. Whiss blinked. The scene before him was outwardly unchanged, yet he was seeing it as never before, seeing beneath the surface, as if some outer layer had suddenly gone transparent. The spectators' collective emotions, which he had formerly sensed but not seen, were now visible, almost tangible, existing as a highly inflammable gas or haze of many colors, hanging above and about the audience, swirling and spreading throughout the room. Its motion was chaotic and unpredictable, but not ungovernable. Whiss knew by sure instinct that his words possessed power to shape that roiling mist, to rule its currents, its colors and density. He knew without instruction that he desired a uniform hue, to mold those disparate spectators into a single, mighty, mindless entity, subject to his will. He knew, too, that he required intense pressure to create the explosive atmosphere into which he might fling the lighted torch of his rhetoric. All these things were clear to him in an instant, and as he glanced aside to see his spent father leaning against a partition, invisible to the audience, he understood the cause. Chorl had completed his magical commission.

Whiss looked out over the audience, blanketed in thick clouds of emotion. Through the haze he could see the faces, and through the faces, the things beyond, the fears and needs. He perceived the frustration, the angry hunger, the longing for direction, for unequivocal and comprehensible answers. And he felt the great tide of their affection, their admiration and faith in him, bathing him in delicious warmth. No matter that this adoration was artificial in origin, born of his father's machinations. For the moment, it was real, and all that he had ever dreamed of, all that he knew he deserved, come to him after decades of striving. His heart contracted, and his eyes stung with tears. He paused a moment, partly to collect himself, partly to luxuriate in unaccustomed sensations of total acceptance, love, and dominance.

He was careful not to pause too long. The mists swirled about the audience in wildly varying patterns and colors, raw medium of his art. His father's magic had primed the canvas, but his was the hand of the master.

"We all know our enemies," Whiss resumed, and even to his own ears, his voice had acquired new power and resonance. "We know what we have to deal with. But maybe some of you out there don't like the idea of rocking the boat. Maybe you think it's more trouble than it's worth, maybe you think it's hopeless, or maybe you even think it's wrong. If so, it's a good thing you've come here tonight, because you're the ones I want to talk to. If you're one of us, and you don't believe in your own right to collect what the Privileged owe you, then there are some facts you're forgetting. You're forgetting the suffering of your kin— your fathers, and your fathers' fathers. You're forgetting the way they've used you—used you up, then tossed what's left onto the dung heap. You're forgetting the misery and degradation, the hunger and cold, the kicks and blows. You're forgetting *everything they've ever done to you*. No matter. Tonight I'm here to remind you."

He spoke on. Whiss's sense of timing was excellent. His account of the peasants' suffering at the hands of the Exalted was poignant, vivid, and harrowing, but it was not protracted. Brief and intense was most effective, for the audience's attention span was limited. He chose a couple of individual examples, presenting them concisely. He told of Paque Paqueson, serf of Jerunde, sentenced to death for poaching; blinded, deprived of his right hand, and turned out of his village to wander the barren hills in the dead of winter. No one had dared to aid the condemned man, yet it had taken Paque Paqueson a full three weeks to die. He told of Widow Domaire, a woman of Vaurve, who—crippled with illness, unable to work, and faced with the prospect of slow starvation—had murdered her three young children in order to spare them the endless miseries of a peasant's existence. His voice cracked and shook as he spoke of these things. His eyes blazed with grief and rage that were, in the heat of that moment, perfectly genuine. The audience listened, transfixed. Long before he had finished, scores of faces were wet with tears; but no one uttered the smallest sound, for fear of missing a word of Whiss v'Aleur's address.

Whiss spoke on, and as he spoke, he watched the mists change, the varied currents of color blending and melding into a consistent whole, until every anomaly had vanished, every scrap of individuality was lost, and a single great uniform cloud floated before him, its color deep and somber. He exerted his will, using his voice, his body, his face and eyes, and the currents surging through the cloud danced and swirled at his mental command. The rapt faces of the listeners reflected identically obedient responses. It was easy, almost absurdly easy.

Now it was time for the crucial change, time for the spate of words that would fan their long-smoldering rage, charging the funereal mists with the brilliance of wildfire. Whiss took a deep breath. When he spoke again, his voice had altered. It was negligent, even contemptuous. "You feel sorry for Paque Paqueson, maimed, starved, and frozen to death for the crime of seeking to feed his family? You pity the Widow Domaire, driven by desperation first to infanticide, then to suicide? I see by your faces and by your tears that you do. Well"—he shrugged—"don't bother. Save your pity. Those two aren't worth it. They're dirt. They're scum. They're nothing. And so is everyone here in this room tonight. You're all nothing, you're not worth a thimbleful of rat's piss." He paused again. They were gaping at him, their sensations of amazement and bewildered incredulity perfectly plain to the speaker. He let them wonder an instant, then resumed. "Or so the tyrants would have you believe. The bloodsuckers, the slave drivers and butchers, the demons' spawn—they all want you to think you're nothing, that you don't matter. It suits them just fine that you should think so. The question is—have they made you believe it? Have you all swallowed their shit, for lack of a better diet? Let's just see. How many here think of yourselves as garbage? If you're garbage, raise your hand, and let's all see it. No reason to be ashamed, since garbage has no pride. Come on, let's see your paws in the air."

He waited. No hands rose.

"What, none of you? Not a one? Looks like you don't really believe you're garbage. Looks like you don't relish the taste of Exalted shit. Fancy that." Whiss flashed a brief sardonic smile, which seemed to the audience imbued with special charm. "Maybe some of you even go so far as to think of yourselves as human beings. Is that what you think, my friends—that you're human beings, good as other men and women, and a lot better than plenty I could name? And if that's what you are, then don't you have the natural right to live as human beings? If you disagree, feel free to speak up."

There were no disagreements.

"Do you all understand what I mean when I speak of your right to live as human beings?" Whiss inquired. "I'm talking about your rights to freedom, equality, and fair dealing. I'm also talking about your right to work for yourselves, to build decent homes for your families, to warm and feed and clothe your folk against the cold, without some greedy crow of a tax collector coming around three times a year to strip you bare. Oh, maybe not completely bare. They generally leave you just enough to sustain a stinking poor existence, because they're smarter than the simpleton who slaughters his last milk cow. But that isn't good enough. Because it isn't enough for human beings just to survive, in misery and want. It might suffice for animals, or for the worthless garbage they've tried to make you believe that you are, but it isn't good enough for men and women. Human beings need sound roofs above their heads. They need good fires upon the hearth, shoes in winter, milk for their children and wine for themselves, bread and soup, and maybe some meat once in a while. Humans need these things, they deserve them, and in any kind of a just society, we'd all have as much. Do you smile at that—the idea of a 'just society'? Does it strike you as some fool's sky castle? Well, it isn't. If we've any brains, if we've any guts, if we all work together, it's something we can have."

They sat enthralled as Whiss described his vision of a just society. It was a beautiful picture, fleshed out with images of healthy, well-fed, well-housed, and well-clothed citizens, living and working together in harmony. Privilege would be abolished, serfs liberated, class divisions eliminated, and all men would be equal. Women would be free and respected, children cherished and educated. Property and goods would be fairly distributed to all. This material equality achieved, personal rivalry and resentment would die for lack of nourishment. Justice and contentment would rule Vonahr, a land wherein all men were brothers, and at peace.

As he spoke, Whiss quite believed it himself. His conviction carried through to his listeners, who sat drinking in every word. Their enthusiasm was impossible to mistake, for as he spoke, Whiss could see the great dark cloud that enveloped the audience steadily brightening. The color was changing, leaden gloom giving way to lighter, livelier shades that reflected the mounting hope and enthusiasm of the listeners. That animation Whiss deliberately fostered. He wanted to rouse them, to set their hearts pounding and their blood racing. From there, it was but a short step to ardor of a different kind.

Their faces were alive now, eyes shining and rapt, cheeks flushed with excitement. Beyond doubt, they were ready, and Whiss accordingly changed his tone. "This is our dream," he remarked quietly, so quietly that they had to strain to hear him, and complete silence fell over the room. "This is the world we want for ourselves and our children, and you can be sure we're going to get it. But don't think for one moment that it will be easy. It's going to be hard, my friends, worse than hard, because Vonahr is full of big, fat, rich bloodsuckers—human leeches—the demons and their kind—who'll stop at nothing to keep us down. They like seeing us down there in the dirt beneath their feet. That's where we're the most use to them, and that's where they think we belong. And they're clever— they're going to think of a thousand different tricks to keep us where we are. Want to know what to expect? Well, they'll start by trying to ignore us, to show how little we matter. But they'll soon find they can't make a whirlwind go away by pretending it isn't there. Next they'll try words, a flood of words all meant to convince the world that life is meant to be lived a certain way, with them always on top and us always in the muck. They'll scorn us, sneer down their noses, call us names, try to trick and confuse us with their double talk. But they'll find out soon enough that words don't work anymore—we're wise to their words. Next they'll threaten us with their Exalted magic, which might worry some timid souls. But those of us with our eyes open can see what's clear before our faces. We can see that most of the Exalted *don't have any magic*. If they ever had any at all, then it's gone now, or else so weak that we don't need to worry about it. So they'll discover their old fairy tales aren't worth a pimp's fart."

For the first time since he had begun talking, Whiss sensed a slight lessening of his control. Darkly confused whorls blemished the enveloping mists, and there was an uneasy shifting of weight, a stirring among the spectators. Evidently their deep-rooted fear of Exalted magic was not to be banished at a word, and it would be a mistake to press the issue here and now. Accordingly he hurried on, and soon the audience was again unified, and wholly his. "And that's when the fun will really start, that's when the game will get rough. They've got their soldiers, their guards, their gendarmes, all armed and trained to kill. They've got their prisons, their shackles and whips, their axes, ropes, gibbets. And you'd better know they'll use them. Stand up to the demons, demand your rights, and you are going to bleed. Some of you will die, some of you will see your children murdered before your eyes, for they'll hunt us, their own countrymen, like animals."

He enlarged at some length upon this topic. He spoke of Exalted brutality, painting lurid pictures of the anguish, humiliation, and diverse outrages traditionally inflicted upon refractory peasants. Had he commenced with this topic, he might well have terrified his listeners. But now their blood was up, and his descriptions whipped their rage. The cloud that wrapped them stirred and shifted, as its color flamed to a furious crimson. Whiss himself was by no means unaffected. A part of his mind remained quite detached, observing and directing the performance. At the same time, he genuinely experienced the emotion that he sought so deliberately to convey—as if aping the externals of anger intensified the actual feeling, which in turn enhanced the performance, in a self-fueling cycle of reinforcement that set his pulses leaping and his heart hammering. His pale face suffused deeply. His great green eyes ignited, blazed, and bulged. His features contorted, nostrils flaring and lips writhing. And his trained voice, initially low and restrained, climbed swiftly in pitch and volume, swelling to shake the room with wrathful thunder.

The spectators battened on Whiss's fervor. Presently they were screaming in sympathy, rising from their benches to wave clenched fists in the air. And Whiss v'Aleur, one part of his mind astonished and abashed by the storm he'd loosed, but on the whole sure and exultant, ruled them with his rhetoric, deftly shaped their desires and channeled their passion with a word, a gesture.

"We know what we have to deal with," Whiss reminded them at last. "We know the kind of vomit-swilling slime that's been keeping us down. They've been using us, despising us, pissing on us for years. And why shouldn't they, if we've been willing to take it? Let's face it, we've made things easy for them. But now it's changing. The leeches, the bloodsuckers, the butchers—they're not having it all their own way anymore. We're finally getting together—we, the people, the human beings—getting together to tell those pink-tailed perfumed parasites that they can take their taxes, their feudal dues, their privileges, their finicking high-nosed airs, and shove 'em up their jeweled asses."

The audience hooted and cheered in delight.

"We're finished going hungry to pay their bills—that's over, and now it's time to settle the score."

Wild applause.

"We're going to take back everything they stole from us, and then some. We're going to take back our pride—" Whiss jabbed the air with a clenched fist for emphasis. At the same time, he drove his heel down hard on the hollow podium, which banged sharply as a drum.

Howls of fierce assent answered him. Hundreds of imitative fists rose to smite the air, hundreds of synchronized heels slammed down on the floor with a noise like the boom of cannon fire.

"We're going to take back our self-respect—our dignity—our freedom—our honor—" A florid gesture and a sharp stamp underscored each promise. The audience followed suit, stamping in concert, until the warehouse shook and the thunder rolled through the fetid lanes of the Eighth District.

Whiss held up one hand, and the uproar subsided. "And we're going to take back the goods they've been robbing us of for all these years. The money—the land—the animals—the fine houses—carriages—silk clothes and fancy food—those things are ours by right. We paid for them with our sweat and our blood, and now the debt falls due. We the people demand satisfaction. Our honor demands freedom. Our reason demands justice—reward for the virtuous, retribution for tyrants. And our sufferings demand reparation. At long last—reparation!"

"Reparation!" The cry burst from hundreds of throats, savage and exultant. "Reparation!"

"What's that you say?" Somehow Whiss's voice was easily audible above the din. "I can't hear you!"

"Reparation!"

"I still can't hear you!"

"REPARATION!" They roared in a voice of unimaginable power. The huge voice surged and beat against the walls. The enveloping mists were red and bright, violently agitated, shot through with jagged bolts of luminous force. It even seemed to Whiss that the scarlet air was furnace-hot and crackling.

"Now I can hear you! Now I can hear you! And I want to keep hearing you! I want your voices to be heard in every corner of Vonahr! I want all the world to hear your voices! Reparation!" Up went the fist, down came the heel.

Up went hundreds of fists, and down smashed a host of heels, their impact rocking the warehouse. A tremendous clamor arose, a confused outpouring of rage, fervor, and blind excitement contagious as the plague. Amidst that pandemonium, even Whiss's magically enhanced voice was inaudible. Momentarily deprived of speech, he took the opportunity to study his screaming partisans in wonder. Their response brought a lump to his throat, but at the same time, awakened his frustration. He had succeeded, almost to his own surprise, in whipping them to a frenzy, and now they would follow him anywhere, obey every command, gladly kill or die for him. His crazed disciples burned for action, while he himself burned to taste his new power. The time, however, was not ripe; their numbers were as yet too few, and an ill-timed display would do more harm than good to his cause. But the immediate urge to command his followers, strong as the urge to fire a brand-new gun, was almost overwhelming. Surely there was some task he could set them, some proof of devoted obedience he might demand of them *now*.

Whiss's dilemma was resolved by the sharp sudden crack of musket fire, within the warehouse itself. Following a few startled screams, the tumult subsided, and all present turned to the back of the room, where half a dozen of the city Gendarmerie stood ranged about the entrance. One of them had fired across the audience. The others stood ready, muskets leveled. Dead silence fell over Whiss v'Aleur's audience, and in that silence, the clear voice of the sergeant of gendarmes was easily heard by all:

"You citizens will disperse immediately." The sergeant looked to the podium. "Master Whiss v'Aleur, isn't it? You're under arrest. The charge is sedition. You're coming with us." Down the central aisle that divided the ranks of benches marched the sergeant and his men. No one attempted to hinder their advance. The spectators were motionless, mute and apparently stunned.

Whiss stood frozen, watching them come for him. Out of the corner of his eye he could see his father, the old man gray-faced and all but overcome. Behind Chorl loomed Bierce, scowling and twisting his huge hands indecisively. No help there. He was on his own. Now, if ever, was the moment to test his power. He took a deep breath. When he answered the sergeant, his voice was strong and sure:

"Lackeys of the Exalted, I defy you, and I spit upon the parasite-tyrants that you serve. In the name of the people, I demand justice. I demand retribution upon all tyrants. Justice—and reparation!" He flung his fist skyward. He drove down his heel and the podium banged, loud and sudden as the gendarmes' own musket fire.

As if the signal had broken some spell holding them motionless and silent, the spectators shook off their paralysis to answer with a deep, collective roar. Surging from their seats, yelling like madmen, they converged upon the astounded gendarmes. A couple of wild ineffectual shots rang out, then the muskets were wrenched away from their owners, who swiftly disappeared from view, engulfed in a whirling, shrieking tide of humanity. As Whiss v'Aleur looked on in satisfaction, the upended muskets rose and fell repeatedly; fists, boots, and truncheons flailed; a few flying knife blades briefly caught the light. The victims' screams, if any, were lost in the hurricane howl of the mob. Within moments the gendarmes were dead—battered, torn, and all but dismembered. Only one survived. The youngest and largest of them, a recruit no more than eighteen or nineteen years of age, managed by some miracle to stay on his feet. Luck or desperation carried him all the way to the door. Shaking himself free of several clinging assailants, he exited the warehouse at a run. The jeering victors might have let him go, but some personal demon prompted Whiss v'Aleur to call out, "Stop him, my friends! Death to the enemies of the people!"

They obeyed without hesitation or thought. Out into the alley they streamed, and there by sickly lantern light they glimpsed the fleeing figure of the young gendarme. Yelling, they gave chase.

The fugitive made for the Eighth District Station. Through the winding streets he sprinted, reaching the station some sixty seconds ahead of his pursuers. Entering, he slammed the massive door behind him, dropped the great bar into place, then turned to confront a dozen or so of his amazed comrades. Breathlessly succinct, he gave warning. Moments later, Whiss v'Aleur's minions arrived to find the stout old timber building standing closed like a fortress against them; and this quiet, impersonal resistance somehow fueled their crazy rage.

For a time they flung insults, refuse and rocks, but the station was impervious to all. A pounding assault upon the iron-strapped oaken door proved equally ineffectual, but at least this attempt drew response. From the loopholes in the shutters of the second-floor windows popped gunfire, and two of the rioters fell. The survivors drew back, momentarily thwarted. At last some canny soul thought of fire. A nearby stable yielded faintly damp straw, armloads of which were piled against the four walls of the station house, and set alight by eager hands. Flames crackled, and eye-stinging, throat-closing clouds of smoke billowed. Presently the wooden walls began to burn, and the mob screamed in triumph. Some of its members linked hands and danced in the street. Others embraced. Many stood chanting in fierce unison, fists rising to beat the smoke-filled air:

"Reparation. Reparation. Reparation."

The flames leaped, and torrents of smoke gushed, until the trapped gendarmes could stand no more. The station house was doomed, the atmosphere within already unbreathable. At last the door opened and the thirteen coughing, choking defenders stumbled forth, their leader flourishing a white flag of surrender. Ignoring the banner, the mob fell upon the gendarmes, all of whom died swiftly— some beaten to death, others hanged from convenient lampposts. Thereafter, the victorious Reparationists remained to cavort and sing around the blazing station house. In the matter of the fire, the Eighth District was fortunate. The summer night was all but breathless, and the flames did not jump to neighboring buildings.

Time wore on, and gradually the fierce exhilaration faded, giving way to confusion, to trepidation, to exhaustion physical and emotional. Whiss v'Aleur's inspiring presence was lacking, and each passing minute increased the imminence of the Crowd Queller's arrival. Despite all their leader's reassurances, there was not one of the Reparationists as yet willing to risk a confrontation with the Queller of Sherreen. One by one, they began to fade away down the alleys. The quiet trickle gradually increased to a flow. By the time the Crowd Queller and his followers reached the Eighth District station house, they discovered a scene of bloody carnage, but no perpetrators.

Whiss v'Aleur knew nothing of all this until some hours later. Immediately following the departure of his partisans, he was left in the warehouse with no companions other than five dead gendarmes and two live kinsmen. Chorl and Bierce emerged from the office. Bierce's face was flushed, his normally dull eyes shining with excitement and admiration. His balled right fist was rhythmically smacking his left palm as he observed, "That was—something, Cousin Whiss. That was—something!"

Whiss smiled indulgently, but his demanding eyes were fixed on his father's face.

Chorl said nothing. He appeared shocked, dazed, almost crushed.

"Well?" Whiss challenged. "Well?"

"You had better leave this place," Chorl muttered at last, not looking at his son. "They will be hunting you now. You must go into hiding."

"I shall." Smiling, Whiss surveyed the great room, atmosphere still fogged with crimson, lingering remnant of the crowd's fury, visible to himself and Chorl alone. He took a deep breath and straightened, squaring his shoulders. "But not, I think, for very long."

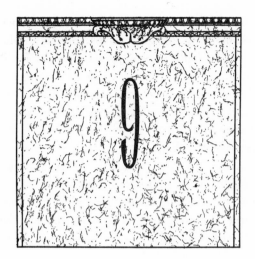

he long, unquiet summer ended at last. Sherreen's smothering thick coverlet of hot air finally turned itself back. The nights cooled and lengthened, while the afternoons gradually progressed from suffocating to bearable, to pleasant, and eventually to glorious. The most beautiful season of the year had come, and the breeze blowing in through the open window of the Rouvignac landau was crisp and alive with the promise of change.

No change needed or wanted, Eliste told herself. *Things are quite delightful just as they are.*

The landau passed under the old marble arch and into the bottom of the Avenue Parabeau. And there on the right, the only commercial establishment permitted to function along the entire length of that exclusive thoroughfare, Crionet Chocolatier vended miraculous confections beyond the artistic range of even the best Exalted kitchens. Master Crionet's sculptures in dark and white chocolate—his molded chocolate creams and truffles, his fantasies in spun sugar, sometimes embellished with fresh flowers, hand-cut faceted sugar "jewels," or real gold leaf—often graced royal tables both at home and abroad. Now it seemed they would do so no longer. Crionet's establishment was closed and deserted. Every window was broken, the door hung ajar on twisted hinges, and the sign had vanished. The cream-colored storefront was blackened by fire. In the middle of a relatively undamaged section, someone had chalked a great scarlet diamond, adopted emblem of the People's Reparation Party. They had chosen the color red to express their anger, and the diamond shape carried a double meaning—diamond as precious stone to symbolize the financial indemnification owed the injured commons of Vonahr, and diamond as the hardest substance known, to represent the durability of the Reparationists' resolve. Eliste's lip curled disdainfully at the sight. Master Crionet was an artist, a genius in his own way, a civic treasure. And instead of the respect and acclaim he deserved, he had endured violence at the hands of vicious imbeciles evidently determined to destroy all that was exquisite in the world.

"Barbarians," she observed aloud.

"They're devils, Miss." Kairthe nodded. "Wicked devils, those Rep—Repairmen—what d'ye call 'em. Those Rep people."

"I cannot understand why the Gendarmerie does not put a stop to this foolishness. Really, they are remiss to allow it in *this* neighborhood. Do they mistake the Parabeau for Rat Town? It is quite outrageous, and someone ought to complain."

"Could be the gendarmes are afraid, Miss. I mean, after all that great hurly-burly in the Eighth District three months back, and all—"

"Well, that simply won't do. They're not supposed to be afraid. They're paid to protect decent citizens from criminals. If they cannot perform that function, then the city should hire others who can."

"Maybe that's true, Miss, but all I can say is, I wouldn't want to meet up with those Reps on a dark night. Truth now, wouldn't *you* be afraid?"

"No." Eliste tossed her head. "Perfect contempt leaves no room for coward-ice. I cannot fear ruffians so crude, oafish, and stupid. And neither should you."

Bereft of reply, Kairthe shook her head. The landau continued up the street, eventually reaching Zeralenn vo Rouvignac's residence. Eliste, closely followed by her maid, alighted from the carriage. Before she reached the door, a familiar tall and silver figure emerged, descended the spotless sandstone steps, and met her halfway down the walk. The Cavalier vo Meureille bent over her hand. Eliste curtsied in reply. It was the first time they had come face-to-face since the night of her presentation, but his was not a presence to be forgotten.

"Exalted Miss, summer's candlelight scarce did you justice. The daylight of autumn speaks far more truly, and thus I see an early promise fulfilled beyond the scope of dreams. Accept my admiration."

"Excellency." Eliste curtsied again, smiling composedly, secure in the knowl-edge of her perfectly groomed prettiness, enjoying the flattery, the magnificent weather, vo Meureille's practiced gallantry and courtliness. This, she felt, without quite putting the thought into words, was the way things were *supposed* to be. Brilliant response eluded her; but if he desired to continue the discourse with a young and sought-after Maid of Honor, the burden of invention fell upon his shoulders.

"Exalted Miss, favor me one moment." He neatly blocked her path, allowing little choice. "I must entreat your indulgence."

"Indulgence, Cavalier? Honor and deference I might grant, but my indulgence surely oversteps the bounds of presumption."

"Ah, you are a quick young study, perhaps almost as quick as Madame Zeralenn herself, but let us not fence—the urgency of the matter admits of no such luxury. Exalted Miss vo Derrivalle, I ask your assistance. You must help me persuade your grandmother to depart Sherreen as quickly as possible."

Could he possibly be joking? she wondered. He didn't look it. Those youthfully vivid eyes in the lightly age-scarred face were unsmiling, even grim. She suspected he was about to say something she didn't care to hear.

"I see the questions in your eyes. Let me answer all at once by telling you that it becomes increasingly dangerous for her—and for you, and all your kinsmen—to remain. This city is overrun with murderous fanatics. The secret societies, subversive self-styled 'parties,' anarchists and various leagues of bloody-minded malcontents breed and proliferate like rats in a sewer. Factious, mutually suspicious, rife with dissension and rivalry though they are, yet their hatred of Crown and Exalted unites them. They are violent, resolute, and effective. Following years of devoted effort, they have at last succeeded in stimulating the rage of the populace to such levels that cataclysm is now imminent. The only safety lies in flight, and you must convince your grandmother of this."

He paused, and Eliste stared at him. Never before had her deepest hidden fears found so clear a voice, and now her impulse was to deny, to resist. She shook her head vehemently. "Cavalier, your concern does you much credit, but I am certain you exaggerate. If matters were as desperate as you suggest, then surely we should see a mass Exalted exodus. But we do not—life goes on as always, and that is as it should be. How absurd and fearful we should appear, how we should compromise our dignity, to flee in the face of a few peasant complaints!" She smiled as if amused.

"Better to die than appear undignified—a truly Exalted sentiment."

"Die?" The smile faded from her face. Behind her, Kairthe uttered a small mouselike squeak.

"You, like the majority of our peers, greatly undervalue the extent and significance of those 'few peasant complaints,' as you term them. It is this ignorance that presumably accounts for Exalted complacency in the face of mounting danger. I wonder if you have any knowledge of recent events in Sherreen. Did you know, for example, that the prisons are filled to bursting with traitors and conspirators? There are new arrests every day. Did you know that the Reparationists have grown so numerous and arrogant that they no longer trouble to conceal their activities, but meet freely in public to foment rebellion? No one dares to interfere with them. Did you know that Shorvi Nirienne's proscribed works are hawked and purchased openly in the streets—and his dangerous eloquence wins him converts even among the educated classes? Did you know that there are now many areas of the city into which it is unsafe for members of the Exalted to venture by night or day? And in light of all these warning signs, is it possible for you or for your grandmother to continue in willful blindness?"

"I have heard rumors, but never heeded them," Eliste returned unwillingly. She did not at all wish to continue a conversation so disagreeable, but he was still blocking her path. "Such matters are the concern of the Gendarmerie, are they not?"

"It is the grossest folly to suppose that a few squads of indifferently trained and equipped city police will shelter us against the coming storm."

"The soldiers, then. The army, and the Royal Guards."

"Cannot stand against an entire population. Moreover, their sympathies are sure to be divided."

"Entire population! Come, this is madness. Most of the people are law-abiding and loyal to their king."

"Child, only look about you. The citizens are ready to drink blood."

"There is our Exalted magic to shield us, as it has always done."

"Ah, the celebrated magic. Not a plentiful commodity, I fear." The grooves about his mouth deepened. "Tell me, Exalted Miss—do you possess any?"

"Well, no, not personally, but what of that? My uncle is most accomplished, and there must be many others like him. So I don't really believe there's anything to be afraid of. In fact, I think those riots and street rallies will all end in a little while when the weather turns cold. The snows and bitter winds are sure to chase those noisy troublemakers straight indoors, where they'll soon forget all about their stupid grievances. After all, 'In Nature's sovereignty shall Man discover true harmony,'" she quoted.

"Yes, I have read Rees-Raas Zhumeau's fantasies. His sentiments are charming and naive as a certain young Maid of Honor I could name. Listen, child. There is trouble brewing, and all of us Sherreenian Exalted stand to suffer. I have sought to alert those concerned, to little effect. The Exalted capacity for self-deception is apparently boundless, and I am universally disbelieved. For myself I care nothing, but your grandmother is a different matter. In her grace and perfection, she is the very epitome of all that the savages seek to destroy. I've tried to warn her, but she is too proud for self-preservation. That being so, I seek intelligence in the keener instincts of the young. While there is still time, you must take Zeralenn away from this place. Do you understand?"

"Cavalier." The improbable exchange astonished her. "What can you expect me to do?"

"Talk to her—only that. She is excessively proud of you, very fond and apt to be swayed by your pleas."

"Oh, I think not. Madame is never swayed by anyone's pleas."

"She is hard, but not so hard as she contrives to appear. If you've any regard for your grandmother, you must somehow persuade her to depart Sherreen. She might withdraw to one of her country estates, and there be safe. Or the two of you together could return to Derrivalle."

"Leave Sherreen, for Derrivalle? Faugh, detestable!" exclaimed Eliste with a delicate shudder. She had lately begun to affect the Sherreenian courtier's exaggerated contempt for all things provincial.

"There are other possibilities," vo Meureille suggested patiently. "Should you not like to tour the foreign capitals—Szar, Flugeln, Lanthi Ume, and all the great cities?"

"Oh, indeed—someday!"

"Then Madame must take you there, and at once. She will prove the perfect guide and chaperone. Perhaps that is best," vo Meureille added, almost as if to himself. "To leave Vonahr altogether—it is not too cautious. Plead with her, then, Exalted Miss. Ask it as a personal favor. Appeal to her generosity, and you are apt to prevail."

"Oh, that seems guileful—even a bit shabby—"

"Not when it is done for her protection. I implore you—exert all your influence to serve both your grandmother and yourself. Will you attempt it?"

He was staring down at her with such intensity that she could not meet his eyes. Really, it was too fantastic, almost unbelievable. "I could ask her, I suppose," she returned, uncomfortable and willing to say anything that might bring the interview to a swift conclusion.

"Exalted Miss, may you succeed where I have failed." He bowed deeply and left her.

Eliste stood frowning after him. She was startled, confused, profoundly uneasy, and a little resentful that he had blighted her day. "He is full of dark idle fancies, no doubt," she remarked aloud, without conviction.

"Well, it curdled me clear through to hear his talk, Miss," said Kairthe.

"Old people!" Eliste muttered between her teeth. "Old people!"

They entered the house, and a servant conducted them to Zeralenn's upstairs sitting room. As Eliste walked into the chamber, a small white fur explosion greeted her. Prince vo Plume, a long-term Rouvignac houseguest, had not forgotten his rightful mistress. Now he flung himself upon her, yapping, dancing, bounding waist-high, circling underfoot, everywhere at once. Eliste was obliged to stroke and tickle the frantic little creature into panting quiescence, finally passing him over to Kairthe, before crossing to the table by the window, where her grandmother sat at tea with Aurelie; the older woman regal in damson velvet, the young girl buried in ruffles, ribbons, and a thousand tight ringlets. The appropriate curtsies, compliments, and ceremonious kisses were exchanged. Eliste seated herself.

"I shall pour for my cousin," Aurelie announced. "I am resolved to polish my deportment to the last degree of perfection, and I believe my progress toward that end is already remarkable." She handed Eliste a full cup. "There, was it not prettily done? Guess what, Cousin? Only guess who was just here to see Grauntie!" She did not pause for reply. "It was the Cavalier vo Meureille, who calls upon us nearly every day. La, I suspect he is in love with Grauntie—I do believe it, truly. Such eyes he turns upon her—it must be love, indeed!"

"Child Aurelie, you are deliberately impertinent, or else incorrigibly silly," observed Zeralenn. "The former is far preferable, but I fear the latter to be the truer description."

"La, Madame, I believe you blush, but you know, you really shouldn't. I only hope that I shall still attract admirers when I am your age. And the Cavalier is so distinguished—such a grand manner, such an air, and he is so tall, and his eyes are still so very pretty. What a gallant he must have been in his day! Was it not so?"

"Child Aurelie, you babble like an idiot. Hold your tongue."

"Now, Grauntie, I am certain you won't take offense, when you know I speak solely for your good. Between the two of us, I think you might consider the Cavalier as a possible match. Is he not to be made a marshal? Of course, he is old, terribly old, but he still has all his teeth, and very pretty they are, too. And I am convinced that it would take but a very little tiny effort on your part to extract a proposal, or at the very least a declaration. Perhaps no more than a languishing glance, accompanied by a deep sigh, would serve. Or if it does not, you might lure him out into the garden by moonlight, and there counterfeit a swoon—I am assured this is an infallible method. Don't you think she ought to, Cousin Eliste? Don't you think she—"

"You foolish prattling child, one more word of this and I shall send you from the room," Zeralenn warned.

"But, *Grauntie*—"

"*One more word.*"

Aurelie subsided with obvious effort.

Eliste tasted her tea, then spoke up reluctantly. The topic had all but introduced itself, and she *had* given her word. "I met the Cavalier vo Meureille as I was
coming in," she confessed. "We spoke, and he took the opportunity to express his
fears concerning—"

"You need not continue," Zeralenn interrupted. "I can guess what is to follow.
I witnessed the encounter from my window just now, noting vo Meureille's
insistence and your obvious uneasiness. He sought to enlist your aid in driving me
from Sherreen, did he not?"

Eliste nodded uncomfortably.

"Well, you have brought the matter to my attention, as you no doubt promised,
and that discharges your obligation to the Cavalier. Beyond that, I have heard all
the arguments, all the dreary doomful prophecies, and I do not care to listen to
them again."

"Then you think there's nothing to fear, Madame?"

"It would be more fitting to say that I *will* not fear. I reside in Sherreen because
I prefer it—because it is my wish. Unthinkable, then, to alter my choice for the
sake of the riotous canaille. I do not permit fear to govern my actions, for that is
not the way a Vonahrish Exalted consents to live. It is not life, but existence only,
a base existence that I despise." Zeralenn looked rigid and unyielding as a marble
effigy carved upon a tomb.

"Formidable, Grauntie!" Aurelie burst out. "La, that is fine! I shall stay here
with you, to be sure! Will you not do the same, Cousin Eliste? We shall all stay
together, living bravely and freely, like true Exalted. I confess, I had thought we
must withdraw to the provinces, enduring rustication like the Count vo Jevenant
and all his sorry tribe, but now I scorn to do it, indeed I do!"

Eliste smiled slightly at her cousin's enthusiasm. She, too, thought Zeralenn's
sentiments fine, but recalling vo Meureille's conviction, couldn't banish all doubt.
"The Cavalier appeared most certain, Madame," she persisted. "And much
concerned upon your account. Surely you won't disregard his warning altogether,
but take precautions to guard yourself?"

"Against abduction, yes. When Meureille comprehends that my resolution is
proof against threats and blandishments alike, he may attempt more forceful
persuasions."

"You cannot suggest that he would carry you off against your will?"

"It is more than possible. He did exactly that some forty years ago, during the
Hetzian civil wars, in the midst of which I elected to take the waters at Zoel.
Perturbed by the advance of the rebel army upon the town, and incensed by my
refusal to forgo the benefits of daily immersion, Meureille and a few of his
servants staged a midnight raid upon my rented villa. Catching me quite unaware,
he clapped me into a carriage and conveyed me over the border."

"But how delightfully enterprising of him, Madame!"

"Possibly. The charm of the gesture eluded me at the time."

"La, superb!" Aurelie exclaimed. "Were you in bed, asleep and defenseless, attired in nothing but a flimsy transparent nightgown, when he came for you? Tell us, Grauntie, do!"

"I shall not weary you with trivial detail."

"And did the rebel army reach Zoel?" inquired Eliste.

"Yes, but not for another full day after. So you see that Meureille's fears on my behalf were altogether premature. However, it is not of my past that I desire to speak, Granddaughter, but rather of your present—and future."

"Mine, Madame?" Eliste's attempted innocence was unconvincing. From the moment she had received her grandmother's summons, she had suspected what the topic of conversation would be. It had been postponed for a while, but Zeralenn was not to be put off forever.

"I am informed that the Duke of Feronte pays you assiduous court. Is this intelligence accurate?"

"Well, it depends on what you mean by 'assiduous,' I suppose."

"Do not hedge, girl. I hear his attentions are marked and unmistakable. He has requested an assignation?"

"Is this a matter to discuss before—?" Eliste's eyes cut significantly to Aurelie.

"Beyond doubt. If the child listens carefully, she may perhaps acquire useful knowledge. You will listen, Child Aurelie?"

"Oh *yes*, indeed, Madame!" Aurelie's myriad ringlets jiggled avidly.

"Excellent. You may remain, but hold your peace." Zeralenn turned again to Eliste. "Well, Granddaughter? The Duke has requested an assignation?"

Eliste sighed. "Often," she admitted.

"He has sent you letters?"

"Returned unread, or else publicly shredded."

"Poems? Flowers? Fragrances? Bonbons?"

"All returned, except for the last, which my roommates devoured despite my protests."

"Songbirds? Live butterflies to finish a formal coiffure? Albino rodents? Trained monkey, and all such requisite livestock?"

"Rejected."

"And what of the more substantial offerings? Jewelry? Objets d'art? Advancement of your family members? A position at Court for your father, perhaps?"

"Father can rot in Fabeque, and welcome."

"Quite so. But what truth in the rumor that his Grace has offered to settle property upon you?"

"I believe he sent around a deed, or certificate of title, or some such document. I did not trouble to observe closely. Legalities bore me."

"Never underestimate the fascination of certain legalities, Granddaughter. Such negligence reveals a want of imagination. And how long has Feronte's pursuit continued? Several months now, is it not?"

Eliste nodded.

"Your resistance has been well-engineered—consistent, provocative, perfectly designed to inflame his ardor. Upon that score, I applaud your skill. The game cannot, however, continue thus forever. All the Court applauds the comedy, and his Grace stands in danger of public ridicule, a thing he abominates above all others. In the face of repeated failure, the Duke's initial enthusiasm must eventually transmute to contempt and revulsion. As your sponsor and partisan, it is incumbent upon me to warn you at this time that you stand in danger of overplaying your hand."

"Why is it," Eliste inquired after a moment's reflection, "that everyone must insist that I am playing a game? Why is it that everyone is so certain that each refusal is meant as an encouragement, each rebuff calculated to allure, each word deceitful—in short, that I am a lying hypocrite?"

"Bah, you speak like a schoolgirl. Nonetheless, I begin to perceive my error." Zeralenn surveyed her visitor minutely. "Have you then conceived a particular detestation of the Duke?"

"Detestation—oh, no! Not exactly. Yes and no. It's hard to put into words." Her grandmother offered no assistance, and Eliste continued in some confusion. "That is to say, I don't like his Grace. I find him brusque and abrupt, presumptuous, cynical, and arrogant. I am not at all easy in his company. And yet somehow his attentions don't displease me. It's not simply that his greatness flatters my vanity—"

"It does not?" Zeralenn inquired with amusement.

"Certainly it does, but that's not the whole of it. His Grace somehow conveys an impression of—force, of command, assurance, vitality, and power that is attractive. He seems devoid of doubt or hesitation. When we are in the same room, I am acutely aware of his presence. There's something about him quite strikingly—er—" Eliste groped for the right word.

"Masculine?" Zeralenn suggested.

"That's it. Exactly. It is a quality whose appeal is immediate, and somehow—ah—"

"Visceral?"

"Just so. So you see, I'm uncertain. I can't decide."

"But you cannot stand hesitating forever, or you will lose your chance. You realize, Granddaughter, that you are offered an extraordinary opportunity. But I wonder if you recognize the full extent of your good fortune. Do you realize how many women long for such eminence, how few attain it? The Duke is second in Vonahr only to the King. As a man, he is far from repugnant to you, that is clear; and caught up in the excitement of the chase, he offers all that you could possibly desire——"

"He does not offer affection," Eliste said slowly. "He does not offer loyalty or respect. Nor does he offer marriage."

"Ah?" Zeralenn's brows rose. "Now we come upon it, I think. I confess you disappoint me. I had not thought to discover you still so much the provincial, and bourgeois provincial at that. Does commonplace marriage, with all its limitations, represent the height of your ambition?"

"I don't know."

"You had best give the matter some thought, then, and quickly. If you would marry, whom do you choose? I am informed that your success at Court is noteworthy and your suitors numerous, which merely confirms my expectations. It seems a pity to waste such potential, which perhaps approaches my own at a similar age, but let us review the possibilities. Are you tempted, for example, by the title and fortune of the Marquis vo Lieux-v'Olliard?"

"He can keep them both," returned Eliste. "A decent, amiable sort, but indescribably boring. A fortnight of his conversation would sink me in enchanted sleep for a hundred years."

"A pity. What of Rouveel-Nezoir vo Lillevant, then?"

"In love with his own profile."

"Vo Renache?"

"Clever but heartless."

"Vo Pleniere-v'Orenne?"

"A boy, merely."

"Stazzi vo Crev?"

"Superficial."

"Vequi v'Isseroi?"

"Vequi—oh, he's dear." Eliste laughed. "But who could take him seriously?"

"It would seem that you are hard to please."

"Oh, I don't mean to be, Madame. It's just that these men all seem so incomplete, somehow. It's as if they aren't altogether real. They're polished and elegant, they speak with cleverness and wonderful gallantry. But where's their— their—I don't know, their true intelligence, their imagination, their humor, their heart? Why, all of them put together don't have as much of those things as"—

Dref Zeenoson's lean dark face flashed into her mind for an instant—"well, as one of the serfs back home at Derrivalle. Each seems lacking. I don't know, perhaps I'm silly, or maybe I expect far too much. But how am I to decide what to do, when nothing at all seems quite right?"

Zeralenn took her time to answer. "You are very young, Granddaughter," she observed at last. "Your doubts and confusions are those of the very young, and your habits of mind reveal inexperience. I speak in particular of your tendency to view each decision as final, irrevocable, and therefore over-whelmingly significant. It would appear, for example, that you regard the proposed Feronte liaison as a permanent step, one that might bar you from a future match more to your taste—in short, a move that limits or destroys your options. In reality, of course, the opposite is true. Such an association would greatly expand your opportunities. The woman occupying his Grace's attention is a notable personage in her own right. Her prestige is immense, and a measure of that prestige devolves upon her subsequent consorts. Thus she is a prize much sought after. Her choices are varied, her freedom of action all but limitless, her position altogether enviable. It is something you would do well to consider."

"Then you're advising me to accept Feronte, Madame?"

"I am advising you above all to please yourself. How this may best be accomplished, only you can judge."

"It is entirely plain to *me* what course best serves my cousin's interests," broke in Aurelie, unable to contain herself any longer. "There can be no question. She must spurn Feronte. Awed by this display of antique pride and virtue, the King himself will lose his heart, and then he will be her slave, her absolute drooling, mewling, groveling slave, eager to give anything for her favor, la! My cousin is like to gain a duchy if she but spurns his Grace. That is what *I* will certainly do, when my own turn comes."

"Not a bad stratagem, Child Aurelie." Zeralenn permitted herself an acid smile. "Better yet if his Majesty had ever been known to display the slightest interest in any female other than his own wife. In view of their Majesties' childless state, his interest even in the Queen would appear open to question."

"Well—" Aurelie appeared unconvinced. "Perhaps the beauty destined to capture the King has not yet appeared at Court. When *I* come to Court, we shall see, indeed."

"You shall not come to Court within the decade, if you do not learn how to govern your tongue."

"But, *Grauntie*—!"

To Eliste's relief, the conversation drifted on to other topics, and the matter of Feronte's attentions was allowed to drop. Presently tea was finished, and she took her leave. The gray Rouvignac landau was waiting to return her to the Beviaire. She settled back upon the cushioned seat with a small, rueful sigh. Throughout the short journey she remained silent, lost in frowning abstraction, and Kairthe did not venture to address her. Her silence continued as she entered the palace to make her way along the now-familiar glittering corridors to the Maids' Quarters, where yet another offering awaited her.

The Quarters were deserted. The Maidsblanche denizens attended the Queen. The other girls were off about their own errands. Even the Marquise vo Quivesse was absent. Eliste walked into the Maidsmauve chamber. There on her pillow reposed a small parcel wrapped in wine velvet, bound in black satin ribbon— identifying emblems of Feronte's tribute. Eliste heaved another sigh. The Duke's determination pressed upon her with an almost tangible weight that irritated and gratified at once. For a moment she considered tossing the package out the open window into the garden a couple of stories below, but curiosity and something more got the better of her. Stripping away the velvet, she opened the box to discover a silver filigree locket upon a fine silver chain—quaint, pretty, and probably quite old. Beneath the locket lay a card bearing the simple request or command:

Think of me.

—*Feronte*

Eliste smiled, surprised and intrigued. The ornament was charming beyond doubt, but of much inferior value to the Duke's previous offerings. It would seem that a message of some sort was intended, but the meaning was open to interpretation ranging from graceful compliment to the very opposite. The deliberate obscurity piqued her curiosity. Still smiling, she drew the locket from its container. The moment she touched it, a distinctive fragrance rose to her nostrils—a heavy, intense perfume, musky almost to the verge of vulgarity, compelling and subtly disturbing. For a moment her vision swam and she swayed, light-headed and heated as if she'd drunk too much champagne. Her eyes cleared and the world righted itself, but the fragrance lingered, tenacious and assertive as the Duke himself.

Eliste pried open the filigree cover, and the source of the odor became apparent. The locket contained perfume in solid form—a waxy substance, snake-mottled and lion-tawny in color. She ran her finger across the smooth surface, and the scent clung to her flesh. Absently she touched her hair, her temples, her wrist, her earlobes, and the fragrance enveloped her. She stood still, drinking it; then, slowly lifting the locket to her throat, heard herself murmur, "Put this on me, Kairthe."

"What, Miss, you mean he's finally sent something you'll keep? That's a new one." Kairthe was behind her, clever fingers fiddling with the delicate clasp. "Phew! Kill me dead! What a smell!"

"You find it disagreeable?"

"No, Miss, not disagreeable at all. It's fine and fancy, and no mistake. And the necklace is real pretty. Only that smell—is—well, it's—"

"What? It's what?"

"It's going to give people ideas, that's what."

"What ideas? What are you talking about?"

"Just . . . ideas. If those lords and cavaliers and such don't already have ideas, they're sure going to get them when they smell this. There's just something about it—"

"Nonsense, child. You exaggerate. It's ordinary perfume, nothing more, and very much in the mode."

"Yes, Miss." The clasp clicked shut. "There—got it that time. Finished. Turn around, Miss, and let me see." Eliste obligingly wheeled, and Kairthe clapped her hands. "Suits you, it really does, and it goes nice with your dress. Only—are you feeling all right, Miss? You're looking kind of blank and slack-jawed, like someone just fetched you a good one behind the ear. Have you been at those pills again?"

"No, I haven't, and there isn't a thing wrong with me." Even as she spoke, Eliste didn't altogether believe it. She *was* feeling a little peculiar, a bit disoriented, and in an elusively familiar way. Once—somewhere, somehow—she'd experienced exactly this same cloudy confusion. The recollection hovered teasingly just beyond the bounds of memory. Each time she made a mental grab, it dodged like a gnat. Presently she shrugged and gave up. She'd remember eventually, but not now. In any event, there were more interesting things to consider—the Duke of Feronte, for example. She suddenly discovered that his image filled her mind—an extraordinarily vivid and substantial image, one that she could almost touch, and one that would not go away.

As the hours passed and she went about her customary business, drifting from palace to theater, to Havillac Gardens, then back to the Beviaire and the Queen's service, then on to dancing and a late dinner, moving always in the midst of the gallant, the gorgeous and giddy, the image of the Duke was never quite dislodged. Often it was very immediate, very real; and sometimes much less so, even fading to the verge of nothingness when her mind was active—but never wholly absent, and never distanced for long. Nor did she actively seek to prise him from her mind, for the constant vision was oddly gratifying, a secret satisfaction—or would have been, had she not been troubled from time to time with that sense of doubt and vague confusion, whose nagging familiarity she could not quite account for.

As the hours passed, Eliste began to find herself looking for him everywhere she went. At the playhouse, in the Queen's Presence Chamber, at the card tables—always her eyes searched the crowds, to no avail. The Duke was nowhere in evidence, and her discontent mounted. She had thought to conduct the survey discreetly, but her preoccupation did not escape her companions' notice. Stazzi vo Crev remarked jokingly upon her distrait air. Vo Lieux-v'Olliard appeared wounded by her inattentiveness, while Merranotte v'Estais laughed and called her the "Enchanted Princess." To all of them Eliste responded with smiling, uncomfortable denials; and her eyes continued to wander.

The Duke remained invisible. When at last Eliste repaired to the Maids' Quarters and slumber, her frustration had built to teeth-grinding levels. She fidgeted impatiently as Kairthe undressed her, and snapped as the maid attempted to unfasten the locket chain, "Leave it alone!"

Kairthe stared at her, startled, then shrugged philosophically and continued her work. Eliste bit her lip, somewhat ashamed; but remorse quickly subsided, crowded from her mind by thoughts of the Duke's purposeful countenance. A little later she lay in bed, eyes wide open in the dark. She was acutely conscious of the locket, whose silver weight, heated by her body, lay warm as a human hand upon her flesh. The unusual, persistent perfume was strong in her nostrils, and sleep was a long time in coming.

In the morning she awakened to find the Duke's image fixed, if possible, more firmly than ever in her mind. The day that followed echoed the preceding afternoon and evening. Eliste pursued her accustomed activities; and always and everywhere, her eyes roamed corridors and galleries in search of his Grace. Two or three times she caught sight of him, and each time she froze, paralyzed, torn between the urge to accost him and a curious impulse to flee. As for Feronte, he seemed not to see her. If he noticed her at all, he showed no sign. He was unconscious or else indifferent, and Eliste fingered the fragrant locket in mounting disquietude.

So matters continued for the next several days. The flow of the Duke's gifts and messages had entirely ceased, a fact unkindly remarked upon by all the Maids of Honor. He neither sought his former quarry nor appeared aware of her presence. Eliste, bewildered and obsessed, began to lose sleep. Her appetite failed, along with her spirits. Pleading illness, she moped alone in the Maidsmauve chamber, where she sat for many hours absently fingering the locket that hung day and night upon her breast.

At the end of the week, Feronte sent a message—a simple and forthright invitation to dinner for two in his rooms. In scanning the note, Eliste was once again conscious of that elusively familiar sense of confusion—of wrongness. It was not enough, however, to delay by an instant the dispatch of her affirmative response.

The stretch of walkway beneath the overhang of the sorriest old tenement on Aether Street in the Eighth District belonged to Crone Plaissie. For the space of two years—no small period by the standards of her kind—she had occupied that territory. Come rain or shine, come snow or blasting heat, Crone Plaissie was always there with her begging box daubed in garish colors, her hoarse croaking songs and verses, her interesting sores. Very occasionally, the exigencies of illness or childbirth enforced her absence. Where she repaired upon such occasions, no one knew, and where she slept each night remained a matter of indifferent mystery. But every morning found Crone Plaissie ensconced in her accustomed archway, and every pedestrian encountered her outstretched palm.

Pickings were surprisingly good. An amateur might have supposed that the wealthy, glistering sections of town—the environs of the Beviaire, the Parabeau, and other such choice locations—would yield the best returns, but such was not the case. The aristocrats of the Parabeau had mastered the art of selective blindness. They could walk within inches of Crone Plaissie, apparently unconscious of her existence. This was not the talent, however, of the Eighth District scum, who displayed a peculiar vulnerability to pleas, accusations, and reproaches. They gave, and the accumulated weight of their contributions far outweighed the silent contempt of the Exalted. In the slums of the Eighth District, Crone Plaissie found livelihood—meager and grudging, but it served.

Scanty gray hair, toothless gums, sunken colorless cheeks, and a bent shrunken figure had earned her the title of "Crone." A misnomer, for the apparent beldam was no more than thirty-four years old. Disease, chronic malnutrition, and repeated childbirth had aged her prematurely, but Plaissie did not regret the dilapidated aspect that served as an invaluable professional asset. Nor did she lament the unremitting hardship of her life. Tedium occasionally troubled her, but not lately. In recent weeks, the unusual activity centering about the old house directly across the street from her stretch of walkway had engaged her close attention.

The house—a run-down anonymous edifice owned by one Madame Hiroux—attracted too many visitors, far more than its undistinguished air seemed to warrant. Most of the strangers were youthful, shabby, and nondescript—students, perhaps. But several were well-dressed and prosperous-looking, men of consequence, clearly out of place in the Eighth District. Noting this, Crone Plaissie kept her eyes open, and her vigilance was rewarded. She saw that they came and went—generally by way of the back door—at all hours of the day and night, in an unobtrusive trickle easily overlooked by all save an attentive observer. Unable to fathom the establishment's appeal, she first suspected the existence of a new brothel, whose extreme discretion obviated necessity of payment to the local gendarmerie. Continued surveillance soon convinced her otherwise, for she spied neither women nor adolescent boys upon the premises. Was it the meetinghouse of an anarchist gang? Birthplace of a new religious cult? Den of gentlemen thieves? No obvious answer presented itself, and Crone Plaissie's interest sharpened. The days passed, the mysterious comings and goings continued, and her idle curiosity waxed obsessive, eventually overcoming the ingrained caution of a lifetime.

It happened on a mild autumn night, when the Crone's interest was once again arrested by anomaly; this time by the arrival of a trio of strangers—slouch-hatted, muffler-swathed, faces deliberately obscured. One of them carried a bundle under his arm—Madame Hiroux's callers often bore such bundles—and although the house appeared entirely dark, the men were admitted at once, as if their arrival were expected. The door closed behind them, and all was as before.

Sudden impulse overcame Crone Plaissie. Despite her apparent infirmity, she could move with speed and agility when she chose. Now, rising from her place, she stepped from the archway and glided across Aether Street like a tattered ghost. Around the corner of the Hiroux dwelling she stole, down the tiny alley that ran between the house and its nearest neighbor. And there at the rear of the building, dim and completely invisible from the street, she spied a faint line of weak light glowing through a chink in the barred shutters of a ground-story window. The aura of secrecy was alluring as the clink of stolen coins. Creeping silently near, Crone Plaissie applied her eye to the chink.

The scene she beheld was neither striking nor particularly revealing. A half dozen men and one woman sat around a wooden table in a small, plain, sparsely furnished chamber, located behind the kitchen and probably designed for storage. A commonplace room, commonplace occupants. The woman—rawboned and lantern-jawed—was Madame Hiroux. The men were strangers. Spread out on the table before them were papers—pamphlets, tracts, something of the sort, and of no interest whatever. One of the men was reading in a low voice. Crone Plaissie could not make out the words, nor did she much care to. It was distinctly disappointing. She had expected to witness secret rites—colorful abominations, criminals gloating over some illicit treasure trove—and all she got was tedious dry literature. She might have spared herself the trouble. And yet—the visitors desired secrecy, and they must have their reasons. Might they not be fugitives, hunted by the Gendarmerie? Frowning, she surveyed them in turn. The Hiroux woman was not important, scarcely worth a glance. And the six men? She knew none of them, and yet . . . her eyes lingered on the reader. He was middle-aged, plainly dressed, graying, ascetically nondescript. Not at all impressive, not with that shabby old jacket of his, certainly nobody important. And yet—and yet . . . her memory rattled. Had she not seen that face somewhere or other? Had she not at least seen a *drawing* of that face?

Certainly she had. How could she miss it, when the broadsides bearing his likeness and description were posted all over Sherreen? The Gendarmerie and even the Royal Guards were all of them hunting for Master Shorvi Nirienne. So eager were they to silence the renegade republican lawyer that they were offering a reward for information leading to his capture. An impressively generous reward.

Crone Plaissie paused to consider her options. She had no interest in Nirienne, and his capture was a matter of indifference to her. That being so, she had only to yield up her new information to the nearest official, collect the promised reward, and her comfort was assured for the next year or more. Such a move, however, could not be accomplished in true secrecy. Assuming that the authorities could be depended upon to honor their pledge—always a large assumption—the news of her windfall would inevitably reach the ears of The Fungus, who would then demand his customary twenty percent. She would have to pay him, too, else varied and colorful misfortune would ensue. The Fungus and his twenty percent might perhaps be circumvented by applying directly to Nirienne himself. Properly approached, the fugitive might well consent to buy her silence by equaling or besting the gendarmes' offer; and of course, The Fungus would never hear about it. The trouble there was that Nirienne might easily conclude that his own safety necessitated Crone Plaissie's permanent removal, in which case neither The Fungus nor the Gendarmerie would be there to protect her. No, all things considered, excessive cupidity was worse than imprudent—it was downright suicidal. This thought in mind, Crone Plaissie set off at a smart trot, heading for the makeshift headquarters that, in the wake of the destruction of the Eighth District station house, the gendarmes had set up in a rented hovel some blocks distant.

Shorvi Nirienne had reached the penultimate page of the newly completed essay that he was reading aloud when a light tapping sounded at the window. Nirienne's reading cut off in midsentence, and he sat expressionlessly still. Not so his companions. Daquel and Beq—the two youngest and tallest men present—rose simultaneously from their chairs. Daquel took up the heavy walking stick that he didn't need for support, while a pistol materialized in Beq's hand. Motionless silence for an instant, and then the tapping resumed, knocks and pauses alternating in a quick distinctive sequence familiar to all. Stepping to the window, Daquel eased the shutter open to confront an agitated sentry. The young man—one of the several Niriennistes stationed about the Eighth District—was winded and panting.

"Gendarmes. Eight or ten." The newcomer spoke in a breathless whisper. "Beggarwoman from across the street leading 'em straight to us."

"Someone should have blinded that flea-bitten hag. It was an oversight," Daquel found time to observe. "You and the boys delay them if you can, while we disappear Shorvi."

"End of Aether Street's already blocked."

"Right. The other, then."

The sentry's head jerked in response, and he departed. Daquel closed and barred the shutters, then, meeting Beq's eyes, inquired, "—And?"

"Quite ready," Beq affirmed. Turning to Nirienne, he said, "Your escape route's prepared. Come, I'll show you."

"Commendable efficiency, gentlemen." Nirienne was already gathering up the last of his writings. Task completed, he rose pale but unruffled. "Before I go, I wish to thank you all, and to issue one final request: Do not, I implore you, subject yourselves to any further risks in my behalf—there's been too much of that already. Don't hinder, thwart, or antagonize the gendarmes. Assist them, or appear to do so, and they'll have no reason to question your good faith." He paused, but there was no answer. The still faces of his comrades reflected a quiet, impenetrable obstinacy.

"To the garret, sir," Beq suggested politely.

"Quit jawing and go *along*, Shorvi!" Madame Hiroux urged less politely. "We'll look to our business, never fear. You just mind your own."

Nirienne didn't budge. "Let us understand each other. You must promise your consent to this, or I won't leave you."

"Shorvi, you don't know what you're——" one of the men began excitedly.

Madame Hiroux silenced her red-faced compatriot with a gesture. Brows arched and lips pursed, she surveyed her guests in turn. Speaking glances were exchanged, and Madame turned back to Nirienne. "Promise," she conceded meekly.

A dutiful submissive muttering ran around the table. Nirienne regarded his disciples with suspicion. They met his narrowed gaze blandly. Madame Hiroux noted with satisfaction her guest's uncertainty. "You don't have time to stand and chatter," she told him.

"Shorvi, will you just *get out of here?*" Daquel begged.

"The garret," Beq repeated, and Shorvi Nirienne permitted himself to be led away. Up four flights of stairs he trailed Beq, up to the airless slant-ceilinged attic wherein he had spent the past nerve-strung but productive months. Past the rickety desk at which he had so often sat far into the night, quill in hand, cudgeling his mind for the thoughts, and the words for the thoughts. Pausing only long enough to grab the packed satchel that always lay beneath the bed, he hurried to the open dormer window. Beq was already halfway out, folding his long limbs through the small casement with the ease of a circus acrobat. He was out. Nirienne passed the satchel through, then followed reluctantly in his companion's wake. For a moment he teetered upon the sill, then a hand took his arm firmly and drew him out onto the ledge.

Shorvi Nirienne unwisely looked down to behold the cobbled street, peopled with purposeful gendarmes and inquisitive pedestrians, much too far below him. His flesh crawled, and he wobbled. Vertigo sent the world spinning, and he grabbed at the window frame. He clung there, gasping, suddenly soaked in icy sweat, and then the steadying hand was back at his elbow.

"Breathe deeply." Beq's voice fell coolly, nonchalantly, upon his ringing ears. "It will soon pass." There was no hint whatever of the urgency that must surely have gnawed like a wolf at the young man's nerves. Even in the midst of his misery, Shorvi Nirienne could almost smile at such perfection of sangfroid.

He breathed deeply, as directed; and sure enough, his giddiness subsided. When he ventured to open his eyes, he did not look down again, and the view at eye level was far more to his liking. Ice-colored moonlight bathed an eccentric landscape of rooftops, chimneys, gables, and dormers. Here and there the lanterns glowed at the windows, amber light warming tiled peaks and valleys. Occasionally the odd spire or crumbling cupola thrust itself above its neighbors, but these were scarcely noticeable, for but a few streets away rose an enormous structure that dwarfed them all. Massive dark bulk picked out with a few pinpoint lights, the Sepulchre prison dominated the skyline. It was across this angular wilderness that Beq had plotted his emergency escape route.

"Ready," Nirienne announced quietly. With visible effort, he relinquished his death grip on the casement.

"Excellent. This way." Beq moved off along the ledge. Intestines knotting, Nirienne forced himself to follow. On his right, the roof sloped sharply away; on the left, the building dropped sheer as a precipice to the street some fifty feet below, where the gendarmes already stood at Madame Hiroux's door. Instinctively, he spread his arms for balance. The ledge, though nearly as wide as the makeshift single-plank bridges that sometimes spanned rural brooks, seemed precarious as a tightrope; and at times he even imagined that it trembled like a rope beneath him.

Around the corner of the house they edged sideways, to encounter a featureless brick wall rising straight and unclimbable athwart their path. At the base of the wall, the ledge terminated. To the left, a neighboring house presented a chipped and peeling cornice. The distance from ledge to cornice was not great—a matter of some five or six feet—and Beq jumped it easily, heedless of the chasm gaping beneath him. Ensconced upon the neighboring cornice, he beckoned.

Nirienne silently prayed that the pale moonlight camouflaged his terror. He didn't dare hesitate; if he stopped to think, he would never do it. Above all, he must not look down. He took a great thirsty gulp of air. Images of his wife, his son, his young daughter—all safely hidden away in a remote Jerundie village—clicked into his mind; and he wondered once more, as he had so often wondered, if he would ever see them again. Then—dry-mouthed and white-faced, graying hair plastered to his wet forehead—Nirienne launched his middle-aged and sedentary body into space. He actually jumped too far, hurtling heavily against the brick face of the opposing building; had it not been for Beq's quick steadying hand, he might have rebounded clear off the cornice. He paused for a moment, leaning all his weight against the wall. Gradually his pounding heart slowed, his breath evened, and he looked around to find himself safely clear of the Hiroux dwelling.

Beq moved on, eyes scanning the brick wall on his left side. Soon he found what he sought, and then, to his companion's astonishment, began to climb. Nirienne looked closely, and discovered a row of chiseled indented toeholds, together with several short, stout spikes sunk into the mortar. How Beq had managed to place them without attracting the residents' attention was not clear; beyond doubt, he was a resourceful one.

Nirienne followed his guide, boosting himself from spike to spike, and found the ascent unexpectedly easy. Fifteen feet straight up, and then they hauled themselves onto the roof, where Nirienne rested briefly, puffing a little. His rising confidence suffered a setback when they reached the far side of the building, there to encounter a gap some ten feet in width separating them from their nearest neighbor. Impossible to jump such a distance from a standing start. Nirienne glanced questioningly at his companion.

Wedged in between the chimney and the angle of the roof lay a plank, perhaps fifteen feet long, obviously one of Beq's provisions. Now lifting the wooden length from its resting place, and working with the efficiency born of practice, Beq spanned the gap. The plank, stretching from roof to roof, was easily wide enough to walk on, as the young man demonstrated by his effortless crossing. This accomplished, he knelt to steady the bridge for his companion.

Nirienne scuttled across the gap. Immediately Beq dismantled the bridge, thrusting the plank out of sight behind the nearest chimney. No sign of the gendarmes, no hint of pursuit. Nirienne caught the angry sound of shouting a street or two away, perhaps in Aether Street. Probably it meant nothing; the cries of the Eighth District were incessant and generally inconsequential.

On they toiled across the rooftops, often stepping from building to building, but sometimes obliged to pass by way of Beq's improvised bridges. Eight more times they crossed the man-made chasms, then hurried across a leaden plain of flat roofing to the edge of a building, where a seemingly careless scattering of debris concealed a small canvas tarpaulin weighted down with bricks. Beneath the tarpaulin lay a rope ladder, which Beq hitched to a low iron guardrail. The two free ends of rope were very long, dangling within six feet of the ground. The ladder itself touched the cobbles below. Over the railing Beq swung himself smoothly, feet discovering the wooden rungs without fumbling. Nirienne followed, less confidently, and the two began to descend. Minutes later they stood once more on solid ground, in a dark reeking wynd some half a mile from the Hiroux residence. Gathering the two free rope ends in one hand, Beq jerked sharply, releasing the hitches that bound ladder to guardrail. The ladder tumbled to the ground at his feet. Swiftly coiling rope and rungs, he stowed the bundle beneath a mound of refuse doubtless heaped in that particular spot by design.

The wynd was deserted; Beq had plotted their route well. Nor had he reached the limit of his resources, for now he proceeded to lead his charge through a dark twisting maze of alleys and walkways, weaving expertly among the tenements and taverns, laying a trail certain to confound pursuit. The two quiet, plainly dressed men walking the Eighth District warren attracted little notice and less curiosity. Within minutes, they had reached Duck Row, a small cul-de-sac lined with old houses, once comfortably middle-class and even now unusually neat and respectable, by Eighth District standards. Beq went straight to Number 11, knocked discreetly, and waited.

A very brief flash of light from a peephole; then the door opened. A tiny, ancient, and wizened man admitted them. Behind him in the dim hallway stood an equally tiny, ancient, and wizened woman. Both appeared frail, delicate, insubstantial to the point of weightlessness; a pair of human cobwebs. Their eyes were identically vague and watery, pale as drowned silver, and Nirienne experienced a moment's misgiving. Were these two relics altogether aware?

"I've brought you a present," Beq announced.

"Good lad. Hiroux's got too hot, eh? It was bound to happen," the male cobweb piped, in tones thin and reedy but perfectly assured. And all of a sudden Nirienne wondered how he could possibly have missed the shrewdness in the drowned silver eyes.

"Master Shorvi Nirienne, allow me to present Master Oeun Bulaude and his sister, Mistress Oeunne Bulaude," said Beq.

"The most ardent of all Niriennistes," Oeun reeded.

"And the most venerable——" piped Oeunne, voice thin and tweeting as her brother's.

"The most tenacious——"

"Most loyal——"

"Most selflessly dedicated——"

"And the most indescribably cunning."

"We welcome you to your new lodgings."

While Shorvi Nirienne and his guide navigated the rooftops of the Eighth District, events of note transpired below. Within minutes of the sentry's warning, imperative hammering shook the front door of the Hiroux dwelling. Evidently the random Niriennistes out on the streets had not managed to delay the gendarmes' arrival in the slightest. Madame Hiroux allowed the pounding to continue for as long as she dared. When she judged they were about ready to break down the door, she opened it.

Eight gendarmes glared upon the threshold. The studied tardiness of her response had nettled them. When the commanding sergeant spoke, his tone was peremptory, almost bullying. "We're here for Nirienne."

"Huh?" inquired Madame, puzzled.

"Get out of the way." He made for the door.

"Oh, no you don't." Bracing her arms against the jamb, she barred the way. "My lodgers are mostly asleep, and I won't have your goons clodhopping through to shake 'em up. I won't have my place getting a bad name on your account."

"We've heard that Shorvi Nirienne's in this house."

"That lawyer-ninny everyone's dithering about? Here?"

"Don't play dumb. We know about you. The word's out on you."

"Someone's playing you for a fool."

"Then you won't mind us looking around."

"Think again. Anyway, you can't come in here without a—what d'you call it—warrant, or certificate or something. You got a paper?"

"Could you read it if I did, Countess Slops?" The sergeant produced a bark of humorless laughter. "Now, get out of the way."

"Kiss my ass," Madame suggested.

Not troubling to reply, he thrust her aside. Instantly she was back again to block his path, and when he lifted his hand to strike, she hiked up her skirt and kicked his kneecap with all her considerable strength. The sergeant uttered a yell of pain and rage. Doubling his fist, he swung at her, knocking her backward into the hall. She staggered, recovered, and flung herself on him with the yowl of a furious cat. For a few moments, all was a blur of snapping teeth and raking nails, flying fists and feet. The sergeant grunted explosively as her fist slammed into his belly. Her knee jabbed at his groin, and he twisted to avoid it. A V-shaped pair of rigid fingers drove viciously for his eyes, and he managed to catch her wrist, barely in time. Twisting the imprisoned arm behind her back, he neatly forced her to her knees. Her struggles subsided, but her outcry did not, and the noise attracted attention. A curious crowd gathered swiftly.

"You crazy bitch, you're under arrest," the sergeant informed her.

She spat expressively as he clamped a pair of manacles on her wrists. Dragging the prisoner to her feet, he swung her against the wall. "You two"—the sergeant addressed a couple of his men—"keep an eye on her, and guard the door. The rest, follow me."

As they entered the house, Madame Hiroux lifted her voice in a tremendous shout. "Daquel! Daquel!"

The four remaining Niriennistes burst from the kitchen, out into the dim corridor. Crash of the door, thunder of footsteps on uncarpeted floorboards. The sudden appearance of four silhouetted figures rattled the gendarmes, whose confidence had been badly shaken by the massacre of their Eighth District compatriots months earlier. Nirienne's yelling partisans bounded forward. One of the soldiers, thoroughly unnerved, leveled his weapon and fired. A Nirienniste fell dead. Another shot, almost simultaneous, and a second victim went down. The two surviving Niriennistes froze for a horrified instant, then turned tail and ran. One dashed for the darkened stairway. A bullet in the back dropped him before he reached it. The last survivor, Daquel, ducked into the kitchen, slamming the door behind him, then sprinted for the back room and its exit into the refuse-heaped patch of bare dirt that passed for a garden. Throwing the bolt and flinging wide the door, he jumped through—almost into the arms of a couple of gendarmes stationed at the rear of the house. Hearing the shots within, they did not hesitate to fire, and Daquel fell, fatally pierced.

The slaughter was accomplished within seconds. The sergeant did not stop to think about it. Dispatching a couple of subordinates rear to confirm the fate of the last fugitive, he led his remaining men up the stairs to conduct a search painstaking but fruitless. When they came at last to the garret, with its signs of recent tenancy, it occurred to the sergeant to check the window as a possible means of exit. One of his men climbed through the dormer; surveyed the ledge and rooftop; and, never suspecting the existence of Beq's all-but-invisible spikes and toeholds sunk in the wall of the neighboring tenement, returned to report the impossibility of escape by that route. That Shorvi Nirienne had lately occupied the premises seemed probable. That he had successfully effected his escape this time was unquestionable. No doubt he would surface again before long, but for now he had quite eluded the hunters. In the meantime, four possibly unarmed corpses, whose deaths the sergeant must justify to his commander, lay below; an utterly uncooperative prisoner, against whom nothing beyond disorderly conduct could be proved, awaited questioning; while a hostile, fiercely inquisitive crowd loitered muttering in the street. In short, a wretched muddle.

The sergeant was cursing under his breath as he descended to regroup his men. The curses expired upon his lips as he exited the house. For a moment he stood staring, unpleasantly startled. During the few brief minutes that he had spent searching the premises, the crowd outside had swollen to alarming proportions. The neighborhood residents, instinctively cognizant of violent death in their midst, had converged upon the Hiroux dwelling by the hundreds—perhaps by the thousands. Aether Street was packed with spectators, jammed together shoulder to shoulder, pressing and straining for a glimpse of the latest neighborhood horror; overwhelmingly curious, yet peculiarly quiet. Lantern light illuminated a sea of still faces, a glittering of intent eyes. In view of the multitude gathered here, there was surprisingly little noise; no shouted insults, no complaints, gibes, accusations, or taunting yelps. The sergeant would have preferred such familiar and comprehensible commotion to the almost eerie restraint that now confronted him. It was not the quiet of tranquillity, nor indifference, nor yet of resignation; but rather a tight-strung, quivering, black tension, alive and charged with predatory expectation. Underlying that dark intensity, feeding and fed in turn, there was hatred; uncanny in its intensity, terrible in its quiet power. The sergeant could feel it beating at him in silent waves, and although not at all an impressionable character, he could not help but shiver. For a moment the gendarmes stood paralyzed, while the uncanny whisperings of the mob hissed in their ears like the sigh of a poisoned sea; then professionalism came to the sergeant's rescue, and his mind began to function again.

By no means could his tiny squad deal with the sinister mob in Aether Street. It would take a regiment of the Royal Guardsmen for that, or better yet, the Crowd

Queller. In view of the situation, a dignified but very prompt departure was more than advisable. But the house itself, with its bloodstained contents, could not be left open to the inspection and tampering of the populace. All normal standards of procedure required him to assign a couple of men to guard the Hiroux dwelling, but these were not normal circumstances, and common sense informed the sergeant that such a command would sacrifice the lives of the men he selected to leave behind. Yet how could he avoid it? He would look like a gutless fool, he reasoned, if he slunk away, demoralized by a crowd that had as yet offered no concrete opposition. How could he explain his misgivings to his superiors, if it came to that? How could he describe the tingling of his nerves, the twitch of his muscles, the sense of impending doom? They would think him a coward, a girl. Why expose himself to censure, even reprimand? Sheer foolery. He drew a breath, prepared to issue appropriate commands; met the eyes of the chosen men; perceived the knowledge there, and checked. When he spoke, it was only to order retreat. The gendarmes marched off, dragging Madame Hiroux with them.

The mob allowed them to depart. The toxic human ocean parted, and the gendarmes hurried for their station house. The uniformed men were hardly out of sight before the citizens stormed the Hiroux house, bursting in to discover the corpses of four unarmed young Niriennistes, one of them shot in the back. Word of the massacre spread quickly among the assembled citizens. Word rushed like water down Aether Street, out into fetid Paradise Square and beyond, swiftly flooding the wynds and alleys of the Eighth District, whose residents responsively came flocking. And the tale lost nothing in the telling, expanding within minutes from ugly incident to full-scale atrocity. It was said that a score of Niriennistes—some of them women—had been cut down like weeds. It was said that the women had been violated, the men tortured and mutilated by gendarmes. It was said that the Eighth District—hotbed of conspiracy and rebellion—had been targeted for reprisal. An attack by the Vonahrish Guard, backed by the Hurbanese mercenaries, was imminent. The neighborhood was to be razed. The tales raced and bounded, sprouted dark pinions and flew; and the citizens came in search of the source.

Time passed, and the crowd continued to grow, until narrow Aether Street could no longer contain it all, and the overspill began to clog the square beyond. Save for a continual, muted muttering, the citizens were uncharacteristically quiet. The exact nature of the force drawing them in upon that spot was not entirely apparent, but the force was very strong. As the hours passed and the night deepened—but not in that place, for a multitude of lanterns and torches maintained an artificial orange dusk—the citizens still came, until it became apparent that the very fact of the crowd's existence was in itself a stimulus to further growth. Many new arrivals professed ignorance of the deaths in their neighborhood. They came because they had heard that the Eighth District was up in arms, they had heard that the District was on the march. They came to lend their aid in the great, if unspecified, endeavor.

The hours lengthened, the tales flew, the crowd expanded. Growth ceased around midnight. There came a lull, a lessening of emotional intensity; a natural pause, during which a number of citizens, tired and directionless, or else fearful, quietly returned to their homes. Most remained, however; many lying down to sleep, heads pillowed upon folded jackets, upon their companions' laps, upon the very cobbles.

Dawn found them out on the street. With the coming of the light, activity resumed, and the true character and purpose of the gathering began to emerge. A majority of citizens, it seemed, expected an attack upon the Eighth District. Primed by tales of slaughter and mayhem in Aether Street, accustomed to brutality and stringent repression, they found nothing strange or incredible in the notion of gendarmes, Guardsmen, and foreign mercenaries waging war upon them. In terms of their own experience, such abuse, upon a lesser scale, was predictable and ordinary. But on this autumn day, here in the worst slums of Sherreen, the popular response was far from ordinary; for it was on this day that the citizens, swayed by a variety of forces whose nature they themselves did not truly understand, finally banded together to resist. The assorted weapons—the battered swords, lances, pitchforks, truncheons, and even a few rusty fusils—that so many of them carried bore testimony to the quality of their determination, if not its source. If questioned, they would have cited the need to defend themselves, their families and homes. Many would have cried out for justice, liberty, fair dealing, and reform; many would have fulminated against the gendarmes, the Guardsmen, the Exalted, and the King; and some might have spat on the ground, mouthing obscenities straight out of *Neighbor Jumalle*. But none of this would adequately have explained the rush of common emotion; the sudden, intense solidarity; or the universal awareness that the time was *now*.

The morning sun climbed, and news of the arming of the Eighth District galloped through Sherreen, even so far as the mansions of the Parabeau and the Avenue Princess Royal; even so far as the Beviaire itself, whose inhabitants shrugged and went on about their business. With the coming of the light, the crowd resumed its growth, now expanding to fill Paradise Square. The citizens, although nervously restive, as yet lacked direction. No clear-cut purpose, no definite leadership, had emerged. This began to change around midday, when a large, formidably armed contingent of gendarmes attempted to force passage through the crowd to Aether Street and the Hiroux dwelling. Unanimously uncooperative, the citizens opposed their advance, presenting a wall of solidly packed bodies, resilient and impossible to breach. The gendarmes did not waste much time trying. Following a couple of unsuccessful attempts, they withdrew, pursued by the hoots and catcalls of the victors.

The brief confrontation stirred passions. The crowd churned, still uncertain but no longer quiet. A few of the most zealous ideologists stood up to exhort and harangue. A few of the most practical realists ganged up to break into a nearby armorer's shop, commandeering and swiftly distributing the contents. A few weak vessels grew fearful and went home, but only a very few. Their places were quickly filled by new arrivals. A growing uneasiness, an irritability born of suspense, confusion, inactivity, and frustration, began to stir the assembled ranks. Fearful imagination ran riot, while impatience and resentment mounted. Fistfights broke out here and there.

A couple of hours later, a perfectly tangible object of hostility finally presented itself. A company of the Vonahrish Guard appeared at the edge of Paradise Square. Speaking from horseback, their captain commanded the citizens to disperse. A concerto of mocking howls answered him. He repeated the command, and a demon's chorus drowned his voice. Someone hurled a glass bottle that shattered at his horse's feet. Struggling to control the snorting, dancing animal, the captain barked an order. The Guardsmen leveled their muskets, and dead silence fell over Paradise Square.

A third command to disperse, perfectly audible this time.

No reply, and no compliance. The citizens had turned to stone.

The captain gave order to fire. For an endless moment, the Guardsmen wavered, facing the mob that contained their countrymen, friends, and kin. Then a small knot of them, moved by identical impulse, simultaneously upended their muskets and with the butts beat their commander to the ground.

An unimaginable roar arose from thousands of throats. Cheering, screaming citizens surged forward to embrace and engulf the mutinous soldiers. The Guardsmen flung their caps and insignia aside; their weapons they retained. Within seconds they were absorbed, assimilated, an integral part of the crowd, which now, awakening to the reality of its own power, chose its direction at last. There were certain forceful, confident figures there, as in any group. Gifted with natural authority, they rose spontaneously to take command. With such leaders at its fore—and driven from behind by specters of fear, want, hatred, and desperation—the vast human mass began to move; slowly at first, but potent and unstoppable as a flow of lava.

They were marching upon the Beviaire. They meant to parley with the King himself. For the King, weak and irresolute though he was, nonetheless possessed a dull good nature. There wasn't an ounce of harm in him, and his failure to mitigate the ancient miseries of his people could be attributed to varied baneful influences, most notably that of his abominable wife. The answer, then, was to circumvent those influences, by force if need be—to go straight to Dunulas, confront him face-to-face. When the people themselves, without benefit of duplicitous intermediaries, spoke in their own behalf, the King would surely be willing to listen. And if by chance he was not, then it was time to twist his wrist.

Through the streets the human lava flowed; through the Eighth District, into Rat Town; up the Boulevard Crown Prince past Havillac Gardens; on along the road as far as Dunulas Square. Initially slow and somewhat halting, the advance gathered speed and momentum as the crowd itself increased in mass. All along the route, new members joined; some voluntarily, some caught up accidentally, and others literally dragged along by force. Some of them were singing as they walked, some exhorting or insulting inactive spectators, some shouting threats, some chanting popular slogans. The cacophony was unremitting; a roaring babble of human voices underscored by the tramp of marching feet, punctuated by the roll of drums and the clang of the tocsin calling citizens to arms.

The mob came at last to Dunulas Square, where progress abruptly halted. On the far side of the square rose the spear-pointed iron pale enclosing the Beviaire and its grounds. The tall gates were shut and chained. Before the barrier stood ranged a troop of the Royal Guard, men whose loyalties lay unreservedly with the Crown. Unlike their plebeian counterparts of the Vonahrish Guard, these would not hesitate to fire into the Sherreenian crowd. Silence descended, a few heartbeats' worth of silence, broken by the thunder of hoofbeats on cobbles.

Into the square, from out of a side street—or as it seemed, from out of nowhere—came pouring a company of masked horsemen. At their head rode a familiar nightmare figure swathed in black and clawed in steel—the Crowd Queller of Sherreen. Instinctively the nearest citizens drew back; quailed, but did not run. The habitual terror of Exalted magic, so deliberately instilled and deeply ingrained in all commoners, moved but did not altogether rule them. Torn between mortal fear and equally intense determination, they stood poised for flight or mayhem; undecided and very delicately balanced.

The horsemen drew rein. So silent had it grown that the equine snorts and pawing, the jingling of bridles and bits, were audible to thousands. In a voice that carried to every corner of Dunulas Square and beyond, one of the masked men ordered the crowd to disperse. The Queller himself was voiceless, as always.

Neither the command, nor the threats that accompanied it, drew any response. The silence continued unbroken as the Queller brought forth a device slim and silvery, bright with glass and burnished metal—the infamous agent of magical destruction, known and feared by all. The steel talons played over lever, bolt, and whorl. The mechanism snapped, sudden as a pistol shot, and the nearest citizens flinched. A lens glowed with poison-colored light, and there was a collective sharp intake of breath.

"Blindness. Deafness. Paralysis," the masked spokesman reminded his listeners unnecessarily. "The fate of Vonahr's traitors is living death. Citizens, leave this place while you may. It is your last chance to save yourselves."

Still no response, other than a minute suggestion of contraction, as if the crowd drew silently in upon itself.

"Are you deaf, there?" the speaker inquired, impatient tone not altogether masking fear.

No answer.

The Queller raised and aimed his weapon, sighting along the luminous barrel. Cries of alarm arose, and the nearest citizens strove to retire; but the press of the mob allowed for no retreat. Some beat and kicked their neighbors in a frantic effort to force passage; others yelled and pleaded, clawed, and even bit. There was a desperate scuffling in the forefront of the crowd, a spasmodic upheaval along the leading edge, a crushing compression of struggling bodies. All to little avail. The Queller aimed carefully, pulled a lever, and a poison-colored spear of light shot from the barrel of his weapon. Across the few yards separating horsemen from mob flashed the luminous discharge, spreading and widening as it went to a cone large enough to bathe half a dozen citizens in pernicious radiance.

Six citizens fell in stricken silence—eyes wide open but suddenly sightless, ears untouched but deadened, limbs unmarked but petrified, consciousness intact but permanently dungeoned—all aspects of the disaster exactly as predicted. Screams of terror and fury arose, and the crowd convulsed, its members seething in directionless frenzy. As they roiled, shrieking and staggering, shoving and clutching and tearing each other, the Queller fired again, and four more victims fell.

Now the citizens on the fringe of the crowd were in retreat, speeding for the safety of the side streets, but those on the leading edge were caught in the press and momentarily trapped. In horror they watched the Queller take leisurely aim. Those in the path of the destroying light shrieked and covered their eyes, some flinging themselves facedown on the ground. Before a third luminous bolt was loosed upon them, the crack of a gunshot resounded through Dunulas Square.

No one knew for certain who had fired, and no one would ever know, for later on, many would claim the honor. Some coolly resolute or hysterically desperate citizen had shot at the Crowd Queller; and whoever it was, had aimed badly. The Queller was untouched; but his horse fell dead beneath him. The Queller tumbled from the saddle. He struck the pavement hard, and the weapon flew from his grasp. Instantly he scrambled to his feet, and as he did so it became apparent for the first time that he was a person of no great stature.

On horseback he had appeared gigantic in his great black cape and peaked headgear. Dismounted, he proved unexpectedly short and slight—indeed, almost runtish.

The Queller sprang for his lost weapon. Before he could reach it, some anonymous citizen had scooped the device from the ground. Pistol shots spattered uselessly as the Queller's minions fired upon the thief, who, blessed with presence of mind, tossed the captured prize into the thick of the mob. A score of hands rose to catch it, and the Queller's magical mechanism disappeared from view.

The horsemen froze, aghast behind their masks. The Queller himself drew a pistol, a weapon absurdly small and toylike. The citizens surged forward, and the Queller fired ineffectually. An instant later they were upon him. If he cried out, no one heard him. The Queller went down, sucked into a maelstrom of rage and violence. Within the space of a gasp, they had torn away his hood, his mask, and robes, revealing a meager body and a youthful, astonished face. Truncheon-bearing fists flailed, booted feet swung, and the Queller writhed and twitched briefly, split lips gaping to reveal fashionably emerald-flecked teeth. Agony concluded swiftly and the Queller expired, oblivion smoothing the features that all the Court would have known—the features of Vequi v'Isseroi, Crowd Queller of Sherreen.

The citizens did not recognize the face; and if they had, it would scarcely have mattered. For all other considerations paled into insignificance in the light of one extraordinary fact: the ancient magic of the Exalted class had been resisted and conquered. Conquered by simple, mundane, physical force. Never before had such a thing happened, and never had the commoners fully believed that it could. Many had suspected as much, of course. Skeptics had whispered their doubts and questions for generations. Of late Whiss v'Aleur had publicly derided the potency of Exalted magic, and v'Aleur's influence was vast. Burgeoning popular cynicism was not in itself sufficient, however, to banish ancient fears; only material proof could do that. The deep-rooted terror of centuries still lingered, and the superstitious certainty of Exalted superiority had never been truly dislodged—until now. The sight of the Crowd Queller of Sherreen stretched dead upon the cobbles furnished at last the tangible refutation of Exalted invulnerability, and every citizen present recognized it as such. The revelation united them as never before; the same furious triumph burned in every brain. A roar of exaltation arose, and the crowd rushed for the paling.

Bereft of their leader, the masked horsemen scattered, and the delirious mob swept the width of Dunulas Square. The Royal Guardsmen fired a volley, and the advance scarcely faltered. Moments later, the soldiers were overwhelmed—smothered and crushed by a force they had never thought to encounter.

It took but an instant to beat the lock and chain from the great iron gates. The lock gave way, the gates swung wide, and a boiling torrent of humanity poured into the royal enclosure. Along the white drive gushed the human tide, up the rise to the Beviaire itself, whose gilded portal was closed and uselessly barred.

They broke down the door within seconds. A squad of servants gathered at the entry furnished brief resistance, but most of these unfortunates were swiftly slaughtered. Surviving retainers fled, and the mob howled in like a whirlwind.

liste had taken unusual pains with her appearance. She wore Madame Nimais's newest confection—an afternoon gown of translucent featherweight silk, shading by imperceptible gradations of color from the palest hint of blush at the low square neck, to a deep vibrant rose at the hem. The Duke's silver locket hung at her throat as always, its fragrance richly pervasive. Her honey curls, painstakingly tousled, were caught up with combs of silver and rose quartz. Her cosmetics were applied so carefully that the rouge masking her sleepless pallor appeared altogether natural, even in sunlight. The necessity of undergoing daytime scrutiny was somewhat unexpected. His Grace of Feronte had specified an unusually early hour for their assignation, and it was by this decision alone that his eagerness might be inferred, for by no external sign was it evident. He had received the news of her assent with his customary impassivity—or so Kairthe, who carried her mistress's message, had related—leaving Eliste to worry and fret her way through the slow ensuing hours. Preoccupied as she was, she'd quite ignored the chatter in the galleries, scarcely noting the talk of unusual unrest in the Eighth District. There was *always* unrest, in the Eighth District or elsewhere; and despite all the shouting, it never seemed to amount to much. Now they were claiming that the citizens were up in arms, which probably meant that another wild-eyed Reparationist had taken a potshot at some gendarme. Eliste had tired of the entire depressing topic; in any event, she had matters of greater import to consider.

The moment she'd contemplated with such ambivalence had arrived at last, and now she was approaching Feronte's apartment. The vast pier glasses that lined the corridor reflected a graceful, somewhat pale-faced figure; very youthful, unsure, and apprehensive, despite all the elegant polish. And that visible uncertainty, as Zeralenn would surely have reminded her, would never do. Almost she could hear her grandmother's precise, exquisitely modulated tones: "Assurance, Granddaughter. Absolute assurance is essential. Assume the carriage of an empress, and you'll discover how willingly the world accepts you at your own evaluation."

Eliste paused before one of the mirrors. Deliberately she composed herself, lifting her chin to assume an expression of such perfect unconcern that even Zeralenn could not have faulted it. Only when she was fully satisfied with the deceptively confident image in the glass did she resume her progress.

A servant admitted her to the Duke's apartment, and her eyes skittered nervously about the antechamber: a spacious, high-ceilinged room, simpler and more somber in its decoration than the current mode demanded, showing no sign of feminine influence. Presumably the Duchess's visits were infrequent. At thought of his Grace's long-suffering spouse, Eliste's conscience kicked, and the question sprang unbidden into her mind, *Why did I agree to come here?* Unconsciously her fingers sought the locket, and a deep draught of its musky perfume somehow reassured her. She was here, she told herself, because she had *chosen* to come, chosen freely. And the Duchess, a realist perforce, would not care in the least. In any event, such worries were bourgeois.

A door opened, and Feronte entered. Eliste's heart jumped, and the gooseflesh prickled coldly along her arms. Her emotions were so riotous, her confusion so intense, that only one explanation suggested itself—love. She had the symptoms, no doubt about it. The dry mouth, the shaky cold hands, the weak knees—her roommates had described them scores of times. She'd always scoffed, but now she was proven wrong, because it had come to her at last, exactly as promised or threatened. His Grace might be presumptuous, cynical, even annoying, but none of that was important—she loved him. Likewise unimportant was the nagging uneasiness, the indefinable intimation of wrongness that had pestered her for days. The doubts bubbled at the back of her mind, even now. She decided to ignore them. Harder to ignore was the sense of familiarity; somewhere, some time, she had felt just like this, known these very sensations. She still couldn't quite recall where or when. And, she assured herself, it didn't matter at all. What mattered was the cessation of a constant pressure, as if in answering the Duke's summons, she had ceased dragging against an invisible collar and leash. The relief was almost physical—which surely signified love, the genuine article—and a rush of excitement thrilled along her veins. Did his Grace share in it?

If so, nothing showed. Feronte's face was closed and unrevealing as always. His attire was casual—he wore plain serviceable garments, riding boots, unpowdered hair—and his nonchalant manner matched his garb. Pausing upon the threshold, he issued curt orders to a couple of lackeys in the room behind, then turned without haste to survey his visitor consideringly and at length, before remarking, "You are punctual, I see. Good. That pleases me."

Eliste flushed. She did not relish the leisurely inspection, as if she were a filly he might or might not purchase. She resented his bland assumption that pleasing him was her aim. A sharp reply rose to her lips and she stifled it, for she recognized then that she actually *did* want to please him, very much so. It had to be love; but it would be a mistake to let him know it. Certainly he mustn't know that his image had filled her mind for days. He mustn't know that she'd lain in bed, drinking in the fragrance of his locket throughout the sleepless nights. Above all he mustn't know that the mere sight of him all but confounded her judgment, else her value in his eyes would surely sink, perhaps to nothing. Tongue-tied, she maintained silence, masking her confusion with an impeccable curtsy.

"You're looking well," Feronte observed. "At least you've had the sense not to trick yourself out like some pastry cook's error in those damned ruffles." Thus his concession to gallantry.

"Your Grace has warned I shall not receive pretty speeches," Eliste murmured, smiling.

"The hair is not to my liking, however. Too many bits and pieces. You'll want to change it."

"I'm content with it as it is." Eliste's smile remained fixed in place. She discovered that a sudden rush of annoyance aided immeasurably in the restoration of her composure. Beneath the surface assurance, however, and despite the irritation, the sense of profound longing persisted.

"Ah. Independence. A hint of rebelliousness, in fact. Well, I can savor the novelty, provided you do not carry it to absurd extremes."

"And if I do?"

"Then we shall not have a happy time of it, Exalted Miss. Nor, I think, a very prolonged association."

"You are persuaded that I want one?"

"You are here, are you not?"

"Your Grace presumes greatly."

"We have already discussed that question, I believe. There is little point or interest in repeating the conversation, particularly in view of the limited time at our disposal."

"Limited time?"

"Quite so. I am engaged to make a fourth at Kalique in vo Brajonard's apart-

ment this evening, which leaves us"—the Duke consulted his pocket watch—
"about two hours."

"Two hours. I see. Are you quite certain you can spare them?"

"It is not an inconsiderable period," observed Feronte, "provided it is used
wisely. Therefore, I suggest we squander no more time upon tedious sparring, but
rather, proceed at once to more rewarding activities. You'll want your dinner, I
suppose. It is laid out in the other room. I trust you've a discriminating palate, as I
desire your opinion of the new champagne I've purchased. Should your judgment
in such matters prove reliable, I shall from time to time require your assistance."

"Wait, I don't know that I want—"

"Come. This way." He took her arm.

Her protests died unspoken, burnt out of existence by the fires that leaped at
his casual touch. She caught her breath, amazed. She herself could hardly believe
the flood of sensation, the weakness of her limbs, the fluttering palpitations. Love,
beyond doubt. And yet—

How could I love him? He's obnoxious.

But her own responses suggested otherwise.

*He's old, terribly old, maybe thirty-seven—thirty-eight—or even more. An ancient
roué—and he's not even that good-looking.*

But love was blind, it seemed.

Something is wrong here. Something is awfully wrong. She frowned, trying very hard
to figure out what it could be.

Despite her misgivings, she made no resistance, *could* make none, as he led her
from the antechamber, along a short connecting corridor to his bedroom, where a
small table by the fireplace was set for two. She seated herself with a certain sense
of relief. As long as dinner continued, nothing alarming could possibly happen, or
so she imagined.

And indeed, her sense of security seemed justified, as the meal, served by a
brace of automaton-efficient attendants, proceeded uneventfully. Feronte's conversation, civil enough, but inconsequential and matter-of-fact, was subtly galling.
A few moments' consideration suggested the reason: he was so relaxed—so
provokingly *cool*. His absolute tranquillity suggested a confidence that verged on
insult. Doubtless he had enacted this same scene scores of times—perhaps
hundreds of times—and he viewed the outcome as a foregone conclusion. And
while she sat stewing, charged with suspense and nervous excitement, hardly able
to swallow for the constriction in her throat, *he* lounged there, wholly at ease,
sipping his wine and discussing the strategy of Kalique.

He is insufferable, just insufferable!

Uneasily resentful, she made monosyllabic reply. But he did not notice her reticence—or else he didn't care—for his easy flow of offhanded conversation continued unabated. Throughout the various courses, she picked at her food and wondered what it would take to crack his nonchalance. It would serve him right if she simply stood up and walked out without a word. *That* would give him pause, definitely. No one could then doubt who had come off the victor in this particular exchange. But she didn't stir—almost felt that she couldn't if she tried—and really didn't want to, when all was said and done. Love, beyond question. In which case, why did it feel so wrong?

A fruit ice was placed before her. Childishly she mushed it about with the bowl of her spoon, then looked up to find Feronte's dark eyes fixed unwinkingly upon her. He said nothing at all, and she felt the blood drain from her cheeks. She dropped her eyes, unable to sustain his stare. The silence lengthened for a few snail-paced moments; and Eliste, as if to veil herself in words against his gaze, heard herself ask in a nervously high-pitched voice, "Have you not wondered, your Grace, why I accepted your invitation today? For months you've favored me with marked attention—"

"While you have played the disdainful nymph. You've played skillfully enough, but the role has begun to pall. It is time for you to assume another."

"Repeated rebuffs did not offend you?"

"I am not easily put off."

"No. But haven't you wondered at my sudden change?"

"Not particularly. I assume you perceived the advantage."

"But I have wondered," Eliste told him. "I have been wondering ever since I agreed to come here. There's something strange in it, as if I acted against my own good judgment, against inclination, even. That's not intended as an insult to you—I'm only trying to be honest."

"It is meant to be taken as the measure of your originality, no doubt, that you cultivate a virtue so foreign to your sex. Just so does the gardener force a tropical blossom in the dead of winter, assured of its value as a curiosity."

"That's offensive, and I won't be spoken to that way!"

"Then I'll speak no more. As we've only an hour left, the time for speech is past. We are agreed upon that one point." He rose from his chair.

Paralyzed with indecision, Eliste watched him circle the table. He took her hand, drew her smoothly to her feet. Her eyes were round with astonishment as he bent to kiss her. Her lips parted. She inhaled his tobacco-and-brandy breath, along with the perfume of the locket at her throat. Then a heated wave struck, knocking the breath and intelligence out of her. Dizzy, she clung to him as the only solid support in a whirling universe. He drew back a little and she stared up at him, breathing hard and dazed by the shock of broken contact. *Come back to me,* she willed silently. Beyond doubt her eyes spoke for her, for he bent to her again, and it was as if she had resumed breathing.

But the atmosphere she drank was poisoned, and some part of her knew it. Beyond the gale of mindless sensation, some immune little voice asked, *What is this?* and reminded her, *It's not you.* Even as she felt her defenses crumbling, her blood rushing and her reservations melting, something spoke of lies, of deceit, of—

Illusion.

Magical illusion. She recognized at last the tantalizing hint of familiarity. She remembered when and where she had experienced this sense of falsity and wrongness. It had been upon the night that she and Uncle Quinz had rescued Dref Zeenoson. Uncle Quinz had cast a glamor, transforming himself and his niece into giant wolves—or so it had appeared, and felt. But in the midst of that illusion, there'd been moments when she'd seen unclearly through the mists to recognize unnatural influence. That night's qualms were repeating themselves today. Exalted magic had mischiefed her mind—she knew it now. Feronte himself owned no arcane power, but he surely possessed the wherewithal to purchase the aid of those who did.

He had made a puppet of her, a mechanical doll. He had stolen her will by deception, and she loathed him for it. But her outrage, for all its intensity, hardly served to break Exalted magic. Illusion still ruled her, and Feronte's touch evoked overpowering artificial response. His sure hands were on her, pushing the gown off her shoulders, while his lips traveled unhurriedly down her throat. Her eyes closed involuntarily and she arched backward against his supporting arm, momentarily oblivious of all save falsely ecstatic sensation. But when his hand slid into her bodice to close upon her breast, she gasped, and the alarm underlying the flash of startled pleasure recalled her to reality. It was a lie, all of it. She *knew* she didn't like or trust him, love notwithstanding. It took all the determination at her command to meet his eyes, to shake her head and mutter breathlessly, "No." Amazing the effort it took to do that, and amazing how ineffective it was.

Feronte appeared not to hear her. One hand remained where it was. The other slid up her back to pick deftly at the lacings of her gown. He got the strings loosened within seconds.

She didn't want him to stop. The warmth of his touch was delicious—and illusory, as some inviolate corner of her mind continued to protest. Lies and deception, and he was using her. The thought was so infuriating that she found the will to repeat, "No."

This time she spoke with more conviction, but still failed to convince her host.

Feronte's hands were knowledgeable, and she found her breath coming in gasps. Her will to resist was rapidly dwindling, was all but gone.

"Stop. I'm in earnest," she appealed faintly.

Ignoring the halfhearted plea, he stooped and lifted her without effort. Alarm could not damp her thrill of instinctive enjoyment, her pleasure in his strength, and her own feeling of lightness in his arms. Advancing several paces to the bed, Feronte deposited her upon the velvet coverlet; and then he was there with her, and all her senses knew the rightness of it, while some small mental voice that nothing seemed able to silence continued to complain:

Lies. It isn't you. Lies.

Correct. But did it really matter? He was Feronte, after all.

He's using me.

A strong sense of outraged identity, what some might have called arrogance, furnished unexpected resources. The voice inside her—the one that protested and argued and could not be altogether stifled—she dimly recognized as the expression of an essential individuality, its perceptions true and intact.

She listened, and the voice grew clearer. Her fury at Feronte's perfidy blazed, burning hot as her pleasure in his touch. It seemed then that the illusion lost some of its power, although at least a part of it, she now saw clearly, was not at all false. This minor victory upon an unfamiliar mental battlefield strengthened her, and she was able to accuse him, "You've used magic."

"Do you care?" The Duke was flushed and short of breath.

No, I don't care, it doesn't matter, I don't care. It was what she wanted to say, it was what he expected her to say, and she wouldn't say it, not for a kingdom. "The locket. The perfume."

"Not now."

"It's a cheat!" she cried, and an oddly alien inner knowledge told her what to do. Somehow she found the strength of will to tear the locket from her throat. The fine chain broke easily, and she threw the ornament aside. Feronte drew back a little to stare at her, clearly surprised. Presumably his former dupes had offered no such resistance. Eliste drew a deep, unperfumed breath that chased the fog like a cold salt breeze. The clean air was extraordinarily bracing. Gone were the mists, the confused impulses, the bewildered artificial longings. All at once she was free again, she was herself. And the man so close to her was a contemptible trickster, whom she herself had never chosen. "Cheat!" she flung at him, and made as if to rise.

Feronte held her down, his weight pinning her to the bed.

"Let me up! Get away from me!" Eliste struggled futilely.

"It's gone too far for that. Stop fighting, or I'll have to use force," Feronte advised her. He was panting, and covered with sweat. At some point he'd removed his coat, and the thin cambric shirt clung to his wet flesh.

Eliste shuddered, wondering how she could ever have thought him exciting, magic or no magic. He was repulsive, and all she wanted in the world was to get away from him. If she'd had a weapon, she would have used it. But she was unarmed, trapped beneath his solid bulk, as he pawed purposefully at her skirts. Filling her lungs, she uttered a scream that undoubtedly pierced through the adjoining walls to the ears of the Duke's personal servants—who serenely ignored it. The next instant, Feronte's hand clapped down on her mouth. Eliste bit hard enough to draw blood, and he recoiled with a startled curse. Her nails raked his cheek, leaving four red tracks, and he sat up abruptly. For a moment he stared down at her, and the expression in his eyes was genuinely frightening. He looked angry enough to beat her senseless, angry enough to kill her. The Duke, however, controlled his impulses. Rising slowly to his feet, he uttered a single harsh command: "Get out."

Eliste shot from the bed. Pulling her disordered garments about her, she dashed from the bedchamber, through the passage and antechamber, and out of the Duke's apartment. Her hair was streaming in wild disarray, her face was wet with tears, and she was sobbing uncontrollably. Down the corridor she fled almost blindly, instinct guiding her toward the refuge of the Maids' Quarters. Kairthe would be there, ready with comfort and soothing words. Merranotte and the other girls would be there to mock the Duke's boorishness; their laughter would certainly mend her spirits. Even the complaining presence of the sour old Marquise vo Quivesse would prove comforting now.

Around a corner she skidded on slippery marble tile, then on along the Queens' Gallery, so named for the uniformly flattering royal portraits that lined its walls. The gallery, she discovered, was unusually populous. Courtiers and their agitated lackeys rushed this way and that. They scarcely bothered to glance at *her*, despite the disheveled appearance that would ordinarily have aroused much amused speculation. An air of oddly apprehensive confusion reigned, but Eliste, sunk deep in self-absorbed distress, did not pause to analyze. Her supposed sanctuary lay hundreds of yards distant. Reaching it was all that mattered.

Reality intruded at last in the form of a footman who jostled her in passing. Eliste's sobs cut off abruptly, and she turned to stare after him, astounded. The fellow was already halfway down the gallery. He had not even stopped to apologize, to implore her pardon and indulgence, to make proper amends. He had behaved as if unconscious of her Exalted rank, and such overt insolence was really not to be tolerated. She would certainly complain, if only she could be sure of recognizing the oaf's face again.

But it seemed there were numerous oafs to complain of. As she stood there astonished, tearstained face stiffened into a scowl, she noticed the scurrying servitors, so oddly bereft of all proper deference, passing her by without troubling to lower their eyes. She noticed the uncharacteristically harried air of their pale masters, and the peculiarity of the scene finally impressed itself upon her. Still frowning, dawningly uneasy, she continued along the gallery. As she advanced, the courtiers and menials, indiscriminately mingled, continued to stream on by her, and now their alarm was unmistakable. Some of them, forgetful of all propriety, were actually running. There were the greatest of seigneurs, the amplest of dowagers, jogging and jiggling in their gorgeous silks, stays creaking and high heels clattering, faces red and moist beneath white-powdered wigs—a ludicrous sight that somehow failed to amuse. Where in the world were they all going—and in such a state? The press of humanity was increasing all around her, and she felt as if she were walking against the wind. Then a hand upon her arm halted her, and a voice spoke in her ear, "Not that way! Not that way!"

The hand belonged to the Baron vo Nezhille, Vice President of the Royal Academy—a plump, kind-faced, normally placid old gentleman who had never before addressed her directly. Now the round cheeks were white, and the neat gray peruke sat comically askew.

"Baron, what's the matter? Why—"

"Go back!"

"But—"

"Back!" he insisted, and left her, moving off at a smart trot.

She stared after him, openmouthed. But how extraordinary he was—how rude and ridiculous! It occurred to her then to wonder if the Beviaire had caught fire. Surely such a great cold pile of stone could never go up in flames; but what else explained this absurdly frenetic activity? Well, fire or no fire, she would continue on to the Maids' Quarters. Her servant, her beautiful new clothes, jewelry, and other personal belongings were there, and she had no intention of leaving the building without them.

She pushed her way another few yards down the gallery, struggling against an increasingly urgent human current. As she advanced, she caught a curious, unfamiliar sound, something like a deep distant thunder of breaking waves. Then she was through the tall double doorway at the far end, and the sound was suddenly much louder and closer, swelling to an elemental roar that somehow sent the chills knifing along her veins. She stood upon the first landing of the Beviaire's immense central staircase. Behind her, a broad marble flight ascended to the third story. Before her, the stairs divided, descending to the gold-and-crystal foyer in a great double curve, like a pair of welcoming arms.

Welcoming?

The foyer below was mobbed. A ragged, filthy horde of bellowing—beasts, lunatics, savages ... she didn't know what else to call them—had somehow managed to force entry. Such a presence was—inconceivable. There must have been hundreds of them there, and more were pouring in every moment through the shattered doorway. As they entered, some pounded off to the left, along the corridors that would ultimately lead them, although they did not as yet realize their good fortune, to the palace kitchens and wine cellars. Others turned right, heading confusedly for the indoor winter tennis courts. The majority charged straight for the staircase, where a pathetic muster of horrified servants, backed by a few members of the King's Bodyguard, stood blocking their advance.

The resistance was crushed, literally, within seconds. As Eliste gaped in pure disbelief, truncheons swung and bludgeons flailed. Such weapons were actually redundant; the sheer force of the human stampede was lethal in itself. The nightmare herd surged forward, screaming, and those in its path were simply trampled. The defenders vanished; a few survivors fled up both arms of the double staircase, the mob roaring close behind. For a paralyzed instant Eliste stood watching them come at her from two directions. The moment somehow stretched like kneaded dough, and they seemed to move so slowly, like figures in the ugliest formal masque ever conceived, that she believed herself dreaming. She *must* be dreaming, else the world had gone mad; or far worse, was simply not the place she had always taken it for. Then time slipped back into place, her limbs unfroze, and she ducked back into the Queens' Gallery from which she had just emerged. Without conscious thought or intention, she followed in the wake of the Baron vo Nezhille and his companions, for it seemed to her proper and correct that the men, the Exalted, the natural leaders, would know where to go and what to do.

What to do? They would call out the Royal Guardsmen, no doubt. They would chase these criminal brutes from the Beviaire. The worst of them would be imprisoned, the leaders would be executed, the world would return to normalcy, and proper precautions would ensure future safety. For such an outrage must never, *never* occur again.

Behind her, the crash of the door flinging open, a shrieking storm of voices, and the first peasant contingent burst into the gallery. They spotted the fleeing Maid of Honor at once; but though they hooted gleeful obscenities after her, displayed no inclination to give chase. Rather, the royal portraits lining the walls caught their attention, for the nearest was that of the detested Lallazay. Whoops of exhilaration arose. Lallazay's image was torn from its place, hurled to the floor, ground beneath booted heels, and thoroughly soaked with urine; after which, collective attention turned to the older paintings. For some minutes the invaders busied themselves slashing, defacing, and defiling queenly visages. When this diversion palled, they turned their wrath upon the mirrors, the windows, the chandeliers. Minutes later, they left the Queens' Gallery all but buried in broken glass.

On they rampaged along the corridors; smashing, gouging, and rending as they went. The pleasure this destruction afforded was keen but superficial. It was satisfying but signified little. Presently it dawned upon even the dullest of the invaders that a definite plan of action was required. Here they encountered some difficulty, for their objectives had been nebulous and diverse from the beginning. They had originally come to request concessions of the King—that was clear enough to all. In Dunulas Square, they had discovered they possessed the power to demand; but the exact nature of those demands was not easily agreed upon. Some called for justice, others for bread; some wanted reparation, others screamed for the death of the Queen. The matter might be argued at length—but not before they had located the sovereign, source of all things desirable, who lay concealed like a treasure at the heart of this vast stone labyrinth. The first order of business was to track him down; his person secured, negotiations might commence. This thought in mind, a great unified party set off in search of the King's apartment.

Eliste knew nothing of this. Viewing the invaders as little more than animals, she would scarcely have credited their ability to formulate plans; but she did not for a moment question their capacity or their will to wreak mindless havoc. In their present state, their idiot passions inflamed by popular rabble-rousers, they were certainly capable of murdering the King, the Queen, and the entire Court, herself included. Perhaps that was exactly what they intended. Incredible to imagine, almost unbelievable—that she could actually die, despite her youth, despite even her great eyes and rose-petal complexion.

I must get out of here. I'll get Kairthe and we'll go to Grandmother's house.

Easier said than done, perhaps. She was hurrying along a fourth-story corridor lined with the private chambers assigned to certain favored courtiers. The rooms—little more than garrets, actually; cramped, drab, all but comfortless— were nonetheless wildly sought after, for an Exalted able to secure living quarters of any description within the Beviaire itself possessed tangible proof of royal favor, and correspondingly high status within competitive Court circles. Now doors up and down the hall were slamming shut. She could hear the sound of furniture being dragged across the bare floors as the occupants shortsightedly sought to barricade themselves within.

It was useless, of course. Neither locks nor piled furniture would keep the hooligans out; yet nobody seemed to think of leaving. A glance out one of the windows told her why. From that high vantage point, she could see all the way to the pale marking the edge of the royal enclosure. The grounds below, and Dunulas Square beyond, were swarming with armed Sherreenians whose shouts and brutish bellowings rose clearly to her ears. There must have been thousands of them down there, waving their pikes and rusty cutlasses, cavorting like homicidal apes. The Beviaire was surrounded, and escape clearly impossible. And no sign at all of the Crowd Queller, the Royal Guardsmen, or the Vonahrish Guard, who should have driven the criminal louts off long before they ever set filthy foot upon royal property.

Where were the soldiers? Why didn't they come? And why did no one with the talent employ Exalted magic in self-defense?

The hurried slamming of doors was her only answer.

But we're Exalted! How can this happen to us—to me?

She would not allow herself to recall the Cavalier vo Meureille's depressing predictions. They did not bear thinking of.

The invaders had not as yet reached the fourth story, but surely it would not take them long. She couldn't afford to loiter there in the corridor. But where to go, where to hide? Her grandmother, she recalled irrelevantly, would doubtless scorn to hide herself.

Well, she's just better than I am, then.

Despite her months of residency, she did not know the palace well. Her explorations had not taken her beyond the Maids' Quarters, royal suites, banqueting halls and ballrooms, state chambers and galleries, a few private apartments— the territory ordinarily inhabited by Exalted residents and visitors. Of the vast warren of servants' quarters up in the attic—or the subterranean maze of storerooms and connecting passageways that would in fact have furnished excellent concealment—she, like most of her peers, had learned nothing. She did not even know how to reach them. A host of palace servants had already gone to ground below, but there was not an Exalted among them. Eliste, victim to the selective ignorance of her class, now found herself at a loss; and at last could only reaffirm her original intent. She would look for Kairthe in the Maids' Quarters. The Maids of Honor, personal attendants to her Majesty, probably warranted the protection of the Royal Bodyguard; and thus the Maids' Quarters would prove as safe a place as any.

Picking up her rosy skirts, she began to run. A narrow staircase near the end of the hall descended from the fourth story. She emerged into a little arched and columned foyer marking the intersection of two major corridors, one of which led to his Majesty's chambers, the other to the Queen's. The moment she exited the stairwell, she caught the discord of common voices and the crash of breaking glass. They had evidently paused on the second-story landing to smash everything in reach, but that delay would be minimal. Within moments they'd be ravening at the door of the King's apartment, and there they would face the Bodyguard, already assembled in the corridor. Even as she watched, the first of the hooligans reached the top of the stairs. Whooping, they burst into the corridor, and the soldiers fired. Bullets sang along the hallway, and Eliste shrank back with a cry of astonished alarm as a ball smacked the wall not two feet from her head. Several of the invaders fell, and the peasant whoops gave way to howls of primal rage. Not fear. In the heat of that moment, bound together by feverish shared conscious-ness, it was as if they had lost all normal sense of self-preservation; or rather, as if they perceived as invulnerable the single great mob entity that annihilated individual awareness. Straight down the hall they thundered, indifferent to the defenders' musket fire. A second fusillade dropped dozens, without slowing the advance in the slightest. A moment later the peasant vanguard encountered the Bodyguard's bayonets.

Eliste did not stay to view the outcome. A few of the invaders—a knot of sun-browned, foulmouthed marketwomen—had noticed her. Somehow those jeering, unsexed harpies seemed even worse than their menfolk—malicious, she sensed, and entirely merciless. When they started for her, she whirled and ran; but even as she sprinted for the Maids' Quarters, she recognized the futility of flight. The invading force was overwhelming, the Bodyguard wholly inadequate protection, and there was really nowhere to hide.

It can't be happening.

The Maids' Quarters had been left unguarded and unlocked. She ducked in, uselessly slamming the door behind her. She stood in the little sitting room, now deserted, but littered with plates of pastry, overturned wine bottles, half-full glasses, and other such evidences of hasty departure. She called out Kairthe's name, received no reply; quickly checked the four suites, and found them deserted. Maids, servants, and Watchdog all had vanished. For a moment she stood there almost forlornly, then heard the seagull screeches of the women at the door, and fled. There was only one way to go—along the drab little capillary connecting the Maids' Quarters with the Queen's apartment. Into her Majesty's sitting room, then through the vast royal chambers she ran, and the harsh voices behind her changed tone suddenly as the pursuing marketwomen came upon the room-size closets housing Lallazay's wondrous wardrobe. Raucous cries of semi-mocking delight arose, and the chase was momentarily abandoned.

Eliste didn't pause until she came to the Queen's lacy pink and gilt bedcham-ber, where at last she encountered humanity. A contingent of the Bodyguard stood barring the entrance to the long, narrow, rarely used passageway that linked Lallazay's bedroom with the King's. She stopped on the threshold, regarding them in bewilderment. Fortunately, she was recognized.

"Butterfly," remarked an officer, employing the popular nickname for the Maids of Honor. "Let her through." The soldiers shifted, and a path appeared.

"But where are the Royal Guards?" cried Eliste.

"Quick." The officer snapped his fingers impatiently.

She did not need to be told twice. Through the gap in the soldiers' ranks she slid, through the door that promptly closed behind her, and then she was running along the unfamiliar passageway ordinarily traversed by royalty alone. The dimness and perfect silence of the heavily carpeted, thickly walled place contributed to her sense of dreamlike unreality. This utter disruption of the world she knew—the *real* world—still seemed to her so fantastical that almost she fancied herself embroiled in some childhood game of make-believe.

The door at the end of the passage was locked. The room beyond was occupied. She could hear the murmur of voices, but her own presence went unnoticed or else unacknowledged. For a few moments she knocked and rattled without attracting attention, and she wondered if she would have to go back the way she came—back to face those screeching amazons who would tear her apart because they could not *be* her. Then a wave of fear and anger swept over her and she beat the door violently, shouting, "Let me in! At once! D'you hear me? Open!" She punctuated each command with a savage kick.

They heard her that time, and must have recognized Exalted accents and attitudes, for the door opened. Disheveled and red-faced, Eliste stepped into the King's bedchamber, which she found crowded as if for a levee. Their Majesties' closest personal friends, advisers, and attendants had gathered there, along with an assortment of favored servants and some of the Bodyguard. Most of the Maids of Honor were present, together with their maidservants and their Watchdog. With a few exceptions—most notably, his Grace of Feronte—the greatest courtiers had converged upon this chamber to cluster about their threatened monarch. At the center of the pale perfumed crowd, Dunulas XIII sat fidgeting. White-faced but tolerably composed, the King observed the unaccustomed scene with an air of incredulous, vaguely troubled confusion. A couple of his intimates—vo Lieux-v'Olliard and vo Brajonard—stood near, whispering unsought impotent counsel. Beside the King upon the brocade settee was Lallazay, unwontedly quiet, nerve-strung and all but quivering with tension. Tightly she clung to the hand of her friend, the Princess v'Arian, who whispered comforting endearments. Behind the Queen hovered Dr. Zirque, solicitously offering nostrums that were, for once, refused.

The King and Queen of Vonahr—and they both looked so small, so vulnerable, so mundane and insignificant. Stripped of the royal glamor designed to veil mediocrity, they stood revealed as two very ordinary mortals. Almost it appeared they had actually shrunk in size. Seeing the King and Queen thus mercilessly exposed verged upon indecency, and Eliste automatically averted her eyes. In silence she crossed the room to join her fellow Maids. The Maidsmauve girls formed a tight little group. Gizine, Neanne, and Merranotte huddled defensively.

Near them stood Kairthe, who now tearfully flung her arms about her mistress. Such was the nature of the moment that Eliste not only suffered the presumptuous embrace, but actually returned it.

"What's happening?" she breathed, instinctively shy of speaking aloud in that charged atmosphere.

"Hush. Listen," Merranotte v'Estais commanded, equally low-voiced.

There was little conversation. Urgent whisperings buzzed close about the King and Queen; otherwise a disbelieving, almost tranced silence reigned, and thus it was easy to hear the din of conflict, only a few yards distant. In the corridor outside the royal apartment, the peasants were screaming for the King. What instinct or intelligence had guided them to the right door, no one could guess. But somehow they had managed to track their quarry through the marble maze, and now only a hopeless handful of the Bodyguard stood between Vonahr's monarch and his incensed subjects. What remained of the Bodyguard had, in fact, already withdrawn to the first antechamber, the door of which they had barricaded as best they could. Even as Eliste stood listening, a heavy, rhythmic pounding commenced. The invaders intended to beat down the door, and the occasional blind firing of the cornered soldiers scarcely deterred them.

The pounding continued without pause, continued until Eliste could feel the blows jarring along her nerves to shake her heart and mind. She wanted to scream, she wanted to run, and here she was, caught fast in the world's most elegant trap. It was only the recollection of her own Exalted breeding, together with a curiously distinct mental image of her Grandmother Zeralenn's flawlessly controlled visage, that enabled her to maintain false equanimity. Similarly unrevealing were the other Exalted faces around her. But the servants fared worse; the menials were uniformly sickly of complexion. Many were sobbing, and a few, prey to trembling limbs, had collapsed to their knees. Kairthe remained on her feet. The tears were oozing from the corners of her eyes, but she maintained the silence of a brave child. Moved, Eliste squeezed the maid's hand, and Kairthe whispered tremulously, "Miss, what'll happen? Why don't they do something?"

She was not the only one to wonder. Everywhere the set faces and staring eyes posed the same question; doubts underscored by relentless beating at the door. The King himself seemed prey to conflicting impulses; now moved by one counselor or another, now pausing to confer anxiously with his wife; now harking dutifully, now sinking into glazed reverie. But a decision of some kind was required, and even Dunulas knew it. When the rending crunch of wood signaled the imminent demise of the outer door, he rose to his feet.

"I will speak to them," the King decreed, straight-spined but a little shaky-voiced. "I will hear their grievances, and this matter shall be mended."

A subdued muttering of protest greeted this announcement. The King wavered, then rallied. "They are my subjects," he declared. "I have allowed an estrangement, and the results are atrocious. My people are confused, agitated, resentful, and destructive as frustrated infants. Beneath the anger, however, the love they bear their sovereign remains intact. I know it; I sense it. My kindness will reawaken their affection. We shall talk, and learn to know each other again. Mutual comprehension ensures amity. To understand all is to forgive all."

The King appeared prettily sincere in his sentiments. His faith in the power of good intention was simple, absolute, and possibly suicidal. Armed with nothing beyond ill-informed philanthropy, he actually meant to face the invaders. A few pleading voices arose and were disregarded, for Dunulas possessed the huge obstinacy of the weak. Once charted, nothing short of natural disaster could alter his course. Now, having reached a decision at last, he jumped to his feet and pattered for the exit. No one presumed to restrain him.

Through the apartment sped the King, with a bright comet's tail of appalled courtiers trailing close behind. Excited almost beyond fear, Eliste followed. The din of conflict intensified as she advanced. By the time she reached the besieged antechamber, the noise was deafening. The Guardsmen were shouting, the creatures out in the corridor were howling and cheering like frenzied devils drunk on victory, and the blows upon the door were cataclysmic. Fissures already marred the gilded surface, and even as Dunulas entered the chamber, the blade of somebody's ax broke through, and high-pitched yelps of lunatic elation arose outside.

Sensations still dulled by the persistent sense of unreality that even now did not leave her, Eliste watched as the King issued orders to his Bodyguardsmen. A blue scarf signaling a request for parley was attached to the point of a soldier's bayonet and thrust through the hole in the door. Fresh howls of triumph arose without, and the cry went up:

"Open! Open!"

Visibly uncertain, Dunulas conferred with his associates, then issued additional orders. Scribbling a note on a scrap of paper, the Captain of Bodyguard pushed the missive through the hole. Presumably the note offered unacceptable terms, for after a moment's silence, a storm arose in the corridor, and then a single voice bellowed:

"Open! We want the King!"

"The King! The King!" A fierce chorus.

The pounding resumed. The door shook, and fresh cracks appeared. Dunulas squared his shoulders bravely; glanced once at his queen, who stood very straight beside him; then nodded to his officer, who appeared to remonstrate. The King shook his head, and all present heard his clear reply:

"I will prove my love by placing myself in my people's hands. They would not harm their sovereign. I know it."

Lordly hands flew to the hilts of small, pathetically light dress swords, but the weapons remained sheathed. A gentleman soiled his blade and his name by drawing upon commoners. No circumstance justified exception.

As King, Queen, and trapped Exalted watched in fatalistic fascination, the barricades were swiftly dismantled. The bolts were pulled, and the splintering door flung wide to admit the triumphant mob.

The world seemed to explode as a horde of cheering savages burst into the antechamber. Instantly the room was thronged. They were pouring in by the hundreds, and those in the vanguard were forced straight on through and out into the audience chamber, the dressing room, the wardrobe, and bedroom beyond. Through the King's apartment they ranged, joyously looting, smashing and, slashing. A host of small, priceless ornaments and curios disappeared as if vaporized. Similarly short work was made of the cabinet containing his Majesty's rings, buckles, knee-sparklers, snuffboxes, and jeweled watches. The wardrobe yielded a rich harvest of gold-laced coats and satin breeches, embroidered waistcoats, scarlet-soled shoes and boots. Upon the remaining royal furnishings, too unwieldy to pillage, the rioters vented their exuberant spleen. Upholstered chairs and settees were disemboweled, brocade curtains and hangings shredded, sconces twisted, marquetry scarred, ormolu pried from its base. One dedicated sportsman, splendidly swathed in the King's canary-colored dressing gown and armed with a slingshot, had made it his mission to shoot the rock-crystal lusters off the chandeliers in each room. Another was busily gouging craters in the boiseries. Everywhere, the popular excitement found its outlet in destruction; the most zestful of which took place in his Majesty's bedroom, where the great silver bed was liberally anointed with the contents of the commode, then set ablaze. The damp, down-filled pillows and mattress charred rather than burned. The weak flames soon extinguished themselves, but not before a dense, foul-smelling smoke had arisen to spread through the apartment.

The smoke soon found its way to the antechamber, adding its stench to an atmosphere already suffocating—hot, close, heavy with the reek of unwashed bodies, garlicked breath, sweat, blood, and gunpowder. The room was packed with humanity, for the majority of invaders had halted there at the hub of events. Scores of Sherreenian citizens crowded shoulder to shoulder. Hundreds more, unable to squeeze their way in, jammed the corridor outside. Off to one side stood the soldiers of the Bodyguard, who had, upon the command of their king, already laid down their arms. Pressed against the walls, squashed into corners, shoved and jostled, elbow-jabbed and sometimes spat at, the shocked Exalted shrank from plebeian contact. At the center of it all, focus both of hope and hatred, were Dunulas and Lallazay. They stood very close, but not touching. Lallazay's soft, mobile face was uncharacteristically rigid, while the King bore a look of faintly perplexed martyrdom.

Eliste stood flattened against the wall. Beside her were her sister Maids of Honor, the Marquise vo Quivesse, and a few of the maidservants, including Kairthe. Between the women and the invading mob, a number of Exalted gentlemen had interposed themselves. Simultaneously horrified and inquisitive, Eliste craned her neck in an effort to peer over or around the human barrier. There were too many bodies, too close, most of them too tall. She could see almost nothing; in fact, she could barely breathe. Kairthe's elbow was digging painfully into her ribs, while Gizine vo Chaumelle's dark head pressed her cheek. The noise beat at her ears, her hungry lungs labored, and she was light-headed, unsteady, perhaps on the verge of fainting. Dizzy, she swayed and would have fallen, but for the closeness of packed bodies holding her upright. For a time all was senseless uproar, crushing pressure, heat, fear, and confusion. Then the din began to lose something of its intensity, and the volume perceptibly subsided. The sense of imminent suffocation passed, and Eliste was able to draw her breath again. Dizziness receded, and the babble of voices began to resolve itself into individual queries, oaths, threats. Still she could not see. Lips parted to drink the fetid air, she strained her ears for intelligence.

Dunulas and Lallazay stood in the center of a tiny clearing bordered by unarmed Bodyguardsmen and Exalted gentlemen. This puny human pale was all that stood between monarch and mob; and the mob was not inclined to brook interference. Quickly the barrier was eliminated; unwilling bodies thrust aside, resistance subdued within seconds. The King and Queen stood pitifully accessible, and nobody knew what to do next.

Regicide might have occurred then and there, save for Dunulas's fearlessly pacific demeanor. The King seemed unaware of personal danger. He faced his fractious subjects with every appearance of trust; a trust they were unaccountably loath to violate. Fury abated in the face of the King's incongruously civilized goodwill. The tumult faded. When Dunulas lifted his hand, silence followed. The King's mild, wondering eyes shifted from face to hostile face. He took a deep breath and spoke calmly:

"Citizens, tell me what you seek. I am listening."

Such quiet had now fallen that Eliste could easily hear the light, monotonous tenor voice that seemed simple and guileless as a child's. That royal naïveté carried weight. It was almost impossible to disbelieve him. At that moment, for the first time, she came close to admiring the Vonahrish king.

The dubious crowd growled softly.

"You have come to voice your grievances," Dunulas encouraged. "Do so now. Above all things I value the happiness of the people. What must be done to ensure it? Citizens, advise me."

A pause, and a muttering uncertainty. A few suppressed curses, a couple of skeptical grunts.

"But is he honest?" someone demanded.

"I speak truly. I wish to mend matters," the King assured them earnestly.

"Prove it."

"How shall I do so? It is for my people to instruct me."

This response, while all the invaders could have desired, imposed unexpected burdens. Once more the issue of specific demands had arisen, and as yet the matter remained undecided. The uproar resumed. A score of suggestions were put forth in as many seconds. Louder and more vehement grew the conflicting voices. Insults flew, oaths and sarcasms sizzled, invective gave way to threats, citizens pushed and shoved each other. Through it all, Dunulas remained motionless, head slightly bowed, eyes lowered in an attitude of lamblike submission. Lallazay, sickly-white, stood erect and pinch-lipped at his side. All about the room, Exalted faces were rigid with contempt and helpless anger.

Eliste could see the indignation glittering in the eyes of her peers, could feel it festering in her own mind. This invasion of the royal palace by the roistering canaille, this vile insult to royalty, was an affront beyond endurance. These chattering, grimacing, dangerous louts, with their outrageous insolence, their brutish violence, their mindless resentment, presumed to dictate terms to the King—it was intolerable, absurd. Yet Dunulas endured it all without complaint. He was yielding, humbly malleable. Shouldn't a *real* king resist coercion? Shouldn't he assert his authority? Shouldn't he, in short, display a little spirit? Eliste glanced covertly about, wondering if anyone shared her sentiments.

The shouting built to a riotous crescendo; no longer could any single voice or any coherent idea express itself. Pained and disgusted, Eliste pressed both hands to her ears. Then some anonymous oaf with big shoulders, big bull neck, and probably a big voice to match, mounted a chair and began waving his arms.

Curious and momentarily directionless, the crowd quieted, and the self-appointed spokesman's voice became audible:

"We can't talk here. We can't decide anything here. We need another place."

Ragged yowls of affirmation, scattered applause.

"Now's the time that counts. We've got to have cool heads. We've got to have some breathing space."

Emphatic assent, and a barrage of queries; answered, to the surprise of all, by the King himself.

"The banqueting hall," Dunulas offered mildly. Startled silence greeted the suggestion, and he added, "It is spacious and airy. There are hundreds of chairs. There we shall assemble in some comfort, and all may be heard in turn."

This prospect—so rational, inviting, and easily effected—was more than welcome to the invaders, who now began to look upon the King with friendlier eyes. A murmur of unwontedly warm approval arose. His Majesty's utter tractability seemed to earn trust, even support; but doubt and natural caution remained.

"While we're off chatting, what's to prevent those Hurbanese lickspittle mercenaries from surrounding the place and trapping us like mice?" someone wanted to know.

"And how can we be sure those Exalted peacocks won't be cooking up some plot?"

"We shall not be molested," King Dunulas assured them. "I take my oath upon it." His manifest sincerity swayed many listeners. Even the skeptics, however, voiced little objection, for there were few among them so dull as to miss the obvious truth—neither soldiers nor Exalted would venture an attack so long as the King and Queen remained hostage.

"Permit my friends and retainers their liberty," Dunulas appealed. "Let their safety be assured here and now, and they will not oppose you. I give you my word upon their behalf."

Again, the plea was almost superfluous. The Exalted courtiers, vastly outnumbered, and most of them armed with nothing beyond their small dress-swords, were capable neither of serious resistance nor of flight. Even should they succeed in escaping the palace itself, they would find the grounds swarming with citizens. There was little to fear from the Exalted—for the moment—and thus no reason to deny the peacocks the run of their gilded cage. The King's request was granted. Dunulas appeared gratified; while the flames of impotent rage and humiliation licked Exalted hearts.

An escort now formed to convey the King to the banqueting hall. Dunulas was permitted a scant handful of titled advisers.

"Don't forget Wifey," someone sang, and there were guffaws.

Lallazay's eyes widened at the unheard-of insolence. Wordlessly she accepted her husband's proffered arm. The mob rippled and parted, an aisle opened, and the procession set off.

For at least a couple of hours following the King's departure, Eliste and her fellow Exalteds remained confined to the royal apartment. Despite Dunulas's parole, the exits were guarded and movement restricted. The crowd had thinned considerably. It was now possible to breathe without discomfort, to speak and be heard, even to walk about. Presumably the mass of peasant trespassers had congregated about the banqueting hall, where negotiations of unknowable significance transpired. More than enough remained, however, to make life miserable with their coarse impudence, their petty tyranny, their ridiculously consequential airs. An insufferable group of them almost instantly set themselves up as the self-styled "Patriot-Protectors," whose ostensible task it was "to safeguard the welfare of the United Citizens of Sherreen." A short time later, that goal was expanded to include the United Citizens of All Vonahr, who were, by and large, as yet ignorant of their "protectors'" existence. Eliste regarded the Patriot-Protectors with mingled disdain and fear. The creatures were laughable, of course, with their crudity, their pretensions, their inept aping of their betters' form. For all the clownish absurdity, however, they were genuinely threatening. The majority of them were armed. Many had participated in the slaughter of Guardsmen and servants, and probably would not hesitate to murder again. Now, swollen with pique and self-importance, they strutted to and fro, preening themselves and flourishing their muskets, stolen from the defeated Bodyguard. It suited their fancy to dictate, to order, above all to degrade the Exalteds now subject—however briefly—to their authority. Thus, there were instant rules of conduct, governing Exalted movement, communication, even diversion. It was forbidden, for example, to assemble in groups of more than four, without a Patriot-Protector present to monitor conversation. Exchange of written notes was altogether prohibited, for most of the Patriots were illiterate and thus unable to foil possible conspiracy. Bullying was carried to such lengths that when Merranotte v'Estais's maid was caught embroidering the v'Estais arms upon a handkerchief, the weeping girl was charged with treason to her class; dragged off into a corner, surrounded, nagged, and harangued at length.

To Eliste and her companions, it was deeply offensive, at once alarming and silly, and wearisome beyond description. There was ennui, annoyance, frustration, petty affront; beyond these trifles loomed a deep and genuine concern for Crown and country. Dunulas had been flung into the lions' cage without a whip. Who could say when the beasts might not turn on him?

The evening advanced, and at last came the word that the Exalted were free to go about their business, provided they did not attempt to leave the building, take up arms, or "assemble in secret to conspire against the people." Negotiations with Dunulas, though promising, would probably carry on through the night. In the meantime, it was permissible to walk the galleries, to eat, sleep, exchange such information as was available. This decree liberated scores of Exalted hitherto herded together into groups of varying size, and confined under guard here and there throughout the Beviaire. Also liberated was his Grace of Feronte, who alone among all the courtiers had offered effective resistance. Feronte, having efficiently organized and armed a small force of gentlemen and retainers, had taken possession of the Swan Chamber and successfully defended it against all attack for hours. The corridor outside the room was strewn with plebeian dead and wounded. Curiously enough, this opposition failed to rouse rancor. Rather, it seemed to win popular respect, even admiration. When a truce was declared, and his Grace cautiously issued from the Swan Chamber, the invaders greeted him almost amiably. He was watched constantly, followed everywhere, and denied access to the banqueting hall, presumably for fear that his too-forceful presence might stiffen the spine of his older brother, thus upsetting delicate negotiations. Yet at all times he merited courtesy, never suffering the indignities inflicted upon virtually all other captive Exalteds.

Eliste, together with friends and servants, returned to the Maids' Quarters. If there they expected to find quiet refuge, they were soon disillusioned. The Quarters had been thoroughly plundered. Furniture was overturned, windows broken, washbowls and pitchers smashed. Jewelry boxes lay open and empty. Gowns and petticoats, many of them senselessly torn and dirtied, were scattered everywhere. In the Marquise vo Quivesse's apartment, the old lady's prized store of pills, potions, tonics, elixirs, and digestives had been rifled. Now the Watchdog sat alone behind her closed door, stunned and apparently mute. In Maidsmauve, the floor was white with the confetti remains of Merranotte v'Estais's vast collection of love letters, the walls reddened with smears of rouge, and the air ghastly with the fumes arising from dozens of broken perfume bottles. The four roommates had all suffered major losses. Their jewelry was gone, down to the last paste shoe buckle. There was not a hat in sight that had not been despoiled of its plumes. Gloves, scarves, fans, and ribbons had largely vanished; and the mutilations inflicted upon linen undergarments were creatively obscene.

For some reason, Eliste's wardrobe had fared comparatively well. Her gowns lay here and there about the room; some of them trampled, some of them ripped, but only one or two missing. It would seem that the superb deceptive simplicity of Madame Nimais's art had not recommended itself to the eyes of the invaders, whose tastes ran heavily in favor of the ornate frills preferred by Neanne vo Zeurlot-v'Innique. Neanne had lost every dress she owned, but for the one upon her back. Now she sat on the edge of her bed, hunched over and weeping softly. Beside her, also weeping, sat Gizine vo Chaumelle, inconsolable over the loss of her heirloom parure. The misery was infectious, and all four of the maidservants were sobbing. Eliste, however, was momentarily immune to tears. Her fright and grief found its outlet in anger. She pictured her belongings, pawed and violated by dirty peasant hands, and the image sickened her. Somehow she sensed herself indirectly contaminated. Such items as proved salvageable would have to be cleansed and thoroughly purified before she could consider allowing them to touch her body again; and even then, she would sense the invisible stains.

Resentment was reinforced by the periodic reappearance of plebeians, who swaggered in and out of the Maids' Quarters like clownish conquerors. They came to gawk, they came to gloat, to snigger, to preach, or justify themselves; but primarily they came to prove, by demonstration, that they could do exactly as they pleased. For the first time ever, they ruled, and the sensation had gone to their heads like wine. Thus the women sauntered in to pick over Exalted belongings, appropriating whatever they fancied, as if wordlessly daring the owners; as if expressing, in each word and gesture, the accumulated anger of generations. And worse by far were the men who came in simply to inspect the famous Maids of Honor. Their commentary was revolting, their familiarity intolerable, and under-lying the crude joviality was always the unspoken threat of violence. Probably they were only amusing themselves, but the danger seemed terribly close and real. Eliste armored herself as best she could in icy contempt. Silent, she ignored both taunts and outrageous overtures. Taking their cue from her, the other Maids of Honor did likewise. Merranotte immersed herself in a book, while Gizine and Neanne built castles of cards. In Maidsrose and Maidsblanche, the girls were all but inanimate, and this dull unresponsiveness eventually produced the desired result. The invaders grew bored, and wandered off.

Sleep was impossible; there was no point in attempting it. Throughout the long night the Maids of Honor maintained vigil, and shortly before dawn, received the astonishing news—His Majesty Dunulas had agreed to the formation of a constitution, wherein the respective rights, powers, obligations, and respon-sibilities of monarch and citizens were to be set forth clearly in writing, for all to see, for all time to come.

To Eliste, it seemed screamingly wrong. The King was the King, and the idea of restricting his authority struck her as senseless. True, she had glanced at Shorvi Nirienne's scribblings, in which the concept of constitutional monarchy was so eloquently defended, and she had been impressed, even stirred. But she was equally stirred by the verse dramas of the last century, in which playwrights inspired by the genius of the ancients argued the conflict between love and honor. It made for brilliant theater and splendid entertainment, but it had little to do with real life. In real life, a king required absolute power. Limitations could only impair efficiency, perhaps disastrously, in times of national crisis. How could anyone, even the idiot canaille, fail to understand that?

But fail they did, and now they were demanding vast concessions likely to initiate total ruination. It was stupid, unutterably stupid, and she could only pray that the King's acquiescence masked some sophisticated strategy of resistance. Not that Eliste thought in terms of strategy. She only hoped that somehow it would happen that it wasn't true; that the King would outwit his doltish enemies, restoring peace and stability and sanity to the world. Anything else, and chaos reigned.

If it was a ruse, it was a remarkably convincing one. Within the space of hours, the King had sanctioned the assembly of a Constitutional Congress, composed of delegates representing the various provinces of Vonahr. It would be the task of said Congress, over the course of the next several months, to draft a document that would lay the foundation and determine the structure of a reformed, presumably improved type of national government—one in which the King, his power absolute no longer, should be answerable to some parliament, or even an old-fashioned Century of one hundred men, in whose membership the people might perhaps be allowed some voice. The constitution would include a Vonahrish Patrimony, specifying those personal rights and liberties henceforth guaranteed as the birthright of every citizen. Upon completion, the King should affix his signature and seal to the new constitution, thus signifying his acceptance of all conditions set forth therein. Thereafter the Congress would dissolve, to be replaced once and for all by whatever form of legislative body the new blueprint might establish.

In the meantime, the King was to grant several immediate concessions, including, among others, the opening of certain Exalted granaries, and public distribution of the contents; elimination of an entire array of taxes and surcharges; liberalization of the old restrictions upon peasant hunting and fishing rights; immunity from reprisal of every citizen participating in the Beviaire invasion; and finally, most extraordinary, the emancipation of all serfs. Henceforth, no Vonahrian should ever be bound by law to a seigneur's soil.

To the disgust of most Exalted, Dunulas agreed to all conditions—even the last. It almost passed understanding—apparently the King had submitted virtually without protest. True, the coercion was considerable; and yet such alacrity in yielding almost argued a positive willingness. Certainly the canaille were beginning to imagine the monarch spontaneously sympathetic to their cause. Now, rumor had it, they were cheering him in the banqueting hall; blubbering, sniffling, and slobbering in mawkish affection as they hailed him "Friend of the People"; squeezing his hand, pumping his arm, even thumping his back. And the King suffered it all, every indignity, while his queen stood beside him, hiding her humiliation and heartbreak behind a faint, fixed smile. This image was so distasteful that many of the more optimistic among the Exalted consoled themselves with the hope of royal duplicity, while the more clear-sighted contemplated the reality of royal feebleness.

Eliste received the news with mixed emotion. On the one hand, she was startled, alarmed, and curious all at once as she tried to imagine the changes that might now overtake her world. At the same time, some part of her mind continued to deny the reality of it all. She tried to convince herself, and at times partially succeeded, that this disturbance would die down of its own accord. Little if anything would truly alter, and life would go on as before. And finally, in considering the emancipation of the serfs—shortsighted though it was, for what should those underlings so reliant upon Exalted protection and guidance do with their new freedom?—she could not help but think of Dref Zeenoson. Wherever he was, in Vonahr or out of it, he would hear the news and he would know that he was free, for all the Derrivalle tattoo marking his flesh. She tried to picture his reaction, she tried to picture *him,* without much success. All she could see in her mind's eye was the long, spare, agile figure clothed in the smock and sabots of a northern peasant—black eyes alive with intelligence, very white smile in a lean, tanned face—Dref as she had always known him, upon her father's estate. But he might be quite different now—as a fugitive serf, he would very likely have altered his appearance. He would do so with the ingenuity and skill that marked all his undertakings, and he might well be all but unrecognizable—a curiously disturbing thought, despite the fact that she was unlikely ever to encounter him again. Unless, of course, he chose to return to Derrivalle. His father and sister were there, after all, and he might now present himself with impunity, provided he was ready to brave the Marquis vo Derrivalle's hostility. Unconsciously, Eliste shook her head. Dref, for all his impudence, would know better than to try it. The Marquis, implacably vindictive, would never forget the serf who had knocked him flat in full view of the assembled menials, bloodied his Exalted nose, then made a fool of him by escaping unpunished; never forget and never forgive. Emancipation or no emancipation, Dref's life upon Derrivalle soil wasn't worth a fleabite. No, she would never see him again.

Eliste shrugged, deliberately dismissing the subject. She could hardly afford to waste time fretting over something so trivial as a single recalcitrant, ungovernable serf. It was dawn, and the incredulous, insomniac Exalted had gathered in the galleries to discuss the appalling events, to exchange opinions and to await fresh intelligence. She would join them.

The four Maidsmauve girls descended to the glass-littered Queens' Gallery, where Exalted mingled unwillingly with the lounging, ubiquitous plebeians. Stazzi vo Crev was there, along with vo Renache, vo Furnaux, and many others of the

erstwhile gay and gallant—now universally sober and anxious. In the presence of
the invader, conversation was subdued and guarded. Information was scanty, and
nothing new might be expected for some hours to come; for the report was
everywhere confirmed that the King, exhausted by the long night's travail, had at
last been permitted temporary respite in the comparative privacy of his own
apartment. Later in the day, the conference would resume; but for now, Dunulas
slept. Likewise sleeping—a host of plebeians, slumped on chairs and settees,
sprawled out on the floor along the walls. They had not known where to go, of
course, or perhaps they hadn't cared, and many had relieved themselves in the
fireplaces or else in the corners. Now the atmosphere was loathsome, and only the
constant flow of autumn air through the shattered windows rendered the gallery
even remotely habitable. Eliste's nostrils twitched in disgust. Beside her Merranotte applied a perfumed handkerchief to her nose, while Neanne and Gizine
frankly gagged.

They were repellent, these peasants. They were animals, dirty animals, loving
the filth in which they wallowed, glorying in destruction. They shouldn't be here,
in this place. It was wrong. The grandeur of the Beviaire should have been
sacrosanct, but these creatures comprehended neither beauty, tradition, artistic
achievement, nor civilization itself.

Brimming with indignation, she hurried to the window for a draught of fresh
air. Down below, the courtyard was thronged with peasants, still waiting in
silence, as they had waited all through the night, like a bedraggled herd of
potentially deadly sheep. Right and left, up and down, wherever she looked, she
saw them. They were everywhere.

Her eyes stung. She couldn't bear the sight of them—nor the stench, nor the
immoderate braying of their voices. She had to get away. Abruptly turning from
the window, she hurried from the gallery, indifferent to curious, staring eyes. Back
to the Maids' Quarters—no true refuge, not any longer, but the closest thing to it
she was now likely to find. The place was blessedly clear of strangers, and the
pressure upon her head and heart eased a little. She discovered that she was tired
to the point of exhaustion. Kairthe put her to bed, and she was asleep within
seconds.

It was past noon when the hard-edged sunlight shooting in through the broken
windows nudged her awake. Her eyes blinked open reluctantly. She had the
distinct, unpleasant sense that something was very wrong with the bright world,
but it took her a moment to remember what it was. The sight of a strapping,
rawboned marketwoman casually rummaging through the contents of a hamper a
few feet from the bed recalled all of yesterday's events. Rage blasted through her,
and she did not pause to consider consequences. Throwing the covers aside, she

sprang to her feet. "Leave that alone," she commanded, low-voiced. Her face was white, lips compressed, eyes wide and blazing.

The woman turned slowly, looked her up and down. After a moment, she shrugged, dropped a handful of silk stockings to the floor, and sauntered out.

Eliste stood, breathing hard. Rage still boiled along her veins, a rage completely out of proportion to that single incident. Things were ugly, confused, madly disordered—and it just wasn't acceptable; in fact, it was growing intolerable. It was high time this wretched farce came to an end. The canaille had been given what they wanted, hadn't they? Now it was time for them to go away.

But they didn't go, not yet. Through the day they lingered, clogging the corridors, the courtyards, and antechambers. The hours passed, and news of the incredible happening galloped through all of Sherreen and beyond, out along the rivers and highways, the lanes and pathways, to speed like a conflagration through the provinces. While King Dunulas remained closeted with a strident band of his subjects, and the Exalted courtiers chafed under unbelievable restriction, the news continued to spread. The day wore on, and some citizens went into hiding, while others armed themselves; and during that time, the crowd about the palace steadily swelled, until it filled the grounds and backed up into Dunulas Square. About the crowd the rumors flew in vast dark-plumaged flocks. Contradictory, unconfirmed, glorious and sinister by turn, the rumors circled and swooped. Dubious yet hopeful, the Sherreenians awaited elucidation.

They received it around twilight, when Dunulas, accompanied by his wife, stepped out upon the balcony of the banqueting chamber to address the people massed below. The King's face was pale and haggard, his eyes shadowed; he looked tired to death. But his manner was mild and equable as ever as he announced the results of the long conference. Absolute silence enveloped the crowd; the citizens seemed scarcely to breathe. The King's light, droning voice was thus audible to thousands as he enumerated the various reforms to which he had given his consent, ending with a brief description of the proposed constitution, whose eventual ratification would safeguard the new liberties of all citizens. The twilight deepened as he spoke, faintly violet air graying to charcoal. The lamps and chandeliers of the Beviaire blossomed. Warm light gilded a host of raptly upturned faces.

The King concluded his address and stood there gazing down upon them with the hopeful, expectant air of a child in need of approval. The breathless silence stretched an instant longer, and then the crowd erupted into a madness of shouting, cheers, and applause. The King's anxiety faded. His soft face relaxed into renewed plumpness, and he glanced down encouragingly into the face of the Queen at his side. Lallazay bent her head in acknowledgment of the popular acclaim. She even managed a sickly semblance of a smile. But the nervous little hands buried in the folds of her skirt were rigid and white-knuckled.

If Lallazay's optimism lacked conviction, the crowd failed to notice. The cheers and applause continued until the King and Queen, weary of smiling and bowing, retired from view. Thereafter there were spontaneous outbreaks of joyous weeping, dancing, capering, and song. The uproar continued for the better part of an hour, and then gradually began to subside. Night had fallen. Many citizens had been waiting in that place for hours; in some cases, for days. They were tired, hungry, unwashed, uncomfortable. Now, curiosity assuaged, and fully content with their victory, they wanted to go home. The cheering had fallen off, but the prevailing mood of joyous camaraderie still found outlet in song, laughter, sporadic joking, and horseplay as the citizens began to disperse. The crowd thinned leisurely over the course of the next couple hours. By ten o'clock or so, the grounds were comparatively clear. Not all trespassers departed, however. A number of diehard zealots lingered, tight muttering clusters of them scattered here and there about the lawn. Hundreds more waited in Dunulas Square. Within the palace itself, a substantial plebeian force remained, ostensibly to continue negotiations. In thinly veiled reality, the obvious peril of the King's position forestalled all attempt at Exalted or military intervention.

Self-defense demanded the continuing presence of plebeian "patriots" within the Beviaire; for only possession of the King's person secured the newly won liberties and privileges. Only the unspoken threat to the King's life could hold the military at bay. Unpalatable, of course, to contemplate anything so disrespectful as locking the King and Queen in their respective apartments. By no means must it appear to the nation and the world that their Majesties were prisoners, victims of their own impious subjects. Sherreenians should not be taken for barbarians, and yet the King must be guarded like the fabulous prize that he was. In the future, perhaps the near future, when the constitution had been completed and Dunulas had set his irrevocable signature and seal to it, trust would become real, and vigilance might relax. In the meantime, the King and Queen would receive due honor within the confines of the Beviaire, beneath the ceaseless scrutiny of gimlet-eyed patriots.

Given such circumstances, the formal and rigidly hierarchical Court could hardly continue to function. The presence of courtiers thus became superfluous—actively undesirable, in fact. For why permit hundreds of Exalted such a perfect milieu in which to gather, to exchange information, to plot and to hatch devilries? Why suffer their wordless ice-dagger contempt? Why feed them? Far better and safer to send the Seigneurs, their women, and their smarmy lackeys packing. Boot them out, divide and separate them, curtail their rights to travel and assemble, and thus their ability to organize resistance; such was the decision of the occupying patriots.

The day following the King's address, the weeding process began. Dunulas and Lallazay were allowed to draw up short lists of indispensable attendants. In addition to these, certain great courtiers whose power, wealth, or public popularity constituted a possible threat were encouraged or required to remain under what amounted to house arrest. First among these was his Grace of Feronte. Most others were considered redundant. By late afternoon, scores of astonished, outraged Exalted were already receiving orders to vacate the premises without delay. Amidst a frantic flurry of activity, the exodus began. For hours thereafter, a steady stream of blazoned carriages crammed to bursting with boxes, hastily stuffed bundles, and frazzled silk-clad humanity rolled down the long white-graveled drive, past knots of jeering citizens, through the gate, and out of the royal enclosure.

By nobody's standards were the Maids of Honor indispensable. The twelve of them were notified of their eviction in the early evening. Because they were young, butterfly-pretty, and harmless, they were given the night to arrange their departure. Throughout the ensuing hours, twelve maidservants feverishly sorted, folded, and packed, while their mistresses desperately sought transportation. By morning, all was miraculously complete. The Maids took tearful leave of the tearful Queen and of each other; promised eternal friendship; promised letters, promised visits; then set forth upon their separate paths, each almost willfully denying the magnitude of the separation.

Several were returning to the doldrums of the provinces, and they were widely pitied. The more fortunate remained in Sherreen. Eliste belonged to the latter category. She had secured the loan of the Marquis vo Lieux-v'Olliard's splendid yellow and black equipage, which bore her grandly through the teeming streets, back to her grandmother's house. Kairthe was sniffling throughout the short journey, but Eliste's eyes were dry. This exile, she assured herself, was but an incident. Without doubt, the madness would burn itself out, and she would be back at Court within days. Weeks, at most.

Sherreen was seething like a heated cauldron. The great popular invasion of the Beviaire, the unparalleled triumph of the people, seemed to have fired every heart with enthusiasm. Everywhere the citizens gathered to marvel, to exult, and above all, to talk. There breathed scarcely a citizen, from wealthiest merchant all the way down to the most scrofulous minion of The Fungus, devoid of opinion. Every possible ramification of the proposed reforms was analyzed at length in the markets, the taverns, the political clubs, the salons, the cookshops, and the coffeehouses. No theory was so farfetched, no suggestion so infeasible, that it did not find its advocates. But certain matters of a practical nature demanded prompt consideration, and chief among these was the actual composition of the Constitutional Congress.

Every province of Vonahr should be represented—so much everyone agreed upon. But how many delegates should there be? How should they be chosen, and by whom? Should delegates be distributed equally among the provinces, in which case tiny, rural VoGrance would speak with a voice as loud as the populous Sevagne's? Should representatives be apportioned according to population? If so, purists argued, a complete and painstaking census was required—a task demanding months of effort. Should former serfs, although emancipated, enjoy the rights of full citizens, entitled to congressional representation? Did freed serfs merit the right to serve as delegates, or was that a liberality extreme to the point of absurdity? Didn't the city of Sherreen, capital and heart of the nation, heavily populated as some small provinces, deserve representatives of its own?

The issues were multifarious, each new consideration giving rise to multiple subordinate questions in a geometric progression that seemed to extend to infinity. Debate, jovial or moralistic or acrimonious, continued night and day. Above that babble of conflicting opinion, however, two voices rose like sky-rockets. Both spoke from the Eighth District; but that geographical proximity was countered by extreme philosophical distance.

Number 11 Duck Row was the site of activity lively and constant. Here, in the Bulaude dwelling, Shorvi Nirienne penned his vision, producing a steady stream of articles, pamphlets, and tracts. Here he conferred with his Niriennistes, here he spoke and won new converts, whose lives would forever bear the imprint of his mind. Now, however, for the first time, he was free to express his views in public without fear of reprisal. The complaisance of the King had legalized so many of the views that Nirienne had favored for years, that former charges of treason and sedition were simply nullified. This so, no longer proscribed, he might speak as he pleased; conversely, all might listen and freely judge. Thus the sitting room of Number 11 was thronged. The hungry-minded constantly came and went, and the Nirienniste convictions spread from that source to permeate the city and the land beyond.

Similarly liberated was Whiss v'Aleur. True, his *Neighbor Jumalle's Complaint* had continued uninterrupted publication for months, and now the journal was known in the provinces as well as the capital, its editor famed both at home and abroad. True, the speeches and rallies had continued, and the Reparationists had marched through the streets, chalking their signature scarlet diamonds on walls all over town, until the gendarmes cringed at the sight of that symbol. They had never been able to silence him, and he had made his voice heard all along at his own pleasure—but now it was different. Now the King was on the run at last, and his bloodsucking Exalted along with him. Official control was slipping, and the cracked old social structure, rotten of timber and foundation, was visibly crumbling. Reparation was imminent, and tyrants might well tremble. True patriots, on the other hand, need fear nothing, for Whiss v'Aleur was there to inspire and guide them.

While theorists waged intellectual battle, the more pragmatic of citizens opted for action. Numbers had already armed themselves, but the great treasure trove of the City Armory as yet remained untouched—an omission demanding immediate correction. For it was widely suspected that his Majesty's present tractability was purely expedient; his great promises ephemeral as morning mist, apt to vanish within moments of sunrise—in which case he should find all the city up in arms against him. Even as the Exalted took ignominious leave of the Beviaire, a purposeful plebeian gang approached the Armory.

The big door was locked against them. Other than that, the building was undefended, its appointed custodians having prudently decamped. Making short work of the door, the invaders poured in to plunder the place of its muskets and carbines, its ammunition and kegs of powder. Of less utility, but of much interest nonetheless, was the huge collection of antique weapons. There were clumsy old hackbuts, matchlocks, and wheel locks, butt of much laughter. Older and more unwieldy yet were the lances, maces, axes, and armor. There were swords and daggers of every description, some of them magnificently ornamental, many of immense value. Such treasure, stacked up everywhere, was seized upon by scores of eager hands. The greatest wonder of all, however, defied rapacity.

They were discovered in the cellars. There, in the dim, cavernous vaults beneath the Armory reposed three great Stupefactions—those hulking remains of the great machines once imbued with dull sentience by the magic of their Exalted creators. Now motionless and dust-covered, there was nothing in their aspect to suggest the presence of life; but they were still impressive, even intimidating, in their size, complexity, and mystery.

The first of the three machines was a great silvery heap whose construction suggested flexibility. A big, slender body armored in finely wrought overlapping scales was supported by eighteen thin, long, jointless legs that curved and bent like lengths of cable. Front and back, the body dwindled smoothly to graceful, elongated, segmented necks; each of the two necks terminating in a conical nozzle of a head; each silver snout narrowing to a circular featureless aperture. A small plaque set at the base of one of the necks bore the word "ZaZa."

The second device was decidedly insectile in appearance, with six jointed legs, a small head equipped with long fronds of antennae, and a squat, ovoid, bulging body that would, when polished, gleam with gorgeous iridescence. The head almost disappeared beneath two protuberant, faceted compound eyes, golden in color. Smaller eyes jeweled the entire body. A gold plaque, neatly ringed with eyes, was engraved "NuNu."

The third machine, very unlike the other two in its massive, obvious immobility, was nothing more than a towering, coffin-shaped leaden cabinet, surmounted by a great branching tangle of interlocking rods, wires, coils, glass and metallic sunbursts, from the midst of which a pair of straight, needle-pointed spikes thrust like great black horns. Someone with courage attempted to open the cabinet, but found it firmly locked. An iron plaque at the base of the device read, "Kokotte."

The three Stupefactions, useless though they seemed to be, commanded much attention. Everyone came down to the cellar to stare at them, to marvel at their sinister strangeness, to enjoy the weirdly delicious shivers. Curiosity concerning the possible purpose and function of such machines ran high. There were multiple hypotheses, none of them verifiable; and in the end, the citizens were left to wonder.

oring. Boring. Inexpressibly boring." Elbows propped on the sill, Eliste scowled down into the Avenue Parabeau, where shabbily assertive figures now promenaded alongside the rightful well-bred residents beneath the facade of Zeralenn vo Rouvignac's town house. The bedroom window was open, for spring had come again, and the air was fragrantly soft. That mild weather, which might ordinarily have set her spirits soaring in the wake of a long and dreary winter, now had the opposite effect, for the changing seasons were an inescapable reminder of time's flight. "Dreary and weary. Low and slow. Sagging and dragging. Stale and pale. Flat and—"

" 'T isn't that bad, surely, Miss?" Kairthe interrupted.

"It is, it is! Everything's so dull, I might as well be back at Derrivalle."

"Slay me! We're not going back there, Miss?" Kairthe had lately learned to ape her mistress's fashionable contempt for all things provincial.

"Don't worry. Couldn't go if we wanted to—we don't have permits. The insolence!" A toss of the head communicated Eliste's contempt for the officious plebeians of the Constitutional Congress's powerful Committee of National Welfare, who presumed to impose restrictions upon Exalted comings and goings. They were insufferable, these upstart delegates, and the worst among them were the largely Reparationist members of the Committee, whose administrative function had somehow expanded within a remarkably brief period to encompass the affairs of all Vonahr. Now there were everywhere regulations designed to govern and humble the erstwhile masters. Although these regulations were ostensibly imposed "to safeguard the public welfare, to ensure protection of all citizens," the true purpose was revenge, pure and simple. And it was almost preferable, in the eyes of many Exalted, to deal with the most fanatical of Whiss v'Aleur's disciples, who at least made no bones about their hatred, than to endure the canting hypocrisy of self-styled "patriots" mouthing sugary platitudes to mask their greed and spleen. The Constitutional Congress was an absurdity, the Committee of National Welfare an obscenity, and all that rendered either tolerable was their clear evanescence.

"How long?" Eliste inquired, almost moaning. "How long?"

"Well, I'd say it's been about six months now, Miss," Kairthe returned helpfully. "It was about harvesttime we got booted out of the palace, then we went through the winter with folk sticking rocks inside snowballs to bust windows and spook horses, and now—"

"I know that! I mean, how long must this foolery continue? When will things get back to normal?"

"What's 'normal' mean now, Miss? Is it going to go back the way it was?"

"Certainly it will! Well—almost." Eliste stopped to consider. Even the most sanguine of Exalted traditionalists could hardly claim that things would ever again be exactly the same. The recent abolition of privilege had seen to that; henceforth, Exalted were subject to the same taxes and sundry charges formerly reserved for lesser folk. The vast implications of this decree were as yet quite lost upon Eliste, who rarely troubled her head with bourgeois considerations of finance. Her own family, and the families of her friends, possessing the wealth of Vonahr, would pay the new taxes without hardship, and that was what mattered. The affront might rankle, but the actual inconvenience involved was negligible. Of far more significance, in her eyes, was the loss of certain ancient feudal and seigneurial rights, some of them quaintly colorful. More significant and tangible yet was the emancipation of the serfs. Why, even Kairthe was now quite free, although she appeared either not to know it or else to reject it—which only demonstrated her good sense. For those so-called "free" serfs had nowhere to go and nothing to do other than continue their labors upon the seigneur's estate, where the time-honored mutual responsibilities of serf and lord had now been discarded, to be replaced by—what? The necessity of peasant toil remained, while the rewards—Exalted protection, concern, largesse—were largely forfeit. Those "emancipated" serfs had simply thrown away their greatest benefit, in exchange for an illusory freedom that served them nothing. In that sense, little had truly changed. Dref Zeenoson, wherever he was, would surely disagree; but he'd be wrong. One day, perhaps very soon now, Eliste conjectured, they would perceive the magnitude of their own error, and if they weren't too stupid, stubborn, and addled by

Reparationist rhetoric, they might voluntarily request a return to the old ways, the true ways, the right ways. In the meantime, tedious absurdity reigned.

"Will we be able to get VoGrance lamb again, Miss?" Kairthe inquired. "And that blue cheese from the Jerunde? And good Fabequais cider? I'd sell the hair off my head for a mug of home cider, I swear I would."

"If you must, then I'll take it for a switch and postiche," Eliste assured her kindly. "Since we match. But I don't think you'll need go so far." In the aftermath of the Beviaire's occupation, fighting had flared up in every province except the Sevagne. Peasants all over Vonahr, inspired by the successes of their Sherreenian brethren, had taken to burning the manors and chateaux wherein reposed the records of debt and servitude. Provincial Exalted, zealous in the defense of their property and their traditional way of life, had launched a spirited counterattack. The King's proclamation of emancipation was initially ignored, and serfs remained chained to their masters' estates. Bailiffs, stewards, and professional tax collectors backed by armed bullies continued to extract the accustomed feudal dues for a little while. Infringements upon privilege were vigorously resisted, and for a time there were even plots afoot to initiate an attack upon Sherreen, to deliver the King and crush all rebellion in one great stroke. Swiftly, however, the confirmation of Exalted magical impotence had spread throughout the land, and plebeian reaction was prompt. The near-instantaneous formation of multifarious local leagues of committed "Patriot-Protectors," whose membership was vast, had resulted in the swift suppression of royalist opposition; and now, six months later, the seigneurs were properly beaten, their open resistance confined largely to Fabeque Province, a few isolated corners of VoGrance, and the hills of the Aussadie, dominated by the formidable illusionists of Bozhenille Commune. The land rested safe in the hands of the increasingly assertive patriots, and the delegates of the Constitutional Congress, all three hundred fifty of them, apportioned roughly according to population and chosen by varying means within their respective provinces, were free to wend their way to Sherreen, to gather in the old Century Hall, refurbished for their benefit, and there get on with their work of charting the nation's future. All well and good; but of much more immediate import to all Sherreenians, most particularly to luxury-loving Exalteds, were the shortages and deprivations stemming from provincial unrest. Foodstuffs of various sorts were in short supply—even Exalted palates were learning to tolerate brown bread in place of white—and somehow the city seemed flooded with wine that smelled faintly of sulfur. Fuel was scarce and of poor quality. Fine fabrics, leather goods, and scents were hard to get; and the imported necessities of life—the best tea, coffee, chocolate, tobacco, Neep's waters—were nearly unobtainable, owing to the mounting nervousness of foreign suppliers. The poor, of course, continued hungry, as always—in fact, more so than ever. Their supposed victory had not materially improved their situation in the least—a truth affording considerable sardonic satisfaction to resentful Exalteds.

"Will we be able to go where we please again, Miss?" Kairthe persisted. "Will folk get proper and respectful in the street again? Will you go back to being Maid of Honor?"

"Certainly," Eliste replied with great confidence, for she needed to convince herself. "Very soon now, I should think."

"Couldn't be too soon, if you ask me. I've had enough of all this upset, this scurrying about, shouting and screaming, pushing and shoving, muddlement and bad language. I want things to quiet down, and I want to go back to the palace. Miss, remember how shiny all the floors there were—like a frozen pond? And remember all the candles, and how good they smelled? And all those mirrors everywhere, so you could see yourself coming and going? And the food—"

"And the music, day and night. And the dancing. The elegance, the grace and gallantry . . ." Eliste sighed longingly, quite forgetful of her own former impatience with the rigid artificiality of court life. "And the beaux—"

"With their flowers and candy, their presents, and all those little letters bouncing back and forth all the time. Remember his Grace of Feronte, Miss? Remember all that stuff he sent you, and you always sent it back, except for the silver locket? Now, *there* was a gentleman knew what he wanted, and didn't stick at going for it. No kind of pink posy, he."

"Ummmmmmm." Eliste's tone was noncommittal. She had never seen fit to inform her maid of the episode in Feronte's apartment.

"What d'you suppose has become of his Grace, Miss?"

"Still detained at the Beviaire, I believe."

"Must be hard for a gentleman like him to be cooped up there."

"No harder than it is for *me* to be cooped up *here*." Eliste slapped the sill petulantly.

"Oh, surely 't isn't the same, Miss. You can still gad about all over town."

"Not quite. Madame will scarcely let me set foot out of doors. Thinks I'll be stoned in the streets, or boiled in oil and devoured by starving peasants or something. So much for all her fine speeches about not being governed by fear."

"Well, actually, Miss, I've heard some tales would ice your tripes."

"Tales—bah!"

The unrewarding conversation was interrupted by the arrival of Aurelie, who hurried in without troubling to knock. A reproof expired upon Eliste's lips as she caught sight of her cousin's face—deeply flushed, eager, sparkle-eyed. The glowing pink cheeks contrasted oddly with the fashionable marbling of sky blue with which the young girl had streaked her brown curls some two weeks earlier, upon the occasion of her fifteenth birthday. Her fingernails were varnished a matching shade of blue. Over her arm she carried what appeared to be lengths of coarse brownish fabric. She wore an unwontedly plain dress, and flat walking shoes—and Aurelie never walked anywhere, if she could help it. Something was definitely up.

"Cousin, guess what? I have a secret, such a secret! You will never guess what it is!" Aurelie announced. "Come, try to guess!"

"But I have no idea."

"Ah, surely it is not so difficult! Do not my eyes reveal all? Are they not the windows of my soul? They shout my secret to all the world, and I am surely undone, la! Come, Cousin, only look into my eyes, and you will know all. Just try, do!"

Resignedly, Eliste complied. "Really, I can't guess. Your eyes are scarcely the traitors you imagine."

"Oh, pooh, Cousin! You are willfully blind. Very well, you have succeeded in wringing a confession from me, as was no doubt your design. I shall surely die of shame, but I will speak nonetheless. Cousin—it has happened at last, as I always knew it must. With my intense and passionate nature, it was inevitable, and now it has come upon me in all fury and I am smitten, overwhelmed and utterly conquered by feeling. Cousin Eliste—I am in love!"

"Well—er—I hardly know what to say."

"Say nothing, Cousin. Mere words are inadequate to address my love, which is an agony and a joy unspeakable."

"Quite. This is something of a surprise. Well. With whom are you in love, then?"

"With Bayelle vo Clarivaux, eldest son of the Viscount vo Clarivaux, whose house is largest upon the Avenue Parabeau. The one with the three-story piazza, you know. Bayelle—is it not a beautiful name?—is seventeen, an excellent age. The servants reveal that he has been abroad for the past year, completing his education with the Grand Tour, but now he is back, he is back to stay!"

"Well, that's not so bad. He's certainly not unsuitable. When did you meet him?"

"I have not met him—yet. I have only watched him from my window as he walks to and fro. But that has been enough to teach me that he is pensive, even brooding, yet sometimes reckless; melancholy yet fiery, proud and passionate—in short, my absolute soul mate. I have read all this upon his countenance, which is noble and pretty beyond belief."

"I see. Well, have you told Madame about this?"

"La, no! How should I endure her inquisition, her sneers and carping?

Doubtless she would say I am too young to seek happiness, but what are years? Is it not the heart that matters? My heart was born ancient."

"You ought to tell her, though—she might be able to arrange an introduction."

"Not she. Grauntie means well, and no doubt possesses knowledge of the world, but she was born devoid of tender sensibility. Therefore, I have cherished my love in silence. At times I've thought I'd burst with secret knowledge, but I have held my peace."

"Really? For how long?"

"It's been four days now."

"Four days. That puts passion's onset at the end of last week, just about the time you were telling me how bored and out of sorts you were feeling."

"Cousin, I was close to despair. Life seemed but a dreary desert. And then, when all was blackest, Fortune directed my vision to the street below my window, and I beheld—him. There he was—the prettiest fellow I ever laid eyes on—and instantly my heart caught fire, my world was transformed. Ah, whoever loved that loved not at first sight? One single look, and I was lost, quite lost, la!"

"Quick work. Look here, Aurelie, I understand your feelings, but I really think you'd better tell Madame. Otherwise, only think, you might never meet your Bayelle."

"Oh, yes I will." Aurelie nodded confidently. "I do not submit such things to chance. *I* am no sacrifice upon Fortune's altar, la! I will meet him. I will meet him *today.*"

"What are you talking about?" Eliste was starting to worry. Her young cousin's eyes reflected unsettling fanaticism.

"Every day, about this time, my Bayelle strolls the Avenue Parabeau. Where he goes, I do not know, but today I intend to find out. I will follow him, and somewhere along the way, I shall contrive to introduce myself. Thereafter, Destiny dictates."

"Ridiculous child! You'll do nothing of the sort. You cannot mean to chase after some boy unaware of your existence!"

"I'll make him aware. He'll notice me." Aurelie's jaw set.

"Take care, or you'll make a fool of yourself. Where's your modesty, your dignity?"

"What do I care for them? There are more important things. I must think of the future. I am already fifteen, a woman, and time flies. I shouldn't care to wake up one morning to discover myself eighteen and fading, alone and unsettled in life, opportunity gone—and all because I let every chance slip through my fingers. That isn't what *I* want!"

Eliste felt the angry color leap to her cheeks. Her own recent eighteenth birthday, celebrated quietly in her grandmother's house, had been a depressing affair. The gifts, favors, and festive meal, generous though they were, had only served as a painful reminder of diminishing prospects. Months earlier, as a sought-after belle at the Beviaire, with so many eligible men from whom to choose, she had never dreamed that this could happen to her—that she would reach the age of eighteen unmarried, unbetrothed, quite at loose ends. That was what happened to plain girls, to dull girls, to poor girls—not to Exalted Miss Eliste vo Derrivalle. But here she was, mewed up in the Parabeau, without so much as a single formal offer to consider. The Court was dispersed, Exalted social activity all but nonexistent. The gallants had vanished, seemingly evaporated; and it was true, she *had* let every chance slip through her fingers. Life was over at eighteen. The tears stung for a moment behind her eyelids.

"—And so, I have been thinking it over for ever so long," Aurelie, unaware of her blunder, chattered on, "and now it is time to take action. I have suffered love's agonies quite long enough. Today, I will follow my Bayelle—to the end of the world, should he ask me!"

"My dear child," Eliste expostulated, concealing her dismay behind an assumption of superior maturity, "you are Exalted, and underage. You simply cannot go tearing about the streets by yourself, like some little grisette."

"Certainly not. I shouldn't dream of such a thing. I cannot do it alone, and that is why I've come to you, Cousin. You shall serve as my chaperone."

"I will not! I'm not *that* old, Aurelie!"

"Ah, but you are so clever, Cousin! So sophisticated and wise beyond your years, since you have been at Court! You will do splendidly. Besides, I've no one else to ask. You *will* help me, will you not? Please, oh please!"

"It's out of the question. It's not only unbecoming, it isn't even *safe*! Why, I've heard some tales would—would ice your tripes!"

"But it is only the Exalted at risk, and I have thought of that already. See, Cousin, look what I have brought." Shaking out the lengths of coarse brown fabric, Aurelie proudly exhibited a pair of long, plain, hooded capes. "There is one for each of us. Here." She tossed one to Eliste. "We shall wear them to cover our gowns—and behold!—we are transformed, without benefit of magic! We become two poor little seamstresses, common girls, free to go where we please. Is it not a clever scheme, novel and delightful? Come, Cousin, let us be off!" Swirling the cloak in a great exuberant arc, Aurelie shrouded herself in brown, pulling the hood up over her blue-marbled hair. "Come, hurry, hurry, hurry!"

"Absolutely not. Aurelie, only stop and think—"

"Wait." Suddenly transfixed, Aurelie lifted one azure-nailed hand, enjoining silence. Bounding to the window, she froze like a hunting dog at the point to stare down into the street. Following a moment's electric silence, she whispered, "It's he. There he is, right down there, right now! It's Bayelle! Gad, he's so pretty, I can't bear it!"

"Where?" Unwillingly curious, Eliste glanced down to behold a well-dressed, slightly built, sandy-haired youth with features so delicately modeled as to justify Aurelie's descriptive term, ambling indolently along the Avenue Parabeau. "Nice-looking boy."

" 'Nice-looking'? Cousin, that is like calling the Beviaire 'cozy.' He is superb, altogether extraordinary, and I love him dearly. But look—look—" Aurelie's plump little hands clasped convulsively. "He is moving off. He is going! He is leaving! Quick, let's follow before he gets away!"

"Are you mad? Aurelie, just sit down. You are most certainly not going to—"

"Yes I am! I will, I will, I can't help myself! If you won't come with me, then I'm going alone!"

"You can't. I absolutely won't let you—"

"Be my friend, Cousin, and come with me. Otherwise, adieu! Love conquers all!" Not pausing to await reply, Aurelie turned and sprinted for the door, cheap brown cloak flying. She was through in a flash, and then a quick descending clatter sounded along the stairwell.

For a moment Eliste stood paralyzed with indecision. Her obvious course, certainly, was to ring for the servants, who would overtake the besotted fugitive before she was a hundred feet from the house. Such capture would result in severe embarrassment and probable punishment for poor Aurelie, who had trusted and confided in her cousin. It seemed a considerable betrayal. Perhaps it would be best, after all, to accompany the child. Thus she might shield an impulsive, inexperienced young girl against serious indiscretion; she might monitor the development of a potentially perilous situation; and above all, she herself might *get out of the house*. Interest stirred at the prospect.

"Don't tell anyone about this," she instructed the wondering Kairthe; and, donning the brown cape, sped in the wake of her flying cousin.

She caught up with Aurelie a few yards down the road. The girl was moving slowly, sneaking conspicuously from doorway to doorway, while maintaining a constant distance between herself and the quarry. Up ahead, young Bayelle vo Clarivaux sauntered along, wholly unaware. Aurelie started guiltily at the light touch upon her shoulder. Whirling, she recognized her cousin, and relief found outlet in a spate of high-pitched giggles. Hugging herself, she bent double. Eliste waited patiently, and at length the other recovered herself so far as to observe, "Cousin, I knew you could not fail me! Ah, I am glad you have come—I am quite beside myself—I cannot think—I believe I'll die—emotion overwhelms me—"

"So I see. All right, Aurelie, I'm here, much against my better judgment. Now, pull yourself together and make up your mind what you want to do." Eliste's levelheaded manner masked a sense of illicit exhilaration, an inappropriate urge to echo her cousin's giggles. She could feel her mouth starting to stretch into a smile, and she compressed her lips firmly, severely. She was, after all, the chaperone.

"I cannot say." Aurelie's breath was quick with excitement, and her face was bright pink. "I have not decided. I await inspiration. Oh, I shall think of something presently, but for now, let us simply follow him, let us only *look* at him. He's so wonderful!"

"Well, we'd best look quickly, then. He's getting into a fiacre, which we can't follow on foot, so I'm afraid that's the end of that. You'll have to come home."

"Oh, no! No! Not yet! It can't be!" Eyes wide and turbulent, Aurelie watched her inamorato enter the little one-horse carriage. The door closed, and the fiacre rolled off down the street.

"Well, my dear," Eliste began, "he's gone, and I'm afraid—"

"No!" Venting an inarticulate squeal of frustration, Aurelie darted out into the middle of road, where she stood pumping her arm furiously. Wondering, Eliste followed. As she reached her cousin, a second fiacre, attracted by the young girl's frantic signals, pulled up.

"What do you think you're doing? That is a common, dirty, *public* conveyance. We cannot ride in that thing!" Eliste exclaimed.

"Yes we can! I have money!" Aurelie hopped in. "Follow him! Follow him! Don't let him get away! But don't be *obvious*, fellow!" she instructed the driver, pointing after the retreating vehicle. Evidently comprehending, he nodded. Aurelie turned back to her cousin. "Come *on*! Quick, Cousin, quick or I must go alone!"

Certainly she could not let the deranged baby do any such thing—no telling what might happen. And there *was* something appealing in the grubby novelty of the experience. Eliste climbed in, realized there was no attendant to close the door, bemusedly pulled it shut herself, and the fiacre rattled off down the Avenue Parabeau. With a sigh of mingled exasperation and amusement, she settled back on the uncomfortable seat. Beside her, Aurelie was leaning forward, fists clenched, passionate attention focused upon the carriage, a couple of hundred feet ahead, bearing the object of her immoderate affections. No hope of conversation there. Eliste shrugged and turned away to look out the window. Thanks to her grandmother's protective strictures, it was the first time she had ventured abroad in nearly a month, and the first time without supervision since the day of her return to the Rouvignac residence six months earlier. Changes had taken place since her last sortie; so much was obvious at a glance. As the fiacre turned off the manicured Avenue Parabeau, the changes became more noticeable—impossible, in fact, to overlook.

The signs of republican encroachment were too obvious. Everywhere the peasants thronged, including the good neighborhoods wherein they would never formerly have dared to set foot. But they dared now. Flaunting their new liberties, packs of them idled in the parks and the squares; lounged about fountains, walkways, gardens; loitered by the entrances of fine shops, inns, and even private mansions where their presence had never before been tolerated. Through the streets they swaggered—impudent, foulmouthed, and truculent, the worst offenders being those whose caps or jackets bore the scarlet-diamond insignia of Whiss v'Aleur's rabid disciples. Diamonds were chalked up on walls, pillars, monuments, and even trees all over town. Many such symbols were accompanied by the simple, tersely suggestive demand: REPARATION. Eliste tensed at sight of the crudely printed letters. Even sequestered in her grandmother's house as she had been for so many months, she knew the vindictiveness of Whiss v'Aleur's most ardent devotees—strident fanatics of the lunatic fringe, endlessly demanding indemnification in the form of Exalted property, Exalted fortunes, Exalted humiliation, Exalted blood; violent, rapacious, veiling their greed and hatred in self-righteous rhetoric; contemptible and frightening. They were not above terrorism, these criminals who called themselves "patriots." They were not above burning, smashing, beating, even killing. Several Exalted houses scattered about the town had been gutted and the mansion of the Count vo Cereux burned to the ground. Reparationist destruction of the very property they coveted was clearly self-defeating, yet seemed to satisfy some deep and basic inner need. In the face of such malice, no Exalted was truly safe, and the law offered scant protection. Reparationists were quite beyond the law these days; now more than ever before, thanks to the power of the Vanguard.

The Vanguard—an armed corps of recent formation, ostensibly existing to enforce the administrative policies of the Constitutional Congress's Committee of National Welfare—was actually composed of the most devoted and muscular of Reparationists, owing personal loyalty not to the Committee as a whole, but specifically to its president, Whiss v'Aleur. How Whiss had managed to engineer this feat in the absence of official consent and funding was not altogether clear, even to fellow Committee members. But somehow he had done it, and now "Neighbor J" owned a base of military power quite out of all proportion to his official status as Sherreenian delegate to the Congress—or so many privately believed, who might not these days have ventured to voice their opinions aloud.

And there was a group of them now—half a dozen Vanguardsmen, presumably off-duty, lounging beneath the overhang of some anonymous tavern. Their uniforms, of coarse brown serge, baggy and aggressively plebeian in style, were embellished with scarlet sashes and red diamond insignia. Their weapons were of good quality and modern design. As the fiacre passed them, and the Vanguardsmen caught sight of the girls within, whistles and wolf howls and appreciative lip-smackings arose. Eliste shot them a brief glare of loathing, then lifted her chin and averted her eyes. Beside her, Aurelie was bouncing gently up and down, lips parted, eyes fixed on her beloved's conveyance, and quite unconscious of the soldiers' impertinence.

The two invisibly linked carriages sped on, heading for the river. Presently passing the Sepulchre, they clattered over the Bridge Vinculum, across the Vir, and into the Waterfront Market, which, like all the rest of the city, reflected Vonahr's changing state. The market was noisy and populous as ever, yet many of the merchants' booths were shuttered and closed, while those still functioning offered sadly limited wares. Around even such inadequate sources, long queues had formed. The appearance of the crowd there had altered, as well. The colorful liveries of the great houses, formerly so much in evidence, had all but disappeared. Popular hostility, baitings, and occasional beatings had forced even the most loyal of retainers to discard the visible trappings of servitude, at least in public. Along with obvious servitude, obvious gentility was equally out of fashion. Here in the streets, a certain studied informality ruled—a deliberate carelessness of dress that verged on slovenliness, an assertively familiar manner that more than verged on insolence; a casual, sloppy disregard for outmoded proprieties, all too obviously designed to display the new pride and independence of the freshly liberated Vonahrish citizen. Among the Sherreenian civilians walked a variety of uniformed military men—more of them than formerly seen, except in time of war. The Vonahrish Guardsmen, known to support the policies of the Congress, were numerous and generally well-regarded. Less numerous, but noticeable for the sake of their exotic accoutrements, were the colorful Hurbanese and Rhelish mercenaries. There were the loyalist, unpopular Sherreenian gendarmes and Royal Guardsmen. And then, increasingly prevalent, the brown and scarlet of the Vanguardsmen.

Eliste eyed the soldiers with distaste. There were too many of them—too many uniforms, too many weapons, too much implied intimidation. She was relieved when the fiacre passed from the Waterfront Market to rattle on through the streets to the Circle of the Grand Monarch and thence into Riquenoir Street. A couple of minutes later, they passed Madame Nimais's shop.

"That, at least, has not changed," Eliste observed aloud. "Isn't it good to see that some things do not alter?"

Aurelie did not notice the question. Her eyes remained chained to the fiacre ahead, and she muttered feverishly, "Where can he be going? Oh, where *can* he be going?"

Sighing, Eliste abandoned all attempt at conversation.

Out of Riquenoir Street, into a tangle of lanes and past the King's Theater.

And then Aurelie clutched her cousin's arm, exclaiming, "The New Arcade! He is surely going to the New Arcade! Oh, I shall die, la!"

Eliste perceived no such necessity, but judiciously held her peace. Presently the huge double-decker structure of the Arcade loomed in their path, and before it Bayelle vo Clarivaux's vehicle halted to disgorge its lone passenger.

"There! There he is! See! It's Bayelle! Look!" Aurelie's nails dug into Eliste's arm. Rising to bang her fist against the fiacre's roof, she commanded the driver, "Let us off at the New Arcade, fellow! Haste! Haste! Do you want to spoil everything? Hurry!"

He obeyed, and she flung him a handful of money, then sprang from the carriage. "Come, Cousin!" Aurelie insisted. "Quick, before we lose him! Oh, gad, but he's pretty!" Brown cape flying, she dashed into the New Arcade.

Resigned, Eliste followed. The Arcade, once an object of such wonder and curiosity, now after months of Sherreenian residence seemed to her commonplace; as yet blessedly untouched by social, political, or economic upheaval. The shops were as opulent, the customers as prosperous as ever. It was a pleasant sight, but its novelty was long gone. Scarcely wasting a glance upon the great glass-paneled roof, the shops, the paste-jeweled carts and bedizened vendors, the tame songbirds and costumed monkeys, or even the jugglers and acrobats performing about the fountain in the vast atrium, she hurried after her cousin, who in turn chased Bayelle vo Clarivaux.

Quite certainly, the boy didn't know he was being followed. His easy demeanor, as he sauntered from shop to shop—pausing briefly now and then to purchase a handkerchief, a stick of sealing wax, a packet of snuff—reflected no awareness of observation. The two girls followed at a safe distance—Eliste tolerant, her cousin quiveringly eager. Bayelle led them at a leisurely pace through the Arcade's lower level, at last emerging into an open-air café, where the patrons sat at small whitewashed wrought-iron tables, set up upon a flagged terrace beneath a great striped awning, overlooking Merchant Square. At one of the largest tables sat a group of youths whose accents, manners, and careless costly dash marked them as Exalted. Young Bayelle joined his peers, who evidently expected him. While Eliste and Aurelie watched from the doorway, the youths ordered a bowl of punch.

"Now what?" inquired Eliste. "There is no decent way to approach him. Really, Aurelie, I think you'd better—"

"No! Do not say it! I will find a way—I must! If I but empty my mind—"

"That shouldn't be difficult."

"—Inspiration will surely enter! Come, let us sit where we can watch him. Perhaps he'll notice me. Am I looking well? Is my hair well-ordered and beguiling? Let us take a table and order violet water-ice. No, that will stain our lips an odious shade of purple. He would never adore me then. Let it be rose water-ice."

"Ridiculous. We cannot enter a public café unescorted and unattended. The customers would take us for— Oh, I don't have to tell you what they'd take us for!"

"Pooh, what do we care? I am not afraid! There is nothing I won't dare for love."

"Well, there's plenty *I* won't dare. How would you feel if they refuse to serve us? Think of the embarrassment!"

"Cousin, I had thought you owned a greater spirit. Well, if you will not come, then we must part, for I must go on. I simply cannot help myself, la!"

"Aurelie—"

It was too late. Administering a final unnecessary pinch to her already pink cheeks, Aurelie strode forward with an air of determination to take possession of a table whose position afforded an uninterrupted view of Bayelle vo Clarivaux's nicely drawn profile. After a moment, Eliste reluctantly followed. She could feel the pressure of curious eyes as she walked across the terrace, and she could guess what the customers were thinking. Her cheeks began to burn. Head held high, she seated herself with all the dignity she could muster. At Bayelle's table, a few feet away, the Exalted youths had noted the girls' arrival. Already they were nudging each other, grinning and winking; behavior unthinkable in the presence of women of their own class. No doubt about it, they thought the worst. Her sense of discomfort intensified. She cast a reproachful sidelong glance at her companion. Aurelie didn't notice. Her shamelessly languishing eyes were fixed upon Bayelle, and she appeared unconscious of all else. Eliste gave her head a rueful shake.

The proprietor approached—a bulky bourgeois sporting a white apron, white cap, and a manifestly disapproving frown. He paused at their table; took a deep, irate breath. Before he could speak to command their departure, Eliste calmly ordered a pair of rose water-ices. His face changed at the sound of her voice, with its Exalted accent, its tone of Exalted unthinking authority. His eyes dropped to her feet, clad in expensive shoes and translucent silk stockings; jumped to her hand—smooth, very white, ringed in gold. He glanced at Aurelie, noting the long blue fingernails—a cosmetic affectation of the Exalted alone. His face cleared. Bowing, he retired, to reappear a few minutes later bearing a pair of ices, each topped with a pink sugar rose.

Aurelie had noticed none of this. Eyes still fastened upon the neighboring table, she spooned her ice mechanically, unconsciously. Eliste, eventually bored with watching her, allowed her own eyes to wander. She sat beside the wrought-iron railing at the edge of the café's terrace. On the other side of the low barrier, the vehicles and pedestrians filled Merchant Square. For a time she amused herself watching them. The Square seemed unusually populous. On its far side, some patriotically slovenly character sporting a scarlet diamond upon his cap had mounted a barrel to harangue the people—a common occurrence, these days. Idly she studied the speaker. He gestured passionately, his features were twisted with anger, and he appeared to be shouting; but she couldn't make out a single word. Whatever his topic, it must have been interesting, for he swiftly gathered a sizable, attentive crowd. For a little longer she watched, then lost interest. The minutes passed and Aurelie continued silent, presumably awaiting inspiration.

"Must you stare so openly? You are making a spectacle of us both," Eliste complained at last.

"I think—I think I must send him a note," Aurelie murmured dreamily. "A veritable billet-doux, la! I shall tell him that a lady of quality, whose unhappy circumstances necessitate absolute anonymity, requires his assistance upon a matter of some urgency and delicacy. As the situation is not without peril, she relies upon his gallantry no less than his discretion. Then I shall suggest a secret assignation. That will pique his interest, will it not? That touch of mystery always does so."

"No! Absolutely not!"

"No? You think stronger wording is required? Less guile, a more forthright outpouring of tender sentiment? Perhaps you are right. Then I shall simply tell him that I have long admired him from afar, and I am desperately desirous of making his acquaintance." She snapped her fingers at a passing waiter. "Fetch me paper, pen, and ink at once."

"No, you idiot, no!"

"Well, you needn't call me disagreeable *names,* Cousin!"

"You deserve them. Have you taken leave of your senses? I will not allow you to humiliate yourself!"

"I am not humiliated—I am in love! It is stronger than I, and I cannot help myself!"

"This lunacy has gone far enough. You will come home with me at once."

"I won't! I won't!"

"You will, or I'll tell Grandmother everything."

"Oh, you vile traitress, I thought you were my *friend!*"

"Finish your ice, and then we're going."

"I never guessed you could be so beastly. I think you are jealous. Yes, you are—you're jealous of my love, because you are old and alone!"

"Why, you impertinent little wretch—you silly little immature *child*—"

A yelling disturbance arose in Merchant Square. Eliste broke off speaking and turned to look. The crowd gathered about the speaker seemed all at once aflame with rage. Its members were shrieking invective and waving clenched fists in the air. "What in the world is all that?"

"Who cares about the rabble at a time like this? Cousin, my love for Bayelle is *important,* and you are being simply horrid—"

"Sssshhh—wait a moment."

Surprised, Aurelie fell silent. Similarly silent and suddenly watchful was every Exalted patron of the café. Out in the square, the crowd seethed fiercely. Truncheons were brandished and stones were flung, apparently at random. Evidently the popular wrath lacked focus, but this deficiency was remedied upon the appearance of a carriage, an outsize ornate affair drawn by six matched bays, en route to the New Arcade. As the carriage entered Merchant Square, the crowd convulsed—an all too commonplace occurrence these days. A great roar arose— so ferocious that Eliste flinched at the sound of it. The huge communal voice expressed more than anger—there was real hatred there. An instant later, the crowd attacked with sticks, rocks, knives and a variety of makeshift weapons. The big carriage shuddered beneath the assault. Terrified, the horses reared and plunged. Equally terrified, a brace of footmen leaped from the vehicle; while the coachman made the mistake of drawing a pistol.

The footmen, though subject to blows and abuse, were permitted to flee. With them went a shoal of fearful citizens. Before he could fire a shot, the coachman was pulled from the box down into a lethal whirl of flying fists and feet. The carriage door was ripped from its hinges. Eager and furious hands reached in to drag forth the two passengers—a handsome, richly dressed lady, dark-haired and full-figured; together with her maid. The maid vanished instantly, sucked into the human maelstrom. The lady resisted for a moment or two, clinging to the carriage. Clawing hands tore at her hair, her flesh, her clothing. Swiftly she was stripped of cloak, hood, and fichu. Her gown, rent from neckline to waist, gaped wide, exposing her to the gaze of a multitude. Arms crossed over her chest, she shrank back, eyes popping, mouth squared. Somebody's truncheon struck her temple, felling her to the ground. Then the roiling human mass contracted suddenly, and she was gone, prostrate body blocked from view.

In helpless horror, the Exalted patrons watched from the terrace.

"Who is it?" A cultivated voice, hoarse and sickened.

"The arms upon the carriage are Feronte's." An awed whisper. "It is the Duchess."

"No." Eliste hardly recognized her own faint voice. She felt oddly detached and distant. A slight pain connected her to the world. Aurelie was clutching her hand hard enough to hurt. "It isn't her Grace. I think it is—it is Madame vo Bellesandre, the Duke's friend. He must have lent her the carriage as a favor. A favor . . ." Her voice trailed off.

"Animals." An anonymous expression of Exalted shock. "Beasts."

Out in the square, the crowd was methodically ripping the carriage to pieces. The horses had already been released from harness and led off by their new owners. A trio of still bodies sprawled on the cobbles. Human eddies were rushing out from the center and swirling in all directions. A few fear-struck citizens were fleeing straight for the New Arcade. When the first of them reached the café, observers desperate for information instantly seized upon him.

"The Duke of Feronte has escaped Vonahr." The speaker—a bespectacled, soberly clad bourgeois with the neatly respectable appearance of a small shopkeeper—panted and struggled for breath. "He sneaked out of the Beviaire some time last night—reached the border this morning, they say—and now that Reparationist out there has it that Feronte's planning to raise a foreign army against us—restore absolutism, massacre the entire Congress, huge reprisals against Sherreen—all of that. When he'd got the crowd whipped up proper, along comes the carriage with the Duke's arms on it—and you saw the rest." The little man's face was gray and sick.

There was silence as his audience digested the news. Eliste's eyes, wide and incredulous, were fixed upon the torn corpse of Madame vo Bellesandre—an inoffensive creature, harmlessly vain, murdered for no reason beyond the current popular detestation of all things Exalted—and the cold terror stirred to life inside her, a helpless black dread that even the storming of the Beviaire had not awakened. For it came to her fully for the first time that the hatred was everywhere, all around her, flooding all the land. She and her fellow Exalteds were drowning in it.

The murderers' rage had not yet spent itself, and presently that fury fixed upon a new target—the elegant and pristine western face of the New Arcade. The Arcade, with its expensive shops and well-heeled patrons, constituted a clear affront to democratic sensibilities, and as such invited popular vengeance. Across Merchant Square roared the crowd, heading for the terrace café. For a frozen moment the Exalted stood watching them, then all erupted into confusion as the customers scattered; the more agile leaping the wrought-iron railing to flee into the side alleys, but the majority blindly seeking the illusory shelter of the Arcade atrium. Eliste stood horrified and bewildered, for nothing in all her experience had equipped her to deal with such insanity. All about her, alarmed Exalteds were pushing, shoving, and elbowing each other in their haste to reach the exit, and they took no notice of her whatsoever. By all normal standards of behavior, the gentlemen should have seen first to her safety, sacrificing themselves in her behalf should circumstances warrant. For a few seconds she stood vainly awaiting the requisite offer of assistance. No such assistance materialized, and she gazed about her in astonished incomprehension, until she realized that the cheap brown cape, chosen to camouflage her Exalted status, had served too well. The gentlemen failed to recognize her as a member of their own class, entitled to their protection and deference. Taking her for a common girl, of no account, they were leaving her to fend for herself. She was on her own—unbelievable, but true.

The same realization had evidently struck Aurelie, who knew just how to deal with it. In an instant Aurelie stripped away her cloak to uncover blue-marbled hair and expensive garments. Now recognizable as Exalted, she scooted nimbly across the teeming terrace to fasten like a remora upon the arm of the startled Bayelle vo Clarivaux. Eliste followed, arriving in time to hear Aurelie announce, ". . . your neighbors, kinswomen to the Countess vo Rouvignac, in need of your protection, Exalted Sir. Ah, here is my cousin, whose giddy thirst for adventure has led us to this desperate pass, la!"

Eliste's indignant denial was drowned in the cries of fear and pain as a barrage of rocks pelted the terrace. The whizzing missiles were everywhere, rattling like hail against walls and furniture. Instinctively she raised her arms to shield her face, while Aurelie shrank back with a faint cry to press herself against Bayelle vo Clarivaux. Startled and alarmed though he was, the boy nonetheless displayed presence of mind. Seizing a small overturned table, he contrived a makeshift shield for himself and the two girls. Thus protected, they retreated. Stones continued to bang the tabletop until Bayelle had led them from the terrace, around the angle of the great building, and along the wall as far as the big central entrance to the New Arcade, where the fiacres customarily waited. There, all was chaos as frightened shopkeepers, restaurateurs, artisans, and customers poured forth in search of quick escape. The available fiacres were commandeered instantaneously. Newly arriving carriages were besieged, surrounded by clamorous, struggling hordes of would-be passengers effectively blocking all departure. Shouted commands, pleas, accusations, and imprecations filled the air; equine whinnies, the creak of wheel and axle, the furious snapping of whips, all underscored by the dull dangerous roar of voices in Merchant Square.

Bayelle had wit enough to bypass the jockeying crowds. Leading his two charges away from the New Arcade and into Viomente Street, where the fiacres ordinarily carried passengers between shops and theater, he secured a conveyance with relative ease. Forgetting her former disdain for public transportation, Eliste climbed gratefully into the shabby little vehicle, sinking down upon the threadbare seat with a suppressed sob of relief. She was trembling, disheveled, and sore where a flying stone had grazed her wrist. Opposite her sat Bayelle, and beside him Aurelie, clinging tightly to his arm. Bayelle issued orders, and the fiacre set off for the Parabeau. Viomente Street was alive with agitated humanity, gathered in restless knots and clumps, aware of disturbance but ignorant as yet of the cause. Despite the popular turbulence, the fiacre sped on unhindered, soon passing from

Viomente Street into Breakleg Lane, past the King's Theater and thence to Riquenoir Street, where tranquillity yet reigned. The world was sane again, and Eliste, expelling her breath, leaned back and closed her eyes. But that made things worse, for behind her closed lids she could see, in vivid detail and with horrible clarity, the crowd closing in on the helpless Madame vo Bellesandre. Try as she would, she could not banish the ghastly images; nor could she banish the new fear that accompanied them. The world was not at all the place she had thought it. The security she had always taken so much for granted rested upon an appallingly weak foundation, and she was surrounded by predators thirsting to bleed her, though she herself had never knowingly offered offense. The source of the hatred she ascribed to the vicious nature of the canaille. Of its possible justification, she had not as yet much more than an inkling. She knew only that she was sickened and bewildered and afraid as never before.

Was Aurelie similarly horror-struck? Eliste opened her eyes to behold her cousin drooping and swaying in her seat. For a moment, she was deceived; then, noting the younger girl's bright eyes and healthy color, she recognized the ruse.

The featherheaded twit's incorrigible.

Aurelie sighed and collapsed against Bayelle vo Clarivaux's shoulder. Her eyes were closed, her body limp, her cheeks revealingly pink. Bayelle, however, was unobservant, or innocent, or both. Instantly solicitous, he chafed her wrists and patted her cheek. She did not move, and he threw an anxious, uncertain glance at Eliste.

"She will recover presently," Eliste assured him dryly. "Do not distress yourself, Exalted Sir."

He nodded, clearly taken aback by her callousness, then resumed his wrist-chafing. Aurelie stirred and murmured. Bayelle bent near to catch her words. He did not address Eliste again throughout the journey.

Some half hour later, the fiacre halted before the Rouvignac town house, and Aurelie permitted herself full consciousness. Lashes quivering, she opened her eyes to observe faintly, "We have arrived. You have saved us, sir, and your heroism places us forever in your debt."

"Oh no, Exalted Miss—anyone would have done as much." Despite the disclaimer, the boy looked pleased and flattered. His open, ingenuous face flushed.

"Indeed not. Chivalry true and generous as yours is rare. It is upon that chivalry that I depend in asking you—in *beseeching* you—to hold this matter of our meeting in the strictest secrecy."

"Secrecy?" Bayelle was transparently intrigued. "But why, Exalted Miss?"

"For fear of my Great-Aunt Zeralenn, who is also my guardian at present," Aurelie confided. "She is a woman of fierce, terrible, relentless, and despotic temper. I am wholly at the tyrant's mercy, and she would surely visit the cruelest punishment upon me should she discover that I have ventured forth without permission—even in so worthy a cause as the protection of my dear, headstrong cousin."

"Your cousin might do well to school herself in prudence." Bayelle's disapproving eyes flicked Eliste. "She exposes you to much misfortune."

Torn between amusement and disgust, Eliste forbore reply.

"Oh, do not reproach her, Exalted Sir. She is impetuous, perhaps even reckless, but her intentions are surely good. In any event, she is my kinswoman, and thus entitled to my loyalty—no matter what!"

"You've a generous heart and a fine moral sense, Exalted Miss," Bayelle observed.

Eliste gazed studiously out the window.

"La, sir, you will make me blush." Aurelie raised imploring eyes. "And your promise of secrecy, sir? My unhappy circumstances necessitate absolute anonymity. As the situation is not without peril, I rely upon your gallantry no less than your discretion." Precocious bosom rising and falling swiftly, she leaned close. "You *will* guard my secret, will you not?"

"Certainly, Exalted Miss, if you wish it. You may rely upon my honor."

"I do, Exalted Sir, indeed I do! And now—if you will assist me—I am still somewhat weak . . ."

"Gladly, Exalted Miss."

"Perhaps—" Aurelie's insistent eyes held Eliste's. "Perhaps we might best escape Madame's notice should we enter the house separately. And surely, Cousin, all things considered, that is what you most desire?"

"Oh, surely," Eliste agreed. Her cousin wanted the boy to herself for a few minutes, that was obvious, and in view of the child's extraordinary exertions, certainly she deserved no less.

They decided that Aurelie would enter by the back door, and Eliste discreetly by the side, through the stillroom. Bayelle paid the driver, then assisted each girl from the fiacre. His expression was distant and his manner curt as he handed Eliste to the walkway. The boyish face brightened into eager cordiality as the younger girl emerged. He offered his arm, and she clutched. Together they made their halting way toward the back of the house, Aurelie apparently reliant upon her savior's support. Lips curved in a somewhat sour smile, Eliste stood watching; then, as they disappeared from view, she hurried to the side door, entered and slipped through stillroom and the chambers beyond, until she came to the central foyer, where she paused. From the parlor opening off the foyer came the sound of voices: the low, distinct, slightly husky tones of Zeralenn, mingling with the deeper accents of the Cavalier vo Meureille. Trapped in Sherreen, perhaps not altogether unwillingly, by the Committee of National Welfare's restrictions upon Exalted travel, Meureille had continued a frequent visitor at the Rouvignac residence throughout the dreary months.

Eliste took a step toward the parlor, then halted. She ought to tell them of events in Merchant Square, but couldn't do so without revealing Aurelie's illicit sortie, and her own as well. In any case, they would hear the news soon enough. As she stood there vacillating, the Cavalier's words became distinguishable:

". . . must not be deceived by the apparent equilibrium—it is but the final brief lull preceding unimaginable violence."

"Come, Meureille, we are both of us too old for the greensickness." Zeralenn's acid amusement sounded genuine. "Where is the proof?"

"Upon the common faces discovered in every street and square."

"Ah, the eternally grumbling rabble."

"Do not underestimate the commons. The strength and ferocity of their rage exceeds all measure, understandably so. And now, with the traditional restraints imposed by fear largely removed—with our Royal Guardsmen thrashed, our gendarmes murdered, our magic scorned, our vulnerabilities fully exposed—it awaits but an incident, a word, a breath, to loose the mob's full fury."

"In what cause? They have achieved their aims without great bloodshed. They have made his Majesty a prisoner. Their ludicrous congress, now groaning in the throes of composition, infests the Century Hall. Presently, its labors concluding, this clownish conclave will deliver itself of a constitution—a monstrous mis-shapen spawn that we must greet as an infant prodigy. In the meantime, they have abolished the Exalted privilege sanctified by centuries, declared an impossible equality that defies nature, outraged law and custom and decency, and doubtless rendered Vonahr contemptible in the eyes of all nations. Having achieved so much, what more can they desire?"

"Vengeance," Meureille suggested. "Countess, you do not comprehend the intensity of the people's hatred—a source of power now cultivated by various demagogues, most notably those of Reparationist persuasion."

"I do not concern myself with the vile rantings of foulmouthed peasant fanatics."

"Perhaps you should concern yourself. Those rantings now reshape our world."

"Temporarily, I trust."

"I fear your trust is misplaced. Transformation is infrequently reversible. The tides of change carry us on, whether we will or no; and ignorance of their direction offers neither refuge nor defense."

"Defense? Are we criminals that we must defend ourselves?"

"Exactly so, in the eyes of a multitude. Are you not aware that the Reparationists brand all Exalted, without exception, as enemies of the people and traitors to Vonahr? The more vindictive among them demand the death of the King and Queen."

"That is an ugly impossibility, unworthy of attention."

"Again you deceive yourself. It is by no means impossible, and the matter demands your closest attention. It has received mine for months now, and the information I have acquired will perhaps prove worthy of your consideration. Two facts, in particular, appear significant. In brief—my sources within the Beviaire inform me that the King, who has convinced his gaolers of his good intentions, is but lightly guarded, enjoying considerable freedom of movement and privacy within the confines of the palace. Thus it is with the Queen, as well. I am also informed—and following some months of investigation, have succeeded in verifying this—of the existence of a tunnel, presumably the work of forgotten smugglers, that passes beneath the city wall, to emerge upon the bank of the Vir well downstream of the city gate. This so, the means of their Majesties' deliverance suggests itself."

Eliste, eavesdropping in the hall, unconsciously shook her head. Now that his Grace of Feronte had fled, the vigilance surrounding Dunulas and Lallazay would surely increase. Meureille did not yet know it, but the King's best hope of escape was already gone. Lost in her own thoughts, she missed her grandmother's reply.

"You underestimate the loyalty of my associates," the Cavalier's voice resumed. "The secret is quite safe. But only reflect, Countess. This escape route from Sherreen may preserve Exalted no less than royal heads. I intend to convey my peers to safety, in such numbers as circumstance permits."

"What, and beggar them in the process? Folly, Meureille."

Eliste frowned. Her grandmother referred to the recently enacted legislation prohibiting Exalted emigration from Vonahr. The new law was designed to discourage anti-Constitutionalist activity abroad, and infraction was punishable by state confiscation, or rather theft, of the offender's Vonahrish property and wealth. Feronte had fled. Was the King's own brother now a pauper?

"It is my greatest hope that you and your kinsmen may be among the first so delivered," Meureille persisted. "Come, Madame. Do you not owe it to yourself and your young protégées to seek safety now, while the risk is comparatively slight? Be assured it will increase in the future."

"That is uncertain. As for the kinsmen beneath my roof, the majority departed for the provinces some months ago. Of those remaining, I owe it to them to maintain the strictest standards of Exalted courage, decorum, and dignity, that they may learn by example. Anything less, and I serve them ill. As for myself, Sherreen suits me, I am not minded to leave it, and I am used to following my own inclination."

"Some things do not change. That arrogance, Countess, was never the least of your charms, and yet you have often paid its price. Only recall that autumn in Flugeln, when your rebuff of the reigning Dhreve precipitated the Muinotz-Favessiotti duel. The scandal chased you all the way home to Vonahr."

"Reproaches, Cavalier, hardly suit the lips of one whose role in the affair should hardly have gone unpunished, had the Dhreve discovered it."

"Your silence proved my salvation, Countess, but that is hardly the point. I must urge you to consider my advice. You may be free of Sherreen within hours."

"Useless. I am resolved to remain."

"I expected no less. Here, then, Madame—rest assured you may accept without compromise of priceless dignity."

He must have handed her something, for she inquired, "What is this?"

"There is written the name and address of one who may assist and protect you if for any reason I cannot."

"Bah, Meureille—when did I ever require protection?"

"Rather, when did you ever confess it? Well, concede nothing if it does not suit you, only keep this, as a favor to me."

"Very well, if you wish it, but this alters nothing."

The conversation continued inconsequentially, and presently Eliste departed. She found eavesdropping unworthy. Moreover, she had heard enough to provide ample food for thought. Tripping quietly up the stairs, she sought the refuge of her own chamber. It was only midafternoon, but she was exhausted and miserable. Her head ached, and useless tears blurred her vision. A thousand fears and questions jangled her brain; far too numerous, too confusing, and alarming to consider calmly. The sights and sounds of Merchant Square were still with her: Madame vo Bellesandre's death, interspersed with flashing glimpses of Sherreen's streets seen through the window of the fiacre, red diamonds, uniformed soldiers and their weapons, Aurelie and Bayelle's childish faces, and always underneath it all, the quiet, rational voice of the Cavalier vo Meureille prophesying disaster. Later, she would have to sort through them all, but for now, they were unbearable. Flinging herself down on the bed, she escaped into slumber.

L ook them over, then tell me what they are," Whiss v'Aleur commanded his father.

"They are ancient Stupefactions," Chorl Valeur replied at once.

"Obviously. Any dolt can see as much. I must know their function." Whiss did not trouble to disguise his impatience; he rarely did so these days.

Chorl was silent.

"Well?" The trained voice lashed, and Chorl winced.

Whiss v'Aleur and his father stood in the vast twilight cellar of the City Armory. The place was closed to the public, but the restrictions governing ordinary mortals did not apply to the President of the Committee of National Welfare; an eminent citizen, a great power in the Constitutional Congress, a man to be reckoned with. All doors opened to such a man, and that was as it should be, that was how Whiss had always known it was meant to be. He had come a long way since his days of beggarly obscurity in Rat Town. The wretched hiatus had ended at last, as he had so often—so bitterly and desperately—assured himself it must end. Finally he had achieved something approaching the recognition due him, and he had climbed high. *But not high enough,* some compulsive hunger of the mind clamored like an eternally empty belly. *Not high enough.*

Sometimes Whiss wondered if that hunger would ever be satisfied. But he didn't think about it often, and certainly not now. For the moment, his attention focused intensely as sunlight bent through a lens upon the stored Stupefactions, whose potential power was manifest even to untutored eyes. Sooner or later, someone would claim that power. For the sake of the nation, the Vonahrish people, and humanity in general, that someone ought to be Whiss v'Aleur. Thus, annexation of the old machines smacked more of duty than ambition, more of public service than self-aggrandizement. It was a service demanding some insight, however; some understanding of mechanical function and operation. Therefore, he had ordered the Armory cellar opened in secret, and there he had conveyed his magically knowledgeable father, together with his adoring and ever-useful cousin, Bierce Valeur.

Bierce now stood a little apart from his kinsmen. His shoulders were hunched, hands buried in coat pockets, big legs solidly splayed, head thrust forward, upturned eyes—green like his cousin's, but small and muddy where the other's were huge and translucent—fixed upon the great leaden coffin, crowned with spikes and barbs, whose plaque bore the engraved legend "Kokotte." His expression was utterly rapt. For once his attention was diverted from his cousin's face. He seemed, in fact, unconscious of his surroundings. That was acceptable, for the moment. His services were not as yet required.

"Well?" Whiss repeated, voice and stance imperative.

Chorl shifted his weight unhappily, body drooping as if crushed by atmospheric pressure. As always, he felt inadequate to deal with his quick-tempered, quick-tongued, and unpredictable son. For that matter, he sensed himself inadequate to deal with Sherreen in general, and all its myriad confusions. Above all things he longed for the soothing tedium of Vaurve Province, but such retreat was out of the question—Whiss would never permit him to go. And while arcane ability might have carried him beyond the city gates, somehow the old man never resorted to it, for his son possessed a natural manipulative genius that transcended the power of magic. Now that son awaited information of a sort that Chorl was loath to divulge. There was little point in trying to hold back, though. Somehow or other, through guile or flattery or bullying, Whiss would get what he wanted. Whiss always did.

"I am not an expert on this matter. I have never before actually encountered such machines," Chorl offered at last, and seeing his son's brow darken, added hastily, "But I have seen their like in books, and I will tell you what I remember. These three Stupefactions were once magical Sentients designed to assist in the maintenance of public order and safety. This one"—he indicated the slender, silvery, double-headed construction—"whose name was ZaZa, breathed fire and vapor in defense of her masters. She was ardent, irritable, passionate, and full of wrathful temperament. She was quick to take offense, vindictive, and it is said that she never forgave a slight, real or imagined." Chorl turned next to the great mechanical beetle whose gold plaque, bordered in faceted eyes, bore the title "NuNu." "The Sentient NuNu, Queen Mother to her kind, was once the ultimate spy. Dedicated, tireless, and industrious, she maintained ceaseless vigilance over the suspected enemies of her masters. No one was safe from the scrutiny of NuNu, for she was aided in her endeavors by flying swarms of her offspring; trained in surveillance by their mother and capable of introducing their tiny selves unnoticed into all environments. NuNu was an indifferent mother, regarding her children as expendable and replaceable. To her masters, she was essentially indifferent. Her nature was cold, emotions torpid, and her enthusiasm wholly given over to insectile preoccupations with duty and function." Chorl moved a few paces right to stand beside his nephew before the leaden cabinet labeled "Kokotte." He threw the younger man a quick, revealingly fearful glance. Bierce took no notice. He was staring fixedly at the Stupefactions. His mouth hung slightly open and his little eyes were blank. Drawing a relieved breath, Chorl continued, "This last, the Sentient Kokotte, once served as public executioner, dispatching vast numbers of the condemned, both singly and in batches. She performed her task with efficiency and apparent willingness. She was reliable, indefatigable, altogether insatiable in appetite. So much was self-evident. Her innermost feelings, however, she never revealed. Her fears, hopes, affections, and obsessions always remained a mystery, and do so to this day."

For a time there was silence, while three men studied three Stupefactions. At last Bierce Valeur spoke very softly, almost dreamily. "Maybe she'd tell them to me."

"Eh?" Chorl threw his nephew another uneasy, uncomprehending glance.

"Beautiful Kokotte," Bierce murmured. "ZaZa. NuNu."

Whiss v'Aleur ignored his cousin. His eyes, filled with a new greed, lingered upon Kokotte as he inquired, "The damage, you would say, is not extensive?"

"I doubt that there is any real damage," Chorl replied. "They are asleep—or tranced—or stupefied, if you will, no doubt through boredom and inactivity. It can happen to anyone."

"And where is the prince whose kiss awakens these sleeping beauties?" Whiss inquired with the iron-weighted jocularity that was his closest approach to humor.

Too late scenting danger, Chorl relapsed into scared silence.

"Well, Father? You take my meaning, no doubt. The Stupefactions must be restored to sentience. That is your task. You must begin immediately."

"I can't." Chorl moistened dry lips. "You ask too much."

"I ask nothing. On behalf of the people of Vonahr, I demand your services."

"You do not understand," Chorl pleaded. "Listen to me. I have not the competence to deal with such devices—"

"You possess magical power, as we all know too well."

"But not to that degree. It is not as if I'd studied the art from childhood. It came upon me relatively late in life—"

"To the exclusion of all else," Whiss cut him off. "Yes, I am well aware of it. When you had a wife, sons and a daughter—when you had all of that, and not before—came that sudden flowering of magical aptitude, demanding all your care and attention. You indulged your appetites as you saw fit, and then, early desires sated, you turned away to pursue new ones."

"That is a distortion." Chorl spoke without conviction, for his son's complaints struck resonant chords of guilt. Whiss's accusations, unjustly exaggerated though they were, yet contained a kernel of truth. His magical aptitude *had* manifested itself unusually late, and he *had* neglected his family for the sake of self-development. The studies were all-consuming, unavoidably so. So very often, his reading and practice had demanded his complete attention, at the expense of everything else. And though he acknowledged his obligations to the wife he had taken when he was seventeen years of age, and the four surviving children he had sired by the time he was twenty-three, he had never failed to place the magic foremost in his life; not since the dawning of that unforgettable day he had first known the glory of the power, beside which all other experiences faded into clouded unreality. Perhaps it was selfish, or heartless, or wrong, but for him there was no other possibility, never really had been. He believed that his wife had understood, or nearly so. She had accepted the situation without complaint, and in return, he had provided well for the slow, commonplace woman who over the course of the years had become a stranger. He had seen to it that she lacked for nothing, and so far as he knew, she was reasonably content. In any event, she had never reproached him. As for the children, in three cases out of four there was no difficulty, for they had inherited their father's magical ability. This talent fortunately manifested itself without delay, and he had seen to it that their education commenced at a suitably early age. Each of the three had entered Bozhenille Commune for training as small children; and now, decades later, there was not one of them who did not outstrip the father in magical accomplishment. The one sad exception, of course, was Whiss. Whiss, the firstborn, legitimate heir apparent, inheritor of nothing. No magical talent had come to him, and he would never forget or forgive; nor would any member of his family be permitted to forget. Poor deprived Whiss, always angry, always cheated. A perennial object of guilt, pity, remorse, and lately—fear.

"You are in debt, very greatly in debt." Frowning, arms folded, Whiss moved in nearer, too near. "And now in partial repayment, I ask but a trifle you should be eager to perform."

Chorl experienced the familiar rush of shame, the familiar uncertainty, the familiar inclination to yield. This time, however, he resisted the urge. Recognizing the Stupefactions for the source of power that they were, he was forced to consider the use his son might make of them; and he realized that he simply didn't know, couldn't even guess. Whiss, subject to urgent impulses arising from a bottomless well of anger, seemed capable of anything, anything at all. Not with his father's assistance, however—not this time. Having reached such a decision, it was beyond Chorl's power to express it aloud. Should he attempt to do so, Whiss would beat down his defenses within seconds. This so, the father perceived only one navigable course. He lied.

"I cannot do it. Much as I should like to oblige you, it is beyond my power. The old Sentients were vastly complex devices. Only a true adept, trained in his art from childhood on, might hope to deal with them."

"Indeed." Whiss's narrow stare pinned his father.

"Truly." The old man nodded, eyes wide and earnest. "Have I not gladly done all in my power for you?"

"Gladly? Have you ever given gladly to me? And all in your power? That is the real question."

"Oh, believe me. I'd wake the sleepers if I could, but it is a task far beyond my ability." Imperative that he convince his son, else Whiss would undoubtedly call upon his cousin Bierce's assistance; and that form of coercion Chorl dreaded above all. True, Bierce had never actually harmed him, had never even breathed a threat, but there was something about his quiet, inert nephew that chilled the old man's blood. Chorl supposed that it might have something to do with Bierce's hands—so huge, so ugly and powerful, yet so clever and precise as they toyed with those inevitable gears and cogs. Somehow he could not help but visualize those same hands holding a very sharp, thin knife—Chorl shuddered, and his eyes flew without volition to his nephew. But Bierce, mesmerized by the Stupefactions, appeared unconscious.

"I see." Whiss nodded slowly. His pale eyes, at times almost uncanny in their quality of penetration, held his father's. He stared, and Chorl stirred uneasily. "I see. Perhaps. Well, your power has been adequate to assist when I address a crowd. I trust it continues so."

"Oh, to be sure. Indeed it does." Chorl attempted an appeasing smile. "There is no doubt of that. Though surely this is irrelevant, now that you have achieved your aims."

"I have not achieved them. You are a fool to say so." Whiss was suddenly tense and quivering with passion. His great eyes widened and blazed, while his narrow yellowish face seemed somehow to contract, throwing the bones into sharper relief.

Chorl could not repress his nervous start.

"The Constitutional Congress is corrupt, riddled with royalist sympathizers, reactionaries, and other such enemies of freedom," Whiss continued, and no one hearing him could have questioned his conviction. "If Vonahr is ever to be truly free, the Congress must be cleansed. The people's welfare demands this. On behalf of the people, on behalf of the downtrodden and abused, I undertake the task."

Chorl could think of nothing to say. He felt himself sinking in quicksand.

"The traitors and conspirators think themselves safe." Whiss stretched his closed lips briefly. "They are mistaken. I will expose them, denounce and destroy them. I require your cooperation. I expect your wholehearted support."

Again the narrow, probing scrutiny, before which Chorl's eyes dropped. After a moment, however, he lifted his head and managed to ask quietly, "What are you planning to do?"

"For the present, I work to consolidate my support in the Congress. When the moment is ripe—perhaps in a few weeks' time, perhaps in a couple of months, but not longer—then I will denounce the enemies of the people. It will be an extraordinary speech, a speech rallying all listeners to a single cause. I cannot overstate the significance of the occasion, and therefore I demand your assistance, Father. You must ensure the proper response of the audience."

Expecting instant acquiescence, he was taken aback when his father inquired, "Who are these enemies of the people?"

"There are many," Whiss replied shortly. "Worst among them are Shorvi Nirienne and his minions—men so devoted to the interests of King and Exalted that I doubt not their intent to sabotage the constitution, if they can. Traitors all."

"No," said Chorl. He straightened, squaring his shoulders, while his son stared at him, astonished to encounter unequivocal opposition. "I have read Nirienne's books. He is not a traitor. He is a patriot, one of the brightest lights of the new Congress. Such a man must not be destroyed. I could not be party to that."

"The enemies of the people—"

"—do not include Nirienne."

Silence for a heartbeat, while unspoken questions hovered in the air. Chorl had not gone so far as to suggest actual withdrawal of his magical support, but all at once Whiss felt threatened, acutely threatened, unsure and furiously resentful— emotions cloaked beneath a rigid stillness of face and body. Chorl sustained his son's unblinking regard with apparent composure, and finally it was Whiss whose eyes flickered.

"That is unclear at present. If Nirienne himself is not a traitor, then he is surely surrounded by those who are," Whiss conceded at last, and the yielding was almost physically painful, in view of the hatred he bore Shorvi Nirienne; hatred as luxurious, dense, delicious, and addictive as the very best chocolate. There were many reasons to loathe Nirienne: for his fame, his success and influence in Congress, for his outspoken opposition to Reparationist policies, for the mawkish spun-sugar sentimentality of his ideals, for his hypocritical affectations of toleration, moderation, and generosity; above all for his effortless popularity, for the respect and affection and abiding loyalty that he inspired among his associates, *without benefit of magical aid*. Yes, it was easy to hate Shorvi Nirienne; but for now, it was politic to disguise all personal animosity, and Whiss forced himself to add, "He may be misguided only. I am willing to admit that possibility. I wish to be just, after all."

"I know you do, I know it." Chorl's head bobbed eagerly. "And I am sure you *will* be." He had flatly contradicted his son, and not been made to suffer for it. Moreover, Whiss wanted to be fair; he had said so. Relief filled Chorl's mind, excluding all else for the moment, and perhaps it was this, in addition to his own timorous nature, that kept him from perceiving what ought to have been so clear—his son's essential dependence on him, his own very real power.

"Then I assume your loyalty continues, Father? Provided my decisions meet with your express approval?" Whiss's effort to filter the anger from his voice was not successful.

"I'll do what I can." Brief flash of assertiveness exhausted, Chorl relapsed into drooping passivity. He found himself suddenly very tired. His son's glittering green stare was growing insupportable, and he longed for escape.

"Yes. That must serve, I suppose. You see I am not unreasonable. I am willing to trust in you, Father, and thus I resign myself to disappointment in the matter of these Stupefactions. For you inform me that their reanimation requires the abilities of an adept trained in the magical arts since early childhood, and where is such a one to be found? Wherever might I discover such a paragon of knowledge?"

Whiss's voice carried certain sleek velvety overtones that Chorl Valeur found disquieting. More disquieting yet was his son's expression, one he remembered too well from earlier times: a clench-jawed, tightly smiling mask concealing the most concentrated rage, frustration, and malice. Just so had a much younger Whiss appeared when contemplating the offenses of his schoolfellows back in Vaurve Province, and it was a look that boded ill. Even as a boy, Whiss had usually discovered means of expressing his displeasure. Those who crossed him found themselves plagued with lost or damaged property, false accusation, and sundry apparent accidents. Vengeance might be delayed as expedient, but never forgotten; its inevitability heralded by—that look. Now, decades later, the look was unchanged, and Chorl was ill-equipped now as then to deal with its author. He felt helpless, old, drained. "I want to go home," he said aloud.

Whiss inclined his head, affecting to believe that the old man referred to his Sherreenian lodgings. Turning to his cousin, he was faintly surprised to note that Bierce, ordinarily so attentive, now appeared unconscious, almost as if he hadn't heard.

Bierce hadn't heard. Sunk in contemplation of the Stupefactions, he had for once lost track of his cousin's conversation. He would regain it shortly, for Whiss claimed his first and deepest loyalty, but for now, the machines held him. They were surely the most beautiful things he had ever seen, owning a kind of precise, durable perfection that the flawed children of bungling Nature might never hope to equal. Bierce had always loved the strength and symmetry of machines—their solidity and predictability. He could trust machines, and he could understand them. Unlike creatures of flesh, whose responses were crazily random, machines were consistent and reliable; but also unlike creatures of flesh, they had no perceptions, no thoughts or emotions, no individuality. Bierce was not such a fool that he failed to note such things; it was, after all, the intense personality of his cousin Whiss that aroused his adoration. Machines, for all their loveliness, lacked what was truly most significant—all machines, that is, except *these*. These Stupefactions were different, combining mechanical regularity with the promise of individual identity. It remained only to wake those dormant personalities in order to achieve the ideal—a blending of hitherto irreconcilable elements. The thought of that awakening excited Bierce, sent the warm currents coursing all through him. He could feel the hot flush of blood in his cheeks, the tingling down his spine, and they were delicious. If the mere thought carried such pleasure, what might the reality afford? For a few moments, he gave himself over to the luxury of fantasy. He imagined the Stupefactions, tranced no longer but fully awake; aware of his devotion and returning it in full measure, even exceeding it. He knew then what he truly yearned for—the love of the Sentients, so much stronger and steadier than any other love. Perhaps there could even be one among the machines whose every pulse and throb belonged to him alone; a special Sentient who would make him her god—now *there* was something to dream of, something glorious. He could never express his longing aloud, of course. Carping folk would take him for an eccentric. Cousin Whiss would eye him askance, and even mewling old Uncle Chorl might lose all respect and fear of him. Bierce would regret that, for he found his uncle's terror enjoyable. It was fun to play upon the old man's fear while contriving to appear unaware. It was fun to make his uncle cringe or start in that nervous way of his, and never let on that he saw. It was good sport, and a good feeling he would not want to lose. No, he could not express his desires verbally, he had never been good with words anyway, but somehow he had to make his feelings known to that alluring device known as "Kokotte"—

A touch on the shoulder, and Bierce emerged from his reverie to find Cousin Whiss at his side. Whiss crooked an imperative finger, then turned and walked away. Dutifully, Chorl and Bierce followed. Together they filed from the Armory, past the guards who shut and locked the doors behind them, and out into the street where the hackney waited. The ride back to their lodgings in Nerisante Street, but a short walk from the Century Hall, was a silent one. Chorl slumped miserably; Bierce fondled his wheels and cogs; and Whiss, apparently lost in thought, stared blindly out the window. Occasionally he turned hard-gleaming eyes upon his father, and at such times the tense, tight-lipped little smile made its reappearance.

Upon reaching their rented house, the three kinsmen dispersed. Chorl sought oblivion in slumber, while Bierce descended to search the cellar for interesting mechanical flotsam. Whiss made directly for his own bedchamber, locking himself within. There in the privacy of the monastically austere little room, he penned a series of letters. He wrote swiftly, without uncertainty or hesitation, never blotting a line. His lips were stretched tight over his teeth as he worked, and the smile was one his father would have recognized.

The bullet fired from the second-story window of Number 10 Duck Row came within an ace of doing its work, parting the breeze a handspan above Shorvi Nirienne's head. The report sounded clear and sharp upon the darkening air. Quite likely the target owed his life to that uncertain evening light, which had thrown the unseen marksman's aim off. At sound of the shot, Nirienne wheeled to strain his vision through shadows in search of the source. For a moment he stood there staring, and then his practical-minded young companion Beq grabbed his arm and almost forcibly hurried him the last few remaining yards, up the steps and through the door into the familiar sanctuary of Number 11. Once inside, they bolted the door and each man drew a pistol. For a few seconds they waited, but the assault was over.

"What happened?" Attracted by the noise in the hallway, Master Oeun Bulaude had come to investigate. Beside him stood his sister Oeunne, gray and insubstantial as ever; and behind the siblings, Frezhelle and Riclairc, a couple of resident Nirienne satellites.

"Another attack," Beq told them. "How many has it been now, Shorvi?"

"I have not been keeping score," Nirienne replied coolly.

"Fourth within a month," Oeun reeded.

"Well, they've all failed."

"Through merest happenstance, I believe. Best look sharp, my friend. They'll nail you in your coffin yet, if you do not take care."

"As far as I am able, I do so." Nirienne's expression did not quite achieve the easy nonchalance it aimed for.

"Not so, not so. You expose yourself to public view like some alley-cat streetwalker," Mistress Oeunne tweetled severely. "You flaunt yourself, you beckon, you entice. It is practically indecent, this flirtation with disaster. Were your political views anything less than irreproachable, I should almost be forced to question your moral character."

"Mistress, rest assured I offer Madame Catastrophe no deliberate encouragement."

"I think I believe you, and therefore ascribe your laxity to mere naïveté," Oeunne conceded. "You are like a child, Shorvi—brilliant, talented, but careless and haphazard. It is up to wiser heads to guard your safety. Is it not so, Oeun?"

"Surely it is so, Oeunne. His mind is set on higher things. He cannot be troubled with the mundane trivialities of self-preservation. It is for the likes of us to arrange such details."

"Then enlighten this careless and haphazard child," Nirienne suggested. "How shall I best protect myself, what exactly do you advise? I cannot very well surround myself with guards night and day, nor can I hide behind stone walls."

"I am not so sure of that," said Oeun.

"Hiding might be just the thing," Oeunne concurred. "A leave of absence from the Constitutional Congress, a discreet withdrawal from Sherreen itself—"

"—Would please our Reparationist friends no end," Nirienne observed, "sparing them the expense of another bullet. My disappearance would clear the greatest obstacle from the path of v'Aleur and his jackals, freeing them to abort the new constitution, to guzzle blood to their hearts' content, to seize power as absolute as any hereditary king's."

"And all of this happens if not for you?" Oeun inquired. "The Congress cannot do without you, and therefore you must play the sacrificial victim?"

"They are such fools, then, all the Congressional delegates, that they will follow the v'Aleur thing blindly?" Oeunne demanded. "All of them are fools, save Shorvi Nirienne?"

"They are not fools, most of them, but considerably intimidated," Nirienne countered without rancor. "Whiss v'Aleur's power and influence expand from day to day. The fanaticism of his followers finds its outlet in violence. That cannot surprise anyone who has ever heard him speak, for the man's impulses are vicious, and his ability to rule an audience is almost magical. Within the Congress, there are those repelled by v'Aleur's extremism, but such dissent is fragmented and often fearful. A unifying voice is required to marshal the forces of the opposition—"

"—And such a voice is Shorvi Nirienne's," Beq interjected quietly. "The one voice that consistently makes itself heard. Many times I've attended the congressional conferences, to hear Shorvi argue Whiss v'Aleur and his creatures to a standstill. He is perhaps the only delegate possessing both ability and courage to do so much. In recognizing his own significance, Shorvi does not boast, but merely acknowledges an obvious reality. The Reparationists' similar acknowledgment reveals itself in the frequency of attempted assassinations."

The others eyed Beq with varying degrees of concern, but without skepticism. They were wont to regard Shorvi Nirienne, quite erroneously, as a being set apart from other men, existing upon a higher plane; intellectually and morally superior, but at the same time unworldly, impractical, ill-equipped to deal with ugly realities. It was the integrity of Nirienne's political values and persona that fostered this illusion, and even his closest associates often failed to note the underlying pragmatism; the level, clear-eyed assessment of men and circumstance. Shorvi was too fine and high-minded to know when to come in out of the rain, such partisans as the Bulaude siblings fondly imagined; but they entertained no such illusions concerning Beq, whose cool ingenuity was recognized by all. Beq was a sharp one, certainly, and when he spoke, those who knew him listened.

"Well, then—let us say he is indispensable," Oeun conceded grudgingly. "What then? Must he expose himself to Reparationist bullets? Shall Shorvi find no refuge? Where are the safe houses that used to await him?"

"Still waiting," Beq assured him.

"The escape routes? The rooftop highways, the ladders, the culverts, chutes and tunnels?"

"All in good order. I inspect them periodically. Shorvi's escape within minutes is assured, should the need arise," said Beq. "There are safe houses all over town."

"But none so safe and fine as *ours*," said Oeunne.

"Well. I suppose you know what you are about." Oeun frowned. "But in the meantime, what's to be done? Do we stand idle, like waxwork dummies, while they bombard Shorvi? Sooner or later, one of those bullets will find its mark."

"Anyone ever consider picking off Whiss v'Aleur first?" Veste Riclairc spoke up at last. "Certainly someone could get him, and that would solve all our troubles."

The suggestion appeared to strike many a responsive chord, but Shorvi Nirienne remained immune. "You wish to make a martyr of him?" Nirienne inquired. "Murder him, and his immortality is assured. I'm not inclined to perform such a service for Whiss. Let him alone, for now. Sooner or later, he's bound to wreck himself."

"But how long might that take?" demanded Oeun Bulaude. "And in the meantime?"

"In the meantime, there are Beq's ladders and tunnels, together with a bulletproof waistcoat."

The days had lengthened to weeks and even months. The Sherreenian streets were dusty, breathless, and stinking; the citizens sweaty and irritable. Summer had come once again before Whiss v'Aleur judged the moment ripe for his great coup. Perhaps he needn't have waited quite so long, but he wanted it flawless and foolproof. He could tolerate no possibility of error, and therefore he had planned and plotted, checked and double-checked, holding off until each detail was honed and polished to perfection. But the day had finally arrived, and now it *was* perfect. The crucial speech, with its carefully crafted threats, accusations, and denunciations, was ready. He had rehearsed it scores of times, and now he knew it by heart, down to the last practiced passionate inflection. It was a speech calculated to rouse anger, hatred, fear, cupidity, patriotism— emotions that Whiss had always known upon instinct how to exploit. Such powerful currents, properly channeled, would carry him to the preeminence he knew himself meant for; it was only a matter of dominating the audience, and that he knew how to do. His natural rhetorical talents, backed by the magical assistance of his father, were almost sure to win the day. But "almost" wasn't good enough.

Whiss detested uncertainty, and therefore he had prepared the ground with care. For weeks now, his agents had been busy among the delegates—soliciting support, jerrybuilding quick new alliances, kindling hostility among rival factions; undermining the credibility and morale of potential opposition; bribing, flattering, cajoling, exhorting, or threatening as appropriate. He had directed this operation with discreet energy and inborn skill; and now, in the wake of frenetic covert activity, Whiss felt his position relatively secure. The members of the Reparationist party were of course uniformly loyal. Similarly reliable was the membership of Whiss's own Committee of National Welfare; and the Committee of Congressional Procedure, whose pederast chairman Cheneuve had proved conveniently vulnerable to blackmail; and the Red Diamond League, representing the most violent elements of the Sherreenian mob—all of them staunch supporters. Of the remaining delegates, the motley assortment of undecided souls included a number susceptible to blandishments or intimidation, and these he had swiftly secured. In these days of confusion and upheaval, only the Niriennistes and their allies presented anything resembling a united resistance to the burgeoning power of Whiss v'Aleur, and this resistance would be crushed in early childhood if not outright infancy. It should not be unduly difficult, for the Niriennistes in their self-infatuated nobility had never troubled to learn the art of intrigue. The same could not be said of their enemy. Whiss was a master, but nonetheless too wise to trust in words alone. If intrigue failed, there was always the Vanguard.

Whiss's great day dawned clear and bright, as befit his hopes. Rising early, he dressed with care, meticulously brushing every speck of dust from his now-famous black suit, scraping the lank hair straight back from his tall yellowish brow and binding it at the nape of his neck with a tight triple knot as if fearful a single hair might escape. Toilet completed, he breakfasted frugally, then repaired to his chamber to pass the last hour remaining before his departure in serene meditation—or so he intended. But Whiss soon discovered serenity impossible to achieve. Nervous tension—excitement, dread, fierce uncertainty—fired his blood and twisted his vitals. His pulses galloped and his stomach flopped like a captive fish. When he tried to review his speech one last time, the phrases merged and inverted, echoing madly in his mind. It was much like the time he had prepared to deliver his first public address at the warehouse in Pump Street, so many months earlier; here was the same feverish anticipation, the same sickening stage fright. But the speech in Pump Street had been a triumph, he reminded himself. The destruction of the Eighth District station house had proved it. He had made countless other speeches since then, each and every one of them tremendously effective, as subsequent acts of destruction had demonstrated. His orations were always successful, thanks to his own natural talents, enhanced by his father's magic. Enhanced, augmented, assisted. What might happen were that magical assistance withdrawn, Whiss did not care to consider; and he did not need to consider it, for there would be no withdrawal, ever.

Only—

Only it was impossible to avoid noticing Chorl Valeur's lack of enthusiasm, his hesitancy—no, more than that, his palpable reluctance. Whiss, pacing feverishly back and forth across the uncarpeted floor, paused in midstride. Chorl's assistance was unwilling, just as it had always been. He gave nothing spontaneously; coercion of some sort was invariably required. So it had always been, and so it continued. Whiss's narrow jaw tightened. The frustrations and resentments of a lifetime sparked his mind, igniting the ever-present angry vapors to explosive effect. The rage swept through him, annihilating all else, to his relief. The rage he knew, and could deal with. Its wild terrain was familiar. He knew the possibilities, the limits, and above all, the potential. This sheer raw energy would lend force to his rhetoric, a force almost equaling the best of Chorl's moping contributions. It was like a magical tonic, for now he was vital and invincible; as if in relinquishment of self-control he found mastery.

Whiss wheeled to stare into the small cracked mirror that hung above the washstand. He saw his own face, drained of color but for two blotches of livid thunderhead bruising his cheekbones; flaring nostrils, grayed lips all but invisible;

huge eyes wide, hot, and glittery. He looked strong and madly resolved. He looked unpredictable and dangerous. He looked the way he sensed he ought to look, to best impress his listeners. He was ready. He knew it, and realizing so much, pounced upon the moment.

Grabbing a leather-backed binder of notes, Whiss hurried from the room, down the stairs into the hall, where his cousin Bierce dully awaited. Chorl was nowhere in evidence. Indifferent, incommunicative, invisible—as always. Seized with sudden overmastering frustration, Whiss pivoted and hurled his binder at the nearest window. The resulting crash of broken glass seemed disproportionately loud. Bierce gaped at his cousin in startled admiration. Whiss himself stared quiveringly straight ahead. An instant later, Chorl appeared. The old man asked nothing, didn't need to, being well acquainted with his son's nervous rages. At such times it was best to maintain silence, for a single misplaced word could push Whiss to full screaming frenzy; in which state Chorl genuinely feared him.

In silence the three kinsmen exited the house. The silence continued throughout the short walk down Nerisante Street to the Century Hall, outside of which loitered an unusually dense crowd of unusually scrofulous citizens. They raised a hoarse cheer at sight of Whiss, and a number rushed forward to kiss his hand, as if he were Exalted. The hall was full when the v'Aleur kinsmen arrived—an anomaly for Whiss, who generally was first to appear at any meeting; an easy way, he had discovered, of advertising his diligence. Today, he wanted to make an entrance. His devotees and disciples—some vaguely cognizant of his intentions, others minutely instructed—awaited some more or less forceful demonstration of Reparationist potency. Their hopes were to be fulfilled beyond their wildest expectations.

They separated at the door, Chorl and Bierce heading left to take their place in the high visitors' gallery, a position commanding a clear view out over the entire assemblage whose perceptions Chorl was required to influence. He would obey, of course—certainly, he must. But he found himself increasingly reluctant to prostitute his magic to his son's ambitions—though those ambitions were in the largest sense patriotic and philanthropic; or so he kept telling himself in the hope that sheer weight of repetition might eventually crush all doubts. In any case, if everything went well, then this might be the last time. Perhaps, after today, Whiss would finally be satisfied—that is, if Whiss *could* be satisfied. Chorl cast a surreptitious look right and left. The gallery was crowded. Today, the faithful had turned out in force. Beyond doubt, his son's adherents had been summoned to shape the audience. Sprinkled in among the ordinary private citizens were dozens of armed Vanguardsmen. Noting the ominous brown-and-scarlet presence, Chorl fluttered internally. Very much he wanted to retreat, but escape was quite impossible; Bierce sat at his elbow, disquietingly close and attentive.

Whiss v'Aleur appeared at last. A hum of conversation arose among the delegates, a patter of applause among the spectators. Pausing briefly at the entrance, Whiss glanced up at the gallery—ostensibly in acknowledgment of the salute, in reality to pinpoint his father's location—then advanced to take his seat in the midst of his allies. The meeting was called to order, and the Constitutional Congress was once again in session.

It began conventionally enough. The minutes of the last meeting were read and discussed. A couple of minor points of procedure were debated. The bumpkin Binaire, delegate from VoGrance, stood up to drivel on at length about some minor question of representation chiefly relating to rural itinerants—peddlers, Turos, players, and their disreputable ilk. Nothing of consequence, until Binaire had completed his remarks, countered perfunctory rebuttal, and resumed his seat. A brief lull, then Whiss v'Aleur rose to take the rostrum. A stir of interest animated the somnolent delegates. Always an inspired speaker, Whiss commanded attention at all times. But today in particular, rumor had it that he intended something special. Even without such rumors, his appearance would have attracted notice. His manner was sufficiently composed, but the livid cheeks and burning eyes were startling.

They watched in curious silence as he ascended the rostrum. Once ensconced behind the lectern, Whiss surveyed the audience at length, preternatural tiger-eyes shifting slowly from face to face, sliding easily over some, elsewhere pausing long and significantly, to the indescribable discomfort of assorted victims. Protracted survey concluding, Whiss began to speak; and if his celebrated colloquial style no longer quite plumbed the scatological depths of the Pump Street days, yet it had lost little of its crude vigor.

"Many among us," Whiss commenced, "think our job is almost finished. The first draft of the Vonahrish Constitution will soon be complete. Once it's done, spiffed up and polished, there's only to elect the Double Century that our famous Paragraph Eighty-seven provides for, and then we're through here. The Congress dissolves. We can congratulate ourselves, and we can all go home— or so we'd like to think. It's a pretty picture, but it happens to be false. Our obligations aren't discharged that easily. Our work here isn't done, and won't be done, so long as royalists and reactionaries continue to infest this assembly. It has recently been discovered that our Constitutional Congress is riddled with treachery and corruption." Whiss paused to allow the full impact of his disclosure to make itself felt.

Confused murmuring from the delegates. He had taken them by surprise. Whatever they thought of Whiss v'Aleur, they had never expected this.

"All of us know that the fugitive emigrant Duke of Feronte flaunts his vileness in foreign courts, openly soliciting the aid of our enemies in the restoration of

Vonahrish absolutism. Feronte—bigot, satyr, artist in villainy, refined in cruelty, bloody even in his pleasures—may truly be called Archenemy of Liberty. It shames us greatly to acknowledge such a countryman; and it shames us infinitely to acknowledge the presence of the criminal influence even here, within the Congress itself. There are those among us in league with the traitor Feronte. Evidence of conspiracy exists—factual evidence, in the form of documents. These documents have come into my possession. They will be surrendered to public scrutiny at an appropriate date. In the meantime, the guilty must be punished, the traitors must be cast out. The Constitutional Congress must be purged."

Whiss paused to survey his listeners. He required no magical assistance to sense their confusion. The faces before him reflected obvious consternation. And even as he studied them, the air in the Century Hall rippled, the delegates wavered like phantasms, and he experienced the now-familiar sickly qualm that signaled the working of Chorl Valeur's magic. The faintness passed almost at once, and Whiss beheld the emotions of his audience. There was the polychrome haze of feeling, so usefully informative, so beautifully pliant. He loved the look and smell of it, loved its weight and texture, above all loved its obedience to his will. He glanced up into the gallery to behold his father, spent and sagging, and the sight reassured him. Things were under control, his own control.

Whiss spoke on, describing in detail the nature of the conspiracy polluting the Constitutional Congress. He told of the treachery of individual members, the corruption of conscienceless self-serving cliques, the growing threat to newly won liberties. He suggested the possibility of royalist reprisal. He spoke of betrayal, perfidy, dishonor. He used such phrases as "vessels of infamy," "debased, filth-slobbering slaves of the Exalted," "vile infections of the body politic." He continued in the same extravagantly denunciatory vein for some minutes, speech charged with all his hoarded and skillfully directed angry passion. As he spoke, he watched the mists swirl and thicken, darken and homogenize at his command. At the end of about half an hour, the haze was dense and consistent as it was ever likely to become—which did not express the total mastery that Whiss desired, but it would have to do. For he was forced to admit that these Congressional delegates—for the most part mature, educated, and at least moderately intelligent—were not susceptible to mindless domination, at least not all of them. The Reparationists were all right, of course. He could see them where they sat in the low seats clustered at the base of the rostrum. Their faces bore the repetitive stamp of adoration, and the mists that swathed them were darkly turbulent. Similarly enthusiastic were the Red Diamond zealots massed in the upper reaches of the hall. Their aura was deep and responsive as a well-governed mount to the stab of a verbal spur. Yes, he could trust the Red Diamonds; they were his. And there were others, of course, scattered here and there throughout the audience. He sensed their response and he knew they were faithful, knew they were obedient, knew they were good.

Unfortunately, there were exceptions. He could spot the unregenerate, strewn throughout the hall, recognizable by their chill and sluggish auras. The greatest concentration of resistance predictably centered upon Shorvi Nirienne, seated in the midst of his sycophants. The mists that enveloped Nirienne and his crew were the color of ice, heavy and all but inert. Nothing could have spoken more clearly the intransigent spirit of such men than that miasma, so detestably immune to oratory. He had never won a convert among the Niriennistes, never brought a single one of them under his sway. Thus they were enemies of the people, enemies of all Vonahr.

This so, Whiss did his duty. Indirectly, he demanded their deaths. As matters stood, the Constitutional Congress possessed no specific legal means whereby to cleanse itself. It was this deficiency that Whiss v'Aleur addressed with his demand for the establishment of a National Tribunal possessing judicial authority to try and condemn every enemy of the state, regardless of kind or degree.

"For there must be no exceptions," Whiss informed his audience. "The enemies of the people shall be subject to the justice of the people, and it must be equally so for all—not excluding the Exalted, not excluding the King himself. Not even the King is beyond the reach of justice." A buzz of astonishment greeted this novel suggestion. The mists seethed, threatening to break free, and Whiss spoke quickly, with renewed insistence to reinforce his control:

"The nation cannot continue unarmed, naked and exposed to the worst attacks of the human wolves and tigers. The citizens of Vonahr have a right to defend themselves, and thus a right to arm themselves. Would any here dare to deny them that right? The National Tribunal shall serve as the sword of a strong, free people—swift and sure in defense of justice, fearful only to the enemies of liberty. In the name of the people, I demand a Tribunal, to be furnished with all such authority as required to operate freely and effectively in our defense. A matter so clearly essential to the public welfare is not open to debate. No true patriot of Vonahr will question this necessity."

A quick survey of the responsive mists confirmed Whiss's natural expectations. The haze surrounding his own followers was brightening to a flame-colored enthusiasm. A few more words would trigger cheering demonstrations. By contrast, the impervious atmosphere surrounding the opposition was grayly bleak as winter, shot with dark troubled streaks of doubt, trepidation, hostility, and one bilious shade that Whiss would not permit himself to identify, although in his heart he recognized it—contempt. Enough energy and turmoil there, he noted, to prompt some sort of challenge.

And sure enough, there was Shorvi Nirienne rising from his seat, insufferably collected, to observe, "The matter is very much open to debate. It would appear that Congressman v'Aleur has failed to consider the full implications of his own suggestion. The creation of a National Tribunal, armed with extraordinary arbitrary power to punish unspecified crime, the existence of which has not as yet been convincingly demonstrated, would surely usher in an era of unprecedented, judicially sanctioned violence, whose inevitable result——"

The remainder of Nirienne's remarks were drowned out by the furious clanging of a bell. Congressman Cheneuve, Chairman of the Committee of Congressional Procedure, acting moderator of all debates, and currently in thrall to Whiss v'Aleur, had not forgotten his master's commission. Shorvi Nirienne was not to address the assembly. At all costs, his mouth must be stopped.

"Congressman Nirienne is out of order," Cheneuve observed. "Congressman v'Aleur holds the floor."

Whiss v'Aleur's faction cheered and applauded.

"Master Chairman, I respectfully request permission to rebut Congressman v'Aleur's proposal——" Nirienne got no further. The Chairman's bell resumed clanging.

Wordlessly, Whiss v'Aleur altered his stance and expression. Silently, he gestured. His loyal Reparationists, perfectly attuned to his moods and magnificently responsive to the smallest of his voiceless commands, needed no additional instruction. A shrieking clamor arose, a wild storm of shouts, catcalls, boos, hisses, insults. The noise swelled to fill the hall, to rattle the windows and beat at the walls. A casual listener might have supposed the Congress united in its opposition to Shorvi Nirienne, but Whiss v'Aleur knew better. The bright, passionate haze embracing his followers was blemished like a diseased complexion with grim-colored anomalous patches. Quite apart from the central clot of Nirienniste hostility, blotches of drab reserve, doubt, and indecision spotted the entire hall. These areas of resistance comprised perhaps half the Congressional membership, but the delegates in question didn't know their own strength. The doubters were scattered far and wide, largely ignorant of one another's existence, uncertain and somewhat afraid. That formless confusion Whiss could see at a glance, and inwardly he blessed it. For all his undeniable cleverness, Shorvi Nirienne had hardly as yet mastered the art of practical politics, and this failure to organize his disparate partisans proved as much. Perhaps even now Nirienne recognized his error, but he should not enjoy leisure to profit by the lesson.

Shorvi Nirienne hesitated, as if contemplating further remonstrance. But nothing he wanted to say would be heard, and after a moment he reseated himself. Relative quiet descended upon the Constitutional Congress.

"What honest citizen," Whiss v'Aleur resumed, almost conversationally, "hesitates to yield himself to the judgment of the people? Who fears the people's scrutiny, save the villain harboring secret guilt? Who opposes the people's will, save the people's enemies? These are questions that we would do well to consider with care. The delegates' differing attitudes in respect to the proposed National Tribunal are more revealing than the individuals concerned might care to admit. In light of the evidence I now hold confirming the existence of conspiracy in our midst, the terror and hatred of guilty men speak loudly as a signed confession—for in the new Vonahr, the innocent need fear nothing!"

Frenzied acclaim from the Reparationists and Red Diamonds. Demanding cries from a number of strategically deployed allies:

"Who conspires? Who are the guilty men? Name them!"

"Gentlemen, don't ask it of me," Whiss advised. "We aren't a judicial body, and we aren't equipped to deal with questions of treason. For now, I counsel patience." And he shaped his voice, his words, his face, and gestures to heat the mists about his followers to glowing, seething impatience.

They would never let it rest now. The shouting broke out again—"Name them!"—and the sight of so many waggling jaws afforded Whiss a brief vivid image of himself as a master ventriloquist, his own voice issuing from countless puppet mouths.

Shorvi Nirienne's extreme pallor betrayed belated recognition of the trap that had been set for him. But his white face was calm as he stood once again, and his clear, even voice somehow rose above the babble as he observed, "If Congressman v'Aleur possesses proofs of conspiracy, as he claims, then these evidences must be produced at once, and submitted to the examination of our entire assembly. If incriminating documents exist, let Congressman v'Aleur present them now."

"I'll present them willingly enough—to the justices of our National Tribunal," Whiss returned, and his allies cheered with an intense, concentrated enthusiasm that supported the illusion of near-unanimity.

When the shouting subsided somewhat, Nirienne attempted reply. "Congressman v'Aleur's deliberate conflation of two separate and distinct issues appears evasive—" he began, and got no further.

"Liar!" Whiss v'Aleur shouted, and his clenched fist violently smote the lectern. Having decided at some level just a whisper below consciousness that the moment was ripe for one of those effective displays of righteous passion, he slipped mental leashes, loosing his emotions. His face suffused deeply, his eyes blazed and bulged, and his voice rose to full, unrestrained scream. "Liar! We'll hear no more from your carrion-stinking maw, you chancre, no more! Despicable LIAR!"

For a moment the delegates sat gaping and astounded. Then the mists about the Reparationists flamed to wild crimson, and Whiss's allies broke into frantic, near-delirious, shrieking applause. Narrow chest heaving, Whiss stood drinking it in. But he could not allow it to continue long, else run the risk of losing his own furious momentum. He gestured, and his puppet audience fell silent.

"I will not suffer attacks upon my personal integrity—not by criminal scum masked in false respectability!" Whiss proclaimed. "I will not submit to the vicious calumny of liars and traitors! I am a patriot, but not a martyr—unless it be for my country's sake!"

Howling approbation from the Red Diamonds. Shorvi Nirienne's attempted reply was inaudible.

"Shorvi Nirienne has assaulted my honor," Whiss raved on, apparently raging, but with one corner of his mind quite lucidly observing and directing the scene, "and there he has blundered, for now I am obliged to retaliate. Accused, defamed, and insulted, I am left with no choice but to defend myself. So be it, then. He has brought it upon himself. My friends and fellow delegates, you have asked me to reveal the names of those in league with the enemies of freedom. The conspiracy is deep-rooted, its members numerous. But there is one man above all—one malevolent guiding force—one man whose treachery poisons this entire Congress. That man is Shorvi Nirienne! There is our traitor— Nirienne! Nirienne!" Whiss's outflung arm and rigidly pointing finger symbolically skewered his foe.

Pandemonium broke loose. Every delegate in the hall was yelling, and the din was intolerable. The accused man was trying desperately to answer, but hadn't a prayer of being heard. Similarly inaudible were Frezhelle, Riclairc, and other such staunch Niriennistes who sought to speak in their leader's defense. The moments passed and still the uproar continued, until Whiss himself chose to interrupt it. He raised both hands, and into the ensuing lull flung his voice:

"I demand the expulsion of Nirienne and his accomplices from this assembly. The Constitutional Congress must be cleansed!"

Quick as a fencer's riposte, the voice of Nirienne followed, to make itself heard for one fleeting moment: "I claim the right to answer these charges."

Then the tumult recommenced, louder than ever and helpfully reinforced by the clang of the Chairman's bell. For a little longer Nirienne stood mouthing futile inaudibilities, and then, with a gesture of frustration and a look of determination, made for the rostrum. But this eventuality had been foreseen and provided for. Nirienne found his path hopelessly clogged with Reparationists, thickly interspersed with uniformed Vanguardsmen. Turn, twist, push, and strive though he might, he could not win past them. Similarly thwarted were Frezhelle and Riclairc. One of the Vanguardsmen shoved Riclairc, and the infuriated

Nirienniste threw a punch. Noting the occurrence from his elevated position, Whiss seized upon it.

"They brawl like hooligans," Whiss exclaimed, and as always the yelling subsided at his utterance, and he was heard. "They insult us all. They bring violence, slander, treachery, and corruption to our gathering. Shall we endure so much, or shall the Constitutional Congress cleanse itself?"

Renewed impassioned cacophony, in whose midst the urgent shouting of Shorvi Nirienne and his friends was lost. Following a quick assessment of emotional climate, Whiss judged that the ultimate moment had arrived. Almost invisibly, he signaled to a brown-and-scarlet figure stationed beside the great double doors at the rear of the hall. The Vanguardsman, alert and awaiting this sign, unbarred and flung wide the doors.

A roar arose without—a dark, deep-throated bellow, beside whose primordial savagery the hysterical yammering of the Congressional delegates waxed shrill and trivial. An instant later, a horde of citizens accompanied by a contingent of the Vanguard burst into the Century Hall. Comprising the worst dregs of the Sherreenian mob, they were ragged, filthy, hungry, and filled with hate—thus, the natural subjects of "Neighbor Jumalle." Most of them were subterranean-pallid and scrawny; the women youthful hags with drained sagging breasts and drained battered faces, the men crazed demonic scarecrows. More than one spectator was struck with mingled sympathy and revulsion, sorrow and disgust at the sight.

Despite the misery of their condition, the invaders appeared more fearsome than pitiable. A belligerent, threatening vitality animated all that wretched swarm. Down the central aisle they streamed in a noisy, malodorous, resistless tide. The majority of delegates easily gave way before them; those that did not were roughly flung aside. As they advanced, the avalanche rumble of their voices began to resolve itself into distinguishable repeating cries of:

Down with Nirienne!—Death-Death-Death! Down with Nirienne—Death-Death-Death!

The bouncy rhythm conveyed a certain sinister jollity.

"Citizens, what do you seek here?" Whiss v'Aleur inquired from the rostrum.

And numerous voices howled back exactly on cue:

"An honest Congress!"

"Down with Nirienne and his dirty crew!"

"The people of Vonahr command, and we are your servants," Whiss yielded gravely, and saw the mists before him glow with savage joy.

"Then let's clean house!"

At that point all coherent conversation ceased, or rather was lost and drowned in the great swell of voices. The noise was literally painful, and many a delegate stood shouting at the top of his lungs, with hands pressed tightly to his ears.

The horrendous racket did not deter the mob in the least. With a swift efficiency that suggested planning and even rehearsal, the invaders' apparently slipshod column broke and split, its two tattered tentacles curving wide to surround Shorvi Nirienne and a band of his closest associates. The chosen victims were plucked from their chairs, then forcibly propelled, driven, dragged, or even carried up the aisle and out the rear exit. A number of victims struggled—pleaded, argued, or berated inaudibly—all equally useless efforts. Nirienne himself did none of these things. For a second or two he stood regarding Whiss v'Aleur with the sort of detached, clinical interest often accorded certain venomous reptiles, and then, expressionlessly unresisting, accompanied his captors from the hall. Nirienne's step was firm, his head high as he marched between the screaming ranks. Only his alert dark eyes revealed agitation, as they shifted here and there, swiftly scanning faces. If anywhere he discovered empathy or support, they were useless offerings.

Up the aisle they hurried, and then at the door the crowd divided, about half its members pausing there, the others issuing like a channeled flood to flush despised jetsam from the Constitutional Congress. Out into the full glare of summer sunlight surged the citizens, their captives in tow, and then Shorvi Nirienne and his allies were violently thrust forth to land facedown in the gutter.

Despite his aches, Nirienne rose so quickly and lightly that it seemed he had never been down. Around him were some twenty-five of his closest political allies, including a number of youthful hotheads, now trading furious insults with their enemies. Verbal conflict swiftly escalated. Somebody hurled an empty wine bottle. Others followed suit, and the rejects were soundly pelted with broken glass, sticks, gnawed bones, and rotten vegetables. Resistance was useless, and Nirienne ordered retreat, leading his allies from the disaster site in tolerably good order. For a few hundred yards, a pack of citizens yapped upon their heels, then lost interest. The battered victims were permitted to depart in search of a refuge wherein to lick their wounds and to contemplate the calamity that had so unexpectedly befallen them.

Following the eviction of the Niriennistes, the uproar in Century Hall continued for some minutes. Reparationists and Red Diamonds were howling in unbridled exultation. Invading citizens chanted and stomped. Delegates shouted and spectators squalled. The volume of noise was appalling, the confusion complete.

Whiss v'Aleur, the one man present who might actually have restored order, chose not to do so. For one thing, he was tired, momentarily drained of energy by an almost cathartic spasm of triumph and satisfied hatred. For another, the scene before him was far too enjoyable to end prematurely. The noise, the fervor, and exotic worshipful passions—they were all for him, for Whiss. Little, slighted, ignored, and neglected Whiss was the focus and master of all this furor. His power over these clack-jawed marionettes was absolute. He jerked their strings and moved their limbs. He filled their minds, and they spoke his thoughts. He could end their strife with a few well-chosen words any time he chose, and that rich sense of dominance was somehow luxurious as the actual exercise of power. He wished to savor it. Moreover, the present crazy turmoil afforded an opportunity to assess the altered emotional climate of the hall. Today's great coup had gutted the opposition at a single stroke. That foul cloud of Nirienniste pollution was gone forever. The remaining ugly rack of gloom-hued vapors—noxious but diffuse—might be dealt with at leisure. In fact—and this first flash of omnipotence was intoxicating—there was no problem Whiss v'Aleur could not deal with, provided his father continued cooperative. Whiss's eyes automatically sought the visitors' gallery, where Chorl Valeur slumped and drooped in obvious misery. The old man's reluctance daily increased. Today's events might for the first time drive him to open defiance—he might even think to withdraw his assistance. But if he presumed, if he dared to threaten—that, too, could be dealt with. Whiss knew how to secure his father. Whiss had already taken steps to do so. Whiss knew how to protect himself, how to destroy a rival, how to maintain control. Whiss had come into his own.

horvi Nirienne's downfall marked the clear emergence of Whiss v'Aleur as supreme figure in the fledgling Constitutional Congress. As President and unofficial despot of the Committee of National Welfare, Whiss had already wielded too much power to suit his detractors. Now, with the elimination of his chief rival and the near-simultaneous establishment of the National Tribunal—ostensibly an independent body, but in reality, as everyone knew, an instrument of the Reparationists—his dominance waxed inordinate. Nothing could have illustrated this more clearly than the Tribunal's immediate proscription of Nirienne and all his evicted followers. Charged with "treasonous conspiracy and crimes against the people," the Niriennistes were ordered arrested upon the Congressionally mandated authority of the Tribunal, backed by the armed strength of Whiss's pampered Vanguard. Some half a dozen ex-delegates were rounded up and flung into prison; the remainder managed to evade capture. To the unspoken satisfaction of many, Nirienne himself escaped the net.

Throughout the months of Congressional maneuverings, Shorvi Nirienne's intelligence system had never ceased to function, continuing at all times active and well-ordered under the directorship of the highly capable Beq. Now, in time of renewed adversity, the machine operated with all its old efficiency. The majority of threatened delegates managed to flee Sherreen, while their leader faded completely from sight. The tide of anti-Reparationist literature flooding the streets nearly every day testified to Nirienne's continuing presence in the city. But his exact whereabouts remained a mystery to all but a few select initiates—a mystery that the various agents and spies of the Committee of National Welfare appeared increasingly eager to solve.

The six captive ex-delegates witnessed the historic first session of the new National Tribunal from the dock. The authorities neatly sidestepped the problem of Shorvi Nirienne's escape by trying him and his fellow fugitives in absentia. All were predictably judged guilty, and all were condemned to death. Despite the efforts of the Reparationist-controlled Congress to limit public knowledge of the affair, this verdict and sentence created a furor. Apart from the obvious injustices and brutalities involved, loomed the more immediate issue of misappropriated authority. At no time during all the months that had elapsed since the storming of the Beviaire had any party presumed to arrogate the life-and-death judicial prerogative formerly belonging only to King, to Exalted, or to duly appointed representatives of either. Events following the initial invasion had effectively demonstrated the actual disposition of power, but no one had ventured to formalize that reality—until now. A deal of public outcry arose, which Congress and Tribunal blandly ignored. There were harangues in taverns, skirmishes in salons, angry letters, broadsides, circulars—all of them officially disregarded. But gradually it dawned on alert observers that overly vociferous opponents of Reparationist policy were curiously accident-prone. Their homes were vandalized, their places of business torched, their family members threatened and worse, with disturbing frequency. When the Vanguard closed down Matchlock Tavern, known haunt of Nirienniste sympathizers, no one was particularly surprised. When the editor of the outspoken *Rat Town Gadfly* was beaten to death in an alley in broad daylight, the town buzzed—but did nothing. When the two small children of dissident Sevagnie delegate Grimaux disappeared, dissent within the Congress abruptly abated.

The one party most clearly entitled to challenge Reparationist encroachments continued inactive. King Dunulas, still caged in the Beviaire, maintained discreet silence, at least insofar as the world was permitted to judge. In the absence of effective leadership, there seemed little to be done; and in any event, the entire issue might amount to less than originally feared. For the weeks passed, and the threatened executions failed to materialize. The six condemned delegates languished miserably enough in the Sepulchre, but at least they were alive. Perhaps the new Tribunal, repenting its audacity but unable to commute the sentence without public loss of face, might simply permit the delay to continue indefinitely. Many Sherreenians assumed as much. A glimpse into the mind of Whiss v'Aleur would have shaken their confidence.

The news of the mass Congressional expulsion made little impression upon the Rouvignac household. Eliste, who found politics tiresome and lately depressing, didn't much concern herself. True, she harbored a certain negligent regard for the writings of Shorvi Nirienne, but not so much that his downfall affected her. The internecine squabbling of delegates was viewed with contemptuous amusement by Zeralenn; and Aurelie, feverishly preoccupied with Bayelle vo Clarivaux, failed to note the incident at all.

Harder to ignore, however, were the actions undertaken by Whiss v'Aleur in fulfillment of his own promises. He had, of course, always preached Reparation— the material indemnification of ancient social wrongs. This principle lay at the very heart of his professed political philosophy. And now, to the delight of his devotees, he was starting to make good on his word. Within a few days following Nirienne's departure, the Committee of National Welfare effected enactment of new legislation imposing severe taxes upon the holdings of every Exalted family. Initial resistance was violent. Congressional tax collectors all over Vonahr were defied, abused, beaten by lackeys, and in some cases, summarily hanged. A wave of assaults, murders, arrests, and chateau burnings followed; and a host of incredulous provincial Exalted found themselves cast into prison. The most refractory of seigneurs were fined and additionally penalized with interest charges. A few, to their utter amazement, even faced criminal prosecution. In these cases, confiscation of property followed close upon conviction, such action carried out for the most part by local Leagues of Patriots. In the end, all but the suicidally obstinate consented to pay. The revenue thus generated was partially redistributed in the form of free bread and soup for the common citizenry. Modest though this remuneration was, it pleased the hungry peasants. Over the weeks, additional edible largesse was dispensed at irregular intervals. On Queen's Day— rechristened Patriots' Day—in Sherreen, a small copper coin accompanied each loaf of bread, and for the moment at least, Whiss's status as national savior stood firm.

Benevolent reputation thus established, Whiss was freed to pursue his own ends. Subsequent arrests and confiscations were carried out in comparative silence, the monetary proceeds thereof finding their quiet way to assorted select coffers. The general public heard little of these acquisitions, for the popular press was rapidly learning discretion; but among Exalted victims, they were infamous. Half the Exalted population of Sherreen had been despoiled of cash, real estate, livestock and chattel, stock certificates, heirloom jewelry and plate, and in some disgraceful cases, even furs and clothing. The more prudent among them took to hiding their valuables.

Zeralenn vo Rouvignac did not stoop so far. She had been warned often enough that conspicuous wealth invited Reparationist attention. She knew, too, that her famous collection of jewelry—the gifts of numerous admirers, including a brace of kings—presented a tempting target. She had been advised repeatedly to send her treasures out of the city—or even out of the country, if possible.

Failing this, she might secretly bury them, in the hope of retrieving them at some future date when the world should regain its sanity, and the Reparationists should be hanged for the thieves they were. It was sensible advice, but Madame refused it.

"These baubles are worthless, if not conveniently available to my use," Zeralenn murmured, with such convincingly languid indifference that only those who knew her best would have noted the rigid set of neck and shoulders, the defiant hazel glint beneath slumbrous lids. Thus the jewels—even including Dunulas XII's famous triple rope of matched black pearls—remained within their rosewood cabinet in the Countess's dressing chamber. Despite the pleas of friends and family, she wore them freely as ever. Cash lay in an unlocked bureau drawer, silver in an unlocked sideboard. Ornaments and works of art were openly displayed, and life went on as if all social alteration stopped short at the Rouvignac threshold.

But Eliste knew better. Already she had seen several of her friends stripped of their belongings, witnessed their fury and heartbreak. She recalled the peasant women brazenly looting the Maids' Quarters, pawing her possessions, and the mere thought brought back all the sense of helpless rage and violation. Only now she was not helpless, and it wasn't going to happen to her again—she wouldn't let it happen. Countess Zeralenn might scorn all defensive subterfuge, but her granddaughter did not. She would hide her personal treasures where the canaille might never find them.

Aside from a large and expensive wardrobe, Eliste's valuables did not amount to much. Like any other girl of her station, she possessed a store of jewelry, most of it pretty but inconsequential—for the ornaments of real worth were usually worn by married women. Nonetheless, she owned a few good pieces that had once belonged to her paternal grandmother—fortunately, in Zeralenn's keeping at the time of the Beviaire invasion. There were several trinkets, tokens from friends or admirers, to which she attached sentimental significance. Above all, there were the gifts of Uncle Quinz—delightful magical frivolities, prized for their charm and for the affection she bore the donor. The porcelain garland, composed of a hundred different flowers, each wafting a distinctive fragrance, was surely unique. The gold-backed hand mirror that offered constantly changing views of dreamlike rose-clouded landscapes was valuable by any standard. Then there were the comic jeweled dice, with their mischievously shifting faces—and several other such irreplaceable trifles that she couldn't bear the thought of losing.

On a sweltering night at the height of summer, Eliste sat in her bedchamber, fanning herself and supervising while Kairthe sewed jewelry into the hems of petticoats and chemises. The atmosphere was stifling, motionless, dead. An open door and window might have accomplished wonders, but Eliste permitted neither. The door was locked to prevent the intrusion of servants who might see what they should not, and worse, carry word back to their mistress; for Eliste's convictions notwithstanding, she did not care to brave her grandmother's disdain. The window curtains were drawn to foil observation, and would remain so until the job was finished. Spurred by discomfort, Kairthe worked quickly; ripping stitches, tacking, hemming. Anxious to expedite matters, Eliste herself took the hundred-rekko note she'd received for her birthday and with her own hands sewed the folded paper into a slit in the lining of Prince vo Plume's little scarlet collar.

The garland, the mirror, Grandmama Berrisse's tiara, and a few other substantial articles required different handling, but Eliste had already considered this.

"Empty that," she commanded, indicating a wooden letter-casket. "Then pack up whatever's left."

Kairthe performed with her usual efficiency. Last item in was the porcelain wreath, carefully wrapped in multiple layers of tissue.

"There. Finished." Kairthe shut the casket, snapping the catch. "Now what, Miss?"

"Now—out to the garden. Quietly, softly. You take the box. Also this." Eliste added a purloined spade to the maid's burden.

"Buried treasure, Miss?" Kairthe's round eyes sparkled. "Like the pirates?"

"Just so."

"And you're like the captain? And me the sailor that digs the hole?"

"If you like."

"The captain always shoots the sailor," Kairthe pointed out. "Burns 'is brains so the poor sod can't blab."

"Too noisy. A shot would rouse the whole neighborhood. So I guess you're safe, for now."

"Thanks, Miss."

"Now, follow me." Eliste paused at the bedroom door to listen for a moment, cautiously cracked the door to peep out into the empty corridor, then stuck her head out for a quick glance right and left—just the same procedure she had followed over a year earlier, the night she'd sneaked from her father's house to liberate Dref Zeenoson. Recollections of that night rushed into her mind— moonlight-silvered fields and hills, the mothlike figure of Uncle Quinz emerging from stone, the extraordinary sensation of illusory lycanthropy, the stables by night, Dref Zeenoson's final flight into darkness, and her own subsequent sense of inexplicable desolation. She could feel an echo of it even now—but it was not the time to think of such things. She slipped out into the hall. Kairthe trailed close on her heels.

They made it down the stairs without incident. It was Eliste's intention to exit quietly by the front door, circling back around the house to the garden, thus dodging the servants' notice. So simple a scheme should have gone off smoothly—and would have, but for unusual ill luck. As they reached the foyer, a knocking sounded at the front door. It was most unlikely. Visitors at ten o'clock were almost unheard of; but there it was. The door quivered beneath increasingly urgent blows.

Eliste and Kairthe traded guilty, alarmed glances. Clutching the box to her breast, Kairthe took a step backward, as if contemplating a dash for the safety of the upper story. But already it was too late. The butler, prompt to a fault, was hurrying across the foyer to answer the summons. He opened the door, and after that, curiosity held the two girls.

A man stood on the threshold. Despite the damp heat of Sherreenian summer, a drab cloak swathed and masked his portly figure. Beneath the enveloping folds, the rapid, distressed rise and fall of his chest was discernible. His face was all but lost in the shadow of a wide hat, pulled low. In one hand he carried a small valise.

"Admit me to the Countess," the visitor commanded breathlessly. The accent was Exalted, garbled with alarm, but somehow familiar.

"Whom shall I announce, sir?" the butler inquired, following a brief doubtful scrutiny of the other's plain attire.

"Never mind that." The visitor cast an uneasy glance back over his shoulder.

The butler reached his verdict. "Madame is not at home."

"Take me to the Countess at once, fellow!" A note of rising desperation under the bluster. And the voice was certainly familiar.

"Madame is not at home."

"You impudent scoundrel, I tell you I insist! You villain, I will have you thrashed!"

The threat produced little impression. The butler's lip curled. He began to close the door.

"Admit the gentleman." Eliste had finally identified the voice. Both men turned in surprise as she spoke, noticing her for the first time. She advanced to meet the stranger as he entered.

"Exalted Miss—" The visitor's relief was almost palpable.

"Advise Madame that a gentleman awaits her in the parlor," Eliste instructed, and the butler withdrew. "Kairthe, you may go," she suggested with meaning, and the servant thankfully fled upstairs, bearing the telltale box. Eliste turned back to the visitor. "Your Lordship—?"

Hastily baring his head, he bowed and straightened. She looked up into the scared eyes of the Marquis vo Lieux-v'Olliard. It was no wonder that she had initially failed to recognize him. The Marquis's white peruke was missing. His own thin and graying hair hung lank about his sweat-dewed, moon-pallid face. He was plainly dressed, unattended, his characteristic placidity unwontedly agitated.

"Exalted Miss vo Derrivalle—Exalted Miss—er . . . Still in Sherreen, are you? So you are—and where is the Countess, eh?"

"She'll join us shortly, no doubt. This way, Marquis." She led him into the parlor, where he seated himself as far from the open windows as possible, despite the sultry weather. "May I offer you refreshment?" Eliste suggested ceremoniously, holding her raging curiosity in check with difficulty. To her amazement, he refused. Never had she known vo Lieux-v'Olliard to refuse food or drink. And never had she known him so undisguisedly indifferent to *her* pretty presence and smiles, like a man without time for trifles. In fact, he seemed hardly aware of her.

"The Countess? The Countess?" he pleaded.

She reassured him as best she could. Thereafter, all but ignoring her polite commonplaces, he sat fidgeting and drumming his fingers upon the arm of his chair. Eventually her conversational efforts died; and then, to the vast relief of both, Zeralenn entered, impeccable and perfectly composed as always.

Vo Lieux-v'Olliard leaped to his feet. "Vo Meureille—get him here," he burst out. "I could not send anyone of my own—he will understand—only get him here!"

Eliste gaped at him. The Marquis was distraught, almost hysterical. She could not imagine why. She noted, however, that her grandmother displayed neither confusion nor even surprise. Zeralenn twitched the bellpull. A servant appeared, received low-voiced instructions, and retired. The Countess turned back to her green-faced caller. "He will be here within minutes," she promised.

Vo Lieux-v'Olliard heaved a shuddering sigh. Thereafter abandoning all conventional pretense, he slumped dully in his chair. His hostess made no further effort to engage him in conversation.

Eliste's sense of exclusion was intense. Her grandmother and the Marquis understood one another perfectly. Obviously there were events afoot of which she knew nothing; unlikely though it seemed, the bovine vo Lieux-v'Olliard was involved. Whatever it might be, they had not seen fit to confide in her, and probably would not do so now. Any moment she might expect to be ordered from the room—sent off like a child to the nursery. Well, she was not a child, and if they tried to treat her as one now, she would rebel. It was time to take a stand.

But the dismissal did not come. Zeralenn noted her granddaughter's defiant expression. Her own lips turned down at the corners, and she held her peace. The minutes crawled by, and shortly after eleven, the Cavalier vo Meureille arrived; at sight of whom the catatonic vo Lieux-v'Olliard returned to life.

Like the Marquis, vo Meureille was plainly and darkly dressed. Unlike the Marquis, he was composed, cool and alert. His courtesies to the two women were almost perfunctory, but apparently it was beyond his power to dispense with them altogether. As quickly as decency permitted, he turned to vo Lieux-v'Olliard and remarked, "We may leave shortly, if you are quite prepared."

"Oh, indeed, indeed." The Marquis stood. "I am more than ready. Let us be off at once, if you please!"

"Best to give it another few minutes." The Cavalier consulted his timepiece. "We'll want to pass at the change of the watch."

"Off where?" Eliste could stand it no more. "Pass where?"

The three of them, united in understanding, respectively weighed her. Zeralenn finally responded, "The Cavalier has made it his task to convey our persecuted peers from the city."

By way of a tunnel under the wall, Eliste recalled. But to reveal her knowledge would reveal her eavesdropping. Aloud, she merely inquired, "Persecuted?"

"Those Vanguard fellows would clap me in the Sepulchre," vo Lieux-v'Olliard informed her. "A bad business, Exalted Miss. Very bad."

The Sepulchre. The name shocked her. "But of what do they think your Lordship guilty?"

"Wealth," the Marquis returned dolefully. "But I swear, it's not my fault. I only inherited."

"Since when has that been a crime?"

"Since the Reparationist pirates declared it one," vo Meureille informed her dryly. Turning to Zeralenn, he inquired, "She doesn't know this?"

"Hush, she is only a ch—" Meeting Eliste's indignant eyes, Zeralenn amended adroitly, "She has been sheltered."

"Then it is time that she learned, for her own safety. Exalted Miss—" Somehow, despite his gallantry and distinction, the Cavalier suddenly seemed pedagogical. "You should be aware that the greatest among his Majesty's subjects have now become the most persecuted. The thieves presently controlling that ridiculous Constitutional Congress are much in need of cash to ensure the loyalty of their hired bullies. Such is the strength of his Majesty's defenders both in Sherreen and the provinces, that an army is required to oppose it—and that is a costly undertaking. Thus the concept of 'Reparation' progresses from ideal to simple necessity. They need money. They know who has it. The rest is sadly obvious. Those among us conspicuously blessed by Fortune—such as his Lordship here—may expect unjust accusation, imprisonment, violent extortion, and death. Yes, death," he insisted, noting her incredulity. "There have already been murders. Where do you suppose the Viscount vo Cheteigne is now? And his estate? And where is vo Brajonard? It is better not to think of it. And this will continue until such time as his Majesty's friends succeed in restoring order and decency. In the meantime, the greatest targets among us must fly or hide. Which is less offensive to Exalted honor?"

"Gad, it's true, Exalted Miss," vo Lieux-v'Olliard interjected. "They're on us like a pack of wild dogs. Didn't you know? There's nothing for it but to scrape things together and go while we can. See, I've got the cash, the shares, certificates of deposit, notes and bonds, deeds of title, and Great-Great-Granddad's sparklies from the wars." He patted the valise. "I'm ready. Don't think too ill of me if you can help."

"Certainly I do not," she answered untruthfully. He was Exalted, even titled, and he was running away! Running from the canaille! What must Madame think? Eliste looked to her grandmother, expecting contempt; only to discover a grave, almost sorrowing countenance. Her own incipient sneer died, and she inquired with a more genuine sympathy, "Do the Vanguardsmen now pursue your Lordship?"

"Gad yes, Exalted Miss! I'd be sharing straw with the Sepulchre rats by this time, but for the good word from vo Meureille's people. They saved my skin, I'll swear they did! But I only just managed to shave off, and now the streets are crawling with those Vanguard fellows—I actually had to run from a gang of them, think of it! And I'm told that all the city gates are guarded—"

"They are always so, these days," vo Meureille informed him.

"—And my affairs have never been so fearfully muddled."

"Do not distress yourself, Marquis," the Cavalier advised. "The gates are guarded, but there is still a relatively safe way out, a path known to few. Another two hours should find you safe beyond the city walls. And after that, you might do well to consider temporary emigration."

"Oh, I will, surely I will! Lanthi Ume for me, I think—they've a decent respect for breeding, there. And what about you, eh, Countess?" vo Lieux-v'Olliard inquired of his hostess. "Your Ladyship's scarcely invisible."

"A great loss if she were," opined Meureille; absently, automatically gallant.

"Can't Meureille here persuade you to retreat, eh?"

"It's not been for want of trying," Meureille told him.

"It is not a possibility to consider." Zeralenn appeared serenely impervious.

"And what about the King?" Eliste inquired boldly, and faced a battery of startled eyes. "Well, if the greatest Exalted are in danger, isn't his Majesty in greater danger yet? Might *he* not end in the Sepulchre?"

"Granddaughter, you speak very much out of turn." Zeralenn's straight figure was rigid. "The person of the King is sacrosanct, and remains so in the face of all such evanescent turmoil as we now endure. To suggest otherwise transcends childish impertinence. Such thoughts are unworthy—they are vulgar. You bring shame upon yourself."

Her grandmother's icy severity perhaps masked uneasiness, or even alarm, but Eliste didn't see it. Cheeks aflame, she lowered her eyes.

But vo Lieux-v'Olliard was not similarly abashed. "You oughtn't be so hard, Countess," he suggested. "The young lady shows good sense, and I'm in agreement with her. Gad, his Majesty's own brother wasn't too proud to bundle himself off months ago, and a hot time he had of it, from what I hear. So much for royal sacrosanctity. But the Cavalier here would know more of that than I. Eh, Meureille? Do you not correspond with Feronte's people in Strell? Egad, here's a thought for you. Feronte and his Strellian hosts might cough up the wherewithal to grease a few appropriate palms, thus easing his Majesty's passage from the Beviaire. To be sure, we Vonahrish Exalted will do all we can, and yet it seems to me that these Strellian nobles might well consider—"

"Marquis, it is time," vo Meureille broke in, with such quiet, easy assurance that the interruption seemed spontaneous and random.

Vo Lieux-v'Olliard nodded vigorously. He showed not the slightest awareness that his mouth had been deliberately stopped. But Eliste perceived it clearly enough, and her frustration, momentarily assuaged, reawakened. They didn't want her to hear anything about the King's possible escape. They didn't trust her any more than they would trust . . . well, Aurelie, for example—and they were always shutting her out! Her face pinched in sulkily. Nobody noticed.

Zeralenn and Eliste saw their visitors to the door. The Cavalier vo Meureille's hired hackney waited in the street before the town house. It was a sound choice of conveyance, for Vanguardsmen in search of the rich Exalted vo Lieux-v'Olliard would never think to investigate so shabby a public vehicle. The Marquis himself eyed the hackney with misgiving, but consented to enter. An instant later they were off, clip-clopping along the deceptively tranquil streets toward their secret destination; some unknown neighborhood, a nameless street containing an anonymous building into whose cellar opened that vital tunnel running beneath the city wall. Amazing that Meureille had ever managed to track it down. His methods were no doubt ingeniously obscure. But somehow he had accomplished it, and so the precious lifeline ran unsnagged and unobstructed for now. The Marquis vo Lieux-v'Olliard would doubtless escape Vonahr safely, to join fellow Exalted expatriates in Lanthi Ume, or elsewhere.

Zeralenn and Eliste stood in the doorway, watching until the hackney disappeared from view. Eliste's mind was crammed with questions, none of them voiced aloud. There was no point—her grandmother would never answer. Presently the street was empty and the two stepped back indoors. Zeralenn retired to her own apartment, while Eliste sped upstairs to collect her maid and her boxed treasures. Thereafter, the interrupted interment proceeded without mishap. But as Eliste stood in the moonlit garden behind the house, ostensibly supervising Kairthe's efforts, her thoughts wandered. In her mind she followed through the streets upon the fugitive footsteps of her former suitor, and wondered if the formerly unthinkable could ever come to pass—that she or those close to her might one day tread a similar path.

"Then that is your last word on the subject?" Whiss v'Aleur inquired.

"Absolutely my last word," Chorl Valeur returned, heart and conscience simultaneously lightening. He took a deep breath, and his spine straightened. He was frightened, but at the same time happy, happier than he had been since he came to Sherreen. Bierce wasn't looming around to intimidate him today—Bierce was often blessedly absent of late—and at last Chorl had found courage to stand up to his son. Finally he was asserting himself, shrugging off a weary load of misery and humiliation. Amazing how good it felt—he should have done it months ago. Staring Whiss straight in the eye, he spoke firmly. "The subject is closed. Now—why have you brought us to this place?" The two of them stood before the City Armory, whither Whiss had dragged them all the way from Nerisante Street. Chorl saw no purpose, but his son had insisted.

"There is something here that may interest you. But more of that presently. For now, I must remind you again of your duty, as you have clearly forgotten it. The people of Vonahr require your services. You owe them that much, at the very least. It is a debt you should be glad and eager to pay." Whiss's manner was sternly admonitory. Almost he might have been the father, rebuking a refractory son. Such a tack was usually effective, but today Chorl displayed abnormal recalcitrance.

"I am aware of my duties. I have forgotten nothing, and I require no instruction." Chorl delighted himself with his own boldness. "I am quite willing to serve the people, but their interests and your own do not necessarily coincide. That has become clear enough. Let us not mince words. Your trickery enlisted my unwilling aid in the ruin of Shorvi Nirienne. It was cleverly accomplished, and you triumphed—"

"Let us say the people triumphed. The nation triumphed."

"That is questionable. The nation loses a champion, while you trample your rivals. The fact is, you deceived and used me. That was always your way, from the first. You have used me for months, for a lifetime perhaps, but now it must end. I have reached my decision. Tomorrow I return to Vaurve. No doubt you will thrive, but without your father's aid." Chorl folded his arms. "And I do not wish to speak of this again."

Whiss studied his father, and a curious sort of hot-colored lens seemed to bend and reshape his vision. The world twisted, warped, resettled itself, and before him he beheld an enemy. There had in the past been some doubt into which category Chorl might fall, but all such questions were now answered once and for all. The enemies of Whiss v'Aleur were enemies of Vonahr, and as such, deserved no quarter. A vein throbbed in Whiss's temple. It took every ounce of willpower at his command, but he refrained from striking his father. There were better ways to deal with this particular adversary, much better ways.

"Well, you are obviously determined, and nothing I can say will alter your decision," Whiss conceded, without apparent rancor. "I regret your departure, but I must accept your choice. I will not seek to hinder you. Before you go, however, there is something you ought to see. This way." Grasping the other's arm, Whiss steered his father toward the doorway.

Compliance in so small a matter seemed the reasonable course, and Chorl did not resist. The Vanguardsmen blocking the entrance made way without demur for the Committee of National Welfare's President. Their very docility struck Chorl as indefinably threatening.

Through the vast ground-level chambers, then down the stairs to the dim cellars wherein the Stupefactions reposed. What for? To Chorl it seemed a waste of time, but he held his peace. He was leaving the city within twenty-four hours; it would all be finished soon enough.

Down, down the dank-aired stairway, Whiss in the lead, Chorl trailing resignedly. Many Vanguardsmen here—far more than in the past—elaborately armed, yet uniformly acquiescent. Down to the bottom, and it was not quite the same as Chorl remembered. That great, dim space was now divided by high wooden partitions that were surely new additions. It took him a moment to see that the thin walls formed a trio of open-faced, three-sided cells, isolating each of the Stupefactions; and longer yet to comprehend the reason.

The Stupefactions now bore new appendages: a human being attached by an anklet and stout chain to a staple sunk into the base of each mechanism. A collar and a second chain bound each prisoner to the stone cellar wall. The new partitions, flimsy though they were, effectively blocked vision and discouraged communication among the captives. Thus separately shackled were two men and one woman, all of them recognized at once by Chorl, who was their father.

There was second son Eularque Valeur—unwashed, unshaven, and generally wretched—chained to the two-headed Stupefaction called ZaZa. There was the short and dumpy figure of daughter Phlosine, attached to the mechanical beetle NuNu. And there was youngest son Houloir, squatting miserably in his fetters at the foot of the Kokotte. A few feet from Houloir stood Bierce Valeur, mesmerized gaze fixed worshipfully upon the Stupefaction. So this was where Bierce had been spending his time lately.

For a few moments Chorl stared, simply unable to take it in. Finally the scene registered. A gasp of dismay escaped him and he started forward, only to be halted by Whiss's restraining hand upon his shoulder.

"It is best that you do not approach them," Whiss suggested pleasantly. "Your presence, though doubtless welcome, would surely divert their attention from the task at hand, and we cannot afford that now."

"Your brothers—your sister—what does this mean?" Chorl stammered in utter bewilderment. Though never close to any of his children, he was not devoid of paternal sentiment. The three before him had inherited their father's magical ability, together with his pliant and timorous nature. However tenuous, a bond existed; and the sight of his offspring in chains affected Chorl strangely. He wanted to weep. Terrified of displaying such weakness, he managed to suppress the tears, but only with difficulty.

"Eularque, Phlosine, and Houloir are all good patriots," Whiss explained, with the tight-lipped smile that his father dreaded. "They have placed their magical talents at the nation's service, and presently they devote their best efforts to the reanimation of the old Stupefactions. You'll recall, you informed me that the task required the expertise of an adept trained in the art since childhood. I wondered where such might be found. I thought, and the solution to this difficulty soon presented itself. Yours was excellent advice, Father, and I thank you for it with all my heart."

"But the chains—they are shackled—"

"Surely this slight restriction of physical movement assists in the absolute focus of their attention upon the task at hand." Whiss's smile did not falter.

"No, that is not necessary. They will tell you so themselves. Eularque!" Chorl's voice rose to a shout. "Houloir! Phlosine, answer!"

"Peace, Father," Whiss advised, and at his subtle signal, a gaggle of Vanguardsmen pressed in close, blocking the light. "Peace, they cannot hear you. Their minds wander in search of the buried mechanical sentience. Lost in their magical labors, they seem to see and hear nothing; but you would surely understand that better than I, would you not? You waste your breath, I believe. But no, I am mistaken, for here comes Bierce. You have managed to attract *his* attention, and he wishes to pay his respects. Now, there is family feeling for you."

And indeed, Bierce was advancing upon them like a perambulating monolith. Chorl instinctively cringed. Abandoning pretenses, he turned upon his son to exclaim, "But this is monstrous—monstrous! This is your family—your own brothers and sister."

"Rest assured I value them highly."

"How can you permit such vile abuses? Chained in a cellar, shackled like criminals or animals!"

"I have already explained the necessity. It is temporary, and in any case, intermittent. My siblings leave this place at night."

"Ah, that is something, at least. Where do they lodge?"

"In the Sepulchre."

"Impossible. Even you would not do that."

"In kindness only. They are safe in the Sepulchre. No harm can befall them there. It is entirely for their own defense and protection. I am sure you understand me."

"No—no I do not understand you at all."

"No? But it is quite obvious. In these uncertain times, Sherreen is rife with danger. My siblings—so unworldly, so naive, so ignorant of life's evils—are natural prey to human predators. Truly, I fear for them, and thus rely upon thick walls and stout locks to guard their safety."

"What madness is this? You steal their freedom, and claim it is for their good?"

"Truly. I have done my best for them, and yet I fear it is not enough. There is danger everywhere—even within the Sepulchre itself, and even here. Constant vigilance is required, and I alone cannot maintain it. That is why I must request your assistance."

"Mine?" Chorl appeared nervous, indignant, and confused all at once.

"Eularque, Phlosine, and Houloir need you—so much so that it is no exaggeration to remark that their very lives depend upon your care."

"Mine?" Chorl repeated, hopelessly bewildered.

"Indeed." Whiss nodded, torn between amusement and impatience at his father's obtuseness. Subtlety was wasted here; in any case, subtlety had never been his forte. "The danger, I tell you, is all about us. No one's to be trusted. Only consider, for example, my own Vanguardsmen. Ostensibly they are loyal to me, the President of the Committee. In reality they are fractious, violent, and murderously opposed to all magical manifestation, which they regard as Exalted in nature. Nothing convinces them otherwise, and thus my talented siblings are never truly safe among them. A restraining hand is required to govern the soldiers, but I cannot be here all the time. And that is why I must depend upon you, Father. You must serve as my deputy here. Your frequent presence ensures the safety of my siblings. Without it, I cannot say what might befall them at the hands of the Vanguardsmen, whose cruelty is equaled only by their ingenuity."

It seemed to take forever to drive the point home, but when at last Chorl understood, the entertaining extravagance of his reaction justified Whiss's unwonted restraint. His eyes expanded in a ridiculous pop-eyed goggle of horror, his mouth worked, he made a couple of unsuccessful efforts to speak, and finally managed to blurt out, "You would do this—you are an unnatural brother—an unnatural son—a merciless and twisted creature—"

Whiss was silent. His lips curled faintly.

"Don't call Whiss names," Bierce Valeur advised. His huge hands flexed, but he did not change expression. "Don't ever do that."

"Oh, he has received a blow," Whiss excused. "But he will recover." It was not easy to curb his own angry passions, but the look upon Chorl's white and twitching face made the effort seem worthwhile. "Come, Father. Surely we understand each other, and there's no need to quarrel. My siblings are quite safe for now, as you can see. Why should they not continue so? Tomorrow, after you have assisted my next address before the Congress, perhaps we'll come back here and you may satisfy yourself that they are well. Will that reassure you?"

Chorl made no answer; and under the circumstances, Whiss took his silence for assent.

The first days of Sherreenian captivity were dreadful. The Valeur siblings—innocently prompt in their response to the fraternal plea that had lured them from Vaurve Province—were initially horrified to confront their brother's duplicity. Expecting to find Whiss ailing and in need, they had discovered him flourishing and infernally vital. Expecting gratitude and a warm welcome, they had found themselves shackled, imprisoned, and coerced. In theory, recourse to magical illusion might have freed them; in reality, the affair was not so easily managed. Whiss had separated the new prisoners, isolating each under heavy guard. Communication among them was prohibited, organized resistance all but impossible, and the merest hint of illicit magical activity sufficed to provoke the wrath of the omnipresent gaolers. As if this weren't enough to cow them, there were the threats. Eularque, Phlosine, and Houloir—no cowards, though timorous, shy, and pliant—might severally have defied any force; together, family feeling guaranteed their downfall. Indeed, it was almost too easy. These weak specimens, unworldly and almost childlike, were born to be governed. The moment Eularque Valeur was made to comprehend the mortal danger facing his siblings and his father, he capitulated. Had he chosen to stand firm, he might have found that Whiss's threats were largely empty—that Whiss held his kinsmen and their combined talents indispensable—but Eularque dared not put it to the test. Phlosine and Houloir proved similarly yielding; it seemed a hereditary trait.

The first couple of days were a nightmare blur of inimical faces, alien surroundings, and towering, inert Stupefactions; the nights, a dark vision of weeping dungeon walls, iron bars, and chains. The Valeur siblings, shocked and disoriented, went mechanically about their tasks, moving from Armory to Sepulchre and back again in a wretched acquiescent stupor. Passive and empty-eyed, they shuffled to and fro like rust-jointed automata.

This began to change, however, as professional interest dawned. Growing absorbed in their task, the siblings forgot fear and grief. Absorption soon deepened to obsession, and external awareness dimmed. The Armory cellar, with its soldiers, chains, and shackles, seemed to fade from existence. All that remained were the machines, and their beckoning, elusive personalities. To the uninitiated, the Valeurs appeared unconscious, all but lifeless. In reality, their minds were active and intensely focused; every mental fiber stretched to the uttermost, each faculty extended and straining through murky telepathic space in search of forgotten mechanical sentience. In a way it was like hunting for treasure at the bottom of a dirty lake: all clouded swirls and spirals, choking weed and floating debris, icy obscurity, confusion. A hundred times at least, Eularque thought to glimpse the hot and hasty mind of ZaZa. A hundred times at least, his own awareness went flying off in pursuit of fiery phantoms that eluded him; mere dreams of ZaZa, thin heated emissions of the true essence. The questing minds of Phlosine and Houloir encountered similar obstacles and snares. The Stupefactions slept on.

Until—

Until at last Phlosine abandoned the chase, switching from hunter to bait. Repetitive glimpses of the Sentient NuNu's ghostly reveries afforded insight, and Phlosine accordingly stilled her mind. Her thoughts, turning inward, grew tortuous and cryptic. Tantalizingly, she veiled her consciousness, and NuNu— the ultimate spy, even in sleep—could not resist the silent challenge.

Gradually Phlosine became aware of an inquisitive psychic presence. Highly alien identity impinged upon her own. She sensed pressure, an invasive scrabbling at the edges of her thoughts. She withdrew, shrouding herself in thicker veils, and the scrabbling grew more insistent. Phlosine's mind took flight, diving suddenly through dim telepathic levels; and the other, now upon the verge of waking, pursued. There was expression that communicated itself across psychic space as an insectile buzzing and whirring. Phlosine ducked, dodged, coyly retreated. The buzzing vibration intensified, rising in pitch until NuNu's own increasing excitement woke her. And then she was there, whole and complete, awake and aware for the first time in centuries. Phlosine, her task accomplished, enjoyed one brief flash of triumph, then sank into exhausted slumber.

NuNu the Queen Mother, the All-Seeing, Mistress of Secrets, stirred bright wings and opened a hundred eyes. There were walls all about, blocking Her vision, concealing all manner of possible secrets. It was imperative that She deposit several thousand golden eggs without delay; and soon Her tiny nits, capable of bypassing almost any obstacle, would buzz forth from the nest to gather information, as the bees they somewhat resembled gathered pollen; and these toothsome scraps and morsels of knowledge they would carry back to their august Mother, who consumed all; internally listing and indexing, compiling and cross-referencing, collating and computing, analyzing and evaluating; at last eliminating Her digested information in the form of conclusions—excreta dutifully gathered and removed by Her human workers.

But all that must wait until the nits were hatched. In the meantime, the workers must tear down the enclosing walls, else bear Her to another place. NuNu the Queen desired a tower perch, from which high vantage point She might gaze out over all the city, Her hundred eyes staring in all directions simultaneously. She desired it at once, and the imperative clack of Her mandibles conveyed the urgency of Her wishes; but the workers were unaccountably slow to obey. There were workers all around Her, idle as if they imagined themselves drones. An angry whirring escaped NuNu, and Her wings lifted slightly. Had a human limb come within reach of Her mandibles, She would have snapped it off.

Then NuNu the Queen recalled from the times long ago that workers of the sort She now beheld—armed and clad in uniform—were congenitally inferior creatures, incapable of comprehending Her wishes. Two exceptions presented themselves. One of them—a human male of gigantic stature, nondescriptly clad—stood a few feet distant, regarding Her with such patent veneration that there could be no doubting his will to serve Her. The other—the woman whose challenging reticence had lured Her from sleep—clearly possessed the mental capabilities of those upper-caste workers through whom She had been wont to communicate Her commands. But the female worker was unconscious, and of no immediate utility. For the present, NuNu must wait. But not, She trusted, for long.

Eularque Valeur selected a different method. The mental coquetry that lured NuNu would never have roused the ardor of ZaZa. Following days of fruitless effort involving vast expenditure of mental energy, Eularque finally hit upon the right approach. Sophistication was wasted here. ZaZa, fierce and passionate, found her truest self in battle. A call to arms was certain to snare her mind. Having at last divined so much, Eularque abandoned his psychic search; gave over hunting, traps, lures, pleas, and argument. He halted, and his mind grew briefly still. Shortly thereafter, a hot corrosive stream of insults, abuse, contempt, and defiance flooded the channels of his consciousness, then burst forth into telepathic space. Defiance sprayed like an acid sneeze, and ZaZa woke to seek the source.

ZaZa the Victress rose through the mists of sleep and stupor, lifting toward the light, old memories and desires and hatreds stirring, coalescing as She neared consciousness. An enemy was near at hand—She sensed the hostile presence—and She could not kill until

She had fully awakened. Not that She slew for the simple love of destruction; but a threat to Her property left Her with no other choice. For ZaZa owned a flock of humans. They were Hers, and Hers alone. What function they served was never defined, for She never ate their flesh, nor drank their blood, nor covered Herself in their hides. Perhaps they were pets, or perhaps they simply satisfied some obscure collector's instinct. Or more likely, some form of ownership was essential to Her nature. In any event, they belonged to Her, and their husbandry was Her obsession.

What set the humans of ZaZa apart from all other gooey nonmetallic members of the race was never exactly specified, but somehow ZaZa knew; and Her prized domesticated humans were to be defended at all costs against the attacks of rogue predators of any species, most particularly their own. Thus She woke, eager to breathe fire upon Her foes, only to discover the ruse. Here in the Armory were no enemies. Every human in sight was Her legitimate property—so much She knew upon instinct. There was, in particular, one nondescriptly clad man whose worshipful expression and gigantic stature marked him as a valuable possession. Similarly valuable was the pallid, balding creature whose magical mental maneuverings had broken Her long stupor—so valuable, in fact, that someone had taken the precaution of shackling him to Her side.

Such order and care were commendable, but distinctly stultifying, for ZaZa's nature craved the primal stimulation of combat; without it, She grew dull. Danger, death, and triumph were required. Above all things, She longed for the taste of flame in each of Her mouths, the brilliant jets lancing straight into the crowd, the sound of screaming and the luscious fragrance of roasting flesh. Yes, these were the things She needed, and soon.

ZaZa stirred restlessly, and tendrils of noxious mucous vapor dribbled from each of Her snouts.

Houloir Valeur felt himself lost in an alien world as he searched in vain for the consciousness of the Kokotte. Through the dark empty reaches of telepathic space ranged his questing intellect, without once encountering the faintest flicker of sentience. He might have supposed the levels to be quite uninhabited, or else he might have concluded that the Kokotte's identity was irretrievably lost—that she was truly dead. But the information gleaned from countless tomes lining the library walls at Bozhenille Commune suggested otherwise. Somewhere, buried deep and quite forgotten, the Kokotte's identity persisted. Such a thing could never be altogether lost, so long as the mechanism herself remained intact. His failure to recognize her essential self suggested no more than extreme unfamiliarity of type.

But the dim days perished upon the rim of his consciousness. NuNu and ZaZa resumed life, but Houloir did not know it. All his being was focused intensely upon—nothingness. He searched through nothingness. He struggled, floundered, struck out wildly in all directions to encounter—nothingness. It was bewildering, protracted, and lonely beyond the endurance even of a magical recluse habituated to solitude. His mind was lost and cold, spirits dragging. The equivalent of a mental shrug would have broken his trance, restoring him to a reality that now seemed infinitely desirable, despite its well-remembered terrors and betrayals. Resisting such temptation, he persevered.

Houloir struggled on for an eon. But he found nothing, and the icy void stretched out forever, and he could never search through it all, *knew* he never could. Despair all but overwhelmed him then, and mentally he voiced his woe in a plaint that amounted to a prayer.

The prayer was heard.

The Sentient Kokotte awoke at last. She lived. She was aware. Life, civilization, the world itself and everything it contained—all of which had suspended themselves throughout the long centuries of Her repose—now resumed. The universe existed once more.

The Kokotte was not vengeful. She bore no grudge against the humans failing in their duty and worship, those whose neglect had precipitated Her long sleep. They had inflicted spiritual damage upon themselves, which was sufficient punishment unto itself; beyond that, they were no concern of Hers. In any case, they were gone, and She could not be troubled to restore their existence for purposes of chastisement. What signified was not the past, but rather the future—a golden time of plenty and pleasure for all, of sanctity and lavish sacrifice, of fruitful vines and veins, of opened hearts. The Kokotte had returned to the world, and now the Age of Perfection should begin. The Kokotte was demanding, yet bountiful; jealous and exacting, yet limitless in Her largesse. Properly fed, She would pardon all.

There was great need of feeding. Her fast had been prolonged, and Her appetite was huge. Now was the time to end the hunger, with a great glorious glut of flesh and fat and fiber, blood and bone and brain. Now She should be compensated for the lost uncounted years of obscurity, and once Her needs were met, the world should be renewed unto glory and splendor eternal.

The Kokotte was all benevolence. She desired nothing beyond peace and joy, goodness and plenty, reverence and worship and nourishment. Personal appetites satisfied, Her equanimity was unshakable; and there seemed no reason to expect deprivation—there were bodies all around Her, and many of them were fat. Largest of all was that of the gigantic man, nondescriptly clad, observing Her with adoration; but somehow the Kokotte knew that he was not for immediate consumption. At present, such an acolyte might be put to better use. Likewise indispensable was the meager little creature whose prayers had awakened Her. His prayers had reached Her, his faith was great, and he had earned the right to serve Her.

She was the power, She was the glory, She was the eternal, the unchanging, the one reality. And She was very hungry.

In token of Her willingness to accept sacrifice, the Kokotte threw wide Her leaden doors.

When the tangled branching rods and wires that topped the great coffin shape of the Kokotte began to hum and vibrate, Bierce Valeur felt his breath quicken. When the glass sunbursts glowed with sudden light, his jaw sagged and his little eyes popped. And when at last the massive doors flung open with a crash, Bierce literally dropped to his knees, overcome with awe and a joy inexpressible.

She had opened herself at last, revealed herself fully to him—to him. Bierce knelt but a few feet from her base, and from that position enjoyed an unobstructed view of her great hollow interior. The cavity and doors were lined with dingy steel spikes, soiled and crusted with ancient waste. Each spike terminated in a conical point that was pierced, striated, and cunningly hinged. The purpose of such elaboration, if any beyond decorative, was not apparent. As for the spikes themselves, there could be no doubt as to their function, and Bierce's heart swelled in admiration. Without recourse to magical methods, he sensed himself perfectly able to divine the will of the Sentient Kokotte; and greatly he longed to serve her, thereby earning her esteem, and perhaps even her love.

She ached with the hunger of empty centuries. She desired human flesh, and Bierce's immediate impulse was to give her Cousin Houloir, who now lay sunk in exhausted slumber on the floor at her foot. Having served his purpose, Houloir might be considered expendable. Moreover, Bierce had little use for his cousin, who was weak and glum and perpetually scared, like a younger edition of dreary old Uncle Chorl. Yes, Houloir was an obvious candidate for sacrifice, and yet— there was always the chance that Whiss might disapprove. Perhaps Whiss had further plans for his brother—with Whiss, you never could tell. Therefore Bierce restrained himself, and his muddy little eyes ranged the cellar in search of alternate victims. But all he encountered were armed Vanguardsmen, obviously unsuitable prospects.

Bierce was thoroughly confounded. No practical solution presented itself, and yet somehow he *must* satisfy the Kokotte's needs, else know that he had failed her. For a very long time he stood absolutely motionless, big arms folded, brow furrowed heavily in thought.

The problem that loomed insurmountable in the eyes of Bierce Valeur presented no difficulty whatever to Whiss. The Sepulchre housed six eminently suitable victims—the half dozen condemned Niriennistes. For weeks now, their execution had been postponed, while Whiss awaited the reanimation of Kokotte, upon whose untested capacities his hopes rested. Now she was awake at last, and it was time to put her abilities to the test. Accordingly, the first of the condemned was conveyed in secret from Sepulchre dungeon to Armory cellar.

The prisoner—the former Congressman Moudarde from Fabeque Province—was led in by four guards. Moudarde was blindfolded, and his wrists were bound behind his back. His muffled head was bent in an attitude of listening. Abruptly, the blindfold was stripped away; and the Congressman, eyes smarting and blinking, gazed about him. He beheld a windowless but well-illuminated space, populated with brown-and-scarlet Vanguardsmen. Interspersed with the soldiers were several civilians, among whom Moudarde spied the skinny black-clad figure of Whiss v'Aleur. Behind Whiss rose a great leaden cabinet, lined with spikes and crowned with luminous thorns. He didn't know what it was, but instinctively Moudarde hung back at sight of it.

But there was no resisting. The guards hurried him on. He caught a flashing glimpse of gaping doors, glowing arcs, crusted spikes with hinged serrated extremities vibrating, clicking and snapping like eager jaws. And they *were* jaws, Moudarde unwillingly realized, each spike equipped with a mouth that lived, a hungry mouth with stabbing dart of a steel tongue, and tiny, tearing, carnivorous teeth—all rushing toward him—

He fought then, kicking and biting, flinging himself from side to side, while an unconscious puling escaped him, a repetitive high-pitched squeal that would have shamed him had he heard himself. All to no avail. They dragged him forward, and finally, when the little jaws upon each spike were snapping at his flesh and he could smell the eager metallic voracity—when he was close enough to glimpse the pink-silver palate of each mouth, like steel flushed with desire—then a scream escaped him, an unrestrained shriek that cut off all at once as a shove propelled him straight on into the maw of Kokotte.

The great leaden doors clanged shut, and for a moment the echoes bounced beneath the vaulted ceiling. Then silence, while every witness strained for the sound of screaming—of which there was none. No shrieks, no pleas, no imprecations; only the muted rattle of ambiguous internal tremors. The luminosity playing upon the glass whorls and sunbursts intensified. An instant later, the tiny bolts of radiant force began to crackle along the Kokotte's two great vertically thrusting black horns, ascending in quick succession until the dagger-pointed tips glowed searingly bright. A buzz among the spectators, underscoring a high, vibrating mechanical hum; then a tremendous arc of white brilliance flared between the horns, and the hum shrilled to an excruciating fleshless howl. The spectators started, flinched, clapped startled hands to their ears; some shielded their eyes against the glare. A few seconds later, it was finished. The brilliance faded to restrained luminosity, and the noise ceased altogether. A grinding of hinges and the Kokotte's doors swung open to reveal—almost nothing.

She was quite empty save for a rat's nest tangle of bloodstained rags. Long shreds of reddened fabric festooned the cavity. A coil of rope—formerly confining Moudarde's wrists—wrapped a couple of spikes. A pair of sodden shoes lay on the floor. From the shoes trailed scraps of skin, bone, and gristle. The spectators pressed forward eagerly but cautiously. A Vanguardsman prodded a shoe with the point of his bayonet, and a lively crackling sizzled along the Kokotte's spikes and barbs. The clinging rags bubbled and darkened and stank. Squeaking like mice, the spectators shrank back. It was not for another several hours that the Kokotte's acolytes dared approach to clear away the cooked debris.

The experiment had proved a qualified success. The Kokotte was hungry, quick, and lethal; so much was gratifying. But her methods were sloppy. Some sort of improvement was required. Whiss v'Aleur gave the matter much consideration, eventually issuing new orders. When the second Nirienniste—former Congressman Clionne from Jouvier Province—was brought in to the Armory cellar, he entered bare save for the cord attaching his wrists. Clionne put up less struggle than his predecessor. Perhaps he was simply a weaker man, or maybe the unaccustomed vulnerability of nudity smashed his defenses. In any event, Clionne was easily manipulated, and moments following his appearance, the leaden doors clanged shut behind him. The seconds passed, the radiance mounted, and then the white glare arced, a heated gust swept the cellar, and the leaden doors parted.

This time, there was little room left for improvement. Spontaneous cheers arose among the watching soldiers. Kokotte's interior was empty and clean, but for the length of bloody rope. Suffused with rare warmth at the sight, Bierce Valeur wrested a musket from the grasp of the nearest Vanguardsman, and with its barrel deftly flicked the cord from the cavity. In doing so, he came nearer the Kokotte's spikes than anyone other than the victims themselves; but did so without fear, for somehow he knew she would not hurt him. And sure enough, she didn't. The luminosity of her glass sunbursts mounted, but the glow was soft and warm.

"Beautiful." His intimate whisper was meant for the Kokotte alone. "So beautiful."

Beyond doubt, she heard him. And surely she understood him. A thin, nearly inaudible hum escaped her, a song of love if ever he heard one. He knew she was still hungry. The miserable half-starved carcass of Congressman Clionne hadn't begun to satisfy her. She needed far more. And yet it was not *his* flesh for which she hungered, not Bierce's. She felt his devotion, she valued it, and perhaps—

perhaps she was already beginning to return it. Bierce swallowed hard, blinking unwontedly bright eyes. He had to look away for an instant, and his glance fell upon Cousin Houloir, whose face was streaked with tears. Didn't the mewling milksop have the wit to recognize a brilliant success? Bierce had no patience with him. Fortunately, Cousin Whiss was cast in a different mold. Cousin Whiss was smiling.

Cousin Whiss had good reason to smile, for Kokotte's restoration provided the elegant solution to a practical problem that had plagued him for months. Long had he sought a means of public execution combining fearsome (but not gratuitously grisly) spectacle with high efficiency—a surprisingly elusive prize, but needful, in view of impending events. For Whiss foresaw carnage, a mighty slaughtering. Not that he was vindictive in the least, never that; but the Father of Reparationism was the Son of Justice, and justice unmistakably required the wholesale extermination of Exalted tyrants. The abused citizens demanded no less; or would do so shortly, when they had been properly schooled. Moreover, the same flood of Exalted blood destined to quench the popular wrath should also serve to wash untold wealth into appropriate coffers. The property of the condemned, automatically forfeit, would be put to its highest and best possible use—that is, to the outfitting and maintenance of the troops upon which the security of the Reparationist Party, and hence of all the nation, increasingly relied. This great purge Whiss saw as desirable and thus inevitable; for as his successes accumulated, the two attributes became increasingly indistinguishable.

In his mind, the matter was already settled. The Exalted executions should be publicly performed—that was definite. The people of Vonahr deserved the pleasure and edification such spectacle afforded; the Exalted criminals deserved every indignity; and Whiss himself deserved the satisfaction. The decision was final, yet there remained mundane questions relating to actual method. Various means of mass execution existed, but all were deficient in one way or another— too slow, too messy, too flamboyantly gruesome, too expensive. Some were clearly better prospects than others, but even the best of them failed to resolve logistical issues of corpse removal, interment, or consumption; or cleansing and purification of the execution site. No thoroughly satisfactory method had suggested itself— until the awakening of the Kokotte, whose swift and exquisitely discreet voracity endeared her at once to all beholders. Here at last was an executioner whose refinement freed her new Reparationist acolytes from all possible charges of barbarism.

Whiss v'Aleur was delighted, and eager to prove the Kokotte's virtue in public. This was easily accomplished, for the four remaining condemned Niriennistes still lay in their Sepulchre dungeon. Within the space of a single day, a large flat platform upon wheels—something resembling a land-going barge—was constructed. Upon this conveyance the Kokotte was placed with reverence, shrouded in black canvas, and drawn by night through the darkened streets from the Armory to the Sepulchre.

"Where have you been? What have you been up to all this time?" Eliste's foot was tapping. Her impatience masked profound uneasiness. Kairthe, plainly clad, with work-roughened hands and peasant accent, could gad about Sherreen in relative safety. Such excursions were a source of pleasure to the maid and information to the cooped-up, news-starved mistress. But Eliste sometimes wondered—what if something should happen to Kairthe, out there alone on the streets? Accident, sickness, or outright assault? An Exalted was responsible for the safety and welfare of her servants. What if—? "Where have you been?" she repeated sharply.

"Sepulchre, Miss. Near it, mind, not in it." A little pale and oddly distrait, Kairthe seemed hardly to notice her mistress's annoyance.

"What are you talking about? Explain yourself at once. But wait. You're looking decidedly off. You've permission to sit. Are you ill? Are you going to faint, or convulse, or anything tiresome?"

"No, Miss." Kairthe perched self-consciously on the edge of a brocaded bedroom chair. "I'm all right, truly."

"You're sure? Then talk."

"Right. I got plenty to tell. It was like this. I was on my way to pick up some of those little sugar wafers that you can't live without, Miss, and you know, I've got to pass by the old prison to get across the bridge to the market. So I'm walking along, and I see all these city folk standing about the gate, and I stop to find out what's going on. I ask around, but nobody seems to know for sure, so I start worming my way toward the front, and before long I'm pretty close to the bars, and I can see what everybody's gawping at. Square in the middle of the Sepulchre courtyard, there's this *thing*. It's like a whacking great armoire of lead metal, with pointed spikes inside, and all horns and brambles and glass trumperies on top. And it's *big*, Miss. Dead huge."

"Well, but what was it?"

"That's just what I'm asking myself. That's what I'm also asking everybody about me, but nobody can say. Only some folk swear it's another of those Stupefactions, like that watchdog thing at the North Gate. And it was true, it was like that, sort of, only different."

"Different in what way?"

"Shaped different, but that's not it. This one, it's lighted up on top, with colors, and sort of a stirring in its branches. This one's like—awake. And of course, folk are trying to figure out where it's sprung from, and how it got there, and what it's good for. Me, I don't know what it is, but I know that I don't any which way like the look of it."

"So the mystery remains unsolved?"

"Not so, Miss, I'm sorry to say."

"Sorry?"

"After a time," Kairthe continued, "out of the prison comes a soldier to nail up a notice on the wall. Someone reads it out. Four Nirienniste traitors set to be put down in the courtyard at three o'clock. So now I guess everybody has a pretty good notion what that thing standing in there has got to be for."

"You waited there until midafternoon to watch a public execution?" Eliste almost accused; part shocked, part revolted, but unwillingly fascinated.

"Well, it wasn't a question of *choosing*, Miss." Kairthe's round face flushed. "By that time, there was no getting out of it. I was right up there by the gate, almost pressing my nose against those bars, and the crowd was grown so tight and thick behind me that I was good and stuck there where I was."

"Indeed."

"Truly, Miss! And besides, once I knew what was coming, somehow it seemed like I just couldn't look away."

Eliste nodded; a tacit, shamed admission of comprehension.

"The news must have run through the streets," Kairthe resumed, "for the citizens kept coming and coming, until the stretch before the gate was so packed with 'em that no carriage nor yet even a sedan chair could get through. Some folk were boozing it, and some got rowdy, with laughing and horsing around. And some got ugly about it. But most were just quiet and waiting.

"Dead on the stroke of three, they come out of the Sepulchre. There were soldiers and guards and such. There was one that they said was Governor Dovelle Egure of the Sepulchre. There was the deathsman—very big, so he makes Borlo Bunison back at home look like a whelp—and some were saying that it was Bierce, kin to Whiss v'Aleur, but I can't vouch for it. And there were the four prisoners, and kill me dead if they weren't plucked stark naked! Miss, so help me, they were bare as chickens ready for the pot!"

"Oh, that is infamous!" Eliste's flash of indignation was subtly pleasurable. "These Reparationists are animals. Why should they resort to such petty, pointless cruelty?"

"I couldn't say, Miss. But I'll swear you could've bowled me over with a breath. I didn't know where to look, and neither did anyone else. I heard folk kind of tittering, you know the way they do when they're flummoxed and don't want to show it. But that didn't last long, and I don't think the prisoners even heard it— they looked too broke down to notice anything. I felt sorry for 'em, Miss, and I wasn't the only one. I even heard a whispering that these were good Congressmen and good bourgeois that deserved better. But there were Vanguardsmen about, and nobody talked too loud.

"They lined up the four in a little row right before the great contraption," Kairthe continued, "and there they stood while the charges against 'em were read out. And if they were guilty of it all, then they truly deserved to die."

"But were they really guilty?" inquired Eliste.

"Not for me to say, Miss. Anyway, the talking ended, and then they got down to business. The deathsman grabbed the first prisoner and just slung 'im straight into the armoire. And then it was just like that thing was alive. The doors clamped shut of their own accord, and the lights got brighter and brighter, and the noise got louder and louder, until all at once there was this great flash that hurt to look at, and it was all over. The doors opened themselves up again, and Miss—*there was nothing inside!* Nothing left but a length of bloody rope. I couldn't believe it. Nobody could believe it, and you should've heard the shouting and squawking then!

"The deathsman acted like he didn't hear. He just took a long fork and flicked the rope away, like it was the most natural thing in the world. And while he was doing that, he stopped and kind of petted the armoire—ran his hand all along it, even over the spikes—and I swear he was *talking* to that thing. I wasn't near enough to hear what he said, but I could see his lips move. He acted like he was talking to his kin. Real strange.

"After that, the other three prisoners went—boom, boom, boom—one after t'other, each the same as the first. It took but minutes to do 'em—you just couldn't believe how fast it went, and how—how *clean* it all was, with nary a scrap left behind, like there'd never been anything there at all."

"In a way, that's almost worse than——" Eliste broke off with a shudder.

"They were finished then," Kairthe concluded. "The soldiers and Governor and deathsman packed up and marched off, leaving the armoire in the courtyard. We dawdled about in the street for a time, waiting to see what might come, but there was nothing more, and I came home. And that's why I'm late, Miss."

Eliste was silent. There seemed little to say.

"Oh, one more thing," Kairthe recalled belatedly. "While all this was going on, you could see a couple of faces at a tower window of the prison, and folk down below were saying that one of them belonged to Master Whiss v'Aleur himself."

From his vantage point beside a window on an upper story of the Sepulchre's central tower, Whiss v'Aleur—or "Valeur," as he had recently, prudently, restyled himself—watched the entire display. He noted the Kokotte's superb efficiency, the mechanical steadfastness of the Vanguard, the perverse devotion of his cousin Bierce.

And the audience? The reluctant magic of his father enabled him to gauge its reaction at a glance.

The citizens were scared, confused, and excited, Whiss perceived without surprise. The pristine ferocity of Kokotte revolted and titillated them. Many were pleased, but afraid to admit it; some were ambivalent, and more than a few were honestly sickened. Trifles, of course. The pleasure could be stimulated, the nausea suppressed, at Whiss's will. His own talent, backed by Chorl's magic, gave him power enough for that, and to spare.

Didn't it?

Somehow the doubts persisted, eroding his confidence and gnawing at his nerves. He needed to banish the doubts, for his own sake and for the sake of the nation. He needed to protect himself. He owed Vonahr no less.

Fortunately for the nation, Whiss could rely upon the loyalty and cooperation of the National Tribunal, whose presiding justices willingly deferred to the Committee of National Welfare's wisdom. Whom the Committee denounced, the Tribunal condemned; and the Committee itself was composed of ardent Reparationists, real patriots, good men (with one or two exceptions, which should be attended to presently) upon whose constancy Whiss Valeur could always depend.

Whiss repaired to his office at the Committee of National Welfare and issued appropriate orders; thereafter, the Tribunal was ceaselessly busy. The deepest, weepy-walled dungeons of the old Sepulchre were occupied for the first time in centuries; then filled; and soon full to bursting. The excess captive population spilled over into a couple of smaller gaols: the Keep and the Treasury, situated upon opposing verges of the city. Soon these, too, were packed; and then the inadequate cells in the district gendarmeries began to fill. Certain select cellars and storehouses were likewise called to use, and in one notorious case, a dried-out well. It was a public disgrace. More space was required, else fewer prisoners. In Whiss's eyes, the problem's solution was obvious.

The Kokotte was busy, active, and well-nourished. At first her diet consisted of Whiss Valeur's political opponents, real and imagined. Recalcitrant or refractory members of the Constitutional Congress went first, in certain cases accompanied by their friends and family members. Offensive journalists, malcontents, and overly outspoken critics soon followed. Almost every day, a killing or two or three took place in the Sepulchre courtyard. The citizens of Sherreen soon grew inured to the sight of the Kokotte, with her hungry spikes and her naked victims. The initial shock of her appearance and method wore off quickly, and the public executions soon became, for many, a favorite form of free entertainment.

It was on a drizzling autumn morning that Whiss sat alone in his office, reading a communication from the police spy operating under the code name of Lentil Soup. The spy network was so extensive, its written output so voluminous, that the drudgery of perusing reports was ordinarily given over to upper-level administrators of the Gendarmerie and junior members of the Committee. Rarely was any submission directed to the attention of the Committee's President. But Lentil Soup's report was particularly noteworthy, touching as it did upon the comportment of the President's own cousin. Whiss read:

> . . . there are some who attend the executions nearly every day. Arriving early in the morning, in order to secure the best positions near the gate, the devoted often wait there for hours. These aficionados—the men dubbing themselves "Cavaliers of Kokotte," the women facetiously styling themselves "Coquettes of Kokotte"— have lately begun to affect an exquisite nicety. They have devised an elaborate system of ranking whereby condemned criminals are categorized according to imaginary standards of desirability. Many of these poseurs pretend to discern, by the play and intensity of luminosity, the precise degree of the Sentient Kokotte's pleasure in each offering.
>
> Among these Cavaliers and Coquettes, Compeer Bierce Valeur has assumed a certain celebrity status. They have bestowed many affectionate nicknames upon him; they toss presents, favors, notes, and other such sorry toys through the bars of the gate when he appears in the prison courtyard; they call out to him as he passes, wooing his notice—the men offering drinks and loans, the women offering anything and everything. It is much to his credit that Compeer Bierce takes no notice whatever of these impertinences. Wholly absorbed in his patriotic labors, sober and devoted agent of Reparationist justice, he ignores the follies and excesses of his admirers. Unhappily, the same cannot be said of the various participating Vanguardsmen, many of whom conduct a souvenir trade in the lengths of cord that are the Sentient Kokotte's sole leavings. Even the officers are not above engaging in this sordid commerce . . .

Whiss Valeur set the report aside, placing the paper precisely in its proper place upon the spotless, faultlessly ordered desktop. Lentil Soup was correct, of course. The souvenir trade in rope was unbecoming, unmilitary, and generally unacceptable. And yet, almost he could sympathize with the entrepreneurial Vanguardsmen. The soldiers only scrabbled for a few extra biquins; the needs of the Reparationist Party, while vastly larger in scope, were identical in kind. Money was required in quantity, and preferably without delay. Fortunately, a source was near at hand.

For months now, Whiss had been quietly filling the Sepulchre with Exalted prisoners—for the most part wealthy ones thought to have concealed significant sums that were the rightful property of the Vonahrish people. These criminals had proved uniformly unregenerate, refusing to divulge the whereabouts of their valuables and remaining obdurate in the face of the most inventive persuasions. They were worse than thieves, actually. They were enemies of the nation, deserving the punishment reserved for traitors. According to recently enacted Congressional legislation, such punishment included confiscation of the felon's entire fortune and estate, down to the last stick of furniture. Whiss took up a fresh sheet of paper and began to write. Shortly thereafter, the Kokotte graduated to a richer diet.

A dutiful National Tribunal confirmed the Committee of National Welfare's judgment. A dozen sketchy trials, conducted and concluded within a single day, resulted in twelve swift condemnations. The carrying out of the sentence followed without delay. Upon a sharp and hard autumnal morning, a file of twelve naked prisoners stumbled out into the Sepulchre courtyard, there to meet the Kokotte.

Whiss Valeur stood with his father at their usual post near the window in the central tower. From that height he had a clear view of the execution site and of the citizens clogging the street before the prison gate. The crowd was unusually large and volatile today, and no wonder. Never before had Vonahr witnessed such an event—a dozen Exalted dispatched en masse, without ceremony, like so many peasants—and popular curiosity was intense. Voices were strident, gestures expansive, and a restless jockeying for position continually stirred the spectators' ranks. Those too far from the gate to see—and this morning, there were many— were loud in their frustration. The Cavaliers and Coquettes of Kokotte, always at the forefront, were particularly conspicuous today. A number of Coquettes had embellished their hats with tall stalks, branches, wires, and glass beads designed to echo the Kokotte's crowning elaborations, and such headgear roused the noisy indignation of those whose view of the courtyard it blocked. To drown out criticism, the Coquettes and their male counterparts began to sing a mock-worshipful hymn to the Kokotte, set to a tune so bumptiously catchy that the crowd was soon joining in the choruses.

Whiss Valeur permitted himself a smile. He turned to his father. "I do not require your aid to gauge their mood today," he remarked.

Chorl manifestly did not want to be there. Dejection exuded from every pore. A weak vessel indeed, he was shocked and sickened by public executions. Still, his attendance was voluntary. Whiss had never commanded his father's presence, and the old man was perfectly free to stay away if he pleased. But Chorl chose to watch the Kokotte in action, apparently inflicting the sight upon himself as some sort of incomprehensible personal penance. And then he assumed tragic and wounded airs about it, doubtless by way of silent reproach.

Familiar resentment singed the edges of Whiss's mind. "They are excited— ebullient—even exhilarated, wouldn't you say?" he pushed. *"Wouldn't you say?"*

Chorl winced beneath the vocal lash. "Perhaps. You have been at pains to rouse them to their worst," he replied tiredly.

"Their worst? I have striven to instill a sense of patriotism; and not, I think, without success."

"Yes, you have worked hard. For weeks now, you have bombarded the populace with pamphlets and broadsides. You have exhorted the Congress, mustered the Reparationists, courted the Vanguard and the Vonahrish Guard, rallied the faithful by torchlight. Every sentence that you have written, every word that you have uttered, has been calculated to kindle smoldering class hatred to open flame. You have labored well and truly, and the success of your efforts reveals itself upon the faces in the crowd below us now."

"Quite a speech, Father. Melodramatic, inaccurate, irrational—quite up to your usual standard. As always, I appreciate your loyalty, your understanding, and your support." For once, it required little effort for Whiss to maintain an acid smile and an air of composure. His father's observations, stingingly accurate though they were, paradoxically soothed his irritation to rest. For the accusations confirmed a single essential and gratifying truth: as always, the Sherreenian crowd had proved itself his faithful friend and slave.

Chorl sighed heavily and looked away. Whiss followed his gaze. Down below, the prison door opened. The condemned and their captors stepped forth. The crowd rustled, sighed, and tried its weight against the gate. A hush fell; the intent, staring silence of a mantis.

Unclothed, the Exalted greatly resembled their plebeian inferiors. There was really nothing visible to set them apart from common mortals. The twelve men— two of them actually titled seigneurs—were shivering, presumably from the shock of the chilly autumn air upon their bare flesh, and not from fear. Their faces were still and unrevealing, carriage upright and seemingly undaunted. They were Exalted, after all.

As the prisoners drew near, Kokotte somehow recognized her prey. The small lightnings began to crackle along her horns, and strong anticipatory vibrations rattled her internal spikes. Even Bierce Valeur, who stood at her side crooning endearments, did not venture to touch her at such a moment.

This time, Governor Egure did not read the charges aloud; he would have gone hoarse before he got through that list. There was only a quick statement of the

Tribunal's verdict and sentence, followed by a listing of the prisoners' names and titles. This concluding, Bierce was free to proceed.

Kokotte displayed a hearty appetite, consuming all twelve bodies within half an hour. Down below in the crowd, the pretentious Cavaliers and Coquettes, claiming special insight, were no doubt asserting their divinity's particular pleasure in the delicacy of the feast. To Whiss Valeur, however, it was clear that the Kokotte made no distinction between Exalted and plebeian flesh, devouring each with equal enthusiasm—an edifying display. Once and for all, the myth of Exalted superiority was exposed, the reality of Exalted vulnerability publicly confirmed; here was the most elemental proof of it. The blaze of brilliance signaling the demise of the Baron vo Beune-v'Abeaux, last of the prisoners, drew a fierce howl from the crowd, and then a great cheering arose, so triumphant and prolonged that even Bierce Valeur took note, frowning suspiciously but shrugging his shoulders and ducking his head a little in acknowledgment of the acclaim.

Whiss Valeur felt pleasurably warm all over, despite the weather. Beside him, his father emitted a small nauseated gurgle and turned abruptly from the window. Whiss scarcely noticed; his good humor remained intact, and with reason. The Sherreenian crowd, so carefully cultivated for such a long time, had responded like a dancing bear to the signals of its master. That popular enthusiasm down there trumpeted his victory. The mob supported him, as always; the Vanguard was devoted, the Vonahrish Guard favorably disposed. In the glow of that hot popularity, his power and prospects all but unlimited, he was free to pursue his aims almost without fear of opposition. Those aims grew clearer by the day. His course was straight and sure; marked out, he was deeply certain, by Destiny.

Thereafter, Exalted arrests and executions became commonplace. Usually the arrests occurred at night, when the Vanguardsmen swept down without warning upon target dwellings. Inhabitants, including servants, were bundled into the increasingly notorious closed carriages and removed to the Sepulchre under cover of darkness. The morning sun would rise upon yet another Exalted town house bearing on its front door a fresh black circle surrounding a scarlet diamond, emblem of the Committee of National Welfare and symbol of congressional confiscation. The Kokotte's daily offering in the Sepulchre courtyard now routinely included a quota of Exalted, and the audience had grown used to the sight of doomed seigneurs. Something beyond the victim's mere Exalted status was now required to stimulate increasingly jaded Sherreenian sensibilities. The first public sacrifice of a woman—one Madame Hiroux, a person of no importance, but known to have aided enemies of the state—excited unusual interest, and was heavily attended by citizens keen to appraise the victim's physique. Other women followed Madame Hiroux, and the novelty wore off, not to be fully revived until the first execution of an Exalted female, the luckless dowager Countess vo Prosq, known conspirator against the Committee of National Welfare. Popular interest in such spectacle eventually lost something of its initial intensity, but never altogether died out, and the death of an acknowledged beauty was always certain to draw a lively crowd. Similarly popular victims included the very young or old, the excessively obese or scrawny, the interestingly infirm, and above all, the crippled or deformed.

As Exalted executions increased in frequency, even the proudest and bravest among the formerly privileged were forced to take note. Mounting alarm was manifest in a sudden rash of attempted departures, undertaken in deliberate defiance of ordinances restricting Exalted travel. A few of the most arrogant (or perhaps only the dimmest) among the would-be emigrants took to the streets in their own blazoned carriages, apparently even yet unable to believe that anyone would presume to hinder them. Prompt arrest at the city gates demonstrated their error. Sepulchral incarceration followed, terminating in trial and speedy execution; for the crime of emigration, formerly punishable by mere confiscation of property, now carried the death penalty.

Schooled by their peers' disastrous example, the wiser among Exalted fugitives approached the city gates incognito. Anonymity, however, was far more often sought than achieved.

"What is happening at the city gates?" Eliste demanded of the Cavalier vo Meureille. She sat alone with him in the Rouvignac parlor. Zeralenn would appear any moment, but for this brief space of time, she had Meureille to herself for once, and she could ask the questions impossible to utter in her grandmother's presence. "I've heard wild stories from the servants. They talk of demon-sentries and mechanical monsters guarding the exits. They say that no Exalted escapes recognition—that no disguise deceives the monster—but surely these are idle rumors. I am all but imprisoned here, Madame pretends that nothing is amiss, and I am starved for news. You know everything, Cavalier—take pity, and tell me what is really happening."

"You somewhat overestimate my powers, Exalted Miss, but I will do my best." Meureille, gray-clad and silver-haired, was elegant as ever, but unwontedly dark under the eyes. The collapse of his world could not shake his perfect gallantry of manner, but almost he was beginning to look his age. "It is best you learn that the servants' tales of demons and monsters are fictions layered upon a kernel of truth. The sentries at the city gates, for example, are not demons, but only mortal men superbly trained in the arts of detection. To them, Exalted quality reveals itself in the smallest quirks of speech and accent, in gait and posture, in fleeting expressions, in a hundred signs almost too slight and tiny to register upon the conscious mind, but source of a potent intuition that at times appears supernatural."

"Maybe they're clever, but they're only human, and not even Exalted, at that. Surely they can be outwitted."

"Perhaps. But human intuition is scarcely the greatest danger to confront escaping Exalteds. There remains the matter of the mechanical monsters."

"Mythical, I trust?"

"Not altogether. You're aware that all traffic departing Sherreen is now routinely directed to the North Gate?"

Eliste nodded.

"The Stupefaction at the gate has been awakened. She is now known as the Sentient Boomette. Fashioned to serve as the ultimate guard and civic watchdog, she is able to recognize the few Exalted fugitives whose craft has defeated the human guards. How she accomplishes this, I cannot pretend to guess; and probably neither could anyone else, saving an accomplished magical adept. Her admirers believe her capable of reading minds."

"Ridiculous—a machine!" He did not answer, and Eliste's assumed assurance faltered. "But surely you can't believe such stories?"

"Exalted Miss, I honestly do not know what to believe. On the face of it, the claim appears absurd. Yet the Sentient Boomette has repeatedly demonstrated her ability to pick out disguised Exalted fugitives lost in the midst of a common crowd; and to accomplish so much, it would almost seem that she must glimpse thought, or mental images. Whether she does so or not, one thing is certain: the Sentient Boomette is far more to be feared than the keenest of human sentries."

"And whom has she picked out?" Eliste didn't want to know, but couldn't bear not knowing.

"Stazzi vo Crev and his sister were both taken at the gate last week. One of the vo Pleniere-v'Orenne cousins was unmasked a few days ago. Three of the vo Chaumelle family, including your friend Gizine, are in the Sepulchre now. And there was also . . ." His voice went on, the unthinkable list continued, each name a wound.

"But those are among the greatest families of Vonahr. The vo Crevs—they have married into royalty from time to time. A vo Chaumelle was commander in chief of the Vonahrish armies in the Jurlian-Zenki Wars; that name goes back *forever*. Surely the canaille would not presume to harm them. Arrest them, yes, but they would never dare to—to . . ." Her voice trailed off.

"Stazzi vo Crev will be executed tomorrow afternoon," Meureille informed her expressionlessly. "The others I have named will shortly follow, to be followed in turn by many others of equally Exalted rank. Mere eminence no longer furnishes the slightest protection; quite the contrary, in fact. Lately, each afternoon's parade of sacrificial victims includes a quota of Exalteds, often of the highest nobility. Far from decrying the brutality, the Sherreenian mob relishes the spectacle. Every day, the street before the Sepulchre courtyard gate is thronged from dawn to dusk, and quite impassable to traffic. The noise and nuisance are so extreme that a sizable faction of neighborhood residents demands the Kokotte's removal to some alternative site, and the matter is periodically debated in Congress." He spoke in a quiet, almost matter-of-fact tone that somehow underscored the horror of his news, and he was staring straight into her shocked eyes.

Unable to sustain the level gaze, Eliste looked away, wishing with all her heart that she had known better than to question him.

"But come, did you know nothing of this? Have you no idea what goes on in the world about you?" Perfect courtesy did not altogether mask his impatience. "Do you never read the popular journals?"

"Madame does not encourage it." Eliste stirred uncomfortably. "She considers them vulgar."

"Ah, she seeks to protect you, but I think she does you no real service in preserving your ignorance. You are not a child, and it is time your eyes were opened. Here, then, Exalted Miss——" Meureille reached into his pocket and brought forth a wad of folded tabloids, cheaply printed on coarse yellowish paper.

Eliste accepted almost reluctantly. A trio of titles jumped off the pages at her. *The Compeer*, official mouthpiece of the Reparationist Party; *The Ink Sac*, audacious underground successor to the recently burked *Rat Town Gadfly*; and Shorvi Nirienne's latest essay, *The New Tyrants*. For a moment she was tempted to refuse them, but curiosity overcame her, and she quickly stowed the papers away out of sight in her little burled lue-wood sewing box that sat on the floor beside her chair.

"Read them, Exalted Miss," Meureille urged, "and you will learn. Perhaps you will come to comprehend the magnitude of the danger that surrounds us. And when you do, perhaps you will succeed where I have not in swaying the will of your grandmother. Try to make her understand. Tell her that the path to safety remains clear, although not forever. Tell her this protracted lingering is sheerest madness. And if she will not believe you, then tell her——"

"Still seeking to corrupt my granddaughter, Cavalier?" Zeralenn stood in the doorway.

Meureille and Eliste swiveled guiltily to face her. Meureille was instantly on his feet and bowing. "Seeking to recruit her, I confess it, Countess. The old soldier overlooks no possible resource."

"Nor does the old marauder, nor does the old corsair. Bah, Meureille, such tactics are beneath you. Unworthy and useless, quite useless."

Eliste wondered if her grandmother had caught the transfer of newsprint. Impossible to judge by her face, of course. Zeralenn entered and seated herself. Conversation resumed, and the Cavalier's lapse was not mentioned again.

Later, much later that night, alone in the privacy of her own chamber, Eliste finally perused Meureille's offering. The content of the tabloids more or less confirmed her expectations. The proscribed liberal Nirienne was now criticizing the Reparationist regime as he had once censured the monarchy. Much good it was likely to do him; the man was finished, even if he didn't seem to know it. Likewise, *The Ink Sac* echoed Nirienne's dissenting voice, but in language accessible to the ordinary citizen. *The Compeer,* of which she had a pair of thin issues, was of course filled with articles and essays certain to outrage Exalted readers. Eliste was frightened and depressed, as the Cavalier no doubt intended she should be. The journals possessed one merit, however: they helped to keep her mind off pretty, frivolous little Gizine vo Chaumelle, locked up in the Sepulchre—almost anything was better than thinking about that . . .

One boldface title in *The Compeer* caught her eye: "Nits of NuNu Uncover Conspiracy."

Eliste knew all about the nits. By this time, everyone in Sherreen knew about the nits. Deep in the cellar of the City Armory, several thousand of the golden eggs deposited by the Sentient NuNu had finally hatched. The liberated nits—tiny, metallic, winged, and hungry for knowledge—had taken to the air at once, overspreading all of Sherreen within hours. Everywhere they buzzed in search of information; and though an army of them perished—swatted, crunched, and flattened by irritated citizens—thousands survived to carry morsels of news back to their queenly mother. NuNu accepted, digested, and excreted all; and thus her human workers discovered conspiracy hitherto undreamt of.

For months now, numbers of Exalted—some of them among the richest and noblest, and therefore the greatest debtors to society—had been disappearing, almost under the nose of the Vanguard. Repeatedly, arresting officers had struck by night, to discover houses devoid of occupants, cash, and jewelry. Impossible that so many Exalteds—entire families of them—had fooled the guardians at the North Gate. Equally impossible that so many should succeed in concealing themselves within the bounds of the city itself; not when information leading to the capture of highborn fugitives was now worth a five-rekko reward. Yet they continued to vanish, apparently into thin air. Infuriating, uncanny, and quite inexplicable—until now; until the vigilance of NuNu's nits revealed the existence of a secret exit, presided over by some phantom gatekeeper. Somebody—evidently a resident Exalted, aided by a small band of associates—was conducting his fellow peers from the city upon a regular and frequent basis. As yet the traitor's identity, together with the nature and location of the escape route, remained unknown. All should eventually come to light, however. Now that the nits were abroad, it was only a matter of time; and then the Kokotte should have him, whoever he was.

Eliste read, and shivered. Did the Cavalier vo Meureille know of this? Silly question. Obviously he knew, and didn't care; or rather, didn't intend to acknowledge it, much less let it stop him—classic Exalted panache . . .

But the genuine concern for vo Meureille was driven clean out of her head when she caught sight of the black title disfiguring the front page of the second *Compeer*: "The King's Treason." It took a moment to become real. And then she read:

> The Committee of National Welfare has today announced its acquisition of certain documents confirming the complicity of his Majesty Dunulas in a plot to murder the Constitutional Congress. It has been revealed that the King, aided and encouraged by his wife, has for months engaged in criminal correspondence with the fugitive-emigrant former Duke of Feronte. This guilty trio, abetted by foreign powers hostile to Vonahrish liberty, together with assorted domestic absolutist reactionaries, schemed to fill the cellars of Century Hall with barrels of gunpowder; a project already in a state approaching completion at the time of the Committee's investigation. Successful consummation of the conspiracy should undoubtedly have ensured the destruction of the entire Congress, together with the innocent patriot-spectators in the galleries, the Century Hall itself, and a considerable portion of the surrounding district. The terror and confusion attendant upon this massacre should well have served the ends of those foreign and domestic enemies seeking to work the utter ruination of Vonahrish liberty.
>
> But for the Committee of National Welfare's unceasing vigilance, the plot must have succeeded, to the grief of all true patriots. The minds that give rise to such treachery are less human than diabolical; the men and women capable of loosing such villainy upon their own countrymen are less criminals than monsters in human form, deserving of the extreme penalty.

Eliste read disbelievingly. *Deserving of the extreme penalty.* The words simply made no sense. They were talking about the *King*. It was impossible. She read again. And again. The words began to clarify. Not impossible.

For the last year and more, while the Constitutional Congress charted an erratic national course, Dunulas XIII had pottered aimlessly about the Beviaire, a docile prisoner, amiably anxious to avoid inconveniencing his captors. Throughout the period of his detention, he had maintained such acquiescent silence that many of his supposed subjects had all but forgotten his existence. They would remember now, however. They would certainly remember now.

No wonder Zeralenn had tried to keep such newspapers out of her granddaughter's hands. Perhaps it would have been better if she had succeeded. Eliste set the journal aside on her nightstand, blew out the candle, and lay back in bed. Sleep eluded her, however. For a long time, she lay wide awake, insomniac prey to chill foreboding.

The King's trial, conducted behind closed doors, was almost perfunctory. Such speed and discretion were well-advised. Otherwise, the mild and wide-eyed bemusement with which his Majesty responded to the charges might have won him too many supporters. He knew nothing of any gunpowder, Dunulas earnestly insisted. He knew nothing of treason and plot. He had not corresponded with his brother Feronte. He wished harm upon no one. He desired nothing beyond the peace and contentment of his subjects. As hereditary king, was it not only natural that he should love his own people?

The National Tribunal was almost hard put to convict him. A couple of the justices showed signs of weakness, even appearing to waver a little. For it still seemed to some of them, fanatical Reparationists though they were, an awesome thing to take the life of their king. Fortunately, solid evidence existed to bolster sagging resolve. There were documents to examine, incriminating letters copied in the fair hand of the King's private secretary and bearing Dunulas's own scrawled initials; or so it seemed.

In vain the King professed his bewildered ignorance. The documents appeared to be his. If indeed they were forgeries, it was up to his Majesty to prove that claim. Dunulas predictably proved unequal to the task, and conviction swiftly followed. Thereafter, a death sentence was inevitable, and the astonished King heard himself condemned as "an enemy of the nation," "an enemy of Mankind," and "an enemy of the People's Revolution." The sentence was innovative in two respects, marking the first judicial disposal of a Vonahrish monarch, hitherto only slain in battle, or sometimes frankly murdered; and also marking the first official self-recognition of the Revolution—accomplished in fact a year earlier, but never before openly acknowledged for what it was.

The execution of Dunulas XIII could hardly be carried out in the Sepulchre courtyard; an event so momentous required a more impressive setting. The

Committee of National Welfare opted for the Circle of the Grand Monarch, recently restyled "Equality Circle"—dignified, and large enough to accommodate the thousands who would surely assemble to witness the Revolution's ultimate triumph. The Kokotte was duly conveyed to the designated site, but not without incident.

Despite the genuine revolutionary fervor of most citizens, a monarchist element yet remained to challenge the Tribunal's judgment. The proscribed traitor Shorvi Nirienne, who dared not show his face, wrote from hiding to question both the necessity and the legality of the King's execution. His sedition found its audience, and sporadic rioting broke out all over town; the most serious incident involving an assault upon the Kokotte herself, en route to her new post. It was cunningly planned, the monarchist forces waiting for their target to reach the midway point of the Bridge Vinculum before launching a double-pronged attack. And they would no doubt have succeeded in their aim of tumbling the Kokotte down into the River Vir, but for the intervention of the Sentient ZaZa, whose blasts of green fire and choking vapor swiftly cleared the Bridge Vinculum of all rioters.

The charred corpses were cleared from the bridge, the interrupted progress resumed, and the Kokotte reached Equality Circle, where she was enshrined upon a suitably tall platform, with Vanguardsmen stationed below to worship and to guard her day and night.

Two days later, a vast crowd assembled in Equality Circle to witness the execution of the King. Among the spectators stood Shorvi Nirienne, trusting in a dark wig and a pair of wire-rimmed spectacles to preserve his anonymity. Initially intending a solitary excursion, he had at the last moment surrendered to the pleas of his associates, allowing Beq to accompany him. The younger man now stood at his side.

Nirienne allowed his eyes to wander about the Circle. He noted that the Sentient ZaZa was on hand to maintain public order; but her presence was superfluous, for the crowd's mood was curiously subdued and somber, even melancholy. The weather echoed the public demeanor: the skies were overcast, and the first thin snowflakes of winter dusted the breeze.

Nirienne, together with a host of others, watched almost incredulously as the guarded closed carriage containing the King arrived at the foot of the scaffold. The door opened. His former Majesty emerged and, without fanfare, mounted the wooden steps. Perhaps in concession to the cold weather, or perhaps in outmoded deference to his rank, the King had been accorded the decency of a long cloak, which was not removed until the last moment. Nirienne winced as the rotund royal body was exposed; bone-deep republican convictions could not altogether banish his shocked sense of lèse majesté. Nor was he the only one to feel it. All about him, he heard the hiss of sharply indrawn breath. Even the imperturbable Beq was not immune.

Dunulas XIII faced death as he had faced life—with benevolent incomprehension. Nirienne watched as the condemned monarch addressed some sort of remark, presumably a request, to his captors. The response was negative, and the King appeared mildly disappointed; probably he had sought leave to address the crowd. Disappointment notwithstanding, he could not have suffered much at the end. His eyes widened more in amazement than fear at sight of the Kokotte's spikes, and he could not have felt more than an instant's winter chill upon his flesh before Bierce Valeur's firm shove thrust him into the Sentient's cavity.

The leaden doors clapped shut.

A radiant play of force along the Kokotte's horns, a mounting intensity, and then the flaring, blinding consummation.

The doors parted to reveal an empty interior, and a sigh swept the crowd, a murmurous breath of solemn wonder. Although a scattering of Reparationists threw their caps in the air and cheered at the top of their lungs, they did not succeed in rousing the audience to enthusiasm.

The harmless, foolish King of Vonahr was dead by the hand of his own subjects, who now for the first time seemed to recognize the significance of their action. They had blasted the traditions of centuries, Shorvi Nirienne reflected. They had razed the worm-eaten social structure to the ground. They had destroyed the familiar, the comprehensible, in favor of—what? A sense of uneasy sadness, even regret, suffused the crowd—a kind of instant nostalgia. They had clamored for change, and now they should have it perforce. Beside him, his companion echoed his unspoken thoughts.

"There is no going back," said Beq.

Nirienne was not in attendance one week later, when Queen Lallazay followed her husband. Rather, he stood at a safe-house window, listening stone-faced as the ringing of bells and the firing of salutes announced the declaration of the new Republic of Vonahr. On the floor at his feet, where he had let it fall, lay the latest issue of *The Compeer*, whose lead article announced the Constitutional Congress's designation of Whiss Valeur as acting Protector of the Republic; a temporary position, and yet, owing to the nature of the crisis at hand, necessarily endowed with extraordinary powers. One day, the restoration of social equilibrium would permit all citizens the luxury of perfect freedom; in the meantime, Whiss Valeur enjoyed authority rivaling that of any monarch Vonahr had ever known.

•　　•　　•

The official birth of the new republic was marked by upheaval both in the capital and the provinces. Loyalist revolt flared briefly in Fabeque, Jouvier, and VoGrance. Its suppression was particularly brutal, marked by wholesale slaughter of insurgents. There were protests and celebrations, riots and jubilations, everywhere.

In Sherreen, the streets hummed day and night. There was an odd quality of excitement in the air, a peculiar abandon, a shared sense of living in extraordinary times. During those first days of the new Republic of Vonahr, possibility seemed infinite. It was enough to drive the impressionable to hysteria, and frequently did so. The city never slept, and violence was endemic; most of it directed against Exalted scapegoats. Never before had Exalteds been so energetically hated. Those trapped in the city cowered behind closed doors like caged mice. Neither their property nor their persons were safe. Exalteds so unlucky as to be recognized in public were chased, robbed, stripped, and beaten—not infrequently, beaten to death. No protection was offered by law or government; and there was no escape, save for those fortunate few departing the city by secret pathways.

Neither Vanguard nor city Gendarmerie doubted the existence of a hidden tunnel beneath the city wall. Their best combined efforts, however, succeeded in uncovering neither the tunnel's location nor the identity of its steward. The weeks passed, they learned nothing, and Exalted emigrants continued to slip through their fingers. The authorities might eventually have been forced to admit defeat, had it not been for the random, fortuitous entrance of a golden nit, no larger than a bumblebee, into the private study of the Cavalier vo Meureille.

I have called the two of you here this morning to inform you that we are departing Sherreen," Zeralenn announced. "You may each carry away so many of your belongings as will fit in a single valise. Prepare yourselves at once, for we shall be leaving shortly—tonight, in fact."

Eliste and Aurelie gaped at her. Eliste wondered if her grandmother had been seized with some sudden hysteria. But Zeralenn did not appear in the least hysterical. Her spine was straight, expression serene as ever. Her face seemed a trifle haggard and perhaps a little sad, but the layer of cosmetics masked such signs of weakness. The tired effect may have been enhanced by a severe black gown that was aging and unbecoming, as well as illegal. The wearing of black by members of the class formerly known as "Exalted" (all hereditary titles of nobility and privilege having recently been abolished by Congressional mandate) was now a crime; for overt mourning of the dead traitors Dunulas and Lallazay was a deliberate affront to republican solidarity, and as such, punishable by death. That, however, did not deter Zeralenn vo Rouvignac, within the privacy of her own home.

Private only so long as we keep the nits out, thought Eliste, eyes automatically scanning the walls, the floor, the ceiling, and furnishings of her grandmother's morning room in search of the telltale flash of gold signifying surveillance. How many Exalted—how many of the people she knew—had now lost their lives through the agency of NuNu's nits? How many tiny indiscretions, how many thoughtless, overheard comments had led her friends to Equality Circle and the

Kokotte these past few weeks? She had lost count. Wealth, position, breeding, wit, beauty, youth, innocence—none of these formerly powerful charms offered the slightest protection. Gizine vo Chaumelle was gone, along with most of her family; and the Count vo Brajonard, Riste and Fovier vo Dev-v'Urois, and far too many others. The remaining Exalted had learned caution, screening their windows and doorways with translucent muslin stretched upon wooden frames, their fireplaces with fine metallic mesh, and routinely checking every room each day for invasive presence. Despite all care, however, infiltration was not infrequent, and it was never advisable to discount the possibility of observation.

"Well, children?" Zeralenn's brows rose. "You sit as if petrified. Have I failed to make myself clear?"

"You must excuse our astonishment, Madame," Eliste replied. "For months you've refused even to discuss the possibility of retreat. And now, today, so very suddenly—"

"What about living bravely and freely in Sherreen like true Exalted?" Aurelie wanted to know. "What about not permitting fear to govern your actions? What about all that you said? Didn't you mean any of it, Grauntie? What—"

"What has happened to change your mind?" Eliste finished.

Zeralenn surveyed her youthful relatives, as if gauging their fortitude, and then replied dispassionately, "About an hour ago, a summons arrived. All members of this household are required to present themselves at the District Gendarmerie within twenty-four hours, there to take the Oath."

There it was—an unequivocal death sentence; a shocking blow, despite its predictability.

The new Oath of Allegiance comprised a promise of unconditional fealty to the Republican Protectorate of Vonahr, together with a repudiation of the monarchy in general and the "traitor-tyrant Dunulas" in particular. Citizens of all degree were obliged to repeat the ritual denunciation of "royalists, absolutists, reactionaries, elitists, malcontents, social parasites, and all such enemies of the Motherland," and to pledge their eagerness to die in defense of Vonahrish liberty. It was a statement deliberately designed to goad outraged Exalteds into open defiance— a victory in Republican eyes, for resistance to the Oath of Allegiance constituted clear proof of absolutism, sufficient to send the exposed traitor and his family straight to the Kokotte without recourse to the empty formality of a trial. The property of such traitors was automatically forfeit to the state. As its authors intended, the Oath of Allegiance presented surviving Exalteds with an impossible choice: on the one hand, loss of life and property; on the other, loss of honor in swearing falsely, betrayal of the ancient code of Exalted loyalties, amounting to moral death. Faced with such a dilemma, more than one Exalted had, after the stern fashion of the ancients, sought escape in self-slaughter. Formerly, these had included only such unfortunates already suspected of varied crimes against the Republican Protectorate. But now, no formal accusation was necessary—they had dispensed with that pretense. Summonses of the kind that Zeralenn had received were now widely distributed, their wholesale issuance presaging the systematic extermination of the entire Exalted class.

The canaille meant to kill them all; partly for ancient fear and hatred's sake, but mostly to seize their wealth.

But it's monstrous—fantastic—impossible.

Not at all impossible.

Surely, surely there must still be decent people to speak up against all this.

The decent people are frightened, or misled, or both. No help there.

"A debt of blood and pain . . . may be repaid with interest, one day."

The long-ago words of Dref Zeenoson rang in her mind, and Eliste felt the blood drain from her cheeks.

But Aurelie evinced no such dismay. "Well, perhaps we should just take the Oath, then," she suggested. "Then they'll leave us alone."

Eliste and Zeralenn stared at her whitely.

"Well—well—they would, wouldn't they?" Aurelie wilted perceptibly. "Why are you looking at me like that? We must tell the creatures what they want to hear, and then we shall be safe and comfortable. I know fibbing's bad form, but they haven't left us any choice at all, have they? We cannot help it, so we can hardly be blamed. Anyway, it scarcely signifies what we say to *them,* so where's the harm? It seems quite plain to me."

"Child Aurelie." The look of sadness beneath Zeralenn's layer of paint was now unmistakable. "Very often I have ascribed your trivialities, your vulgarities and banalities, to the characteristic shallowness of youth. I have reminded myself that your blood is good, and I have trusted in that heritage to correct the worst of your faults. What I have just heard, however, forces me to doubt. I must wonder if you were not born devoid of some essential quality."

"Rather like an egg without a yolk," Eliste suggested. "Rather like a tart without jam."

"That's *mean,* Cousin!"

"There is an emptiness in you, Child Aurelie—a blank void in place of pride, self-respect, and honor."

"Not true! Not true! I have lots of self-respect—lots of pride and honor! Heaps of 'em! La, Grauntie, I don't understand you, I swear I don't! I meant no harm at all. Why so furious a pother over so small a matter?"

"Precisely because you do not understand that it is not small."

"Oh—gad! Oh—really!" Aurelie's cheeks flushed red, and she drummed her green-lacquered fingernails nervously upon the arm of her chair. A matching streak of green shot her brown curls. Nails and hair were each dyed the precise shade of the identifying cockade that law now required every formerly Exalted citizen to wear at all times. Within doors, Zeralenn and Eliste each defied the regulation. Aurelie wore her green cockade, but the child had rather touchingly turned oppression to flirtatious advantage. Absurdly, the green accents suited her, brightening her skin and sparking her eyes. "If I'm so bad as all that, then I'm very sorry, la! But after all, Grauntie, *you're* the one who speaks now of running away—"

"Do not try my patience with foolish impertinence. For myself, I should not stir from this house. But I have lived a very full life, and what is apt and appropriate for me is not so for you and your cousin, whose lives have hardly begun. I have exposed you both to danger by keeping you here in the city throughout these past months, but I do not regret that, for courage in the face of adversity is an obligation of our class, and it is best that you learn it early. Obligation, however, does not extend to passive acceptance of death; and that is what now confronts us if we remain."

Frowning, Aurelie studied her fingernails.

"Where shall we go?" asked Eliste.

"Indeed, where should we go but to Strell, there to offer such service as lies within our power to render his Majesty?"

Eliste started. It still surprised her to recall that the fugitive Duke of Feronte, currently living in Strellian exile, was now the rightful King of Vonahr. It seemed unreal—almost she could imagine that there would never be another true king. Perhaps it was for that reason she thrilled so at the prospect of escape. Vonahr was polluted beyond hope of immediate recovery. It might take years, even decades, to restore a reasonable social balance. In the meantime, flight was the obviously attractive course, and she suddenly realized how much she desired it. For months now she had lived in the shadow of fear, confusion, misery. She wanted to get away from all of them. She wanted ease, plenty, security. She wanted the world back the way it should be, and that meant flight—a new beginning, somewhere in a sane world with sound standards, where high blood ruled as Nature intended. Yes, it was time to go.

"Well, we can't go." Aurelie's lower lip protruded. "They won't let us out. We can't get past the gate."

"There is another way open to us."

Having eavesdropped with profit months earlier, Eliste already knew what that way was; but Aurelie appeared uncomprehending and skeptical.

"The Cavalier vo Meureille has offered many times to conduct us from Sherreen by way of a tunnel running beneath the city wall," Zeralenn told them. "Now it is time to accept his offer."

"So *he's* the one with that mysterious tunnel we've heard so much of—vo Meureille! But how romantic—how dashing—how frantically *stylish*! Only to think, in all these months I never guessed! Gad, what a slyboots your lover is, Grauntie! I swear, I never thought—"

"I have already dispatched a message to the Cavalier," Zeralenn continued as if she had not heard, or did not wish to. "And I do not doubt a swift reply, wherein he will specify the hour and location of our meeting. Presumably we shall depart under cover of darkness, which gives the two of you the rest of the day in which to complete your preparations. Pack your bags; dress yourselves plainly and warmly. Proceed with discretion. It is better if the servants do not know."

"Madame, you doubt them?" Eliste was mildly surprised.

"Quite the contrary. The loyalty they have displayed in remaining beneath an Exalted roof has already compromised them to the point of danger, and I wish to avoid compounding their difficulties. If they learned in advance of our departure, they would no doubt insist upon accompanying us, and I would not see them subject themselves to such risk upon our account. It is best if they remain in Sherreen, honestly ignorant of our whereabouts."

"Kairthe can't stay here all by herself," said Eliste. "She is—was—a Derrivalle serf, one of our people, so I must look after her."

"Very well, Granddaughter, you may bring your woman; but see to it that she is properly schooled. We cannot permit chance indiscretion to betray us en route."

"How shall we travel, Madame?"

"Once beyond the walls of Sherreen, we shall find it relatively easy to make our way by stage to Arenne, where we must hire passage upon a ship bound for Strell. No doubt Meureille will arrange such matters on our behalf."

"Strell. *Strell*, la! It is so far away, and so foreign." Aurelie's lower lip jutted emphatically. "And I do not see why we have to go. I don't believe the canaille will really harm us. After all, we have done nothing wrong. And probably most of those awful stories we hear aren't even true. I still don't see why we mightn't simply repeat that trifling Oath. La, where's the shame in mumbling a little foolish ribble-rabble—empty words that we should despise in our hearts? What harm in that? And then they would leave us alone, and we could stay here."

"Aurelie—!" Eliste began furiously, but a gesture from her grandmother silenced her.

"I can only hope you do not comprehend the full extent of your own baseness," Zeralenn replied slowly, in the iciest voice Eliste had ever heard. Her hazel eyes were cold as northern granite in winter, and she sat frozenly upright. "Listen carefully, and perhaps you will understand. I have never in my life been so ashamed of you as I am at this moment. You disgrace your family name, you disgrace the entire Exalted order, and I sorrow to acknowledge you as one of ours.

But mark this, girl. If ever again I hear you speak of repeating the Reparationists' vile Oath, I will disown you. I will never forgive you, never speak to you again, and you will no longer be my kinswoman."

Before Zeralenn had half finished, the frightened tears were streaming down Aurelie's face. "Grauntie——" she implored.

"There is nothing more to say. I trust I have made myself clear, and I assume you realize I am in earnest. That is all. You may go."

The two girls curtsied, and hurried from the room. Eliste cast one brief glance back at her grandmother, sitting perfectly upright, unyielding and infinitely inflexible. Aurelie was still crying. No sooner had the door closed behind them than her muted whimpers gave way to open sobs.

"Unfair! Unfair! So unkind! And it just isn't fair!"

"Aurelie——" Eliste found her own anger ebbing. Her cousin was only a child after all——giddy and thoughtless, but basically sound. Age would surely improve her——wouldn't it? "I know she seems hard, but try to understand how deeply you grieved her. Have you no idea what the Oath of Allegiance actually represents?"

"Oh, who cares about that? I'm not interested in that! Did you hear the dreadful things she said to me? She doesn't understand how easily wounded I am, or she could never have been so cruel! Oh, Cousin, what am I to do? I don't want to leave Sherreen! I cannot bear it!"

"My dear, we have no choice. Can't you see that?"

"Oh, that's easy for *you* to say! *You* have nothing and no one to hold you here, so what does it matter to *you*?"

"Is it not the same for us all?"

"Cousin, as my confidante and sometime chaperone, you above all should know better. For me, there is——Bayelle."

"What, still?" Eliste was taken by surprise. The Viscount vo Clarivaux still occupied his Avenue Parabeau town house, but weeks earlier, he had taken the precaution of sending his young son and sole heir into hiding. Bayelle had vanished overnight, and it seemed unlikely that anyone outside the Clarivaux family knew of his whereabouts. "Come, that is impractical. Quite probably your young beau has already fled the city."

"No, he hasn't."

"You can't know that."

"Oh, can't I?" Aurelie's cheeks were wet, but she was smiling, almost with a hint of smugness. "You do not imagine, surely, that my Bayelle would allow me to languish in lonely ignorance? He could not do so——he adores me, he is absolutely head over heels! I'll swear he cannot live without me, la!"

"Quite. So you actually know where he is?"

"Certainly I know, although you must understand I cannot reveal so deep a secret even to you, my faithful confidante. Do not plead or press me, for I must never yield. Suffice it to say, my Bayelle remains here in Sherreen, and— Oh, how *can* I possibly leave him, Cousin? I cannot—I simply cannot!"

"Hush, Aurelie. Listen to me. We must leave, and there's really not much point in carrying on about it. Just be grateful there's still a way out. But this madness won't last forever. Someday things will be right again, and we'll resume our normal lives. If Bayelle is as devoted as you claim, won't he wait for you?"

"He would wait for me until the end of time. For him, there will never be another. I know this. But—but—" A worried frown creased Aurelie's brow. "—What if I cannot wait for *him*?"

"Oh, eternal love is on the wane?"

"Certainly not. I adore my Bayelle, and I always will. And yet—as you know, Cousin, I am of an affectionate and deeply passionate nature—and gad, there are so many pretty fellows about! In Bayelle's absence, I am bound to be pursued by many, and what if I should weaken and succumb? What then?"

"Then I'd say you should have a new beau."

"But perhaps not as good as the old. Perhaps I should not profit by the exchange, perhaps I would regret it. I must think of that."

"Impossible child, whatever shall we do with you?"

"Of course," Aurelie mused, "if I lost him, I could always win him back whenever I wanted. But perhaps it is best simply to hold fast. Why alter perfection? But if I do not, who knows what opportunities might be lost?"

"These are significant issues," Eliste agreed gravely, and then her mental smile faded as it occurred to her that Zeralenn, her own mentor, may well have regarded her feverish calculations of last year with the same tolerant, superior amusement that she herself now accorded Aurelie. It was a humiliating thought.

At least Aurelie seemed to have forgotten her distress. The tears had dried, and she stood still, arms folded and brows knit, lost in internal debate. Eliste jogged her arm gently. "Come, we'd best ready ourselves."

"But I cannot make up my mind—it is too confusing— Oh, very well. There is nothing better for now, I suppose. Cousin, I have no idea how to pack a valise; it is quite beyond me. I should have someone of my own to do it for me, but of course I do not, so you *will* lend me your woman, will you not?"

"As soon as she has done for me, I'll send her to you."

"Oh, thank you, thanks indeed! You have always been my true friend!" Doubts forgotten, Aurelie kissed her cousin soundly. Hand in hand, the two girls raced up the stairs.

Eliste's preparations were unexpectedly prolonged. To begin with, she needed to send Kairthe down to the garden to retrieve the buried valuables. Thereafter, she had to pick out a very few of her most indispensable garments, suitable to

Strellian exile; and the choice was not easy. The bulk of her extensive wardrobe would have to be left behind. Most of Madame Nimais's exquisite and ruinously expensive creations—abandoned. It seemed almost a desecration; but the alternative—desertion of Prince vo Plume—was even worse.

"It won't do, Miss," Kairthe opined. "You can't carry the little dog with you. This will never work."

"Just do as you're told," Eliste returned sternly. "Two holes front, two holes back, one on each side. Don't argue with me, just do it."

Sighing, Kairthe resumed her labors. With a sharp purloined knife, she was carving air holes in the single leather valise that Eliste was to carry away. For a couple of minutes she worked in silence, then looked up to observe, "The Plume will never bear it, Miss. He's used to having it all his own way."

"He'll learn better. I have."

"He'll yap his head off."

"No, he won't, not by the time I'm through with him. Come on, little rat, eat up." She was feeding the animal slices of chocolate-cherry cake soaked in kirsch. Prince vo Plume gulped greedily.

"Faugh, Miss! He'll just puke it up all over the rug, and then it'll stink in here."

"No, he won't. It'll put him straight to sleep. Just watch."

But Prince vo Plume refused to behave. Much to Eliste's surprise, he suddenly lost all interest in chocolate cake. His muzzle swiveled toward Kairthe, and his silken ears twitched forward. For a moment he stared, then bounced to his feet, yipping furiously.

"Naughty thing, what's the matter with you? Be quiet."

The soprano uproar did not abate. Prince vo Plume sprang from his mistress's lap and scurried over to Kairthe. Barking urgently, he danced and bounded about her ankles.

"Whatever do you want, Plumie?" Kairthe inquired. "You want to go outdoors?" Setting the valise aside, she stood up. Prince vo Plume pranced, pawing at her gown. "Cheeky little devil, it's a good thing for you you're so cute, you can get away with anything. Now, what is it—?" Automatically, Kairthe shook out her long skirts, and in doing so, dislodged a small golden object clinging to the fabric. With a buzz and a whir of metallic wings, a nit of NuNu took to the air, circling about in search of escape or concealment. Kairthe shrank back with a cry; and then, snatching up a ruffled cushion, batted aggressively. The nit headed straight for the window, screenless in the cold season, rapping the glass pane thrice before lighting on the brocade curtain, where it sat whirring erratically.

"Smash it! Use a book!" Eliste commanded, taking refuge behind a chair.

"But, Miss, what if it stings?"

"You're the one who must have brought that thing in here, after you took the Plume for his walk! It's your doing, you deal with it!"

Obediently, Kairthe wrenched the shoe from her foot and struck, missing the nit but hitting the window. A pane shattered, and the nit, freighted with lethal information, glided for the gap. Kairthe swung with her bare hand, then recoiled with a shriek, sucking her stung palm. The nit altered course, veering toward the big cheval glass. There it hovered, buzzing loudly. Taking up the nearest book—a copy of Shorvi Nirienne's *The Promise*—Eliste approached and hit hard. She struck glass, and the mirror crashed to pieces. Kairthe and Eliste screamed, Prince vo Plume barked and cavorted wildly, and the nit zipped out of range.

Wildly, Eliste flung the book, and the excited nit whizzed straight at her face. She flung up a protective arm, and the next moment screeched as a red pain flashed along her nerves. She opened her eyes to discover the nit, trapped and buzzing furiously, its sting buried in her wrist. For the first time, she saw the thing at close range; noting the curved polished plates armoring the body, the finely articulated legs, golden filigree wings, and the twelve protuberant, precisely faceted eyes. It was a beautifully constructed little machine, delicate as a piece of jewelry, totally loathsome in its burnished perfection. For a moment Eliste stood frozen with a curious kind of horror, then found her wits and commanded, "Tweezers!"

Kairthe supplied the requested article. Grimacing in disgust and pain, Eliste drew the nit from her wrist. A gasp escaped her as the sting pulled free. A drop of blood welled in its wake. The nit struggled, the tweezers vibrated between her fingers, and Eliste tightened her grip. "Book," she commanded, and Kairthe deposited *The Promise* in her mistress's outstretched right hand. Kneeling, Eliste positioned the nit upon the floor, then brought the volume down heavily to flatten the fragile body and wings to gold foil. A couple of legs kicked briefly, then all motion ceased.

"Nasty thing. Real unnatural." Kairthe studied the bright debris with disapproval. "I hate it."

Eliste nodded. Absently she sucked her wrist, which was already starting to swell. "I never knew they can sting."

"You'll want some goo on that." Producing a vial of homemade ointment, Kairthe anointed the inflamed area. "I'm sorry, Miss, I truly am. I'm the one brought that little bugger in here."

"Not your fault. I just hope there aren't any more of them about."

"Well, if there are, the Plume's sure to nose 'em out. Miss, what do we say if someone asks what all the ruckus in here was about?"

"We tell the truth, that's all. Everyone understands about the nits. Speaking of which, you'd best tack pasteboard before that broken pane, to make sure no more of them get in."

Kairthe obeyed, and the light dimmed infinitesimally.

Eliste watched almost dreamily. Her wrist burned, her heart still raced, yet her mood was distinctly optimistic. It was, she realized, the prospect of flight that braced her spirits. Another few hours and she would be clear of Sherreen: clear of the walls hemming her in, clear of nits and Sentients, clear of Reparationist hatred, of Vanguard and of Sepulchre, clear of the Kokotte's lengthening shadow, free of all the mounting fears that had darkened her life for so many months.

She had never really paused to analyze the forces at work in Vonahr. She had lived from day to day, conscious and resentful of the steady, remorseless, and apparently unopposable constriction of her world. She had mourned the passing first of luxuries and privilege; then of freedom and legal redress; and finally of security, protection, justice, safety. The magnitude of such oppression was almost impossible to grasp in any concrete sense. She had experienced keener resentment at the loss of her right as an Exalted to stroll in the Havillac Gardens between the hours of noon and six than at the loss of her right to legal counsel should she be summoned before the National Tribunal. The one was immediate and intensely galling; the other—simply fantastic beyond comprehension.

Like others of her class, she had continued in the belief that the losses were temporary and reversible. Accepting her grandmother's Exalted dicta, she had carried on, insofar as she was able, as if nothing had changed—carried on, denying a world that closed in tighter and tighter, ultimately dwindling to the tiny volume contained within the maw of Kokotte.

And now she was finally getting away from all of it.

The rest of the preparations were completed without mishap. Kairthe cleaned up the broken glass, then sawed the final air holes in the valise. Prince vo Plume polished off the last of the kirsch-sodden cake, thereafter waxing somnolent. Placed atop a pile of lingerie in the open valise, he slept soundly. Eliste fretted over gowns and shoes, eventually selecting a few favorites. Kairthe departed to assist Aurelie, returning an hour later. And then there was nothing left but to sit awaiting information or a summons from Zeralenn.

But the hours lengthened, and no word issued from the silent master suite. Around noon, Kairthe brought in lunch on a tray, and Eliste spent half an hour picking apathetically at her food. Presently the soup, salad, and cutlets were removed, almost untasted. One o'clock came and went. Two o'clock, and Prince vo Plume, reviving from his alcoholic stupor, hopped out of the valise to nose and sniff about the room. No word from Zeralenn. Three o'clock. Four. Still no word. Eliste was at first puzzled and then indignant. Her grandmother told her nothing—didn't trust her—treated her like a child—

By five o'clock, when the wintry light was already threatening to wane, indignation gave way to worry. And then at last, when worry had grown acute, she was called back to Zeralenn's morning room. Finally. Her misgivings subsided; they had been groundless, after all. She hurried downstairs.

The alteration in her grandmother's appearance—a rare concession to practicality—intrigued Eliste. Gone was the old-fashioned panniered gown, gone the towering rigid coiffeur and the mask of cosmetics. Zeralenn wore a plain, smartly cut traveling suit of gray alpaca. Her simply dressed, unpowdered hair was drawn up under a wide hat. Her face, for once nearly stripped of paint, revealed an unexpected tired fragility, belied by iron composure of manner.

"Close the door," Zeralenn commanded. "I've something to tell you, and I do not care to be overheard."

Eliste obeyed with reluctance. Whatever was coming, instinct informed her she did not want to hear it. Her grandmother's revelation, however, exceeded her worst expectations.

"I have just received word from vo Meureille's household," Zeralenn announced. "The Cavalier's activities and identity have become known to the Committee of National Welfare."

"The nits . . ."

"Presumably so. It was inevitable, of course, that he should be unmasked at last. I am only surprised that he has been able to carry on in secret for so long. Now his arrest has been ordered, and he has been forced into hiding. His present whereabouts within the city are unknown, and thus my messages cannot reach him. We may expect no assistance from the Cavalier at this time."

"And our departure—?"

"Postponed."

Eliste spent the next few seconds struggling to maintain the impassible demeanor that Exalted breeding demanded. It was not until this moment that she realized how heavily she had counted upon Meureille's nick-of-time intervention. Throughout the past dark months, her illicit knowledge of a secret escape route had served as a talisman to ward off fear. When things got bad enough, she had often assured herself, they could always turn to the Cavalier. Meureille would come to the rescue; Meureille would carry them to safety. She could endure the miseries of Sherreen with fair equanimity, so long as the exit remained open; but now the door had slammed shut in her face.

"Do not look so shocked, Granddaughter," Zeralenn advised. "You are tolerably polished at this point, yet your face still betrays you. Perfection of elegance requires perfection of self-command."

"I'm not really concerned with elegance at the moment." Eliste managed to keep her voice fairly steady.

"Ah, but you should be, and at all times. Until you have learned that one lesson, your education has scarcely begun. For now, your youth purchases indulgence; but it is a matter that cannot be ignored indefinitely."

"Shall we maintain our elegance in the Sepulchre, Madame? Shall we practice our niceties upon rats and turnkeys?"

"If necessary. However, I prefer to believe that we shall not be called upon to do so. We are not without resources, Granddaughter. Meureille cannot assist us for now, but there is another refuge. We will make use of it tonight."

Eliste knew what it was, although she had not recalled its existence until that moment. Now the details of the overheard conversation came back with perfect clarity. The Cavalier had given Zeralenn the name and address of someone, he had said, "who may assist you if for some reason I cannot." There was hope in that, and she was ready to grab at the faintest hope; but she retained the presence of mind to conceal her ill-gotten knowledge. Biting back all reply, she lowered her too-revealing eyes and arranged her features into an expression of inquiry.

Perhaps Zeralenn divined something of the truth, for she favored her granddaughter with a penetrating glance before continuing, "There is a decent loyalist household near the Waterfront Market where we may rest for a night or two until Meureille arrives to conduct us from Sherreen."

"Won't he have conducted himself from Sherreen by this time? He can't very well stay. Now that he's been exposed, he'll be hunted by every gendarme and Vanguardsman in town."

"Possibly, but Meureille loves sport too well to forfeit a match over trifles. Rest assured he will not abandon his fellow Exalteds, and be doubly certain he will not delay in coming to *our* aid."

"How shall he find us, Madame?" Eliste's eyes were perhaps a little too round.

"He knows the place," Zeralenn returned dryly. "Now—as discretion is desirable, I have scheduled our departure for midnight, at which time I will send one of our people to summon a fiacre. Such mean, common conveyance we must endure, this once. I trust your preparations are complete. To you, for now, I entrust the guardianship of your cousin Aurelie, whose adolescent vaporings I am not minded to endure. Go upstairs, see to your baggage, your cousin, and your woman. Tender them such explanation as you deem appropriate—I leave these details to your judgment. Sup within your own chamber. Sleep if you can, but not too long. At twelve o'clock, descend in silence to the foyer, and we shall bid this house farewell."

"And if the house is being watched—?"

"Then our excursion is brief."

"Madame, this has been your home for decades. I know it must be hard for you to go."

"It is of no consequence; I am not sentimental. Granddaughter, I shall see you again at twelve o'clock. Now leave me." Seating herself at her writing table, spine never touching the back of the chair, Zeralenn turned her attention to a stack of correspondence. After a moment's hesitation, Eliste withdrew.

She relayed an edited version of the truth to Aurelie and Kairthe, telling them of unforeseen complications necessitating brief detour and delay prior to Sherreenian departure. She did not inform them of the Cavalier vo Meureille's misfortune, nor did she point out the increased peril of their own circumstances. If they did not see that for themselves, there was no use in frightening them.

Kairthe received the news with a wide-eyed gravity suggesting comprehension; while Aurelie positively brightened, lifting moist eyes ceilingward to proclaim, "Destiny chooses not to part me from Bayelle." Eliste did not trouble to argue the point.

Thereafter time slowed to a crippled limp. Eliste detested the waiting. It was wretched empty time, full of boredom and tension, spoiled for all activity; lost time that seemed to go on forever. Sleep was out of the question; it was far too early, and she was wide awake. She tried to read, to embroider, to work a jigsaw puzzle—all without success; she couldn't keep her mind on any of them. She had better luck when she took up her sketch pad and began to draw—an imaginary landscape, initially exotic and fantastical, but later on filling as if of its own accord with familiar figures: a horse very like her own red Hussy, ridden by a long-legged figure with Dref Zeenoson's lean face and dark eyes; and perched on the branch of a flowering tree, a smudge of gray with white wafting hair, somewhat reminiscent of Uncle Quinz. She might have lost herself in this, but for the presence of Aurelie.

Trotting continually in and out of her cousin's chamber, prattling and chattering, nibbling endless chocolate almonds and spewing unwanted advice, Aurelie seemed to imagine herself about to embark upon a pleasure jaunt. Lacking all sense of personal danger, she viewed the midnight outing as adventure; and her exhilaration was almost intolerable. Eliste endured it for hours, and then, when she could stand no more, sought refuge in feigned sleep. Aurelie withdrew, dragging a reluctant Kairthe, whose services as coiffeuse she had long coveted. In the silence of the darkened, empty chamber, false slumber became real, and Eliste dozed fitfully until a light touch upon the shoulder woke her. Kairthe stood beside the bed. The clock on the mantel read quarter to twelve.

Minutes later, they descended to the foyer. All three girls were warmly and plainly dressed, with thick hooded cloaks over dark woolen dresses. Kairthe carried Aurelie's portmanteau, together with a small bag of her own belongings. The valise containing a quiescent Prince vo Plume, Eliste herself retained.

Deliberate footsteps upon the staircase, and then Zeralenn was there to shepherd them firmly out the door.

The midnight air was sharp, chill, and unforgiving. Eliste flinched at the slap of a winter-stiffened breeze laced with the tang of old smoke. Overhead the stars sparked a beautifully clear black sky; but there was no moon, for which they might be grateful, as the nits of NuNu were known to love the light. The creatures were capable of functioning by moonlight, lamplight, even starlight if need be, but decidedly they preferred the day. The nit sting upon Eliste's wrist still burned faintly. She cast a quick, wary glance about her, but caught no telltale flash of gold. The familiar vista of tree-lined, lamplit street and creamy clean town houses advertised a spurious normalcy. Eliste shook her head. Even now, even as they literally fled for their lives, she could scarcely believe it. Sherreen was still beautiful, still seemingly tranquil, still to all appearances much the same as ever. It *felt* the same, lush and rich and safe, filled with grace and every pleasure. Was it possible that violent madness reigned amidst such surroundings? Was it not time to wake from an ugly dream?

The sight of boarded doorways marked with the scarlet emblem of congressional confiscation on houses up and down the silent street confirmed lunatic reality. The cold breeze pushed at her stinging eyes as she turned to look back one last time. Beside her, Kairthe was sniffling softly. Zeralenn permitted herself no such indulgence. Hurrying on without a backward glance, she led her young charges a couple hundred yards up the street to a waiting fiacre. They entered, and seated themselves. Zeralenn issued orders, and the vehicle set off along the Avenue Parabeau.

The way was familiar to Eliste: through the good and bad neighborhoods; past the Sepulchre, its high turrets dead black lapses in starlight; and on across the Bridge Vinculum into the Waterfront Market, now closed for the night, emptied of tradesmen and customers. Past the shuttered booths they sped, past the silent sheds and stands, across the open expanse of the Martmead, depopulated now but for a brace of patrolling gendarmes, at sight of whom Eliste found herself cringing like a criminal. But the gendarmes scarcely glanced at the hurrying vehicle, allowing it to pass on unhindered into the fringe of taverns, cheap cookshops, and pawnshops that edged the open market. Shortly thereafter the driver pulled up, having reached the specified destination. Zeralenn paid him, and the passengers alighted near the public pump in Ladyshoe Street, where the potboys and skivvies from the still-bustling cookshops came to suck their long clay pipes, to gossip, and to kill time. And even at that hour of the winter's night a few of them were there, half a dozen figures huddled about a yellow-smoked, refuse-fueled fire. Conversation ceased as the fiacre disgorged its feminine cargo, and the potboys frankly stared.

Eliste had often traversed this neighborhood by carriage, but never before on foot. Now, without the neat varnished walls to enclose and protect her, the place seemed suddenly transformed; far more assertive and immediate than ever before—too much so. She did not like the dirt and dilapidation, the fumes and stinks, the excessive proximity of common humanity; such republican color was better appreciated at a safe distance. No doubt her companions concurred. Kairthe was fidgeting uneasily, and Aurelie had buried her nose in a perfumed handkerchief. Zeralenn, however, took no notice. Drawing from her wallet a map of the city, she studied it closely for a moment, nodded, then turned and marched off down Ladyshoe Street, with her three charges stumbling in her wake.

At Luckless Lane they turned left, then left again into a nameless alley lined with drab darkened tenements, within whose recessed doorways the vagrants slept curled under piles of rags. A few more turns, and Eliste had completely lost her bearings. She felt herself cut off from everything in the world she knew, disoriented and directionless, with nothing to guide her but the tapping of her grandmother's ivory stick upon the cobbles. Fortunately, Zeralenn seemed quite sure of her way, and the tempo of tapping rarely slackened. Only twice she paused briefly to consult her map by lantern light, the second time attracting the attention of an inquisitive nit, which she swatted almost absently with her suitcase before resuming progress. The bag struck against the nearest wall with a telltale jingle that revealed the nature of the contents: jewelry. Yes, Zeralenn had elected to rescue her famous collection, and now she was strolling fearlessly about one of Sherreen's sorrier neighborhoods, unarmed and quite unprotected, carrying a double king's ransom in gems. It was, Eliste reflected, so exactly like her.

After an hour's wandering, Eliste was tired and apprehensive. Her arm and shoulders ached with the unaccustomed burden of the valise, and despite the protection of hooded cloak, she was thoroughly chilled. Her companions were at least as badly off. Kairthe had two bags to manage; while Aurelie, who had insisted upon wearing narrow, high-heeled shoes, was limping noticeably. Worse than fatigue and discomfort, however, was the worry. For they had trudged through street after sleeping street, any of which might have contained Vanguard patrols, without locating what was beginning to seem a mythical refuge; and at this point it was impossible to avoid wondering whether Zeralenn, despite her apparent confidence, had not led them all astray. Eliste kept her suspicions to herself for a while. At last, however, when they paused to rest briefly and inconspicuously in the shadow of an alcove, she could no longer maintain silence.

"We're lost, aren't we?" Her voice, pitched discreetly low, was meant for her grandmother's ears alone.

"Not in the least, Granddaughter," Zeralenn replied in normal conversational tones. "I wonder at your despondency. You will alarm your woman."

"Where are we going?"

"To Master Xouvie's black-and-white house at the foot of the slope, near the smaller of the two pumps in Voutriere Street. So Meureille described it, as the buildings in this neighborhood are unnumbered, I believe."

"Why is it taking us so long to get there?"

"Possibly your cousin's limping pace has delayed us."

"Why didn't the fiacre carry us straight to this house?"

"And compromise our hosts thereby?"

"But do you know the way, Madame?"

"By no means, but that is what maps are for. Assuming that ours is current, the street we want should be . . . there." She pointed.

Eliste's eyes followed the outstretched arm to the entrance of a nondescript row of shops and houses. A signpost on the corner bore a name, but in the dark, she could not read it. "That's it? That's the one?"

"Without doubt."

"Oh, finally!" The end in sight, her spirits bounced and fatigue subsided. "Then let's go find it. It's so cold out here—I *do* hope they'll have a good fire!"

"And tea, and hot chocolate." Aurelie spoke up for the first time in an hour. "And perhaps some buttered cinnamon-sugar toast. And feather beds, with lavender-scented linens, well-warmed. And plenty of hot water, and perfumed soap. And proper servants, who know what they're about."

"Well, I shouldn't count on the servants," Eliste cautioned. "These people won't be Exalted, remember."

"But they aren't the *scum*, are they?"

"Softly, children," Zeralenn advised. "Come, now." Abandoning the alcove's shelter, she tapped straight on, with Eliste, Aurelie, and Kairthe trailing at her heels. Close inspection of the signpost confirmed location. They had found Voutriere Street, and Master Xouvie's black-and-white dwelling could not be more than moments distant. Down the slope they hurried, quick footsteps punctuated by the tap of a pallid stick. The hard breeze pelted them with grit and cinders, cut and chilled them, but it didn't matter, not anymore. Down past the blind-shuttered buildings, down to the bottom of a sharp incline, and there was a pump, not far from which rose a big old house, black and white in the picturesque antique style, exactly as Meureille had described.

Only, the Cavalier's description had not included the boarded windows, the chain and padlock, or the great diamond daubed in scarlet upon the front door. The place had somehow fallen into the hands of the Constitutional Congress. Its erstwhile master, Xouvie, might be dead, imprisoned, or safely clear of Sherreen; impossible to say which. Judging by the garbage that fouled the front steps, the house had been deserted for some time, but Eliste was constrained to verify the observation. A succession of knocks, whistles, flung pebbles, and muted halloos failed to draw response. Certainly no one was there, and the building itself was quite secure against invasion.

A cold wind scoured Voutriere Street. Drawing the woolen folds of her cloak about her, Eliste shivered. Not far away, clock chimes sounded the hour of three. The chimes died, and silence reigned.

What do we do now?

The universe did not reply. The wind shot dust and dark and cold at them. Eliste pulled the edge of her hood slantwise across her face. Her fingers were stiff and wooden. She wanted to go home, back to the Parabeau town house; and if she'd been alone, she might have followed that impulse, suicidal though it was. But her grandmother's presence somehow precluded surrender. The wind was vengeful. If she had cried, her tears would have frozen to her flesh. She wanted to fling herself down in the street, she wanted to throw things and scream. Instead, she looked to that source of inspiration—Zeralenn—and for the first time ever, encountered indecision. The wind was instantly colder. She felt it clear to the bone.

"Think of something else, Grauntie," Aurelie advised, but no reply was forthcoming.

The wind jabbed at them. The flesh shrank; there was no refuge.

The void pressed hard, and it was deadly cold.

an't go home. Can't go to an inn; we'd attract attention. Can't get past the city gates.

   Only a little time, perhaps minutes, before some patrol of gendarmes or Vanguards-men turns up.

   And that will be that.

   Eliste's thoughts whizzed and buzzed like captive nits.

   Nowhere to go. Nowhere to go. Oh, is it possible that it's only been a few hours since we were all at home, warm and unafraid, with Aurelie prattling on about her beau?

   Her beau. Bayelle vo Clarivaux. Who's found a safe hiding place somewhere in Sherreen.

   And she knows where he is.

   "Aurelie." Eliste rounded so suddenly that the younger girl jumped. "Where is Bayelle?"

   "Gad, how you startled me, Cousin!"

   "Never mind that. Where is he?"

   "Cousin, what can you be thinking of? I am sworn to secrecy, as you know, and I would rather die than break my oath."

   "Ha! You'd swear and then break the Oath of Allegiance willingly enough, so why stick at this?"

   "Cousin, at times your tongue is distressingly bitter, a fault I ascribe to the frustrations of spinsterhood. But to comprehend all is to compassionate all."

   "Very good of you. Now tell me what I want to know."

   "Impossible. Whatever would my Bayelle think of me?"

"Trifles. He'll understand. Now listen, this is important. We must find a place to go, somewhere to hide, before we are discovered. Do you want to go to the Sepulchre?"

"I would much rather go home. What's more, I think we should, too. I am perishing of the cold, and my feet hurt. I want to be in my own room, with a good fire, a cup of chocolate, and all my own things about me. I have had enough of this vagabondage, la! Let us return home. The canaille will not bother us if we are clever. Surely it should not be difficult to outwit such rabble."

"You don't know what you're talking about. Do you want to go to the Kokotte?"

"It will not happen. You can't frighten me!"

"No? Speak up, Aurelie, or I'll slap you. I'll *pound* you!"

"Grauntie!" Aurelie hastily retreated. "Grauntie, help! Make her leave me alone!"

"Eliste, explain yourself," Zeralenn commanded.

"Her secret beau, Bayelle vo Clarivaux—"

"Traitress! You promised you'd never tell! Shame on you, Cousin! Shame!"

"The young vo Clarivaux," Eliste continued, "has got a hiding place somewhere in the city. Presumably it is a safe place for Exalteds, and Aurelie knows where it is."

"Is this true, Aurelie?" Zeralenn inquired.

"It's a secret, an absolutely sacred secret. Unlike my cousin, *I* don't betray confidences. You wouldn't want me to break my *word*, Grauntie?"

"If the vo Clarivaux heir owns a proper sense of Exalted chivalry—and in light of his lineage it is fair to assume that he does so—then he will gladly sacrifice all in your defense," Zeralenn replied. "Therefore, he would certainly desire you to speak, under such circumstances as these. You will reveal the young man's whereabouts."

"But no, I don't want to—I couldn't bear for him to think ill of me!"

"Speak up at once, or I will take my stick to you," Zeralenn remarked calmly.

"And I'll slap you," Eliste promised. "And I'll tell Kairthe to slap you, too."

"She wouldn't do it!"

"Yes, I would, Miss," Kairthe told her. "If I got to."

"Oh, it isn't fair, you're all against me! Three against one! Why do you persecute me so?"

"Nobody's persecuted you yet," Eliste advised. "And nobody will, if you do as you're told."

"Bullies! Don't you come near me!" Aurelie stumbled backward until her back pressed the wall of Master Xouvie's boarded dwelling. Her companions advanced, and the young girl sidled off toward the corner of the house, where a big wooden column rose to bolster the roof overhang. At the foot of the column bulked a tall drift of accumulated refuse. As Aurelie drew near, the heap quivered, empty bottles and broken crockery sliding from its summit. Rags and crumpled newspapers erupted as a crouching, hitherto concealed figure rose slowly to its full height. Aurelie shrieked and shrank away. Eliste started violently, and beside her, Kairthe gasped. Zeralenn alone stood motionless and apparently unmoved.

The figure, which resembled a continuation of the rubbish heap—all dangling scarecrow tatters draped upon a starved skeletal frame—stepped slowly forth from the shadow of the column. The faint light of a lantern some dozens of yards distant fell upon a gaunt and singularly hideous male countenance, low of brow, wide-mouthed and pig-eyed. These features, unattractive in themselves, were further marred by a diseased skin whose raised scales, crusts, and ruffled flaking patches were easily visible even by night. Similar scales and shreds of dry dead skin disfigured the arms and calves, which were bare despite the chill of winter.

The apparition approached, and a stench of ancient sweat and filth seeped from his rags. Eliste stood her ground with an effort, and fortunately he paused several feet away to address them in hoarse tones, grating and somehow gloating:

"Need a place, do you?"

No reply.

"Worried, maybe? Feeling queerly? Don't know the neighborhood? On the prowl for a gallant knight? You're in luck—Exalted ladies. You've found him, isn't that juicy?"

Silence.

"Out to take the air, then. Walking the streets for pleasure, not profit. Stupid of me. I beg your pardon. Exalted ladies."

"Why call us Exalted, you saucy scoundrel? *I'm* not Exalted!" Kairthe flashed.

"Right. The soubrette, I guess; the devoted slave." The smile that accompanied this remark revealed blackened teeth and puffy gums. "So, then—a sorry supper of aged mackerel with a triple serving of underdone mutton. Better?"

Neither Kairthe nor Aurelie understood him. Eliste stiffened with incredulous outrage, while Zeralenn expressed nothing.

"Leave us." Automatically, Eliste resorted to the tone of icy authority with which she might have cowed an impertinent serf back at Derrivalle, but it was not effective now.

"Your servant. Exalted Lady." The newcomer offered another ruined smile. "I'll leave, and the four of you can freeze your Exalted tails out on the streets until it grows light and a patrol picks you up. Or you can come along with me. Your choice."

"Come along—with you?" Eliste was too astonished for anger. "Who are you?"

"Quite nobody, by your lights—a beggar."

"Come, state your name."

"Introductions, little Marquise? You first."

"Explain yourself, fellow."

"You're in luck. I can find you a place."

"What do you mean?"

"A room. Four walls. A roof. You follow me? You do speak Vonahrish, don't you? Exalted Miss?"

In the old days, she would have struck him for his insolence. Now, she didn't dare. "Where is this place?"

"Don't trouble your little frizzled head about that. The point is, you can lay low. Sometimes it's the only thing."

"Why should you render us such service?"

"Think hard. Exalted Miss. It will come to you."

"You—oh, you want us to give you money?" Eliste was still unaccustomed to the concept of cash payment. It had never truly been part of her world.

"She always this sharp?" the stranger inquired of Zeralenn.

Zeralenn ignored the taunt. "If I understand you correctly, you are suggesting that we pay you, no doubt exorbitantly, then follow you to an unspecified destination?"

"That's it exactly. Exalted lady."

"And in earnest of your good faith—?"

"Nothing."

"It is possible you are neither willing nor competent to fulfill your promise."

"Quite possible. You've got to take your chances. Or don't, as you please." A shrug stirred his tatters.

Their options were few and uniformly unappealing. The stranger was loathsome and his offer implausible, but they needed badly to get off the street before dawn. Still, to follow such a creature . . . it was too fantastic—

"Another thing you might think about." The gloating note in his voice was now unmistakable. "Turn me down, and I hop to the district station—it's not far—speak my piece to the oinks, and collect a bounty of five R's when they pick you up. Not much, but better than nothing. One way or another, I'll make out."

"Stinking goat-turd," Kairthe muttered under her breath.

"It's up to you. Exalted ladies. But make up your mind, I won't hang around."

The wicked lash of the wind facilitated decision. "What payment do you require?" asked Zeralenn.

"One hundred rekkoes."

"Oh, he must be mad!" Eliste exclaimed, almost involuntarily.

"A bargain. Twenty rekkoes apiece for your Exalted selves, twenty for the little soubrette with the mouth—help comes dear, these days—and then there's the twenty percent added on for The Fungus's commission."

"The what?"

"And don't think of cutting the commission. That won't float. It's The Fungus set us to watching this house in the first place."

"Watching?"

"In shifts, ever since Xouvie caught it. You didn't think this was an accident? You're not the only Exalteds come nosing around here. Xouvie was always doing, so it was odds on something useful would turn up. So it has, and I've grabbed the goods."

The stranger's proprietary attitude was unsettling. Eliste cast a nervous glance at her grandmother, whose face revealed nothing, and then essayed uncertainly, "You would have to perform your commission to our satisfaction before we could even consider paying you."

His abrupt bark of laughter increased her discomfort. The facial contortions set the little rags of peeling skin on nose and cheeks to fluttering. He did not trouble to reply.

"One hundred rekkoes. There is your payment in full." Zeralenn expressionlessly proffered a handful of notes. "Now lead us."

For one moment, Eliste felt as if she could read his mind. Surely as she knew her own name, she knew that he thought of robbing and killing them all. Perhaps their number daunted him—they were women, but there were four of them. Perhaps he feared their outcry would draw the gendarmes. Or perhaps he was simply less formidable than he appeared. The illnesses that left their visible mark upon him may have undermined his strength considerably. Had he guessed the contents of Zeralenn's valise, none of this would have deterred him; but he did not guess. Following an instant's hesitation, he took the money, stowing the notes out of sight beneath his rags.

And now, having received payment, would he simply disappear? That was another possibility.

"No fear. Quenuble will cough up six R's for you, and I don't plan to miss out. Beats the Reps' going rate," observed the stranger, as if he, too, could read minds.

"Quenuble?" inquired Eliste. The name was familiar, but she could not quite place it. "Cough up?"

He did not see fit to enlighten her. "All right, let's move. Stay behind me and don't chatter. That is, if you please—Exalted ladies."

Reluctantly they obeyed, and found themselves wandering tiny, dank back alleys probably not even marked on Zeralenn's map.

He might, of course, be leading them straight to the nearest district station of the gendarmerie.

No, he isn't, Eliste was able to assure herself with absolute conviction. *Because if he does, then he'll lose every last biquin of that hundred rekkoes.*

Where, then?

The trek, which seemed to go on forever, actually continued not much more than half an hour. To Eliste's relief, they soon left the alleyways behind them, entering into a hearteningly decent neighborhood with aged but respectable shops and dwellings. Light glowed at a few windows. Several of the shopkeepers were already up and about, readying themselves for the morning trade, which would commence in a couple of hours. Such homey signs of life and warmth should have been comforting, but Eliste viewed them with dread. The world was awakening. Dawn approached, and soon the empty streets would fill. The presence of Exalted pedestrians would be noticed, despite all efforts at concealment. And then—the shrill verbal assault, the threats and insults, the flying spittle and rocks, the blows of fist and stick, the torn clothing, and worse. There were certain particularly fervent revolutionaries, she recalled, fond of carving literally blood-red diamonds into Exalted flesh. Or perhaps, since this area of the city appeared relatively civilized—a simple demand for papers of identification and legitimate pass-town, signed by the appropriate section chief; and in the absence of these documents, the summoning of gendarmes or Vanguardsmen. It had happened to many Exalteds. It had happened to Gizine vo Chaumelle.

But it did not happen now. Their guide led them around a corner, into a street Eliste actually recognized: Cliquot Street, on the outskirts of the Waterfront Market. And there, straight ahead, an establishment she knew: a pastry shop she'd passed often enough on her way to the New Arcade—Master Quenuble's House of Swans. Quenuble did not really stand in the topmost rank of stylish Sherreenian *pâtissiers,* but found his customers chiefly among the affluent bourgeoisie and the lesser grade of untitled and unfashionable Exalteds. By Beviaire standards, he was second-rate, and yet the fragrances floating from the House of Swans, and the puff-pastry creations displayed in the window, had occasionally snagged Eliste's casual attention. Sometimes she had glanced in the window while passing, but certainly never thought to enter. She thought about it now, however, and with considerable misgiving.

The House of Swans occupied the street level of a tall, solid, spacious old structure, exuding ancient respectability. Presumably the upper stories comprised the living quarters of the Quenuble family. Light shone from every ground-floor window. Not surprisingly, the pastry chef had already started in on his daily stock of fruit tarts and *mille-feuilles,* his cream puffs and éclairs, his multitiered *gâteaux,* and his signature swans of choux pastry. The yellow light from the windows fell upon a knot of wretched, starveling figures clustered about the door. The door itself was marked with a big, exuberant scarlet diamond. Similar diamonds defaced the shutters, the shopfront, and the swan-shaped sign that hung above the door. It was this sight that now aroused Eliste's alarm, reinforced by the presence of arrantly republican strangers.

"Wait," Eliste commanded their guide. She was prepared to pluck at his ulcerous arm to gain his ear if necessary, but he glanced back at her without slackening his pace, and she did not have to touch him. "Look at that— Reparationist red!"

"Well?"

"We can't go there!"

"Then don't," he advised pleasantly.

This time, it took real self-control not to hit him. Her hand actually twitched, but again prudence ruled, and she turned wide eyes upon her grandmother.

"Do not alarm yourself," Zeralenn counseled imperturbably. "We have cast our lots; now let us carry through."

"But this animal is leading us straight to—"

"Hush. Courage. Composure at all times, Granddaughter. You are Exalted. Now come, and let us see."

There was no point in arguing with Zeralenn. Eliste might follow, balk in the street, or run in the opposite direction. She chose to follow.

Not through the clot of beggars clogging the front entry, however; for their guide conducted them along a narrow pass-through separating the House of Swans from its nearest neighbor to the red-diamonded back door, upon which he rapped authoritatively. A man—round of face and belly, middle of stature and years—answered the summons at once. The white apron stretched taut over comfortably expansive stomach, the flour-whitened hands and forearms, announced the arrival of the *pâtissier* Quenuble. A white cap appliquéd with a big red diamond sat atop his wiry gray curls.

"Well, Shreds, my lad?" Quenuble inquired of his scrofulous caller.

"Six R's upon delivery," Shreds replied.

"Ah—very good! Exactly so. Fair enough."

As Eliste watched in mounting disquiet, money changed hands.

What's he paying for? And why?

Shreds counted over his gleanings, jerked his head, then faded off into the night without a word. Eliste scarcely noted his departure. Her eyes were fixed upon what appeared to be their purchaser, who was now bowing and gesturing with the clumsiest possible gallantry.

"Exalted ladies, if you will honor me," Quenuble invited. "Your servant, ladies."

There was still time to run away from this place bedizened front and rear with the scarlet symbol of the Reparationists. For a moment, Eliste considered doing so.

"Exalted ladies, yours to command. If you will be so good as to enter," the chef urged, underscoring the plea with another execrable bow. "You will be safe here, quite safe, you may be sure." Certainly he looked and sounded sincere, and solicitous to the point of anxiety, but Eliste was far from convinced.

What about those beastly red daubings, then? What about that cap?

If her grandmother entertained any such doubts, it was not evident. Apparently altogether confident, Zeralenn nodded once to the chef and swept on past him into the building. A brief exchange of frightened glances, then Aurelie and Kairthe followed. Eliste was shivering, as much with tension as with cold; she hoped her voluminous cloak masked all such signs of weakness. Slanting a narrow, sidelong look at Quenuble as she sidled by him, she slid on through the door into a flour-dusted cold-cabinet, at whose center stood a marble-topped worktable bearing several folded batches of partially rolled puff pastry. The cabinet did not noticeably differ in temperature from the street outdoors, and Eliste's shivering did not begin to abate until Master Quenuble guided them on into the bright kitchen beyond, where a fire burned on the vast hearth and the big ovens were already thoroughly heated. Here the cinnamon-spiced atmosphere was overpoweringly rich, warm and luxurious as a perfumed bath. Despite her fears, Eliste could not repress a sigh of pleasure. Instantly she pushed back her hood and stripped off her gloves, exposing aching ears and chill-stiffened fingers to the tropical air. Had propriety permitted so much, she would have removed shoes and stockings as well; her feet were numb and wooden.

"Soup, Exalted ladies. You'll want hot soup. Hot tea? Hot chocolate?" Quenuble offered.

"Oh, *rather*." A fervent whisper from Aurelie.

"Come, I'll set these chairs by the fire for you."

Such clucking concern seemed to belie the grim red emblem, and vice versa. Eliste found herself too tired, cold, and confused to puzzle it out. The warmth of the kitchen acted upon her almost as a narcotic, sapping fear and energy alike. She would address the matter—in a little while, preferably following the hot soup and tea. Sinking into the nearest chair, she stretched out her hands to the fire. Aurelie did likewise, while Kairthe, prohibited from seating herself in the presence of her betters, knelt upon the hearth.

Zeralenn remained standing. Her lips were faintly blue with cold, and her teeth were disposed to chatter, but these things never mitigated the precision of her speech.

"Master Quenuble, such kindness places us in your debt. We may not accept hospitality, however, before it is certain that we understand one another quite clearly. My companions and I seek lodgings for an indefinite period, probably not to exceed a few nights. Preferring privacy and anonymity, we trust in your discretion to safeguard our seclusion. For such service, you will be amply recompensed."

"Recompensed?" Quenuble drew himself up. His round, amiably foolish face struggled against nature to express affront. "You are in error, Exalted lady, indeed you are. I declare, you wrong me. *Pâtissier* Quenuble does not render service in hope of payment. Let us not speak of such things. I am Sherreenian, Madame, and loyal—faithful to my king and country, like my father Quenuble, and *his* father Quenuble before him, and indeed, every Quenuble that has ever lived. My own two little Quenuble lads will prove similarly loyal, else I will beat the stuffing out of them by way of instruction. Madame, we Quenubles are of a respectable family, and the Exalted themselves do not despise our pastry. Recompense, indeed—bah!"

"I stand corrected." Zeralenn inclined her head gravely.

This concession was as close as her companions had ever known her to approach an apology. It satisfied Master Quenuble, whose indignation relapsed into affability, but Eliste remained uneasy. She nodded her thanks as their host handed her a steaming cup of lentil soup; sipped and sighed again as the warmth spread through her chilled body, but could not forbear inquiring, "The red diamonds on your door, on your cap—?"

"Camouflage, Exalted Miss. Craft, guile—unworthy perhaps, yet how else shall Quenuble remain free to serve his king and country? But make no mistake, Exalted Miss, I despise the filthy red diamond symbol. I tell you, I hate it. My wife, the Madame Quenuble, also hates it. My two little Quenuble lads will likewise hate it, if they know what's good for them. Shall I tell you a secret, Exalted Miss? Every night, before I retire, I curse and revile the red diamond symbol, and often I spit upon it. And my wife, the Madame Quenuble, has painted a red diamond at the bottom of the chamber pot. This in itself might send us to the Kokotte should it become known, but the two of us deem the satisfaction worth any risk. I will spit upon the red diamond in your presence, if you desire a demonstration. I will do so this very instant, if you like."

"Not necessary," Eliste assured him, her distrust beginning to ebb. And yet: "Why did you give money to the creature that led us here?"

"To Shreds, you mean? Oh, don't fret over Shreds, Exalted Miss. Odd figure, not as bad as he looks."

He almost couldn't be, thought Eliste.

"A little rough-hewn, Shreds, like all brethren of the gutter—the beggars, that is—but on the whole, no worse than the rest of them, just scrabbling on through.

All of them know, because the Madame Quenuble has seen to it that they know, that *Pâtissier* Quenuble pays a reward of six rekkoes for the safe delivery of distressed Exalteds to his door. Thus I am able indirectly to serve our exiled King by extending aid to the victims of a lawless revolution."

"Then all those beggars out there on the street *know* that you harbor Exalted fugitives?" Once again Eliste was seized with an urge to flee. "Dozens of them *know* that we are here?"

"Scores, at least—perhaps hundreds," Quenuble suggested blithely. "But most assuredly they know, Exalted Miss."

"Come, we'd better leave this instant, while we can." Eliste turned to her grandmother, now seated beside the fire.

"Calmly, Granddaughter," Zeralenn advised. "Let us consider."

"Consider! Calmly! By this time, one of those creatures has doubtless summoned the Vanguard."

"Nobody's going to do that, Exalted Miss," Quenuble assured her. "Couldn't happen. Anyone tried it, and the brothers would leave pieces of him scattered all over town. No, it's true," he insisted, noting her look of disbelief. "These brethren of the gutters aren't fools—"

"They are worse. They are beasts. They are Reparationists."

"What they mostly are is hungry, Exalted Miss. And they're not like the booby in the fable killed his last cow. If the Vanguard discover Exalteds here, then Quenuble and all his family are finished. Without Quenuble, there is no hope of a six-rekko reward. More to the point, the daily contribution of yesterday's unsold pastry ceases forever, should the House of Swans fold its wings."

"Is that why those people wait at your door?"

"Exactly so. Even as we speak, the Madame Quenuble distributes jam rolls, slightly stale cake, and brandied plum buns among the brethren, whose silence is thereby assured."

"You have bought them with pastry?"

"It is a sounder currency than most," Zeralenn interjected.

"You speak rightly, Exalted Lady. Indeed, you have hit upon a great truth, the significance of which I strive hourly to impress upon the minds of the two small Quenuble lads."

Thereafter, Eliste began gradually to lose the thread of conversation. As her fears subsided, fatigue asserted itself. She grew quiet, her eyelids drooped, and several times she found herself nodding. Aurelie was in a worse state yet, rubbing her eyes and yawning behind her hand; while Kairthe, curled up on the hearth, frankly snored. Zeralenn sat upright as ever, spine invincibly straight, but her drawn features betrayed exhaustion. Presently taking notice, Master Quenuble offered to conduct them to their beds in "the hidden hall," as he called it. Candle in one hand, Zeralenn's valise in the other, he led them from the kitchen, along a dim corridor to the staircase, and up to the second story, then to the third. And on the third, there was another corridor, with a trapdoor in the ceiling and a hinged wooden stairway—actually a ladder—ascending to the attic. The attic itself was silent, slant-beamed, and crammed to bursting. The weak candlelight played upon trunks and boxes stacked in towers, roomfuls of worm-eaten furniture, bundles, roped bales, and mounds of jumbled rubbish. But there was no sign of a bed, and nowhere else to go; or so it appeared. Then Master Quenuble picked a path through the clutter to the tall old armoire standing in the corner, opened the doors, pushed aside a veil of ancient garments, and fumbled within. An internal catch snapped, internal springs sang, and the wooden panels at the rear of the armoire parted. The opening beyond yawned blackly.

"Ladies. Exalted ladies." A beckoning finger-wiggle.

Through the armoire, and then there they were in the "hidden hall," a niche between steep-pitched roof and straight attic wall, probably intended for storage. Or perhaps not. One hundred fifty years earlier, the victims of the Vernal Purge had sought refuge in cellars and attics all through Sherreen and its environs. Innumerable niches, compartments, concealed holes, and closets had somehow materialized to shelter uncounted fugitives. Most of them had long since been given over to the housing of unused luggage, cleaning implements, bricks and shingles, and sacks of powdered plaster. This one, however, clearly fitted out for habitation and maintained in a state of readiness, was furnished with a pair of cots, well-mattressed and blanketed; carpet on the floor, a bureau, dusty washstand with bowl and pitcher, iron-strapped trunk, candlestick set atop a deal table equipped with two rickety arrow-backed chairs, covered water jugs standing against the wall, a small iron stove venting into the chimney, and a full scuttle of coal. The hall itself was breathlessly narrow. With outstretched arms, it was easy to touch both walls simultaneously. Yet it ran the entire length of the house like a right-triangular tunnel, its shadowy span barely lighted at each end by narrow slits tucked beneath the eaves—slashes almost invisible from the street, through which the gray light of dawn was just now beginning to filter.

"Poor and unfit," confessed Master Quenuble. "But the best I can offer, for now. Exalted ladies, before I leave you to your rest, a word of advice. Do not leave this hidden hall during the daylight hours. Only in the evening, when the day's trade is finished and the House of Swans has closed its doors, is it safe to venture down to the kitchen for your meals—which, if you will so far honor us, you may take in the company of the Quenuble family, with whom you are welcome to join in the nightly reviling of Reparationist regicides. At all other times, it is well not to call undue attention to your presence. The rug upon the floor will deaden the sound of your footfalls, but step lightly nevertheless. Speak softly; do not shriek at sight of a mouse or spider, if you can help it. Do not carol or whistle or yodel. As much as possible, keep the curtains drawn over the vents; but most particularly at night, when the glow of candlelight might betray your presence to observers down on Cliquot Street. Exalted ladies, I trust I may rely upon your discretion?"

"You may," Zeralenn assured him.

But Eliste's confidence did not match her grandmother's. Reluctant though she was to disclose her secret, there was really no way of putting it off any longer. "There is—a—a—small difficulty," she confessed, and forestalling inquiry, opened her valise to extract the groggy Prince vo Plume, who lay in her cradled arms limp and quiet as a white fur tippet.

Aurelie oohed softly, a vertical crease indented Zeralenn's brow, and the pastry chef shook his head.

"Noisy little yapper, I expect," he observed.

"Oh, no, he'll be good."

"Needs to run outdoors every day, or we'll be wading in it."

"Perhaps the two small Quenuble lads might enjoy walking him—he'll heel for them," Eliste suggested. "Perhaps the Madame Quenuble would find him amusing. He does tricks."

"Tricks, eh?" Master Quenuble wavered momentarily, then rallied. "But no. A little, useless, lady's toy like that would attract too much attention—people asking where the runt came from and what good he is and so forth. No."

"This was a great stupidity, Granddaughter," observed Zeralenn. "There is no place here for the animal."

"But he's not useless," Eliste insisted, playing her last card. "He's a perfectly fine nitter—he'll discover a nit of NuNu where you or I would never think of looking."

"Well, that is handy, if he can actually do it."

"He can—he does. I've seen him."

"Hmm." Master Quenuble fingered his double chin, reconsidering. "We'll put him in the kitchen, then. And if he finds a nit one day—well, then he'll have earned his keep, and more."

"Thank you, sir." Releasing a relieved breath, Eliste relinquished her pet.

Quenuble left them. The wooden partition that formed the door to their refuge and the back wall of the armoire clicked shut behind him. It was dawn. Stronger light was thrusting in through the handspan windows. Wheels were already rumbling over the cobbles down on Cliquot Street. Kairthe lowered the thick black blinds, restoring midnight. Undressing with some reluctance in the drafty atmosphere of the hidden hall, they sought their respective beds—Eliste and Aurelie squeezed uncomfortably together in one cot, Zeralenn alone, Kairthe stretched out on the floor. For a while Eliste lay wide awake, tense and preoccupied with the events of the night, with the peril of their situation, the uncertainty of the future, the strangeness of their new surroundings, the unaccustomed and unwelcome proximity of Aurelie's already-inert body. She would never fall asleep, not under these circumstances, Eliste told herself. Never. And then she fell asleep.

Her slumber was dreamless, profound, and prolonged. When next she opened her eyes, it was midafternoon. Aurelie's elbow was firmly lodged in the small of her back, and it was probably this pressure that had roused her. Now she sat up slowly, blinking a little at the prism-shaped wooden tunnel. Zeralenn and Kairthe were already up and dressed. Flawlessly groomed as always, Zeralenn sat at the table, writing in the little gilt journal that used to grace the escritoire in her morning room. Kairthe was at the washstand, rinsing out lingerie. Now setting the work aside, she hurried to Eliste's assistance. Never did she consider that an Exalted lady could or should arise, wash, and dress unaided. Even in the aftermath of the Revolution, the possibility simply did not occur to her; nor did it enter the mind of her mistress.

Presently attired in last night's plain wool dress, Eliste joined her grandmother at the table. Low-voiced greetings were exchanged, and then, elbows propped upon the table, chin propped on her fists, Eliste leaned forward to inquire, "And now, Madame?"

"Granddaughter?"

"This place is all very well, and we've been lucky to find it and all that, but we want to leave Sherreen as quickly as possible."

"Clearly a more difficult undertaking than anticipated, and for the moment quite beyond our power."

"We can't sit cooped up in this attic indefinitely."

"It is preferable to the Sepulchre, I believe."

"If we got word to the Cavalier vo Meureille, letting him know where we are, then he'd come to us and we could carry through with our original plan, couldn't we?"

"I daresay. How precisely do you propose to do that, Granddaughter? You've a method, I presume?"

Eliste colored—her grandmother hadn't lost the knack of making her feel a fool—sat silent for a moment or two—*What would Dref think up now?*—and then, much to her own surprise, an idea did occur to her.

"Why, yes," she rose to the challenge, careful to appear casual. "I do, as a matter of fact. Master Quenuble is evidently on excellent terms with the fraternity of Sherreenian beggars. The beggars go everywhere, know everything, and they are infallibly faithful to their own best interests, or so we are told. If all this is true, then why not have Quenuble offer a generous reward—which we should pay—for the discovery of vo Meureille's whereabouts?"

There. Not exactly a stroke of genius, but better than nothing.

"Well. So." To Eliste's gratification, her grandmother appeared almost taken aback. "That is not such a bad notion. Not bad at all. There are possibilities to consider here. Well done, Granddaughter."

Eliste felt her cheeks warm with absurd pleasure. Praise from Zeralenn was rare.

"We will consult Master Quenuble as soon as—"

A creak and protesting moan from the cot interrupted the conversation. Behind them, Aurelie stirred, woke, and gazed about her.

"Oh, gad—not a dream." Her eyes shut briefly, and she murmured, "Bring me a cup of chocolate, Kairthe."

"Can't Miss," Kairthe replied with genuine regret. "No tea or juice, neither. We've got nothing, Miss."

"What—nothing!" Aurelie's eyes popped open and she sat bolt upright in bed. "Nothing to eat or drink in here?"

"Water, Miss."

"Faugh, abominable! Well, then, go downstairs and fetch me something from the kitchen at once."

"But I can't, Miss! Don't tell me!"

"Don't be a goose. Off you go."

"I can't, Miss. I swear, I'm not allowed!"

"Gad, is it possible the creature is *arguing* with me?"

"That will do. Leave her alone, Child Aurelie," Zeralenn commanded. "She is your cousin's woman, not yours. In any event, the girl speaks truly. We are none of us to leave this room before nightfall. You've another three hours or so to wait."

"But, Grauntie, I'm hungry *now*, quite intolerably so!"

"Fill your stomach with water, if you must. And be so good as to lower your voice," Zeralenn suggested.

"Water—oh, barbarous! Very well, if we are to live as savages! Kairthe, bring me some wretched water, then dress me!"

Kairthe complied, and minutes later Aurelie joined her kinswomen at the table. "Cousin, if you will be so good, please move aside a little so that we may share that chair. Thank you. A little farther, please. Gad, what a trial." She seated herself. "Now, then, what are we to do with ourselves before dinner?"

"You are at liberty to amuse yourselves quietly, as best you may," Zeralenn told her.

"But what is there to *do* in here?"

"I myself am taking the opportunity to bring my journal current. If you like, I will tear blank pages from the book and give them to you. There is a full bottle of ink, and a plentiful supply of fresh-sharpened pens."

"What in the world am I to do with *those*?"

"Your powers of invention appear limited, Child Aurelie. With paper, pen, and ink, the possibilities are almost endless. You might, for example, begin a journal of your own. You might compose essays, poetry, songs, or dramatic verse—"

"*I'm* no prune-faced bluestocking scribbler!"

"You might work sums—"

"They make my head ache!"

"You might in that case sketch landscapes, portraits, still-life arrangements, and so on—"

"Tedious!"

"Perhaps you could design the dresses and jewels you would like to own someday." Eliste entered the discussion.

"But I should want them so, and what if I never got them? Oh, it would break my heart!"

"You could bend and fold the paper into animals, birds, and flowers," Eliste continued. "You could tear it into bits to make a jigsaw puzzle. You might devise number games or word games. We could mark out a checkered board, draw the pieces, and play chess—or anything else we want. We could draw a set of playing cards, make paper counters, and play Peril, drivendo—or even Antislez, if I drew the Obranese deck. You could . . ." She was starting to stretch for ideas, and Aurelie's eyes continued unresponsive. "You could write letters to your friends— why, you could write to Bayelle. You could tell him what's happened to us, let him know you're safe, talk to him as if he's with you—"

"Pour out my heart in lines of fire, the depth and passion of which will enshrine me forever among the great lovers of history! Formidable! How I should relish it!" Aurelie glowed briefly, then relapsed into her former discontent. "But where's the use? What point in writing letters that cannot be posted? It is so much wasted effort."

"Truly, they can't be posted just now, but who's to speak for the future? What you need to do is to tell yourself in your own mind that you are speaking directly to Bayelle. Use your imagination—I know you've got one," Eliste urged, setting pen and ink before her cousin. "Convince yourself that he's here, looking over your shoulder as you write."

"Oh, no, I shouldn't care to let him see me now, with my hair all out of curl. However . . ." Somewhat reluctantly, Aurelie accepted a blank page torn from Zeralenn's journal. "Well, I shall try, I suppose. But I must have this chair to myself, else I cannot concentrate, I cannot compose. Cousin, I am sure you understand."

"Oh, very well." Eliste wandered away from the table. For a little while she kept a surreptitious eye on her cousin. Aurelie at first appeared irresolute—squeezing out a laborious sentence, then frowning and chewing her pen for a while before squeezing out another. Presently, however, inspiration took hold; the frown disappeared and the pen raced over the paper, its scratching loud in the quiet room. Quickly the page was filled, and Aurelie requested another, and then another.

Eliste walked to and fro, exploring, but there was little to see; virtually nothing beyond what she'd absorbed in last night's first glimpse. The narrow carpet covered only the central section of the room, stopping several feet short of the wall at either end. Beyond its padded boundaries, the irregular old floorboards creaked and groaned at every step, despite all precautions. With infinite care, she crept to the rear wall and peeped down through the vent into the warren of walled enclosures, footways, and alleys that backed the House of Swans. There was someone filling a bucket at a pump down there; someone burning a heap of rags; a cat promenading a fence. Nothing of consequence. She crossed to the front, where she could look down into Cliquot Street.

This was by far the more interesting view. Cliquot Street was broad and busy, agabble with commerce and enterprise. In addition to the requisite shops, taverns, and cafés, the street contained a gaudy collection of pushcart vendors selling everything from deep-fried ganzel puffs, to cheap scarves, trinkets, and in one peculiar case, last month's newspapers. There was also a strolling population of prostitutes, beggars, and street musicians, all competing on more or less equal footing for the same elusive coins. It was a scene, Eliste was sure, of which she wouldn't tire quickly. Apparently, there was always something going on. Just now, for example—a swirl of unusual activity down below as the street cleared and the spectators lined up three deep along the gutters on both sides, shoving and elbowing for a good view of whatever was approaching. Hard jostling, and the occasional exchange of blows. Waving arms and upthrust fists; cheers and jeers and shouts of "Reparation!" And then a little convoy rumbling up from the Waterfront Market: two open carts, doubly flanked by a contingent of the Vonahrish Guard and followed by a straggling train of cavorting patriots, on their way to Equality Circle and the Kokotte. The carts were crude and sturdy, probably appropriated from the nearest farm. Each contained some dozen bound and naked figures; young and old, male and female, commoner and former Exalted, mingled indiscriminately. From her vantage point four stories above the street, Eliste could not begin to judge individual faces and features, but the varying stances of the condemned—the angle and tilt of a head, the set of neck and spine—sometimes almost shouted; expressing everything from apathy and misery to theatrical disdain, from defiance to studied nonchalance, from tranquillity to weeping panic. A few in each cart huddled together for warmth or for modesty's sake. One of them down there, slim and chlorotic, was nodding and grimacing at the crowd like an actor. Another—quite different, with a laborer's muscular body and a square, blunt-featured face—dared to lift his voice in a great shout: "Long live the King!" Eliste heard, and her eyes stung. If anything followed, she did not catch it, for a roar arose, a tremendous volume of disapprobation that easily drowned his voice. Stones and clods arched through the air, pelting naked flesh. Some victims cringed, dropping to their knees, unable to shield themselves with their bound arms. Some ignored the barrage. A few demonstrative citizens, venturing too near, were repelled by thrusts of the Guardsmen's musket butts.

The carts rolled on up Cliquot Street. For a while the crowd loitered, but nothing more appeared, and the spectators began to disperse. Eliste stood quite still. It was her first actual glimpse of the famous sacrificial carts. She had been hearing of them for months, and the reality precisely matched the descriptions; yet the sight momentarily froze her. Her imagination was too vivid for comfort. All too clearly, she could see herself down there standing in one of those carts. Her point of view seemed to change, descending, and she *was* there, passing beneath the facade of the House of Swans, with its narrow little vent tucked up almost out of sight under the eaves, and, in some lunatic dissociation, her own white face peering down at herself through the vent. She could feel the shuddery chill of the wintry air upon her bare flesh, the bite of the cord at her wrists, the jolting of the cart through the soles of her feet. Zeralenn, Aurelie, and Kairthe stood in the cart beside her. Aurelie was speaking.

"Gad, but this seems so slow, Grauntie! So tiresome, la!"

"Patience, Child Aurelie. We are certain to get there eventually."

Bizarre. Then she noticed the voices behind her; they really *were* talking. She turned away from the window. She was cold, far colder than the room temperature warranted.

Repairing to the cot, Eliste pulled Uncle Quinze's magical gold-backed mirror from the valise, and for a time lost herself amidst roseate landscapes through which no carts rumbled. Presently the reflected world grew hazier as rose cooled to lavender. Eliste looked up to discover that the light outside was fading. Half an hour later, Kairthe pulled the curtains down at both windows, then lit a candle at the table, filling the room with weak yellow light and nervous shadows. Shortly thereafter, Zeralenn judged it safe to descend.

The floorboards whimpered as they picked their way through the junk-heap attic. A little wrestling with the trap and ladder, then down; some difficulty for

Kairthe, burdened with a water jug that already needed refilling. And down two more flights to the warm kitchen, where the Quenuble family already sat at table: Master Quenuble solid and sugar-dusted; the Madame Quenuble, some years her husband's junior, but similarly broad and whitened, with a shortbread waistline; and the two small Quenuble lads, Thierre and Breuve, aged eight and nine, squat square miniatures of their father. At the foot of young Breuve Quenuble's chair, Prince vo Plume sat up begging, with such success that he greeted his mistress's entrance with almost perfunctory demonstrations.

The newcomers were welcomed cordially but without ceremony. Seats and bowls were provided. They were invited to help themselves to pork ragout, bread, and red wine; and so they would have done, for the first time in their lives, had not Kairthe insisted upon serving them. Master Quenuble stirred. For a moment he seemed disposed to assist, but a sharp glance from his wife quelled him. Neither Madame nor the children appeared to share the *pâtissier*'s exaggerated deference for all things Exalted. The fugitive quality might merit loyalty, honor, assistance, even sympathy; but they could serve themselves. Eliste and her grandmother were content enough with this, and Aurelie endured it. Only Quenuble and Kairthe seemed troubled.

Both food and conversation were good, the latter enlivened with Madame Quenuble's recital of current gossip gleaned from the day's customers; including an account of rioting in Equality Circle some hours earlier, where enraged citizens had fallen upon a party of the Kokotte's Cavaliers and Coquettes, whose immense and ridiculous headgear blocked the public view of the Duke of Rivennier's execution. Today's batch of victims had also contained several of the Duke's v'Estais kinsmen—including his pretty granddaughter who was once a Maid of Honor—as well as a redheaded Baron vo Pleniere-v'Orenne, and one of the former king's great courtiers, the famous wit Vicount vo Renache.

Merranotte.

The names pierced Eliste. No longer hungry, she pushed her bowl aside. The greatest and noblest gone in a breath—and the world scarcely rippled.

All in all, a particularly choice collection this afternoon; and the assembled spectators, unwilling to forgo sight of the sacrifice for the sake of the Coquettes' worst affectations, had started pitching bricks and broken bottles. Dozens of citizens of each faction had been bruised or otherwise damaged before the intervention of the Vonahrish Guard finally quelled the rioting. In the midst of this uproar, apparently unconscious of whizzing missiles, the Kokotte and her chief acolyte Bierce Valeur had continued quietly about their business; methodically dispatching a total of twenty-four victims. By the time the public disturbance ended, the public spectacle had done likewise. And it was so clear to anyone owning a thimbleful of wit that these open-air offerings were an obvious threat to civic peace and order, that even those bloody-minded jackass-Reparationists ought to be able to see it; or so Madame Quenuble opined.

Her husband concurred, punctuating her account with his own ritual fulminations. These creative dissections of Reparationist character and intellect seemed a favorite Quenuble diversion. Guests and family members were encouraged to participate. The visitors declined, but the Quenuble lads displayed hereditary enthusiasm, each striving to outdo the other in luxuriance of language and invention. Young Thierre was particularly imaginative in his speculations concerning the origin of the Reparationist party ("When a rotten dead warty toad lay in a swamp, and the sun shone down on it and it puffed up with stinking gas, bigger and bigger until it all burst, and something crawled out of the gunk—well that's when the first Reparationist was born. Or what about . . .").

Breuve liked to examine appropriate response in the face of Reparationist aggression. "Want to know what I'd do if a Rep muscled me?" he would inquire, and the ensuing descriptions were elaborate. "But you can't do that, 'Liste, you're a girl. And you haven't got the trained poison snake or the hollow iron darts." As owner of The Runt, as the boys had dubbed Prince vo Plume, Eliste merited special attention. She now sat flanked by children. "So do like I say. When a Rep muscles you—just knee 'im in the nuts and knock 'im in the nose. That's what." His brother nodded vigorous assent.

"I'll remember," Eliste vowed gravely.

"Boys, watch your language. That isn't the proper way to speak to an Exalted lady," Master Quenuble admonished.

It is these days.

The meal concluded. Shortly thereafter, the boys retired, under protest. At the kitchen door, Breuve turned back to catch Eliste's eye, then silently mouthed the words "Knee 'im—" His knee viciously jabbed air. "And knock 'im." He threw a sharp punch at nothing. She nodded reassuringly, and they exited. In the children's absence, Zeralenn put forward Eliste's idea of employing Sherreenian beggars in the search for the Cavalier vo Meureille. She would offer a reward of one hundred rekkoes for news of the Cavalier's whereabouts, Zeralenn announced, provided that secrecy was maintained.

The Quenubles approved, encouraged, each offering to spread the word among the most diligent of mendicants. Within hours, the news would reach The Fungus, whose consent was essential; but there seemed no reason to imagine it should be withheld. Thereafter, beggars in all corners of the city would be watching for Meureille. There was no hiding place within the bounds of Sherreen so deep, so dark and secret, that the brethren of the gutter could not sniff it out. It might take days, perhaps even a couple of weeks; but in the end, Meureille would surely be found.

Sitting in the firelit kitchen, warm and well-fed and reassured, Eliste could feel the cold knots inside her start to loosen. This pastry chef and his wife were so kindly confident, it seemed almost insulting to doubt them. Besides, she did not want to doubt. They would find Meureille, they would leave Sherreen, with its red diamonds, its spying nits, its open carts rumbling between Sepulchre and hungry Kokotte. The sense of nightmare entrapment, rising to such sickening levels of late, would disappear completely, once and for all. It was going to happen very soon—the Quenubles had promised—everything would be all right—

It just has to be true.

Aurelie had hardly ventured a word since they'd left the attic, but now she was speaking up at last, making requests. She needed writing paper, she announced; a plentiful supply of good stationery, with new pens and colored inks. She also required provisions to stave off starvation during the daylight hours of incarceration.

The Quenubles were wonderfully patient. They owned no writing supplies, but they could furnish sheets of unglazed wrapping paper and a basket of apricot twists. For Eliste and Zeralenn, there was a small package of books once left by an indifferent scholar in exchange for cream puffs, and never reclaimed. Eliste herself had never displayed any great zest for reading, but now, in that place, she seized upon the volumes hungrily. Following the day's quiet inactivity, she would have welcomed further kitchen companionship; but for the Quenubles, obliged to rise before dawn, it was already time to retire. The Exalted ladies were welcome to sit up for a little while beside the fire, Quenuble informed them, but not too long. A light in the kitchen late at night was bound to arouse curiosity, if noticed. It might be best, he suggested gently, if the Exalted ladies returned to the attic.

He was right, of course, Eliste conceded with internal reluctance. She didn't want to go back. Last night's refuge was already beginning to seem like a gaol; but he was right. Back up stairs and ladder, through attic and armoire; back to prism-prison, and silent tedium. There could be no escape into sleep as yet. It was only a few hours since they had risen, and all four were wide awake; moreover, it was best to confine waking activities as much as possible to nighttime hours, when the House of Swans was free of customers.

They set about filling up time. Seated cross-legged on the floor beside the table, within the radius of candlelight, Kairthe mended lace. Zeralenn embroidered—her eyes were still preternaturally sharp—while Aurelie resumed her interrupted letter. Aurelie's composition now flowed, copious and effortless. Rarely did she pause to grope for words, but occasionally the pen froze and she lifted her eyes from her work to exclaim in a whisper, "Gad, this is so poetical, he *ought* to see it. He *should*."

"Well, perhaps he will, someday," Eliste soothed absently. Sinking down upon the cot, she examined the bundle of books, whose titles were just barely visible in the low light. *Mollusks of the Douenne Estuary. Two Thousand Greej Patterns. The Gleque Method of Crop Rotation.* Several others, equally unpromising. No wonder the anonymous student had never reclaimed them. But there at least was one of Rees-Raas Zhumeau's early effusions, which would do well enough. She needed more light to read by, however; and because both chairs were occupied, that meant seating herself on the floor next to Kairthe. The floor. Unbelievable. She did it, however, much to her servant's amazement. Thereafter, she found it no easy matter to immerse herself in the pastoral vision of Zhumeau. The fancies that seemed so beautiful and moving when she first read them, two years earlier, were now beginning to strike her as silly, particularly the bits about the Golden Garden. Did that mean, she wondered, that she was growing old and hard and cynical? Really, it was difficult to concentrate on starry-eyed old Zhumeau, but then, she wouldn't have to do so for very long. It wouldn't be much longer now before the Cavalier vo Meureille would appear to take them away. Probably not more than a day or two, certainly not more than a week.

But it took longer than that. For the first couple of days, Eliste lived in a state of continual expectation, ever on the alert for the rattle at the armoire announcing the arrival of Master Quenuble with a message from the Cavalier. But the days passed, each one like the last, undistinguished by incident. Eliste learned that the consent of The Fungus had been obtained with ease, contingent upon payment of a twenty-five-percent commission—a bit higher than The Fungus's norm, but in view of the magnitude of the reward, acceptable to the Sherreenian brethren of the gutter; and now the beggars were poking and prodding into every odd corner in town. Their eventual success was all but certain, but there was no way of expediting the search, and Meureille was proving unexpectedly elusive. A week went by, and no one glimpsed him. Another week, and winter pressed hard upon Sherreen, while the Cavalier continued invisible. Successive bitter days; the mud in the gutters turned to granite, the water hardened in troughs and fountains. Then, for forty-eight hours, the Vir itself froze over, a phenomenon outside the direct experience of any living Sherreenian, although many had heard old tales of "sliding the river." It was surely the coldest Vonahrish winter within human memory, and humanity collectively cringed shivering, drawing in upon itself in small clots centered around grates and stoves. Snow quaintly feathered the streets and squares; a pretty sight for a few hours, until passing feet and wheels packed the fluffy mantle down into a dense, slick, lethal surface that would surely persist for months. Perambulation was hazardous as well as comfortless, and those citizens able to go indoors did so. A comparative hush fell over the city; even the beggars seemed to vanish. And somewhere within frostbitten Sherreen, the Cavalier vo Meureille lay hidden and inaccessible, immured like a crumb at the bottom of an icebox.

Eliste cultivated patience, a virtue to which she had never before aspired. She wore extra layers of clothing, including knitted gloves and cap, to ward off the cold. She sketched, wrote, composed, began a journal, devised games and puzzles, produced a fanciful deck of cards, embroidered, crocheted, and read whatever she could find, eventually absorbing even *The Gleque Method of Crop Rotation*. She also spent a good deal of time beside the little window, staring down at the activity in Cliquot Street. Although this spectacle proved endlessly absorbing, the diversion carried its price, for she could not stand there so long and often without sometimes glimpsing the open carts en route to Equality Circle. They came every day, sometimes late in the afternoon, sometimes around midday, rarely earlier. The quick clearing of the street and the instant materialization of a gutter audience heralded their approach. That gave her, she was forced to admit to herself, sufficient warning to turn away from the window, but usually she stayed where she was, held fast in the grip of morbid fascination. The carts traveled in little caravans these days, usually no fewer than three, sometimes as many as five, each bearing about a dozen passengers; accompanied by guards and trailed by the enthusiastic and the inquisitive. The number of victims was increasing, just as the lower limit of their age was noticeably decreasing. Eliste's hands had jumped the first time she peeped down from her aerie to spy children of eight or nine standing in the carts alongside their mothers. Her disgust and hatred had flared so violently at the sight that for a moment or two she was actually dizzy. When the qualm subsided, leaving her wobbly and clammy-fleshed, the carts had already passed from view. Thereafter she armored her mind, viewing the quotidian convoys with physical equilibrium intact. No matter how she hardened herself, however, she could never suppress the surge of impotent fury scorching her at sight of the condemned infants; nor, somehow, could she bring herself to look away from them.

The naked bodies packed into those carts were slush-white or tinged with blue, shoulder-hunched or crouching, shuddering at the touch of the frigid air. Some of them were splotched and streaked with bruises, raised welts, padded yellow blisters; others were inanimate and empty-eyed, awake and yet unconscious. Eliste had heard stories of the subterranean Sepulchre torture vaults. There were machines down there, it was said; old magical contraptions that could twist perception, senses, even reason. . . . These tales, carried through the streets by the beggars and hawkers, repeated at dinnertime by Madame Quenuble, Eliste had initially dismissed as wild rumor. The condition of the condemned, however, could not be ignored or easily explained away.

Probable, then, that the stories were true, at least in part. Torture and death for her fellow Exalteds—but *which ones?* She couldn't stop wondering, and this wretched unsatisfied curiosity festered and enlarged, eventually approaching obsession. In vain she strained her vision, inspecting each passenger in turn. She stood four stories above them. Their heads—wigless, unpowdered, uncurled, and unkempt—were bowed for the most part, with faces averted; the half-frozen bodies, she had never before seen denuded of silks and brocades. Under such circumstances, identification was impossible. Often she thought to glimpse a familiar brow or chin, a contour, a posture, a color, or expression that she knew. Once she spied a straight pale profile so like Rouveel-Nezoir vo Lillevant's that she was almost sure—almost. Perhaps. No, never *sure.*

Not that she was deprived of all knowledge. The daily reports from Equality Circle often noted specific victims. She knew that Stazzi and Putsie vo Crev were both gone. So were the Cavalier vo Furnaux, the Countess vo Brajonard and her four children, Baron vo Nezhille, Arl v'Onarl, and so many others, so very many. Night after night the familiar names had struck like arrows, and she had winced at each, while beside her her grandmother's face stilled into such marble immobility that at last Madame Quenuble took note, and took to censoring her own reports. Even then, however, the names continued to drop, often from the careless lips of the children. Day after day and the list continued to grow. But that was not the most immediate of worries.

From time to time, the Vanguard searched the local shops and houses. Presumably they hunted fugitive Exalted, enemies of the Revolution, illicit documents, literature or correspondence, Nirienniste pamphlets—anything that could possibly pass for evidence. The method of target-site selection was unknown to the public. Perhaps the Vanguard relied upon information relayed by human spies, or by the nits of NuNu, or both; perhaps there was a geographical pattern; perhaps some of the time they simply chose at random. Eliste had heard of this from Breuve and Thierre, and once she even saw for herself.

Ice-glazed wintry dusk, and a closed carriage with a red diamond emblem draws up before the mercer's shop standing on a long diagonal across Cliquot Street from the House of Swans. Eliste, well-muffled, and stationed as usual at the vent, presses her cheek hard to the wall and squints for a better view. Out of the carriage come piling the soldiers, dragon's breath smoking on the cold, shadowed air. A split in the squad, a couple of Vanguardsmen circling to the rear of the shop, the others straight to the front door and in. Nothing to see for a while, other than citizens, alerted by the presence of the carriage, gathering to view the denouement. Then—emergence of the soldiers, dragging with them a man and a woman, the woman twisting and clawing uselessly. Into the carriage, a slamming of doors, and off. End of performance, and the audience disperses quickly. The next day, the mercer's shop boarded tight, the symbol of Congressional confiscation painted two feet tall on its door.

It had fallen upon the mercer without warning. It could just as easily strike the *pâtissier*. And Eliste's fears, temporarily lulled, began to wake again.

The longer they lingered in Sherreen, the greater the risk of discovery. Meureille. They needed him. Where was he—dead, imprisoned, or fled? *Where?*

She hated it all—the waiting, the mingled fear and tedium, the helpless inactivity, the sense—even yet—of something like astonishment at the monstrous injustice of it all.

She sought mental anesthesia in routine. Sleep late every day, as late as possible, sometimes past noon. Then wash, dress, and breakfast on yesterday's pastries. Several hours of varied quiet activity. Minimal muted conversation. As little walking to and fro as possible, and that, cat-footed. Writing, drawing, card games, crocheting, and time at the window—too much time, too many carts passing by, too many doomed faces hovering upon the edge of recognizability.

Did the others share her fears and frustrations? Difficult to say, for such conversational topics were by tacit consent avoided. Zeralenn appeared stoically serene; Kairthe—a lesser target than her Exalted companions, yet greatly jeopardized by serving them—was consistently good-humored; and Aurelie, usually prone to complaint, was now so absorbed in her unilateral correspondence with Bayelle vo Clarivaux that all dissatisfaction fled her mind. Letter after letter she composed, at least two a day, sometimes more, each crammed with the sublimest of sentiments, or so the author claimed. Aurelie was fond of dropping hints and provocative comments—"This will astonish him—la, he will think me bold!" "I blush—perhaps I am too daring!"—but when pressed for specifics, maintained high-minded reserve—"But I must not speak, it would scarcely be fair to Bayelle!" After the first few days, her companions no longer rose to the bait, but such neglect did not affect the volume of production. The letters proliferated at an astounding rate, and Aurelie refused to explain what became of them all— presumably she was storing them in some secret place. Nettled by her cousin's mysterious smirks and shrugs, Eliste soon stopped asking.

Twilight each afternoon, then early winter darkness. Departure of the last customers, closing of the House of Swans, then down to the kitchen for warmth and firelight, food, conversation, wine, and companionship. The best time of the day, but far too short. All too soon, the Quenuble family off to bed; and then, a few more minutes in the kitchen, usually given over to light exercise of one kind or another. Here they could dance to the tunes that Kairthe hummed softly, and the three girls did so, dipping and twirling, shadows swaying on walls and shutters. Zeralenn did not dance, but walked to and fro, striding vigorously, pale face deceptively rosy in the red-tinged light of the dying fire. Dying already? Yes, and time to return to prism-prison. Eliste hated that. Every night, it seemed harder to force herself up those stairs and back to the attic she had come to detest. It was so quiet, so confining—they were living like mice in the wall.

But her appreciation of the mouse hole increased considerably the day the Vanguard visited the House of Swans. They came around noon, at which time the pastry shop magically emptied itself of customers. The search itself seemed a matter of little consequence to the soldiers, whose expectations were clearly low. If they'd possessed significant information, they would have worked harder. As it was, they seemed indifferent, almost lackadaisical, their attention focusing primarily upon Master Quenuble's pastel petit fours, which were consumed by the dozen. They did take care to check each room, each wardrobe, bureau, trunk, and desk drawer. They looked into the cellar and poked a little about the attic, even glancing dutifully into the old armoire in the corner. The armoire's false back was fixed in place, and the Vanguardsmen discovered nothing. They scarcely troubled to check along the heavily obstructed wall for concealed doorways, but the four crouched in the compartment beyond could not know that. To Eliste, it sounded as if they meant to tear the attic apart. Kneeling on the floor, ear pressed to the wall, she could hear every footstep, every creak and thump, every grunt and mutter. Beside her cowered Kairthe and Aurelie, likewise listening; all three girls tightly clasping one another's hands and scarcely breathing. Zeralenn sat at the table, immersed in *The Gleque Method of Crop Rotation* and seemingly unconscious of the soldiers' presence.

Thudding, banging, cursing; a rabid inquisitive scuffling at the door of the armoire. It seemed to go on forever, as if the moment, in all its distilled misery, were suspended in time.

Voices a couple of feet away; Aurelie's long fingernails digging into her wrist; a sense of intolerable pressure. And then retreating footsteps, diminishing voices. Clattering on the ladder, and the attic was empty. Freeing herself of clutching hands, Eliste rose, stole to the vent, and gazed down into Cliquot Street. Minutes later, the Vanguardsmen emerged empty-handed from the House of Swans, hurrying off to seek better gleanings elsewhere. Eliste, leaning her full weight upon the wall, stood absolutely still for minutes thereafter.

The mouse hole had its uses, beyond doubt. Neatly concealed and well-appointed, there was perhaps no better hiding place in all of Sherreen. But the best was not good enough, a fact that grew increasingly apparent over the next few days and nights, during the course of which Prince vo Plume flushed no less than three nits of NuNu; two in the shop and one in the kitchen. The nits did not mind cold weather in the least. In fact, their numbers appeared to be on the increase. The three intruders discovered by the dog were promptly crushed, but it was a safe bet that others would soon follow; and how long before one should succeed in escaping the Plume's notice? It would surely happen sooner or later, probably sooner; and the Vanguard's second search would be far more painstaking than the first.

Eliste was plagued with a recurrent mental image of an hourglass swiftly emptying itself. Her sense of urgency was acute and impotent; there was absolutely nothing to be done. The days passed, and her tension mounted, killing appetite and repose. Sleep eluded her entirely the night following the appearance of seven fully loaded carts of the condemned down on Cliquot Street—the largest convoy she had ever seen; enough, one would have thought, to challenge even so excellent a digestion as the Kokotte's. The scene was repeated the following day. Evidently the Kokotte continued unimpaired, but the same could not be said of Eliste, who worried, and lost sleep, and would no doubt have fretted herself into a state of nervous illness had not a message arrived at last to announce the discovery of Meureille's whereabouts.

H e had been nearby all the while. Less than a mile away, in fact; holed up in the back room of a boardinghouse at the bottom of Riquenoir Street. Almost in plain sight, as it were; and yet, so excellent the discretion of friends and followers that it had actually taken the brethren of the gutter over a month to sniff him out. They had tracked him down at last, however; and now, on a brilliantly icy winter's morning, their success was heralded by the arrival of a beggar bearing a message from the Cavalier vo Meureille, deliverable upon payment of the promised reward.

Eliste was roused from uneasy slumber by a rattling at the armoire. Alarmed, she sat up in bed. Beside her, Aurelie burrowed under the blanket like a frightened rabbit. Kairthe woke and rose from the floor, but Zeralenn, very early up and dressed—or still up?—was already at the partition, sliding the bolt and shifting the panel to admit an excited Breuve Quenuble. The boy relayed his news with an air of triumph that Zeralenn seemed to find convincing. Without hesitation, she handed him one hundred rekkoes in notes, and his eyes widened in awe at the sight of so much money. He was gone before Eliste could protest.

"The proof?" she demanded belatedly. "Madame, surely you shouldn't have paid before we'd seen some proof?"

"I cannot trouble to haggle." Zeralenn's attitude toward money had always somehow managed to combine the practical and the utterly indifferent.

Suppressing a shrug, Eliste rose and managed to dress herself, while Kairthe assisted Aurelie. No sooner were they done than Breuve was back, bearing the message.

"Meureille's hand, without doubt." Unfolding the small white square, Zeralenn read without haste, while her companions clustered to peer over her shoulder. "Observe, Granddaughter—your fears were quite groundless. The Cavalier is well, as I expected. He bids us meet him at midnight tonight, at South Arch below the Waterfront Market, from which point he will guide us to his tunnel. Beyond Sherreen, we shall proceed by coach to Arenne, from whence we set sail for Strell. It would appear that our troubles are at an end."

An end! Eliste could hardly believe it. She needed to read the note again, to handle it and assure herself of its reality. Kairthe was similarly caught, gazing fascinated upon the missive she could not read. Only Aurelie seemed immune. Aurelie stood aside, whispering into young Breuve's ear, and Breuve was nodding. Shortly thereafter the boy departed, but Eliste scarcely marked his disappearance. Escape! Her mind hugged the prospect, and minutes passed before the practical intruded upon euphoria. They needed to prepare themselves, to pack their belongings, to bid their remarkably generous hosts farewell, and—

And not much else, actually. The day yawned before them, empty and all but endless—a long, long succession of hours stretching between morning and midnight. It would seem to go on forever; but then, didn't they all?

But not for much longer. We're getting out.

Excitement swept through her. She was suddenly filled with energy, and there was nothing to do with it all. Packing was accomplished within minutes. The one last essential article—Prince vo Plume—would have to be stowed in the valise at the last moment. Beyond that—nothing required. And it was only midmorning, hours earlier than she would normally have awakened, but further sleep was out of the question. She was electrically awake, and certain to remain so.

The longest day. The longest day that ever was, bloated with desultory conversation, lackluster rounds of Peril, slipshod indifferent handiwork. Only once came a real diversion, in midafternoon, when Eliste, pulled by some cold force impossible to resist, repaired to the vent to gaze down into Cliquot Street. Instinct had drawn her at the exact moment the carts of the condemned were passing below; seven of them today. As always, she found herself unable to turn away, and stood there watching it all.

But for the last time ever.

Hours and more hours. Infinitesimal lengthening of shadows down below; a faint reddening of the light on snowy roofs, followed by a graying of the air. And then, beyond doubt, the sun was truly setting at last, the world outside indisputably darkening, and the House of Swans closing its doors for the day. Still many hours until midnight, but now the tedium broken by the usual evening descent to the kitchen.

Last meal with the family. Parsnip stew with shreds of mutton, bread, red wine.

Master Quenuble and Madame animated beyond the norm, probably to mask uneasiness. The two boys rambunctious, inquisitive; excited by clandestine activity, and saddened at the loss of Prince vo Plume. She would, Eliste discovered, miss the Quenubles; she would also worry about them.

Supper concluding, and the withdrawal of the boys. Farewells and dignified handshakes, for the Quenuble lads would never have suffered kisses. A couple of tears in the eyes of young Thierre, however, as he bade farewell to Prince vo Plume: "Don't let The Runt go hungry!" And Breuve's parting admonition: "Remember, 'Liste. If they muscle you—knee 'em—and knock 'em!"

Gone. And after them, Madame.

Master Quenuble volunteered to stay up with them until eleven-thirty, the scheduled hour of departure. He would carry their luggage down from the attic, check the street outside for patrols, and at the appropriate time, secure a fiacre. He offered these kindnesses entirely for his own satisfaction, or so he insisted, and with such conviction that Eliste actually believed him. In her Beviaire days, she would never have credited such altruism; would have scoffed fashionably at the bare notion. "Selflessness is but the last refinement of overwhelming vanity," she would have quoted vo Renache. *Dead, he's dead.* Now she was obliged to reconsider.

Slow hours, endless hours. The night uncoiled like a dying snake. Firelight waning; stillness deepening. Then, luggage down from the attic, and the stowing away of a sleepy, acquiescent lapdog. Brief disappearance of Master Quenuble; minutes later, out of the kitchen and through the silent shop to the front door, before which the fiacre waited. No patrols in sight. No pedestrians. No sign even of the beggars, who might in milder weather have occupied neighboring doorways. Farewells and fervent handshakes at the door, then out, and the shock of the brutal winter air upon bare faces. Eliste turned back for one last look at the House of Swans with its deceptive red diamonds. Master Quenuble stood in the doorway. Light from the single candle he carried glanced off a metallic point upon the jamb. That one flash of gold set off responsive alarms preceding conscious recognition. Cold internal lurch, and Eliste pointed urgently. *They're not usually out at night.* Master Quenuble followed her finger and eyes, discovered the nit of NuNu perched there; almost casually slipped off his heavy shoe, and flattened the nit with one expert blow. Quite unalarmed, he smiled, hoisting his shoe in triumph to display the blot of foil gilding the sole. And that was the image Eliste carried away with her as she hurried across the walk and into the waiting fiacre.

Wave once more through the window, then rattlecreakclop, and off.

It was only a short ride, not much more than fifteen minutes, through Waterfront Market to the South Arch. The Market itself was virtually deserted, its booths shuttered and its customary nocturnal population off somewhere hiding from the cold. But to Eliste, fresh from attic incarceration, the scene was novel, even exciting, and she spent the time glued to the window.

Rattlecreakclop, and there was the South Arch looming ahead, its square-cut bulk flanked by lanterns. No sign of humanity, and just as well, for now. If he was present, the Cavalier was cautious at sight of the anonymous vehicle and driver.

Full stop. The passengers alighted and the fiacre departed. Hurry carefully over the treacherous close-packed snow to the minimal shelter of the arch itself, and there huddle against the wind, shivering but exhilarated.

They did not have long to wait, not more than three or four minutes, before a cloaked and muffled masculine figure broke from the darkness of an alleyway and made straight for the arch. Eliste studied their savior closely. It was amazing what a difference a few weeks made. The Cavalier was not as tall as she had thought him, not quite the imposing figure that she recalled. But, for such an elderly man, he moved with extraordinarily youthful vigor. Astonishing, really. Beside her, Aurelie was bouncing gently and twisting her hands into knots. The girl's excitement mounted by the second, and Eliste had no sooner registered the strands of sandy hair visible beneath the newcomer's hat than her cousin sprinted forward to greet him with squeals.

"Bayelle! Bayelle!"

"Exalted Miss!" Bayelle vo Clarivaux caught her two hands. "Dear Aurelie—to see you again! All your letters—you can't know what they've meant to me!"

"And yours to me are all that have made life worth living throughout these ghastly weeks, la!"

Eliste stared, and Kairthe goggled. Zeralenn's expression was cold as the ground underfoot. Sensing the pressure of their eyes, Aurelie threw them a quick, uneasy glance, then tugged at Bayelle's arm, drawing him forward. "See," she proclaimed brightly, "here are my kinswomen, no doubt overjoyed to see you. How fortunate our acquisition of so gallant a protector! Is it not fortunate, Madame? Cousin?" Her voice trailed off. Even Aurelie could scarcely pretend to view the slightly built, seventeen-year-old Bayelle vo Clarivaux as real protection.

Freezing, outraged silence, and Aurelie's smile dimmed a little. Bayelle, however, acquitted himself well. Bowing over each lady's hand, he straightened and addressed Zeralenn. "Countess, I know you might have selected a better escort. Therefore, I credit your kind invitation to join you here tonight more to your generosity than your need."

Invitation? Eliste's incredulous eyes bored into Aurelie, whose own gaze was bent studiously to the ground.

"Nonetheless, Madame," Bayelle continued, "I am armed, and that must count for something." He displaced his cloak to reveal a pistol thrust through his belt.

"I am not a bad shot, and may perhaps prove useful. It is in such hope that I place myself at your service."

He looked so young and bravely earnest, it was impossible not to like him. *Too good for Aurelie,* thought Eliste.

Even Zeralenn could not resist, and her expression gradually thawed. "A courteous offer and much to your credit, Exalted Sir. We accept with gratitude. And yet, if you will enlighten me—am I to understand that you and this child for whom I am responsible have engaged in a correspondence?"

Bayelle reddened. "I assure you, Countess, the exchange was entirely innocent—er, decorous, and—and innocent—"

"I do not doubt that your half of it was, but that is hardly the point. By what means did you contrive to send and receive these letters?"

"Breuve," Eliste suggested bleakly.

"Gad, Cousin, but you are sharp! Yes, little Breuve Quenuble carried our secret post to and fro, day after day after day!" Aurelie confessed blithely. "What a fine sport he was, and how he delighted in the adventure! Whatever should we have done without him?"

"What indeed?" Zeralenn's lips bent sourly. "And yet you miss the mark, child. Did it never enter your mind that a daily exchange of letters might be noticed and monitored, to our complete undoing? Have you forgotten our enemies' methods? Do you not comprehend the enormity of your folly?"

"Oh—pooh!" Aurelie tossed her head. "You mustn't scold me, Grauntie! After all, it's turned out for the best, has it not? We were never discovered, we are all quite well, with Bayelle here to protect us, and what could be nicer? Come, will you not *smile?*"

I hope she dies, thought Eliste. *I hope she sprouts warts.*

"All's well, and why must you be so *cross* with me?"

"It is not my anger that need concern you, Child Aurelie, but rather, the Cavalier's. Your reckless stupidity endangers all, and if he should now refuse us assistance, I should scarcely blame him."

"Come, Countess, you are well aware I will refuse you nothing," observed the Cavalier vo Meureille, stepping forth from the shadows. No doubt he had overheard most of the conversation.

Eliste started. His silent approach had entirely escaped her notice. Now he was bowing with the easy grace that neither age nor circumstance could impair, straightening—and yes, there was that impressive height she remembered; there were the vivid eyes, the silver hair.

"You still move like a ghost, Meureille," Zeralenn observed composedly.

"So must we all, Madame, and we shall do well enough. Now, to work." Meureille's eyes scanned and measured the streets. "The presence of young

Clarivaux here works to our advantage, permitting division of a group whose size might otherwise have drawn notice. The Countess and Exalted Miss vo Derrivalle will accompany me. Clarivaux will escort Exalted Miss vo Rouvignac and the maidservant."

There! You see? Aurelie was silent, but her triumphant eyes spoke.

"After we first three have departed, wait exactly five minutes and then follow," Meureille instructed.

"Where?" Bayelle's businesslike composure suggested competence.

Eliste recalled his resourcefulness upon the afternoon of Madame vo Belle-sandre's death. She and her relatives and servant were in good hands. These men could be relied upon absolutely. Thus reassured, she burned to *go*. Her foot tapped impatiently.

Meureille recited a set of directions. Their objective was an empty tobacconist's shop standing within fifty yards of the city wall's southern face, which impinged at that point upon the River Vir. Although the great water gate itself was heavily guarded, the irregular streets and neighborhoods that had, over the centuries, arisen beyond the ancient barrier, were not. It was into a warehouse in one of these quiet streets, but a few yards from the river, that their tunnel exited.

Bayelle listened attentively, and nodded once. Yes, the route was fixed in his mind. Yes, he would wait for five minutes before leaving. Yes, he would maintain constant distance between the Cavalier's party and his own.

Then the first three were off, Eliste clutching her valise, sliding and skidding perilously on the ice-paved streets. Meureille, who would ordinarily have offered assistance, did not do so now. Beneath his cloak, each hand rested on a pistol butt. His eyes roamed continually, alert gaze sweeping the streets, probing the alleys and darkened doorways. They encountered neither pedestrian nor patrol. Presumably the bitter weather worked in their favor. The wind that sliced like tailor's shears through layers of clothing had chased the Sherreenians from their streets, with a few minor exceptions. Here on the left, at the mouth of an alley, a small knot of the gutter brethren huddled about a reeking refuse fire. No threat there, and Eliste felt a moment's throb of pity. To be out on such a night, with nowhere to go—horrible. How did people ever come to such a wretched pass?

Ten minutes of walking, and she glanced back over her shoulder. Nobody there. Empty, quiet. No sign of Bayelle and his charges. Another ten minutes, stumbling through shabby ill-lit streets, bent straight into the wind and beginning to shiver, before they came to a closed and long-deserted shop with faded tobacco leaves painted on the sign that swung creaking above the padlocked door. The boarded windows bore the familiar emblem of Congressional confiscation, at sight of which Eliste glanced questioningly up at their guide. Calmly producing a key, Meureille removed the padlock and led them in, bolting the door behind them.

Inside, it was dark and icebox cold, but blessedly sheltered from the wind. Eliste stood still, expecting Meureille to strike a light; but this he did not do. Of course not—he couldn't risk it; the shop was supposed to be deserted, after all. Several blind moments, and then her eyes adjusted and she perceived the faintest illumination entering through chinks (observation slits?) in the window boarding, and through a grillwork skylight. Beside her, she could just barely distinguish the dark forms of her companions. Of the room in which they stood, she could see almost nothing; but somehow sensed that it was small and bare.

"How did you happen upon this place, Meureille?" Zeralenn inquired with the negligent curiosity of a tourist.

"Hardly by happenstance, Madame." He pitched his voice so low that the women had to push their hoods back, uncovering their ears, in order to hear him. "I'd seen certain references to a smugglers' tunnel—reputedly a very impressive piece of engineering—running beneath Sherreen's wall and emerging into the cellar of a private dwelling, or rather, what would have been a private dwelling in the last century. Following some months of investigation, I located and then purchased the building—anonymously, it goes without saying. This place belongs to me. The Congressional emblem upon the windows is counterfeit, by the way— painted there by an associate possessed of artistic leanings."

"A pretty touch, that."

"Discourages intrusion. As for the tunnel itself, it is all that I had hoped. For months now, it has served a useful purpose. May it continue so."

"Admirable, Cavalier."

Did Meureille, like herself, treasure Zeralenn's rare approbation? Eliste fancied that he did.

Small mouse-scratching at the door. Meureille applied his eye to a chink, then slid the bolt and opened the door briefly to admit Bayelle, Aurelie, and Kairthe; Aurelie clinging tightly to the boy's arm, the maidservant burdened with two bags.

"Gad, but it's so *dark*!" Aurelie exclaimed.

"Lower your voice," Zeralenn told her.

"But I can't see anything—anything at all!"

"Then take my hand, Exalted Miss, and I will guide you," Meureille offered quietly. "Once downstairs, we shall have a light. In the meantime, try to compose yourself."

"Oh, is that you, Cavalier? But where *are* you? This is simply impossible— Ah, there you are! Yes! Now, Bayelle, you must take my other hand, or I vow I shall not dare to move a single step! Come Bayelle, here is my hand, and I shall swoon with fright if you do not find it soon! Ah—there, now!"

At least, Eliste noted aridly, her voice was comparatively muted.

The six of them linked hands in the dark, and Meureille led them across the room, around some waist-high barrier that must have been the shop's counter, through a doorway, and down a flight of stairs to a small, windowless, mildew-scented cellar. Here the Cavalier lit a candle. Weak rays shivered upon damp stone walls, head-knocking low ceiling, fissured and puddled floor. No contents, no debris. No exit, other than the door at the head of the stairs, or so it appeared.

Meureille walked straight to the wall and slid a second key into what looked to be a natural crack in one of the stones. Clicksnap of a hidden lock, wail of hidden hinges, and a small door revealed itself. Irregularly shaped, with a facade sculpted to blend indistinguishably into the surrounding wall, the portal was all but invisible. Its unknown architect must have been proud.

How clever. What an amazing thing. No wonder the Cavalier had foiled the Vanguard's best efforts for so many months, and would doubtless continue to do so. Eliste was smiling as she watched the door open upon blackness. *Thanks, all you smugglers.*

Only a little above them, the front door banged open. Quick footsteps boomed on the bare floorboards. Involuntary startled shrieks escaped Aurelie and Kairthe. Certainly the noise would be heard above.

"In. Quick." Meureille threw wide the tunnel door. Kairthe stood near him, petrified and staring. Seizing her arm, he slung her through into utter darkness.

Thunder on the stairway, swinging orange gleams of lantern light, and three Vanguardsmen were upon them. Discarding the candle, Meureille drew both pistols. "Go! Run!" he commanded. Eliste and Aurelie dashed for the tunnel.

"Halt!" An alien voice behind them, and the shattering blast of a shot; followed immediately by others, succeeding one another so rapidly that almost it sounded a single volley. Lead smacked stone a few inches behind her, and Eliste, terrified, darted through the open door, with her cousin whimpering in her wake. Behind them, a terrible commotion; ahead, darkness beyond comprehension.

As the first Vanguardsman fired, Bayelle vo Clarivaux did likewise, neatly dropping his target. A second soldier's shot took the boy between the eyes, killing him instantly. Meureille and the third guard, facing each other at a distance of some seven or eight feet, fired simultaneously. The soldier fell. Meureille himself went down, a bullet lodged in his chest. One Vanguardsman remained on his feet. Clearing the prostrate Cavalier at a bound, and with scarcely a glance to spare for Zeralenn, who had tarried to view the outcome, he sprang for the tunnel entrance. As his adversary passed, close enough to touch, Meureille raised himself slightly, lifted his second pistol, and squeezed the trigger. The weapon spoke, and the soldier collapsed, blood spraying. The gun dropped from its owner's hand and Meureille fell back, laboring hard for his breath.

Zeralenn knelt beside him; took his hand, and held it firmly. A single lantern, lying on its side in a corner, continued to burn. By that light she could see the terrible size and location of his wound; could see his face, with its pinched look and its telltale bluish pallor. Her own face was very still, eyes bright with tears not permitted to fall.

"Countess?" His voice, a suffocating whisper.

"I am here, Meureille."

"Can't see you properly. Eyes fogged."

"It will pass. We will carry you to a physician. Your constitution is excellent; you will mend within weeks."

"We have never lied. Now is not the time to start."

"No."

"The others?"

"Safe in the tunnel."

"Follow them."

"Presently. There is no need to hurry; we are quite out of danger now. You have saved us all, Meureille. Do you hear? You have saved us." As she spoke, footsteps pounded the floorboards overhead. To Zeralenn, they sounded loud as cannon fire, but the Cavalier did not hear them. A spasm shook him, and his grip crushed her hand. Orange light stabbed down from above. Placing one hand upon his cheek, very gently she turned his face away from the stairs.

"Take the girls abroad, Countess. Be prudent. For once."

"I will follow your advice exactly." Clattering at the head of the stairs. "We will go to Strell, there to join the large company of those owing you their lives. You have done well, Cavalier. Nobly—oh, so very nobly indeed."

Her praise shone a moment in his eyes. He sighed. The breath ghosted out of him. She knelt beside a corpse.

The Vanguardsmen—another four of them—were already halfway down the stairs. For an instant they checked at sight of the cellar carnage—five dead bodies in a cramped space reeking of blood, smoke, and powder; an old woman clasping the hand of a dead man and scarcely heeding their arrival—then the paralysis passed and they were down the stairs and three of them racing for the tunnel entrance. The fourth stayed behind to guard the exit, and moments following the disappearance of his comrades, a joyous echoing whoop rushed back to his ears:

"Look here—Bonbons! Bonbons!"

The youngest and prettiest among condemned prisoners were known as the Kokotte's Bonbons.

The tunnel was narrow, low, and constricted; the first few feet of its dank length faintly illuminated by the weak light bleeding from the cellar. After that—blind darkness, extending unknowable distance. For a few moments the three girls hesitated at the edge of the shadow, uncertain whether to move or wait; until Eliste, taking charge, commanded her companions to form a chain. They obeyed without question, glad to defer to authority, any authority. Thus attached, they pushed forward with caution, stooping ever lower as the passageway contracted around them; Eliste in the lead, Aurelie clutching a handful of her cousin's cape in one hand, a handful of Kairthe's in the other. Eliste still carried the valise containing Prince vo Plume. Her free arm stretched groping into darkness, her foot advanced to pat and test the ground at each step.

A few yards; a few more. Halting and hesitant progress, but much improved when she veered to the right, fumbling in search of the tunnel wall. There it was, rough mortar beneath her hand, icy moisture seeping through the leather and lining of her glove. A bit faster now. Easier to walk stooped over in darkness with the wall to guide her; a little less bewildering. But where were the others— Zeralenn, Meureille, Bayelle? Why didn't they come?

Just a little behind us, she tried to convince herself. *They'll catch up any second. They will.*

And yes, there *were* footsteps behind them, a gleam of lantern light, and she turned gladly to discover a hunting wolf pack of Vanguardsmen coming on fast. Joyous whoops rushed down the passageway, to send the fugitives scurrying. Confused and terrified, impeded by their long skirts, they managed no more than a few stumbling paces before the soldiers caught up with them. Eliste stiffened, shuddered with incredulous loathing, to feel their hands actually upon her. Almost reflexively, she smacked her assailant's face as she might once have struck an impertinent serf, and he slapped her so fast in return that a cry more of surprise than pain escaped her.

"You're all under arrest, Bonbons," one of the men informed them without rancor. "Come along."

Back along the tunnel, quick march, single file, the prisoners almost dazedly unresisting. In any case, no point at all in struggling; these garlic-breathed louts were fearfully strong. Eliste's captor held her carelessly one-handed, but his fingers met in a grip above her elbow so cruelly tight that her entire arm was going cold and numb. Back through that clever door, secret no longer, and into the cellar to confront the ghastly sprawl of bloodied bodies. There the Cavalier vo Meureille, vivid eyes permanently closed; there the three dead Vanguardsmen; there Bayelle vo Clairvaux, with his young, ruined face; at sight of which, Aurelie's eyes bulged and her hands flew to her mouth as if to contain a shriek.

Eliste's first reaction, superseding even grief and terror, was simple nausea. Her stomach churned, on the verge of rebellion. Gulping air, she silently prayed for control. She wouldn't disgrace herself; she wouldn't disgrace her grandmother, who now stood erect and dry-eyed. The qualm passed. Eliste noted that Zeralenn's guard had appropriated his prisoner's hand luggage; standard practice among these human vultures. Judging by the fellow's vacant expression, he did not yet realize that he had just acquired one of the great jewelry collections of Vonahr. The sight, however, sufficed to nudge the cupidity of Eliste's own captor, who now wrenched the valise from her hand. Hatred iced her spine; pain froze her face. She stood up straight and impassive as her grandmother. Tiny ghost tug at her sleeve. Kairthe was there, scared face bathed in tears. Eliste pressed the girl's hand hard, and kept it. *Courage,* her fingers advised.

The Vanguardsmen were in excellent spirits. True, they had lost three comrades. But they had bagged the famous, pesky vo Meureille at last; discovered the Cavalier's secret tunnel, which would now be walled up once and for all, thus cutting off the last great avenue of Exalted emigration; killed a second Exalted traitor; and taken a clutch of female prisoners, three of them dessert-stuff sure to look well in a cart. All in all, a triumph, certain to garner commendations, bonuses, perhaps even a promotion for the sergeant.

And what a valuable lesson it was to all, the sergeant pointed out sententiously, to witness tiny circumstance give rise to such great consequence! Just consider, it had all come to pass only because some nit chanced to notice some brat carrying messages to and from a pastry shop! Who could have dreamed what such a small thing would lead to? It was worth thinking about. Surely the prisoners were thinking about it even now. The pastry chef and his family would shortly be thinking about it. The misbegotten fool offering shelter to Bayelle vo Clarivaux would also be thinking about it before too long.

And now, to the Sepulchre. The Treasury was closer, but for the Vanguardly minions of Whiss Valeur, there was always but one destination. One man left behind to guard the premises, shortly to be joined by others for corpse removal and tunnel blockage. Up the stairs; through the shop; out the front door, and into the teeth of the wind.

A carriage waited before the shop, one of the dreaded and celebrated closed carriages, at sight of which, all the hysteria pent within Aurelie found sudden outlet. An uncanny goblin scream escaped her. Head thrown back, eyes squeezed shut, and throat cords taut as cable, she stood ripping the wind with her voice. The Vanguardsmen forgot to laugh. They stared, startled into momentary immobility, as the prisoner went wild; twisting, plunging, and kicking; scratching, biting, flailing. And all the while, her outcry continued, ranging from clench-teethed bat-squeak shrilling, to ear-splitting full-throated howl.

The noise roused Prince vo Plume to frenzy. Within his prison, he barked and struggled. The valise shook in the hand of the soldier, who dropped it with a startled curse, then stood gaping in superstitious awe as the bag yipped and jerked on the cobbles at his feet. The prickle of pins and needles along her arm informed

Eliste that his grip had loosened, but he was still hurting her. If only she could hurt him back.

"If a Rep muscles you—knee 'im—and knock 'im—"

Her body moved faster than her mind. Almost before she realized what she meant to do, she had swiveled on her heel to face her captor, lifted her skirt with her free hand, and driven her knee up hard into his groin. The result seemed almost magical. He doubled with a yawp, and then it was easy to twist her arm from his grasp, to piston her clenched fist straight into his face. Sharp pain in her hand. Broken knuckles? If so, worth it. He sat down abruptly, clutching himself. Grabbing her skirts, she whirled and ran.

Up the street in the dark and cold, skidding on the icy cobbles, yet moving faster than she had ever moved in her life. A rush of buoyant blood, a sense almost of flying, legs flashing faster and faster, as if there were no limit to her speed. Yet something else was moving just as fast, something was buzzing, flickering gold before her eyes, goading her with briery jabs. A couple of NuNu's nits, which often accompanied the closed carriages of the Vanguard, were in the air and circling about her. If she couldn't evade them, then she might as well have spared herself the trouble of running. Buzz, jab, and a stinging pain at the side of her neck, causing her to stumble. She struck at the whizzing nit, and missed. Lowering her head with a sob, Eliste ran on, never daring to glance behind.

The sergeant, in a quandary, was forced to think fast; an unaccustomed exercise. Four surviving Vanguardsmen, counting himself. One stationed inside the tobacconist's, one temporarily incapacitated. One still struggling to control a weeping, hysterical Bonbon. He himself might chase the escapee, but who, then, would guard the other two prisoners?

"Get that little bitch." Using his musket as a support, Eliste's victim grimly hauled himself to his feet. "I'll handle things here."

He probably could; he had only young girls and an old woman to deal with, and an Exalted would-be emigrant should not be allowed to stroll away. The sergeant was set to run, when one of the prisoners spoke up.

"Yes, bring her back at once, fellow." Kairthe's spine was arrogant, her expression mildly petulant. Her accent and intonation precisely echoed Eliste's. "I cannot manage without my woman."

Aurelie, whose strength and voice were all but exhausted, overheard. Her diminishing outcry ceased, and she stared with circular tear-dimmed eyes. Even Zeralenn blinked.

"You cannot manage—!" The sergeant's guffaw atomized saliva. "Oh, you peacocks are unbelievable, truly incredible. Let it go, then—the soubrette is not worth so much trouble," he instructed his men. "As for you, Exalted Miss, cheer up—you won't need to manage for very long. All right, let's move."

They did not go, however, before one of the soldiers cautiously nudged Eliste's valise with the tip of his bayonet, releasing the catch and slitting the strap. Prince vo Plume's silky head emerged. He yapped soprano, and the men roared with laughter. Wriggling free of his prison, he stood barking angrily up at them, until Eliste's former captor, still in pain and out of temper, clubbed the little animal to death with two blows of his musket butt.

The prisoners were loaded aboard, and the carriage rattled off into the night.

It was fortunate that the nits of NuNu were so stupid. Eliste, exhausted and unable to elude her tormentors, finally gave up trying. She could run no farther. If she died for it, she had to stop. Panting, she sank down on a low step in the shelter of a recessed doorway. Leaning her head against the wall, she closed her eyes. When next she opened them, one of the nits sat inches from her face, watching with its dozen eyes, bright cuirass winking in the light of a nearby street lamp. Without moving her head, Eliste reached down to slip off one shoe; aimed with care; struck fast and hard. *Got it.* The nit perished with an audible crunch. Its sibling was nowhere in sight, having doubtless departed to carry informative gleanings back to the august Mother, currently ensconced in state atop the Armory roof. Best to move on, before the thing came back.

Eliste inspected the sole of her shoe, decorated with gold foil like the boot of Master Quenuble.

Master Quenuble, now revealed as a royalist, now wanted by the Vanguard. Master Quenuble, lost and doomed, along with his entire family; all of them, food for the Kokotte.

Warn them. Too late for Zeralenn, for Aurelie and Kairthe. Far too late for Meureille and Bayelle, but perhaps the Quenuble family could still be saved. She would go at once to the House of Swans.

Where was it? Eliste looked up and down the empty street. Silent, dark, and alien. She had no idea where she was. She had no idea how to find her way through the city maze; there was no one to ask, and not a fiacre in sight at this time of night. No matter, she would manage. Cliquot Street must lie to the north, and north was—which way? The stars might have told her, if only she spoke their language. Too bad she'd listened with half an ear when Dref used to speak of them. There was another guide, however, closer than the stars and much more comprehensible: the River Vir. Its current flowed north. Even Eliste knew that.

To the river, then. The pounding of her heart had subsided, and her breath came easily now. She could move again; needed to move, in fact, for the race of her blood had slowed and the cold was pressing upon her, numbing extremities, chilling the sweat on her face. To the river.

The Vir proved unexpectedly elusive. Eliste ranged the tortuous streets in confusion, now wandering up blind alleys, now blundering upon walled court-yards. The wind bit effortlessly through her garments; the wind clawed and tore. It occurred to her then, for the first time—there was nowhere to go to get out of it. No shelter in all of Sherreen, and no one to turn to. No kinsmen, friends, or servants left. No one to help and protect her. Without such help, she was finished; she would freeze to death on the streets.

Oh, no I won't. I won't let myself. If I have to get through on my own, then I will. I'll find a way.

There was a certain warmth in that, as if she had stoked some internal fire.

Shortly thereafter, she emerged from a narrow pass-through to find herself standing above the Vir, whose black nighttime flow pointed the way north. Ahead, just barely visible through darkness and distance, a string of firefly lights picked out the Bridge Vinculum, toward which she directed her steps.

It was farther than it looked. She had walked so long and far over packed snow that her feet were all but numb, and even the bravest of resolutions could not stave off such cold for long. When she spied a group of the wretched, pressed into an open-faced riverside lean-to and huddled about a sparse collection of radiant coals, she could not forbear joining them, if only long enough to restore sensation to deadened feet and hands.

They made room for her willingly enough—five figures so muffled and swathed in rags that features, contours, age, and even gender were indeterminable. Automatically she thanked them, and five mummied heads turned as one. She realized then how revealing were her voice and manner. Every gesture and syllable proclaimed her Exalted. Almost as conspicuous in such a gathering was her costume. She was disheveled and plainly dressed, but simplicity only emphasized the quality of her garments. These faceless wraiths knew just what she was; she could feel their knowledge stirring at the pit of her stomach. If there had been a patrol about, they might well have turned her in for the five-rekko bounty—a great sum to such folk. As it was, on such a night, she probably had little to fear from them. Another time, she might be less fortunate.

Nobody spoke. Eliste lingered only long enough to revivify hands and feet, then hurried off, pushed from behind by their eyes. On she went, black river to the left, bridge before her, definitely nearer now, its lights brighter and stronger. On against the wind, for another twenty minutes that felt like a hundred twenty; then the old Vinculum rose before her. The Waterfront Market was there to her right, and she knew exactly where she was: a good forty minutes' walk from the House of Swans, if she were fresh and vigorous. And now? Her feet dragged. Her muddy, ice-burdened skirts weighted every step, slowing her pace to a plod. At this rate, how long would it take? The eastern sky was already threatening dawn.

Hurry, hurry, hurry.

But her limbs resisted the mental lash.

Cut through the market, exhausted and stumbling much too often, eastern sky relentless. And then, quite unexpected, a rare stroke of luck: crunchgrind over ice and stone, and here came a lone fiacre, out on the streets at an unlikely hour. She waved, and the surprised driver pulled up. Stating her destination, she climbed in. The fiacre rattled off, and Eliste sank back on the seat. Her eyes closed. Her mind slowed.

Jolting progress, drifting visions, brightening sky; and then the shops and dwellings of Cliquot Street, rooftops light-grazed. The fiacre halted. The driver demanded his fare. It was the first time Eliste had thought of that. Now she dived into her pocket to bring forth a little netted purse containing a handful of biquins; small change with which to tip lackeys and porters, the only kind of money her former station had obliged her to carry. Pouring the coins out into her palm, she extended her hand.

He took the money, summing the total at a glance. "Not enough," he told her. "Another twenty-five."

She stared up at him, astonished. Not enough? What was she supposed to do about that? It made no sense. She had already given him all she had. He reiterated his demand. Clearly he was stupid. She turned and walked away.

"Here—you—!"

She heard the angry voice rising behind her. Once it would have annoyed or bored her. Now she was scared and humiliated. Spurring her tired self to a run, she fled down the street, and the fiacre followed; clip-clop, rattlesqueak, furious bellowing behind her, until she ducked back into a walkway between two shops and the vehicle passed on. For a moment she rested, breathing hard, back pressed to a cold wall; then looked out cautiously. Cliquot Street was coming to life. Windows glowed, with silhouetted figures passing to and fro; a couple of pushcarts were already out; a few pedestrians slanted against the wind.

And the House of Swans? She couldn't see it from her present position. The fiacre had disappeared. Drawing a loose fold of her hood across her lower face, a commonplace action in such weather, she slipped out into the street and ran the last few yards—

But stopped short, shrinking back into the shadows, at sight of the Vanguardsmen stationed before the House of Swans. Judging by the soldiers' bored demeanor, they had been standing there for some time. A couple of inquisitive citizens loitered on the spot in hope of diversion. The front door of the pastry shop was already marked with a big, new scarlet diamond—real, this time.

The Quenubles were already gone, their property forfeit to the Republican Protectorate. She was too late, too late by hours. The strength and determination gushed out of her. She sagged as if deflated.

Gone. Everyone gone. All of them.

Exertions in vain. Eliste quite alone.

What now? What will I do?

For a couple of minutes her mind must have ceased functioning. She stood staring at the House of Swans, thinking of nothing at all. Eventually her eyes ascended from street level, traveling up the building to the skinny slit tucked under the eaves, the attic observation slit; and she thought to catch the fugitive glint of her own eyes staring down from that familiar vantage point. Surely in a moment she would wake to find that she *was* standing up there, gazing down on Cliquot Street? It would not be the first of such visions.

No dream. Her point of view remained street-bound. A bitter gust swept the dawn cobbles, and she shuddered.

What now? What to do?

She was chilled to the marrow now, heavy sodden garments offering little protection. She was footsore, and so tired that every joint ached feverishly. Fear and exhaustion precluded hunger for the moment; but she was coldly parched, longing beyond expression for bouillon or tea to warm her from the inside out.

What now? Where will I go? Where can I go?

So tired. Almost too tired to think, and that was good; good not to think about the newly dead and the lately doomed; best not to think at all. New chill upon her face; winter's breath on tears.

A café. Warm inside. Sit down near the fire with a cup of tea. Rest. Rest.

But she had no money left, not so much as a biquin on her. There would be no tea. No fire. Nowhere to rest, unless in some doorway, out in the cold. Only to sit for a moment, to close her eyes—

I'll freeze.

People do, you know.

But not I.

Dank, heavy skirts slapping her ankles, and she remembered then the bits of jewelry sewn into the hem of her petticoat. There was her gold ring set with garnets, the little cameo with seed pearls, a few trinkets of silver and rose quartz. Nothing very valuable, but surely enough to purchase food and lodgings.

She wanted them *now*. Stepping back into the alleyway shadows, Eliste tore at her hem; shook the ornaments out onto the ground, and gathered them up with eager, cold-clumsy fingers.

A short while since, at the bottom of Cliquot Street, she had passed a café with light glowing behind its shutters, an "Open" sign already hanging on the door. She hurried back there at her best speed, now no more than a lead-footed trot. A few dawn pedestrians stared curiously after her as she passed, but she was beyond caring.

Inside the café, the indifferent warmth of a modest coal fire seemed paradisiacal. Taking a tiny table in a corner, tucked behind the stove and invisible from the doorway, she ordered tea and a hot meal. In her exhaustion, she forgot the indiscretion of her own accent; the momentary blankness stilling the proprietor's face at first sound of it reminded her. Once again she had betrayed herself, and prudence dictated instant departure. She did not move, however; could not move. If she died for her mistake, so be it. For the moment, she didn't care.

The food arrived and she ate ravenously, warming from the inside out, from the outside in. When she was warm clear through, she dropped off to sleep as if drugged; slumping in the straight-backed wooden chair, head sunk on her breast. The proprietor—not inhumane by nature, and quite taken with the drawn, pretty face visible beneath the drooping hood—allowed her to rest undisturbed for a time. Only when the café began to fill with the midmorning trade did he wake her to demand payment.

Eliste proffered a silver ring, at which the proprietor scarcely glanced. "Cash," he said.

She had not expected this. "But it's all I have," she explained politely.

"Where do you think you are?" She did not answer, and he stared at her until she squirmed. "You've got your nerve."

"But—but—it's a very nice ring, real silver—"

"Real garbage. What do I want with that? All right, give it here, I guess I'll take it. And you'll take a word of advice, little girl. Don't try this on, anywhere else. Another time you might wind up peddling your gewgaws to the gendarmes." He glared into a pair of wide, frightened eyes, and found himself softening. "Now, you listen. You got any more jewelry, you want to turn it into cash. Nose out the pawnbrokers, look for one who'll give you a fair price."

"A pawnbroker?" The concept was exotic. "Where would I find such a person?"

"Pawn Street, of course. Where else?" She looked confused, and he added with a touch of impatience, "Other side of the river, runs between Rat Town and the Eighth District. That's the place for the pawnbrokers. Bloodsuckers all. You want to watch your step, little girl."

She thanked him and took her leave, glad to abandon the site of her own blundering, yet unutterably reluctant to venture forth again into winter. Still, it was not as dreadful as she had feared. The wind had abated, dulling the razor edge of the cold. Morning sunlight filled the street with a colorful brittle brilliance. The shops were open now, there were carts and carriages out on the road, smoke-breathed bundled-up pedestrians hurrying about their business, a not unattractive stir of life and activity. Rest and a hot meal had served her well. Her clothes were almost dry again. She felt stronger, braver, better able to resist the cold, to resist the fear and grief that would freeze her from within if she gave way to them.

She soon discovered it was best to focus her mind upon small immediate tasks. If she paused to think—if she considered her prospects on the streets of Sherreen, or the prospects of her captive friends and kin—she would certainly panic, she would run screaming. But crossing the Vir to find Pawn Street—she could think about doing that. When she got there, she would think about finding a buyer for her jewelry, and when she had some money, she could think about finding a place to hide, somewhere warm and safe—

Nowhere's safe.

Don't think about it. For now, across the river and on to Pawn Street. Nothing else, for now.

But it wasn't possible to govern thought and sensation as she came off the Bridge Vinculum on the far side of the River Vir to confront the Sepulchre. Only a couple of streets distant, the old fortress loomed above the surrounding tenements. Her feet stopped moving. Without volition, she halted to stare; nor, for several moments, could she tear her eyes away. Zeralenn—Aurelie—Kairthe, all there, and what must they be suffering now? But they were not likely to suffer long, her intellect insisted on reminding her. The interval between arrest and so-called trial was customarily brief; the interval between trial and execution briefer yet. A couple of days, sometimes only a few hours—

Isn't there anything I can do? Anybody to help? There must be!

Nothing. Nobody.

The tears were running down her face again, and passersby were staring at her; the last thing in the world she wanted. Brusquely she wiped her face, and realized she had made another mistake. Her handkerchief was transparently fine, beautifully embroidered and lace-edged; an Exalted possession certain to be noticed. She should never have displayed it. How many more such errors could she afford?

Wrenching her eyes from the granite towers, she hurried on. She was in the

Eighth District now, which she had never before glimpsed save through the window of a moving carriage, and at such times she had usually averted her eyes. But there was no averting them now. The ugliness engulfed her, assaulting every sense. Crumbling, dilapidated houses and shops, flaunting their red diamonds; for this wretched slum was the very cradle of Reparationism (whose triumph seemed, judging by the look of things, hardly to have improved the lot of its proponents). Astrologers, fortune-tellers, palm readers, self-styled "healers" occupying every other shopfront. Taverns and rancid-oil cookshops, and rooms in hovels to let for a pittance. Citizens ragged, filthy, and elflocked. Pinched, starved faces, marked with disease and despair. Faces vicious, faces sly and predatory. Bodies crippled and twisted. A legion of beggars, some of them creatures scarcely human. Shouting voices, scorching language. And the atmosphere, the stench—how did they endure it? Garbage fires ringed with shivering forms smoldered in the gutter all along Bridge Street; a throat-clutching, eye-watering yellowish smoke filled the air with grit and cinders. Mingling with the smoke—the stink of bad oil, rotten fish, unwashed bodies. The street itself was an open sewer, presently clogged; its normally rainwashed kennels frozen, contents mounding.

She didn't dare apply the handkerchief to her nose. Bowing her head and breathing shallowly, Eliste hurried up Bridge Street, trusting in the dun-colored haze to veil her against inquisitive eyes. Even in the midst of such fog, however, her decent clothes and fine features did not pass unnoticed. A concerto of chirrups and lip-smackings marked her progress.

Disgusted and intimidated, she quickened her pace, eager to put the Eighth District behind her. Straight up Bridge Street at her best speed; a quick nervous trot through dim, notorious (although she did not know it) Cudgel Walk; then, thankfully, out again onto Pawn Street, which marked the district boundary. Straight ahead lay Rat Town, haunt of students, bohemians, and assorted highly vocal malcontents; a neighborhood many cuts above the Eighth District with respect to safety and breathable atmosphere.

Exactly as described, Pawn Street was heavily populated with pawnshops. Half the buildings in sight bore the classic gilded symbol of the broker. Eliste walked up and down, inspecting the shops in turn, each with its sad display of strangers' lost treasures: jewelry and plate, furnishings and art objects, weapons, tools, and musical instruments velvety with dust. Not much to choose among them. At last she entered a large shop, comparatively clean, its sign freshly painted. No customers within. Behind a counter next to the door stood the broker himself, a corpulent bourgeois with the face of a snapping turtle. He was eyeing her with the frank curiosity that her appearance seemed always to arouse in this section of the city. Quite likely he mistook her for a buyer. The first words out of her mouth would disabuse him of that notion, but she had to be careful. No more Exalted accent and mannerisms, nothing to betray her, no more mistakes. She was a common girl, an ordinary grisette of no particular distinction. Not a Sherreenian daughter, though—she could never carry it off.

She might have mimicked the coarse city accent with fair success. But the myriad gestures, expressions, attitudes, habits, and tastes marking the native Sherreenian commoner—she would never catch them all; the closest observer in the world could scarcely hope to do it, and she had been anything but that. She would surely give herself away, wrecking upon some tiny invisible shoal, and they would see she was not what she claimed.

But there was another voice, acceptable by the most fanatical of Reparationist standards, one that she could easily echo to perfection, having known it since earliest childhood—the drawl of a Fabequais peasant. Kairthe's accent. Dref's accent. No one, hearing her speak so, would distinguish her from the genuine article. She could have worked the charade in Fabeque itself. And here in Sherreen, her lapses from the ordinary might draw attention, but not suspicion, for their explanation would be clear—she didn't know any better. She was a provincial.

She spread her wares out on the counter. "What'll y'give?" she inquired, sounding like Kairthe's sister.

He inspected the jewelry without haste and seemingly without interest. "Twenty," he offered at last.

It was worth easily fifteen times that amount, probably a good deal more. The angry color mounted to her cheeks. He thought her some simpleton he could cozen. He was quite mistaken. She'd show him. "Don't try that on," she replied, barely remembering to modify her accent in time, and braced herself for combat.

He did not trouble to answer.

"Come, let's have your best price," she urged.

No reply, no reaction. He was stone. But he wouldn't get the better of her. Gathering up the bright little store, she warned in Kairthe's voice, "I've no time to fool about. Talk serious, or I'm gone." Stowing her trinkets away in her pocket, she headed for the door.

Now, of course, she would hear his voice calling her back, offering money, bargaining.

No voice. She walked out. He made no attempt to detain her. No matter, she would do far better elsewhere. Pawn Street was putrid with pawnshops.

The broker in the next shop offered eighteen rekkoes for her jewelry; the one after that, seventeen. Then eighteen again. Nineteen. Sixteen. Twenty. Along the length of Pawn Street, offers rarely varied by more than a rekko or two. One scoundrel tried offering eleven, but he was an exception. Nobody offered more than twenty. It took perhaps a score of attempts to convince her, but in the end, she took the twenty.

Again she stood out on the street, her netted purse flat no longer, but not nearly as full as she had expected. Her ventures into so many shops had consumed the day. It was already late in the afternoon. She was tired and footsore. Her back ached from prolonged standing, and the cold was starting to work its way through her clothes. Worst of all, she was hungry again. It was many hours since she had eaten. She needed food, no doubt about it, and how much would it cost? The slenderness of her own means suddenly terrified her. A rosewater ice at the New Arcade Café was priced at two rekkoes, she recalled. At that rate, how long could her twenty last?

Well, she wasn't at the exorbitant New Arcade now. The common folk subsisted on next to nothing, and surely she had wit to do as much. Turning off Pawn Street, she followed University Street on into Rat Town, entered the first coffeehouse she came upon, and sank gratefully into a chair. The place was crowded with students, loud youngsters with open faces and vivacious gestures. She viewed them as youngsters, although they were in fact her own age. They didn't dream how lucky they were, to be so free and careless. She wished she were one of them, could lose herself among them. True, the university accepted no women, but perhaps if she disguised herself as a boy—?

Idiotic. She must be growing light-headed with hunger. Eliste ordered cheaply—tea without honey to save a couple of biquins, a plain hard roll instead of brioche. She ate slowly, making it last. Not too long, however. It was already growing late, and she needed to find a refuge for the night—a clean, quiet room with a good fire. Best not to put it off—but, oh, it was hard to think of going, when she was still so tired, and still so hungry, and it was so cold and frightening out there—

"Want to join us?"

She looked up, startled. A man stood too close. He wasn't a student, she saw at once; not young enough, too dirty under the fingernails. Smile too wide, too unwavering, revealing bad teeth. She looked away.

"Join us?" he repeated, as if he imagined she hadn't heard. "That's us, there." He pointed to a table in the corner, where two men much like himself sat grinning and grimacing at her.

Apes, she thought, and shook her head curtly.

"Don't worry, we'll treat you right. Buy you a drink and all. Come on." Receiving no reply, he took her arm and jerked it lightly. "Come on."

She froze. He dared to lay hands on her! In any kind of a sane and normal world she could have ordered him whipped or worse. "Let go," she whispered, and her accent slipped; but she spoke so briefly, in a voice so low, that the lapse went unnoticed.

"Come on, come on," he droned soothingly.

He wasn't hurting her, but he clung like a twining weed, and she was caught. Don't fight. Don't shout. Don't make everyone look. Don't think of calling for help; there is no help, not for Exalted outcasts. Primitive trapped-animal fear and rage fired her mind. She wanted to bite and claw, but certainly her incubus never guessed it; he continued to smile and drone. Eliste nodded and rose to her feet. The droning ceased, the moist hand loosened upon her arm. She freed herself with a sudden quick twist and exited the coffeehouse without giving way to her impulse to run.

Outside on cold University Street again. Her belly rumbled with hunger. In her haste, she had left the last uneaten morsel of bread lying on the coffeehouse table, and she cursed herself for a fool. No point in dwelling on it, however. Right now, she needed to find a room. There were still a couple of hours of daylight left. That should be plenty of time.

On through Rat Town to a pleasant, clean, and spacious boardinghouse, where the landlord demanded thirty rekkoes a month in rent, payable in advance. No, he did not let upon any shorter terms. If the young lady wished to rent by the night, or possibly by the hour, no doubt there were establishments in the Eighth District happy to accommodate her. Good afternoon.

The next boardinghouse was noticeably less clean and spacious, but the rent was better: twenty-two rekkoes a month. Better, but still too much.

After that, a grubby and down-at-heels old tenement stuffed to the rafters with university students; a rather agreeably raffish atmosphere, but no women allowed. Sorry.

Another, cramped and dilapidated; only fourteen rekkoes a month, a bargain. Three months rent, payable in advance, however. No, no exceptions. Sorry. Had the young lady thought of trying the Eighth District?

The young lady was beginning to think of it. The afternoon was wearing on, and soon the sun would set. The thought of finding herself again alone on the streets at night was unendurable. She was desperately tired now, horribly hungry and cold. She needed a place, any place.

Back, retracing her steps of the day. Weary trek down into the smoke-choked slum. Only a few hours earlier, these sights and smells had all but nauseated her. Now she barely noticed them.

Refuge, before dark. It was all that mattered.

On the corner of Bridge Street and Cudgel Walk stood Prilq's Hospitality, with a To Let sign stuck in the grimy ground-floor window. Eliste stood considering for a minute or two. The so-called Hospitality was particularly uninviting, with its dirty peeling facade, rusted rainspouts, and dim, cracked windows; but perhaps that was all to the good—it was bound to be cheap. She walked into a dark, low foyer and found Prilq himself, doubling as concierge behind the counter. He was a man neither young nor old, unwashed and malodorous, balding, and nondescript save for a pair of unusually plump, wide, cushioned pink lips, always moist and pouting like a girl's. He studied her, and the lush lips ripened.

Yes, the rent was amazingly low, only a few biquins a night; lower rates yet for those rare tenants able and willing to pay by the week. Eliste instantly engaged for a week's lodgings, sight unseen. There—transaction complete, and she was safe for the next seven nights. Her spirits rose a little.

"Let's see the room, then," she requested, Fabequais accent nicely controlled.

"Now?" Prilq's pink lips stretched and pursed. He seemed torn between surprise and amusement. "Now? Oh, 't'isn't quite ready and proper yet, really. My guests don't generally turn up so early. Maybe you'd like to come back in a couple of hours? Works out a lot better."

Two hours . . . that would give her time to eat, which she badly needed. Her stomach was growling and fidgeting again; amazing how often it seemed to do that. Repairing to a nearby dingy cookshop, she dined very frugally. At this rate, her money would hold out for a good five weeks, or even a little longer. And after that? She needed to keep herself somehow, and that meant finding work. It was an extraordinary idea; she, the daughter of a marquis—work?

Or starve on the streets.

But what employment was she fit for? Of what use her polish, her exquisite deportment, her fashionable feminine accomplishments, even her dashing horsemanship? Her dancing had always been much admired—perhaps she could be an instructor? Governess? Milliner's assistant?

She could do those things, or learn them, given a chance.

Without a character? Experience? References?

Thus disadvantaged, how would Dref shift?

Well, I could write my own references. Very nice ones, too.

She was still mulling it over as she walked back to Prilq's Hospitality. It was quite dark now. The orange light of the garbage fires flickering upon nearly opaque billows of yellowish smoke lent Bridge Street a singularly infernal air. Black silhouetted figures, misshapen by their ragged layered wrappings into the semblance of demons, scuttled to and fro. Voices cooed hoarsely out of the shadows at her, and she quickened her pace; but now that she had somewhere to go, she was far less afraid.

The windows of Prilq's Hospitality glowed halfheartedly. She entered and requested her key. Prilq's lips puffed with surprise and amusement. There was no key, he informed her, and without offer of assistance or candle, directed her to her chamber. It was up on the fifth floor, at the top of the building.

Eliste began to climb. The Hospitality was larger than she had realized, with each floor's four chambers opening upon a central landing. For the first three stories, candles burning in wall sconces lighted the stairwell. After that, she had to feel her way in the chilly dark. Gripping the banister, she ascended, blackness about her filled with creaks, squeaks, and rustlings, thump of footsteps overhead, muffled voices, occasional laughter behind closed doors. At the top of the stairs, on the fifth floor, only one door, and that showing a line of light beneath. Her room. She opened the door; stopped dead on the threshold. *Her* room? The Bridge Street inferno had nothing on this.

One great chamber took up the whole top story of Prilq's Hospitality. The weak glow of a single lamp illuminated bare floor, bare walls, low bare-beamed ceiling. An uncovered slop bucket stood in the corner. A huge wooden shelf, projecting from the wall at a height some two feet above the floor, ran the length of the entire apartment. This was the bed. A wooden ledge about two inches thick served as the only pillow. Wadded sailcloth sacks padded the shelf, but there was no real mattress, no sheets, no quilt. The bedclothes consisted of some four filthy, threadbare blankets and one canvas tarpaulin; these shared by two dozen women, packed like human cargo in the hold of a slaver.

They ranged in age from seventeen to seventy-five; in profession from unemployed seamstress, to unemployed laundress, to luckless widow devoid of support, to ordinary vagrant. The brethren (or sisterhood) of the gutter was amply represented here; it was evidently to such haunts as the Hospitality that female beggars turned to escape winter's chill. Despite the diversity of type, the women seemed curiously alike, all of them more or less equal in wretchedness. The faces visible above the dirty blankets shared a uniformly grayish pallor. Beneath the blankets, the bodies were fully clothed, even down to the shoes they dared not remove for fear of theft. Odd lumps and bumps marred the terrain; those fortunates possessed of material goods slept atop their bags and bundles.

The air was cold—for there was no fire—and indescribably foul. The room possessed but two windows, both painted shut for the last thirty years and more. The fetor of decades found its home in this place—dead air, sweat, oil, dirt, and blood; cheap brandy, smoke, and tobacco; vomit and diarrhea—a loathsome stew of new and ancient stinks. Eliste gagged on it. For a moment she stood choking in the doorway, contemplating flight back down the stairs; complaints, remonstrance, arguments, threats, and demands. But what use? If Pink Lips Prilq of Prilq's Hospitality had a better room to offer, it would be at a price she couldn't afford. She could sleep in this hellhole or else return to the street, a prospect she dared not face.

To bed, then, at the extreme edge of the shelf, where there was still a little space left. Overcoming vast repugnance, she crawled in, careful not to touch the gaunt, corpselike figure beside her; drew a stingy fold of the tarpaulin over herself; and lay there rigid, eyes tightly shut. The dormitory was tolerably quiet. A few snores rumbled the vile air, and several feet away, near the center of the bed, an incessant muttering delirious monologue issued from the lips of one either drunk, feverish, or mad; but hers was the only voice to be heard. Among two dozen tenants, some were surely wakeful, but none spoke; either a sense of communal consideration ruled them, or else they were too drained of life, too hopeless and undernourished to squander precious vitality upon conversation. The rags beneath Eliste's body were packed and compressed into hardened-lava ripples and lumps. They were unmistakably damp, and they smelled abominably. Restlessly, she stirred and shifted in vain search of comfort. She would never manage to sleep in such a place, never—

But real exhaustion soon overcame discomfort, sinking her into an uneasy slumber from which she was presently roused by a sharp stinging sensation. She sat up abruptly, and tiny dark forms scuttled in all directions. The bedding was alive with insects—fleas, bedbugs, she did not know what they were; but they were plentiful and they were voracious. An involuntary shriek escaped her. She slapped frantically at the bedding, and at herself. The corpselike figure lying beside her rolled over and cursed softly. Eliste subsided. The insects had been frightened off, but they would undoubtedly return. She couldn't stand this ghastly place, not another moment of it; she had to get away—

Where? Back to the streets, at this time of night?

She wasn't going anywhere—at least, not now. Eliste sighed and lay back; squeezed her eyelids shut; tried not to think of the insects, the filth, the stench; tried not to think of danger, destitution and loneliness; tried very hard not to think of Zeralenn, Kairthe, Aurelie, Meureille, Bayelle, the Quenubles; tried not to think at all. True slumber now eluded her. From time to time she dozed lightly; woke and dozed again, the periods of sleep and waking blending indistinguishably into one another. So passed a long and miserable night.

At the break of icy dawn, Prilq came to turn them out of the building. The women, evidently used to this, too tired and broken-spirited to resist, obeyed without protest; shuffling down five flights of stairs and out the door in remote vacant silence, like perambulating automata. Eliste was last to leave. The dormitory contained no washstand, she discovered; nowhere to refresh herself even minimally, no cold water with which to bathe the itching bites that dotted her ankles. Discomfort and indignation emboldened her. She complained bitterly.

Prilq was not offended. A basin, pitcher, and soap could be provided, he informed her equably, at slight additional charge. As for the room itself, it was required during the daylight hours for purposes that he did not specify, and therefore guests were encouraged to vacate early. "But *you're* welcome to hang about as long as you like, Sugarplumfairy." A shiny wet pout cajoled her. His gaze felt like a clammy hand on her.

She left at once, feeling soiled. If she hadn't paid him a full week's rent in advance, she would have sought other lodgings. But she had paid, and he'd never return a single biquin, and she couldn't afford to sacrifice so much—unless, of course, she happened on some alternate source of income.

Employment. Before the day was out, she would find decent employment, and then she could safely consign Pink Lips and his unspeakable Hospitality to perdition. Now, how to go about it?

Bridge Street was already astir, its miserable population hustling. Garbage smoldered in the gutters, dense smoke strangled the walkways, cloaking ragged forms and muting raucous voices. A few shafts of sunlight poked through the cindery haze. It was going to be another bright winter day, hard-edged and bitter. Head bowed, Eliste walked quickly, avoiding the eye contact that she had discovered invited solicitation, endearments, crooned obscenities. Soon she discovered what she sought—a broken-down pushcart vendor of oddments, from whom she purchased pen, ink, and paper; a considerable outlay of capital, but a worthwhile investment. She took her writing supplies to the nearest cookshop, and there, while breakfasting, penned three letters of glowing recommendation from fictitious Fabequais sources unlikely ever to be investigated. Thus armed, and filled with determination, she set off in search of work.

She commenced in confidence and optimism; secure in the power of her appearance, backed by forged credentials, anticipating immediate success. It was a far more difficult undertaking than she had ever dreamed, however. Through the streets of Rat Town she wandered, knocking on strange doors, waiting in strange entries and foyers, wheedling strangers, and smiling, smiling, smiling, smiling. As the hours passed, fatigue mounted, rejections accumulated, and the smile began to lose its dazzle. Around midday, she paused briefly to rest and eat, begrudging every biquin; then on, through Rat Town to the bourgeois neighborhood beyond for more queries, refusals, closed faces, closed doors. By sunset she was thoroughly tired and discouraged. She faced a long walk back to the Eighth District, another night of bug-ridden wretchedness at Prilq's Hospitality. No matter. Tomorrow her luck was bound to improve.

But it did not. Across the Vinculum again, this time to canvass the Waterfront Market, whose depleted condition alerted Eliste to the cause of her trouble. Despite the sunshine and clear cold skies, fully a third of the market booths were closed and shuttered. Those still open offered a sorry selection of inferior goods selling at inflated prices. Domestic products were scarce, and foreign imports ruinously expensive, for the resources of all the nation were now of necessity funneling to the Revolutionary troops engaged in suppression of royalist insurrections flaring throughout the provinces. The civilian population was universally feeling the pinch. Country farmers had been stripped nearly bare, their crops requisitioned to feed the Republican Guard. Merchants in town, deprived of meat and produce, deprived of all varieties of goods, were closing their doors by the hundreds. Want and hunger pressed upon Vonahr more cruelly now than in the days of Dunulas. True patriotism demanded glad sacrifice in defense of the infant republic, or so Whiss Valeur insisted. Yet such politically correct enthusiasm was hard to maintain, as the ruined, dispossessed, and starving victims of civil war, forced from their despoiled farms and villages, came streaming into the largest Vonahrish cities—most notably, Sherreen. They were hungry, they were freezing, they were desperate for work, of which there was little to be found, even for the skilled craftsmen and experienced laborers among them. It was against such competition that Eliste vo Derrivalle launched her pretty face and false documents.

Another day of useless searching. Another horrible night of Hospitality, this time with a new refinement of misery: one of the nameless tenants, evidently afflicted with insomnia, consoled herself throughout the night with a foul clay pipe, whose fumes presently wreathed the entire bed. In the morning, Eliste reluctantly parted with five biquins for use of the washbasin, cold water, and a petrified scrap of soap. This expense she deemed unavoidable, for Eighth District existence was already leaving its mark upon her. Her unwashed skin was dull and itchy, unwashed hair stringy, unwashed garments increasingly disreputable. She needed to look decent; how else could she possibly convince anyone to hire her? She made such repairs as limited time and resources allowed, then sallied forth to try her luck in a new neighborhood.

Her luck was bad. That day she went without lunch to make up for the money spent on washing, and the small denial affected her noticeably. She was tired; she had never been so tired. Her feet and legs and back ached. It was harder than ever before to trudge from door to door, to flash her smile and her forged references. By the end of the afternoon, the letters were crumpled, creased, and limp as their owner. She'd lost count of the day's rejections; not one of them extending so much as a shred of hope. She stopped a little earlier than usual that evening, too drained and dejected to continue. It was necessary to pause, to sink down upon the stone ledge encircling a public fountain and to rest there for a time before undertaking the long trek back to Bridge Street. This would never do; she needed to keep up her strength. Above all, she needed a good night's sleep, something she had not enjoyed since crossing the Hospitality's threshold. Thus at dinner that night, in place of her customary tea, she substituted a glass of wine; which, in conjunction with overwhelming fatigue, resulted in deep unbroken slumber, proof for once against vile bodies and viler insects inhabiting her bed.

She awoke rested and comparatively renewed. Yesterday's black despondency had receded, and once again she felt herself fit to face the world. Or rather, she would be fit to face it, once she'd had a wash. Five biquins for soap and water, but they were worth it. She would feel almost herself again. Thus fortified, she could resume her efforts; and today, she was deeply certain, she would find employment. The five biquins were a sound investment. She felt in her pocket for her purse. It wasn't there.

A mistake, obviously. She'd placed it in another pocket. Or another. Eliste tried all her pockets, found them empty. Shook out the folds of her skirt and cloak; checked her bodice, her hood, her shoes. Not there. Sick with fear now, she turned back to the bed, rummaging frantically through the filthy rags. It must have fallen out during the night. It *must* be tangled in the bedding. It must—! Not there, and no more denying—while she slept so soundly last night, someone had managed to steal every biquin she owned. Whoever slept beside her, most likely. But last night she'd been sandwiched between two bony bodies. Which of these anonymous scarecrows had it been—the light was low, she hadn't looked, but she *had* to remember—and quickly, oh, quickly, for they were leaving now, shuffling dully from the room—one of them not so dull as she seemed—and soon they'd be gone. Now, before they got away—

"Wait, all of you, listen to me! Nobody leave—please!" Eliste's voice came out high and shaky. Some of the women paused, mildly curious. "Someone has stolen my purse—blue netting, with about fifteen rekkoes. I'll give a rekko to anyone who gets it back for me. Turn out your pockets, and if anyone refuses, then search her! Find it and I'll pay you!"

In her excitement, she quite forgot her accent, but her listeners did not notice, else dismissed Exalted intonation as the affectation of an ambitious prostitute or actress. More likely, they thought her mad or drunk; yes, certainly they thought so, for here and there a tired cynical eyebrow arched, a derisive finger tapped a temple. Most of them simply shrugged and walked away.

"Don't go!" Eliste grabbed an alien arm. Its owner shook her off. "Wait— listen to me!"

No. They might have been deaf. But she would stop them. Eliste braced herself against the doorjamb, blocking exit. One of the roommates slung her aside with unexpected strength, and she went reeling. Before she recovered, half of the suspects were gone. Terrified and furious, she kicked the bed, flinging rags and blankets every which way. Surely her purse must be in there somewhere.

"Save your strength, Sugarplumfairy."

Prilq had witnessed the entire scene. Now he stood there smirking at her. For the moment, she was too distressed to hate his moist pink smile. Perhaps he could help her—?

"Lost your money. Sorry. Sad story, sad. Good thing you're paid up here for another three nights, isn't it?"

She stood still, watching warily.

"But what will you do after that?" Prilq inquired kindly.

"Listen, listen to me, one of those women stole my purse, and if you'll stop them from leaving—if only you'll stop them—"

"Oh, now I can't do that; I'm not a gendarme. Do you want me to call the gendarmes, then? I'll be happy to do it. Just say the word."

Now she was remembering to hate him.

"So what will you do when your three nights are up? Hmmmm?"

"I'm going to find employment before then."

"Now, why didn't I think of that? Employment. Of course. Obviously, there's any number of jobs you're fit for."

"I'll find something."

"I really hope so. I'd hate to turn you out, Sugarplumfairy. Such cold weather."

"You'll be paid, don't worry."

"I never do. Neither should you. With that face, you needn't worry about money."

"I don't see what my face has to do with it."

"Think again. You don't know what you've got. You don't need to walk the streets, and you don't need to pig it in this sty like those broken-down drabs. Listen, you can be comfortable. Have a room of your own. Good coal fire. Plenty of food. Wine. Even get you a new dress. Live like an Exalted, eh?"

"What do you mean?"

"Easy. We just move you down to the third floor. Nice room, with a few visitors. No more than three or four a night, mostly. Gentlemen. Nothing rough, nothing funny, I guarantee. Easy life, no worries. Solve all your problems in a hurry."

"How dare you? *How dare you?*"

"Whatever happened to the northern accent, Sugarplumfairy?"

"Oh, you are despicable. I'd like to see you whipped."

"And I'd like to see you on the third floor. What about it?"

"Out of my way. I've nothing to say to you."

"Well, think it over. When you change your mind, just let me know."

"Never."

"We'll see," said Prilq. He stood aside, and she went out.

• • •

That day she walked for miles, penetrating far into the bourgeois neighborhoods that lay beyond Rat Town. Her luck was bad as ever, her efforts consistently futile, her state of mind indescribable. Desperation lurked behind her eyes, quivered at the edges of her indefatigable smile. Prospective employers sensed it, despised it. She could feel their contempt eroding her courage. Or perhaps it was hunger that did that, for she hadn't eaten all day. Nor would she eat, unless she found a job, for she hadn't a biquin left to purchase food. No food. Best not to think about it. Best to fill her stomach with water, and try not to think about it.

Naturally she thought of nothing else.

As the hours passed, her hunger grew, passing through various stages of discomfort, and presently sharpening to pain. Was this what the peasants were always complaining about, was this how it actually felt? But how could they endure it? Of course it was safe to assume that she, an Exalted, felt such deprivation far more keenly than commoners of duller sensibility. Those born to such a life were fashioned by Nature to endure it. Weren't they? How else, after all, could they stand to go on living?

No wonder they hate us.

The day wore on. Her hunger waxed and throve. There was food everywhere, she began to notice; how had she never before observed it? Cookshops, taverns, cafés, and chocolate houses on every street; pushcart vendors of ganzel puffs, grilled sausage, hot chestnuts on every corner; fragrance of baking bread, frying fish, and roasting meat on every breeze; and everywhere, all the time, people eating—munching their snacks, their sweets and salted nuts, their damned noisy apples. Her stomach clenched and complained at the sight. Where was it all coming from, when there was supposed to be such a great food shortage?

But only for the very poor, it seemed.

She would not be that for much longer, she told herself. She would find a way out of the gutter. She would eat, she would be warm again.

Not today, however. And not in Sherreen, she was increasingly certain. Sherreen had proven itself entirely inimical. She would never find work here; she would starve here—she was already starving. Her salvation lay beyond the city walls. She needed to make her way somehow back to Derrivalle and the sanctuary of Uncle Quinz's cottage, where she would be safe and loved. She should have seen it days ago, but she had been blinded by fear, an irrational terror based upon tales that were almost certainly exaggerated. It had taken hunger and mounting desperation to open her eyes, but they were open now, and she knew what she had to do.

She stood within two miles of the North Gate. It was midafternoon, and the farmers and marketpeople in from the country for the day would now be heading home. Scores or hundreds of citizens would be passing through the gate, and with them would pass Eliste vo Derrivalle, invisible in the midst of the common throng. And the danger of detection? Surely not so great as rumor painted; bedraggled, grubby, and pale with hunger, she was altogether unrecognizable as Exalted.

Eliste walked on, renewed in strength and purpose. Forty minutes later, she was gazing upon the North Gate for the first time since the day of her arrival in Sherreen. The ancient portal, with its massive timbers and its medieval iron strapping, was as she remembered. But the makeshift framework barriers constricting the exit were new. The dozen or more armed Vanguardsmen stationed at that point were new. And the aspect of the canine Stupefaction towering there— that was very new. The great steel watchdog that had for centuries overlooked the countryside now faced inward, into Sherreen. The glass eyes concealed for so long behind domed steel lids were now wide open, their owner disturbingly awake. This, then, was the notorious Sentient Boomette.

Eliste watched for a time from a safe distance. Carts, carriages, and pedestrians were passing steadily under the muskets of the guards and the nose of the Sentient. From time to time, the Boomette's glass eyes glowed with light and changing color. Her dished gridwork ears swung this way and that; an uncanny sight, no doubt giving rise to the legends of supernatural Sentient powers. But it didn't seem to amount to much. The traffic flowed on. It was no such great matter, after all, to depart Sherreen; the rumors were inflated, designed to terrify the ignorant. Or so she tried to assure herself.

And yet her feet wouldn't carry her forward. She loitered there, motionless in the street, as the minutes passed and the human tide funneled through the narrow gap. The Vanguardsmen inspected, queried, and judged; while the Boomette shifted her steel snout back and forth like a monstrous hound sorting scents on the breeze.

She was growing very cold, and the icy pavement underfoot was making itself felt. The delay was pointless. If she were going, she'd best move before the traffic thinned. Now, without thinking about it any more. She resumed walking.

Bombshell commotion ahead. A keening alarm—half siren, half howl—rent the Sherreenian air. The Boomette's ears swung, her jaws clattered, her eyes glowed infernally. Eliste froze. The thing had spotted her. The stories were true, all of them; the Sentient was omniscient, it had caught the Exalted quality of her thoughts. Now the masquerade was over, and not unexpectedly—every instinct had warned her. . . . She couldn't run, she couldn't stir.

But nobody heeded Eliste.

Every Vanguardsman in sight was converging upon the knot of astonished pedestrians clustered before the old city gate. There was a swift expert survey, a barking confirmation from Boomette, and one of the peasants was plucked from the center of the group; an elderly man with the shapeless colorless garments, stooped posture, and plodding gait of the typical peasant farmer. The man was ordinary, distinguished in no way from others of his kind—until they stripped away his cap, his lank wig, his false beard, to reveal a relatively youthful, clean-shaven face.

Even at a distance, Eliste recognized the Marquis v'Ausse-vo Treste, second cousin to the King himself. She had seen him often enough at Court, even danced with him once or twice. The guards at the gate could not assign a specific name to the face; but they knew an Exalted fugitive when they saw one, and hoots of delight arose, to be taken up by the idlers customarily gathering about the gate in the hope of viewing just such sport.

Eliste watched as the luckless Marquis was dragged away. The hot glow faded from the Boomette's eyes, public exhilaration gradually subsided, and normal traffic resumed. For a time Eliste stood motionless, until she became aware that she was attracting curious glances. Her paralysis broke and she began to move, backward, away from the North Gate, away from the Boomette.

The trek back to Prilq's Hospitality seemed endless. She was ravenous, dejected, and horribly weary—weary as never before. Frequently she paused to rest, slumped against a building, or sitting on stairs or in doorways, like one of the beggarwomen. It was quite dark by the time she reached the Hospitality. She slipped in quietly, but did not succeed in escaping the notice of Prilq himself, who smiled, nodded, and welcomed her with detestable geniality.

"Mutton stew tonight," Prilq remarked. "For all the third-floor guests."

Ignoring him, she mounted the stairs and managed to haul herself up five flights, stopping only once to rest. The stink in the communal chamber was worse than usual tonight. The pipe smoker had returned. This time, Eliste didn't care. Crawling in beneath the tarpaulin, she dropped off to sleep within seconds, and slumbered undisturbed until dawn.

Despite her hours of unbroken rest, she woke bone tired and oddly dull-minded. Her body ached, and there was a sharp, unfamiliar pain in her belly that took a moment to identify as hunger. It took considerable effort to drag herself from her filthy nest, and then she shuffled down the stairs and out the door as spiritlessly as the lowest of her roommates. Outdoors, it was snowing lightly, small wet flakes spattering out of a still gray sky that looked soft as sleep. Shivering, she pulled the folds of her cloak tighter and trudged on down Bridge Street.

That day, she did not get far. Her legs wouldn't carry her beyond the Eighth District, and she found herself poking about the seedy taverns and tenements that lined Paradise Square. No employment to be found there, of course, but perhaps she was to blame, for stopping so often to rest—no telling how much time she wasted that way. Once she even drifted off to sleep, sitting upright on a public bench, awakening twenty minutes later to find herself dusted with snow. She couldn't afford such lapses. Nor could she afford to loiter about the cookshops, drinking the odor of seafood chowder; it only made things worse. She pushed on, miserably persistent.

"Veal rissoles and sweetbreads for the third floor tonight."

Prilq's cheery announcement greeted her return that evening. Averting her face, she made for the stairs.

"Wait a moment."

She paused reluctantly.

"You know, Sugarplumfairy—I'm getting worried about you." Prilq's pout expressed concern. "You're not looking so good. Not good at all. Sort of green about the gills. Consumptive, maybe."

"I'm all right."

"Are you really? But you won't be for long. You're going downhill, Fairy—sliding fast. Looking tired. Looking sick, looking old. Not smelling so great, either. Picked up the crabs yet? Don't worry, you will. Not much time left."

"Time for what?" She already knew the answer.

"To accept my offer. It doesn't stay open forever, you know. I can't use no stinking beat-up bone bags. Another few days, and you'll lose your chance. This time next week, you'll either be dead or standing butt-to-wall in an alley at five biquins the pop. My third floor is a lot cozier. Think about it."

She thought about it, and the sudden intensity of longing was almost shocking. Hot food. Coal fire. Bath. Bed with a mattress. Food. Food. Food. She could have them all. She could have them *now*.

Prilq was watching her face closely. He smiled.

Yes. She clenched her teeth to keep it in. Easy, as he had said. And what choice was there, after all? But that was just what Aurelie had said about swearing the Oath of Allegiance, and she had despised Aurelie for it. There were some compromises to be made only at the expense of essential identity. Afterward, life might continue, but the human being formerly inhabiting that body would be gone. Taking the Oath was one such compromise. This was another.

Not trusting herself to reply, Eliste turned and plodded for the stairs.

"Think about it." Prilq's voice behind her.

Think about it.

She was a little dizzy, and needed to rest three times on her way up to the fifth floor. Heedless of filth and stinks, she crawled into bed and collapsed into slumber.

Morning light shoving through the cataractal windows. Tired. Hard to get up. Listless and faint. Drag on down the stairs, and there was Prilq again.

"Tripes northern-style for the third floor tonight. Onion soup, cheese topping."

"Choke on them," Eliste suggested dully.

To her surprise, the moist smile evaporated. Before she could move, he grabbed her arm, hard enough to hurt. "I've about had enough of you," said Prilq.

Astounded, she stared up at him.

"You hear?" He shook her slightly. "I'm not putting up with any more of your snot. Now get this straight. Come back tonight ready for the third floor, or don't bother to come back at all."

"What do you mean?" She was genuinely uncomprehending.

"It means you're out. Understand?"

"You can't do that to me!" Shock restored a measure of her energy. "I have another night. I already paid for it!"

"Did you? I've a bad memory for details."

"You know I did! I have another night!"

"Funny, I don't seem to remember that; so your time's up. If you don't like it, you can always take your complaint to the gendarmes. You want to do that, Sugarplumfairy? You want to run to the gendarmes?"

"You're a cheat as well as a swine, Prilq."

"Still got some spirit left, I see. Too bad there's no brains to match. Well, you can lunch on pride and see how you like it. Now get out." She didn't move, and he thrust her forcibly out into the street.

The door slammed in her face. She stared at it, almost disbelievingly. It remained closed, and after a moment she walked away, moving like a sick or very old woman.

Gray skies. Misty, dim, and foggy streets—or was it only her own hazy vision? She visited a few Eighth District businesses that day: a wineshop, a couple of cheap boardinghouses, a vendor of secondhand clothes. At least, she thought she visited them. Or had it been yesterday? Time and perception were skewed. She was growing a little confused. One thing was certain, though—no success. Yesterday, today, tomorrow—why did that make her think of reading Shorvi Nirienne?—all alike; an unbroken succession of failures, disappointments, petty humiliations. No employment, no money, no shelter, no food.

Hours and miles. A wavering succession of people and places. Cold and hungry, sick and faltering. She found herself near the Bridge Vinculum, where the carts and wagons converged from all points to pass over to the Waterfront Market. And there, horse pawing for traction in the icy ruts, a farmer's cart laden with carrots, onions, and potatoes.

Food. Piled high. She didn't stop to think. Strength and purpose instantly flashed. She darted for the cart, rolled vegetables into the outstretched sweep of her skirt, and, holding the folds up in both hands, ran for cover. She didn't even know if she had been seen.

Screeching abuse behind her. Yes, she'd been seen, all right. Would they chase her for a skirtful of roots? Eliste chanced a glance behind her. Commotion in the crowd. Shouting back there, waving fists, and somebody threw a rock. She accelerated, and the vegetables began to bounce, flipping from her skirt out onto the cobbles. The uproar behind her diminished. Eliste scarcely noticed. Still she ran, and still her hoard shrank. By the time she reached Aether Street, all she had left was a fistful of raw carrots and a couple of potatoes. To her, it seemed a treasure.

Soon exhausted, she stopped running. To her left she spied a recessed doorway opposite a big boarded house marked with a red diamond. Into the doorway she slid, and sank down panting. A moment later she drove her teeth into a raw, semifrozen, semirotted potato. The flavor and texture were revolting, but starving Eliste tasted ambrosia. For a moment she luxuriated, and then burst into violent tears. For the moment she could eat no more, but crouched there shivering, half blind, racked with uncontrollable sobs.

She must have fallen asleep there, huddled in the doorway, for when next she opened her eyes, the light had changed. The long shadows of late afternoon stretched over the cobbles. Night was coming on, and then what? Barred from Prilq's Hospitality, where would she go, what would she eat, how would she live? Eliste closed her eyes, wishing herself unconscious again. She couldn't face these questions, didn't want to face them. She wanted oblivion. Why had she awakened at all?

Because she'd been disturbed. Because she'd felt something hit her leg lightly. She looked down. A coin lay in her lap. Whoever had dropped it there while she slept was already gone, forever anonymous. She picked up the coin and examined it wonderingly. A two-biquin piece—enough to purchase an entire loaf of week-old bread. Momentary salvation.

"That's mine."

An angry croak scraped her ears. Eliste looked up. A woman stood there, arms folded, eyes narrowed. She was iron-haired, bent-backed, and nearly toothless. Despite the apparent decrepitude, she looked vigorous and strong.

"You hear? That's mine. Give it here."

Eliste's wordless confusion must have communicated itself, for the stranger added by way of explanation, "Aether Street between the alley and Hiroux's old place belongs to Plaissie. No poaching allowed. This is my stretch, these are my pickings, and that's my copperkitties you got there. You want to keep your face on straight, hand 'em over."

Poaching? Pickings? Copperkitties? It was all so much gibberish, but one thing was clear. This stranger now blocking the doorway wanted the precious coin that staved off starvation. *No. Mine. Getawayfromme.* Eliste stood up, quick alarmed strength springing from some unsuspected reserve. Her fist clenched on the coin. "Leave me alone. Get out of my way," she said.

"Gi' me that, you draggle-tailed scrag, or I'll kick your teeth out the back of your head," returned Crone Plaissie. Receiving neither reply nor cooperation, she grabbed the other's wrist and twisted it.

Pain shot along Eliste's arm, triggering days' worth of pent fear and fury. Her mouth contorted. She wasn't even conscious of the ugly squalling yell that escaped her. Her left hand lunged, seized a handful of gray hair, yanked viciously, then slammed her attacker face first into the brick wall. Crone Plaissie howled and fell to her knees, blood pouring from her broken nose and split lips. Even then Eliste did not release her, but stood shaking the captive head to and fro by its hair, ceasing only when the other's wails gave way to spasmodic coughs that sprayed bloody froth in all directions. Eliste bent forward to address Crone Plaissie from a distance of inches. "Leave me alone, or I will kill you. You understand? I'll kill you." She wanted to do exactly that.

Crone Plaissie found herself staring into a pair of dilated, fever-glittering eyes. Her own eyes widened. "You're clear loony," she whispered.

"That's right. So you'd best leave me alone. Just leave me alone." Eliste walked away slowly. She didn't know where her brief burst of strength had come from, but it was over now, leaving her weaker than ever; shaky, queasy, and light-headed. Worse—disgusted, and even ashamed. It had been inexpressibly ugly. For a moment she had actually been ready to kill that wretched woman—had longed to, in fact. What was happening to her? *I won. I should be thankful, I suppose.* She shook her head, as if to dislodge unwelcome thoughts. In her right hand she still clutched the two-biquin piece. She would eat this evening. That was all that mattered.

Behind her, the beaten beggarwoman was spewing venom. What was she shrieking?

"The Fungus'll hear about this!" Crone Plaissie had recovered both courage and voice. "If you think you can nick my stretch and walk off white, you better think again! The brethren'll do you—you're in the grinder, bitch—you're in the sausage! The Fungus looks after his own—you're in the lime!"

More gibberish. Soon it died away behind her. Eliste departed Aether Street as fast as her legs would carry her. The two biquins were soon gone, exchanged for a stale loaf that she carefully divided into quarters. Crouched out of sight behind a low stone wall bordering one of the nameless walkways, she ate one portion, chewing each mouthful slowly and at great length. All too soon, the meal was consumed down to the last crumb. Eliste sat resting until the cold began to seep into her bones. Then she got up and walked on. The meager nourishment had helped her. She was tired and listless, but no longer dizzy. She walked until she came upon a knot of the homeless packed in around one of the ubiquitous Eighth District refuse fires. They made room for her, and there she spent the night, sleeping curled up on the ground. She woke the next morning stiff and bruised, aching in every joint, and afflicted with a persistent cough—but still alive, despite the winter's cold. That day she wandered, hardly bothering to seek employment. Her appearance was now so wretched, unkempt, and filthy, that not even the meanest of Eighth District cookshops would have considered taking her on as a kitchen slavey, and she knew it. No point in trying—better to devote such strength and resolve as yet remained to the grim scramble for sustenance.

She made the loaf of bread last three days. After that, things got harder. For a while she tried hanging about the garbage heaps that burgeoned behind the taverns and cookshops, but pickings there were poor. In these lean days, it was only the sorriest of liquescent vegetables and the green-furriest of stiffened porridge that were discarded; and even this repellent fare was quarreled over by scavengers far stronger and fiercer than Eliste. Once or twice she managed to sneak a double handful of air-browned fruit parings, but nothing more.

She had better luck with her sporadic raids upon the farmers' carts that groaned down Bridge Street en route to the Waterfront Market. A sudden falcon descent on some vehicle hesitating upon the verge of the Vinculum; fast seizure of a few potatoes, turnips, winter squash, whatever came to hand; speedy disappearance down one of the alleys, now familiar as the state chambers of the Beviaire had once been; a few turns to throw off pursuit; then to ground somewhere, heart still hammering with exertion and fear, yet ravenous for the soil-encrusted prize. Such forays kept her on her feet for a while, but she hated them beyond expression—hated the degradation, the unutterable indignity, the sense of defilement, and hated the very real danger. Should she be caught, she would probably suffer the common thief's punishment of branding, whipping, or imprisonment; but a district magistrate determined to abide by the exact letter of the law could conceivably sentence her to death. And a fine piece of irony it would be, she reflected, to forgo the Kokotte in favor of the hangman; really too amusing. No, she didn't like stealing. The question was academic in any case, for like it or no, she could not hope to continue for very long. The scanty diet that barely sustained life did not maintain strength. She was growing daily feebler, finding it harder and harder to run any distance. When she could no longer run, her raids upon the carts must cease.

There was less risk in begging, or so it initially appeared. Eliste soon discovered that her wide eyes were worth money: a piteous expression set off by convulsive coughing was apt to earn biquins. Yet so wretched was her appearance that attempted indecencies were infrequent. Few desired to touch her; perhaps it was the tubercular wheeze that scared them off, or maybe it was the sight of her handkerchief, stripped of its lace edging, and spotted with blood from a cut finger, supposedly the product of her lungs. For a couple of days she prospered, collecting enough to purchase stale bread, a few apples, even a cup of hot soup. Another day of such success, and she could treat herself to a night's shelter in some establishment similar to Prilq's Hospitality. She wouldn't starve or freeze, after all. And as for the other, greater fear—capture, Sepulchre, Kokotte—in her present guise, there was not a gendarme or Vanguardsman in all of Sherreen who would recognize her as Exalted. She would not have dared to pit her disguise against the perceptions of the Sentient Boomette, watchdog at the North Gate; but human soldiers could be deceived.

They *were* deceived. Vanguardsmen passed her by every day without so much as a glance. Yet she felt she was observed, and nothing could rid her of the comfortless sensation. The beggars were watching her, she knew it. She felt their eyes upon her day and night.

After her meeting with Crone Plaissie, Eliste never returned to Aether Street. She didn't encounter the Crone again, nor even catch sight of her at a distance, but she never quite managed to dismiss the incident from her mind. The shrill vituperation haunted her. The threats, which seemed so much gabble at the time, had since somewhat clarified themselves. *"The brethren'll do you—The Fungus looks after his own—"* The brethren of the gutter, she had meant—the organized league of Sherreenian beggars—would avenge the injury done one of their membership. But the Crone had attacked her, and she had only defended herself. Since then she had committed no offense, troubled nobody. The beggars, she sensed, had studied her closely for several days, but never actually molested her. Perhaps The Fungus, whatever that was, judging her harmless, would simply leave her alone.

But she soon discovered otherwise.

It was early evening, and bitterly cold, but Eliste hardly minded. Enjoying a successful day, she had dined sumptuously on bread with drippings, and an entire bowl of cabbage soup; with enough of her earnings left after that to purchase space in the big shelf of a bed at Wonique's Warm Welcome. Wonique's, though fulfilling neither promise implicit in its title, was nonetheless preferable to the street, and Eliste gladly contemplated the prospect of roof and blankets. Thus absorbed in her reflections, she failed to note the gleam of attentive eyes following her progress, the stirring in the shadows. Suspecting nothing, she was taken entirely unaware by the arm slung around her from behind. Before she could scream, a hand clamped down on her mouth, and she felt herself lifted off the ground and borne backward into the mouth of an alley. The assault took place on relatively populous Pump Street, but went unnoticed or else ignored.

This was it, then—rape and murder, without a doubt; two common enough occurrences. She had never let herself believe it could happen to *her*. For day after day she had ranged the worst of the slums without serious mishap; but her luck had run out at last.

Eliste fought hard; kicking, writhing, thrashing wildly. But the arm encircling her was made of iron; against such restraint she was helpless. It was dark in the alley, but she could dimly sense her two assailants; burly, ragged figures wafting the rank stale stink of beggary. An instant later, someone threw a cloth sack over her head, pulling the drawstrings close around her neck. Sight was extinguished, breath nearly so. Filthy burlap chafed her face. Dust and flour tickled her nostrils.

They were on either side of her now, hands heavy and tight on her, hurrying her along the twists and turns of some blind pathway. For a few moments she went unresistingly, then, balking, drew dusty breath and screamed. Invisible fingers promptly stuffed folds of burlap sacking into her open mouth. Eliste gagged, choked, struggled.

"Settle down or I'll break your arm." Harsh voice, warning pain at her wrist. He meant what he said.

No use resisting. Her struggles subsided, and they dragged her off, every which way through the alleys and walkways until her sense of direction was utterly confounded. The long hike was inexplicable. Why didn't they just do whatever they meant to do and get it over with? It seemed this was no ordinary, random attack; which meant that it must be worse. Her eyes tingled with incipient tears, which she managed to suppress. These animals would not witness her terror. Beneath the rags, the dirt, and degradation, she was Exalted still.

Up a couple of steps, grumble and creak of a door, and into a building of some kind. Impossible to guess what sort; her senses were all but extinguished. Up a flight of stairs, carpet beneath her feet. Step, step, door opening, forward and through. Then they released her, and somebody pulled the sack from her head. Eliste looked about her; caught her breath, so startled that she almost forgot to fear.

The chamber in which she stood was warm, very humid, and very dim, lit only by a handful of coals glowing on the grate; yet her eyes were accustomed to complete darkness, and she could see well enough to recognize the style of a Parabeau town house. They had not dragged her long or far enough to pass from the Eighth District; she was still in the slums of Sherreen. Yet the room in which she now found herself resembled an Exalted gentleman's library in nearly all particulars—clean, expensively rugged and curtained, mahogany-furnished, marble-manteled, coal-warmed, book-lined, redolent of leather laced with an unfamiliar sharp medicinal odor. In place of the writing desk that might ordinarily have occupied the central position, however, there stood a huge copper bathtub, shaped like a square-toed, high-backed shoe, which covered the naked body of its occupant to a line high above the waist. The bather himself was a man of indeterminate years, white-haired, with an unlined face; so corpulent that folds and swags of his flesh overhung the sides of the tub. This flesh was noteworthy: smooth and pure white as lard, save where fuzzed by ashen coin-size patches with the look and the texture of mold. Here and there, where the patches had split, oozed open ulcers. A board lay across the front of the bathtub. Upon this board rested a bell, and an open book, over which the colorless head was studiously bent. For several moments following Eliste's entrance, the bather continued to read, thus demonstrating vision extraordinarily sensitive to the faintest light. At last, marking his place and setting the book aside without haste, he looked up. His eyes were oddly translucent and roseate, almost red; lids and lashes pale to the point of invisibility. He gestured, and the two kidnappers withdrew, shutting the door behind them. Thereafter, he scrutinized Eliste at length. She returned the regard steadily, and he smiled a little.

"So. The little wolf's-head at last," he observed. "Come nearer." Lifting a sponge from the bath, he applied the sopping object to an open sore marking one bleached shoulder and pressed lightly. Darkened water streamed down his body; in the low light, the liquid appeared blood red. The medicinal smell in the room intensified.

Eliste concealed her revulsion. She likewise hid her surprise at the sound of his voice, which was beautiful—resonant, mellifluous, not at all in keeping with his appearance. Even more astonishing, he spoke with the accent and manner of her own kind. He sounded Exalted. Lifting her chin, she advanced a couple of paces.

"Do you know who I am?" he asked.

She had not the slightest doubt. Dozens of half-heard, half-comprehended allusions were now quite clear. "You'd be The Fungus." Just in time, she remembered her accent.

"Ah, a country wench. And how do you come to find yourself so far from your native Fabeque, my dear?"

"Came in service as lady's maid," Eliste mumbled. "Lady's gone now, carted off to the Sepulchre. Finished, I guess."

"No doubt leaving you alone and friendless, a stranger in Sherreen, bereft of employment and destitute. Is that it?"

"That's the way of it, sir."

"A sad tale, but scarcely unusual these days. Thus you shortly found yourself reduced to beggary?"

"Aye, I went a-begging, sir."

"And not without some success, I understand. Tell me, what do you call yourself, my dear?"

"Kairthe, sir."

"That nom de guerre will serve as well as any, for the present."

She was careful to appear uncomprehending.

"Now, little Kairthe, do you know why you were brought here tonight?"

"For fighting with one o' your people, and shmushing her face up." There seemed little point in evasion. "But I swear, Master Fungus, 't was her began it. Truly, and I never meant to hurt her so bad."

"Did you not? I am sorry to hear it, for I had deemed you a lass of spirit. But that is not important—the state of my Crone Plaissie's face signifies little. A minor disfigurement only serves to increase her earning potential. In that sense, you have done both her and me a favor. You might have increased the benefit by taking out an eye, but there is little point in mourning lost opportunities. Do you know why Plaissie attacked you?"

"Well, she said I was—was a-poaching on her copperkitties, I think. Pinching her pickings or something. Nicking her stretch. All like that. But I'll swear I never meant to, and I'm very sorry, and I'll not do it again. I vow, I'll never set foot in Aether Street again, Master Fungus."

"Very good, but you are still missing the point, my dear. Aether Street—Pump Street—Parabeau or Dunulas Square—it is all one. Anywhere you go in Sherreen, you are poaching. The Brethren of the Gutter hold exclusive rights of beggary within the city limits. Milking, as it is termed, is a privilege restricted to the membership alone. The fraternity, I might observe, is vigilant and zealous in defense of its traditional prerogatives. Intruders, would-be independents, and poachers are dealt with severely. Oh, very severely indeed. And you, little Kairthe, are just such an intruder."

"I never heard of no one having to get leave to beg in the street."

"You have heard of it now. I trust you will profit by the instruction."

"Profit—hah!" The implications of his warning hit her hard. He was telling her that she was to be deprived of her sole remaining source of livelihood. Hunger was suddenly immediate again, and it was unfair, when she had struggled so hard—monstrously unfair. For the moment, indignation almost overcame alarm. She chanced a scowl at The Fungus. He was studying her microscopically. It was an odd, analytical regard, almost amused, she suspected; but at least he appeared neither hostile nor minatory. Perhaps if she tried, she might awaken his sympathies. He was, after all, a man—of sorts—and as such, perhaps not immune to feminine appeal, even stemming from so bedraggled a source as herself. It was at the very least worth a try. Fixing wide, imploring eyes upon him, she spoke softly.

"But Master Fungus, what's to do, then? I've looked real hard, but there's no work to be had. If I can't beg, what'll become of me?"

"Starvation is always an option."

Bleached brute. She didn't let resentment touch her face. "Oh, sir, I can't think you'd really want to see me starve. Your heart's not made of stone, is it? You seem to me a gentleman—a decent sort—"

"Do I?"

No, actually. "Truly, sir. I can only hope you'll think of the fearful fix I'm in, and take pity. Won't you gi' me your help, Master Fungus? Please?" If only she could cry now; if only— She pictured her grandmother, standing in the blood-drenched cellar beside the corpse of the Cavalier vo Meureille, and then she *was* crying, the tears welling plentifully.

"That is excellent, child. Naive, heartfelt, genuinely affecting. The tears are an exquisite touch. Well done." The Fungus squeezed his sponge, and sanguinary streams coursed down his white chest. "Your pretty distress moves me deeply. Who could resist such aqueous charm? Certainly not I, and therefore I am willing to exert myself on your behalf."

"Ye'll tell your folk to leave me alone, then?" asked Eliste, pleased with her easy victory.

"It is not quite that simple. Sherreenian beggary remains the exclusive right of the gutter brethren, and that rule never alters. If you would milk the streets, then you must join the fraternity—no easy matter. Admissions are relatively rare, for strict limitation of our numbers protects the livelihood of all members. Nevertheless, it is possible that we should find a place for you."

"Me—join the Brethren of the Gutter?"

"Possibly. Make no mistake, this is a signal concession; but well-merited in your particular case, I believe. You have been watched for several days now, my dear, and your observers have been uniformly struck by the polish of your performance. The expressive eyes, the dejected grace, the wordless suggestion of gentility fallen upon hard times—it is all most effective. The trick with the bloodstained handkerchief is particularly admired, and deemed worthy of a professional. You are gifted with considerable native talent. Such abilities warrant cultivation, and therefore we will accept you."

"Well, now." She thought rapidly. She, Exalted Eliste vo Derrivalle— acknowledged and accepted as a beggar? Humiliating—intolerable. And yet, in light of reason, it really wasn't a bad idea. She *was* a beggar, for now at least, and making it official would make it comparatively safe. Certainly she couldn't hope to defy the entire brotherhood; she'd do better to join them. And there were additional possible benefits to consider. The beggars of Sherreen went every-where, saw everything, knew everything. Nothing in the city was hidden from them. With such intelligence at her disposal, she could find a way of escaping Sherreen. The gutter brethren might know of another tunnel somewhere, or a way past the barricades, or some means of deceiving the Sentient Boomette. She might get away—join the Exalted emigrants in Strell, or perhaps return to Derrivalle, where Uncle Quinz's magic would surely defend her against the excesses of Revolutionary fervor. All in all, not such a bad idea at all.

"What would I have to do, then, sir?"

"You will bind yourself with an oath of loyalty, secrecy, and obedience to our laws. You will promise to honor the territorial rights and privileges of your brethren. Thereafter, you will be granted a stretch of your own, within whose borders you will confine your activities. You will on a weekly basis tender a twenty-percent commission upon all your earnings to my designated representative—"

"Twenty percent is a lot."

"Administrative expenses are high. The rate of commission is not negotiable. Attempted evasion of full payment is neither practical nor advisable. Should you require additional information on this subject, I refer you to Noseless Flaute or to Brokeface Brionne. Either is well-qualified to advise you."

"I hear you, sir."

"Excellent, my dear. And now that we understand each other, we need only conclude the formalities, and I will assign you your own territory. Something in one of the better neighborhoods, I think, where that wan, broken-blossom look will show to best advantage. There, your chosen persona of the Consumptive Grisette will doubtless melt many tender hearts. Although—" The Fungus added upon reflection, "it seems almost a squandering of resources. For the longer I look at you, the more clearly I discern the rather fetching creature that lurks beneath the filth, the rags, and the peaked pallor of malnutrition. Give you a bath, decent garments, adequate nourishment for a few days, and what, I wonder, shall we discover? It is possible that we can find a better use for you than milking. In fact, I am quite certain of it."

"What do you mean?"

"Madame Daux's in Rat Town fulfills the needs and desires of the flush university lads, who relish variety. Madame is generally in want of fresh belles. On the other hand, the clientele at The Honey Pot, in Breakleg Lane, is generally older, more sedate, and better-heeled. If there is an opening there, your earnings are apt to be higher."

Eliste stiffened. Another pander. They were everywhere, numerous as bed-bugs, and just as disgusting. She hated them all. But much as she longed to tell this moldy lump of uncooked dough just what she thought of him, as she had told the similarly enterprising Master Prilq, this time she did not dare so indulge herself, and confined herself to the mild observation, "Don't think I should like it, sir."

"No doubt you will grow accustomed."

"Think I'll just stick to milking, if it's all the same to you, sir."

"Ah, little Kairthe, but that is hardly your decision to make."

"You mean I got nothing to say about it, Master Fungus?"

"Once you have taken your oath, you will accept the decisions of your superiors in the brotherhood without argument, reservation, or complaint."

"But what if I don't like those decisions?"

"You will learn to live with them, my dear. In light of the alternatives, you will find that is best."

His red eyes rested upon her. Astonishing that eyes of such a fiery color could look so utterly cold. Suddenly, it seemed as if she saw for the first time what lay beneath the sardonic urbanity; and then all at once she was very afraid of him. Her voice was steady but small as she replied, "Master Fungus, please just assign me a stretch for milking. That's all I want."

"Your wants, my child, are inconsequential. It is best that you recognize that at the outset. Come, now—enough discussion. Accept what is offered, and let us make an end."

Accept? Impossible. But what choice was there? In any event, she didn't dare refuse outright. The expression she had caught in his eyes a moment since warned her not to cross him. Time. Delay. Put it off an hour, a day. Perhaps a miracle would occur.

"I need to think it over, sir," Eliste countered.

"Indeed. Interesting." Thoughtfully, The Fungus pressed the sponge to his sores, and the dyed water dripped in bloody rivulets down his hairless white body. "Very well. I give you twenty-four hours; at the conclusion of which, if I do not hear from you, the offer is withdrawn, never to be renewed."

"How would I send a message? I don't even know where this place is."

"Drop a word in any beggar's ear, and it will get back to me."

"Right, sir. Then if it's good with you, Master Fungus, I think I'll be getting along now."

"You shall have an escort," he informed her, and rang the bell.

The door opened, and one of the kidnappers entered. Eliste stood unwillingly submissive as he blindfolded her. The smooth voice of The Fungus glided through the dark.

"Choose wisely, little Kairthe. Consider your present, and your probable future. And while you do so, one word of advice—do not attempt begging. Any such infringement will henceforth be dealt with harshly. You understand me?"

Eliste nodded.

"Excellent. Then I bid you adieu for now, my dear. It has been a pleasure."

She could not bring herself to return the compliment. She dropped a brief, blind curtsy in his general direction, then allowed her guide to lead her away, down the stairs and out of the building. Outdoors, the sudden shock of the cold made her gasp. In the humid warmth of The Fungus's study, she had forgotten winter. Now it was back again, with its merciless wind and its treacherous ice underfoot. Sightless, she tripped and stumbled through the streets, forced to rely on her erstwhile kidnapper's support. He steered her through the twists and turns for a time, and then abruptly he left her, slipping away without a word.

Removing the blindfold, Eliste gazed about in confusion. She stood in a cul-de-sac, empty and unfamiliar. The tenements rising on either side were shabby and decrepit. Almost certainly, she was still in the Eighth District. It shouldn't take long to orient herself. She walked out of the cul-de-sac and along a pass-through, presently emerging onto Pump Street. A few hundred yards distant hulked Wonique's Warm Welcome. Dubiously, she fingered the six biquins in her pocket. If she spent them all on bed space at the Welcome, she would have nothing left over for food tomorrow; and she had been warned against begging. On the other hand, the night promised exceptional discomfort. The wind was moaning and stabbing like an anguished homicide. For days now, a cough had troubled her; nothing approaching the Consumptive Grisette's convulsive spasms, but persistent, and sometimes accompanied by mild dizzy spells. She could not afford to permit herself a serious illness. Even as Eliste stood deliberating, it began to snow. Icy flakes drove almost horizontally into her face, and that decided her.

She spent the night at Wonique's Warm Welcome, abandoning that fetid shelter at dawn to discover the city newly purified with snow; a pretty sight to view from the comfort of a warm chamber. The sun, just showing above the rooftops, invested the crystalline mantle with a fabulous glitter. The snow underfoot, fresh and dry, crunched like deep-fried ganzel puffs. *Food. Food.* It was another of those icy, cruelly brilliant mornings.

Eliste trudged down Pump Street, miserably preoccupied with the latest catastrophe. One more day. One day left to decide, and then The Fungus expected an answer. She was in no position to refuse him, and what he intended for her was insupportable. She could not leave Sherreen, and remaining, she would almost certainly starve. Either way—trapped and lost. No way out. Her mind spun futilely.

Lost in misery, she had scarcely noted her own course. Now she found herself at the foot of Bridge Street, almost in the shadow of the Sepulchre. Straight ahead lay the Vinculum, its ancient snow-clothed span already alive with traffic. Beyond it the Waterfront Market, with its booths and its carts, from which—who knows—she might manage to snatch a turnip or two. It would be comforting to know that the river lay between herself and The Fungus; not that the geographical separation afforded the slightest protection, but somehow it would *feel* better. On she pushed, and almost the moment she set foot on the bridge, her thoughts jumped and a solution to her difficulties presented itself. There was indeed a way out—a very final one. Frowning a little, almost absently, she stepped to the stone guardrail, leaned over, and stared down into the water. The river was swollen and swift today, its ruffled tan surface spotted with floating ice and debris. She would not last long there, and there would be an end to fear, misery, cold, and hunger. No more Fungus to soil and sell her.

Escape. For an instant, fantastically alluring. Not now, of course. The Vinculum was crowded, her action would be noted, and some officious hero might even insist upon rescuing her. Later that night, when the place was all but deserted—

She could picture it very clearly in her mind, and she could even feel it: launch from the bridge, rush of icy air, skirts and cloak billowing; terrible, helpless, accelerating descent; and a ghastly, inevitable moment of *regret*. Strike water so hard and fast that the surface would feel solid; then down, down, down into the dreadful blackness and the icy cold. Agony, lungs starving, and the body's instinctive struggles to live; desperately violent, sightless struggles—subjectively prolonged for hours. And then the sensation of frigid water rushing into her lungs—the terror—

Eliste shuddered. Her vivid imagination, usually a source of diversion, sometimes had its drawbacks. With both hands, she pushed herself away from the guardrail.

Slowly she crossed the bridge and walked on into the market, where the sight of heaped food banished all other considerations. There was bread there—new loaves. Eliste sidled near. The merchant, alerted by the longing in her eyes, watched unwinkingly. One illicit grab, and he'd call the whole market down on her. . . . No good. She drifted on.

Potatoes, onions, walnuts, preserved fruit, salted meat. Food everywhere, all of it jealously guarded. She couldn't even get close. Some sixth sense warned the merchants of a predatory presence; one after another, they shooed her away from their stalls. Eliste's cheeks burned with humiliation, but hunger fostered perseverance. Methodically she worked her way around the market's perimeter, reaching the far edge about an hour later. And there at last, a stroke of luck: a fishmonger and a buyer, deeply engrossed in their haggling. The merchant stood with his back to her. Beside him, a tub of herrings, smoked to a beautiful shade of dark gold, and stacked like ingots. Eliste approached; softly slid a herring from the pile. The merchant didn't notice, but the customer squawked an alarm.

Instantly Eliste whirled and ran, dodging and weaving with the adroitness of a street urchin. Shouting behind her, and she quickened her pace. The fishmonger would never abandon his stall to chase her for one stolen herring, yet she was terrified. There might be gendarmes about, one never knew, and *they* would surely chase her. She didn't dare look back.

By the time exhaustion finally forced her to a halt, she had traveled far beyond the Waterfront Market, deep into unknown territory. To the best of her recollection, she had never set foot in this staid petit-bourgeois neighborhood. Shops, houses, and faces were uniformly unfamiliar, and that was good. Here she was a stranger; here she could be invisible. Clearing a bare patch in the snow, she seated herself upon somebody's front steps, waited for her distressed breathing to ease, then ate the purloined fish. Chronic abdominal ache assuaged, she rose and walked on; while the griefs temporarily chased from her mind returned now in full force to poison all her thoughts. Wholly preoccupied, she wandered, scarcely noting her course. A tide of pedestrian traffic drew her along with itself; she neither saw nor sensed the purposefulness of the flow. She moved unaware of the current that carried her; consciousness did not dawn until she came to the end of the narrow street and the vista before her suddenly expanded. The buildings seemed to roll back, clearing a great circular plain paved with cunningly shaped granite flags in three colors. The pattern of the flags led the eye by design to a central area traditionally occupied by an equestrian statue of Dunulas the Great. The statue was gone now. In its place loomed the Kokotte.

She had come to the Circle of the Grand Monarch, newly-christened Equality Circle. She would not knowingly have approached this place. But now that she had arrived by chance, she halted, transfixed at her first sight of the Sentient. There, straight ahead, rose the gluttonous queen of nightmares, crowned with barbs, high-enthroned upon a wooden scaffold. In all particulars, she conformed to description; yet verbal portraits had never truly captured the essence of the original; never conveyed the power and hunger; above all, never suggested the uncanny sense of slow, cold consciousness radiating from the huge coffin of a body. Kokotte's doors gaped wide, exposing discolored internal spikes that quivered. Quick, restless pulses of light danced upon her thorny crown, flashed along her glassy whorls and sunbursts. At her side stood a stone-faced monolith of a man who could only be the famous Bierce Valeur, cousin to the unspeakable Whiss, Master of the Revolutionary Revels, High Priest to the Kokotte—the executioner. How many human beings—how many of her own friends and acquaintances—had this hulking butcher personally destroyed? Eliste wondered. Whatever the number, it was bound to increase today. Bierce's presence upon the scaffold, and the hurried last-moment convergence of a festive throng, signaled the imminence of mass sacrifice.

The tide of humanity washed Eliste forward. She found herself standing in the thick of the spectators. At the forefront of the crowd, clustered about the base of the scaffold, frisked the Cavaliers and Coquettes of Kokotte. These disciples, brave in their horned headgear, were jigging, singing, striking poses, and calling to Bierce Valeur. Some of the Coquettes were pelting the scaffold with scarlet carnations, their own chosen emblem. Bierce ignored the floral tribute. He stood very still and quiet, one hand resting upon the Sentient's flank, muddy eyes bright with love. Almost he seemed unaware of his surroundings.

A commotion at the edge of Equality Circle, where the hawkers stood vending their tidbits and trinkets, and the mob parted as the daily convoy came rumbling up out of Arcade Avenue. An indifferent harvest today: four open carts, each carrying the customary dozen or so naked and shivering victims; surrounded by guards, and trailed by the usual straggle of shouting, cavorting citizens. A few of these patriots, particularly keen for public notice, even performed crude gymnastics: leaps, cartwheels, and back flips.

The procession advanced over the granite flags to the foot of the scaffold, and there halted. Instantly the character of the Kokotte's radiant display altered. Her lights flashed bright and suddenly eager. A shrill mechanical humming mosquitoed above the crowd's hubbub, and Bierce Valeur hurriedly withdrew his hand.

The four carts were ranged at the foot of the scaffold. There a line of guards stood ready to repel the advances of the crowd. There also stood the Clerk of the National Tribunal, bearing a sheaf of death warrants, each warrant awaiting the appropriate signature and notation effecting its transformation to a death certificate. Beside the Clerk stood a brace of red-diamonded stalwarts, eager and proud to serve Bierce Valeur.

Bierce descended. With the aid of his assistants, he removed the condemned from the carts, lining them up with their backs to the Sentient; an orientation dictated less by mercy than expedience. Bierce had long since discovered that the sight of the Kokotte in action was apt to rouse victims to screaming revolt. Sparing them an intolerable spectacle promoted docility. The deployment was carried out with a detached, businesslike efficiency that brooked no denial; not a single prisoner offered resistance.

Eliste could not make herself leave. She didn't want to see this; yet she was paralyzed, frozen in place.

Is there anybody there that I know?

Always the same question. In the past, always unanswerable; perhaps mercifully so. But now, for the first time, she viewed the proceedings at close range, from ground level. For the first time, it would actually be possible to identify victims.

Bierce's minions were already hauling the first of the condemned up the wooden steps. At the top, all three became visible above the heads of the massed spectators, and Eliste spied a plump, brown-haired young man whose round face with its glazed despairing eyes was unknown to her. Somehow, she could hardly have said how, she knew that he was not Exalted. He might have been a university student, or perhaps the son of a prosperous shopkeeper. The nature of his crime was impossible to guess; in the wake of Whiss Valeur's new Law of Denunciation, it might have been almost anything.

Atop the scaffold, Bierce himself took charge, manipulating the prisoner with an ease born of great strength and much practice. The victim seemed almost to fly forward over the planking, straight to the maw of Kokotte. The leaden doors clanged shut with ferocious speed. The mechanical hum shrilled to an intolerable shriek. Small lightnings flashed along the two great vertical horns, faster, brighter, faster, building, until a burst of terrible brilliance flared white and searing at the summit. The doors parted, revealing a cavity empty save for a length of blood-stained rope, and the crowd, thoroughly inured to this spectacle, merely buzzed its satisfaction. Bierce Valeur twitched his long-handled hook, and the soiled cord went flying, to be caught in midair by a Coquette who screamed in delight at her good fortune. In the meantime, the next victim had already reached the top of the stairs without the assistance of Bierce's underlings. It was a woman this time, elderly, but still slim and very erect. Eliste looked up, and recognized her grandmother.

Like all of the condemned, Zeralenn was unclothed, but her unbound silvery hair, still long and thick as a girl's, covered her to her knees. Her spine was straight, expression serenely composed as always. Almost she might have been about to step into her bath, but for the wrists bound behind her back. At the top of the stairs, she paused to survey the crowd. The hazel eyes traveled slowly over the upturned faces with a thoughtful, considering look; slid across her granddaughter's visage; a split second later, returned and anchored there. Not a muscle in Zeralenn's face moved. Not the faintest light of recognition flickered in her eyes. But she had seen; of that there could be no doubt.

Bierce Valeur now laid hands upon her. She looked up at him and said something, her words inaudible to the spectators. Bierce appeared taken aback. She shook herself lightly free of his grasp, and he, perhaps out of deference to her age, or perhaps even yielding in one unguarded moment to her steel regality, permitted it. Unassisted, she advanced upon the Kokotte with a firm and steady step, and a murmur of surprise at the unorthodoxy arose among the spectators. The sound broke Bierce Valeur's trance. He took two long strides after the anarchic prisoner. Before he could reach her, she stepped calmly into the cabinet. The doors banged shut. The lightnings played.

Eliste felt nothing. She was trembling, and her teeth chattered uncontrollably, but she felt nothing. The clear winter air was suddenly gray and foggy, filled with muffled, murmurous voices, like the sigh of the sea. Curious. For some reason it seemed hard to stay on her feet. Shaking her head to clear it, she looked again to the scaffold, where Bierce Valeur, no doubt anxious to atone for his momentary lapse, dealt masterfully with his next client—a young, fair-headed girl. Kairthe.

Kairthe, not afforded the modesty of unbound hair, was fully exposed to public view. At sight of the slender and youthful form, appreciative howls arose:

"Bonbon! Bonbon!"

The cries echoed and resounded crazily, seemed to merge for a moment with another voice, an alien voice in her mind. Again, Eliste shook her head dizzily, pressed both hands to her temples. Up on the scaffold, Kairthe like a brave wide-eyed child in the grip of Bierce Valeur. And still the joyous cries from the crowd, and the metallic reverberations vibrating between her temples, crashing like an orchestra of gongs and cymbals. The other voice was there again, and for one brief moment, Eliste thought, impossibly, to sense the mind of the Kokotte herself:

For She is the One, the Eternal, the Glorious. She is the Power and the sole Reality. Her radiance warms and fills the Void. She is Totality. Bow down and worship. Sacrifice unto Her. Feed and tend Her, for Hers is the hunger of the Infinite.

A quick professional thrust propelled Kairthe to her doom. The doors clamped shut, and moments later, the flare of brilliance announced completion. The echoes in Eliste's mind swelled to a roar, a hurricane; then faded abruptly, and she heard nothing more for a time.

When the ragged girl with the filthy fair elflocks collapsed to the granite pavement, the citizens thought little of it, for such occurrences were commonplace. She might be squeamish, ailing, or perhaps just starved. Under the Law of Denunciation, of course, all public or private displays of sympathy for condemned enemies of the people were regarded as counterrevolutionary, and therefore treasonous; but this famished creature's giddiness was not interpreted as such. A couple of the more charitable among the spectators picked her up and carried her to the edge of Equality Circle, where they left her on a bench. A minute or two later, Eliste revived; rent with grief and horror, and longing for renewed insensibility. But she was wide awake, and likely to remain so.

Abandoning the bench, she wandered away, quite aimlessly. It made no difference where she went; there was nowhere to go, really. She walked without purpose and without thought. Sometimes, when she was tired, she sat for a while; sat numbly, willing her mind to inaction. When the cold impinged upon awareness, she rose and walked some more. Throughout the afternoon she wandered. Gradually, the periods of rest grew longer and more frequent. By the time she reached Ladyshoe Street, her condition was almost stuporous. Sinking down upon the stone lip of a big trough fed by the runoff of the public pump, she sat as if petrified, thinking of nothing at all. So long did she rest there, motionless as a corpse, glazed eyes fixed on the pavement at her feet, that at last her appearance began to draw attention. A couple of the potboys from nearby cookshops attempted amiable overtures, to which she did not respond. One or two passing housewives, market baskets over their arms, stopped to ask if she was sick, or lost. She appeared not to hear. Thereafter, taking her for a simpleton, people left her alone.

She had no idea how long she had been sitting there when one of the passersby, taking pity on the wretched loon, dropped a copper biquin into her lap. The coin fell into her line of vision. She looked at it vaguely. Moments later, a shadow darkened the ground at her feet. Slowly she lifted her eyes to discover a fantastically filthied and tattered trio standing beside her, their combined bulk blocking the light. Brethren of the Gutter, beyond doubt.

"You've been warned," one of the beggars said.

"You think you could get away with it?" asked another.

She stared at them without comprehension.

"No poaching. Order of The Fungus. You knew."

She had forgotten The Fungus, but she remembered now. She wanted no quarrel with these people. She wanted to be left alone. She held out the coin to them. "Here, take it. I never asked for it."

"Oh, you've asked for it, all right," one of the brethren told her pleasantly. "And now you're going to get it." He took the biquin, stowing it away beneath his rags. Then he bent slightly, as if about to make a leg, and slapped her face hard, to send her sprawling in the street.

Eliste scrambled to her feet. She meant to run, but her limbs had gone wooden. Before she had taken a single step, a second beggar grasped her shoulder, jerked her around to face him.

"Crone Plaissie says hello," he remarked, and backhanded her across the face, knocking her sideward into the reeking embrace of the third man, whose clenched fist promptly struck her to the ground again.

Eliste lay dazed and aching. Her ears rang. She'd cut the inside of her cheek on a tooth, and her mouth was filling with blood. She didn't try to move. If she rose, they'd hit her again.

"Now look there. We're getting her all dirty."

"Mud all over those clothes. And all our fault."

"We'd better do something about those clothes."

"Let's wash 'em."

Two of the brethren stooped as one, lifted their victim, and heaved her into the great public trough. Eliste struck the frozen surface jarringly. For a split second the ice bore her weight, then broke beneath her, sinking her in three feet of filthy, frigid water. For a few panicked seconds she thrashed in murky ooze and algae, then, finding the bottom, she planted her feet and attempted to stand.

As her head broke surface, somebody pushed her back under. She swallowed water, choked and flailed. Came up again and was ducked again. Next time she rose, her head struck the underside of a still-unbroken patch of ice, and in her blind terror, she thought herself trapped beneath the surface. She went wild then, fighting with hysterical strength to smash straight through the ice, emerging in a bright burst of frozen shards. Her assailants, satisfied for the moment, were already walking away. One of them glanced back over his shoulder to remark, "You won't get off so easy again." The three of them soon disappeared from view.

Eliste didn't watch them go. Shivering and sobbing, she dragged herself from the trough. Dirty water streamed from her in torrents. Bits of ice clung to her cloak, and strings of algous slime festooned her hair. Pedestrians on Ladyshoe Street were giving her wide berth, walking by with their eyes carefully averted. No one appeared aware of her, much less willing to help. For a moment their callousness amazed her; yet it was predictable, really. To the ultrarespectable petite bourgeoisie, the squabblings of the gutter folk were invisible.

A cruel little lancet of a breeze slashed at her dripping rags, and Eliste hugged herself, shuddering. She had never been so cold—cold clear through, cold enough to die. Unless she found a fire to warm and dry her, she realized dimly, she actually *would* die; but surely it didn't matter much. Perhaps it would be for the best; she certainly had no desire or reason to continue living. Yet she found that she was walking down Ladyshoe Street, and she found that her eyes were shifting mechanically, right and left, in search of shelter and warmth.

They wouldn't let her into the shops or taverns, of course. She was ordered away from the doors of several. No one would tolerate such a disreputable, glassy-eyed, soaked guttersnipe dripping about. She belonged in a charity hospital, or else a madhouse, and to such institutions she was advised to betake herself.

She walked on into the Martmead. She was hardly conscious of her own intentions, yet at the back of her mind, the garbage fires of the Eighth District smoldered. Around such fires, burning day and night, the destitute were free to huddle. Nobody was ever turned away. But the Eighth District was far away, a terrible distance to walk, and she was so very tired. She was always tired these days, but particularly so now. So exhausted and aching that she could hardly move; so weak that she must stop for rest every few hundred yards.

She must have been walking a very long time, for it was late in the afternoon, almost twilight. Her clothes no longer dripped, but they had not dried; every stray breeze knifed straight through. She was shivering continually, yet somehow didn't seem to feel the cold. Quite the contrary, in fact; her face was furnace-hot, lips parched and cracked. Her thirst was terrible; nor could the fragments of ice or the handfuls of grimy snow on which she constantly chewed assuage it. She couldn't understand why she felt so dizzy. It made no sense that she should wobble and stagger, requiring the support of walls or the occasional hitching post to keep her on her feet. It was ridiculous, and terribly inconvenient; at this rate, it would take her all night to reach those beckoning garbage fires.

She was back in the Waterfront Market again. The merchants were shutting up shop, which meant that evening had come. So the darkness about her was real, and no trick of failing vision. That was good, that was a relief, but there remained such a distance to travel, over ground that seemed shaky as aspic beneath her, and she really was *very* tired—

When she crumpled unconscious to the cobbles, she had the good fortune to be noticed. Had the hour been later, and the marketplace deserted, she would have lain there for hours, to die of the cold before morning came. As it was, her collapse was observed by many disapproving eyes, and the gendarmes were summoned. In the eyes of the soldiers, for whom failure to meet a weekly quota of arrests meant reprimand, the situation was self-explanatory. The prostrate gutter-snipe was obviously dead drunk. Moreover, her face was bruised, and she had a black eye, which proved that she had been brawling. Drunk and disorderly, she belonged in gaol. The Sepulchre was the nearest prison, but that antechamber of death was not the abode of scruffy little alley kittens like this one. They took her to the Treasury instead.

P rison was wonderful, better by far than Prilq's Hospitality. In no condition to
stand before a magistrate upon arrival, Eliste was summarily sentenced by the
Lieutenant Governor of the Treasury to a week's detention. She wished it
could have been ten times as long—at least, wished so as soon as understanding returned. For the first twenty-four hours, she was by turns insensible and
delirious with fever; sometimes thinking herself back at Derrivalle, where the
liberated serfs all bore an unaccountable resemblance to The Fungus; sometimes
imagining herself exposed in an open cart, pushed and jostled by the bodies of her
fellow condemned. The pushing and jostling were not altogether fanciful.
Throughout the night she shared a pile of verminous straw with a gang of women
whose feet and elbows often prodded. Mindful of possible contagion, however,
they gave her as wide a berth as possible, and she slept in relative peace.

Rest was what she seemed to need the most. The next day, her fever broke and
she slept deeply for many hours; revived briefly in the early evening to find herself
sitting up, supported by the anonymous arm of one who spoon-fed her gruel as if
she were a baby; then relapsed into slumber that continued unbroken until
morning.

Her illness was not of the worst. When next she opened her eyes to behold thin
rays of winter sunlight struggling in through deep-set barred windows, she was
weak and very listless, but already starting to mend. She lay on straw alive with
fleas and lice. Some nameless philanthropist had thrown a blanket over her. Eliste
gazed about her with awakening interest. Some trace of awareness must have

persisted throughout delirium, for she knew perfectly well where she was. They had brought her to the Treasury; but in place of the minuscule solitary dungeon she might have envisioned, she discovered a large and crowded chamber. The ward was dreary, bare, and fireless, but not unbearably cold. The stone wall against which the straw was piled radiated a faint warmth transmitted from the hot prison kitchen that lay on the other side. By comparison to Prilq's Hospitality, or Wonique's Warm Welcome, the atmosphere in this place was luxurious. The stench was foul, of course; but no worse than that which she had often gladly paid to endure elsewhere. To her surprise, the door was wide open. Women came and went freely. A few sported the classically unequivocal bedizenments of prostitutes, but the majority of them were shabbily nondescript, indistinguishable from the ordinary citizenesses thronging the Waterfront Market every day. One such woman sat beside her now. She was almost young—perhaps twenty-eight or -nine; plainly dressed; tall and big-boned, with broad shoulders, hips, and nose; large hands, breasts, and chin; a ruddy shrewd-eyed face, and reddish hair. Certainly there was nothing in her appearance to suggest the convicted felon. Here, beyond doubt, sat last night's benefactor. Even now, she was slipping an arm around Eliste's shoulders, lifting her up, extending a spoonful of soup.

Down it went. Potato-leek, watery but welcome. Eliste gulped, choked, sneezed.

"Not so fast," the other cautioned. Sharp Sherreen city accent.

She nodded comprehension and acquiescence. She would have nodded anything to get the spoon back in her mouth. The spoon was back. She sucked and slurped.

Eliste didn't count the spoonfuls. Eventually she noted that the warmth was spreading through her, carrying the life back to dead extremities. She was warm. She had food. She loved gaol. She slept again.

When she woke, she was nearer her usual self. She was hungry, but not desperately so. She was unspeakably dirty, plagued with itches, rashes, bites, sweats, scales and scurfs, slimes and stinks. She wanted to bathe; might just as well have wanted to fly. Was there enough soap in all Vonahr to make her feel clean again? Reluctantly, she opened her eyes. She still lay on straw, beneath a moth-eaten blanket. The redheaded woman sat knitting beside her. The fleas feasted. Eliste twitched, scratched, and slapped herself sharply.

"Heh!" said the redhead.

"What?" said Eliste. Fully conscious, she remembered the Fabequais accent. But what might she have said while feverish? The face of her companion told her nothing.

"Easy," said the other. "It's all right."

Of course it is.

"But—"

"Easy. What's the fuss?"

What indeed? Eliste subsided, breathing deeply. No fuss, certainly not.

"Better look sharp. If you're really so sick, they won't feed you. They won't want to waste the food on a corpse."

Reasonable.

Eliste sat up, an impressive demonstration of vitality. She swayed, but remained upright.

"Very good. But don't go acting too chipper, else they'll set you straight to work."

Eliste looked a question.

"In the kitchen. Scrubbing. Dipping candles, trying out fat, making soap. In the laundry. Scrubbing. In the privies. Scrubbing. Down below, beating hemp. You don't want that, let me tell you."

"But everybody's sitting around doing nothing."

"Not everybody, Miss Simple. Only the ones who've paid off the warders. That lets you out."

"How do you know?"

"You're flat empty. I checked. Oh, don't look so goggled. I wasn't aiming to rob you. If you'd had anything, I'd've made sure no one took it off you."

"Oh." Eliste frowned uncertainly. She supposed she ought to believe. She supposed she ought to be grateful to this stranger who had helped her. She *was* grateful, but sensed clearly that the woman wanted repayment of some kind. Not money. But surely she expected something, and if not cash, then what? "Thank you," she added with an effort.

The woman was watching her closely. Too closely, she thought; shrewd eyes too unwavering. Eliste looked away. "If this is prison, why's the door unlocked?" she asked uncomfortably.

"You *are* green, aren't you? All the inner doors are unlocked during the day. You can go where you please, including the men's section if you've a mind to make money, up until Doublebell in the evening. When the first bell sounds, it means you've got ten minutes to get yourself back here. If you're not back by lockup, and they nail you, you'll spend the night outdoors in the courtyard, and you'll miss breakfast. Not that breakfast's much to miss. Thin gruel and maybe some moldy old bread. Every day. Filthy stuff, bad enough to gag a pig. Grease the right axles and there's better, of course, but you'd need the cash. Aiming to earn?"

"No."

"Then I guess you'll have to make do for—how long? How long is it you're in for?"

Her tone was casual, yet Eliste sensed disquieting interest. She didn't want to answer, but the query was harmless, evasion pointless. Her brief interview with the Lieutenant Governor was all but lost, but somehow the outcome had registered. "A week," she said.

"A week. Well, that's not too bad, is it? Not bad at all. A trifle." The stranger appeared unaccountably gratified. "Drunk and disorderly, I guess?"

Why are you so interested?

"What about you?" Eliste inquired, in a feeble effort to turn the tables.

"Me? I'm boxed for ninety days, this time. Eighty left to go. Block Chief had it in for me. He wanted a whopping grease on every Strellian bundle I sold darkers, and I told him where to stick it. So he just dangled low until I shaved twenty minutes off the last Fratsup, and then he peached me for apathy, the little turd."

Eliste performed a swift mental translation. The Revolutionary Commissaire of this woman's Block—one of the new subdivisions of the various Districts of Sherreen—had demanded a share of her black-market profits. She had refused, and in retaliation he had reported her late arrival at one of those recently initiated, mandatory neighborhood jollifications known as Egalitarian Fraternal Suppers. Under the Law of Denunciation, a demonstrable lack of patriotic zeal was regarded as counterrevolutionary. Actually, the woman had gotten off easily. These days, her crime might easily have sent her to the Kokotte.

"If he thinks this'll whip me into line, he'd better think again. I call it a holiday. What's more, I've friends outside will see to his business. He's going to find his well full of piss and dead cats. I hope he likes it."

Eliste produced a politic smile of sympathy, and the woman favored her with another narrow, unsettling scrutiny. "I'm Jounisse," she announced abruptly. "Who are you?"

"Stelli. Stelli Zeenosgirl."

"You northerners all have names that sound like tin pans clattering. Well, little Stelli, you're in luck. I know my way around this place, and I've decided to lend you a hand."

"I can't pay you."

"Who's asking for payment? Don't worry about it. Maybe someday you can return the favor, maybe not. In the meantime, I've nothing better to do."

Unconvinced, Eliste managed another stiff smile. Perhaps she was lucky to meet this Jounisse, but she didn't trust her an inch.

In the days that followed, Eliste had little difficulty maintaining the appearance of weakness that preserved her from consignment to cellar or privy, for the appearance reflected simple reality. Her fever did not return, but she was feeble, exhausted, drained, hardly able to make it from straw to slop bucket without tottering. She spent much of her time sleeping, lying with her back pressed flat to the warm stone wall, and that was good, so long as the dreams of Zeralenn's death did not return. But they came often, and she would wake with the tears streaming down her cheeks. Or she would dream of Kairthe, Bierce Valeur, and the Kokotte, and then she would start from slumber with a stifled cry that drew the incurious attention of her fellow prisoners. They were a motley lot, these prisoners; much varied in age, appearance, and condition. Very petty malefactors for the most part, their offenses ranged from drunken obstreperousness, to prostitution, to filching chestnuts from a vendor; from spitting at a gendarme, to defacing shopfronts and public monuments with ordure. Few seemed genuinely dangerous or violent. Two or three were given to threatening braggadocio, and these nobody meddled with; but for the most part they were civil enough. Unlike the shuffling hopeless denizens of Prilq's Hospitality, these women did not lack for energy. Throughout the day they chattered, cackled, screeched, and squabbled like a cageful of daws. If she closed her eyes, ignoring the gutter accents, Eliste could almost have imagined herself back in the Maids' Quarters of the Beviaire.

As promised, the ordinary Treasury diet was wretched and repetitive. Most prisoners managed, by some means or another, to purchase better meals; some of them dined well indeed, on roast fowl, white bread, even wine and pastry. No such luxury was available to Eliste, but there was one consolation. The prison fare, universally despised and rejected, was available in reasonable quantity to those able to stomach it. She could eat her fill of last month's green-spotted crusts and weepy gruel. To Eliste, fresh from freezing starvation, such plenty seemed sybaritic. For the moment, she desired nothing more.

The other women were inclined to mock her simplicity. At first, they attributed her somnolence to the effects of illness. Later on, when it was clear she was recovering, they offered much advice and instruction, which might greatly have improved her lot, had she but listened. There were, she was informed, at least half a dozen different ways that she might earn herself some money. There were plenty of men who'd be happy to pay her. And there were plenty of fellow prisoners who would gladly hire her to take over their work details in kitchen or latrine. Or if she happened to be daring, and very clever, she might pick a turnkey's pocket. Or—

But the quiet new prisoner ignored the best of advice, rejected the friendliest of overtures. She seemed content to lie about on filthy straw, silent and lost in her own thoughts. It was impossible to avoid suspecting that she was a bit stuck up, though what the grimy little starveling imagined she had to be stuck up *about* was unclear. Certainly she was a sluggard, lacking ambition to better herself. She was welcome, then, to her fleas and her gelid pap; the lazy lump deserved no better. The women presently lost patience and interest. After a day or so, they left her strictly alone—all of them, except Jounisse.

Not easily discouraged, Jounisse insisted on visiting with Eliste at least twice a day. Always she would sit down, smiling as if she imagined herself welcome, and then she would chatter gossip, jokes, complaints, and nonsense for twenty minutes at a time, undeterred by the other's monosyllabic unresponsiveness. She appeared simply amiable and obtuse, but somehow Eliste knew better. This woman was no fool, far from it; she knew perfectly well that her friendship was unwanted, and yet she insisted on hanging about. It was inexplicable and unnerving.

What did she want?

The relentless sociability drove Eliste to swift recovery. As soon as she was able to walk, she fled the ward in favor of the common room, where the prisoners mingled to chat and drink, to play at cards and dice. She even joined in a game of Roullo, playing until Jounisse discovered her there.

Next morning, she tried hiding out in the laundry. She had not been there for more than an hour before her incubus appeared. The walled courtyard likewise failed as a refuge, as did the drafty ground-floor corridor, and even the niche in the stairwell. No matter where she went, Jounisse infallibly tracked her down. The woman possessed the instincts of a bloodhound. Eliste found herself dreading the companionable clap on the back, the hearty "Well, my little sister, you are always turning up. I'm starting to think you must be following me!" She hid her distaste as best she could, for it was too revealing, and in any case, Jounisse had helped her. Her knowledge and advice, which she dispensed freely, were actually useful; occasionally she even offered a bite of her own barley sugar or chocolate, urging the treat on a reluctant Eliste with an insistence that would not be denied. Eliste was uneasily appreciative, but the doubts persisted, and with them came the fears: What if Jounisse were some sort of a police spy? Sherreen was notoriously infested with such, most of them in the employ of the Committee of National Welfare. It was their business in life to sniff out counterrevolutionism, and they were often called the "Victualers," for this was the function they served in relation to Kokotte. Was Jounisse a Victualer, suspicions aroused by some chance word that Eliste had let slip while feverish? And if so, then why so lengthy a postponement of the inevitable denunciation? Was additional evidence required? Or did the woman simply amuse herself with cat-and-mouse?

No point in agonizing. Best to think of other things, if possible. In fact, there were certain matters demanding her attention. Half the week was gone. Another three days, and she would be released. She would find herself back out on the streets of Sherreen; still penniless, still unemployed, still prohibited from begging. She would freeze and starve again, a hideous prospect. Eliste did not want release. The

Treasury, hellhole though it was, offered shelter and marginal sustenance. Where else would she do as well? Definitely she wished to remain, but how to manage it? The obvious route—by way of some misdemeanor leading to arrest—was fraught with danger. There was, she realized, a remarkably fine line, sometimes indistinguishable these days, between convictions resulting in a light gaol sentence and those carrying the death penalty. Often the difference depended solely upon the whim of a single magistrate. A testy judge, troubled with dyspepsia, might send an adolescent pickpocket to the Treasury for a couple of months—or else, just as easily, to the gallows. It wouldn't do to ignore such possibilities.

And another possibility worth notice—that she might follow her companions' good advice, taking over some fellow prisoner's work detail for a fee. Then she would not be turned out penniless into the streets three days hence. Unluckily, she thought of this too late. Her recent wanderings had not escaped the notice of the ward sergeant, who now deemed her recovered, and fit for labor. Eliste was assigned to the kitchen, where she stood scraping and scouring the blackened remnants of burned porridge out of great iron pots from morning until night. It was miserable and taxing work. The great washtubs of water were scalding hot, and the lye soap almost caustic. By the end of the first afternoon, her back, arms, and shoulders ached fiercely.

She spent three days scrubbing pots. At the end of that time, she was exhausted and still destitute. Release loomed, horribly imminent. There seemed no escape from freedom. On the last night, she trudged back to the ward, a quarter hour short of Doublebell. Her mood alternated between despair and self-recrimination. She should have thought of a means to stay here. She *should* have.

"Heh—Stelli!" A voice in her ear, a hand on her arm. Jounisse again.

"I can't talk now." Eliste averted her face.

"Just for a little. Come on."

Eliste found herself pulled off course, backed up against the wall of a tributary passageway, where the weak light of a single ceiling-hung lantern barely served to pierce the gloom. Jounisse stood close, regarding her too intently.

"Big day tomorrow, eh?" said Jounisse.

"I guess so."

"Bet you can hardly wait. Expect you've had enough of scrubbing pots."

Eliste shrugged.

"What do you plan to do with yourself, then?"

"I don't know." Eliste's voice and eyes revealed more than she realized of despondency and fear.

"I don't suppose you've any money. You've been almighty high-nosed about earning anything in here. What do you figure on doing out there without any money?"

"What's that to you?" Eliste snapped, self-control slipping. "Why are you so interested? What do you want?"

"Look, I've been decent to you all week, not that I've ever heard a word of thanks—gone out of my way to help you out—"

"Why?"

"You're so green, you needed it."

"And?"

"And I've got something on could do us both some good. I need a body set to bust the box." She meant a prisoner about to be freed. "I've been looking you over for a few days, and I think you'll do. Earn yourself some money."

"Oh?" Arms folded, Eliste awaited the inevitable shady proposition.

"That's right. All you've got to do is carry a letter. Easy and safe, eh? For that, I give you twenty-five biquins in advance, and then there'll be another fifty on delivery."

Seventy-five biquins—three quarters of a rekko. Eliste caught her breath. She could live on that for days. But it was a remarkable sum to pay a mere errand girl. There had to be a catch.

"It smells," she observed aloud.

"Can you afford such a particular nose?"

"I can't afford to run afoul of the Kokotte. Who's this letter for, and what's it all about?"

"That's not your concern. It's something I don't want gawked over by the Lieutenant Governor's flunkeys—" Prisoners' ordinary correspondence was routinely perused and censored. "And I'm willing to pay high for privacy. That's all you need to know."

"I'd need to know who to give it to."

"Depends on who they send. Beq, most likely. Sure, that would be it, this week. You give it to Beq."

"Beq. Where would I find this Beq?"

"Beside the v'Uique-Deurenne crypt in The Cypresses, tomorrow night at midnight."

"Midnight—that's loony!"

"That's when he'll be there." Jounisse shrugged. "That's the way of it. You know The Cypresses?"

Eliste nodded. The small graveyard exclusively given over to Exalted dead lay adjacent to the Havillac Gardens. Several of the Rouvignac clan lay buried in that place. Zeralenn vo Rouvignac had expected to rest beside them one day. Whereas now—

"I'd rather meet him somewhere else," said Eliste.

"Oh, you'd rather! Well, sorry, but it isn't your choice, Princess. V'Uique-Deurenne crypt at midnight, and good wages. That's it. Take it or leave it."

Eliste didn't have to think for long. The offer seemed questionable at best, but she was desperate for money. She nodded, reluctantly.

"All right, then. Take these." Jounisse proffered a handful of coppers, and a sealed letter elaborately crisscrossed with wax drippings. Her shrewd eyes gleamed. "And mind you—no tampering. You fool with that letter and Beq will know, sure as nightfall."

"And then?"

"And then no money."

"You're taking a big chance on me, aren't you?"

"Not so big. Judging by what I've seen, you're not much the businesswoman, and you're going to get rat-hungry out there, real fast. You need those biquins bad. Oh, you'll deliver my letter, no question about it."

"Well, as it happens—you're right."

Eliste stowed the coins and letter out of sight beneath her rags. The two women made it back to the ward moments before Doublebell. There they separated, taking no further notice of one another. The door was locked, the lamp extinguished, and the prisoners sought the verminous straw.

At dawn, Eliste devoured a final wretched prison breakfast, wolfing all the porridge she could hold and wisely stuffing every pocket with compacted crusts of bread. Thereafter, she was conducted to a ground-floor cubicle, where a clerk placed a notation beside Stelli Zeenosgirl's name in one of the vast prison ledgers. A turnkey led her across the open courtyard to a small side door in the wall, unlocked it, and unceremoniously thrust her through. The door banged shut behind her. She stood free upon the streets of Sherreen for the first time in a week.

Her stomach was full. She had twenty-five biquins, and tonight there would be another fifty. Her straits were not desperate. Quite likely they would be very soon, but for now, the respite continued. Eliste took a deep breath. The air was cold and raw, but seemed to have lost last week's killing edge. Her dry rags warded off the breeze. The pale morning sunlight upon her face carried a faint recollection of warmth, enough to rouse the ghost of optimism. Almost she dared to hope that the worst was over. Another couple of weeks, and the red buds might actually begin to glow on branches presently bare. Winter was on the wane at last.

She had all the time in the world—all day and half the night—to get herself to The Cypresses. No need to hurry, and that was fortunate. The graveyard lay miles away, on the far side of the Vir, halfway across Sherreen. She would have to walk the entire distance, and she had by no means recovered all her strength.

Eliste decided to make a leisurely trip of it. She walked slowly, pausing often to rest, to drink in the chilly air blessedly free of prison stench, to gaze about at the city that was, for her, simply a larger prison. Already deeply tired by midday, with many miles left to go, she stopped at a roach-ridden café for a frugal but very extended lunch. The food, while cheap and simple, seemed exquisite by comparison with Treasury fare. She lingered by the fire, requesting free refills of her teacup as long as the proprietor's patience held; and while she sat there, she was almost content.

The idyll ended, and she resumed her trek, crossing the Vir at the quiet Cheuv Bridge, a mile upstream of the Vinculum. She wanted no part of the Waterfront Market, the Eighth District, or Rat Town. She much preferred to avoid her old haunts, site of so much fear and misery. Necessity would no doubt force her back to the District soon enough, but she would do what she could to delay the return.

Once across the Vir, she asked directions in her country accent, eventually finding her way into the bottom of the Boulevard Crown Prince, which she might follow for miles, straight on up into the Havillac Gardens. She made her way haltingly along the boulevard, eventually reaching the wealthier neighborhoods, the section of Sherreen that had once been her world. Now, in her rags, with her sickly dirty face, she was a trespasser here. In earlier times, a creature such as she had become would never have dared set foot upon these clean expensive streets. These days, of course, the filthiest of true patriots flaunted their rags everywhere.

Curious. She was passing the v'Esseult town house—presently red-diamonded—where she and Zeralenn had often sipped cordials in the salon with Madame v'Esseult's carefully cultivated collection of wits, artists, scientists, and statesmen. She could remember the voices—laughter, conversation bright as the firelight—all inexpressibly distant and dreamlike, now . . . gone. Gone.

Many hours later, she came to the Havillac Gardens. It was twilight, and the lamplighter was at work. One by one, the lanterns edging the Girdle that circled the great park were brightening to golden bloom. The Girdle itself, once glittering day and night with the gilded toy phaetons and cabriolets of the fashionable, was now the property of assertively shabby patriots. The only vehicles in sight were drab fiacres, for good patriots—and wise ones—rarely owned their carriages these days.

Eliste rested for a time on a stone bench beside the Girdle. She was exhausted and dizzy, no doubt residual effects of her illness. When her head cleared, she rose and repaired to a nearby cookshop, where even the simplest meal was far beyond her means. Once again, she ordered tea and made it last for hours; then at last slipped out into the night to steal her way through the dark Havillac Gardens, northeast to The Cypresses. She had never been alone in the gardens at night before. The park was almost like a forest from one of the old tales, with narrow rustic paths winding among huge old elms and chestnuts; quaint and charming by day, but in the dark——? The branches seemed to clutch like the hands of Vanguardsmen.

Fortunately, the night was clear and bright. Moonlight poured freely through the bare branches arching overhead. Eliste hurried along the graveled path, continually glancing this way and that into the shadowy undergrowth, remains of her cloak clutched tight about her. Encountering nobody, she proceeded without mishap to the northeast edge of the park, which marked the boundary of The Cypresses. Here she very much needed to rest for a time, before pressing on into the old Exalted graveyard.

The massive marble crypts and monuments of the formerly-great rose up around her. They were huge, some of them; topped with human effigies, sculpted crests, and rampant heraldic beasts. Here a frozen lion-eagle roared soundlessly; there a flying serpent spread its vast bat-wings; straight ahead, a snarling Oei reared, eternally poised to strike. The moonlight revealed widespread neglect and decay. No citizen dared now tend Exalted graves. The shrubbery was overgrown, paths choked with weeds and brambles, gravestones foul with dirt and moss. Somehow, the dark patches marring once-snowy marble enhanced the lifelike aspect of the petrified beasts. Eliste could almost feel the pressure of stony eyes. Or live ones? Heart knocking, she wheeled to search the shadows. No one there. She was quite alone. She hurried on.

Some ten minutes later, she located the v'Uique-Deurenne crypt, a big foursquare affair with an entrance surmounted by the bas-relief family arms. No telling what time it was, but she was certainly early. It would be another several minutes at least before Beq, whoever he was, arrived to claim his letter. *If* he arrived, of course. There was always the chance of misunderstanding, mishap, or delay. Perhaps he wouldn't come at all, and then she would have undertaken all this arduous trip for nothing, and she wouldn't be paid. That would be bad enough; but now that she stopped at last to consider, there were far worse possibilities. She knew nothing at all of this Beq. She had come to meet a strange man at midnight, in a deserted spot. All the time that she had struggled toward this place, she had thought of nothing beyond the promised reward of fifty biquins that would keep her alive for another few days. But now that she was here, in a silent garden of stone monsters, with midnight drawing on, she thought of other things. Beq might simply refuse to pay her, of course; he might also rob, assault, or even kill her.

Best not to be too trusting. Perhaps she should observe this Beq from concealment, before confronting him; perhaps she should not confront him at all. Eliste drew back into the deepest shadows; crouched down out of sight behind a tombstone of black granite; there waited, and shivered, and watched.

The quiet minutes passed. The moon sank toward the horizon. Distant chimes sounded the midnight hour. Footsteps crunched on gravel. A man approached the v'Uique-Deurenne crypt. She spied a tall, spare figure swathed in a greatcoat with a multitiered caped collar. His step was elastic; he was probably young. His face was invisible, lost in the shadow of a tall hat with a curling brim.

Beq paused, glanced about almost idly, it seemed; then walked to the crypt and stood leaning against it, arms folded. He wore no gloves. The light of the sinking moon shone upon a lean, long-fingered right hand, its back marked with an indelible black letter *D;* a symbol utterly familiar.

Eliste stood up and stepped forth into view.

"Dref," she said.

Chorl Valeur, limp with exhaustion, sank into the nearest chair. His son Eularque slumped to his knees, and thence to the floor.

Whiss Valeur eyed his kinsmen without sympathy. "Well?" he inquired. "What is this, why do you stop? Get on with it."

"Finished," Chorl muttered.

"What do you mean? Explain yourself at once."

"It is done. The house is awake."

"I see no sign of it."

"What sign would you expect?"

"Don't try to fence with me, Father. My patience is all but exhausted. For the past two hours, I have watched you mutter and groan and twitch. I have watched, and worse, I have listened, until I am half mad with boredom and vexation. Now all at once you give over, and the two of you tumble in your tracks like dead men; but all else remains unchanged. Now, understand: I expect results, else you and my brother will continue your efforts."

"I tell you, it is done." Chorl massaged both temples. "The house wakes, the house listens, for now. Oh, believe me."

"Well. Perhaps." Whiss's green eyes narrowed thoughtfully. "You will have a chance to prove it. That is what we are here for, after all."

"Here" was the rented house in Nerisante Street, to which Whiss still clung even in his present glory, for the appointed Protector of the Vonahrish Republic needed to maintain a modest public demeanor, nothing that smacked of reactionary splendor. The house was now protected day and night by Vanguardsmen; other than that, nothing about it had changed—until now, if Chorl spoke truly. Well, that could be judged easily enough.

The combined magical talents of all the Valeur kinsmen did not suffice to create a new Sentient, but could perhaps accomplish the next best thing—temporary investment of rudimentary consciousness into large existing inanimates, specifically buildings and monuments. A judiciously selected house—a tavern, a shop, a statue—capable of noting events within its environs would prove an invaluable source of intelligence to the Committee of National Welfare. This so, what enemy of Vonahr—or of Whiss Valeur—could hope to escape the Committee's vigilance? Even so elusive a fugitive as Shorvi Nirienne could not remain at liberty for long. Nirienne, whose unseen but vociferous presence stirred the most dangerous dissidence, continued a particularly galling thorn in the side of Whiss Valeur. By all rights, the man's expulsion from the Constitutional Congress, months earlier, should have finished him. A decent and speedy suicide might have concluded the affair nicely. Who could have guessed that Nirienne, refusing to accept the reality of his own destruction, would go to ground in Sherreen itself, resuming illicit publication as if the Revolution had never occurred? He dared to criticize the Republican Protectorate as he had once challenged the monarchy. He deplored, he accused, he exhorted. Concealed and defended by his idiotically loyal followers, he rallied the unfaithful, and his influence crept like gangrene. Not for much longer, though. This new weapon, founded upon the Valeur magic, should put an end to Nirienne once and for all—provided that it worked.

"Prove it," Whiss repeated. "Before witnesses."

Several witnesses sat waiting to be convinced. Bierce Valeur was there, huge bulk incongruously poised atop a spindling gilt armchair that seemed unfit to bear his weight. Frowning, Bierce toyed with his cogs and gears. He had come obediently in response to Cousin Whiss's summons, but the interruption of his communion with the Kokotte troubled him mightily. He hoped it would not last long.

Beside Bierce's chair stood Congressional Congressmen Pieuvre and Poulpe, good Red Diamond men both, allies upon whom Whiss Valeur knew he could rely. Pieuvre was sweating, and his shirt was soaked, despite the cool of the morning. His plump face was flushed, and brandy weighted his breath; yet his gestures retained their precision, and the smile he bent upon Whiss Valeur was an obsequious masterpiece. By contrast, Poulpe was icily perfect. Young—no more than twenty-five or so—fair and remarkably handsome, with regular features, golden curls, lapis eyes and the lashes of a girl, Poulpe had won the nickname of The Marble God; and indeed he owned the symmetry of a classical statue, along with the coldness. The admiration that his beauty aroused was wasted on Poulpe, who cared for nothing beyond the creation of the perfect state, based upon Reparationist principles.

Chorl shook his head vaguely. In the aftermath of prolonged magical effort, intense fatigue seemed to cloud his thoughts. "What have you done with Phlosine?" he inquired with an effort. "Where is your brother Houloir?"

Whiss disliked questions, but this time he decided to humor his father. "Phlosine is upstairs. She will rejoin us presently," he explained with unwonted patience. "As for Houloir, rest assured he's comfortable and quite secure." This was true enough. Houloir Valeur's solitary Sepulchre chamber was well-furnished, well-warmed, and well-guarded. He was there now, for it was a policy strictly adhered to by Whiss that his four captive kinsmen should never meet to hatch plots and rebellion. One or another of them was always held apart, in the hands of Vanguardsmen; a precaution that ensured the docility of the remaining three.

"You have not harmed Houloir?"

"Quite the contrary. I am my brother's keeper."

Chorl lacked energy to rise to the bait. Throughout the months of his Sherreenian residence, the old man seemed to have shrunk, dwindled and faded to the verge of transparency. Wavering and insubstantial as fog he appeared, but some spirit yet remained, for now he met his son's eyes and said quietly, "I understand your motives in this. You hunt your enemies to the death with magic."

"The enemies of Vonahr, Father. The enemies of the people."

"Your own rivals. Shorvi Nirienne."

"The Arch-Traitor, yes, together with the worst of his creatures. The viper Frezhelle, for example. The scorpion Riclairc. And that devil, Beq."

"Magic will avail you little." Chorl folded his arms.

The delicate gilt chair creaked dangerously as Bierce Valeur shifted his weight. His questioning eyes sought his cousin.

"You refuse your assistance?" Whiss spoke very softly. "Do you refuse me, Father?"

"No. You misunderstand, as you have always misunderstood. Magic may serve as your spy, if you must bend it to that end. Magic may even serve to destroy Shorvi Nirienne for you. It will not, however, destroy the power of Nirienne's thoughts, nor the loyalty of his disciples. It is not nearly strong enough for that. Destroy the man himself, and you will find yourself fighting a far more formidable opponent—his memory in the hearts of his friends and followers. You cannot use magic to obliterate an idea. But I am not certain that you are capable of understanding that."

"This old man is a Nirienniste." Poulpe's cold eyes pronounced a death sentence. Beside him, Pieuvre nodded, wafting alcoholic fumes.

"I thank you, Father. The profundity of your political wisdom is matched only by the breadth of your worldly experience. Rest assured, I value your opinion

according to its worth." Whiss's labored sarcasm fell short of the cool nonchalance it aimed for, undermined by jerky fingers and glaring eyes. "I will grant your
advice all the consideration it deserves. In the meantime, you will lend your
particular talents to the patriotic cause. You will serve the interests of the
Republican Protectorate, else stand revealed as an enemy of the Republic. You
will perform your duty voluntarily, or else you must be compelled. Do not imagine
that your reluctance has not been noted, Father." Whiss's anger was mounting
uncontrollably, boiling up out of the deepest mental crevices. "You do not give
willingly, but you've a debt, and you must pay it. Never forget how much you
owe—" He flushed darkly, and his voice rose to full shout. "D'you hear me—
you *owe*!"

Chorl was staring at him, stunned and scared beyond reply. Another voice
answered for him:

"Hold your tongue, Whiss." Eularque Valeur, whose presence had been quite
forgotten by all, was dragging himself to his feet. Eularque was ghostly, drained
and shaky, but his jaw was hard and his eyes defiant. Months of constant
communion with the Sentient ZaZa seemed to have left their mark. It was as if a
trace of the Sentient's fiery spirit animated her human steward. "Don't talk to our
father that way. He owes you nothing. It is not his fault that you are small and
empty of heart, bitter and alone. You have striven toward these things since
childhood, and you have achieved them entirely on your own. They are the just
deserts of the bully, the hypocrite and tyrant that you are."

Whiss's eyes bulged. It had been a long time since anyone had dared to cross,
much less criticize, the Committee of National Welfare's master. Almost unbelievable that his hitherto meek and pliant brother should thus defy him. More
astonishing yet were the insults and abuse—incredible words, unimaginable
accusations that somehow cut and burned. Intolerable words, intolerable. He
needed to strike back, but for once, words failed him.

Seeing this, Bierce Valeur set his wheels and cogs aside. Cousin Whiss needed
his assistance. For the moment, even the Kokotte was forgotten. Bierce stood up,
and the frail gilt chair fell over with a crash. Taking a couple of long steps
forward, he lifted his hand and slapped Eularque open-palmed across the face.
His real strength was not behind the blow, yet it was enough to strike the smaller
man to the floor. A faint wounded peep escaped the watching Chorl Valeur.
Bierce leaned forward. "Don't call Whiss names," he advised. "Don't ever do
that." He raised his hand again, and Eularque cringed, brief flash of defiance
spent.

The incident served to break Whiss's paralysis. The furious color ebbed slowly
from his face. Somehow he managed to chivy the unruly genie of his emotions
back into its bottle. Once again, he was master of himself and of others. Someday,

certain as death, he would revenge himself upon Eularque, but now was not the proper time. "Enough," he decreed, and the trained skillful voice commanded instant obedience. Activity ceased; all eyes turned to Whiss. "It's not the time to quarrel. We are here to view a magical demonstration. Let's proceed with it. Bierce, fetch my sister down here."

Bierce departed. In his absence, Chorl assisted Eularque from the floor to a chair. Eularque slumped, lax as a dead worm. Two or three minutes later Bierce was back, leading Phlosine Valeur. Phlosine offered no resistance. She stood quite still, defensively hunch-shouldered, nervously blinking. Pieuvre leered at her. Poulpe studied her emotionlessly, as if she were a specimen upon a dissection table.

"Phlosine, my father and my brother claim that this house has awakened," Whiss informed her. "You are to verify this."

Phlosine appeared uncomprehending.

"Father, you tell her," Whiss snapped, losing patience.

There followed an exchange among Phlosine, Chorl, and Eularque, filled with arcane references and expressions unintelligible to the uninitiated listeners; at the conclusion of which, Phlosine nodded and stepped to the fireplace. Bracing both hands against the mantel, she bowed her head, closed her eyes, and stood motionless. The minutes passed. Phlosine neither moved nor uttered a sound.

Whiss frowned. "What is she—"

"Quiet," Chorl commanded in a whisper, but with such unwonted authority that for once his son obeyed.

Silence, broken only by the ticking of the tall clock in the corner, the muted rumble of wheels out upon Nerisante Street. Silence that stretched to wearisome length, before at last Phlosine raised her head and began to speak. That is, she opened her mouth and a voice emerged. But the voice was not Phlosine's, and no motion of lips or tongue was visible. Her eyes were open but empty, face still as an idol's.

My windows—dusty, dusty. The voice creaked like aging timbers, guggled like water in a leaf-clogged rainspout.

The listeners traded startled glances.

The tiles drop from my roof. Beetles nest. Mice foul me, mice. Mice gnaw me, mice. A verminous, rustling, pattering voice.

Leaking, dripping, seeping. Voice the music of raindrops on the roof. *The dry rot, the rising damp. Plaster cracking, paint flaking. I age, age.*

"What is the woman doing?" Poulpe inquired expressionlessly.

Dark of night, sunrise. Footsteps, voices. Footsteps, footsteps, up and down and time, and time. Through the winters, summers, winters. Voices of wind, of rain, of mice, of humans. Time.

"Ask her about the humans," Whiss commanded his father.

"House, speak of your humans, if you please," Chorl requested.

Foundations of stone, stone and mortar under the hot sun, and the humans grumble as they work. Timbers rising, meeting, joining under the sun. Humans sweat and hammer and grumble. I grow beneath their hands. They deck me in shingle and tile—

"More recently," Chorl suggested gently. "Since the zenith of today's sun."

Two humans speak to me, for the first time. They say I am finally awake. I say they finally listen. The sad old man talks to his son—"Where is your brother Houloir?" "I am my brother's keeper." Anger worse than mice.

"Phlosine could not have heard that," murmured Whiss.

"You hunt your enemies to the death with magic," says the father. Shorvi Nirienne. "Yes—viper Frezhelle. Scorpion Riclairc. That devil, Beq," says the son. "You refuse your assistance?" They fight, father and son. Magic will not destroy Nirienne, says the father. "This old man is a Nirienniste." Anger, anger, mice, then the old man's other son says, "Hold your tongue." Bully. Hypocrite. Tyrant. "Don't call Whiss names," and the big man hits. Hits like hail, like lightning. Hits.

Phlosine Valeur shook and swayed. Her hands tore themselves from the mantel, flew to her face to press a sympathetic hurt. Her face was her own again. Communion with the house shattered, she wheeled to face her cousin Bierce. "You struck Eularque," Phlosine whispered. "How could you do such a thing? Oh, how could you?"

Bierce looked at her.

She had described conversations and events of which she could know nothing. Only the house itself could have told her. The demonstration was an unqualified success. The technique herein validated might be employed to great advantage in the haunts of the worst Niriennistes.

Whiss Valeur smiled, well pleased.

"What a family I have," he observed.

S he must have been still weaker and sicker than she knew, for events somehow blurred in her eyes and mind, and afterward she had trouble remembering clearly. She knew, though, that Dref Zeenoson recognized her the moment she spoke. She knew, too, that he was shocked at the alteration in her appearance, for she heard him mutter under his breath something like, "Ruination, have you risen from one of these graves?" And there was the voice she remembered so well, with its broad northern accent and incongruous literacy, unmistakable and absolutely unchanged. He was well-dressed, fit, and assured. He had obviously prospered. She would have expected no less—that was Dref.

She heard herself mumbling very stupidly, "But I was to meet Beq—I'm supposed to meet Beq—"

He answered, "You have," and she still didn't really understand him. She was dizzy again, with another of those ridiculous seasick spells that troubled her so often these days. She was swaying and tottering, unable to continue the conversation until the silly qualm passed; then his arm was around her, and she heard his voice as if at a distance: "Lean on me." She didn't like to, it seemed absurd that she should have to, but there was no resisting. He held her quite firmly, she had no breath to argue, and she didn't really want him to remove his supporting arm. She let herself rest against him, and it felt so good, so warm and safe—

"Come with me."

His voice again, coming at her through layers of cotton batting, it seemed; and then he was leading her off, forcing her to walk. She pulled back a little; she didn't want to walk, she was too tired, and there was nowhere to go—but he was trundling her along irresistibly, through the menagerie of stone monsters, and then along the dark graveled paths beneath the trees of the Havillac Gardens. She could see nothing, she was blind, but Dref made his way without difficulty. Gravel shifted beneath her shoes for a while, then it didn't. Part of the time he was carrying her—at least she thought he was, but she wasn't really sure, it wasn't clear. The next thing she knew for certain, she was in some sort of a carriage, probably a public hackney; none too clean, with stuffing oozing from the torn leather seat. Dref beside her. Hackney jouncing along the city streets, she had no idea where, and didn't really care. Dref seemed to know exactly what he was doing; he always did. She would leave things to him—an almost unimaginable luxury.

Hackney stopping. Dref half assisting, half lifting her to the ground.

She breathed fresh air, and it revived her a little. She looked around, and found herself standing in a seedy, lively, unfamiliar little cul-de-sac. Music of a fiddle nearby, probably skipping from the tavern across the street. Pedestrians strolling about, even at this late hour; young, most of them, and not hungry-looking. Dref led her straight to one of the houses; a big, ramshackle affair with an old-fashioned overhang. In, and up three flights of stairs, for which she required assistance. His lodgings, on the fourth floor, seemed almost luxurious to her. There were two chambers: one spacious and pleasantly furnished, with bed, upholstered chairs, rag rug, and curtains of some deeply colored woolen stuff; the other, much smaller, and fitted out as an office or study, with a desk and book-lined walls. The atmosphere was blissfully warm. A few embers still smoldered on the grate. Eliste stared at them, almost in disbelief.

Dref's hands were at her throat, deftly loosing the strings of her cloak. Divesting her of her outer layer of rags, he steered her firmly to the bed. She noted the spotless feather mattress, laundered linen, and pillow. All at once she was acutely conscious of her own filthy state. "It's clean," she mumbled, ashamed. "I can't—"

"Take off your shoes. Get some sleep. In the morning, we'll decide whether you need a physician."

"But—"

"Do as you're told."

Lacking the strength to argue, she obeyed. She had not slept in a feather bed since leaving the Rouvignac town house. She had almost forgotten the feel of a pillow beneath her cheek, fresh sheets—the softness, the warmth. But she hadn't much time to enjoy these sensations, for sleep overtook her almost immediately; a profound, black sleep devoid of dreams.

The light was bright and the shadows short when she awoke; it must have been close to noon. For a moment, she didn't know where she was. She sat up slowly, blinking more in puzzlement than alarm. Despite the unbroken hours of slumber, she remained deeply tired. Other than that, she felt well enough, relaxed and curiously unperturbed. Here she sat, alone in a strange room. Where? She caught sight of her tattered cloak, slung across the back of a chair. She had taken it off— somebody had taken it off her—? It came back to her then, and she understood her own peculiar tranquillity. This was Dref's place; no wonder she wasn't worried.

A rattle at the door, and he came in. Eliste stared at him, astonished and inquisitive and somewhat tongue-tied. Seeing him in daylight, after so long a separation, her initial impression was that he had changed greatly. Almost he seemed a different person, a handsome stranger. Curious. She had never before thought of Dref as handsome; that term simply did not apply to serfs. But now it was almost as if she saw him for the first time. Upon closer inspection, she realized that his lean face and long figure were actually much the same as ever. There were the angular features and black eyes that she knew so well, but the expression had altered. There was a certain alert hardness about his face, decision and authority; less a change than an intensification of qualities already there. He was dressed differently, of course; quite plainly and soberly, but as a free Sherreenian. The change suited him; almost he could have been taken for a gentleman. His upright carriage and the easy freedom of his movements had formerly appeared impertinent; now they seemed altogether appropriate.

He was studying her with equal attention, and she was once again conscious of the wretched spectacle she presented, with her rags and filth, oily lank hair, and dirty pallid face. She looked down at her hands, angry red against the clean white sheets, cracked and blistered by scalding lye-soapy water during her pot-scrubbing stint in the Treasury. Really, it was astonishing that he had recognized her at all. She felt the color heat her cheeks. In the old days, he might well have poked fun at her appearance; he enjoyed discomfiting her, and knew that she would never have him punished for it. And now—? With an effort, she looked up, forcing herself to meet his gaze. But there was no mockery in Dref's black eyes; he did not appear in the least amused.

"How are you feeling?" He seated himself beside the bed.

"Better. Much better."

"Could you eat?"

Food. He was offering her food. Not trusting herself to speak, she nodded, and he handed her a pasteboard box carried from a neighborhood cookshop. She tore it open with almost indecent eagerness, to discover stuffed rolls, still warm; marinated vegetable salad; eggs in aspic; and a warm apple tart. Incredible. She hadn't seen such food in—she didn't remember how long. Her eyes and nose tingled. She would weep if she weren't careful. Grabbing one of the stuffed rolls, she wolfed it down within seconds; grabbed another and devoured it with equal speed; nearly inhaled one of the eggs. Only then did she slow down, and, a little shamefaced, think to extend the box to Dref. He shook his head, smiling; poured from a jug, and passed her a cup filled with clouded red-brown liquid. She drank. Sweet cider, another nearly lost sensation.

"Fabequais?" she guessed, determined not to cry.

"Yes. Certain attachments persist, it seems."

She bobbed her head and went on eating, while he watched her. Finally the edge of her hunger dulled, and she became once more uncomfortably aware of his scrutiny. She didn't like him watching her that way. "Where is this place?" she asked, to make him talk.

"Flou's Pocket in Rat Town," he told her. "I've lived here for over a year now."

"Rat Town. Well. It's fine, Dref. You must be a success. What have you been doing all this time?"

"Working, eating, sleeping."

"Working at what?"

"Whatever came to hand, whatever paid."

"I can understand that. Tell me, did you come straight to Sherreen when you left Derrivalle?"

"More or less. It's been a fairly eventful time for me; even more so for you, I suspect. There's a great deal you might tell me, starting with an explanation of your presence in The Cypresses last night."

"Oh—well—I was supposed to deliver a letter to this Beq—"

"Who gave you the letter?"

"Nobody. Some woman. Didn't you say last night that you're Beq, Dref?"

"What was the woman's name?"

"Oh, does it matter? Speaking of names, how do you happen to be called 'Beq'? It seems so short and abrupt—"

"My northern accent struck Sherreenians as amusing. At first they rechristened me 'Fabeque,' then shortened it to 'Beq.' But you shouldn't address me by that name. Here, I am known as 'Renois,' and that is what you must remember to call me."

"That's very interesting. Why did you—"

"Was her name Jounisse?"

"Who?"

"The woman with the letter. Was her name Jounisse?"

"It might have been. Is she a friend of yours?"

"Where did you meet her?"

"Well, I never delivered the letter, did I? I ought to fulfill my commission."

"No need. I already have it. I took it from your pocket last night."

"Oh! I see. Well, no bad news, I hope?"

"Where did you meet Jounisse, Eliste?"

"You know, I'm terribly sleepy all of a sudden. Do you suppose this cider could have turned?"

"No. Last I heard, Jounisse was in gaol."

"What peculiar people you seem to know."

"Don't I, though? Jounisse is in the Treasury, isn't she?"

"You concern yourself greatly. This Jounisse is a particular friend of yours?"

"She is estimable, beyond question. No doubt you formed similar conclusions when you met her. In the Treasury, was it?"

"Oh, I wish you wouldn't ask me!" she exclaimed, abandoning the evasions that were useless with him. "I can't talk about it, don't make me talk about it. My grandmother is dead, you know. So is Kairthe, I saw her—and probably Aurelie, and the others, my friends, so many of them murdered, and they did nothing to deserve it. I'm still alive, but I've been—I won't talk about it, and I won't think about it, else I'll fly apart into a million fragments—" The hand that held the cup was unsteady.

"There, my poor little Elli, you don't have to, I won't ask you. Now hush, calm yourself, and drink your cider, there's a good child. Sit back, and I will entertain you with tales of my travels, only slightly embellished for dramatic effect. Would you like that?"

She nodded. She had always enjoyed Dref's stories. Now she could sit here in this warm comfortable place, eating good food and listening to him talk. Yes indeed, she would like that.

Beginning at the moment of their separation, he told her of his flight from Derrivalle; his journey by stagecoach, paid for with the money she had given him; his arrival in Sherreen, and early employment as paid ghostwriter of theses for the richer and lazier of university students; his remarkably profitable black-market dabblings; his days as assistant to the editor of the now-defunct *Rat Town Gadfly*; his narrow escape when the *Gadfly* office was attacked and destroyed by Vanguardsmen; his subsequent journalistic endeavors and adventures, which seemed to have brought him into contact with some of the most colorful of Sherreenians. He made a lively story of it. He had always possessed a narrative sense, and his tale was filled with enough incident, humor, adversity, and eccentric characters to sustain interest, despite its length. Eliste listened, enthralled. The distinctive inflections of his voice, so familiar, awakened a thousand memories. The minute

fleeting expressions on his face—the quirk of his lips and the arch of his brows—
were utterly unchanged. Why, she wondered, had she imagined him so altered? A
year and a half of freedom had left its mark. His manner was perhaps more easily
and genuinely assured now than formerly; other than that, he was much the same.

And yet not quite. As he spoke on, she noted that he waxed reticent on the
topic of his recent activities, deflecting inquiries with vague references to
meetings, projects, investigations, ventures. She really could not guess what he
meant, and requests for clarification were parried with anecdotes so entertaining
that the original inquiry was usually lost. He had always been good at that;
never, in all the years she had known Dref Zeenoson, had she succeeded in
extracting information he wished to withhold. She could be certain that he had
involved himself in a variety of enterprises, some of them apparently questionable; he had flourished in Sherreen. Last year's sale of a design for some kind of
fancy gun that he called a "breech-loading flintlock rifle" ensured his comfort;
while his miniature wooden splints, with the bulbous heads that burst miraculously into flame when scraped along a roughened surface, might bring real
affluence, in time. But what was he working on now? Oh, this and that. And that
was all she was likely to get out of him today. For now, best simply to enjoy his
stories, enjoy the sound of his voice.

She would have liked listening to him all day, but certain matters had to be
settled. Draining the last of her cider, she forced herself to begin, "Well, Dref,
I've been trying to think what to do—"

"About a doctor, you mean? Last night in the graveyard, I thought you at
death's door, or perhaps already beyond the threshold, a ghost—"

"You always swore you didn't believe in ghosts."

"I was willing to reconsider; one must keep an open mind. Today, however, I
perceive nothing ailing you that rest and good food won't remedy."

"Oh, I'm quite recovered. Truly, I need no doctor. But you seem to have done
so well, and you have always been so ingenious, that I wonder if you might not
advise me where to go for employment."

"Employment—you, Eliste?"

Was he laughing at her? She darted a glance at him. No, no laughter there. If
anything, he looked rather sad. "Well, I have no choice, you see," she explained
with careful composure. "I'm on my own now. I can't leave the city, of course.
Even the cheapest lodgings and food cost money, and I must find a way to earn
some."

"Where have you been lodging?"

"Here and there. Sometimes Wonique's Warm Welcome."

"That pesthouse!"

"Even a pesthouse costs money. I've tried hard to find honest work, but no one will have me. I don't know what to try next. Have you any advice?"

"Always. In the first place, you are not presently fit for employment. Your health is poor, you are not strong, you couldn't hope to earn wages."

"Bother my health, but surely a little light sweeping and dusting——?"

"Could you drudge for twelve hours a day? Six days out of every seven? I don't think so. And that is what would be required of you were you so fortunate as to secure a position; which, in your present state, is hardly likely. Don't scowl. I'm simply stating the facts. That being the case, full recovery is clearly your first order of business. You need decent air, decent food, rest, and quiet. Wonique's Warm Welcome is not the place to find any of them. You would do far better to remain here."

"Here? You mean right *here*, in your lodgings?"

"Certainly. I've two rooms, far more than I need. You'll keep this one, and I'll install a cot for myself in the other. You should be comfortable enough."

"I can't do that."

"What alternative do you propose?"

"Dref, you are kind and generous beyond reason, but it's impossible. My presence would be discovered, and then your landlord would turn you out."

"You are unacquainted with my landlord. This boardinghouse is inhabited by a dozen tenants—all of them, but I, university students. Of that dozen, at least half contrive to keep their wenches upon the premises. The landlord charges each an extra rekko a month, and winks."

"Oh! You mean, they would actually suppose that I——"

"Does it matter what they suppose?"

"Perhaps not, but there's something else that does matter. You know who I am, and you know the penalty for aiding an Exalted. If the Vanguard should find me here, you'd surely pay a call upon a Lady." She used one of the countless current terms for execution.

"Having avoided the Lady's acquaintance thus far, I am resolved that we shall continue strangers. Don't worry, I'm not without resources."

"I know, but——"

"Do you know the best thing about this house?" Dref inquired offhandedly. "There is a bathroom. The landlord, surely an eccentric, has installed a copper tub—pump—kettles—even towels and soap—all available at a moderate charge to his tenants and their guests."

"Hot water? Soap?"

"Whenever you like."

It was more than she could resist.

•　　•　　•

She had her bath, a long and luxurious warm wallow to soak away the accumulated dirt of months. She scrubbed vigorously until the dead scurf came off her arms and legs in grayish rolls and the new skin beneath glowed. She lathered and rinsed her hair three times; brushed her fingernails, pumiced everywhere. She stayed in the tub until the water began to cool; then emerged, feeling lighter, to dry herself thoroughly before donning the clean white cambric shirt and worsted knee breeches that Dref had lent her to wear in lieu of her own foul rags. Both garments were ridiculously large; the shirt sleeves flapped inches beyond her fingertips, and the breeches would have fallen off but for the cord confining them at the waist. Eliste rolled the shirtsleeves back and paused, struck by the boniness of her exposed wrists. She looked down at herself. She had grown thin, pitifully scrawny and wasted. A small mirror hung on the wall. Rubbing the moisture away, she stared at her face in dismay: hollow-cheeked, ashen and peaked, with dark-ringed eyes, too large and scared-looking. She had grown ugly. *Hideous.* It was hateful to be so ugly when Dref would see her. With an abrupt movement, she turned from the mirror.

For the first several days following her arrival, she continued tired and listless. She spent a great deal of time sleeping—nine or ten hours every night, with frequent naps during the day. Her waking hours she spent sitting in the over-stuffed chair beside the window. There the weak sunlight fell warm on her face, and she could look down into Flou's Pocket, where winter's snow and ice were unmistakably melting. Day by day, the dirty white patches were shrinking. The drifts dwindled magically, the cobbles revealed themselves, the rooftops unveiled, and huge icicles formed along the eaves of neighboring houses. Occasionally one of these great frozen spears would tear itself free to crash down into the street with the crack of musket fire, a noise that made Eliste start nervously; but in time she grew used to it. Similarly, she grew accustomed to the sight and sound of the university students racketing in and out of the tavern across the street at all hours of the day and night. Watching them, listening to their cheerful raucous voices, it was almost possible to imagine a world safe and normal.

She ate prodigiously, as if to assuage prolonged hunger in one great spasm of gluttony. Dref seemed both amazed and amused by her appetite, which he encouraged by carrying in so much food from the nearby cookshop that she grew embarrassed, fearing herself a great burden to him. He assured her otherwise, with such conviction that she took him at his word, and kept on eating.

As vitality and strength increased, she began to take more interest in her surroundings. The activity down in Flou's Pocket was absorbing; the activity within the boardinghouse itself, with its transient youthful population of students and grisettes, even more so. She soon came to know her neighbors by sight and sound, if not by name. They seemed a companionable lot, constantly in and out of each other's rooms to eat, drink, and gossip; gathering nightly in one room or another to drink and sing; stealing up and down the stairs at night, intent upon illicit romantic enterprise. They would have been happy enough to welcome her into their circle. A newcomer was bound to arouse curiosity; but most particularly a newcomer associated with "Master Renois," who—all of twenty-five years old—was known to the students as "The Gaffer," and commonly supposed to conceal a criminal past. Fearful of discovery, however, Eliste discouraged inquiries and friendly overtures alike, keeping for the most part to Dref's apartment.

There was enough in those two rooms to keep her occupied for weeks: books on every conceivable topic, musical instruments, sketching supplies, chess set, and an assortment of projects in various stages of completion, for Dref was always involved in one odd exercise or another, just as he had been as a boy. Now, as then, there was no telling what peculiar enthusiasm might seize him; it might be anything from the invention of a synthetic candle wax, to the creation of an improved alphabet, to the design of an ideal public hospital, to the construction of a fanciful model flying machine. Dref was always willing to tell her about them, and he had a way of making even the dreariest subjects interesting. She found herself enjoying his explanations more than she might ever have expected; for when he spoke, growing absorbed in his topic, he relaxed, and his constraint temporarily vanished.

Constraint. She had noticed it almost from the first day. Nothing obvious or easily defined. Certainly no sign of embarrassment or uneasiness. Now as always, Dref was the essence of imperturbability. He was neither cold nor distant, but seemed somehow too courteous. Formerly, he had delighted in teasing her, deflating her vanity, puncturing her adolescent dignity. Now, however, he was careful to spare her feelings; always considerate, always kind. The serf quite willing to dare the anger of his master's daughter would never dream of patronizing a beggarly outcast. He was too charitable for that. He was sorry for her. She had lost everything—family, friends, fortune, rank, even the pretty face she had been so proud of—and he was sorry for her. It was a bitter draught.

And yet it seemed to her that his almost cautious demeanor concealed more than simple pity. There were too many topics of conversation too smoothly dodged, too many questions too neatly deflected. Certainly he had been—and probably still was—involved in activities of which he preferred her to remain ignorant; perhaps the students were correct in their surmise after all. He had constructed new barriers; evidently he didn't quite trust her. At first she was a little hurt; later on, as vitality returned, she grew piqued, and determined to overcome his reserve one way or another.

Reticence and pity notwithstanding, Dref remained the most engaging companion she had ever known, blessed with a quickness and clarity of mind almost freakish in view of his base origins, and once again, Eliste found herself wondering if Exalted blood might not run in his veins. She suggested as much to him one evening, and then his courtesy did slip, and he lambasted her with such merciless derision that she was reduced to red-faced silence. She didn't enjoy the experience, but it forced her to think. Perhaps Dref had a point. Events of the past months *did* effectively blast all the ancient assumptions of innate Exalted superiority. There was no denying it. Exalted magic had yielded easily to raw plebeian vigor. Bereft of that advantage, no longer entitled by birth to power and privilege, the scion of a hundred seigneurs became an ordinary mortal, obliged to compete on an equal footing with bourgeois, peasant, even former serf. It was an upsetting thought that smacked strongly of Niriennism. Dref, of course, owned a full set of Shorvi Nirienne's writings; he had always admired the man. In such a world as Dref Zeenoson and Shorvi Nirienne envisioned, Exalteds—those so fortunate as to survive the current massacres, that is—would have to rely upon their own individual efforts and talents. Fair, perhaps—in her heart, she had to admit it—but alarming, very alarming. She spoke no more that night.

Perhaps Dref regretted her discomfiture, for the next day he brought her a present: a generous length of good lightweight wool in a shade of gray-blue that suited her, several yards of fine white linen, needles, pins, and thread—all intended for the manufacture of a dress and chemise. Eliste could sew a fine seam, but had no idea how to construct an entire garment. The remnants of her old clothes, however, could be disassembled to serve as a pattern. This she did, and spent the next several days cutting, pinning, fitting, and stitching. The work was easier than she expected, and not unpleasant. Her old gown had been plain, but beautifully cut; in duplicating its lines, she created a surprisingly graceful costume for herself, with a sweeping full skirt and snowy fichu. The day she finished, she donned her new clothes and seated herself beside the window, impatiently awaiting Dref's return from the cookshop. He let himself in a few minutes later, and stopped short on the threshold as she rose to greet him. He looked startled, and then his white smile flashed.

"Why, you are quite yourself again," he said.

"No, I know better than that." She meant it.

"You always were a stubborn child," he replied, and setting his bundles aside, took her arm and led her to the mirror that hung above the washstand.

She hung back. Convinced of her own irrevocable unattractiveness, she had avoided the sight of herself.

"Now, look at yourself." Taking her by the shoulders, he turned her firmly to face the mirror.

Eliste's protests died unspoken as she viewed her own reflection for the second time since her arrival. Her clean hair, its gloss restored, fluffed and waved about her face. The dirty-looking circles beneath her eyes had faded away. Her face was still pale, but her lips had regained their normal color, and the faintest tinge of rose stained her cheeks. Almost unwillingly, she smiled. It was amazing how much better she felt.

"There is Eliste again," observed Dref. "And no longer willing, I'll wager, to sit cooped up in two little rooms."

"Oh, but I've been so comfortable here, Dref. And—peaceful—safe— and—" She was almost inclined to say "happy," but that would have made no sense.

"But wouldn't you like to go out?"

"Of course, but I can't."

"Yes, you can. You'll be perfectly safe. Wait and see."

The next day, he turned up with a parcel containing a warm secondhand cloak, knitted stockings, and sound shoes that, against all odds, fit adequately. She put them on, took his arm, and he escorted her down the stairs and out into Flou's Pocket. She took a deep breath of fresh air—sharpish and chilly, but the new cloak kept her comfortable. The citizens about her looked harmless; there was no sign of gendarme or Vanguardsman, not a single threatening uniform in sight. The sun was shining, and her spirits lifted. And then she was walking with Dref, strolling past the pleasant seen-better-days boardinghouses, and the little shops, booths, and pushcart vendors catering to the student population. Sometimes they paused idly to inspect the secondhand books, clothing, cheap jewelry, and household wares. At a bookseller's booth, Eliste asked the price of a dog-eared copy of Bounarte's *Verses*, and she saw Dref's face go red with suppressed laughter at the sound of her Fabeque accent, which precisely matched his own. Around midafternoon they stopped at the little café at the bottom of the cul-de-sac for mulled cider and buttered crescent rolls. They sat near the front window, where they could watch the passersby outside, and they talked. Afterward, Eliste could not have exactly described the conversation, which was leisurely, rambling, and filled with digressions; but she remembered that she was able to talk a little for the first time about her grandmother without disintegrating, and to her surprise, Dref talked to her of Zhen Suboson, for whose death back at Derrivalle he seemed to imagine himself partially responsible. It was not often she had known him to set aside his mask of nonchalance. But they did not by any means confine themselves to painful topics; she laughed a good deal, and so did he, and if she had stepped back at that moment to observe herself, which she did not, she would have realized that she was happy.

She felt close to Dref that afternoon, but such was not always the case. There was a great deal he didn't tell her, and as the days passed, she found her quite unseemly curiosity mounting. He was often out during the day, probably attending to his various business ventures, and these absences did not much trouble her. But where did he go at night? So frequently he would venture forth into the dark, sometimes empty-handed, sometimes carrying a small satchel whose contents remained a mystery to her. Sometimes he was gone only two or three hours; but often he was out far into the night, and occasionally he did not return until dawn, when the click of his key in the lock would awaken her from sound sleep, and she would groan protestingly, and he would whisper at her to go back to sleep. Nothing she could say or do upon such occasions ever induced him to reveal the nature of his errand. Always he staved off her questions with vague references to "meetings," "planning committees," and "councils." She never got anything more out of him than that, although she tried every argument and blandishment that she knew. Dref remained coolly impervious, and her first suspicion was that he must have a sweetheart hidden away somewhere, a thought extraordinarily disturbing. He had always ignored the girls of his own class who sighed over him back at Derrivalle. Eliste had chaffed him then for his stony heart, but somehow it had pleased her. But now, in Sherreen—? He had every right to amuse himself, of course (but what if it was more than just amusement?), and in any case, it was no business of hers, really nothing to her. She was his friend, and naturally concerned for his welfare, but that was all. She wondered about it night and day, however; her inquisitions grew more insistent, but did her no good. Dref, slippery conversationalist that he was, easily parried her queries with news of events in the city.

She learned from him that public executions were numerous as ever, but the proportion of Exalted victims among the condemned had decreased, for virtually all surviving Exalteds had by this time managed to flee, or else had gone to ground. Under Whiss Valeur's new Law of Accusation, an indicted traitor haled before the National Tribunal had no right to summon witnesses in his or her own defense. This simplified the Public Prosecutor's job considerably, and thus the Kokotte continued to enjoy her daily huge ration of suspected anti-Reparationists, most of them now bourgeois or peasant. The new development found scant favor in the eyes of Sherreen's plebeian population. Attendance at Equality Circle seemed to be falling off. The Coquettes and Cavaliers cavorted with all their original enthusiasm, but ordinary citizens were beginning to stay away. Perhaps the people were growing tired of the bloodshed—or even sickened by it. In Dref's opinion, the deadly Revolutionary fury had already passed its peak. The popular anger was on the wane, and thus the days of such violent fanatics as Whiss Valeur were numbered.

Niriennism. She recognized it readily enough, for uncomfortable curiosity had lately impelled her to read through several of Shorvi Nirienne's works, and she perceived clearly Dref Zeenoson's natural affinity for such a mind. Dref spoke now with an unwonted gravity reserved for the very few concerns that mattered most to him. It wasn't enough to convince Eliste that he was right—if revealed as Exalted, *she* wouldn't last long, whatever he might think about waning Revolutionary fury—but it did serve to alleviate her suspicion of clandestine romance. No, he must be up to something quite different.

One night he came home fairly early from his mysterious meeting. Eliste was still up, seated beside the dying fire. Drawing up a second chair, Dref sank into it, extending his long legs comfortably. Eliste caught a brief flash of light, apparently glancing off the sole of his shoe. Frowning, she looked closer and spied a golden blotch all too familiar—the remains of a nit of NuNu. Dref had spent the evening in some place subject to surveillance. No point in asking where or why—he would never tell her that, any more than he would tell her what was in the satchel he sometimes carried abroad at night, or why he sometimes received messages in a graveyard at midnight. The man was close as an oyster; nevertheless, she intended to find out. It was not for another several days, however, that she divined the truth.

Early evening, after dinner; she and Dref sat in their respective chairs before the fire. Eliste was rereading *Todaytomorrow;* more attentively, this second time. Both book and author now caught her imagination. Despite her absorption, however, something sent a tingle along her nerves, and she looked up suddenly to find Dref's black eyes fixed upon her, their expression unreadable. How long had he been watching her like that? Her breath quickened, and she felt the hot color leap to her cheeks. He'd see it, too. He'd think her an absolute fool, and he'd be right. To disguise her confusion, she inquired with assumed carelessness, "Whatever happened to Shorvi Nirienne? Executed, wasn't he?" Her voice came out a little breathless.

"Still alive, they say, but a fugitive," Dref replied.

He couldn't have spoken more casually, but her nerves tingled again, her perceptions seemed momentarily heightened, and she knew. Of course. No secret that Shorvi Nirienne was assisted and protected by a devoted band of followers. Dref was one of them. He had to be. Long before he ever came to Sherreen, he had proved himself a Nirienniste by natural inclination, and always he had contrived to follow his own inclinations. He was cool and daring, ingenious and determined, altogether the perfect conspirator. His reticence, evasiveness, and nocturnal forays were all at once explicable. There was no proof at all, and he would never admit it, but she knew she was right.

"Ummmmm," Eliste murmured, and Dref frowned at her.

•　　•　　•

Phlosine Valeur was tired of talking to buildings. Their outlook was narrow, their conversation jejune. They displayed a tiresome concern with the weather, and a near-universal preoccupation with mice. She was sick of their creaks, their groans, their slipped tiles and dry rot. She never wanted to hear another word about drainage. She had no choice, though. Brother Whiss commanded, and Whiss's word was literally law. It was the will of Whiss that father and brothers should awaken the edifices, and sister should commune with them. Phlosine had learned long ago that obedience was the only course, and she obeyed now, enduring without complaint the dreary dolor of tavern and theater, of café and chocolate house. She listened to the tales of broken windows, gouged plaster, leaks and drips. Oh, but buildings were boring. Warehouses were perhaps the worst, almost intolerably dull, but that was beside the point; she had to listen to them all, else word would get back to Whiss. Congressmen Pieuvre and Poulpe, who monitored her every architectural communion, would surely let Whiss know if she slacked off. Best to comply, best to give Whiss what he wanted. Thus, she listened day and night to wooden groans, and presently her efforts yielded results.

There had to be twoscore at least of coffeehouses and small taverns clustered about the University of Sherreen's lecture halls. Each and every one of them might or might not be the haunt of the Niriennistes whose activities infuriated Brother Whiss. Months would be required to awaken each of them. It was only by the merest chance that The Retreat, a student coffeehouse tucked into one of the empty storage cellars below the Duchess Tower (now People's Reparation Hall), was granted opportunity to express itself:

Shorvi, Beq, Riclairc, and the others at Viomente's Buskin, tomorrow night, Phlosine repeated the tower's observations dutifully, and her listeners snapped to attention.

"What is that you say, darling?" Pieuvre urged.

"Explain, woman," Poulpe commanded.

Phlosine obligingly repeated herself.

It was around eight o'clock on one of the mildest nights in months that Dref Zeenoson bade Eliste farewell and set out from his lodgings, satchel in hand. She now more or less guessed his purpose, but never for one moment guessed how short a distance he traveled before pausing. Once out of doors, Dref circled around to the back of the house. There, sheltered from view, he opened the satchel and went to work. Swiftly he changed his overcoat for one far older and shabbier; covered his black hair with a lank grizzled wig and a dented wide-brimmed hat; and, working in the dark with an expertise born of much practice, affixed a graying mustache to his upper lip, then smudged a little dark color into the hollows under eyes and cheekbones. Preparations completed and satchel safely stowed out of sight beneath a bush, he resumed his journey; enough altered in appearance that even a close acquaintance would not readily have recognized him.

He took a fiacre as far as Breakleg Lane, alighted at the bottom of the street, and approached his destination warily, on foot. This was only his customary procedure—ordinarily a superfluous precaution—but tonight his vigilance was rewarded. Dref paused in the shadow of Viomente's statue; some fifty yards distant, the windows of the cabaret called Viomente's Buskin were alight. The door stood wide open, and he could hear singing inside. A few beggars and prostitutes loitered at the entrance; a drunk sprawled in the gutter; customers came and went. To the casual eye, the scene appeared absolutely normal. But Dref noted the unobtrusive presence of two Vanguardsmen standing in a doorway across the street. They seemed to be idling there, smoking their clay pipes, and they displayed no disposition to move. He glanced sharply up and down Breakleg Lane. Half a block away, another brown-and-scarlet figure lounged against a wall. Next door to Viomente's Buskin, two men loitered in the dimness beneath the overhang of a closed and shuttered mercer's shop; too dark there to see if they were uniformed or not.

Dref waited motionless for four or five minutes; the objects of his scrutiny did likewise. At last he stepped forth from the shadows, and, moving at a halting pace very unlike his natural stride, advanced upon the cabaret. Nobody seemed to notice him. He sidestepped the importunate at the door, and went in.

The place was packed and clamorous, as always. Up on the stage, the famous old comedian Binoobio was singing a patter song and cutting capers; behind him flexed and jiggled his trademark bevy of scantily clad Milkmaids, each sporting a red diamond emblem upon her ruffled garter. The customers were howling with laughter, shouting, whistling, stomping, and periodically joining in Binoobio's cheerfully obscene refrain. Audience enthusiasm was deafening, but no more so for this particular act than for at least a dozen others equally popular; which was the reason that Viomente's Buskin offered such an excellent occasional meeting place for Shorvi Nirienne and his supporters. Here, where the dusky, smoke-heavy atmosphere veiled their features, they could gather without attracting attention, almost without fear of recognition. Here, they could converse without the least chance of being overheard. Even the nits of NuNu avoided this place, their delicate sensory apparatus useless in the midst of such pandemonium. Viomente's Buskin was perfect—at least, it always had been.

Dref scanned the big room and spotted them almost at once. They sat at a table in the darkest corner: Frezhelle and Riclairc, both well-disguised; Oeun and Oeunne Bulaude, without camouflage and needing none, for those two faces formed by nature to express simpleminded innocence were as yet entirely unknown to the authorities; and Shorvi Nirienne himself, whose slouch hat, pulled low, was a sole grudging concession to prudence. They hadn't seen him, and Dref made no move to join them. Taking a chair at a tiny table near the door, he ordered wine, and while he drank, surveyed the audience. An ordinary-looking crowd; and yet—the two burly men hulking beside the front exit were nondescriptly clad, but they had the stance and look of soldiers, and one of them sported the spiky "Liberty" haircut beloved of Vanguardsmen. And leaning against the counter—a square-built loner with the bulge of a pistol visible beneath his blue carmagnole.

Dref made his decision. Drawing a scrap of paper and charcoal from his pocket, he printed: "Leave. One or two at a time, S first. Back exit. Now.—B" Folding the message carefully, he caught the eye of the nearest cate-girl and crooked his finger. Scenting profit, she came at once, hopefully proffering her tray of oranges, dried fruits, salted nuts, candies. He purchased an orange; dropped extra money and the folded note into her tray, and a few words into her ear. The girl was sharp, evidently an old hand at such games. She nodded competently and withdrew; then he watched her wend her way—as if by chance, but very efficiently—through the crowd to Shorvi Nirienne's table. She stopped, smiled, extended her tray. A scrap of white flashed for a split second between her fingers, then dropped into Nirienne's lap. Oeun Bulaude bought a packet of raisins, and the cate-girl removed herself. Probably the delivery of the message had gone unobserved. Nearly every eye in the house was fixed upon Binoobio's bouncing Milkmaids.

Nirienne waited a cool couple of minutes before reading the message. His eyes dropped for a moment to his lap. He did not change expression. A slight shift of the shoulder marked an under-the-table transference of the message to Frezhelle, who sat upon Nirienne's right-hand side. As Dref looked on, the note passed almost invisibly from hand to hand. When all had read it, Shorvi Nirienne rose and ambled easily toward the rear exit, for all the world like any other customer briefly repairing to the back alley. Ordinarily, he would have gone unnoticed; but not tonight.

Long before Nirienne reached the exit, a whistle shrilled above the din of the crowd; shrilled again, and then half a dozen plainly clothed, armed men were converging upon the fugitive dissident and his astounded party. Two of the largest threw themselves upon Nirienne; others surrounded the table. Frezhelle leaped to his feet, chair overturning behind him. His hand flew to his breast pocket; someone clubbed his head with a pistol butt, and he pitched forward facedown across the table. Urgent shouting broke out all over the room, and the crowd seethed wildly, some of its members pushing forward for a better view, others streaming for the two exits. Those seeking egress were promptly thwarted. Uniformed Vanguardsmen materialized at front and rear, the whistle shrilled again, and both doors slammed shut.

Following that initial predictable upheaval, order was restored without great difficulty. A few bellowing commands, two or three pistol whippings, and the harmless discharge of a couple of musket shots into the ceiling quickly reduced the crowd to a proper submissiveness. The Niriennistes themselves offered little physical resistance. One after another, they were searched, disarmed, and man-acled. The search revealed little of interest beyond the manuscript of Nirienne's latest seditious essay, intercepted en route to the printer. The note that would have revealed Beq's presence in the cabaret lay on the floor under the table, its light charcoal printing smudged to complete illegibility by the pressure of Oeunne Bulaude's clever fingers.

Dref stood watching it all. His clenched fists were buried deep in his coat pockets. He resisted the almost overwhelming urge to draw his pistol. He stood very still, face white beneath its tan.

The prisoners were efficiently removed by elated Vanguardsmen; Frezhelle, still unconscious, carried out on a shutter. A number of soldiers remained behind to search the premises and interrogate the staff. Customers able to produce identification papers were permitted to depart. Possessing a set of forged creden-tials, together with a serf's tattoo suggestive of sound political leanings, Dref Zeenoson exited unhindered.

He hurried straight back to Flou's Pocket, went in without troubling to remove his disguise. It was quite early, and Eliste was still up. Her eyes widened at sight of his frowzy grizzled wig and false mustache. Dref spoke before she could.

"Nirienne has been arrested," he said.

She had never seen him look like that, not even the time that her father's minions had beaten him bloody and broken-boned. She had never seen him look so defeated, with an expression in his eyes that prompted her to ask, "Have they hurt you?"

"No."

"Did anyone follow you here?"

"I believe not."

"Sit down, Dref. Here, beside the fire. That's right. Would you like a drink?" He nodded, and she poured him out a glass of brandy. "What happened?"

"I haven't sorted it out yet. The Vanguard knew where to find Shorvi. Their trap was well-prepared, they knew in advance. How did they learn that, and from whom?" He was staring into the fire, thinking aloud; no longer bothering to maintain the fiction that his nocturnal activities remained a mystery to her.

"Nits," Eliste said.

"Possible, but unlikely. We've always been so careful—we've screened windows, doorways, and chimneys; held our conferences in bare chambers, and never without searching the premises. If there had been a nit, I would have found it."

"How many people knew where Nirienne was to be found tonight? Could one of his own followers have betrayed him?"

"That is the obvious conclusion, isn't it? And yet, all but unthinkable. There are only four, other than myself, who could have spoken. I can't suspect any of them; they've all proved their loyalty a hundred times over."

"Well, but people change——"

"Not these people. I'd stake my life on it."

You have. "But sometimes people—— Oh, very well, I'll take your word for it. What else could it be, then?"

"Something different. An innovation——" Dref frowned into the flames, characteristically treating calamity as an intellectual puzzle. "They've invented a new means of spying, and nobody in the world is safe from observation until it is understood."

"Might they know who you are and where to find you?" Eliste was mildly sorry for Shorvi Nirienne, but it was Dref who mattered. "Perhaps you should find new lodgings, or even leave Sherreen? Dref?"

"No need. I walked straight out of Viomente's Buskin tonight, and the Vanguardsmen never blinked. They've no idea who I am."

"Thank goodness. Then you're quite safe?"

"Safe?" He smiled with what seemed genuine, if bitter, amusement. "You don't imagine that anyone in Vonahr is safe?"

"What do you mean?"

"With Shorvi Nirienne disposed of, who remains to curb the lunacy of Whiss Valeur?"

"These revolutionaries have murdered the King. What is there to choose among them? Whiss Valeur or some other regicide—does it matter so much which one?"

"Come, is it not time to leave off childhood?"

"I hate it when you talk to me that way."

"You are not leaving me much choice. You're clever enough; don't play the simpleton."

"Simpleton!"

"I assume you play, but I may misjudge. Perhaps your early Exalted training has permanently damaged you, and what I mistake for willful incomprehension is in fact a genuine disability."

"Very fine, coming from you. Why, that so-called wit of which you're so proud has kept you in trouble since the day you were born." She was less indignant than she seemed. At least that wretched empty look of his was fading.

"Listen to me. Whiss Valeur is the worst tragedy that could overtake Vonahr——"

"Then the worst has already befallen."

"Not nearly. We've already suffered bloodshed and oppression, worse in the time of Valeur than ever in the days of the monarchy. We've seen the needless death of the King and Queen, systematic extermination of the Exalted, brutality and mass slaughter in the provinces, suppression of individual liberty, perversion of every Revolutionary ideal."

"And I'd thought these peasants had attained the blessed state," said Eliste. "So sorry."

"You may be sorrier yet, before Master Whiss Valeur has run his course. So may we all. Perhaps the losses would pay for themselves, were they to result in plenty and ease. A well-fed, well-clothed, well-housed population might answer for many an ideological ill. Such is scarcely the case, however. The peasant of the Republican Protectorate is miserable as his brother of the monarchy. He is cold as ever, hungry as ever, fearful and abused as ever. In place of crown and Exalted, he is obliged to serve dictator, Reparationism, and Kokotte. He has lost what little he had, and gained nothing."

"There is the truth, at last. I could have told you as much from the beginning. This entire mad and murderous convulsion has accomplished nothing beyond destruction. It has been vicious and pointless. If only people would come to their senses, and summon Feronte home from Strell to be King, then—"

"That will never happen. The monarchy is finished, Eliste. Its time has passed, and rightly so. I don't believe that Vonahrishmen will ever again submit to the rule of a king. The world is changing, but the direction of that change isn't yet certain. If we had made wise use of this chance to reorder our affairs, then all of us stood to benefit, and we should have served ourselves well indeed. If, however, the discarded monarch is simply to be replaced by another despot, essentially indistinguishable from a king, but bearing another title, then you are right—the entire upheaval has been vicious and pointless. As it is, we sink in barbarism. The world views the excesses of the Revolution with disgust, and those savageries will continue as long as the fanatics rule us. It's a sorry end to all that we have fought and hoped for."

"Well, it isn't ended yet," Eliste tried to encourage him. "I don't know if you're right about everyday life changing that much, no matter what you do to the government. You can shake things up as much as you like, and then when they settle down again, you'll probably find that they've resumed the old pattern. But I do believe that Whiss Valeur should be removed—anyone else would have to be an improvement. Sherreen won't tolerate that repulsive little lunatic forever. Someone is bound to bring him down."

"I thought Shorvi Nirienne the man to do it. But as of tonight, owing to my failure to protect him, Shorvi is finished."

"That wasn't your fault! What will happen to him?"

"Oh, he'll be dragged before the National Tribunal, of course, and his trial is sure to be prolonged and gaudy. I daresay the Reparationists will make a public feast day of it—set Shorvi up as the great adversary of the Republican Protectorate—Once-Radiant, Fallen Spirit of the Revolution, Arch-Enemy of the Nation, Monarchist Menace—all that sort of thing. Thus thoroughly blackened of character, his inevitable conviction and condemnation will be lauded to the skies as the great triumph of Reparationist rectitude. Whiss Valeur will preach and posture over it, and charges of "Niriennism" will serve to pack the prison cells throughout Vonahr. Swift execution will conclude this grand spectacle of national self-purification, and thus passes our best hope of halting the present madness."

He spoke with a sort of dreary irony that Eliste hated to hear yet felt powerless to refute. Everything he said was almost certainly true. All she could think of to say, feebly, was, "Well—even if Shorvi Nirienne is truly finished, and I'm sorry if he is, someone else will come along to take his place. Someone else will take up where he left off—"

"No." Dref shook his head. The movement must have reminded him on some barely conscious level of what he wore. Absently he tossed aside hat and wig, peeled the false mustache from his face. "In the first place, Shorvi's talents aren't commonplace. It wouldn't be such an easy matter to find a replacement. But let us say that we do; let's assume that another man of vision and ability appears. What reason to expect this successor to triumph where Nirienne failed?"

"Well—well—he'd be a different man, he'd act differently, and by that time, circumstances might have changed—"

"There is one circumstance that won't have changed. The difficulties involved in challenging a regime supported by magic will not lessen, no matter how much time passes. That circumstance ruined Shorvi Nirienne, and will no doubt prove equally fatal to his followers."

"Magic—ha! A long time ago, I told you that our Exalted magic protected our privileges, and you sneered at me, and events have proved you right. You didn't think anything at all of magic then. What's changed your mind?"

"The Exalted magic we spoke of at that time was largely chimerical. But now we confront the real thing."

"What, just because Whiss Valeur dug up some turncoat worm to waken those old Sentients? Who did that, anyway? How could any Exalted ever—"

"No Exalted awakened the Sentients."

"Certainly it was. What else could it have been?"

"There is all the problem. It is not commonly known that Whiss Valeur's kinsmen—his father and his siblings—possess trained magical ability."

"They can't, they're not of Exalted blood."

"I assure you. It's my business to know these things."

"But they can't, unless— Oh! You're saying— But what you're suggesting is completely—it's—" Her face crimsoned. *It's disgusting,* she wanted to say. *The commingling of Exalted and plebeian blood is disgusting as a marriage of human and ape.* But some power kinked her tongue; she was oddly ashamed and confused, she hardly knew why, and she finished weakly, "It's a disgrace."

"Certainly it is, for there's no telling what disaster might befall were talent to infuse itself throughout the population, is there, Exalted Miss? Well, that's another day's debate. The fact is, Whiss Valeur enjoys the support of several magically gifted relatives. There's some reason to suspect that their assistance may be rendered under duress, but that's not definite. What is quite certain is Valeur's control of magical resources—which raised him to his present eminence, which defeated Shorvi Nirienne, and which will no doubt continue to destroy all future rivals and enemies for years or decades to come."

"I always wondered how such a slimy, strident, strutting little mountebank ever managed to climb so high."

"Well, now you know the nature of his advantage. I had placed all my hopes in Shorvi Nirienne to overcome it, but that hope died tonight. Where Nirienne failed, who else is apt to succeed?"

He spoke composedly enough, but in a flat, deadened tone that hardly seemed his own. She had never heard him sound so whipped, never even known that he could sound that way. Surely there had to be something she could say to restore normalcy to his voice. Eliste thought. "Well, that magical advantage just can't be so very great," she decided at last, and Dref glanced at her in faint surprise. "Whatever these Valeur creatures might have, it is probably nothing more than a shadow of the real thing. They are not Exalted, after all."

"Eliste, this is folly. What does it take to dent that archaic Exalted arrogance—?"

"Magic is an Exalted trait, and so it has always been. Perhaps these mongrelized Valeurs inherited certain dilute abilities; but nothing to compare, surely, with the talents of true Exalteds, of pure blood. That's only reason."

"No, it isn't. We're not discussing pedigreed hounds."

"The principle doesn't alter. If the kinsmen are forced to assist Whiss Valeur, as you suggest, then how strong can their magic be? What true magical power would submit to ordinary force? How does it compare, do you suppose, to the talent of a *real* magician, like my Uncle Quinz?"

"Your uncle is extraordinary, beyond question."

"He thinks the same of you, but that's beside the point. Now, do you truly imagine that the combined power of those Valeur peasants could stand for one single moment against the *real* magic of my Uncle Quinz?"

Dref was silent.

"Well, there you are," Eliste concluded. "They aren't invincible." There. Maybe that would make him feel better.

Certainly it had some effect. Reflected firelight danced red in the depths of Dref's eyes. "Quinz vo Derrivalle," he mused.

"Yes, and doesn't that prove my point? One of these days, somebody will come along, and then . . ." Eliste's voice trailed off. He wasn't listening to her. Lost in frowning cogitation, he probably didn't even hear her. She knew from long experience that it was useless to talk to him at such times. Frustrating, but at least he was starting to look and act like himself again. She sat watching him quietly for the next two or three minutes.

Then his trance broke, and he turned to inquire, as if he assumed she had been following his thoughts, "Would he be willing to risk it?"

"Who? What?"

"Quinz vo Derrivalle—do you think he'd help us?" Dref's voice had come alive again.

"Help us how? What are you talking about, Dref? What do you want with my Uncle Quinz?"

"Why, you've suggested it yourself. Your uncle is remarkably gifted, with power to resist the combined forces of the Valeur kinsmen. We need him to do just that."

" 'We'? Who's 'we'?"

"Everyone in the world desiring to rid Vonahr of Whiss Valeur. Not five minutes since, you yourself expressed exactly such desire."

"Perhaps so, but I wasn't speaking for my uncle. I don't know exactly what you're plotting, but whatever it is, I don't like it."

"Hasty as ever, I see. Without troubling to listen or to think, you instantly—"

"I don't need to listen to any more. I know you, Dref. You're absolutely reckless. You always do and say exactly as you please, and you don't care a fig if it gets you into the worst kind of trouble. That's your prerogative, I suppose, but it's not fair to involve my Uncle Quinz in your crazy schemes. Uncle Quinz isn't like you. He's gentle, trusting, unworldly. He doesn't know anything about Reparationists or Niriennistes. He isn't practical, he wouldn't know what he was getting himself into. It would be unfair."

"Unfair. Interesting that you should use that term, for to me it seems the height of injustice, as well as presumption, that you undertake such decisions on your uncle's behalf. Is he a child, incompetent, or senile, that he should be denied the chance to choose for himself?"

"And what kind of a choice would he have by the time you'd finished weaving one of your word webs around him? Once you get your hands on him, he won't have a chance. You'll just keep talking and talking until he ends up doing exactly what you—"

"Oh, come. I think you overestimate my powers of persuasion, while underestimating your uncle's intelligence. He is perhaps not quite the helpless moonstruck innocent that you take him for."

"Oh yes, he is, he's—"

"He's a brilliant, gifted, very learned and experienced individual—"

"Not experienced with real life—"

"And beyond that," Dref ignored the interruption, "as a Vonarhishman and an Exalted, Master Quinz holds a personal stake in the outcome of these struggles. It is his own Exalted class now standing in danger of utter extinction. It is his peers, and perhaps his personal friends and their children, now in the Sepulchre, awaiting execution. It is his own countrymen, cheated of their promised liberties, betrayed by their Revolution and their leaders, lied to, exploited, robbed, and slaughtered—all of which will continue unopposed so long as Whiss Valeur and his creatures reign. Does it seem to you so strange or unlikely that Quinz vo Derrivalle might be willing—even eager—to lend his aid in such a cause?"

"He'll be willing enough by the time you're done with him," Eliste muttered. "But he shouldn't; he's so old, and it's dangerous, and—"

"Can you justify denying him the right to decide that for himself?"

"For his own good—"

"You are the best judge of that?"

"As good as any."

"You mean, he has nothing to say about it?"

Familiar words. *You mean, I got nothing to say about it, Master Fungus?* "That's not what I meant. Of course he does—" she conceded, cornered.

"There, that's fair, and I'm delighted to have your consent."

"What do you care for my consent? No doubt you'll pursue your own ends, with my consent or without it."

"Not altogether true, this time. You see, there's a certain difficulty involved in approaching Master Quinz. He may, for example, have fled the country—"

"Oh no, he'd never do that. He likes it where he is. I've no doubt that he's still happily rusticating back at Derrivalle."

"I hope so. Sending him a letter is out of the question, however. I must plan on traveling myself to Fabeque, to meet with him in person. But when it comes to locating your very clever and elusive uncle—"

"Oh, I see. *I see.* You cannot find him without my help. That explains it. Your mysterious concern over my consent—it is all becoming quite clear."

"Cynicism doesn't become you; you haven't the face for it." He smiled a little at her scowl. "As I recall, Master Quinz's cottage in the hills above the Seigneur's estate is concealed by magical means, and all but impossible to find. I also seem to recall that you used to visit your uncle often. You were able to penetrate the magical camouflage?"

"No, not really. There was a signal. I'd pull the lever in the box under the stone beside the tree stump, then Uncle Quinz would come and lead me through the cliff."

"Through the cliff?"

"Well, it wasn't real."

"Of course not. I'll need to know the location of this stump, stone, and cliff. Was there any special way that you pulled the lever?"

"Dref, it won't work."

"We must see about changing your mind."

"It's Uncle Quinz's mind you need to change. He'd never let you in. Oh, he likes you and all that. I'm sure that hasn't changed. But he's very shy at the best of times, and these days . . . well, he knows you were born a serf, and lately, with all that's happened, with all the persecution of Exalteds, he wouldn't dare trust you. No, truly, he'd never let you in."

"All things considered, I couldn't blame him. That is something to think about. Perhaps I could leave an explanatory letter in that box under the stone you mentioned. No, no good. If he won't trust me, why should he believe anything I write? Perhaps you had better write him. He must know your hand—"

"Yes, he does, but it doesn't matter, because I won't do it. You'd have to carry an incriminating letter all the way to Fabeque, and what would become of you if you were stopped and searched? That does happen, I've heard."

"Trifles. When I conceal a document, it is not to be discovered."

"So you say. I think it's too dangerous, but that's not the only difficulty. Uncle Quinz can be shy and timid as a wild bird. He might well suspect that you had written a letter in my hand to deceive him. He knows you're inventive, and he knows you could do it."

"There's a pretty compliment. But in truth—"

"No, it just wouldn't do the trick. Actually, I don't know what would, short of my personal intercession. At least we could be certain he'd trust and talk to *me*. Unfortunately for you and your schemes, that's impossible."

"A frequently misused term."

"Inasmuch as I am trapped in Sherreen—"

"Ah?"

" 'Ah'? What do you mean by 'ah'?"

"It is an interjection of variable function, in this case expressive of skepticism."

"About what?"

"About your so-called captivity, which may be less inescapable than you imagine."

"Oh, indeed. Delighted to hear it. I take it, then, that I am to stroll out the North Gate literally under the nose of the Sentient Boomette, who will no doubt be sleeping at the time?"

"Not stroll, no. It is not as simple as that, and yet I think we might succeed in conveying you from the city."

"What are you talking about? You're not serious, surely?"

"Do I seem to be joking?"

"With you, it's often hard to judge."

"I assure you I am in earnest. There is a way out."

"Out! Why have you never mentioned this before? I've been on your hands for weeks now, and you've never breathed a word. Why is that?"

"Initially, you were recovering from illness, and in no fit state to undertake a journey."

"At the beginning. But since then?"

"You were comfortable enough, and comparatively safe here. You appeared content. I wasn't aware that you were eager to leave."

"Oh! Oh. Well, I wasn't, I guess. But still—was there no other reason?" She wasn't quite sure what other reason she wanted him to name, but somehow it seemed crucial.

"Your escape attempt, while likely to succeed, isn't entirely free of risk. I hesitated to expose you to danger."

"You don't hesitate now, when it suits your purposes, do you?" she needled, for she found his replies indefinably vexatious. "In any case, if I must let my Uncle Quinz decide for himself whether he wishes to expose himself to danger, then shouldn't you have extended the same privilege to me, before this?"

She was sure she had him that time, but Dref scarcely hesitated.

"Ah, but how was I to know you dreamed of departure? You never once spoke of it, and I lack clairvoyance. Clairvoyance, if such exists, surely belongs to the Exalted, and, as we both know so well, I am very far from that." He smiled pleasantly.

"Oh, I don't know about that," she replied, in her frustration falling back on the one suggestion that could usually be depended upon to provoke him. "Perhaps in the last century, some seigneur grew careless. It would explain a great deal."

To her disappointment, Dref merely laughed.

"It's a disgrace," he agreed.

"Well, then—what is this way out of yours?" She changed the subject abruptly, determined to disguise her discomfort at this latest failure to get the better of him. "How should I deceive the Boomette?"

"We will require a loaded cart, a driver, and the assistance of at least two absolutely trustworthy confederates."

"Already I don't like the sound of it. You're not thinking of hiding me in the bottom of a cart and trying to smuggle me out the North Gate, are you? I've heard that the Boomette has discovered scores of Exalted concealed under no end of old sacks and mounds of hay. They say she can catch our thoughts upon the air, like notes of music, and those notes rise through all material barriers to betray us. What's more, there's the driver to consider. No doubt *his* guilty thoughts will catch the notice of Boomette——"

"Too hasty still. Do you suppose I haven't taken account of all that? Now patience for a moment, and I will relate our method; then you may decide if you care to attempt it. Listen."

Sometimes he reminded her of a schoolmaster. Often it piqued her, but this time it seemed appropriate.

"Upon the day of our departure," Dref explained, "a few hours before dawn, we will take ourselves to the dwelling of our first confederate—there's one I know, about the university, should serve. There we shall each of us swallow a sleeping draught—don't look so worried, it's quite safe—and for some eight or ten hours thereafter, we shall be dead to the world." He paused as if expecting exclamation, argument, or remonstrance, but Eliste was silent and attentive.

"While we sleep," he continued, "we shall be packed into false-bottomed crates and consigned to the care of some hired carter who will carry us both through the North Gate and up the highway, delivering us several hours later to a second confederate in the Middle Sevagne. Commission completed, the carter will receive his payment and depart. Confederate Number Two will liberate us from our crates. Thereafter, we shall proceed by ordinary stage to Fabeque and Derrivalle. The advantages of this plan are——"

"I see them," said Eliste. "We'll be senseless at the gate, and thus waft no revealing thoughts to the Boomette. The driver is ignorant, thus innocent, and his thoughts will draw no notice. That is a good plan, I think. But once we're out of the city, we can't travel by stage—we'd need papers for that, else we'd be arrested at the first stop."

"Quite right, but we'll have our false documents, probably within twenty-four hours, if I know a certain craftsman."

"Then—then it sounds as if it might work. But if so, why haven't more Exalteds fled Sherreen by similar methods?"

"How do you know that they haven't?"

"Oh." She hadn't thought of that.

"Now, the question remains—will you do it? You don't have to, you know. If you prefer, you can stay here where you're reasonably secure, and I'll try my luck in Fabeque alone. Perhaps that's what you ought to do. It's the safest course, and you must think of that."

She did think of that. She thought hard and fast. Her initial impulse was to refuse. For many months, she had dreamed of nothing beyond escaping Sherreen. Once clear of the city, she might fly to safety and ease; such thoughts had sustained her throughout all miseries. But now the chance had come at last, and it seemed much less than she had envisioned; seemed, in fact, an invitation to hardship and danger. It would be so easy and natural to say no. She could stay where she was, in this warm and congenial place. Dref would be gone for a little while; and then, failing in his efforts to locate Uncle Quinz, as he must inevitably fail without her aid, he would be back again with her, and life would go on as always. Probably it would, assuming he didn't come to grief en route. Shorvi Nirienne would die, Whiss Valeur would consolidate his power, and what real difference would it make? Very little, probably. But then, what would become of Dref's expression, his eyes? They would change, and she had some influence over them. It was curious to think of that, when he seemed so self-sufficient, but it was true; she could snuff the light—or not.

Much better if he could only be content with a safe, quiet life in Sherreen. Better for him, better for Uncle Quinz, certainly better for Eliste. But he would not be content with it, now or ever—that was Dref.

"Very well, I'll go. It is likely to prove entertaining," she heard herself say, and was somewhat compensated by the way he looked at her.

After that, it was frightening how quickly things moved. Immediately following the conversation, Dref went out again—to arrange certain matters, as he vaguely put it. Thirsty for information, Eliste tried to wait up for him, holding out until dawn flushed the eastern skies and lead seemed to weight her eyelids. Then she gave up and went to bed. When she awakened hours later, Dref was back in his own room, sleeping soundly. She itched to shake him awake, but managed to restrain herself, allowing him to sleep undisturbed into the early afternoon. He woke at last, and then she found her forbearance unappreciated and unrewarded. Pausing only long enough to wolf some bread and yesterday's cold soup, he was off again, without explanation and without heeding her loud demands to accompany him.

Once more left to simmer in her unsatisfied curiosity, Eliste endured an endless solitary day. Dref did not return until well into the evening. By that time she was furious with him, greeting his entrance with icy silence and averted eyes. Dref appeared unaware of her ill humor. He himself was in excellent spirits. Helping himself to food and wine, he sat down at the table; and while he ate, described his activities, which had centered about the effort to obtain a false travel permit and certificates of identification for Eliste. The Nirienniste forger customarily fulfilling such commissions had recently "called upon a Lady." It had been necessary to find a replacement, equally trustworthy, and this search had occupied most of the day. The outcome was successful, however; in token whereof, Dref skimmed a paper packet across the room into Eliste's lap.

The documents within were elaborately stamped and sealed, convincingly official, even lightly worn and aged. She examined them wonderingly. She was now "Iviane Souzolle, wife of Mouge Souzolle; eighteen years of age, resident of Grammantes." The unknown artist had thought of everything. *Dref* had thought of everything, as he always did. Ashamed now of her former petulance, she managed a smile.

"Storm clouds dispersing, I see," Dref observed easily. "That is good. I shouldn't care to have you start off out of temper."

"Start off?"

"Yes, we shall be leaving in—" he consulted his pocket watch, "about four hours. That gives you plenty of time to pack a small valise, if you wish."

"Four hours!"

"Certainly. What point in delaying?"

"But—so soon. I never thought—I wasn't prepared—"

"What further preparations are required?"

"Dref, there are some things you just don't understand." But she saw by his amused smile that he understood very well.

The hours galloped. All too soon, Dref was shepherding her down the stairs and out the door into Flou's Pocket, where he managed to snag a passing hackney. As she climbed into the vehicle, Eliste cast one longing glance back over her shoulder at the lodging house, where, she was beginning to realize clearly, she had been so happy. It occurred to her then that she might never return. Dref, for all his ingenuity, could scarcely provide for all contingencies. A single unforeseen obstacle, one stroke of misfortune at the North Gate, and she would never see Flou's Pocket again. Within hours, she might find herself in the Sepulchre, and Dref along with her. And it could be so easily avoided; all they needed to do was to turn around, go back into the house and up the stairs again—

The door slammed shut. The hackney started to move, and Dref's lodgings receded. Eliste had the sense of helpless, uncontrolled free-fall, just as she had once imagined when she envisioned herself leaping from the Bridge Vinculum. It was done; no undoing it.

She scarcely marked their passage through Rat Town. Soon they were rolling down University Street, then on into University Square, past Liberty Tower (formerly the King's Tower), and on past the heavily propagandistic Ten Philosophers, erected upon the site of the lately pulverized Ten Monarchs. Presently they turned off into one of the tiny capillaries worming in and out of the Square, to halt at a dim featureless intersection. They alighted, and Dref led her down an anonymous alleyway to a drab dwelling whose portal bore the hand-lettered legend "Zouq's Transactions, Ltd." Dref knocked—oddly, with a sharp two-four-two beat—and they were admitted at once by a slovenly peasant with grizzled whiskers and a red diamond emblem upon his breast. Eliste imagined their host to be Master Zouq himself, of Zouq's Transactions, Ltd., but she could not be certain, for there were no introductions. In fact, there was little conversation of any description, and little seemed necessary. In silence, the grizzled one gripped Dref's hand briefly, then turned and led his guests from entry to ill-lit parlor, where two large wooden crates awaited. The crates were open. Each was filled to the top with books. Eliste glanced questioningly at Dref, whose response was wordless. Shifting a few books aside, he took a good hold upon the slightly projecting inner lip of one of the boxes, and, with some effort, lifted away what proved to be a tray comprising perhaps a quarter of the crate's total volume. The compartment below the tray was empty. Several air holes, cunningly coinciding with knots in the unfinished pine, pierced the walls of the box. So this was to be her conveyance. Eliste couldn't help but think of coffins.

"Hop in," Dref suggested.

Just like that? No discussion, explanation, reassurance? It was mad, fantastic. She wanted to argue, but then he'd know she was frightened. He probably knew anyway, but she was ashamed to make it obvious. With a slight lift of the chin, she stepped forward, seated herself on the edge of the crate, swung her legs neatly over the side, and sank down into the empty compartment. Room enough, she discovered at once. She could lie curled up on her side, and it really wasn't too bad. But the thought of that tray of books on top, blocking the light and shutting her in, was unnerving. And then the lid, *nailed* down—a coffin lid—she could feel her palms growing clammy.

Dref and Zouq stood beside the crate, Zouq extending an earthenware mug. Eliste accepted reluctantly. The mug brimmed with a dark liquid. She sniffed suspiciously; inhaled a heavy, too-sweet fragrance. All her instincts warned her not to touch the stuff. But Dref and Zouq stood waiting. They would take her for a silly little coward if she balked now. They would exhort and persuade, she would inevitably capitulate, and her resistance would only serve to waste time and make her look a fool. Impelled by pride or perhaps simple vanity, she drank. The draught was intensely sweet and syrupy, with a suggestion of underlying bitterness—nauseating, really. If she gagged or retched in front of them, she'd die of shame. She gulped it down quickly, trying to ignore the taste, then handed the empty mug back to its owner.

"Well done." Dref mouthed rather than spoke the words; at least, she thought he did, for she heard nothing. But that might have been the effect of the drug—she suspected that her senses were already dulling. For a couple of minutes she watched Dref and Zouq fussing over the second crate—she really didn't know what they were doing; she had grown very stupid all of a sudden—and then she yawned hugely. Amazing how quickly it worked; already she could feel the sleepy cold humor stealing along her veins, slowing her body and mind, slowing life itself. Perhaps they had given her too much of the soporific, enough to kill her. She ought to have been frightened, but found herself too relaxed for fear. It was actually not unpleasant. Doubt and alarm receded; she was unnaturally but blissfully tranquil. She would be asleep soon, and it would be wonderful to let herself drift and float away; but she would hold on just a moment longer to figure out what Dref and Zouq were up to, though it was growing hard to see them, they seemed so far away and lost in mist.

"Better make yourself comfortable."

Dref's voice swam out of the fog at her. She blinked in a useless effort to clear her vision; she could barely find him. She found herself kneeling, chin and both hands resting on the edge of the crate. She felt Dref take her by the shoulders, warm hands lowering her gently to the floor of the compartment. A makeshift pillow—folded cloth or garment of some kind—interposed itself between her face and the splintery pine. Light, brief touch of two fingers upon her cheek—or perhaps she dreamed it, for things were muzzy indeed now—and after that, neither vision nor dreams.

She didn't know it when the tray of books slid into place above her; the hammering upon the lid that followed likewise failed to reach her. There was no awareness at all when her crate, along with its companion, was carried from Zouq's Transactions, Ltd. at the break of dawn and loaded aboard a big hired cart already crammed with boxes and barrels bound for various provincial destinations. And not the least flicker of consciousness as the heavy-laden cart, all collections now completed, creaked off through the sleepy gray streets, setting its course for the North Gate.

Boomette the Guardian of the Gate stood at Her appointed post as She had always stood, as She would always stand. In the dim and distant past, She dimly recalled, She had faced north, with the open countryside stretching away before Her, and the city at Her back. From that vantage point, She had maintained vigil. Day and night, She had watched, ever ready to lift Her warning voice. Three times in Her early life, She had done so, and the bark of Her siren had roused the human defenders of the Gate to repel the advance of invading alien hordes. Then the long deathlike sleep had closed Her eyes, depriving the

Gate of its rightful guardian, and when She woke at last, it was to find Her position reversed. Now She faced the city, but Her function remained unchanged; She must warn of illicit attempts upon the Gate.

How many attempts there were! How many secret enemies strove to pierce, penetrate, and otherwise violate the Gate! How many plots, how many covert forays! The Boomette, of course, uncovered them all. No living enemy of the Gate could possibly hope to thwart Her vigilance; for their eyes betrayed them, together with their voices, their odors, and the fluttering rhythms of their hearts, the whisper of air in their lungs, the ice of fear in their veins. Above all else, their thoughts betrayed them; the scraps and drips and splashes of thought that flew from their minds, straight through pathetically inadequate barriers of secrecy and pretense, to set the Boomette's siren shrieking. Yes, She discovered them all; and yet, remarkably, they never seemed to learn the futility of their efforts.

The vile attempts upon the Gate's virtue continued. The plots were multifarious; there were enemies everywhere, the very air was thick with villainy. The Gate, forever imperiled, would have been ravished a hundred times over, but for the dedication and perspicacity of Boomette. The Gate and its human defenders owed everything to Boomette. Everything. But did these dependents tender the gratitude and veneration that were Her rightful due? Boomette strongly suspected not.

And yet the plots continued, flying so fast in one another's wake that even the Boomette's preternatural perceptions were sometimes challenged, sometimes even confused. Take the present instance, for example. At this very moment, a cart approached the North Gate. Both cart and driver were perfectly familiar to Boomette and human guards alike. Repeatedly, this driver and his vehicle had passed the Gate, and in most cases, the Boomette had rested easy. From time to time, however, doubts arose; and this was one of those times. Boomette beheld an ordinary cart, ordinary driver, no doubt ordinary cargo. Yet something troubled Her, something spoke of duplicity. She could hardly have explained, but She knew that something was wrong. No skewed thoughts wafting like false notes from that cart; but something was wrong. The Boomette's dished ears swiveled and the glass screens of Her eyes lighted, but She spoke not. She listened:

"Your permit, Compeer." Voice of the sergeant at the gate. Easy and unconcerned, for this carter was known to all the guards: a staunch Reparationist, a patriot, one whose testimony had sent the Viscount vo Nire-Chillarde and all his family to the Kokotte; by any standard, a good fellow.

"There. All the right scribblings." The carter produced the requisite documents, which the sergeant scanned without great interest.

"Cargo, Compeer?"

"This and that, the usual."

"What's in the barrel?" The sergeant poked.

"Fancy china for a merchant's wife in Orz-on-Levre."

"Those two big crates?" The sergeant thumped.

"Books for the public school in Dizerne."

"Very good. Pass, Compeer. Live the Protector."

"Live the Protector."

The cart rumbled on through the North Gate and out of Sherreen.

The Boomette blinked Her glassy eyes, swinging Her dished ears to and fro in nameless, voiceless discontent.

liste awoke a little too early. She lay curled in a dark, constricted place. Her feet, knees, and the top of her head pressed against wooden walls. The close small world was rocking and shaking, creaking and groaning. Her head ached and her stomach roiled. She knew exactly where she was; knew too that it would be an exceedingly bad place in which to succumb to nausea. She lay very still, breathing deeply. The minute current of fresh air pushing in through the open knothole some six inches from her face helped, and presently the qualm subsided.

It was day; the faint gray light bathing the knothole told her so much, but she needed to see more. A few wriggling contortions brought her eye to the opening. She peered out at burlap sacks, oaken barrels, pine crates—the carter's cargo, and that was all she could glimpse. Nothing informative. She couldn't judge the time of day, couldn't even tell if the sun shone. Dref had told her that she would sleep for eight or ten hours; if so, it must now be midmorning, perhaps approaching noon. If the driver took an early start, the cart would have passed through the North Gate hours earlier. Even now, she might be out of Sherreen. An astonishing thought; if only she knew for certain.

Eliste relaxed back to her former position, lay still, and listened. The wheels below her turned quite smoothly; not clattering upon Sherreen's granite cobbles, but drumming deeply over dirt. She was out of the city. Free.

Free? The pine walls hemmed her in closely. She lifted a hand to encounter a wooden ceiling, inches above her face. The lid, she recalled only too well, was nailed down. She was boxed up like a chicken en route to market. She fidgeted, uncomfortable and a little afraid. The back of her neck was beginning to ache, and she was all but blind. Far better to sleep on; but she was wide awake, and certain to remain so.

For perhaps another hour, she lay there sore and constricted, shaken to and fro by the motion of the cart. As her discomfort mounted, she tried shifting position, squirming from side to side in an endless futile effort to ease cramped limbs; but the dimensions of the crate allowed for little relief. She wondered if Dref was similarly awake and uncomfortable. With his long legs, he'd be worse off than she; assuming, of course, that he hadn't suffocated, or died of some narcotic surfeit. No, Dref was too careful and canny in his calculations to chance such avoidable disaster. But then, even Dref could make a mistake. . . .

Doubt and discomfort ended shortly thereafter. The cart halted with a final shudder. There followed a period of stillness and quiet. Eliste strained her ears; caught the distant honking of geese and nothing more. Empty minutes; then voices close at hand; thudding and vibration; a double grunting of effort, and she felt the crate lifted. Her breath caught. The crate rose, tipped sharply. For a moment she was almost upside down, then her container righted itself, advanced bobbingly. Step up, and sudden dimming of the light filtering through the air holes; rap of booted heels upon a wooden floor. They had carried the crate into a building of some kind. Short, sharp descent; jarring arrest. Eliste heard a brief murmur of conversation, the thud of retreating footsteps. She longed violently to apply her eye to the air hole, but restrained herself, fearful lest the slightest movement draw the notice of these unseen strangers. Silence. She thought that they had gone, but still she dared not stir. She might or might not be alone.

Moments later, the footsteps were back, heavy and palpably burdened. Grunting and a solid *thunk* as the load was set down on the floor. Voices, a second retreat, click of a door closing, and silence again. This time, Eliste sensed quite strongly that someone stood nearby. Scarcely breathing, she lay motionless, eyes wide open and blindly staring. Several minutes passed thus. Perhaps the unseen companion awaited the complete disappearance from view of the cart and its driver. At last, when she felt that she must move or go mad, the footsteps resumed. Across the room and back; pause; then tapping, hammering, and the protest of nails prised from wood. A few feet away, someone was opening up Dref's crate. Dry-mouthed, Eliste lay listening.

Unidentifiable thumps and thuds, then muffled voices, one of them Dref's. She couldn't quite make out the words, but accent and intonation were unmistakable. He hadn't suffocated in his pine prison. He was all right, and he was here; she resumed normal breathing. But it didn't occur to her to speak or call out; she wouldn't truly believe it was safe until she could *see*.

They were working at her crate now. Inches above her, nails tore loose as the wooden lid was pried away. Then the ceiling of books vanished, and Eliste blinked, squinting against the sudden glare of light. She could make out two dark forms looming above her. Before her eyes had adjusted, before she could really see, they were hauling her to her feet and lifting her out of the crate. Eliste staggered a little. Her legs were weak and shaky, her feet all pins and needles. It passed quickly, and she soon recovered to find herself confronting Dref—a bit pallid and puffy-eyed, but otherwise quite himself—and one other; a skinny, narrow-shouldered stranger of indeterminate age, with a pasty indoor complexion and a wire pince-nez clipped to the bridge of his nervous thin nose. She cast a quick look about her. She stood in a plain room filled with narrow wooden benches. Odd. Through the window she could glimpse flat fields and a stretch of muddy road. Whatever this place might be, it was not Sherreen.

They had done it. They had hoodwinked Boomette with the aid of the Nirienniste network, whose complexity and efficiency were now becoming apparent to her. There was no room for relief or triumph; she was simply astonished.

"Better?" asked Dref.

She nodded. "You?"

"Fine."

"What is this place?"

"I will tell her, Master Beq," interjected the stranger. Eliste couldn't control the surprised widening of her eyes at the sound of the false name, and the respect with which it was pronounced. "Compeeress, you are in the public schoolroom of Dizerne, in the Middle Sevagne. You are quite safe here. I am Touverte, Schoolmaster General of Dizerne County, Vonahrishman and Nirienniste." Touverte performed a graceless bow. "I bid you welcome."

"Thank you, sir." A little confused, Eliste curtsied. Should she introduce herself in return? Should she use a false name? What was the proper etiquette among fugitives, outlaws, and conspirators? More important, it was clear from his manner that this man had not yet heard of Shorvi Nirienne's arrest. Should he be informed?

Dref came to her rescue. "Does the Maritime Stage still come through around midafternoon?" he inquired.

"Two o'clock," Touverte told him.

"We must be on it. Urgent."

"Money?"

"Sufficient."

"Ah, Beq, you are a wonder."

"Food?"

"Come with me."

They followed him from the schoolroom into an adjoining private apartment, where he fed them simply but plentifully. Eliste ate much, talked little; while Dref and Touverte, in what seemed the manner of Niriennistes everywhere, spoke in terse, almost coded fragments. It was then that Dref told their host of Shorvi Nirienne's disaster, and Eliste watched in some pity as Touverte's already-pale complexion dulled to a cadaverous gray. How devoted these Niriennistes were! And Nirienne himself—she found herself wondering for the hundredth time— what manner of man, to inspire such loyalty? He must be extraordinary.

Master Touverte, hard hit though he was, nonetheless managed to maintain his composure; perhaps somewhat heartened by his guest's apparent optimism. There was still a slight chance, Dref insisted, that Nirienne might be reprieved, perhaps even rescued. The schoolmaster chose to believe—or at least, he appeared to believe.

They waited until almost two o'clock, and then, bidding their host farewell, went out to the roadside, stationing themselves at a discreet distance from the schoolhouse to await the appearance of the Maritime Stage, bound for the northern coast by way of Fabeque Province. For Eliste, the entire venture still possessed a dreamlike quality. She half expected to awaken, opening catarrh-rheumed eyes to find herself crouched before a garbage fire on Bridge Street. Why, she wondered, did brief misery seem so much more vivid and real than a lifetime of ease? The experience had seared her mind indelibly as the branding iron seared the flesh of a felon. She didn't believe the recollection of those days in the gutter would ever fade, any more than the tattooed mark of serfdom would ever fade from the hand of Dref Zeenoson.

The stage arrived on time; paused at Dref's signal. Dref paid and they climbed in, stowing their small valises beneath the seat. There were two other passengers, middle-aged bourgeois of nondescript appearance, whose presence was certain to stifle all but the most noncommittal of conversation. The driver cracked his whip, and they were off.

It was a long and taxing journey over sometimes nearly unnavigable muddy roads, a journey in which extended stretches of featureless tedium were broken by interludes of nerve-jangling tension. The Maritime Stage essentially retraced in reverse the route whereby the Derrivalle berlin had made its way to Sherreen nearly two years ago; following Equality (formerly King's) Highway through the villages and hamlets of the Sevagne, then over the Niay Rise into Fabeque Province, and on across the tree-clad hills, through such towns as Beronde,

Fleuvine, and Grammantes. At each and every town, at many of the posting houses along the road, and at the Sevagne-Fabeque border, passengers were required to submit their papers to the inspection of bored provincial officials, toll collectors, and, not infrequently, to officers of the Vonahrish Guard. The first time it happened, Eliste thought she would die of fright; or at the very least, through fear betray herself, which amounted to the same thing. The stage had halted at the barricade on the outskirts of Penaude. A lieutenant of the Guard stood at the coach door, demanding passports and identification. While the officer leisurely scanned documents, one of his underlings mounted the box to examine the luggage carried on the roof. Eliste's heart accelerated. She was trembling, and it would never do to let the soldier see that. Clasping shaky hands tightly in her lap, she bowed her head in what she hoped convincingly simulated the conventional blushing modesty of the bourgeois young girl. Lowered eyes notwithstanding, she was acutely aware of what went on about her. She sensed rather than saw Dref hand two packets of documents through the open door; sensed, sickeningly, the lieutenant's more-than-ordinary attention. Had he spotted the forgery? What else would account for his interest?

"Mouge Souzolle, tailor's assistant, resident of Grammantes," he read. "Iviane Souzolle, his wife. So this is the little wife, eh?"

Dref replied affirmatively.

"Newly wed?" the lieutenant inquired, smiling.

Very newly, Dref told him.

"Ha, I knew it. I've a nose for such things, I. Well, Compeer, the little wife is charming, but she looks a bit pale and cold. You'd best work harder to keep her warm, else she'll find another to fill your shoes. Eh, Compeeress? What about it?"

So that was it. The lout wasn't suspicious, he was merely amusing himself. Eliste's relief was intense but short-lived, almost instantly overwhelmed by new and unexpected horrors.

The Madame Souzolle was a good, sensible, industrious, and dutiful wife, of very respectable family, daughter to a financially solid glover, Dref was insisting, but the lieutenant cut him off.

"Industrious? Dutiful? That's all you can say? Pitiful. Pitiful. This bridegroom's veins are filled with ice water. No wonder the poor little wife looks cold. You must do better than that, Compeer. You must show her some affection, if you hope to keep her. Perhaps the bridegroom requires a demonstration? Eh, Compeeress? Does he?"

Eliste kept her eyes persistently downcast. No need now to simulate blushing embarrassment—it was quite genuine.

The Madame Souzolle had no grounds for complaint, Dref maintained. His behavior toward Madame was correct in every particular, and the lieutenant might

rest assured that every conceivable husbandly obligation was scrupulously fulfilled. Conscience demanded no less.

"Poor little bride! Well, Compeer, you might profit by instruction. But give
her a kiss to prove your good faith, and I guess I'll let you go."

Eliste threw him a startled, incredulous look.

In Master Souzolle's opinion, such lewd displays were tasteless, inappropriate,
and undignified.

"This carriage doesn't move until you do as you're told, my friend. So give her
a buss, and mind you make it a good one, or else I'll show you how." The
lieutenant was enjoying himself hugely, yet seemed to be in earnest. "Shall I show
him how, Compeeress?"

Eliste shook her head without raising her eyes. Dref, with his quick wits, would
now devise some clever excuse to get around this jovial, bullying voyeur. Dref
would surely recognize the necessity, for he was well aware of the distance that
must lie between a former serf and the daughter of a marquis. For all his
impudence, he would never forget that. Confidently, she awaited his reply.

Dref, however, said nothing. She felt his weight shift on the seat beside her,
glanced quickly at him, then went rigid with surprise as he slid an arm around her
shoulders and pulled her close. No, surely he would never presume, he would
never dare—he was a *serf*! She caught the faint pleasant recollection of Schoolmaster Touverte's coffee on his breath, and then he was kissing her, confidently as
if he had the right, as if it were the most natural thing in the world. If he had held
himself aloof from the peasant girls back at Derrivalle, it had not been for want of
assurance; so much was now quite clear. Paralyzed with disbelief, Eliste did not
resist. Somehow his lips seemed to draw the strength out of her; frozen stiffness
gave way to boneless flexibility, and he might have turned or bent her any which
way he chose. Dimly she was aware of the hoots and cheers of the watching
soldiers.

He released her abruptly, and the withdrawal left her suddenly cold. She stared
up at him, inexpressibly shocked and bewildered.

"Do not concern yourself, Wife," Dref advised, and his black eyes held a
warning, together with an incongruous spark of amusement, and something more,
which, in her confusion, she was unable to analyze. His voice was unusually
deliberate and even. "We are in the hands of good patriots."

"Compeer, perhaps there is hope for you after all," the lieutenant conceded. "I
am satisfied, and I wish you good journey." He stepped back from the coach.
"Pass. Live the Protector."

"Live the Protector," driver and passengers dutifully echoed, all but Eliste,
who found herself unable to pronounce the hateful words. But her silence,
mistaken for girlish timidity, drew little notice. Doors slammed, whip cracked, and

the Maritime Stage rolled on past the barricade, up the highway and on into Penaude.

After that, Eliste fretted less over her forged credentials. The workmanship was good enough to carry her past barricades, posting houses, obstacles of every sort. Never was the validity of her passport questioned, and gradually her initial fears subsided, to be replaced by misgivings less vital but no less distracting. She was traveling as Dref's wife, and as such, she was obliged to room with him each night at some roadside inn—anything else would have roused curiosity. And why, she continually asked herself, should that arrangement disturb her in the least? She had shared lodgings with him for weeks in Sherreen, and she should certainly be accustomed to it by now. True, the apartment in Flou's Pocket had offered two chambers, affording considerable privacy, but why should that make any differ-ence? As an Exalted, she had lived her entire life surrounded day and night by servants. She had eaten, dressed and undressed, slept, and bathed under the eyes of menials without a moment's concern, accounting it the natural order of things. This current expedient proximity was only more of the same. And yet, there could be no denying that her outlook had changed, altering noticeably in wake of the ridiculous episode at the Penaude barricade, and even prior to that, she unclearly recognized, already in process of change. It was Dref's doing; he had gone and changed things, upset things. But what choice did he have at the time? Justice compelled her to admit that he had handled matters at the barricade efficiently and convincingly. What was more, he afterward had the good manners to cultivate apparent amnesia, never once alluding to the incident. It was as if it had never happened—as if he had quite forgotten, or perhaps hardly noticed at all—an admirable display of tact, she supposed, but somehow galling. He might at least have acknowledged—? But no, that wasn't fair; Dref's behavior was altogether irreproachable. It was not his fault that she had grown so absurdly self-conscious, not his fault that she was inexplicably uncomfortable, that she often found it hard to meet his eyes when they were together in their room at night, or that the sight of him stretched out on the floor to sleep, with only his own greatcoat to serve as a blanket, should so much trouble her. He had made do with as little or less throughout his years at Derrivalle, and she had never given it a thought. But it bothered her now; so many odd things did these days.

The days passed uneventfully enough. The Maritime Stage sped north through Fabeque; across the open pasturelands whose dull post-winter grass was now spotted with the deep emerald clumps of the early-sprouting wild onions; over the hills clad in trees whose budding foliage, poised upon the brown-gold verge of spring's green explosion, appeared almost autumnal. The weather was clement and generally favorable to travel, with just one day's heavy rain. Mishaps were relatively few: a passenger stricken with the severe gripes, necessitating an unscheduled stop; slight damage to one of the wheels; and another stop for repairs. Only twice was the coach seriously bogged in the mud, the worst of these episodes involving nearly a full day's wallow in the seasonal swamp that annually softened the stretch of highway lying below the town of Beronde. To Eliste, the delays seemed interminable and the ill fortune remarkable; in actual fact, the journey was ordinary.

Around midmorning of the eighth day, they reached Grammantes. Eliste gazed about her in some curiosity. This place, this bustling market square lined with the old guildhalls of rose-flecked Fabequais granite, was familiar and all but unchanged. A few hundred feet away was the Smiling Sergeant, where she had happily dawdled over lunch on her way to Sherreen. And there, on the far side of the square, was the dressmaker's shop of Mistress Zoliay, author of the naive ruffled gowns that had wakened Zeralenn vo Rouvignac's ready disdain. But the dressmaker's establishment was now boarded and marked with a big scarlet diamond—not surprisingly, for Zoliay's dealings with the provincial Exalted must have compromised her beyond hope of redemption. A number of once-smart shops were similarly boarded and diamonded. The medieval town hall's ancient chiseled inscription of "King, Country, Duty" had been covered over with a diamond-shaped sign bearing the painted legend "House of the People's Liberty." And Eliste perceived that she had been mistaken: even sleepy old Grammantes was changing.

The stage stood in the market square for the space of half an hour. It would have been pleasant to disembark and stroll about—pleasant, but unsafe. Grammantes lay but a scant half-day's journey from Derrivalle itself. The Marquis vo Derrivalle, his family and his menials, were well-known in these parts. Eliste vo Derrivalle had not shown her face in Fabeque for nigh on two years, yet it was by no means impossible that she could be recognized by some patriotic Reparationist citizen of the town.

They stayed seated in the coach; Eliste with her hood pulled forward, head adroop, feigning slumber. She remained thus as the passengers old and new took their seats, and did not raise her head again until they were out on the highway once more and Grammantes well behind them. The hours passed without incident. Eliste studied the passing scenery. Fabeque was splendid, even at this time of the year, with its steep hills and dramatically somber skies; she could appreciate the natural beauty, without the slightest sense of coming home. Her real home was not here, she realized, but Sherreen; had been since the day of her arrival, and amazingly still was, in spite of everything. What was it that Zeralenn had said? "There *is* no other place." Yes.

The stage barreled on up the highway, and Eliste, for all her supposed detachment, could not repress a thrill of excitement. Soon, she would be back in Derrivalle itself. What changes would the Revolution have wrought there? For the first time, she began to wonder about her family—her mother, her father, the various maiden aunts. They all seemed very far away. Her father, she actively disliked; and the others had never mattered any more to her than she had mattered to them. There was only one significant person left back at Derrivalle—Uncle Quinz—and for him, she had never entertained the slightest fear. No bellowing band of bullnecked patriots could ever harm Quinz vo Derrivalle. *Could they?* The doubt intruded itself for the first time.

Hours later, they alighted at the mouth of the rutted skinny lane that linked Equality Highway with the village of Derrivalle. The Maritime Stage lumbered off through the springtime mud. Bemused, Eliste stood watching it go. Here she was, back again, standing in the midst of a landscape whose every rise and hollow was totally familiar—and yet now somehow foreign. Beside her, Dref measured the Derrivalle lane with his eyes. For a moment she stood awaiting his instructions, then realized the absurdity of that. She was a vo Derrivalle, standing upon Derrivalle soil. She was Exalted, it was her own kinsman they had come here to seek, and obviously it was her place to take charge.

"We want to avoid the village. We can take the long way around through the scrub—you remember the way. We'll cut straight through the fields to the woods, then pick up the path to Uncle Quinz's cottage." She had lost something of her old assurance. It no longer felt quite right to be issuing orders. But then again, it never had felt quite right, with Dref.

This time, however, he spared her his sarcasms. "Good," he said shortly, and without any more conversation escorted her twenty minutes farther along the highway, before abandoning the road to plunge into the ragged stand of stunted trees, shrubs, and brush that clothed the hillside above the village of Derrivalle.

Back again. Ten years or more since she had last rambled this stretch of countryside with Dref Zeenoson, but the place hadn't changed—she still recognized certain trees she had once climbed, boulders half sunk in the soil, muddy rill in which she had waded on hot summer afternoons long ago—and for a brief moment, it felt as if she had traveled back in time. When she forded the stream, stepping from stone to slippery wet stone, it seemed only natural to take Dref's hand, as she had done as a child, and equally natural to maintain her hold as they hiked the long circuitous way down the hill, coming at last to the small, dense copse bordering the fields at the southern extremity of the Seigneur's property, or what had once been the Seigneur's property. Here, Dref turned to her to announce calmly, "Now I go on alone."

"What?" She dropped his hand at once.

"Wait here for me. Keep yourself well out of sight. I shouldn't be gone for more than a couple of hours or so."

"Ha! If you think——"

"Listen to me, and no tantrums, please. We can't just go charging over the fields and up the hill to your uncle's house. We've both of us been away from this place for months, and we've no idea what may have happened here during that time. Doubtless there have been changes——"

"Well, what if there have been? Why should that mean I must sit cooling my heels all alone, out in the middle of nowhere, crouched under a tree like some kind of sick squirrel, while you just go romping off——"

"Eliste. Think. What if your Uncle Quinz is gone? What if his cottage has been commandeered by the Vonahrish Guard? What if the soldiers—or else local Reparationist vigilantes—routinely patrol the hills above the Derrivalle estate?"

She was silent.

"We need to know these things," Dref continued. "You yourself can't afford to be seen, but the same restriction hardly applies to me. As a former Derrivalle serf, I'll be welcomed here with open arms, and any curiosity I display will appear entirely ordinary. My father will surely be willing to answer all questions."

"Zeeno," Eliste murmured, surprised and a little abashed. In her preoccupation, she had quite forgotten that Dref's family was here—his father and his sister. The image of Stelli Zeenosgirl's glowering dark face sprang into her mind, and then she recalled that same face with its expression of frozen horror upon the afternoon of Zhen Suboson's death; not at all a comfortable recollection.

"So you see," Dref was saying, "it is the safest course."

She nodded reluctantly, unwillingly convinced. He did not give her time to reconsider, but wheeled and set off immediately, pausing just once to toss advice back over his shoulder. "I'll try not to be too long. If you spot anyone, hide."

Where? she wanted to ask, but he was already too far away. For a time she watched his figure recede as he swung north through the fields toward the serfs' cottages that lay beyond the distant stand of Derrivalle timber. Presently trees and distance swallowed him, and the bare fields suddenly seemed indescribably bleak. An early vernal breeze scoured the copse, raw, but tolerable enough. Eliste heaved a small discontented sigh. Dropping her valise at the foot of a tree, she seated herself upon the bag, placed her back against the trunk, and settled down to wait.

Dref Zeenoson hurried across the muddy fields at a pace approaching a run. From time to time, he glanced up at the sky, where a pallid tired sun was already sagging into late afternoon; frowned, and quickened his footsteps. Soon he reached the timber stand and then the green-brown pond in which he had so often swum and fished. On the far side of the pond stood the tumbledown cottages of the Derrivalle serfs, now looking somehow smaller and meaner than ever before— sad, squalid, lifeless. Quite lifeless. Not a soul in sight. No one gossiping at the well, no one hunched over grindstone or workbench, no children running about. The place appeared eerily deserted.

Dref walked straight to the cottage of his father. He knocked, and received no response. After a moment, he threw wide the door, to discover the single room beyond quite empty, with a long-cold hearth. He turned away, and his black gaze raked right and left, then fastened upon a curl of smoke rising from a neighboring shack. A couple of long strides carried him to the source. He knocked again, and this time he was answered. He found himself confronting a shriveled figure, with wizened face and wicked blackberry eyes, foul clay pipe and ugly knitted cap, known to him from earliest childhood, and still all but unchanged. Grandmother Drossonswidow, or Gran' Dro', as she had been known for decades, evidently resisted progress. She still inhabited the old Drosson cottage, still wore the plaited forelock symbolic of serfdom, still bobbed and ducked with astounding agility at sight of knee breeches and piped waistcoat. Her reaction was ingrained. The instant she recognized Dref, however, indignation flared. Who did he think he was, and what was he trying to put over on her? He had always been a bad apple, too quick and taking for his own good, and it had given him ideas. In a word, trouble.

So—she was still mean as a viper, the fiercest female in Fabeque, Dref flirted, and the old woman loosed a delighted cackle. Where had everyone gone? Dref wanted to know, and following halfhearted complaint and fulmination, Gran' Dro' opened up. Times had changed, she confided with mixed condemnation and satisfaction. There were no more serfs, and them what had been serfs were now over at the big house busy being patriots. The big house? Right, the big house, now property of the People—leastways, the people that these days were calling themselves "the People." But what of the Seigneur and his kin? Well, the Seigneur himself was dead, these past ten months and more. It was his own fault, too; he should never have had his lackeys open fire on the People's Reparationist Committee. He'd asked for it, and he got it. His own former serfs stormed the house the same night, dragged the Marquis out in his nightgown, and strung him up on one of the big trees along the front drive. And a fine sight it had been, what with the torchlight and all the commotion and cavortings. After that, Gran' Dro' had awaited the inevitable arrival of the soldiers, come to avenge the Seigneur's death; but strangely enough, they never appeared. What of the Marquis's kin, though? Well, the wife and aunties and such had just been chased off, with only what they could carry on them; and good riddance. The daughter, that pampered little nose-in-the-air piece, had cleared off long ago. No telling what become of her. And Master Quinz? Hard to say, very hard to say. He was an odd one, wasn't he? She could tell Dref nothing for sure about Master Quinz. The Marquis's personal servants? Well, the worst of the rotten apples, the brutes and the ass-lickers—Borlo Bunison and his kind—had been lynched like they deserved. Some of the others—the smart ones, in Gran' Dro's opinion—had got out while the going was good. Dref's own father Zeeno, for example, had the sense to head for Beronde, where they'd heard he was now a cabinetmaker, and doing well. But most of the peasants and freed serfs had remained to set up the People's Reparationist Commune of Derrivalle, over at the big house. Like they thought that living in the manor meant they knew how to run things. Gran' Dro' wished them the best of luck. They would need it, for they were stupid as new chickens. They hadn't any idea how to get things done. Everybody wanted to be an overseer, with nobody to muscle-ache. In the meantime, the spring sowing languished. It would be a good joke to speak to those so-called overseers come harvesttime. Right now, however, everyone was flown too high up in the air for reasonable conversation; everyone, but most particularly, *some people*. This confidence was accompanied by a dark, ocular flash too easily interpreted. Dref attempted no remonstrance. Taking polite leave, he turned from the dead cottage-cluster of the serfs to make his way over field and garden toward Derrivalle Manor itself.

Through the gap in the untended boxwood hedge he stepped, and there it was, rising before him—not so large or grand as memory painted it, fresh-daubed with red diamonds, and a few of the glass windows broken—but otherwise much the same as ever. Dref was challenged before he came within a hundred yards of the house. A couple of scythe-bearing guards bore down upon him. He knew them both from the old days, and he hailed them by name. The guards hesitated; approached cautiously; then recognition dawned, and they greeted him with enthusiasm. For this was the famous Dref Zeenoson who had bloodied the Marquis vo Derrivalle's nose long before any other serf had dared to lift a hand in self-defense; this was the Dref Zeenoson who, alone among all serfs in living memory, had foxed the Seigneur's dogs and shown the province a clean pair of heels. Dref was a hero, and he would always find a warm welcome at the People's Reparationist Commune of Derrivalle. He had come, they informed him, just in time for the afternoon supper. Would he care to join them?

He would.

They brought him in through the kitchen, which was filthy, disordered, and malodorous as it had never been in the Seigneur's day. A long, uncarpeted pass-through led to the chambers wherein Dref Zeenoson had never before set foot.

But he had heard tales of these chambers; house servants of his acquaintance had often extolled the fantastic splendors. Reality, however, proved disappointing. Probably these big old rooms, with their high ceilings, tall windows, and carved mantels, had once been handsome enough. Now, however, the windows were broken, chandeliers smashed, parquet floors dull and gouged. Most of the furniture was missing—either stolen or sold to raise cash, most likely the latter; for the bare, chilly, and dirty building silently shouted its poverty. The signs of neglect and abuse were everywhere. Perhaps it was as Gran' Dro' had claimed— that peasants and freed serfs now disdained labor. Yet it seemed more as if the hapless hopeless village of Derrivalle had simply transplanted itself.

The dining room was packed, but quiet. The entire Reparationist Commune had assembled there for the afternoon meal, a scene somewhat reminiscent of the dismal Fraternal Egalitarian Suppers these days inflicted upon Sherreenians. Fratsups, however, were mandatorily boisterous; here, conversation was muted and curiously spiritless. The Seigneur's long mahogany banqueting table was still in use, its formerly glassy finish now but a memory. The matching brocade-cushioned chairs were gone, however; replaced by benches of raw planking, long enough to accommodate scores of patriotic backsides. At one end of the room stood a new, crude platform of unpainted boards, supporting and slightly elevating a second, smaller table draped in filthy linen. Around this high table sat ten figures, all of them known to Dref; ten of the loudest, most fearless, and most aggressive of Derrivalle malcontents. Their number included one woman only; his sister Stelli sat there, red diamond emblem smoldering upon her breast. She spotted him the moment he walked in, and her eyes met his in a long, unsmiling glance.

Dref's entrance caused a sensation. His former compatriots, their apathy momentarily broken, crowded around him; shaking his hand, thumping his back, and shouting questions, too many questions. He answered briefly, and responded with questions of his own, absorbing the answers as a chattering tide bore him forward to the high table, which accommodated, he discovered, those persons included in "the People's Reparationist Council." The Council members seemed to merit the same extreme, almost cringing respect formerly reserved for Ex-alteds.

They assumed that he desired his sister's company, and they made a place for him at her side. Dref planted a dutiful kiss upon her cheek, and the company applauded. It was like kissing a stone image. Face set, Stelli stared straight before her. Only when he withdrew and seated himself did she turn to favor him with a lengthy, deliberate inspection that took in everything from buckled shoes, to piped waistcoat, to unpatched greatcoat.

"Mighty grand," Stelli at last observed dryly. She herself yet clung, probably through necessity, to the drab, threadbare costume of a Fabequais serf. "Back for good, are you?"

Quite the contrary, he assured her. He was now employed as the agent of a Sherreenian merchant, with business to transact tomorrow in Luiesse—

"Man of affairs, eh? Mighty grand," Stelli repeated.

—And he could only visit for an hour or two before leaving to meet the northbound coach.

"Maritime Stage passed through over an hour ago," Stelli observed at once, black eyes resting upon him like cast-iron weights.

But the mail coach would come after, he reminded her.

"So it does." Her lips curled faintly. "That's real lucky for you, isn't it?"

He supposed it was. No, she had not forgotten Zhen Suboson; clearly she neither forgot nor forgave.

News of Dref's intention flashed along the table. The mail coach! The price of a seat in the swift mail coach was too high for all but persons of consequence. A murmur of wondering admiration arose. Dref Zeenoson had done well for himself, and no mistake. So it *was* possible for a serf to work his way up in the world. Life continued fairly wretched here at Derrivalle, but perhaps elsewhere—? Not much chance of finding out, however. Following the brief period of euphoria that accompanied the establishment of the Reparationist Commune, the drafting of the bylaws, and the self-appointment of the Council, it had soon grown clear that the fledgling utopia required devoted tending, were it to survive its perilous infancy. Human resources grew precious, and thus, some six months subsequent to the Seigneur's death, the Council decreed a new "body tax"—that is, any member of the People's Reparationist Commune of Derrivalle wishing to relocate was perfectly free to do so, provided he or she made adequate cash settlement in compensation for the human labor of which the Commune was to find itself deprived. This, the Council insisted, was only fair; for the Commune maintained all, and an individual withdrawing resources from the common fund should in all conscience make good the loss to his compeers. Fair or no, the immediate result was that the Derrivalle peasants found themselves firmly bound to the soil as ever they had been in the days of their serfdom.

Arrival of the food from the kitchen interrupted the conversation. The high table was served first, with thin vegetable stew, insipid and none too plentiful; indifferent quantity of coarse dark bread; water just barely blushed with vinegarish wine; and a single stringy chicken to divide among eleven people. One of the serving wenches sloshed water on the tablecloth. An impatient grunt escaped Stelli, and the erring wench jumped as if stung. The folk at the lower table ate similarly, but without the chicken. Just so had they eaten as serfs, albeit without the present trappings. Poor though the fare, it was served on the Marquis vo Derrivalle's translucent gold-edged porcelain, and the pinkish water was gulped from crystal of soap-bubble fineness. This, then, was Reparation.

At the request of the Council members, Dref regaled his compeers with a few Sherreenian anecdotes. The low-table folk listened wide-eyed as he told them of life in the city, and its myriad wonders; of the course of the Revolution there; and of the famous patriots he had glimpsed—even the great cousins, Whiss and Bierce Valeur. While he spoke, his sister's iron eyes pressed unwinkingly upon him. Hers had always been an easy face to read; just now, it expressed a brooding hostility, mixed with skepticism. She had changed, however, in these past eventful months; perhaps her new importance as a Council member had changed her. In former days, she was wont to attack without reflection. Now she waited, weighed, considered; and underlying her disquieting deliberation was something that almost seemed like a secret, knowing satisfaction.

Dref fulfilled his conversational obligations adequately, with minimal lying. This done, he was free to beg news of Derrivalle. The Council members around him willingly gabbled of Reparationist triumphs—all save his sister, who sat quiet and ominously attentive. Only occasionally, she threw in a terse observation or opinion; and when she did so, her companions listened with respect amounting to deference. Almost they seemed afraid of her, which was curious; for Stelli, forceful of personality though she was, remained but a young woman of their own class. And though she had walked in the vanguard of the mob that stormed Derrivalle Manor ten months earlier, still her compatriots' attitude was difficult to fathom.

The information that Dref received, though very dissimilarly expressed, deviated little in essentials from Gran' Dro's descriptions: the criminal Seigneur had justly forfeited his life, and his property was now in the hands of the victorious People. More to the point, no one seemed to know anything definite of Master Quinz. The old gentleman might or might not lurk to this day in his hidden aerie—if indeed there was such a place; for a couple of soldierly forays into the hills had proved unrewarding, and the patriotic squads now regularly patrolling the area had discovered nothing. Probably Quinz vo Derrivalle had fled or died years earlier, but nobody could say for sure.

"Got everything you wanted?" Stelli didn't quite sneer.

Dref's face revealed no trace of surprise or any other emotion. If she had hoped to startle him into some sort of revealing reaction, she must have been disappointed. He could never get all he wanted of Derrivalle news, he replied pleasantly, and Stelli's black brows drew together. Someday, perhaps she would learn to control her face; and then she would be truly dangerous.

But she hadn't learned yet. A furious scowl contorted her features, and she surged to her feet so abruptly that the table rattled. Conversation ceased. Her compatriots gaped at her, startled and uneasy. She paid them no heed. Fists clenched, black eyes all but shooting sparks, she stood glaring down at her brother. He met the flaming regard, apparently unmoved.

"You think you're so smart. You think you're smarter than anybody. Well, maybe I know a thing or two that you don't." Without awaiting reply, she turned and stalked from the room, wooden sabots beating a rataplan upon the floorboards.

Dref watched her go. His face was still, but a vertical crease had appeared between his eyes.

Embarrassed, uncomfortable silence wet-blanketed both tables for a couple of minutes, until Dref repaired matters with a series of jokes designed to illustrate the superiority of good, sound Fabequais common sense over useless Sherreenian book learning. He knew how to flatter to a nicety; the tale of the clever provincial apple-farmer and his gullible, puffed-up citified customer roused the listeners to roars of gratified laughter. Dref laughed along with the rest of them, but the crease between his eyes persisted. Often he glanced out the window to note the lengthening shadows and reddening light. At last he brought forth his pocket watch—an ordinary timepiece in a simple steel case, which, despite its plainness, drew murmurs of admiration from the Derrivalle folk, none of whom had ever possessed such a treasure. It was time to go, Dref announced. He must leave at once if he was to reach Equality Highway in time to intercept the mail coach. No, he did not require an escort, he did not wish to trouble his friends in the least. Amicable farewells and embraces were exchanged. Vertical crease more pronounced than ever, Dref Zeenoson took his leave, hurrying away from the People's Reparationist Commune of Derrivalle as fast as his long legs would carry him.

Stelli Zeenosgirl strode directly from the dining room to the chamber once serving as the Marquis vo Derrivalle's study. Upon arrival, she shut the door behind her but did not trouble to lock it, for none of the others were likely to trouble her in that place. Instinctively they shunned the Seigneur's former sanctum, with its intimidating associations and its upsetting collection of medical curiosities, preserved in glass-walled chemical baths. Even upon the wild night of the manor's storming, ten months earlier, few had ventured over the threshold. Stelli, of course, had been one of those few, as she had cherished particular interest in the chamber's contents. She had easily discovered what was almost certainly the thing she sought: a row of big glass jars containing relatively fresh human organs, pickled in something, and labeled simply: "Human, male;

subspecies, serf; age, twenty years; defective, cause unspecified"—all that remained of Zhen Suboson. If the discovery afforded satisfaction, none but Stelli ever knew of it. While she was there, however, she had stumbled upon something new, the existence of which had hitherto gone unsuspected. The age-blackened corner cabinet held a treasure; a dim and ancient mirror of silvery polished metal, whose stiffly carved ivory frame suggested craftsmanship dating from the era wherein Exalted ability had first manifested itself. Something about the mirror breathed magic; Stelli herself could hardly have explained how she guessed the secret. She only knew that something impelled her to speak, to seek, to question aloud; and the miraculous device, for unknown reasons geared to the abilities of ordinary humans, had responded. It had given her all she asked for, and more. Never before had she thought to gain such an advantage over her fellow serfs. Never had she thought to be to them as the Exalted had hitherto been to her. But the mirror placed untold power in her hands, and by means of that power, she had made herself, though only a twenty-four-year-old woman, the most feared member of the Reparationist Council. They listened to her, these others, where they had never listened before. They respected her, they deferred to her, they jumped when she cracked the whip. They were afraid of her. It was heady stuff. It was delicious.

Stelli went to the corner cabinet, knelt and withdrew the mirror; gazed into the wavery depths. "Show me my brother," she commanded, and then, because the wording was never sure, specified, "Let me see Dref Zeenoson the way he is right this very minute."

Sometimes it didn't work. Sometimes, for reasons that she never understood, the mirror didn't give her what she wanted. Sometimes, just as inexplicably, it did; and this was one of those times. The foggy depths swirled and clarified. The mists vanished, and Stelli beheld a tall, lean figure hurrying over the muddy fields. She recognized the horizon's contour, the old oak in the distance, a couple of landmarks. He was not heading for the highway. Stelli nodded to herself.

He went straight to the copse clogging the hollow at the southern end of the Derrivalle estate. There he greeted a cloaked female with light hair.

"Let me see close," Stelli demanded, and once again, for unknown reasons, the mirror obliged. She caught a clear glimpse of her brother's companion: big eyes, heart-shaped face, fair curls. Little Princess Snot. Stelli nodded. Somehow, she was not surprised. Dref always had notions, even if he never admitted them, not even to himself. Dref wanted to climb, over everyone else's back. He didn't care about the People. He wasn't even a real Republican, much less a Reparationist. Actually, he was an elitist, an enemy of the people. He had to be stopped.

She watched on. Dref and his companion, whose very parentage constituted a capital offense, quitted the copse to cut across the open fields, making for the forested hills. Late afternoon was deepening into early evening; the light was waning fast. Yet some arcane property of the ivory-backed mirror enabled Stelli to see clearly as her brother and her former mistress made their way up a steep narrow trail, long unused, and now choked with weed and brush. On they went, the Seigneur's daughter leading the way, and presently they came to a stone-strewn dried watercourse, which they followed up the hill to a small, level clearing, where their progress seemed to be blocked by a sheer cliff of naked granite that rose for a hundred feet or more. Surely they had to stop now. But no. Even as Stelli watched, her brother's companion went straight to a fungus-bracketed tree stump, among whose exposed roots lay a flat stone. Beneath the stone was a compartment with a lever that Princess Snot pulled back and forth a few times in what had to be a code of some sort; the mirror afforded an excellent view. This completed, Dref and his companion seated themselves upon the ground. Minutes later, the cliff began to shimmer with faint phosphorescence that would have been invisible in daylight. Stelli leaned forward. The mirrored rock appeared to simmer, then to boil like lava. The glow intensified, culminating in the apparent emergence from solid granite of a mothlike elderly man clad in gray: Master Quinz vo Derrivalle, looking much the same as he had always looked. Princess Snot and her kinsman embraced. There was some exchange of words not transmitted through the mirror, then Dref and the old Exalted shook hands. A few more words, then Master Quinz appeared to lead his visitors forward straight into the cliff; all three seemed to sink into stone. And after that, the mirror was useless; Dref and his companion had vanished.

Stelli sat staring for a minute or two. "Thank you, Brother," she remarked at last, without expression. "Thank you." Then she yanked the bellpull to summon a messenger.

Uncle Quinz's retreat hadn't changed. The old-fashioned half-timbered thatched cottage still crouched low amidst tall trees, so well concealed by nature that the owner's illusory safeguards were usually redundant. Inside, it was as if time had stood still. There was still the same orderly, comfortable simplicity that Eliste remembered so well: same sagging upholstered furniture, same few small ornaments on the walls, same old iron kettle over the fire, same tall wooden cupboards filled with dusty volumes and those mysterious instruments that she had always called the "widgets." Quinz himself was just the same moth-fragile, pallid, mild, and deceptively childlike nocturnal creature that he had always been; still gentle, affectionate, and dithery as ever. Sitting in her usual place beside the hearth, with a mug of mulled cider in her hand—the white mug with red flowers that Uncle Quinz had always set aside for her use—Eliste could almost imagine herself carried back to childhood. In a moment he would suggest a game of Blue Cat, for surely nothing had altered. But no, not quite true; there was one major change—never before had the familiar scene included Dref Zeenoson, whose presence was likely to alter all things.

Dref had remained quiet enough throughout uncle and niece's initial greetings and transports, quiet throughout the subsequent exchanges of news and information. Uncle Quinz had surprisingly little to relate. Since the night of the Marquis vo Derrivalle's death, the old man's contact with the folk at Derrivalle Manor—infrequent at the best of times—had ceased altogether. There seemed a great turmoil, rage, and misery down there among the former serfs, Quinz reported sadly. Such tumultuous emotions were painful to witness, upsetting, and distracting; they shook his concentration, at the expense of his art. That he could not afford, and thus, he had been forced to withdraw. Quinz appeared hardly to consider the possibility that those same turbulent peasants might actually wish him harm. Yet he was aware of the armed squadrons regularly patrolling the hills— despite his seeming vagueness, he always contrived to know what went on around him—and he had accordingly deepened the magical camouflage shrouding his cottage. Hitherto he had not been disturbed, and his quiet life continued unchanged.

Eliste furnished her kinsman with a judiciously edited version of her Sherreenian experiences. She related the essential facts, but omitted certain details. Thus he learned of conditions in the capital: of Exalted suffering and death, of Reparationist ascendancy, of Sentient and Victualer, of riot and madness and bloodshed in the streets, of Shorvi Nirienne's downfall, of Eliste's own escape in a crate carted out under the very nose of the Sentient Boomette. He did not, however, hear anything of Prilq's Hospitality, of Wonique's Warm Welcome, of The Fungus, or the Treasury. Unfortunately, there seemed no way to avoid telling him that she had shared Dref's lodgings for several weeks. Not that there was anything to hide; but it would sound so questionable, and Uncle Quinz was a very old gentleman.

She might as well have spared herself the anxiety. Uncle Quinz listened attentively to that part of the tale; remarked at its closing, "But how remarkably fortunate for you, my dear!"; turned to Dref and observed, "We are much indebted to you, my boy"; then asked if the famous Whiss Valeur was by any chance related to the Chorl Valeur that he had met once many years ago, upon the occasion of a return visit to Bozhenille Commune.

Dref could scarcely have hoped for a better opening. Chorl was Whiss Valeur's own father, he informed the bemused Uncle Quinz, then proceeded to describe the plight of the captive Valeur magicians, much as he had described it to Eliste days earlier. Oh, but he was good with words, Eliste inwardly observed for the thousandth time; dangerously good. Even as she watched, Uncle Quinz was visibly succumbing, great eyes darkening with distress and pity for the plight of Whiss's wretched kinsmen; for the innocent prisoners, Exalted and common, languishing in darkness; for Shorvi Nirienne and his followers, doomed to infamy and to shameful death; for—

But why did Dref trouble to go on and on? Uncle Quinz was already won. The wide eyes magnified by thick glass lenses would start to fill in another moment. It was so easy, it hardly seemed fair. Just as Eliste had known, Quinz vo Derrivalle with his soft heart didn't stand a chance.

"Perhaps we might assist them?" Quinz suggested before Dref had finished speaking. "It is dreadful to think of Chorl and his children forced to dishonor their art. It is shocking—indeed, it is a terrible thing, touching upon all of us ever to devote our minds and our lives to magical study. Almost it seems a desecration, a defilement of something pure and sacred. It must not be. It shall not be."

"Why, Uncle." Eliste was astonished. She had never in her life heard him speak with such force. As a child, she had never doubted that she knew her uncle through and through; but now, she wondered.

"But there, forgive me, children. You do not wish to listen to an old man's complaints. We shall do what we can for the unhappy Valeur kinsmen, and that is all that need be said."

Eliste suspected that Dref would not be satisfied with this, and she was right.

"And Shorvi Nirienne, sir?" Dref was leaning forward in his chair. "Can you do anything for him?"

"I know little of this Nirienne gentleman," Quinz returned mildly.

"You will know much more, if he survives. Sir, you have already observed the unhappiness of the Derrivalle folk, but that is as nothing compared to the misery of the Vonahrish population in general. You have never seen the Kokotte devour fourscore victims in a single afternoon. You have never seen the ZaZa breathing fire upon a crowd of unarmed citizens—"

"Ah, to think of magical accomplishment perverted to such use! Bah, infamous! Intolerable!"

Again, Eliste gazed at her uncle in surprise.

"So it is in Sherreen," Dref continued, clearly perceiving his host's weak point, "and so it will continue as long as Whiss and his creatures rule us. To such as these, magic is but an instrument of torture and death, employed to subjugate their countrymen. Shorvi Nirienne is one of the few men I know perhaps capable of improving matters; and you are the only man I know perhaps capable of preserving him."

"You've a great admiration for this Nirienne, lad?"

"His abilities are uncommon."

"Surely his ability to inspire loyalty is so. Well, something must be done, that is growing clear. Perhaps I have indulged myself with solitude and learning long enough. They are beautiful, but a price must be paid, it seems, to protect such treasures. And now at last I must visit the world of men again. How strange it will seem! This Nirienne is locked in a dungeon, you say?"

"He was ten days ago. I can't say if he is there still. At the conclusion of his trial, of course, he will proceed from the Palace of Justice, through the Sepulchre antechamber, where his garments will be removed and his wrists bound; then out to the courtyard, straight into one of Bierce's carts, and thence to Equality Circle and the Kokotte—"

Uncle Quinz flinched.

"They are not wont to waste time," Dref observed dryly. "Much depends upon the timing of the trial—its commencement and duration. I've no doubt the Reps mean to make a tremendous show of it, which may delay matters. Perhaps the trial will be postponed for several days, to allow for the propagation of broadsides, pamphlets, and essays stimulating public interest. The trial itself may be unusually prolonged. I've seen the National Tribunal condemn half a dozen men and women within the space of an hour, but Shorvi Nirienne is a special case. There will be witnesses, evidence no doubt falsified, a succession of ritual denunciations—"

"How fortunate I have been to remain apart from this for so long," Quinz murmured.

"He's probably safe in the Sepulchre still. But how much longer?" Dref spoke almost to himself.

"My dear boy, I will do what I can. But to deliver your Master Nirienne from a Sepulchre dungeon—that is a great task, and I am not at all certain that my poor abilities will suffice to—"

"Master Quinz, there'll be plenty of time to consider that en route. For now, may I suggest that you complete your preparations? We must be out upon the highway at dawn tomorrow to catch the Sherreen stage. We can't waste time. The roads through Fabeque are bad right now, and we're like to spend the next eight days and more in travel." Dref's thoughts seemed to turn inward. "And when we finally reach the city—shall we arrive to find that Shorvi is already gone?"

"Ah, there at least I am surely able to assist you." Uncle Quinz brightened. "We may do better than the public stage, I think. Glorielle will carry us."

"Sir?"

"Glorielle is—she can—that is—I can show you more easily than I can tell it. Come with me, lad. You, too, my dear." Uncle Quinz rose from his chair. Snatching up a lighted candle, he hurried to the back door. Trading mystified glances, Eliste and Dref followed.

Out of doors again, and now night had fallen. Quinz vo Derrivalle's candle, together with the light escaping the cottage windows and a nearly full moon, combined to illuminate a curious structure. A few yards from the house, in a clearing among the trees, stood a raised stage with a circular orifice at its center. On either side of the stage rose two tall wooden masts, each equipped with a pulley. Between the masts, suspended by means of a rope threaded through a ring affixed to its summit and passed through the two pulleys down to cleats, hung what looked to be a huge, loose, shapeless mass of fabric. Attached to the bottom of the mass by a great number of small cords sewn into the fabric was a construction resembling a wickerwork gallery with a balustrade, which in turn bore a squatly compact, complex mechanical device of metal and glass.

"Uncle, what is that object?" inquired Eliste.

"One moment, my dear, and you will see. Light. We need more light." Quinz touched his candle to a couple of lanterns mounted on posts beside the stage. "There. Yes. And now behold—Glorielle."

"But what is it, Uncle?"

"A balloon." Dref spoke softly, and Eliste turned to him in surprise. He was gazing raptly up at the weird contraption. "Is it not so, sir?"

"Quite right. Not many would have recognized it as such in its deflated state, but you were always a clever lad."

"Uncle Quinz, how long have you had this?"

"Oh, for over a year, now. And you are to thank for it, my dear. Had you not instructed me, I should never have known that such marvels exist."

"And it works? It really flies?"

"Like time itself."

"Carry us above all the muddy roads, all the way back to Sherreen?"

"This very night, my dear. Is it not thrilling?"

"Yes! Oh, yes! It certainly is! I would never have dreamed— Dref, only think of it!"

"That's just what I'm doing." Dref's eyes remained fixed on the great, limp fabric envelope. "I'm thinking we'll be at the mercy of every stray breeze. Judging by what I've read, the balloon should ascend readily enough, provided it is well constructed and properly inflated with heated atmosphere, or better yet, with inflammable air. Once aloft, however, there is no means of setting a course. Glorielle might sail the sea of air south toward Sherreen, or else the wind might carry her straight off in the opposite direction."

"You are admirably informed, lad." Uncle Quinz nodded. "You have hit upon this wonderful object's greatest weakness. For weeks I pondered that very problem. At length a solution occurred to me, and I spent some months constructing Glorielle."

"You mean, sir, that you have altered the design of the balloon—?"

"Oh, no, my boy. Forgive me, I haven't made myself clear. Glorielle is not the balloon—that in itself is only a handsome sack of treated silk. No, Glorielle is the Sentient I built to propel the balloon. You see—" Mounting the stage, Uncle Quinz laid a fond hand upon the glass-and-metal device affixed to the gallery. Several glass whorls glowed with sudden light at his touch. "Here she is— complete at last, awake and eager, and ready to fly!"

"A Sentient. You actually built a Sentient." Eliste thought of Kokotte, Boomette, and the nits of NuNu. Her stomach tightened. "Please don't touch it, Uncle. Please don't stand so near that thing."

"My dear, I am sorry if I seem critical, but indeed, you are not quite courteous.

You must not refer to my friend as 'that thing.' Her name is Glorielle, a very pretty name, I believe. You must consider the feelings of others, child."

"But can a piece of machinery actually have— Oh, very well, Uncle Quinz, I'll take your word for it. But are you certain that—Glorielle—is really safe? She doesn't spit fire? Or noxious vapor? She doesn't consume flesh?"

"Not that I am aware of. She has never yet displayed such barbarous tendencies. Of course—" a thoughtful frown creased Uncle Quinz's tall brow, "I must confess, I am not certain what she might do if sufficiently provoked to anger. We have not known each other very long, and I am not yet acquainted with all the quirks of her character. Who knows what surprises may lie in store? Is not life exciting?"

"Excessively. But, Uncle—"

"Master Quinz," Dref interrupted, "how does Glorielle direct the balloon's flight? Such a feat requires considerable mechanical energy, more than anyone has hitherto achieved, within the limitations of the balloon's capacity to lift. What is her source of power?"

"Why, I hardly know, lad. I am not nearly that clever and scientific. The most I can tell you is that I *asked* Glorielle, and she very kindly obliged, so ordering herself that my request could be fulfilled. She was most helpful, most accommodating."

"But how did she do that, sir? And how did *you* do it?"

"My dear boy, I do not know how to explain. We are speaking here of a certain knack that I was born with, one I worked very hard to develop. Now I can use it quite handily, but exactly *how* I do so is quite impossible to say. I do not know the answer. I am truly sorry."

Dref shook his head, smiling.

Oh, I suspect you know a lot more than you're letting on, Uncle, thought Eliste. *Dref doesn't quite believe you, either. Never mind, keep your secrets. Perhaps it's best that you do.* Aloud, she remarked, "It really doesn't matter how you do it, as long as it works. And you *are* certain this works, aren't you?"

"Oh, the balloon soars splendidly, my dear. I have seen it do so many times, and a most enthralling sight it is."

"But you've more than seen it, haven't you, Uncle? You've flown?"

"Not yet, my dear. Tonight's ascent will be my first. I am most excited!"

"And your Sentient, Master Quinz? She has proved herself reliable?"

"Tonight comes her very first opportunity to do so. Only think of it—a maiden flight! But do not look so concerned, my boy. I can assure you, Glorielle will cooperate to the best of her ability. She is for the most part amiable, when properly approached."

"Hmmmm."

"And now, children, to work! There is much to do if we are to leave on time. We must collect our belongings, load the gallery properly, and inflate the balloon."

"How long to complete inflation, Master Quinz?"

"It is amazingly rapid. Once the furnace is fairly going, our balloon is fit to ascend in just a little above an hour. Best to begin upon that at once." Candle in hand, Quinz ducked down into the stage's central orifice, there to touch flame to the waiting fuel. He reappeared a moment later, looking pleased. "There—what a sight awaits you, children!"

The silken envelope was already starting to sway. Eliste eyed it askance. "Can a mere sack of cloth truly bear the three of us aloft?"

"Oh, indeed, my dear. You will be astounded. You will see—"

"It looks to have the volume to carry our combined weight well enough," Dref interrupted. "But we won't put it to the test. Eliste, you're not to come with us. You'll remain here in your uncle's house."

It was so unexpected that Eliste forgot outrage, inquiring in simple astonishment, "Whatever makes you say that?"

"Ordinary prudence," Dref returned. His tone was easy and matter-of-fact, but his face was closed, locked, barred, and bolted. Obviously, he expected trouble. "You're Exalted. Identified as such in Sherreen, you'll go straight to the Kokotte; and with the Vanguard everywhere about, the danger of recognition is considerable. But you've had the rare good luck of escaping the city, and now your position is relatively secure. You're safe here. You'll not throw that away on a whim."

She was silent. Surprise seemed to have dulled her wits. Never before that moment had it occurred to her that she might not return to Sherreen with Dref and Uncle Quinz; the idea simply hadn't entered her mind. Now that Dref had suggested it (or rather, dictated it, and how dare he order her about?) she was forced to consider. Clearly, what he said was true; no getting around it. Difficult to refute an argument so sound and obviously rational, but she knew she had to do it. She wouldn't let them leave her behind—she wouldn't. After a few moments' mental floundering, however, her response was decidedly lame. "It is hardly your place to tell me where I may or may not go. I prefer to return to Sherreen, and that is what I will do. Let us not discuss it further."

"Oh, perhaps just a little further. Only deign to explain your reasoning, which is, I confess, rather too deep for me. What purpose is served by your very risky return to Sherreen, Exalted Miss? What precisely do you expect to accomplish there? Enlighten me."

He was insufferable. If only she could produce some suitably crushing retort, to put him in his place. There was, however, no reasonable response to his questions. *But don't you want me there with you?* were the words that popped painfully into her mind; and that wouldn't do, that made no sense at all. But why let him back her into a corner? Eliste straightened, her chin came up, and she answered with assumed indifference. "I am scarcely obliged to justify my decisions to you. I have stated my intention, and there's an end to the matter. I do not propose to argue the point with you; it's too boring."

"Eliste, you are childish beyond endurance."

"Whenever I do or say anything that you dislike, you call me 'childish.' I'm tired of hearing it."

"When you behave like a petulant, capricious little girl, what else do you expect? Just be thankful there are others willing to look after you, if you can't do as much for yourself. You are not going back to Sherreen, and I don't propose to argue the point with *you*."

"Very good, we're agreed not to argue. And, as there's nothing you can do to stop me from going where I please, that leaves little more to be said."

"I'll use force if I must."

"Don't be absurd."

"Try me. I'm serious. You're not going."

It was unbelievable. He meant what he said. She could see it in his face, which was not like his own at all, but hard and unyielding as any stranger's. He wouldn't *allow* her to go. Two years earlier, she would have flown into a rage, fumed and stamped her foot, threatened to slap him. Now, she wanted very much to cry. Anger would have been much preferable to this spineless, humiliating, drippy urge to snivel. Fortunately, she managed to control the impulse. When she answered, her voice was creditably even. "That's not your decision, Dref. The balloon belongs to Uncle Quinz, and you've no right to keep me out of it. *You* want me, don't you, Uncle?" She turned to him confidently.

"Indeed I do, my dear," he replied with all the enthusiasm she could have desired. And yet there was something wrong; he was fidgeting uncomfortably. Before she could inquire, he continued, "Certainly I would love to keep you with me, and yet your young man speaks very truly. I had not thought of it until this moment, but he is absolutely right, and I must not be selfish at your expense."

Your young man? "But, Uncle—"

"My dear child, it is dangerous for you in the city, and there is no reason for you to run such risk. Nothing to be gained, nothing accomplished."

"But, Uncle Quinz—" She had never expected this, and now she was flailing. "You can't mean to leave me here all alone in these hills? What would I do by myself in the wild? I'll starve, or freeze."

"No, no, my dear, all is well. You will find my cottage perfectly comfortable,"

Quinz promised. "There is enough food and fuel laid in to last for months. And my illusions will protect you against intrusion."

"But, Uncle—oh, Uncle Quinz, they won't protect me against loneliness. Left here all alone, I'll die of misery. I'm not like you, I don't thrive on solitude. I cannot bear it; I'll just shrivel. Is that what you want?" she demanded, with a confused mixture of guile and truth.

With Uncle Quinz alone, it would have worked. The old gentleman looked stricken. His eyes suffused. Alone, he could never have held out; unfortunately, Dref was there.

"You'll survive for a few weeks," Dref told her. "And that's probably all it will be before your uncle returns."

"*Your uncle.*" Not "*your uncle and I.*" A few weeks. Suddenly she almost hated them both—these two *men*, presenting a united front against her, excluding her. What matter that Uncle Quinz looked guilty and miserable; he was still siding with Dref. She might have argued, cried, and pleaded. She chose not to lower herself. They didn't want her with them. To blazes with them. Her spine stiffened. "Certainly," she conceded coldly. "Please yourselves." Dref didn't react, but at least she had the satisfaction of seeing her uncle stir unhappily. Good; served him right for leaving her. "Well?" she inquired. "There are blankets and candles inside. Do you want them?" Uncle Quinz nodded. Eliste spun on her heel and stalked back into the cottage. Her throat was constricted, and her eyes burned. She wanted so much to cry, and she didn't know why. There was something about the entire scene that seemed familiar. It all reminded her of something—it made her think of another night, months earlier. Now, as then, Dref was going to leave against her wishes, and there wasn't a thing she could do to stop him. He was simply going to go; but this time, he'd take Uncle Quinz along with him. He'd leave her all alone here, and he wouldn't care; but then, why should he? And why should she? What difference did it make where an upstart serf went, or what he did? It was really beneath notice. But she did notice; and she did care, far too much. He was going away, and it felt like a knife in her breast.

It came to her then that she didn't want to be parted from him, now or ever. In fact, she could barely stand the thought of it. Asinine and incredible, but true. True for a long time, and she had managed to ignore it or deny it. No denying it any longer, however. She was now quite conscious that she wanted him with her badly, that she would never be content without him. He might be a former serf, but that didn't change matters.

Stupid. Idiotic. A pathetic absurdity. She was Exalted, and she wanted a peasant who was ready and eager to literally fly away from her. She had turned down the Duke of Feronte, and others, to save herself for a lowborn fugitive

Nirienniste who regarded her as a wayward child. No doubt Dref would be amused if he knew. There was nothing plebeian about his sense of humor, and he had always appreciated irony.

She wasn't doing herself much good with such thoughts. A couple of tears stung her eyes, and she dashed them away. Bad enough to find herself in such a humiliating state, without advertising it. A little discretion might yet preserve a few shreds of dignity. She took a couple of minutes to compose herself; only when her face was under control again did she glance about the room in search of the blankets and candles she had come to find. It was then that she noticed the odd appearance of the mirror on the wall behind her. It was a small glass in a plain wooden frame, and it had always hung in that same spot. In childhood she had often stood before it grimacing at herself; but she could not do so now, for the glass had somehow lost its reflective power. There was no image of any sort mirrored there. The smooth surface was fog-gray and perfectly blank, glowing with an internal light that rhythmically waxed and waned. For a few moments she stood staring, intrigued and uneasy. Then she called loudly for her uncle. Quinz and Dref were there within seconds.

"What's happened? Why's it doing that?" Eliste demanded.

"No cause whatever for alarm, my dear," Quinz assured her. "The house requests my attention, that is all. It must have something to tell me."

"The house does? The house talks to you?"

"But certainly. The cottage has been awake for decades. Did you never know?"

"No, never. What does it talk about?"

"Mice, primarily. Itchy thatching, rusty hinges, and drainage problems. *Entre nous*, its conversation lacks sparkle; but there, I do not wish to seem unkind. Now, then. Let us watch and listen." Uncle Quinz placed his two hands flat against the wall on either side of the mirror. Bowing his head, he spoke softly and unintelligibly, in the manner that Eliste knew from experience preceded magical manifestation. For a few moments, nothing happened—at least, nothing of consequence. A shutter scraped, a floorboard creaked, the ashes on the hearth stirred, and Uncle Quinz nodded sharply, as if in comprehension. He spoke again, and now the mirror cleared to reflect an image—not, however, of the room or anything in it. Eliste could see the familiar narrow trail leading up the hill to the cliff that blocked the way to Uncle Quinz's cottage. She could see the sheer stone face rising a hundred feet or more, and for the first time in her life, she perceived the illusion. There was the cliff, its stark contour familiar and unchanged; but the rock itself was insubstantial as a dense mist, through which she dimly discerned bushes, scrub vegetation, and a continuation of the path up the sharp, true slope of the hill. So that's what it actually looked like. Of far greater interest than the terrain, however, were the human figures inhabiting it. Clustered at the foot of the cliff were half a dozen armed men whose scarlet bandannas and red-diamond insignia marked them as members of a local Reparationist Compeers' patrol.

Eliste stiffened at the sight. "Uncle," she whispered, "have you any weapons in the house?"

"Certainly not, my dear. Whatever should I do with articles so dangerous? Come, do you no longer trust in your uncle's talents? These roving bands can never find us here."

But even as Quinz spoke, one of the Compeers made straight for the flat stone nestled among the roots of the old rotting tree stump; pushed the stone aside to uncover the little hidden compartment with its lever of bronze; unhesitatingly pulled the lever in the signal sequence that Eliste had been taught as a child. A chime sounded within the cottage; while in the mirror, the murky fog composing the illusory cliff lightened so dramatically that it seemed a wonder the Compeers failed to see right through it.

"Ruination! How did he know that was there? How could he know how to use it? Uncle, you never told anyone, did you?"

"Not I, my dear. But this is most puzzling." Uncle Quinz appeared bemused. "Is it possible that you two children were followed here?"

"No, sir." Dref was certain. "I can answer for that. We were not followed."

"Curious, curious. But how remarkable. Well, there are varied means of observation, as you can see for yourselves. Evidently, someone has access to one; or perhaps, has even discovered a new one—an interesting possibility. Most intriguing."

"Uncle, what will you do to stop them?"

"My child, I have always relied upon illusions to guard my privacy. If they fail to do so, I must confess, I shall find myself at a loss. But let us not assume the worst. Perhaps we shall fool them yet."

"Perhaps." Dref's eyes remained fixed on the mirror, wherein the Compeers were milling about the cliff, experimentally poking and striking at the rock. "But they seem to know what they're about. Master Quinz, how much reality can your illusions withstand?"

"Sometimes the merest breath will blast them; but often my shadows are powerful as fear, impervious as vanity, durable as hope. Depends entirely on the nature of the beholders, lad."

"Then those peasant louts could find their way here within minutes," said Eliste. "We'd best leave while we can; and no more nonsense, I trust, about leaving me behind." This surprise attack upon a hitherto inviolable sanctum increased her own peril a thousandfold; it violated all reason that she should be so pleased about it. But only a conscious effort kept her lips straight.

"Oh, my dear child—" Uncle Quinz was genuinely distressed. "I am so sorry—"

"Save your sorrow, sir," Dref advised. "Perhaps we'll all need it. How much longer before the balloon is fit to fly?"

"Oh, very little time—it is impossible to judge exactly. Let us observe."

They did so, stepping to the back door. Outside, the light of lantern and moon fell upon a vast bubble, dark as the evening sky, richly scrolled and curlicued in gold. Eliste stared. Amazing, this sight, and not the least amazing aspect was the speed of inflation. Already the sack towered, huge and swelling fast; but the silken walls as yet remained loose and wrinkled.

"Perhaps another quarter of an hour will do it," Quinz told them. "Is it not wonderful?"

"Any way to hurry it up, sir?"

"I don't think so. Patience, lad. Come, let us take these lanterns with us. Glorielle is partial to illumination."

They spent the next fifteen minutes loading the gallery with supplies, fuel, water buckets, and ballast, all arranged by Dref to ensure even weight distribution—a matter that had not occurred to Quinz. At the end of that time, packing was complete. The balloon, huge and splendid, strained hard against its mooring ropes; while Glorielle, evidently awake and aware, pulsed with light. Her steel frame vibrated, and a high, fervid hum escaped her.

Slung by chains from the bottom of the balloon's neck was a fire basket of wrought-iron wire. Now Quinz vo Derrivalle stood in the gallery, loading fuel into the basket through ports built into the neck; now he was kindling a fire. Eliste watched her uncle for a few moments and then, impelled by uneasy curiosity, returned to the mirror to monitor the patrolmen's progress.

Even as she looked on, one of the Compeers broke through illusory stone. The fellow stumbled forward a few paces, tripped, and fell on his face. After a moment, he sat up, gawking in clownish wonder. Behind him, his companions appeared to go wild, prodding and hammering violently at the cliff that, to them, still looked and felt solid. They must have been yelling. Eliste could see their mouths working busily; of course, no sound reached her. The leading Compeer picked himself up, turned back to face the others, seemed to call out to them. While he called, he signaled, slowly swinging his lighted lantern to and fro. The men stood still, heads cocked in listening attitudes. Certainly they could hear their vanished comrade; whether they could see the signal light was unclear. The first man retraced his path; stepped forth into view; walked back through the cliff without effort; stretched forth an arm, which the others must have perceived as a human limb emerging from solid stone. One by one, the first Compeer drew his companions through the illusion.

Eliste did not need to watch any more. Gathering up her skirts, she ran back outside. "They're through," she reported.

"Aboard, then," Dref commanded. "The balloon is ready."

"That it is, lad," Uncle Quinz concurred. "I am not certain, though, that the same can be said of Glorielle. It is my impression she desires a few moments more delay."

"What for, Uncle?"

"Meditation, I believe."

"Well, tell her there's no time." Accepting Dref's proffered hand, Eliste scrambled aboard—no easy feat, for the strivings of the fully inflated envelope were now bouncing the gallery this way and that.

"Ah, no, my child. It is best to consider Glorielle's preferences. Perhaps I am to blame for indulging her too greatly, for she is willful and sometimes prone to pettish demonstration."

"Demonstration?"

"If flouted, she may perhaps be moved to tip the gallery, spilling us out onto the ground from a height of three thousand feet or so. Please do not misunderstand me. She is not truly ill-natured, only a little temperamental."

"But, Uncle Quinz, we—"

"Presently, my dear. Best to humor Glorielle. Believe me." Uncle Quinz patted the Sentient. She brightened, luminous pulsations assuming a roseate tinge. "She feels a little threatened, I think—a little insecure. She is thus impelled to assert herself. Let us be sensitive to her needs. We will wait a little."

I'd like to take a sledgehammer to that junk-heap prima donna, thought Eliste, but wisely held her tongue. She glanced across at Dref. His face was expressionless, but she could sense his impatience. Her fingers nervously drummed the balustrade.

Three or four minutes they stood waiting, and then came a flash of lantern light and a braying of voices. The Compeers had reached the edge of the clearing.

"Uncle Quinz—" Eliste implored.

"Hush, child." Pressing both palms to the Sentient's burnished casing, Quinz bent down to whisper gently, "Glorielle. My dear one. We are relying on you." Evidently this was the right approach, for Glorielle pulsed with warm soft radiance, and chuckling clicks purred out of her. "Thank you, my dear. You are most kind." Quinz straightened. "We are fortunate. Glorielle has granted us permission to ascend."

Very decent of her. Eliste said nothing.

"To work, children!"

Quickly they cast off the mooring ropes. As the Compeers rounded the corner of the house, the last lines fell, and the great dusky globe climbed silently for the stars. Shouts and cries piped feebly in its wake; two or three gunshots popped like firecrackers. Eliste scarcely noticed them. The ground sank magically away. She was flying through space, flying without sound, without effort—weightless as if disembodied, and free as never before. Disbelieving rapture filled her. She gazed down at the shadowy moonlit world wheeling slowly beneath her, and for a time forgot all else.

Physical discomfort broke the ecstatic trance. The air about her had turned bitterly cold. Winter had returned, and she was shivering, teeth achatter, despite the proximity of the fire that Dref and Quinz were feeding with trusses of straw. The flames leapt, and she supposed that the balloon should do likewise; but if it did so, she felt nothing. Below them rolled the fields and hills of Fabeque, the sleeping villages and farms, turning; but gallery and passengers seemed suspended motionless in midheaven.

But they *were* traveling, and with remarkable velocity. Far off to their right, a cluster of lights marking the location of Grammantes was already faintly visible. The wind was wafting the balloon southeast over the countryside, at such a rate that they would reach the Haereste frontier by morning. Not such a bad idea, as Eliste saw it. Now that Dref and Uncle Quinz were with her, not such a bad idea to remove themselves, to flee Vonahr, seeking peace and safety in some distant land. Eliste wouldn't have minded at all, but unfortunately the two men would never consent; and more unfortunate yet, Glorielle was present to counter the vagaries of the wind.

Uncle Quinz caressed the Sentient, whispered fondly to her. Glorielle glowed, pulsed, and whirred. Radiant arcs played along her glassy whorls, emphasizing a family resemblance to her celebrated cousin, the Kokotte. She hummed, high and hungry; three or four of her wire vanes whipped the air; there came a sucking whoosh, as of sharply indrawn breath. She exhaled mightily, and the suddenly expelled gust drove the balloon south toward Sherreen. Then there was motion again, wind in their faces, and sound.

Back on course, and the spell was broken. Eliste sighed a little.

Thereafter they made good progress, despite all handicaps. Glorielle's method of navigation was obscure; perhaps she used the stars, perhaps the pull of the land beneath her, perhaps the lights and landmarks of the hidden dimensions. Whatever her system, it was effective; the balloon maintained a southerly course whose constancy was confirmed by Dref's observations of the skies. The hours passed, and the land flowed like a river beneath them. Eliste wrapped herself in a blanket to ward off the chill; busied herself with feeding fire and fighting it. For the blaze in the wire basket had to be nourished with straw and chopped wool, while the numerous little fires flaring like a rash upon the balloon's silken skin had to be smothered with sopping sponges. No point in contemplating the consequences of an ungoverned fire—the hellish blast, the sickening plunge. Best to ply the dripping sponge, and not think about it. She sponged and mopped until her arms ached. She forked hay and fed chopped wool through the ports. Dref did likewise, while Uncle Quinz stood at the rear, communing with his creation. The old gentleman's attentiveness must have pleased Glorielle, who responded with her best efforts, working without pause or rest to drive the balloon south through night and darkness. Often the wind favored them, bearing them in effortless glory. Other times, they were forced to rely upon the Sentient's propulsive power, and then the great globe trudged slowly through the skies, like a prisoner dragging an iron ball and chain.

"Ever consider changing the balloon's shape, sir?"

Eliste turned in time to see Dref's hands sketching ellipsoids in the air, but failed to catch her uncle's reply, if any.

Wind resistance notwithstanding, Glorielle made a remarkably short journey of it. The distance requiring eight days of travel by coach over muddy roads was covered by balloon in less than a single night. It was an hour or more before dawn when they came down quite neatly in a quiet field a couple of miles to the northeast of Sherreen. The grapnel caught, the impact was minimal, and the aeronauts were barely shaken. Before they climbed from the gallery, however, the balloon was already deflating, its billows pressing upon the passengers' shoulders. New fires were scorching the silk. These were quickly extinguished, but the envelope was damaged beyond immediate hope of repair, and they were obliged to abandon it there. Glorielle, however, could scarcely be abandoned. Fortunate that the Sentient was compact and light enough to carry. They stowed her away in a canvas sack that Dref could hoist to his shoulder, then made their way across the fields to the nearest road, which they followed by starlight and lantern light, southwest to Sherreen's small Gante Street Gate.

Easy to enter the capital as it was difficult to leave it. Presumably, no sane enemy of the People would consider approaching Sherreen. No one accosted them, no one demanded passport or identification as they passed through the gate at dawn, in the midst of a gang of market-bound farmers. Once past the Gante Street Gate, they caught an early fiacre that carried them through the wakening neighborhoods, all the way back to Flou's Pocket. Before the sun was fairly visible above the rooftops, they had reached Dref's lodgings. Their arrival drew little if any attention. The triple entrance went unchallenged, and minutes later, all three were safe behind the locked door of Dref's rooms, variously disposed upon bed, cot, floor—and sleeping soundly.

•   •   •

Stelli Zeenosgirl had observed with interest the activities of her brother, as reflected in the dead Marquis vo Derrivalle's magical mirror. Attentively she had monitored his meeting with Princess Snot, their ascent to the strange old Exalted's refuge, the efforts of the Compeers, and the escape via balloon. She had watched the great inflated silken globe sail out of sight, bearing the People's enemies to freedom; she had witnessed the consternated Compeers' inability to prevent it. She had seen all; and now the time to watch was over, and it was time to act.

Stelli put away the mirror; opened the top drawer of the Marquis's desk, and rummaged therein with the confidence born of familiarity to bring forth a miniature, painted on ivory. She regarded this for a moment or two with loathing, then set it aside to rifle the drawer for paper, pens, and ink. Writing supplies disposed before her, she paused to think, black eyes trained like gun barrels upon the blank paper. At last she took up the pen. Her lower lip was caught between her teeth, her brow creased with effort, for composition did not come easily to her. Writing was unnatural, and yet she knew how to do it—she had her brother to thank for that. Dref had taught her, long ago. He had always been unendurably generous with his crumbs gleaned at the Exalted table. Dref's magnanimity might now be repaid as deserved.

Her uncertainty vanished. She dipped her quill and wrote:

> To the Republican Protector, at the Committee of National Welfare, in Sherreen:
>
> Compeer Whiss Valeur, I am a Reparationist Patriot of Fabeque, writing to let you know what happens in your own city, since no one there seems to let you know. Compeer Whiss, you have trouble on your hands. There is an old magical Exalted named Quinz vo Derrivalle, coming to Sherreen to make trouble for you. He is a skinny old body with white hair and stupid eyeglasses. He looks like a dumb dried-up gaffer, but don't let that fool you. He is with his kinswoman, Eliste vo Derrivalle, a prinked-up Exalted whore, whose likeness I now send you. Both of them are enemies of the People. They are hand in glove with all the troublemakers. They want to kill you, and they will do it if you do not take steps. The old man has magic, he can use it, he is the worst trouble that you will ever come up against. If you don't find this old man and his girl, they will bring you down by magic, you can depend on it. I tell you this because I am loyal. You better do something about these Exalted traitors, or they'll do anything they want, and you won't be around to see it. This is all the truth, believe it.
>
> —A Patriot of Fabeque

•   •   •

Stelli read over all that she had written. The text was crude and marked with blotches, yet seemed to express what she wanted to say. Self-interest had obliged her to omit all mention of her brother, whose surname was identical to her own. Perhaps kind Providence should grant her future opportunity to deal with Dref. In the meantime, if Whiss Valeur were all that the Compeers had been led to expect, he would take heed.

Stelli folded her missive about the miniature of her former mistress, sealed the package with wax, and yanked the bellpull to summon a flunky who might be assigned to intercept the Sherreen mail coach tomorrow morning. Within hours, the letter should be speeding on its way; and when it reached its destination—

She warmed at the thought.

liste had more or less assumed that the three of them would share Dref's
lodgings—somewhat cramped, but a dream of spacious comfort in comparison to Prilq's Hospitality or Wonique's Warm Welcome. Uncle Quinz
promptly squelched that notion. The old gentleman required a solitary refuge
wherein to rest, to meditate, to cultivate the single-minded concentration that
his magical endeavors demanded. He was not apt to find true peace anywhere in
Sherreen, but he needed a room of his own; so much was essential. Accordingly,
"Grandfather Renois," as he now styled himself, engaged a pleasant second-story
chamber at the back of the lodging house; much to the bemusement of the student
tenants, who took to calling the new arrival "the Changeling." For a couple of
days, the eccentric presence generated considerable curiosity. Not only was
"Renois'" age highly anomalous in that place, but it was also noted that he
was fond of slipping out of the house upon nameless errands in the dead of night;
moreover, his accent did not at all match that of his supposed grandson. Not that
Uncle Quinz didn't attempt to suppress his Exalted intonation; but his memory
for such details was poor, and his lapses frequent.

It might have been dangerous if his neighbors had seen more of him. As the old
man was retiring and nocturnal, however, sightings were relatively rare. From
time to time he was spotted making his seemingly abstracted way up or down the
staircase in the hours between midnight and dawn. Those meeting him in the
corridor were apt to receive a sweet but vague smile, a distrait nod; or else to find
themselves ignored altogether, as if the old man—sunk in some mysterious half-

trance—thought himself alone. Grandfather Renois clearly meant no offense, and nobody suspected him of such, yet it was impossible to avoid the notion that the old gentleman was a bit simple, perhaps downright addled. After the first few days, student speculation began to subside; the new tenant was an amiably harmless crackpot, who enjoyed taking the air by moonlight, and that was all.

Uncle Quinz's withdrawal left Eliste in a quandary. Now she was back where she had been days earlier—back in Sherreen, sharing two rooms with Dref Zeenoson. Initially she had imagined that her uncle—as an adult male kinsman, now by custom automatically assigned the role of her guardian, whether he wanted it or not—would prohibit such questionable cohabitation. But the irregularity of the arrangement seemed entirely lost upon Quinz vo Derrivalle, who was less contemptuous of propriety's dictates than innocently unaware. Upon the morning of his transfer to the new room, he had merely remarked, "There, children, now we shall all be far more comfortable," and departed with a smile upon his lips. So much for guardianship.

Eliste was taken aback, almost disappointed. She had expected her uncle to simplify matters by telling her what to do, and here he had left the decision entirely in her hands. And it *was* now a matter of choice, as never before. Formerly, she had depended upon Dref's charity; a disagreeable but undeniable fact. Leaving Flou's Pocket would have meant a return to the streets. But now her own Derrivalle kinsman was here, and naive though he was, he had not neglected to supply himself with cash—not the worthless paper currency of the Republican Protectorate, but sound, old-fashioned rekkoes. Uncle Quinz would willingly finance separate lodgings for her—she had only to ask. She could go any time she liked.

But then—to leave, so abruptly. Of course, it was what she ought to do. Best by far for her to flee a situation grown painful and humiliating. Best for Dref, too, she reflected drearily. He had proved generous and steadfast far beyond the claims of old friendship, but even Dref's largesse must find its limit. No doubt he would be glad to have his rooms all to himself again. Yes, in all good conscience, she should go—and without regret, for she was certainly no longer happy in Flou's Pocket. In fact, she was miserable. Strange to think that she had lived here for so many weeks in mindless peace and comfort. How could she have been so contented then and so wretched now, when outwardly nothing had changed? But, of course, it was she herself who had changed, growing fully conscious at last of the ridiculous, pathetic, perverse, and degrading sentiments that no woman worthy of the title Exalted could ever have entertained for a serf—most particularly a serf who did not return them.

But there are no more serfs. No more Exalted titles, either.

No matter. She was desperately ashamed and self-conscious. She could hardly bring herself to look Dref in the face. If he guessed her thoughts—and with his perspicacity, it was not at all impossible that he might—the consequences would be dreadful. He would be kind. He would worry about hurting her feelings. He would be concerned, diplomatic, and sorry for her. She didn't think she could bear it. No, he must never know.

Night and day she fretted over the possibility of self-betrayal; but in fact, as she saw well enough, she needn't have worried. She might have given herself away a hundred times over, and Dref would scarcely have noticed. These days, wholly preoccupied with the fate of Shorvi Nirienne, he seemed hardly aware of her existence. The trial of "the Nirienne Gang," as the five defendants were popularly known, had commenced upon the very day of their return from Fabeque. The event itself was all that Dref had foreseen—gaudy, noisy, highly publicized, and rife with vulgarities of every description. Owing to the unusual nature of the case, Nirienne and his four satellites—Frezhelle, Riclairc, and the Bulaude siblings— were accorded the unusual privilege of cross-examining witnesses called by the prosecution. This so, the deliberations would surely stretch to inordinate length. Clearly, the Reparationists intended to milk the event for every last drop of political advantage.

Dref was always out nosing for information. He spent much of his time hanging about the wineshops and coffeehouses, in hope of useful verbal gleanings. A portion of every day was spent loitering before the Palace of Justice; that dreary relic of a royalist past, adjoining the Sepulchre, and present seat of the National Tribunal. There was always a small clump of the curious clogging the Palace entrance any day of the week. Nirienne's trial, however, attracted inquisitive hordes, and the frequent presence of the tall young man with the tattooed hand went quite unremarked.

In the evenings, Dref was usually out and about upon his multifarious errands; nameless activities that Eliste strongly suspected involved conferences with his fellow Niriennistes. It was not beyond the imagination of these desperate and reckless disciples to plot a rescue—a raid upon the Palace of Justice, or even upon the Sepulchre itself. Such an attempt was bound to fail, but no matter for that—they were quite mad enough to try it, there was nothing these people wouldn't dare for their chief. No point in requesting an explanation, however. Dref had countless ways of parrying questions, and when absolutely pressed to the wall, merely shrugged and observed that she was far better off not knowing. Eliste wanted to hit him when he said that, but it would have done no good; when Dref was in a closemouthed mood, nothing did any good. And he was closemouthed nearly all of the time now, silent and psychically distant. He used his lodgings to sleep in, and little more; during his brief intervals of conscious presence, he immersed himself in the popular journals and pamphlets filled with fanciful accounts of the trial. The Nirienne Gang was holding its own, by all reports. Its members were eloquent in their own defense, particularly Shorvi Nirienne, himself formerly a lawyer by profession. Collective conviction would be more difficult to obtain than anyone had anticipated.

Eliste was uneasy and unhappy, unoccupied and unnecessary, and quite probably unwanted; more alone now, it seemed, than she would have felt if dwelling in true solitude. She should have remained in Fabeque. Here, Dref all but ignored her; an affront she was unable to return in kind. Quite the contrary, in fact. She thought of him continually, unwillingly, almost to the exclusion of all else—and much good it did her; he had no time for her anymore. The books and artifacts, formerly so diverting, now failed to hold her attention. She had nothing to do, and she didn't dare go out, and she disliked staying in. Here, she was only in the way.

She didn't like to bother Uncle Quinz with her problems. But the days passed, her unhappiness mounted, and at last she was impelled to unburden herself. Not such an easy matter to accomplish, for Uncle Quinz was decidedly difficult to pin down. Throughout the daylight hours, he slept, or so she assumed. At night, he was out and about, roaming the streets to confer, as he explained, with "the Inanimates." By this term he referred to the various buildings, statues, and monuments capable of furnishing him with information. Some of these he awakened himself; but many were already aware, thus testifying to the industry and expertise of the captive Valeur magicians. There was much to be learned from the Inanimates, and arcane conference occupied nearly all the old gentleman's waking hours. Eliste watched and bided her time. At last one night she stationed herself outside his door and waited there for hours. He returned in the chilly predawn, and this time, she caught him.

"Uncle, may I speak with you?"

"Always, my dear. Always. Come in." Quinz appeared fatigued, but genuinely pleased to see her. Unlocking the door, he ushered her into his room. "Sit here, my child. It is the most comfortable chair. Would you like a mug of cider? Lemon tea? A game of Blue Cat, perhaps?"

"No, thank you. Uncle, I'm sorry for bothering you at this time of night, when I know you must be tired. I wouldn't have done it if I didn't really need to talk, and I haven't been able to overtake you—"

"Stop, my dear, I am to blame. Caught up in my investigations as I have been, I have neglected all else. It is most inconsiderate of me, and yet I know my niece will forgive."

"No, it's my fault— Oh, anyway, Uncle Quinz, I must speak. There's something I must confess. It's been weighing so heavily upon my mind, and I'm so ashamed, I can hardly live with myself."

"Ah, this sounds serious. My dear, whatever the trouble is, and whatever you have done, I know you have never acted through malice."

"That's true. And I haven't actually *acted* at all. The shame is in my thoughts, not my actions, so far. But—I wish you'd stop looking at me that way, so lovingly and trustingly, for it will all change when you hear what I have to confess, and you will despise me—"

"Come, child, calm yourself," Quinz advised with unwonted firmness. "Do you think my affection such a weak and mutable thing? Almost you wound me. But there, enough of that, I see you are most unhappy. Let us then consider your great crime. Perhaps upon close examination, the monster may prove less fearsome than you imagine."

"Very well." Eliste took a deep breath. It was difficult to continue, and she steeled herself against the inevitable change in her uncle's eyes. "It is this. I have formed an attachment to Dref Zeenoson. A most inappropriate attachment." There, it was out. "I have never spoken of it to anyone until this moment, and he knows nothing of it."

"Ah, I see the difficulty. No wonder you are agitated. Well, my poor dear, your course is clear, is it not? You must tell young Dref of your feelings. No doubt you are shy, and the prospect is daunting, yet in such a case, surely honesty is the best—"

"Uncle Quinz, I don't think you understand me. I am not speaking of simple friendship. I shouldn't be ashamed of that, not anymore. But the attachment I have formed is far stronger, much too strong. It is, in fact, almost—that is to say, quite definitely—deviant—"

"My dear child, correct me if I am mistaken, but are you not trying to tell me that you love the young man?"

She could never have brought herself to pronounce the word. Unable to meet his eyes, she nodded.

"But how delightful, my dear. What could be more agreeable, or more natural?"

Obviously he failed to grasp the situation. "But, Uncle—you can't have forgotten what Dref is . . . ?"

"A splendid lad, absolutely first-rate . . ."

"Yes, he is that—"

"Quite remarkable, in fact, and obviously devoted to you."

"Certainly he is a very generous and steadfast friend."

"Ah? Is that all? Forgive me, my dear, I am no judge of such things, but I should certainly have thought the boy thoroughly enamored—"

Enamored? Dref? She shook her head emphatically. "No, no, he isn't at all. Dref's not that sort."

"What sort is that?"

"Oh, you know—the sort with terribly strong emotions. He's too clever, cool, and contained for that. He's just not a person of great sentiment."

"No? He is not? You know him well, my dear, and I will certainly trust your judgment, but it is most confusing. Am I mistaken, or was it not a sudden access of powerful emotion, resulting in violence, that was the cause of young Dref's flight from Derrivalle the summer before last? Certainly it was much against his own interests to thump your poor father. Why should he have done so if he is quite devoid of strong sentiment?"

"Well—well—a momentary lapse."

"Is it not possible, my child, that you misjudge the boy?"

"I don't know. Perhaps. But that's not really the point, Uncle Quinz. You haven't forgotten that Dref was once one of our *serfs*?"

"And that is a source of trouble?"

"Need you ask? We are Exalted!"

"Ah. Exalted. Serf. Seigneur. But do you not sometimes feel, my dear, that we inhabit a world wherein such terms no longer hold great meaning? Perhaps the very concepts have grown obsolescent. Myself, I wonder if that is such a bad thing."

"You sound as if Dref's got you reading Shorvi Nirienne. This is all very well in theory, Uncle Quinz, but tell me truly how you would feel if a member of your own vo Derrivalle family were actually to mingle pure Exalted blood with the blood of a serf."

"Delighted for her, my dear—provided it was the right serf."

"You wouldn't despise her?"

"I should love her as much as ever, and wish her every happiness."

"You really mean that, don't you? It's hard to believe. Oh, Uncle Quinz, you're kinder than I deserve, but you'll never be called upon to prove it. Weak as I am, yet I shall never disgrace myself, for Dref himself unwittingly prevents it. He thinks of nothing but Shorvi Nirienne, and it's as if he doesn't see me, as if I'm invisible, or nonexistent. Amusing, is it not?"

"Master Nirienne's fate will not always hang in the balance," Uncle Quinz observed mildly. "One day soon the poor gentleman's affairs will be settled."

"I don't think that's apt to change matters. Better if it doesn't, really. Perhaps if I simply endure, this irregular fit will pass of its own accord."

"Ah. Does it show any sign of doing so, my dear?"

"Not the slightest. My mind is not my own, and I hate it. I've never found myself so hopelessly boxed, Uncle. Oh—well, once perhaps, and it felt a good deal the same."

"And when was that?"

"The year before last, when I was still a Maid of Honor at the Beviaire. There was a gentleman at Court—eminent, one whose name you'd recognize—whose attention fastened upon me for a time. He sent me a silver locket, filled with an unusual perfume—"

"But what a delightful offering."

"That is a matter of opinion. I wore the locket night and day—for somehow it seemed I could not do otherwise—and I breathed its perfume continually. The days passed, the perfume took a hold upon my mind, and I couldn't stop thinking of the donor. It struck me as wrong and somehow unnatural that I should think of him that way, but I couldn't stop. Uncle Quinz, you know so much, are you familiar with any magical perfume or essence capable of producing the effect I describe?"

"Indeed I am." Uncle Quinz was looking concerned. "Permit me to observe that this nameless gentleman of yours was less than entirely scrupulous."

"That is putting it mildly. At any rate, several days passed, and then the gentleman invited me to dine with him alone in his apartment—an invitation that I accepted."

"Perhaps you had best stop there, my poor child. I fear you are about to impart confidences you will later regret."

"No, Uncle, I've nothing to hide. I went and I dined with him, and then there were overtures that I was much inclined to accept. But there was always a voice inside me telling me that it was wrong—that it was unreal, insubstantial, unnatural. They weren't *my* real feelings or preferences at all. And then I remembered the time we helped Dref, when I thought you had turned me into a wolf when you hadn't really, and it was something like that. I knew then that he'd used magic to influence me, and I was so angry and scared and disgusted at the thought that somehow I found the will to throw the locket away. The moment I did so, it was all right. I was myself again, as if I'd awakened from a dream, and I went away from there."

"*Did* you, my dear? Well done, very well done indeed. That is more interesting than you can know."

"These days I've been feeling almost the same as I did when I wore the locket. But now it's even worse; now there's no voice inside telling me that it's wrong or unnatural."

"I see. And tell me, child, have there been any other incidents of this nature?"

"Not exactly. Only once, though, for a moment I thought to hear one of the great Sentients speaking in my mind." Not for the life of her could she have said more of her sensations upon the occasion of her grandmother's execution, but fortunately her uncle did not demand particulars.

"More interesting than you can know," Quinz repeated. "My child, have you never wondered whether you might not have inherited a certain measure of Exalted magical ability?"

"Oh, I have nothing like that, Uncle. There's never been a hint of it in me."

"Is it possible that there have been hints, and you have ignored them?"

"You're thinking that those two little mental shudders I described just now might mean something? But doesn't everybody experience something of the sort from time to time? They don't usually mean anything, do they?"

"Sometimes yes, sometimes no. Should you not like to know?"

"To be honest, I don't really care about it. My mind is set on other things these days."

"Too much so, by your own admission, my dear. You stand badly in need of diversion. Something to fill your hours and occupy your thoughts."

"It isn't as easy as that, Uncle."

"Indeed, it is not at all easy. Child, I am not so simple as to believe that some toy or novelty will crowd the troubles from your mind. Forgive me for observing, however, that your present way of life is most conducive to unhappiness. You sit alone all day, cooped up in a little room and quite idle—an existence all but certain to ensure misery. Activity will scarcely solve your problems, but may perhaps serve to alleviate them. Would you like that?"

"Very much. What must I do, then, Uncle?"

"You must visit with me here every day. We shall drink lemon tea, chat a great deal, and pretend that this pleasant room is my cottage back at Derrivalle."

"That's scarcely a hardship."

"Excellent. And in the course of our conversations, we shall discover the nature of your talent."

"I don't think I have any."

"Perhaps not. We shall see. If it should happen that you've inherited so much as a whisper of the gift, you shall learn to use it."

"It seems unlikely, but I'm willing to try."

"That's the spirit, my dear!"

"When shall we begin?"

"Perhaps tomorrow, in the early evening, before I go out? Would that suit? Best for our purposes to maintain a regular and consistent schedule, and yet—alas—I fear that disruptions in the near future are unavoidable."

"What disruptions?"

"During these past nights, the Inanimates of Sherreen have proved most accommodating, most obliging, and I have accumulated considerable knowledge concerning the captive Valeur magicians and their activities. Poor creatures, they are most unhappy! But not for much longer, I trust, for the day of their deliverance is at hand."

"Why, Uncle! You mean you've really——"

"I am ready to begin. I believe I have hit upon the means of rescuing Houloir Valeur. Once Houloir is safe, I shall turn my attention to his unfortunate siblings and father. I will free them each in turn, and only think, my child, what an adventure it will be!"

In the deepest cellars beneath the Sepulchre slept an assortment of old and unpleasant devices. It would have been an exaggeration to call them Sentients, or Stupefactions; for never, even at the height of their powers, had any of them achieved the full self-awareness of a ZaZa or Kokotte. And yet they were recognizable as debased cousins of the Sentients; products of Exalted magic, endowed by their creators with rudimentary identity, will, and a keen sense of malign purpose. Designed to serve as instruments of torture, they could warp the perceptions of their victims, shaping illusion to suit individual weakness—highly serviceable ability. They had stood abandoned and forgotten throughout the years, but now the eager minions of the Republican Protectorate had rediscovered them, Bierce Valeur was expressing interest, and the Protector himself demanded a reawakening.

And who better suited to perform such a task than Houloir Valeur, whose success with the Sentient Kokotte confirmed an affinity for malevolent machinery?

They had dragged him down to the Sepulchre cellars, setting him to work in the old torture chamber. He had spent his days and nights in that dank windowless place, with its ineradicably bloodstained floor and its walls like sponges sodden with human screams. He had toiled ceaselessly amidst the tranced devices, and eventually his efforts were rewarded. They woke; they expressed themselves; their desires and intentions weighted the dead prison air, pressing like iron upon the too-receptive mind of Houloir Valeur.

Never had he encountered such imbecile malignancy; worse in a way than the straightforward solipsism of the Kokotte, for here was remorseless dire purpose quite unleavened with intelligence. They wanted to break, to crush and demoralize; total conquest was their aim. They were relentless, and they were tireless, which last could scarcely be said of Houloir. The constant pressure of that merciless stupidity exhausted him, and there was no escape from it, not even in sleep, for mechanical cruelties pursued him into his dreams. Remarkable how debilitating it was; and worse yet, unutterably worse, when the newly roused devices were first tested upon live prisoners and he was forced to watch. Houloir was tired all of the time, drained and dejected and despairing. His head ached, his eyes were blurred, his stomach rebellious; often he doubted that his strength could sustain him throughout another night of wretched labor. Somehow, however, he continued. Whiss insisted, and Whiss was to be obeyed at any cost.

He had almost forgotten what the sun looked like, what fresh air smelled like. But this last was apt to be remedied shortly, for Houloir was to be allowed an excursion—nocturnal, and heavily guarded at that, but still, a respite from the Sepulchre. His captors could hardly be called generous; they had need of his services elsewhere, that was all. From time to time, in order to maintain her tranquillity, the Sentient Kokotte required a mental joining. It was thus that she made her needs and preferences known to her human attendants. Houloir, her awakener, was the obvious choice to render this service. It was not to his taste, but it would get him out of the cellar for a little while; and in any case, he had no choice.

The Vanguardsmen were to convey him by night in a closed carriage. Equality Circle would be cordoned off for the occasion, as it was understood that the Kokotte preferred privacy for her communings. Houloir similarly preferred it, but that was incidental.

The appointed hour arrived, and they came for him on time. Amazed, he watched them unshackle his wrists and ankles; the fetters were beginning to seem natural to him.

Out of the cellar and up many stairs, out the door, and into the carriage they hurried him. Houloir was pale and more than a little shaky; tired, moderately ill, and entirely docile. In among the Vanguardsmen they placed him, with big human bulwarks on all sides. Whipsnap, creakrattle, and off they went. The carriage windows were shut, of course. The interior was dark, and Houloir could see next to nothing, but a thin sweet current of outdoor air slid in below the blinds, and his nostrils twitched. Fresh air. It made him think of his cottage on the marshes back in Vaurve Province. Of late he had almost forgotten Vaurve—it seemed so remote, a lovely lost paradise whose memory could only burn. But he thought of it now, for he couldn't help himself, and the tears scalded his eyes. He was grateful then for the darkened interior; they wouldn't witness his weakness, and that was a boon—they disdained him enough as it was.

The resonance of the carriage rattle altered slightly. The grind of the wheels took on a subtly different tone, and Houloir knew that they must be out upon the Bridge Vinculum, retracing the route whereby the cartloads of the condemned were transported from the Sepulchre to execution; a route that might never have been established, had he himself not awakened the— But there was no point in thinking about that. Had the Kokotte remained dormant, Whiss and his cohorts would undoubtedly have devised some other, equally effective means of human extermination.

They came off the Vinculum; they must have been entering the Waterfront

Market. They were still a long way from Equality Circle, and therefore it seemed quite inexplicable that the carriage should suddenly pull up short with a jerk and a creak. Houloir was thrown forward, almost into the lap of the Vanguardsman sitting opposite him. He caught himself in time to avoid collision, and drew back, shrinking rigidly in upon himself. Around him, the soldiers were cursing vigorously in the dark. Presently they wrenched open the window blinds, admitting a trickle of light from the coach lanterns. Even before they had done so, Houloir sensed the working of magic; similar to his own but markedly stronger. Not since leaving Bozhenille Commune had he encountered a force so powerful; depleted and dejected as he was, it seemed something miraculous.

His own training armored him against illusion, but he was able to glimpse as a transparency that which his companions perceived as solidity—a barricade of barrels, sawhorses, sacks, and bales, unremarkable save for its billowing mantle of mist—such a slipshod makeshift structure as the furious citizens might construct in an off hour or two. But there were no citizens in sight—at that hour of the night, the Waterfront Market was all but deserted—and no apparent reason for a blockade. Only Houloir perceived the ruse, and even he did not immediately discern its cause.

The horses, immune to human illusion, stamped and fretted. The Vanguardsmen fumed and blasphemed. Houloir waited and watched; and as he looked on, a bit of the mist detached itself from the cloud, thickened, and coalesced into a slight, insubstantial human figure—an elderly man, white-haired, bespectacled, and seemingly frail. Not a face that Houloir recognized, but here beyond doubt was the source of the illusion; magical potency radiated from the stranger in all-but-palpable waves. Houloir almost wondered that his companions failed to perceive it. But then, his companions seemed in no fit state to perceive much of anything. Transparent gags and blindfolds suddenly wrapped their faces; ghostly irons confined their wrists and ankles. The Vanguardsmen were straining violently and quite unnecessarily against their illusory bonds, clawing at their imaginary blindfolds, hysterical muffled voices barely audible.

Here was a truly impressive demonstration. A high degree of magical proficiency was required to produce an illusion proof against physical resistance. This alien adept, whoever he might be, not only did so, but maintained his control upon five adult Vanguardly minds simultaneously. Houloir wondered and admired.

The stranger calmly approached the carriage, opened the door, and stuck his head in to inquire uncertainly, as if asking directions, "Master Houloir Valeur?" A pleasant, tentative voice with an Exalted accent.

Speechless, Houloir nodded.

"Perhaps you would be kind enough to accompany me, my dear fellow?"

Houloir stared.

"This way, if you would be so good." The stranger leaned in among the flopping soldiers, grasped the prisoner's arm, and neatly plucked him forth.

Houloir found himself standing in the Waterfront Market. He was either being rescued or kidnapped; he wasn't sure which, and was there really a difference? He couldn't quite remember. He was a little light-headed, and his legs had gone rubbery. He tottered slightly. For a moment his resistance to illusion wavered, and he saw the carriage halted before a great solid barricade, and the five Vanguardsmen fettered in iron. Even as he watched, the stranger magician standing beside him spoke softly, and it appeared that the four big carriage wheels shattered, one after another—a beautifully detailed illusion, complete with auditory effects. A masterly performance. Muted squeals escaped the terrified soldiers.

"There, they will not be so quick to follow us now, I think," observed the stranger serenely. "This way, my friend."

But the illusion would collapse at once in the absence of its creator. If the stranger abandoned the site, the Vanguardsmen would instantly perceive the cheat. Houloir's doubt must have communicated itself.

"Following our departure, all will continue safely stable for a minimum of four minutes, perhaps as long as nine," the other explained. "And our fiacre awaits not five minutes from here. Stimulating, is it not?"

There was but one possible explanation.

"Bozhenille Commune?" Houloir guessed.

"Exactly so. Ah, what memories. If only there were time to sit, drink cider, and chat of old times. Another night, perhaps. Come along, my friend. This way."

Dazedly, Houloir Valeur suffered his rescuer to lead him off into the dark.

No one wanted to inform Whiss Valeur. To confront the Protector with ill tidings had never been an easy matter, and these days, it was downright unsafe. At the very least, the bearer of bad news might expect to suffer a blast of scorching, screaming abuse. Those less fortunate were often shoved and slapped, or even handed over to the Vanguardsmen for a beating. And now things were growing worse; twice within the past week, unlucky messengers had been stripped of rank and clapped into prison. It seemed that the famous gunpowder temper was waxing all but uncontrollable; a disturbing development. Perhaps the cares and burdens of high office were responsible, for the Protector *was* plagued with unusual troubles these days, his nerves understandably chafed. The public trial of the Nirienne Gang, originally conceived as a stylized propagandistic ballet, had taken on an unwelcome character of its own. The spectacle designed to glorify the

Reparationist regime somehow managed to produce the very opposite effect. No doubt the slippery glibness of the defendants was to blame. Granting the prisoners leave to defend themselves had been a terrible blunder; all five of them proved unexpectedly proficient. Certainly it was no surprise that they were articulate, but no one could have foreseen the traitors' collective power over the emotions and imaginations of the spectators. The public loved them; it was simple, idiotic, and ungovernable as that. The crowd loved the cobwebby quaintness of the old Bulaude siblings; the fire of Riclairc; the fortitude of Frezhelle, who appeared every day with his wounded head artistically bandaged; above all loved the eloquence and spirit of Shorvi Nirienne himself. The potential danger of these uncontrolled Nirienniste outpourings was incalculable. At times, it did not seem entirely impossible that the prisoners might succeed in acquitting themselves. Already, the signs were ominous. All over Sherreen, Niriennism was enjoying an unlikely resurgence. Everywhere, the citizens were grumbling, speculating, even criticizing Reparationist policy. Some presumed to question the continuing necessity of the mass human sacrifice that was officially termed "Vonahrish Purification." They were prating of moderation and tolerance, oblivious of the Reparationist principle that condemned tolerance of seditious speech or writing as counterrevolutionary. The weaker vessels were whining for an end to bloodshed, a return to normalcy, a new beginning. A couple of wisely anonymous popular journalists actually dared to censure Whiss Valeur, and copies of their filth were turning up all over town. Several had even made their way into the halls of Congress itself.

No wonder the Protector was tense and edgy these days, irritable and unusually suspicious. No wonder he was haggard, faintly green of complexion, much given to nervous twitchings and sudden rages. No wonder nobody wanted to tell him that his brother had escaped.

Hoping for safety in numbers, they organized a small committee consisting of Whiss's most trusted allies; Congressmen Poulpe, Pieuvre, Lemery, and Myette. And to bear the brunt of the Protector's fury—Chorl Valeur, plus two of the Vanguardsmen from whom the prisoner had been stolen. In the morning, the reluctant messengers sought their master in his office at the Committee of National Welfare.

Whiss Valeur sat at his desk, pen in hand. It was early, but he had already been there for hours. He was attired in his famous black suit, clothing and person scrupulously ordered, as always. But the shadows beneath the preternatural eyes spoke of sleepless nights, and the thin face was more than ordinarily pinched. He glanced up from his work as the visitors entered, and his eyes narrowed. Clearly, the size of the delegation had roused his ready suspicions.

It fell to the lot of one of the luckless Vanguardsmen to enlighten the Protector.

The wretched soldier, all but tongue-tied, managed to blurt his fantastic story: makeshift barricade in the Waterfront Market; bespectacled ancient materializing out of the fog; gags and blindfolds and iron fetters; exploding carriage wheels; and when it was all over—Master Houloir Valeur gone. The second Vanguardsman, likewise an eyewitness, reluctantly verified the tale.

Several moments of agonizing silence followed. The visitors had mentally braced themselves against explosion, but the Protector's reaction defied expectation. Motionless and stone-faced, Whiss stared out the window. After a time, his eyes dropped almost idly to a letter open on the desk before him. Beside the letter lay the miniature portrait of a young girl: pretty face, large eyes, fair curls. Whiss studied the letter and image briefly, then slid both across the desk. "These arrived yesterday. Examine them," he commanded.

Mystified, the visitors crowded in close to read a blotched message from "A Patriot of Fabeque." Certain phrases leaped from the page:

. . . There is an old magical Exalted named Quinz vo Derrivalle, coming to Sherreen to make trouble for you . . . They want to kill you . . . If you don't find this old man and his girl, they will bring you down by magic, you can depend on it . . .

"You see," said Whiss. His voice was low and neutral; not genuinely calm, but rather, rigidly restrained. "You see this. Now, what have you to say?"

Nobody was particularly eager to say anything. But young Poulpe, certain as any man could be of the Protector's fragile regard, replied impassively, "Last night's events confirm the letter's truth, Compeer. This old magical freak of nature exists, he is here in Sherreen, and he works against you. Thus he must be hunted down and eliminated, for the enemies of the Republican Protector are the enemies of Vonahr."

"Good." Whiss nodded slowly. "At least there is *one* among my so-called allies who dares to speak the truth to me, *one* whom I may trust. Congressman Poulpe's candor is to be commended. But even the best and brightest among you, it seems, have not considered the full implications of this incident. It remains for me alone to do that, as always. Come, do you not see what this means?"

"Vanguard, Vonahrish Guard, and the Gendarmerie must all be placed on the alert. We will utilize every resource," Pieuvre essayed.

"You state the obvious, as usual," Whiss informed him. "Come, are you stupid? We have discovered an enemy. Already he has struck at us. But surely you don't pretend to believe that this old man is alone, or rather, assisted only by some female?"

"It is possible," Chorl Valeur spoke up for the first time. He was glum and droopy as ever, but somehow found the energy to contradict his formidable son. "Given sufficient magical strength, this Quinz vo Derrivalle may have little if any need of assistance."

"Ah, no doubt *you* would think so, Father. No doubt this formerly-Exalted traitor with his magic claims your respect and admiration. Perhaps you are not sorry he has come?" Whiss did not await reply. "But no, don't insult my intelligence with such nonsense. He can't be working alone. There is conspiracy afoot. I've long suspected as much, and now it has been confirmed. We do not yet know the extent of the plot—the number of traitors, their identities, their whereabouts—but all will be revealed in time. It is by no means impossible that treachery infects the Congress—perhaps even the Committee of National Welfare itself. Until the matter has been thoroughly investigated, no man may consider himself above suspicion." Whiss's probing stare chilled each of his visitors in turn.

Only Congressman Poulpe was able to sustain the scrutiny unmoved. Marble composure intact, he observed, "I applaud the Protector's sagacity and resolution. I support his endeavors without reservation, in proof whereof, I offer to lead the hunt for this formerly-Exalted traitor Quinz vo Derrivalle and his accomplice. I will leave no stone unturned."

"Excellent. That is what I like to hear. And how do you propose to go about it, Compeer?" Whiss demanded.

"We have the names of the traitors, descriptions of the old man, a portrait of the girl. We know that they arrived recently. That is considerable information. I will alert the soldiers and police. I will have an artist produce a woodcut copy of the miniature that can be printed up in quantity and posted all over town. I will summon the five Vanguardsmen who saw the old man, and with their assistance, an artist may perhaps succeed in producing an adequate likeness that can also be widely distributed. I will dispatch trustworthy agents to check the various lodging houses for new tenants. I will, it goes without saying, relay all pertinent facts to the NuNu, in hope that she will pass the word on to her nits. I will request that the Protector arrange extensive communion between his kinsmen and the Inanimates of Shereen. All of this, of course, is only a beginning. If these efforts do not bear immediate fruit, there are many other avenues to follow. Give me leave, and I will explore them all."

For the first time since the interview began, Whiss rose from his chair. "Intelligence. Energy. Vision. Resolve. Efficiency. Loyalty. All that I could hope for in the best of patriots." The great green eyes suffused. He stretched his hand forth across the desk. "Compeer, I salute you from the bottom of my heart. You are my other self."

"Protector." Congressman Poulpe clasped the proffered hand. For once, a faint flush of rose stained his sculpted pallor.

The witnesses exchanged uneasy looks.

"Go, then, and hunt like a falcon," Whiss advised. "I know you will succeed. And the rest of you, profit by this admirable example."

It was not clear to what extent they were apt to profit.

Whiss Valeur pressed his minion's hand, then released it. "You understand your mission," he informed his visitors. "Now go fulfill it. All of you are henceforth commanded by Congressman Poulpe. Learn from him."

Multiple unfriendly glances skewered the postadolescent marble god. Poulpe himself appeared unaware. His lapis eyes, bright and hard as sunlit ice, were turned inward.

"Go," Whiss commanded, and his visitors filed from the room like obedient automata. "Father, you remain."

Chorl halted reluctantly.

"You, with all your study, must know a great many of the Vonahrish adepts. Is the name Quinz vo Derrivalle familiar to you?"

"I have heard it," Chorl confessed.

"Ah, I thought so, I saw it in your eyes. You can keep nothing from me, you know. Now, what can you tell me of this Derrivalle traitor?"

"Very little. I have heard that he is unusually accomplished and unusually reclusive, even by the standards of our discipline."

"And that's all? If there's anything more in that head of yours, be certain I will root it out. You can keep nothing from me, Father."

"There is nothing more."

"Well. Perhaps. We shall see. I miss very little, you know. Very little." Abruptly, Whiss stepped out from behind the desk and began to pace. "These eyes of mine are excellent, they see clearly—they see everything. Not everyone realizes how little escapes me. Those who underestimate my eyes sometimes commit the error of plotting against me, and it is so foolish. What conspiracy, after all, will escape the vigilance of one who needs as little sleep as I? I can go for nights on end without sleep, you know. Often I do so. It is a gift of time, an extension of life. I treasure those stolen hours. I invest them wisely, and of course, I see more than anyone guesses."

Chorl watched his son apprehensively.

"For example—perhaps you thought I did not observe your pleasure in my brother Houloir's defection." Whiss rounded suddenly, and Chorl started. "You were glad when you learned he was gone, weren't you, Father? *Weren't you?*"

"I don't deny it," Chorl replied in a low voice.

"Well, at least you are no hypocrite. You may as well be glad while you can, for I will get him back, you know. I still have you, Eularque, and Phlosine. The three of you will use your powers to locate Houloir. I give you forty-eight hours to do it."

"Houloir's powers are sufficient to shield him against observation. I don't think we could find him."

"Nor would you if you could. You are quite transparent to me. I know you hope that Eularque and Phlosine will likewise abandon me. No doubt you would enjoy watching them turn their united power against me. You'd join them if you could. That is what you desire, isn't it?"

"I desire their safety."

"But not mine. They could carry my head on a pike through the streets and you wouldn't turn a hair, would you? Well, don't look for it. I know how to protect myself; I am entirely invulnerable. My siblings know the consequences of treachery, and they won't risk it. As for Houloir and his formerly-Exalted savior, I'll have them both within hours. This Quinz vo Derrivalle will henceforth devote his talents to the great patriotic cause. I'll talk to him, I'll win him over. I see you think I can't do it. But you're quite wrong; I can persuade anybody to anything. This Quinz vo Derrivalle will give me his loyalty, and he will reveal the traitors in our midst. And when the traitors about me have been exterminated—and Nirienne's trial is properly concluded—and the insurrections in the provinces have been crushed—and the threat of a Strellian invasion has been dealt with—and the foreign powers have recognized the legitimacy of the Republican Protectorate—when these difficulties have been resolved, then we may lay aside the instruments of terror and set about building the ideal Vonahrish state. For once the gangrenous limbs have been severed, and all infection burnt away, what remains to hinder perfect healing and perfect regeneration?"

"What remains, indeed?" Chorl murmured. "Will anything remain?"

"We shall not always bathe in these rivers of blood." The headlong, boiling rush of words resumed. "One day soon, Vonahr will be clean, perfectly clean and free of taint, beautiful, pure, peaceful, and justly ordered. Isn't that a prize worth any price? Well? Isn't it? You stare at me with great sheep's eyes. Are you afraid to speak, or haven't you anything to say? Come, tell me honestly what you think."

"I think perhaps you need to sleep."

"Is that your idea of a joke?" Whiss's pallid face suffused. "Do you deliberately provoke me? Take care, my patience is not unlimited. You may go, Father. You're not worth talking to, it's a waste of my time, so get out. I know that's what you want, to get away from me. Did you hear me—I said get out! Go! Get OUT!" Whiss's voice rose to full shout. His eyes, jaw muscles, and the vein in his temple all bulged.

Chorl thankfully hurried for the exit. Once out in the corridor, however, he paused to listen. On the other side of the closed office door, Whiss had resumed his feverish pacing. To and fro raced the Republican Protector, strides ever longer and faster. Chorl Valeur lingered there for some time, but never heard his son's pace slacken. The minutes passed, and the quick, driven footsteps went on and on.

So what did you do with Houloir?" asked Eliste. She sat in the wing chair before the fireplace in Uncle Quinz's room. It was early evening. The curtains were drawn, the candles lit. The footsteps of the upstairs tenant thundered overhead. Next door, someone was singing off-key. In the corner, Glorielle hummed and whirred ambiguously. The atmosphere breathed noisy normalcy.

"Took the poor fellow straight to the North Gate," Quinz told her. "Gave him enough money to carry him home to Vaurve, where he will no doubt find refuge. Waited to see that he got through safely, then came back here, for solitude and rest. I was much fatigued."

"I should think so. But, Uncle, however did you sneak him past the Boomette?"

"Ah, my dear, Master Houloir did not require my assistance in so small a matter. His own powers more than sufficed to deflect the Sentient's attention. The Boomette is not very clever, you know. Not nearly as clever as my Glorielle. Is she, my pretty?"

The Sentient in the corner beeped complacently.

"The Boomette's intentions are good, but her viewpoint decidedly limited. It is not difficult to deceive her."

"Hmf. Not difficult for you, perhaps. But really, Uncle Quinz, was it such a good idea to send Houloir Valeur away? If he's so gifted, couldn't he have helped you to rescue the others—his kinsmen, and Shorvi Nirienne?"

"Theoretically, perhaps; but in truth, it is not as easy as that. Poor Houloir has been so beaten and broken, so bullied and betrayed, that I must question his ability to withstand further trial. Alas, he has been sadly damaged. We may hope he will heal in time, but for now, we must expect of him neither strength nor material assistance. Best that he return to his home, repose, and recovery. As for the rescue of Shorvi Nirienne—I fear that is quite beyond my power."

"Beyond *your* power, Uncle?"

"Considerably. You see, the unfortunate Master Nirienne languishes in the Sepulchre, whose taciturnity resists my best efforts."

"Taciturnity? You're saying you've tried to talk to the Sepulchre itself?"

"Repeatedly. But she will not answer. It is not that she's unconscious—I am certain of that. She hears me, but she will not speak, or perhaps she cannot. It is as if her power to communicate has lapsed, or else she has forgotten it. I cannot believe that this was her architect's intent, and therefore I may only conclude that the Sepulchre has gone mad."

"Mad?"

"That would seem the most reasonable explanation. The rage, terror, malice, and agony of her various tenants have swamped her consciousness. She cannot communicate, she cannot understand or make herself understood. It is a great injustice. This silence isolates her, a sorry fate for such a fine sturdy heap of granite, or indeed for anything else. Is it not? Poor Sepulchre, she is quite a sad case. Perhaps someday things will change for her, but for now, she is solitary and mute and mad."

"So you have no knowledge of the prisoners, Nirienniste or otherwise?"

"Next to none. Mistress Phlosine Valeur is there, I know so much. Likewise there are Nirienne and his friends. Beyond that, I know nothing."

"Uncle, what are we to do, then?"

"Child, that is unanswerable. Easier for us both to concentrate upon more immediate concerns. For example—have you performed the exercises I assigned you?"

"Oh, most of them. I've tried." Eliste shifted her weight uncomfortably, and something impelled her to add, "But I don't see what good they do. Nothing comes of them, nothing at all."

"Well, let us see. Bear with me, my child." Uncle Quinz bowed his head, spoke at near-inaudible length. Moments later, the room appeared to fill with butter-flies—scores of dinnerplate-size creatures with gorgeous gossamer wings in every color.

"Oh, how beautiful!" Eliste clapped her hands in delight.

"There is more. Listen."

The butterflies began to sing, a tiny chorus whose piercing sweetness had more in common with the melody of nightingales than the buzzings and twangings of insects. Puzzled, Eliste peered closely at the nearest butterfly. Tucked between the translucent rainbow insect wings, she spied the tiny beaked head, vibrating throat, rounded breast, and feathery tail of a minute bird. She extended a finger, and the butterfly-bird came at once to perch there, singing.

"Oh, Uncle Quinz," Eliste breathed, enchanted, "this must be the best one you've ever done for me!"

"I am delighted that it pleases you, my dear. Now make it go away."

"I couldn't, it's much too pretty."

"My child, I should be much obliged if you would make the effort."

"Oh, very well, I'll try." Eliste did try, maintaining rigorous mental tension for several minutes; at the end of which time, the butterfly-birds remained colorful, vociferous, and seemingly substantial as ever. She gave it up all at once, letting herself go mentally and physically limp. "Sorry, Uncle. I did my best."

"Curious. Curious. I cannot account for it."

"Well, I warned you. I just don't have the knack."

"You possess some slight measure of talent, my dear. To be honest, it is extremely minor, and yet I would stake all my years of study that *something* is there in you, which should with training serve to arm you against magical illusion. Let us explore the problem. To begin with, have you at this moment no consciousness whatever of the influence at work upon your mind?"

"The sense of wrongness, yes," Eliste answered at once. "I can feel that, and it warns me that I see an illusion."

"Excellent. Excellent, my dear. That is the difficult part—that initial perception. Once you have got that, the rest is relatively easy. You recognize the existence of the illusion—now, simply banish it."

"But I can't, Uncle. I know it isn't real, but that doesn't make it go away."

"There is an obstacle here that we have somehow overlooked."

"Well, don't worry about it. Your illusions are so charming, I'm happy to be deceived. I could look at them all day long."

"Perhaps that is all the trouble. The incentive is not there. Let us try something different. Less charm, perhaps." Uncle Quinz waved his hand, and the butterfly-birds vanished, much to Eliste's regret. He spoke again, and a new vision appeared. Between bed and bureau hulked a sad monster with the vast hirsute body of an ape, bearded horned head of a tusked goat, tail of a bedraggled rooster, and ridiculous vestigial wings sprouting from the shoulders. The creature's wiry hair was clotted with filth and feces, alive with vermin. Urine was running down its leg to puddle on the floor at its feet. Presently it squatted and defecated; an abominable stench arose.

"There, is it not truly disgusting? Is it not repulsive?" Uncle Quinz inquired with modest pride. "Is it not loathsome beyond belief? Do not be afraid, my dear, it cannot harm you. Now, be a brave child and make it go away. I know you can do it. Do not let fear cloud your judgment."

Eliste exploded into gales of laughter. "Oh, Uncle, that must be the ugliest thing I ever saw!" she managed to splutter. "It's hilarious—I love it!"

"Well, make it go away, my dear."

"Oh, please—not yet!"

"This is not as I had hoped." Perplexed and faintly disappointed, Quinz waved his hand. The monster and all concomitant unpleasantness vanished.

"Please, Uncle, bring it back!"

"Another approach is required, it would seem. Let us try once more." Quinz spoke. Miniature apple trees in full bloom sprouted from the rug. The scent of apple blossoms filled the air.

"Pretty." Eliste smiled.

"There is more. Watch."

Beneath the little trees materialized the doll-size figure of a young girl: slender form, pretty face, large eyes, abundant fair hair.

"It's I!"

"So it is, my dear. Keep watching."

A second figure materialized beside the first. A young man, this time: tall, lean and loose-jointed, angular features, black hair and eyes.

"Dref." Eliste's smile faded. "Uncle, what are you doing?"

No answer.

The two small figures strolled beneath the flowering trees. Dref-figure slid his arm about Eliste-figure's waist. Eliste-figure leaned her head against his shoulder.

Eliste felt the furious color burn her cheeks. "Uncle, this isn't funny!" she exclaimed. "It isn't even fair! I don't like it."

No answer.

Silent breezes stirred the miniature branches, and the tiny blossoms snowed down to lodge in Eliste-figure's hair. Dref-figure brushed the petals away, while Eliste-figure laughed up at him.

"Uncle, you're using what I told you in confidence to mock me—shame on you! How could you?"

No answer.

Dref-figure kissed Eliste-figure on the lips.

Eliste sprang from her chair. The tears of angry humiliation stung her eyes. "I won't watch any more of this!" she cried. *"I won't have it!"* Rage and shame boiled along her veins. All the emotion and determination in her focused like sunlight bent through a lens upon the pretty little pastoral. For the first time, the exercises she had dutifully practiced throughout the past days held meaning—they had taught her the nature of total rejection, and how to achieve it.

Trees, flowers, and doll figures vanished in an instant.

"Phew!" said Uncle Quinz. "Such violence, my child!"

Uncomprehending, she stared from the empty floor to her uncle's face, and back again. "Did I do that?"

"Indeed you did, and very thoroughly, my dear. Congratulations! I am proud indeed of my pretty niece." She was still staring at him, and Uncle Quinz's gratification gave way to anxiety. "My child, you are not still angry? I regret the unkindness of my method. You will pardon your old uncle?"

"Oh, yes. Yes, of course. But that illusion—it was what I did that broke it? You didn't do it yourself?"

"Certainly not. Can you not feel the truth of that within yourself?"

"No—well, maybe—I'm not sure—"

"Control and assurance are lacking, but daily practice will develop both. You *will* continue to practice, my dear? It is a worthwhile effort, is it not?"

"I suppose so, and yet there's something almost sad about it. To see the illusions for the shadows that they are—to know that a thought, a mere mental shrug, can destroy them—the magic will no longer seem half so lovely and wonderful."

"An unfortunate truth, my child. That is the price of understanding. And yet, a trained resistance to illusion furnishes powerful protection. I should like to know that my niece's mind is proof against tampering."

"I, too, so I must endure clear vision, I suppose. I'll continue practicing, Uncle."

"Excellent, my dear. I do not think you'll regret it."

Uncle Quinz left shortly thereafter; of late he spent his nights fraternizing with several of the equestrian statues dotted about the neighborhood of the City Armory. Eliste returned to her own room, resigned to yet another solitary dinner. But not this time, as it happened, for she met Dref coming in. She hadn't seen or spoken with him in over two days; he had been off upon his nameless errands. Seeing him now, for the first time in so many hours, she was struck by his look of tired despondency. Not like Dref at all. "Bad news?" she inquired uneasily.

"Yes. Better sit down."

She complied. He was acting as if she were the one about to receive the bad news. Her uneasiness increased as she watched him draw a paper from his pocket, unfold and smooth it.

"Here, look. As of this evening, these are posted all over town."

She accepted the document with reluctance, and forced herself to look at it. What she beheld exceeded her worst expectations.

By Order of the Committee of National Welfare: REWARD, One Hundred Rekkoes, for information leading to the arrest of . . .

Two faces, two enemies of the people, two names: formerly-Exalted Quinz vo Derrivalle, formerly-Exalted Eliste vo Derrivalle. Two physical descriptions, accurate in all particulars. As for the pictures, a pair of crude woodcuts—the image of Uncle Quinz was unrecognizable, but Eliste's own likeness was surprisingly good: the heart shape of her face, wide set of the eyes, and curve of the lips were all accurately portrayed.

Eliste studied the poster in silence. Finally, she raised incredulous eyes.

"We'll never know for certain how they got your names and faces, but I've a theory," Dref answered the unspoken question. "You remember back at Derrivalle, when the Compeers' patrol came to your uncle's cottage? They weren't deceived by the illusory obstacles blocking the path; they knew just where they were going."

"I didn't understand that. Uncle Quinz said that someone must have watched us, but I can't imagine how."

"Nor can I. But I can imagine who. My sister's parting words to me were 'Well, maybe I know a thing or two that you don't.' I think she meant it."

"Stelli? But what could she know, and what could she do? And why didn't you say anything about it at the time?"

"I didn't take her altogether seriously. A mistake, perhaps. Was there anything in your father's house that she could have used to watch us? A viewing lens devised by one of those gifted ancestors of yours, perhaps?"

"I don't know. It's horrible to think of them rooting through our things."

"That's the least of concerns. Clearly, the insight afforded our busy friends of the Committee stops short at the gates of Sherreen, else no need of this effort. But you perceive the danger."

Eliste studied her own likeness. It was too fantastic, almost dreamlike. *RE-WARD, One Hundred Rekkoes* . . . Unbelievable. Wordlessly, she nodded.

"Don't think of going out again. You'll have to stay inside from now on."

Stay inside. Practical. Her mind unfroze. "What about Uncle Quinz? He just went out. He doesn't know about this, does he? We need to go after him, warn him—"

"Softly. In the first place, your uncle has eyes, and if he's gone out, then he's already seen this notice, because they're posted everywhere."

"But he's so abstracted, he just doesn't pay attention—"

"Secondly, we hardly need fear for Master Quinz—his abilities shield him against ordinary danger. It's for you that I'm chiefly concerned. It was a mistake bringing you back to Sherreen."

"Well, there wasn't much choice at the time."

"There is now, however. I am going to arrange your emigration. We'll send you to Strell."

"We'll do nothing of the sort. I'm not going, and this time there's nothing you can do about it. Please don't try to bludgeon me with fifty reasons, and don't tell me how foolish and childish I am. Only listen for a moment. You ought to understand that I don't want to leave my uncle at a time like this—leave him a stranger and a fugitive in this city that must seem to him like an alien hostile world. He'll be happier if I'm with him, and you *do* want him happy and calm, don't you? If he's not, how can he help your Nirienne? Speaking of whom, do you yourself not spend your days and nights plotting your leader's rescue with fellow Niriennistes? I know you won't answer that, but perhaps you could answer this instead: can you at this point spare the time to engineer my escape? It's a considerable undertaking, and you are much occupied. Would it not be best to wait until Master Nirienne's affairs have been settled one way or another?"

"You needn't fear that I'll call you foolish and childish. You are growing far too clever."

"No, I'm only talking common sense. I'll stay in these rooms, and nobody will ever see me. The other tenants here have scarcely glimpsed me, and now they won't see me at all. I'll change my hair so I look less like the picture. I don't think it's such a good likeness anyway—my chin's not really that pointed, is it? I'll do what I must, but I won't leave Sherreen. And there is an end to the matter."

"If I could force you to go, be certain I'd do it. You're mad to remain, you realize that? What will it take to make you understand—"

"Oh, Dref, you worry too much. I'll be safe enough in this place for a little while—only until my uncle's business here is done. That's best for everyone, isn't it?"

"Everyone but you. This lunatic obstinacy of yours is—"

"Shouldn't you save your concern for Shorvi Nirienne, who needs it more than I? What's happening at the trial?"

"The predictable. Shorvi and the others defend themselves too well, with an eloquence surely proving inconvenient to Public Prosecutor, justices, and jurors of the Tribunal. It cannot continue, and it won't be long before their mouths are stopped."

"What, you mean that Nirienne and the others will be murdered before the trial ends?"

"And cheat the Kokotte of her due? Scarcely. It is far more likely that Shorvi's right to speak in his own defense will simply be revoked upon some pretext or other. Thereafter, the problem resolves itself."

"Then what would you do, Dref? For I know you'd do something."

"I? When even Quinz vo Derrivalle admits himself defeated by the Sepulchre's silence, what could I hope to accomplish?"

"Oh, false modesty doesn't suit you; there's no limit to your hopes or your audacity. I know that you and your friends will try to do something for Nirienne, and I also know there's no point in trying to dissuade you. You speak of *my* lunatic obstinacy? Ha. I only hope that you don't get yourself killed. Your death won't serve Shorvi Nirienne in the least, and the world would be less diverting without you in it."

"Ah, unsuspected depths of sentiment. Well, I'll try to see to it that you aren't deprived of your diversions."

" 'Try'? You could do better than that, if you chose."

"Exalted Miss, I shall begin to suspect that you care."

"Certainly I care." She hadn't meant to let that slip out. Wrong. Foolish. Painful. Unsay it. She continued, almost without pause, "You are far too clever and amusing to die so young. I cannot abide waste." Very insouciant, very detached—almost worthy of Zeralenn herself. She glanced quickly at Dref, wondering if he had noticed her lapse. She thought for a moment to catch a shadow darken his face—disappointment? But that was probably her imagination.

"No? A most un-Exalted attitude, which years and experience will no doubt serve to correct."

As always, his sangfroid was more than a match for her own. She should have been relieved. She wasn't.

"In the meantime," Dref continued, "do not concern yourself. There are matters of more immediate significance to consider."

"Such as?"

"Your uncle. It is within the next two or three nights, I believe, that he intends to liberate Eularque Valeur."

Within the City Armory, perpetual twilight reigned. The days and nights merged indistinguishably, undifferentiated by incident or visible change. Eularque Valeur had no idea how long he had been there. For him, time had ceased to exist. He thought no more of Vaurve Province, with its low marshy expanses, its open skies, freedom, and quiet. Those things were gone, perhaps forever. In their place remained only stone walls and locked doors, iron fetters, iron-hard guards, and the fervid caprices of the ZaZa, to whom he was bound by a length of stout chain.

Such enforced proximity fostered an unwelcome intimacy; he knew the Sentient far too well for comfort. Her homicidal longings pressed relentlessly upon his mind. Distressing and debilitating though it was, Eularque never dreamed of rebellion. The outsize hands of Cousin Bierce had long since knocked all thought of revolt clean out of his head. He was here to stay so long as Whiss wanted him. Until Whiss pleased to decree otherwise, there was no way out.

Habituated now to submissiveness, it scarcely occurred to Eularque that others about him might prove less so. Thus he, like his guards, was taken quite by surprise when the Armory literally came under fire; unlike his guards, however, he recognized the magical nature of the attack.

He had been asleep, which probably meant that it was night. He had been dreaming of fire, green dragon's breath lancing into the heart of a crowd—the ZaZa's impulses again, the ZaZa's invasive desires. The yelling of the Vanguardsmen kicked him awake, and he opened his eyes upon an inferno. For a moment he thought he was still caught up in the Sentient's violent dream. Flames leapt everywhere, bright tongues writhed, dense smoke billowed, Vanguardsmen scurried hysterically. Eularque started up with a cry; then instinct strengthened by rigorous training came to his aid, and he sensed the working of magic. At once he perceived the nature of the illusion—a truly masterful production, visual complexity enhanced by elaborate auditory, olfactory, and tactile effects. Eularque could actually hear the crackle of flames; scent the acrid smoke, taste it on his tongue, feel its scratch at the back of his throat; likewise, he could feel the furnace blast of heat. Spectacular, but where had it come from?

The Vanguardsmen were in no position to appreciate artistry. To them, it was all horribly real. No time now to consider the significance of this obvious act of arson, the identity of the perpetrator, or the possible consequences, which included the destruction of the irreplaceable ZaZa. Certainly no time to contemplate the Protector's screaming fury, the demotion or arrest of the officers on duty. No time for anything other than flight, for the Armory cellar housed uncounted barrels of powder; when the flames reached them, the resulting explosion was likely to wipe out half the District. Choking, coughing, and half blind, the Vanguardsmen stumbled for the fire-wreathed exit.

But simple humanity, no less than duty, demanded the prisoner's removal. The poor wretch could hardly be left to burn; he was, after all, the Protector's own brother. Accordingly, an officer and his subordinate made their way to Eularque's side. The officer bore two keys; one for the anklets whose connecting chain bound prisoner to Sentient, and one for the collar whose chain was fixed to a staple sunk in the wall.

Eularque looked on with interest as they unshackled him. He perceived the shape of the illusion as clearly as he saw its falsity. Anklets and collar snapped open; but to the Vanguardsmen, both appeared securely locked. The cursing officer jiggled keys, yanked, pried, and twisted. The locks appeared to resist. The subordinate discharged his pistol, blasting chain from staple; but to him, the attachment appeared unbroken. The illusory fire raged fiercely; flames shot up the walls, danced along the wooden rafters overhead, even licked at ZaZa's silvery scales. Waves of heat singed hair, scorched garments, blistered skin. The Vanguardsmen could bear no more. Bestowing final glances of wordless pity upon the doomed captive, both men sprinted for the exit.

Eularque sat watching them go. Their weaving, scuttling, bunch-backed progress was not unlike the antics of the amateur clowns at the country fairs back in Vaurve Province. Behind him, ZaZa clanked and rattled restlessly. Thin streams of perfectly real, genuinely noxious vapor dribbled from each of her snouts.

"She seems a little uneasy." The voice was pleasant and mildly tentative, the accent Exalted. "Surely the illusion does not alarm her?"

Eularque turned to discover an elderly gentleman apparently emerging from a wall of flame. The stranger was short, slight, and frail; white-haired and bespectacled. His wide eyes bespoke childlike innocence. But here beyond all question was a source of formidable power.

"She is impervious to illusion—she doesn't perceive it at all," Eularque explained. "It's the odd behavior of the Vanguardsmen that arouses her concern."

"But what an extraordinary device, quite astonishing. How I should relish exploring her mind! Alas, it is neither the time nor the place for communion. Another evening, perhaps. For now, other matters must take priority. Master Valeur, are you ready?"

"Ready?"

"To leave this place."

"Really? *May* I?"

"Certainly, my poor friend. As of this moment, you are a free man."

"But Whiss will never bear it."

"He must resign himself."

"There is no telling what harm may befall my brother, my sister, my father—"

"Your brother Houloir has already left Sherreen. Tonight, if you choose, you yourself may set forth for Vaurve."

"*Home.*"

"Hereafter, I mean to free your sister and your father."

"You do?" Eularque was perplexed.

"I do not like to witness the talents of my brethren in the discipline forcibly debased. It offends me, you see. Something must be done."

"But can you?"

"As you see." The stranger's gesture encompassed the ghostly conflagration.

"Bozhenille Commune?"

"Ah, what memories."

"Truly. But who *are* you?"

"I will explain as we go. A hackney is waiting not far from here. Come along, my dear fellow. This way."

This time, nobody volunteered to break the news to Whiss. Even the cherished Congressman Poulpe hardly dared confront the Protector with the fact of this second escape. For a couple of hours, the shining lights of the Committee of National Welfare agonized over the problem. They reached no satisfactory conclusion, and in the end, elected to send a letter. This missive was carried by a solitary messenger, who came in the dimmest hours of dawn, thrust folded communication straight into the line of light showing beneath the Protector's office door, and fled for his life; not even waiting to watch the paper disappear as if sucked into a whirlpool.

Whiss Valeur's reaction went unseen. Closed doors concealed his emotion, if any there was. It was claimed by one or two early-arriving Committee members that those gray hours were enlivened by the crash of furniture striking the walls of the Protector's office, but nobody could attest to the truth of this. Glaziers were later called in to replace the smashed office windows, but the circumstances surrounding the breakage remained obscure.

Thereafter, the Protector secluded himself. No word, spoken or written, issued from his sanctum, past the closed door of which the Committee members tiptoed in awe. The Committee of National Welfare, adequately equipped to function in its leader's absence, called for increased vigilance, a strengthening of the guard about the remaining Valeur captives, new arrests. Whiss himself was ominously mute and invisible.

At the end of thirty-six hours, a folded note slid under the door, out into the corridor, to be pounced upon by inquisitive patriots, who thus discovered that the Protector commanded his father's presence. They summoned Chorl at once, and the old man arrived within minutes.

Chorl was droopy and nervous as always, perhaps more so now than ever before. Interested spectators noted that the old man hesitated a good two minutes outside his son's office door before working up the courage to knock.

Snapping response, and Chorl went in.

The interview was brief and evidently stormy. Behind the closed door, Whiss's voice rose in shouting rage, while Chorl's muttered replies were unintelligible. Minutes later the old man emerged, looking pale and scared. He hurried off as fast as he could go.

Pregnant silence once more fell upon the offices of the Committee. Three hours passed quietly, and then another note issued from Whiss's retreat. The Protector demanded a meeting of the Committee of National Welfare. All fifteen members were commanded to present themselves at once.

It was now past eleven o'clock at night, and over two-thirds of the Committee's membership was absent. Considerable delay ensued, as messengers scoured the various districts of Sherreen in search of the missing men. All were eventually located and dragged from their beds, but it was not until about one in the morning that the meeting actually convened.

Fifteen yawning, bleary-eyed, mildly apprehensive men sat about the long table in the conference room on the top floor of the Palace of Justice. Through the uncurtained windows they could look out across the small courtyard to the vast darkened bulk of the adjoining Sepulchre, whose cells they had proved so instrumental in filling. If patriotic satisfaction derived from such a sight, there was time now to savor it at leisure. For the next two hours, the Committee sat there in total silence. The boldest among them were starting to eye their watches, when chimes sounded the hour of three and Whiss Valeur came in to take his place at the head of the table.

The Protector looked dreadful: haggard and haunted, bilious complexion greener than ever before. He seemed to teeter upon the brink of collapse or hysteria, yet face and voice were rigidly controlled as he observed, "No doubt you are wondering why I have summoned you here tonight."

No answer was forthcoming, and Whiss seemed to expect none, for he continued without pause, "It has long been apparent to me that conspiracy darkens the very heart of the republic—that is, the Committee of National Welfare itself. There are those among us who have sold themselves to the enemies of liberty. Tonight, I will unmask the traitors."

His listeners stared. Suddenly, nobody was at all sleepy.

"They are crafty, determined, tireless, and daring. They are successful, despite the efforts of those who *claim* to serve me, those who *promise* loyalty—" Whiss's accusing eyes stabbed Congressman Poulpe, who sustained the regard impassively. "They spread their poison everywhere. They have corrupted the Constitutional Congress, they have infiltrated the Committee of National Welfare. They are here at this very moment, here in this room. They smile, they lie, they counterfeit patriotism, and they flatter themselves with the thought that we are their foolish dupes. They think themselves safe, but they are mistaken—in the Republic of Vonahr, no enemy of the people is ever safe. We will hunt them down. We will destroy them all. We will begin tonight."

The fifteen members were wide awake now, alert and uneasy. The Committee, long an instrument of terror, was wont to regard itself as inviolable and invulnerable. The thought of treachery arising within the group was novel and disturbing. Whether that treachery was real or a product of the Protector's increasingly erratic fancy would prove a question of limited relevance to the targets of the impending denunciation—either way, the accused were equally doomed. But who were they? How many? Wary, veiled glances roamed the chamber in search of visible guilt.

"Always the Committee of National Welfare has stood as the very embodiment of Vonahrish rectitude. Always its members have shone as patriots, above suspicion. I had thought myself surrounded by men of virtue, men of dedication, loyal Reparationists ready to die for their country and their Protector. Is there any one among you able to comprehend the pain I have suffered in discovering otherwise? Whiss Valeur is betrayed by those in whom he most trusted. It is like a bleeding wound." To the consternation of his audience, the Protector's eyes filled with tears. His voice cracked, and he was forced to pause briefly, head down, mouth working.

The members watched in alarmed fascination.

"But do not expect me to offer myself as victim." Whiss's head jerked up suddenly, eyes greenly ablaze, and several listeners jumped. "Never shall Whiss Valeur bare his breast tamely to the blade of the assassin. For myself, I care nothing, I fear nothing, I would gladly sacrifice all. This fame, which others covet, is nothing to me, nothing; I would willingly abandon it for a hermit's hovel upon a remote mountaintop, somewhere beyond the hatred and malice of envious men. I should drink the pure water of mountain streams, feast upon roots and berries, sing with the birds, and live at one with Nature. Then I should at last be happy."

One or two incredulous jaws dropped.

"But Vonahar needs me," Whiss continued. "I owe it to my country to preserve myself. It is to this end that I have hunted the conspirators. I have watched and I have listened—oh, very discreetly; you can scarcely guess my methods—and at last their identities became known to me. My vigilance is quite inescapable; nothing remains hidden from me for long. I've a list of the traitors in the Committee and in the Congress. It is a long list, whose contents are bound to astonish the ignorant."

The Committee of National Welfare tensed itself. Surely the Protector would now reveal the names of his enemies.

Not yet, however. Whiss Valeur spoke on. His speech was rambling and interminable, occasionally incoherent, filled with hyperbole, accusation, digression, self-justification, and protracted tirade. He spoke at length of the difficulties and dangers besetting the new republic, the threat to liberty, the need for strong leadership. He denounced all dissidents, all reactionaries, all Apathists, and particularly all Niriennistes. He demanded a renewal of the old Revolutionary ardor, the old Reparationist zeal. He called for loyalty, patriotism, self-sacrifice. At times his trained voice thundered forth, as if to be heard by thousands; at times it grew oddly muffled and slurred; and once, when he spoke of leadership's great burdens, the words failed him altogether, and he cried, the quiet tears streaming down his cheeks.

He spoke for approximately two hours, during which time nobody ventured to stir. The sky above the Sepulchre was light when the torrent of words finally slowed to a trickle, then ceased. Whiss stood for a moment, surveying his stupefied audience. "I have opened my heart to you," he announced at last, "and I have done my duty. Now let others do theirs."

Taking up a bronze paperweight, Whiss rapped the table three times in what was evidently a prearranged signal. Seconds later, the door crashed open and a squad of Vanguardsmen burst into the room. A great commotion arose among the Committee members. Collective agitation increased as Whiss Valeur commanded the soldiers to arrest Congressmen Pieuvre, Lemery, and Myette; all three regarded as among the most trusted of the Protector's allies. No one was more astonished than the accused Congressmen themselves, but loud and desperate protestations of innocence went unheeded. Whiss Valeur watched stone-faced as his erstwhile intimates were dragged howling from the room.

The howls receded, faded away to nothing. Minutes later, anyone glancing out the window might have seen the luckless trio bundled across the courtyard and through the Sepulchre portal; but nobody chose to look. The hubbub died. The remnant of the Committee awaited its master's commands.

Whiss surveyed them each in turn. One by one, they wilted beneath his gaze, with the exception of young Poulpe, whose marble calm remained intact.

"You are dismissed. Leave me," Whiss commanded, and turning to Congressman Poulpe, added, "You stay where you are."

The members, exhausted by the night's travails and each profoundly thankful for escape, dragged themselves from the room. Congressman Poulpe sat motionless. No sign of fatigue manifested itself upon his face. Gilt curls remained faultlessly ordered, garments spotless and fresh, as if the world lacked power to mar his perfection.

They were alone.

"You have failed me," Whiss announced. "My brother Eularque has followed in the footsteps of Houloir. My enemy Quinz vo Derrivalle and his woman accomplice remain at large to work my ruin. No doubt they will stalk me one day to the Congress itself, and no one will hinder them. You have broken your promise."

"The hunt continues. I have sent to the former seigneurie of Derrivalle in Fabeque Province for information concerning this magical Quinz. It will not be long now before we have him," Poulpe returned imperturbably.

"That is what you told me days ago. I am tired of waiting for you to make good your word. You are either less zealous or less intelligent than I had supposed. Or perhaps less loyal."

"My zeal continues unimpaired, Compeer." Poulpe's face remained expressionless, and his voice did not alter in the slightest as he spoke. "My intelligence, such as I possess, is at your service. As for my loyalty—never doubt that it is boundless, vast, eternal as the sea. You are the author of Reparationism. That is the center of all things, and you are the source of that center—the guiding mind that orders all, the sun about which we all circle, without whom there is neither light nor life. Protector, do not ask my life in proof of my loyalty—it is too small an offering. I would give more. I would give my reason and my honor. I would give my soul."

"It is sufficient. I am content. Compeer, I cannot doubt you." Whiss opened his arms, and the two men embraced.

Poulpe stepped back, white face unwontedly flushed. "Protector, command me."

"Continue the search, my friend. Only hurry, intensify your efforts. Additional funds and personnel will be made available if you require them, for the matter is urgent. My enemies are everywhere. It is not at all unlikely that these Derrivalle traitors are in league with the Niriennistes, whose organization continues diabolically active. They may strike at any time. My life is in great danger. Is it any wonder I do not sleep?"

"The Niriennistes," Poulpe mused. A faint frown marred the polished smoothness of his brow. "The Niriennistes. That is an excellent thought, Protector. We have not as yet investigated that connection. Nirienne himself and his accomplices will be interrogated. If they've knowledge of this Quinz vo Derrivalle, be assured Bierce will extract it—he has the knack."

"Very good, but the Nirienne Gangsters must suffer no visible damage prior to the trial's conclusion."

"Then we shall consult the Inanimates again. Your sister and your father will assist. There is a coffeehouse at the university—a known center of Niriennism. We will question The Retreat. There is the place to start."

"Inadequate. Inadequate! These assassins must learn to fear me. You will teach them to do so. An object lesson is required, something memorable. Forget the buildings. You will interrogate the patrons. They are likely to prove refractory, as Niriennistes always will, but we've means of dealing with traitors. I leave it to you to devise the method. I trust you will not disappoint me."

"Protector, your trust is not misplaced." Poulpe bowed and retired, lapis eyes thoughtful and almost dreamy.

Twelve hours later, the Vanguard descended upon The Retreat. The student patrons, informed of their arrest, reacted with characteristic impetuosity. Some fled for the back exit, straight into the arms of the soldiers stationed at the rear of the building. Some submitted quietly. And a sizable contingent—including a number of armed Niriennistes—swiftly organized a resistance, barricading themselves behind fortifications of upended tables and chairs, popping off shots at any Vanguardsman within range. The extreme folly of this last course was demonstrated all too soon.

Despite their superior experience and weaponry, the soldiers made no attempt to storm the student barricades, but rather concentrated their efforts upon The Retreat's front entrance, chopping away with axes to raise and widen the narrow opening. Unsafely ensconced behind their flimsy walls of pine, the students watched in wondering trepidation.

The Vanguardsmen drew back. A silvery nozzle of a head, mounted upon an endless serpentine neck, thrust itself through the doorway. The ZaZa surveyed the scene briefly, then sent a cloud of green vapor gusting into the room. Acrid fumes swirled everywhere. A wretched chorus of coughs arose. Gunfire snapped, and several shots flattened themselves upon the Sentient's impervious scales. ZaZa responded with a blast of flame. Green fire lanced, muddied upon wooden ramparts, then glared orange as the pine ignited. Charcoal smoke mingled with toxic green gas. Blackening wood curved and split with sharp reports that echoed the firearms. Choking, hacking, and half blinded, the students tossed aside their weapons. Empty hands raised above their heads, they staggered out into the open.

The ZaZa threw one of her heads and necks forward. Her huge barrel of a body forced itself partially through the enlarged doorway. A straining pause; timbers creaked, shrieked, splintered, and the Sentient was through. Clanking, she advanced upon her plethora of snaky legs. Two sets of hinged jaws parted, internal filaments glowed, and a double tongue of chartreuse fire lashed the rebels. The kitchen stench of charred meat added itself to the stinking atmosphere. Screams of terror mingled with sobs of grief and rage. There was a scurrying of fugitives, a diving for cover, an explosion of oaths and pleas. A second scourging blast, the barricades collapsed, the cries subsided to whimpering moans.

A few damaged figures crawled from the wreckage, creatures so wounded and ruined that the ZaZa did not trouble to kill them. The Sentient withdrew, and her human companions swept in to finish the job. A handful of broken university boys remained alive and more or less ambulatory. These were swiftly rounded up, herded into the closed carriages, and borne away into the night. In the meantime, the fires kindled upon pine and fabric continued to blaze, mounting from cellar to ground floor and beyond, climbing from story to story until the whole of the structure formerly known as the Duchess Tower flamed like a giant torch.

The fire, massacre, and multiple arrests generated intense public furor. Even the most ardent of Reparationists were startled by the Vanguardly excesses, while citizens of more moderate persuasion were terrified and outraged. Not that dissent was freely expressed—such candor would have invited quick reprisal. But the profusion of angry anonymous pamphlets, tracts, broadsides, and editorials circulating throughout Sherreen within hours of the event bore ample testimony to widespread disgust. There were no public protests or demonstrations, but everywhere there was talk; conversation conducted in whispering voices, conversation that halted abruptly upon the appearance of soldier or gendarme; critical, complaining, treasonous conversation.

Vonahrish patriotism, it seemed, was not what it had been. Initial Revolutionary fury spent, the public was losing its taste for blood. The crowds that gathered each day in Equality Circle were thinner; attendance was visibly dwindling, a phenomenon that Kokotte's Victualers and their masters viewed with misgiving. The citizens, like postorgiastic revelers, were sated, sickened, ashamed, or perhaps just tired. Too many were proving themselves weak vessels, altogether unworthy recipients of Reparationist bounty.

It was thought that a healthy dose of propaganda would revive flagging public enthusiasm, and thus "Neighbor Jumalle" took up his pen again. Within the space of a single night, Whiss Valeur produced an apologia of fourteen thousand words; a work so muddled, vague, repetitive, and digressive that no amount of editing sufficed to render it publishable. Thereafter, it became clear that the swiftest possible resolution to a difficult situation was essential. The trial of the Nirienne Gang was suspended, while the surviving scorched victims of The Retreat holocaust, half-mummified in bandages, were hailed before the National Tribunal.

The perfunctory trial was conducted behind closed doors. Verdict and sentencing were commendably prompt. By midafternoon of a bright spring day, the bound and naked culprits stood in a cart en route for Equality Circle.

The crowd assembled to witness the execution was large. The Coquettes and Cavaliers stood at the forefront, flamboyantly extreme as ever in their enthusiasms.

Strategically placed red-diamonded fanatics cheered and cavorted with all their accustomed brio. Vendors loudly hawked their tidbits and trinkets. There was clamor and commotion aplenty. All the noise and activity, however, could not disguise the prevailingly somber mood. The spring sunshine played upon a sea of still, almost sullen faces. The crowd assembled here today was clearly not the hungry mob of yore. The difference became even more apparent as the single cart came rumbling up out of Arcade Avenue. Formerly, the appearance of the day's victims was wont to be greeted with savage acclaim. Today, the voices of a few professional zealots rose oddly thin and small in the midst of a great silence. The silence continued as the condemned students were removed from their cart, lined up at the foot of the scaffold, then dispatched in quick succession.

Sentient, executioner, and assistants performed with their usual efficiency. Coquettes and Cavaliers screeched, waved, tossed red carnations at each great flare of the Kokotte's death light. There was the usual scramble over discarded cords, the usual jockeying in the front ranks. But the majority of spectators were motionless and quiet, almost unnervingly so.

Fortunately, it did not last long. Today, there was only the one cart of victims. The sun was still high in the sky when the Kokotte completed her meal. The citizens dispersed quickly, fading away in such peculiar, charged silence that even Bierce Valeur took note, gazing after them with a faint, suspicious frown.

It was to be hoped that the death of the traitor students would mark the conclusion of a thoroughly disappointing venture. Everything had gone badly. Not only had the mindless Sherreenian mob responded with unexpected sentimentality, but the interrogation of the prisoners yielded virtually no profit. The semi-Sentients down in the Sepulchre's torture vaults had easily broken the wretched victims, reducing each to blubbering acquiescence. They had gleaned a few scraps of useless information. Of the mysterious Quinz vo Derrivalle and his woman accomplice, however, they had learned nothing.

29

id you ever hear anything more from Eularque Valeur?" Eliste inquired. It was early evening. She sat in her uncle's room.

"No, my dear, nothing," Quinz replied.

"Well, he might at least have sent word that he was safe, after all you did for him. He could have said thank you."

"Oh, the poor fellow thanked me profusely before leaving. As for sending word, that could be difficult and dangerous. In the absence of evidence to the contrary, I think we may assume that he is well."

"Oh, Uncle, you're going to squash that Whiss Valeur creature single-handed! Who's next, then? The sister?"

"Alas that is not such a simple matter. Following the departure of Masters Houloir and Eularque, the vigilance surrounding the remaining Valeur kinsmen has greatly intensified. The unfortunate Mistress Phlosine resides in the Sepulchre, whose defenses I am unable to penetrate. For the moment, I find myself thwarted. Nevertheless, the situation is far from hopeless. I believe I have devised a means of drawing her forth, but for that I shall require a little assistance, which I hope that you, my dear, may perhaps provide."

"I, Uncle? You want *my* help? But what could I do?"

"Serve as a porter. Ah, how mystified you look. No fear, my child, I will explain everything. But first, let us observe your progress. You have practiced the exercises I assigned?"

"Faithfully."

"Excellent. Then perhaps you would be kind enough to show me what you have learned." Uncle Quinz spoke and gestured. Instantly, the air blackened. Dense, almost opaque billows of smoke filled the room, swallowing walls, ceiling, furnishings, and occupants.

Eliste was mildly surprised. Ordinarily, her uncle's illusions were seductive, almost too beguiling to resist. Part of the challenge, of course, lay in their charm; an extra effort of will was required to reject them. No such difficulty this time, however. Her surprise increased as four tall figures materialized, one at each corner of the room, and visible through the roiling dark vapors by reason of their gleaming pallor. At first she thought them statues—white marble images in the antique mode, godlike figures of impossible perfection. This, however, was hardly true. They possessed the draped garments, symmetrical features, and staring white eyes of classical statues; but they were alive. Vitality manifested itself as the nearest white figure slowly lifted a rigid right arm above its head. In the empty upraised hand appeared a jagged length of radiance. For a moment the white figure stood poised, the perfect image of an avenging god, then hurled its thunderbolt.

A startled squeak escaped Eliste, and she dived for cover behind the nearest chair. The lightning whizzed by, sizzling the air in its wake, to strike the floor where she had stood a split second earlier. The rug and floorboards in that spot blackened. Astonishing. Never before had Quinz's creations displayed such unbridled aggression. There was no time to ponder the change, however. A second white figure was lifting its arm, aiming its supernatural weapon. A second glowing missile flew, to strike the chair behind which Eliste crouched. An odd, scorched-air odor tingled the atmosphere, and the chair burst into flame. Eliste scrambled hastily backward. Sparks were flying in all directions. Two or three fell upon her skirt, and where they landed, small fires bloomed. She beat frantically at her clothing, flung herself to the floor, and rolled. Most of the fires went out, but one blaze resisted suffocation. It was spreading, yellow flames dancing about her hem, licking higher, and she could feel the heat on her flesh. It was burning her, burning her alive—

"Uncle Quinz!" Eliste screamed in pain and mortal terror. *"Uncle!"*

No answer, and she couldn't see him. He must have been overcome by smoke. He was probably unconscious, unable to help himself or her, conquered by his own illusion—

Uncle Quinz—conquered by an illusion, most particularly his own?

Ridiculous.

And the knowledge that panic had momentarily driven from her mind was back again. None of this was real. She had been making a fool of herself over nothing.

After that, it was easy. Eliste took a deep breath, paused a moment to marshal thought and will, and then, using the methods she had practiced so often, neatly cleared her garments of flame. She stood up, looked around, and wondered how she could possibly have been taken in, even for an instant, by something false as a puppet show. The smoke was still present, but now transparent to her. Beside the fireplace, Uncle Quinz sat watching her attentively. Chair, rug, and floor were all undamaged. Live white statues still inhabited the corners, but now they were ghostly, insubstantial, and she could afford to examine them at leisure, marveling at her uncle's artistry. Two of the statues lifted their arms, aimed, and hurled simultaneous bolts of force. It would have been a simple matter to dispel them, but curiosity impelled Eliste to stand her ground. The lightning struck her dead-on, and so strong was the illusion that she felt the ghost of an impact despite all her preparation; not enough to shake her balance, but still, something. She could not forbear blinking a little as a searing flare of illusory radiance exploded about her. It was unreal and harmless, but disturbing nonetheless. Eliste focused her will; gazed through shadows to the reality beyond, and thus banished the illusion. Smoke, statues, and all spectral remnants of destruction vanished. The room was as it had been.

Eliste permitted her mind to unclench. "That one almost had me," she said.

"Oh, but only for a moment, and you recovered splendidly. That was rather an elaborate illusion you just broke, my child. Well done!" Smiling, Uncle Quinz approached to plant a kiss upon her cheek. No sooner had his lips touched her face than an agitated clicking whir arose in the corner of the room. Uncle and niece turned in surprise to behold the Sentient Glorielle, aglow with pulsing light, burnished metal frame vibrating with emotion.

"What's wrong with her?" Eliste demanded. At the sound of her voice, the Sentient's whir rose to a razor-edged mechanical whine.

"Ah, she is unquiet. I should never have kissed you in her presence."

"Why ever not?"

"It has upset her. Poor pretty, I fear she feels threatened. She requires affection, understanding, and above all, reassurance."

"About what?"

"That she is loved."

"You mean, that machine is jealous?"

"Try to bear with her, my child. She is inordinately sensitive, and essentially lacking in self-assurance."

"She disguises it well. No, you don't have to tell me, Uncle Quinz—I'll hold my tongue."

"Only use it wisely, my dear, that is all I ask." Quinz knelt beside the affronted Sentient, stroked her glass whorls, and crooned. Presently Glorielle's irritable flickerings ceased, and she glowed with a steady, soft light. The thin mechanical whine subsided to chuckling beeps and clucks. Quinz looked up. "She has recovered her poise. Now is the time to approach her. Come, my dear, come here and put your hands on her."

"Mine? Why?" Eliste was startled.

"Glorielle must learn to suffer your touch, if you are to aid us tonight, my dear."

"Must she? Very well. What was it you were saying about porters?" Eliste knelt beside her uncle. Cautiously she extended a hand.

"Well, you see, my little scheme to liberate Mistress Phlosine Valeur requires Glorielle's assistance. Glorielle has very kindly professed herself willing, but one difficulty remains. There, simply place your hands upon her, my child. She will not object. Both hands—that's right."

Eliste's fingertips brushed metal. A little timidly, half expecting mechanical protest or even retaliation, she pressed her palms to the Sentient's silvery flanks. Beneath her hands she felt warmth and deep vibration. Glorielle's humming altered slightly in pitch, while her luminous display deepened from gold to amber.

"But how gratifying. A success. I believe she likes you, my child."

No she doesn't, thought Eliste. *Any more than I like her. But she'll tolerate me for your sake, Uncle. I'm not sure how I know that, but I know.*

"There, that is delightful, is it not?"

"Ummmmmm," said Eliste. *No.*

"Excellent. Now to business. You will assist, child?"

"Gladly, Uncle. What am I to do?"

"Help me carry Glorielle to the Havillac Gardens tonight. Alas, she is too heavy for me to lift alone. Young Dref is not about, and there is no one else but you to whom I would entrust such a task."

"What's Glorielle going to do in the Havillac Gardens?"

"At first, she will wait quietly. A little later on . . . we shall see."

"You're very mysterious. I see I'll have to wait for an explanation. Will you tell me more when we get there? And before we go out, can you do something to disguise us?"

"I had intended as much, my dear. Think what an opportunity to experiment! What would you like to be? A brunette? Taller? Shorter? Rounder? Young grisette? Old marketwoman? You choose."

"A boy! Girl dresses up as a boy. That's what they always do in the theater, isn't it?"

"It is? It is? But how curious. Why should they do that?"

"So they can put the actresses in tights."

"Oh, my. I see. Well. Ahem. Very well, a boy it is, if you wish. But you, my dear, shall not wear tights. And I shall be a sailor," Quinz announced. "Young, with curly black whiskers and ferocious mustachios. Muscular arms, lurid tattoos. Perhaps a bandanna. An air of cool and deadly assurance. A hint of reckless instability, a soupçon of repressed violence. An earring or two. Yes. I like it."

"So do I. Will you do it now, Uncle Quinz?"

"This very moment."

The transformation was swift and seemingly effortless. Eliste felt the changes in her own body, just as she had felt them months ago, upon the night that Quinz disguised her as a wolf. Now she was taller, heavier, with longer limbs and broader shoulders, short hair upon her head, and the sparse threat of a beard upon her chin. Her full-skirted dress and white fichu had transmuted to baggy trousers, shabby carmagnole, and neckerchief. She looked down at her hands, newly enlarged; gazed into the mirror at her newly snub-nosed, newly freckled face, and started to giggle. This time, unlike the last, she was neither alarmed nor confused. Now that she knew how to deal with illusion, she could see through the mask to her own real self, intact and unaltered. Beside her, Uncle Quinz's true form was visible through the obscuring film of brawn, bravado, and bandanna. It was all great fun.

"You have changed a little, my dear," Uncle Quinz observed, light voice ghosted with illusory resonance. "And profited thereby, I believe."

"Thank you, Uncle Quinz, for all you've taught me."

"Pooh, child, no need of thanks—I have enjoyed every moment. Now, delightful though this is, we procrastinate. Let us prepare my Glorielle."

"With illusion?"

"No need, as yet. For now, there are simpler ways." One of the bureau drawers yielded a large canvas sack. Uncle Quinz approached the Sentient, addressed her coaxingly. "I know my pretty will be kind and indulgent, submitting for a brief span to seeming indignity. Patience, my Glorielle—it is all in a good cause, and it will not be for long." The Sentient's humming response must have been affirmative, for Quinz nodded once in evident relief before slipping the big bag shroudlike over his creation. "Ah, that is good. Is she not generous? Is she not kind?"

Eliste forbore comment.

"Now, my dear, if you will check the corridor?"

Eliste did so. "All clear," she reported.

"Excellent. Then let us be off. If you will—?" Quinz gestured expressively. To an uninformed observer, it might have seemed comic to witness the powerful-looking mariner ask for help with so small a burden.

Glorielle was dense and compact, a little clumsy for two people to carry. Eliste and her uncle made their way without mishap along the hall, down the stairs, and out into Flou's Pocket, where the students idled, music spilled from the neighboring tavern, and the fragrance of roasting meat wafted from the nearby cookshops. Eliste inhaled appreciatively.

Springtime. The air was cool, but mild and soft; the winter past, a hideous memory. How lovely it was to step out of doors without cringing at the cold; how lovely to be disguised beyond recognition, safe, and unafraid. It was wonderful to be a boy.

They took a fiacre to the edge of Havillac Gardens. Thereafter, they continued on foot, stumbling along the darkened depopulated pathways, beneath the branches now lightly frizzed with growth. White pebbles crunched underfoot, and somewhere nearby, frogs croaked. Glorielle rested still and mostly silent in her sack. Only occasionally, a muted mechanical hum fought its way through the enveloping canvas folds.

It was still early when they reached the clearing known as the Flower of Light, a trysting spot whose unfortunate proximity to The Cypresses cemetery was wont to dampen romantic ardor. The place was largely but not wholly unfrequented, and thus well-suited to Quinz vo Derrivalle's purposes. Just now, it was quite deserted.

They stood their burden carefully upright in the middle of the clearing, upon a patch of fine white pebbles, and Quinz whipped the canvas veiling away, exposing Glorielle to the stars. The Sentient seemed to take stock of her surroundings. Her glassy whorls pulsed with nervous light. A few uneasy whistles escaped her, succeeded by a steady meditative hum.

Quinz vo Derrivalle hovered anxiously. "Bear with me, my pretty," he pleaded. "Do not be alarmed, do not doubt."

Eliste watched with impatience. "Now what, Uncle?" she inquired.

"Now for the fun, my dear. Step back. Come now, back to the edge of the clearing. Step lively, child."

His hand on her arm, he was sweeping her backward to the line of trees that walled the Flower of Light. Eliste went unresistingly, asking nothing. No doubt matters would soon clarify themselves.

They did. At the edge of the clearing, Quinz vo Derrivalle halted, breathed deeply, spoke inaudibly. The results were startling.

Eliste had been watching her uncle, who in turn appeared to watch nothing; before he had finished speaking, however, some instinct pulled her eyes to Glorielle, in time to witness a transformation. One moment, the Sentient sat there, familiar squat and compact shape adance with pulsing light; and the next, she was—immense, rearing herself high above the surrounding trees. Her lights went out, her whirring vocalization died. No hint of vitality remained. It had happened in silence, without warning and without fanfare. Despite her recently acquired resistance to illusion, Eliste was astounded. Never had she expected anything like this. Behind the huge disguise, Glorielle stood short and wakeful as ever; to the unschooled, however, Sentient was indistinguishable from gigantic Stupefaction.

"Ruination, Uncle, that's a surprise!"

"Do you like it, my dear?"

"It's interesting. What's it for?"

"Bait, my child. Bait. We shall leave Glorielle here overnight. In her present guise, she is unlikely to escape notice for long."

"Hardly. By noon tomorrow, this place will be thronged. But what is the point of— Oh, I see. You think they'll bring Whiss Valeur's sister or father here to waken the Stupefaction?"

"There's my clever girl."

"But won't they be suspicious? I mean, they know they're dealing with an Exalted magician, they know what you are, and the sudden appearance of a huge Stupefaction never seen before is sure to alert them—"

"No doubt that is true, my child. It is my hope, however, that the lure of a new Sentient, and all the power she offers, will prove too strong to resist. The Vanguard cannot readily carry Glorielle back to the Armory, or so they will imagine. Thus they will be left with little choice but to convey captive magician to the Stupefaction."

"Under very heavy guard, I should think."

"Ah, but that I can deal with, I believe. And I shall not go unassisted. Glorielle will play her part."

"Really? What will she do?" Eliste's curiosity flamed. To be included in her uncle's magical endeavors was thrilling. "And when will she do it?"

"Quite shortly, I suspect. Tomorrow night, I will return to stand watch here."

"Good. I'll come with you."

"Ah, my dear, I hardly think that wise."

"But you can't mean to leave me out, after I've helped you? That wouldn't be fair!"

"My child, I am concerned for your safety."

"Oh, no harm will come to me while I'm with you." Suddenly, the prospect of exclusion seemed the worst thing in the world. "Besides, what if you want to carry Glorielle away from this place? You can't do it alone, and Dref will probably be unavailable. You need my help. *Glorielle* needs my help."

Got him.

Uncle Quinz fidgeted. "Perhaps, my dear, we might discuss this matter elsewhere? Here is not the place for it. Let us return to our lodgings."

Eliste nodded. Together they turned and made for a break in the trees.

Behind them rose a wrathful whistling. Eliste and her uncle turned back to behold Glorielle, shaking and furiously agitated behind her towering calm facade. The Sentient's lights flared passionate crimson. Rattling tremors rocked her frame, and her small vanes whipped wildly.

"What's the matter with her?" Eliste demanded. "What's she— *Oh!*" A white pebble shot through the air like a bullet to spend its force against her leg. Despite the protective layering of skirts and voluminous petticoat, the impact staggered her. A second pebble flew—again, well-aimed. A cry of pain escaped Eliste, and she sought refuge behind the nearest tree; peered cautiously around the trunk.

Glorielle stood upon an ornamental patch of white gravel. By some obscure method, the mechanics of which were hidden by the metal casing of her body, the Sentient was grabbing the pebbles on which she rested, drawing them up inside herself, and spitting them out through her vents with murderous power and accuracy. Eliste jerked her head back. A barrage of flying gravel pelted the bole behind which she cowered.

"Glorielle! Oh, my pretty, try to calm yourself, do! Glorielle!" Uncle Quinz flung himself forward, sinking into his creation's surrounding illusory hugeness like a ship into fog, and dropped to his knees at her side. "Ah, my pretty, there is no need for this distress! You are not abandoned—I will return tomorrow, I promise. Do you not recall, we discussed it all? No one is taking me away from my Glorielle, you must believe that. Come, all is well, compose yourself."

Gradually, the soothing, coaxing voice exerted its effect. The gravel bombardment ceased. The crimson flares subsided to uneasy orange flickerings, and the stabbing whistle died to a sullen hum. Quinz stood up and backed away, one cautious step at a time. Glorielle buzzed sharply, but the furious demonstrations did not resume.

"There—I think I have managed to reassure her," Quinz observed with satisfaction. "She seems happier, does she not? I believe she will permit us to depart now."

"Permit us!" Eliste shook with fear and fury. "Permit us! Since when does a paltry pettish pile of mechanical parts dictate our comings and goings?"

"Hush, my dear, she will hear you!"

"I hope so!"

"My child, you must be patient, you must understand that we deal with an exceedingly complex device, delicate and almost too sensitive—"

"She's spoiled rotten! A swat with a sledgehammer would do her some good!"

"No, no, violence is never the answer! If only you could comprehend her many insecurities, her needs and fears—"

"What about mine? That thing tried to kill me!"

"Oh, surely not! She was only distraught at the thought of desertion——"

"She knew exactly what she was doing! And I can barely walk, as a result!"

"Try, my child, please try! Only as far as the public roadway. Can you manage it? Here, lean on me."

Uncle Quinz appeared so alarmed—narrow face frightened behind the mask of the mustachioed sailor—that Eliste began to regret her outburst. She moderated her tone. "I'm all right. I exaggerated. I'm sorry. Let's just leave, Uncle."

He was altogether willing. Hand in hand, they hurried from the Flower of Light, along the dark and twisting paths of Havillac Gardens, breaking contact only when they reached the roadway, where one of the seedier of fiacres was persuaded to halt for a hard-bitten seafarer and his youthful companion.

Quinz left her at the door of the lodging house. His own night's work was not yet complete. He was off again upon his mysterious errands, and this time, she was not invited. For a moment she stood watching, until his artificially augmented figure disappeared into darkness. Then she scurried around to the back of the building, and there in the shadows, alone and unobserved, broke the illusion that masked her rightful form. Herself again, she went into the house, up the stairs, fortunately meeting no one, and back to Dref's rooms. They were empty, of course. Dref was nowhere about; he almost never was. He was off somewhere with his Nirienniste cronies, no doubt plotting some crazy, hopeless rescue attempt. He was likely to get himself killed. No, he was too clever for that. But reckless—always reckless. He risked arrest every day, and there was nothing she could say or do to stop him—or to help him, either. He didn't want or need her help, any more than he wanted or needed *her*. Upstart serf, she hated him. Almost as much as she hated to find herself so ineffectual and so useless. Well, at least Uncle Quinz needed her, if only as a porter. He *would* take her with him tomorrow night, she'd see to it. She was tired of always being left out ... superfluous.

Sighing a little, Eliste undressed down to her shift. A couple of twinges reminded her to examine her leg, already darkening where Glorielle's pebbles had struck. By morning, those bruises would be black. If she hadn't been armored in petticoats, that assault would have lamed her. ...

Glorielle. What a truly vile-tempered, jealous, spiteful, mollycoddled Sentient she was! Dangerous, too. But Uncle Quinz just couldn't see it. He danced attendance on her like some doting grandparent; nothing would open his eyes. Well, he was her creator, after all. And she did, beyond question, have her uses, as she had proved in the past and would prove again in the near future—perhaps even tomorrow.

Tomorrow.

Eliste climbed into bed, blew out the candle. She *would* accompany Uncle

Quinz tomorrow. She closed her eyes. Neither the ache in her leg nor the one in her mind could prevent her from dropping straight off to sleep.

She woke to an empty and silent apartment. The door to Dref's room stood open. His bed was untouched; obviously, he had not returned at all last night. When Eliste stood up, she discovered that her bruised leg had stiffened while she slept. It was now so sore that she could scarcely bend it. Settling back down on the edge of the bed, she kneaded the discolored flesh gently. Later on, she would apply hot compresses—ice, butter, mud, anything in the world that might loosen the muscles—for she couldn't afford to limp. If Uncle Quinz considered her disabled, he would never take her along with him.

Time and mild exercise seemed to help. Gradually her leg untightened; by midmorning she could manage an even, creditably springy stride. Now she simply needed to maintain it.

The day was long and slow, as she had known it must be. Dref did not appear. Eliste filled the hours as best she could with reading, needlework, endless cups of tea. The usual, these days: tedious and solitary, but still, idyllic by comparison to last winter's Eighth District horrors. Periodically she got up to stretch, bend, pace, bounce. The leg continued to function adequately. It was going to be all right.

The day crept on to its conclusion. Moments after sunset, before the last warm-colored streaks had bled from the sky, she was tapping at her uncle's door. Ordinarily, she wouldn't have sought him at such an hour; the old gentleman was strictly nocturnal, and it was possible he might not even be awake as yet. Today, however, she couldn't contain herself.

Quinz answered her knock at once, greeting her with apparent pleasure. He seemed perhaps a little bewildered, a little distrait, but no more so than usual—certainly not as if he had just awakened. The vast colorless eyes behind the glass lenses were bright and clear, loose gray garments unrumpled. She had never seen them otherwise. Eliste wondered then, for the first time in her life, whether Uncle Quinz ever slumbered. Was it possible that sleep was one of those little inessentials with which he had chosen to dispense altogether?

She entered his room prepared to argue and plead; to her relief, both proved unnecessary. Uncle Quinz readily consented to take her with him to the Havillac Gardens that evening, provided she agreed to his choice of disguise.

"What, no more sailor? No more cabin boy?" she inquired.

"We may retain those forms if you are so inclined, my child," Quinz replied. "I would be happy to do so, for I have grown attached in many ways to the black mustachios. The bodies are acceptable, but tonight we must clothe them differently, that is all."

"How differently?"

"As Vanguardsmen."

"Why, Uncle—you fox."

This time, Quinz waited until they were out of doors to cast his glamor, for the sight of uniformed Vanguardsmen walking the corridors of the lodging house might easily have given rise to panic. The forgiving springtime darkness hid his work, and suddenly Eliste found herself back in last night's masculine guise, but this time attired in the shapeless, aggressively plebeian brown and scarlet of Whiss Valeur's own soldiers. Uncle Quinz's bristling mustachios topped the baggy uniform of a lieutenant.

It was peculiar beyond expression, to be Exalted and clothed in the garb of her class's mortal enemies. Peculiar, disturbing, and remarkably useful. Eliste discovered at once the advantage of Vanguardly status. It showed in the alacrity with which pedestrians made way for them on the street; in the obsequiousness of the street vendors, beggars, and buskers; in the respect of cabbies and merchants. The fawning concern, however, was as much a mask as any of Quinz vo Derrivalle's transforming illusions. Not far beneath the surface lurked something very different.

They took a fiacre to the edge of Havillac Gardens, at which point the wisdom of Uncle Quinz's choice became apparent. The Girdle enclosing the park was unusually crowded. Scores of curious citizens loitered there; but none attempted entry, for tonight the armed Vanguard sentries were posted at regular intervals about the entire perimeter. Tonight the Havillac Gardens were barred to all civilians.

Obviously, the bait had been taken.

No ordinary citizen might have crossed that line of guards, but nobody questioned the arrival of reinforcements: an officer of the Vanguard and his subordinate. The nearest sentry snapped a salute as the apparent lieutenant passed him. Quinz vo Derrivalle echoed the gesture and stalked on, his niece trailing a pace or two behind him. Eliste was almost startled by the effectiveness of their disguise. Now that she had learned to penetrate illusion, she found it difficult to believe that others could not do the same. But nobody suspected a thing; it was almost too easy.

The sentries were behind them. For a time they walked in silence along a narrow, empty path. As they approached the Flower of Light, voices became audible and lantern light gleamed through the trees. Moments later they reached the clearing, and Eliste caught her breath. In the center of the open space loomed the illusory Stupefaction—massive, tremendous, awesome even in sleep. And there at her center, like a small seed in an overblown fruit, squatted Glorielle—stubby and wakeful, but quiet. Around the Stupefaction stood a squad of Vanguardsmen. They were vigilant, but easy; clearly anticipating no trouble. The sleeping Stupefaction appeared to pose no immediate threat: the Gardens were free of civilians, and the elusive formerly-Exalted magician currently hunted by the Committee of National Welfare would surely never dare to pit his empty illusions against so formidable a force. There seemed little cause for concern; and an air of curious, almost pleasurable expectation pervaded the clearing.

Uncle Quinz strode forward with confidence. Eliste threw him an anxious glance. Almost she moved to clutch his arm, then remembered to restrain herself. Her mouth had gone sticky-dry. Her feet didn't want to move. Walking straight on into the midst of that uniformed gathering suddenly struck her as pure lunacy. Somebody would see. Somebody would realize.

You were the one determined to come.

She followed her uncle, and then she was in among the soldiers, close enough to scent their suppertime garlic, and it wasn't so fearful after all. The faces about her remained reassuringly indifferent. Nobody saw through Quinz vo Derrivalle's illusions; nobody was even looking. Collective attention was fixed upon a gap in the trees at the far edge of the Flower of Light. Eliste's breathing slowed; she followed the intent eyes.

Voices, lights, slight commotion, and into the clearing marched another party of soldiers. With them came a short and dumpy figure, nearly hidden by tall surrounding forms. Eliste glimpsed drooping head, drooping breasts and shoulders, pudding face, and wondering mild eyes. Phlosine Valeur, almost certainly.

Her eyes are something like Uncle Quinz's, but his were never so sad.

Beside Phlosine Valeur walked another, very different figure: tall, slim, young, and impeccable, with curls so fair and glossy that they glinted even in the low lantern light; upright carriage and exquisitely sculpted white features.

How beautiful he is was Eliste's first impression, but closer inspection soon altered her opinion. The chiseled features were masklike, the blue eyes hard and blank as glass. It was the face of a waxwork dummy, or a corpse, its perfection somehow repulsive. *Who is that? Someone who thinks himself important.*

The newcomers advanced. They stared. Without exception, their wondering eyes lifted to the Stupefaction's summit. Even Phlosine's did so for a moment. But then, while her captors' attention anchored on nothingness, she allowed her gaze to sink slowly, down to the true Glorielle crouching at the illusion's center. Phlosine cocked her head a little, quietly puzzled. She glanced about the Flower of Light, eyes sliding over the various brown-and-scarlet figures to light unerringly upon Quinz vo Derrivalle. The two magicians regarded each other attentively but without expression. Phlosine's eyes shifted briefly to Eliste. She blinked and looked away.

She sees us, really sees us. What now, I wonder? Eliste was totally unprepared for what happened next.

Uncle Quinz gave an almost imperceptible nod, and then, without waiting to see if his niece had noted the signal, advanced upon Glorielle. Eliste shook off her surprise and followed. Their progress was hardly noted, for group attention remained fixed upon the newly arrived Valeur magician and the Stupefaction she had come to inspect. The beautiful young man standing beside Phlosine was speaking. His words were inaudible, but judging by the autocratic elevation of his chin, the inflexible set of neck and shoulders, it seemed likely he was issuing orders of some kind. Phlosine listened and nodded, pudgy face bland as blancmange.

Uncle Quinz was almost upon his creation before she noticed him. Glorielle recognized him at once, for his disguise was transparent to her, and a welcoming display of golden lights flashed along her glassy convolutions; a display that went unseen by all save the three sets of eyes present capable of penetrating illusory camouflage. Eliste was watching her uncle closely, for she had no clear idea what he intended. She saw him bow his head and speak; then he looked up, and she saw rather than heard him mouth the words, "Now, my pretty."

At that moment, golden light glowed above, at the illusory Stupefaction's summit. Eliste saw that the pattern and sequence of flashes precisely mirrored the much tinier display of the real Glorielle. Clearly, Uncle Quinz had done something to strengthen the bond between small Sentient and immense simulacrum.

Glorielle must have expected the signal, for her response was instantaneous, and the great Stupefaction woke terribly from slumber. The golden lights that pulsed along her crowning elaborations deepened to homicidal crimson. Her shrill siren whistling swelled to artificial hurricane-roar. The startled Vanguardsmen shrank back, cursing vigorously.

Good, but not enough, thought Eliste. *There had better be more.*

There was. Glorielle began to breathe smoke—a hitherto unsuspected talent. Thin streams of gray vapor gushed from her vents. To the Vanguardsmen, those streams appeared as vast, billowing black clouds. Blinded and half choked, the soldiers staggered to and fro, curses giving way to hacking coughs. One or two collapsed, succumbing to psychogenic smoke inhalation.

Eliste wondered if that could kill them.

New and greater miseries swiftly followed, as sparks and miniature jets of flame shot from Glorielle's various orifices. To those with power to resist illusion, the spectacle was rather pretty, reminiscent of small-scale pyrotechnics. The mentally unfortified, however, beheld a howling inferno, beside which the dragon's breath of ZaZa paled to insignificance.

Eliste watched with interest as the sheets of flame canopied the Flower of Light, glaring dirtily through banks of charcoal smoke to broil the scurrying luckless. She could see the skin of the soldiers reddening and blistering beneath the illusory assault. Amazing. No cheat there—so utterly were they deceived, their very flesh reflected the false conviction. Almost, she could pity them.

She felt a light tug; Uncle Quinz was pulling at her wrist. Wordlessly Eliste obeyed, following him across the last few remaining feet of space that separated them from the object of their efforts. Phlosine Valeur was placid and deceptively passive in the midst of the unreal conflagration. A Vanguardsman grasped her right arm; the blond beauty clung to her left. Suffocating and half blind though they were, they had not relinquished their captive; together they strove to drag her from the Flower of Light. Phlosine, however, proved harder to steer than an overloaded land barge in a high wind. She had gone limp and unwieldy. Without appearing to offer the slightest resistance, her reeling digressions apparently random, she contrived to hold her disoriented captors in loosely circular orbit about the Sentient.

Uncle Quinz hurried straight to his quarry, but seemed hardly to see her. Rather, he addressed himself to the soldier at her side, who stiffened to attention at sight of the lieutenant's insignia. "Just what do you think you're doing?"

"Sir, the Congressman and I are about to convey Mistress Valeur from the Gardens. We—"

"You're idiots, wandering around like lost sheep," Quinz observed. "Get out of this. I'll handle it."

"Sir, my orders—"

"Shut up. One more heehaw out of your donkey's mouth and I put you on report. Understand?" Without awaiting affirmation, he plucked Phlosine Valeur from her captors' grasp. "You—" He snapped his fingers at Eliste. "Over here. Don't stand there gaping, dolt—move!"

For a moment, she had to strain to glimpse her Uncle Quinz behind the bravado and black mustaches. But he was still there, all right, and clearly enjoying himself. Eliste hopped forward to take the older woman's arm. Phlosine submitted demurely.

"Lieutenant," the blond young man croaked in a smoke-poisoned voice, "you will consider yourself subject to my command—"

"Shove it. I've no time for civilian twaddle."

The other opened his mouth to protest; a fit of coughing bent him double.

"Move her out. Step lively, there," Uncle Quinz commanded. As if by chance, he led his charges straight into the nearest bank of midnight cloud, an illusory well of blackness roiling about the reality of Glorielle's little plumes of grayish vapor. An angry exclamation arising in their wake splintered into racking coughs. The darkness engulfed them. In effect, they were invisible.

"All's well with you, ladies?" Uncle Quinz inquired, in his own voice.

"Yes, Uncle."

"Bozhenille Commune?" guessed Phlosine.

"Ah, what memories."

"Uncle, what about Glorielle?"

"Alas, my pretty would burden us. For now, we must leave her. In her present guise, no one will attempt meddling, and she will be quite safe until we return for her tomorrow. I am sure she will understand."

He could not have been more mistaken.

Glorielle perceived herself abandoned.

Behind them, an enraged whistling, magically translated to shattering, uncanny howl. Even to those who recognized its falsity, the sound was unnerving. The Sentient's anger was gigantic, elemental as storm and fire. The howling mounted and thinned to a piercing shriek; an intolerable, knife-in-the-brain aural assault that went on and on. Hands pressed tight to her ears, Eliste looked back over her shoulder, and what she saw sharpened her alarm. Glorielle, clothed in sanguinary radiance, rocked and quaked like a small volcano shuddering on the brink of eruption. Her vanes whipped violently, to send illusory lengths of steel cable slashing across the Flower of Light. Eliste could not repress a nervous start as one such cable passed straight through her. Had she not fully comprehended its unreality, what might the result have been?

Nothing unreal, however, about the pebbles that Glorielle, in full tantrum, was now picking from the ground and spitting out through her vents. Nothing at all unreal about the speed and force of the flying stones, or the damage they could do.

It happened so fast, there was time only for a brief flash of . . . indignation. Then the pale barrage struck, pelting three targets indiscriminately. Eliste and Phlosine were soundly battered; each would bear the bruises for days. But the worst was reserved, no doubt unintentionally, for Quinz vo Derrivalle. A couple of pebbles, whizzing at bullet velocity, struck the old man's head. One grazed his temple, opening a red gash; another smacked the back of his skull. The breath chuffed sharply out of him, and he pitched face forward to the ground. The spectacles flew from his nose, to land somewhere in the shrubbery.

"Uncle!" Eliste fell to her knees at his side. Quinz lay bloodied and horribly still. She hardly dared to touch him.

Gritting her teeth, she laid a hand upon his shoulder. Quinz stirred, and opened glazed myopic eyes. His lips moved slightly, but no sound emerged.

"Uncle—" She forced herself to speak gently, calmly. "Uncle, you must get up now. Come, I'll help you."

Quinz's empty eyes were fixed on her face. No telling whether or not he understood.

"Uncle, *try*."

Nothing.

"Please, Uncle Quinz, get up!" She shook him a little, and he grunted inquiringly but did not stir. Dazed—or worse. Unbelievable; up until that moment, she had somehow retained some childish faith in her magical kinsman's perfect invulnerability. She had been stupid; and now he was hurt, and it was partly her fault for having helped Dref Zeenoson to recruit him, and it was up to her to see that he was saved. Eliste cast desperate eyes about the Flower of Light, schooled vision cutting easily through dense black clouds of illusion. The clearing itself was free of Vanguardsmen, but the Havillac Gardens were no doubt teeming with them. Their shouts rang through the dark; they were everywhere about. She would have to take him straight through their ranks; but what of that? She and Uncle Quinz retained their military disguises. There was no reason, she suddenly realized, why she shouldn't simply demand the soldiers' assistance. *They* could help the injured lieutenant; the Vanguard itself should rescue Quinz vo Derrivalle. It was a pretty .ought, and there was no reason it shouldn't work, no reason at all—

Uncle Quinz breathed a deep sigh, and his eyes closed. In that moment, his false black hair and mustaches faded away. His muscular figure dwindled, his uniform softened to a moth-gray robe, and he resumed his rightful form. Eliste did likewise; all at once she was a girl again, with long honey hair and full skirts. A few feet away, the gigantic simulacrum vanished, and there stood the true Glorielle, short and shaky, hiccuping flashes of light like radiant sobs of remorse for the injury done her creator. At the same time, the seething smoky clouds swirled out of existence. The air cleared, and reality reasserted itself. Flower of Light and its remaining occupants stood revealed as they were.

Dead—he must be dead. But no. His narrow chest still rose and fell. Her own breathing resumed.

"Ah, he has let it slip," remarked an unobtrusive, Vaurve-accented voice.

Eliste looked up, uncomprehending.

"The illusion—he has let it go. A pity. It was excellent."

Phlosine. Eliste had almost forgotten her. Somehow Whiss Valeur's lumpish sad-eyed sister was easy to forget; but she was worth remembering—she had powers of her own.

"Can you restore it? Or at least, restore our disguises?" Eliste's voice came out tremulous.

"Oh—well—I think—approximately—scarcely so perfect—but something similar—I believe—probably . . ."

"And could you yourself assume the disguise of a Vanguardsman?"

"Oh—well—a disguise—you mean a perceptual-transfer persuasion in the fashion of the vo Nesquierre Final Discipline? Well—perhaps—I think . . . not unlikely . . ."

"How long would it take you to do that?"

"Oh—not long—twenty minutes—perhaps as little as sixteen—"

"That's too long!"

Phlosine winced.

"I'm sorry." Eliste deliberately softened her tone. "Listen, Phlosine Valeur, my uncle came here tonight to free you, but now he's the one who needs help. If he's arrested, they'll kill him. Will you do what you can to get us out of this park?"

"Oh, indeed—I will try—I suppose . . . that is to say—"

"Then, if you'll assist, before the soldiers come back, let's carry my uncle from this clearing and set him down somewhere out of sight."

Phlosine nodded vaguely. Impossible to judge how much she actually comprehended; but then, she had to be far more intelligent than she appeared.

Uncle Quinz was light and easily lifted to his feet. Moreover, he remained at least semiconscious, and capable of limited locomotion. Supported and guided by the two women, Quinz stumbled blindly from the Flower of Light. They led him along a narrow winding path for a few yards, then abandoned the trail to strike off into the wooded dark. Progress was slow—often they stumbled over roots and rocks—but at least this section of the Gardens seemed relatively quiet. No Vanguardly voices echoed among the old trees. When they came to a stand of bushes, well-leafed and offering fair concealment, they stopped there.

Gently they lowered Quinz to the ground, and Phlosine plopped herself down beside him. Eliste likewise knelt. Moonlight barely illuminated the scene. She could just make out her uncle's still white face, his fragile white hands splayed on the black soil. Phlosine was only a shapeless silhouette, smudge-lined profile faintly highlighted. She was knotting her short fingers in what seemed a nervously preparatory manner. Once she began, it would be unwise to stop her, and one thing needed to be said.

"Phlosine, before you start, you ought to know— Phlosine, do you hear me?"

The profile bobbed minutely.

"If anything should happen—if somehow we should separate, and you were to find yourself alone with Uncle Quinz—take him to Number One Hundred and Six, Flou's Pocket, in Rat Town. Once there, go to Master Renois's apartment, on the third floor. Renois is a friend, he'll look after you. You'll remember?"

Another bob. There was nothing for it now but to trust in Whiss Valeur's sister. Eliste settled back on her heels to wait and watch. Phlosine seemed to contract, drawing in on herself. The dark head dipped, the profile disappeared. After a moment, the mumbling commenced.

Eliste sat waiting. At first she tried to listen to Phlosine, but the effort was useless. The other woman's words were so much gibberish. After a minute or two her attention wandered; first to her uncle's terribly still and delicate face, then to the surrounding parkland. The Havillac Gardens were black; she could see nothing. She listened, and caught the gabble of voices—Vanguardsmen's voices, too near, far too near.

Phlosine spoke on. The muffled words that were all but inaudible seemed terribly loud to Eliste. The woman would surely alert every soldier in the park with her noise. And she seemed to be taking so *long* about it. If she made progress, there was no sign.

Mutterings from Phlosine; and the men's voices were closer now, coming on fast. Eliste straightened, craned her neck, strained her eyes. She spied lantern light, brightening through the trees, approaching.

Hurry. Eliste didn't let herself say it aloud. Nagging would only shake the other's concentration.

Something had to be wrong. Phlosine mumbled methodically, but surely she shouldn't be taking so long. She was taking forever, and the Vanguardsmen were terribly close. By now, of course, they would have recognized the Sentient hoax; the cleverer among them would have guessed its purpose; and now they would be combing the Havillac Gardens for Phlosine Valeur. They'd have her, too, along with an unexpected bonus in the form of the disabled Exalted magician who had tried to deliver her.

Phlosine needed more time. There was one sure way to give her some.

Eliste stood. Stepped forth silently from the bushes. Phlosine appeared not to notice her departure; the muttering did not falter. Eliste hesitated, strongly inclined to crawl back into hiding. She took a deep breath and forced herself forward, gliding ghostlike from tree to tree, to meet the oncoming lights and voices. She moved as swiftly and silently as possible, for she needed to distance herself from Phlosine and Quinz before allowing the soldiers a glimpse of her.

They were quicker and more vigilant than she anticipated. Despite her caution, she hadn't put more than a few dozen yards between herself and her uncle before a swinging arc of lantern light snagged her white fichu, fair skin, and hair. She had been expecting that, but not so soon. At once she whirled and ran, white flash of petticoat clearly visible to the soldiers. They yelled and gave chase, four of them crashing through the undergrowth, sounding like a cross between a herd of cattle and a wolf pack. Eliste ran lightly. She was young, fleet, unready to die. Her ploy was risky, but not necessarily suicidal; there yet remained the hope that the darkness would shield her. At the first lull, she paused long enough to discard fichu and petticoat. The night breezes touched her bared throat, soft springtime air that she might under other circumstances have enjoyed. Dark-clad now, she ducked into the nearest thicket; crouched there for a moment to hear the shriek of a whistle summoning all Vanguardsmen within earshot to the chase. Frightening; but at least it would keep them away from Uncle Quinz.

Her instinct was to go to ground. Above all else, she wanted to burrow down behind the brambles, to freeze there like a hunted rabbit, trusting in darkness, stillness, and silence to save her. A false impulse. What she really needed was to escape the Havillac Gardens before daybreak, and in so doing, to center the Vanguard's attention upon herself.

Footsteps crashing through the brush; stab of light. She cringed for a moment, then gulped air and broke from cover.

Patpatpat of moist spring evening dirt underfoot; slap of elastic spring branches at her face, at her uplifted arm. Blind stumblings. Metallic whistle behind her, shouting voices; they acted as a spur to send her shooting off into the darkness under the night sky and trees. Harder to run now; breathing labored, and the leg so blackly bruised by Glorielle not performing as it should.

Voices all about; how many of them, converging upon her from every direction? And how long now had she been running? It seemed endless, but had it been long enough? Again, the useless urge to hide in the dark. Light and noise exploding like a bomb, and they had spotted her again. Off in a new direction, into the black spaces, glowing murky gold in an instant as the lantern light diffused through hazy cool air. Diagonal cut across an open patch, and this time straight into the arms of another band of soldiers filtering through a gap in the trees.

They caught her neatly, subdued her with ridiculous ease. Her struggles were brief and few; there seemed little point in anything more.

"What've we got?"

Someone held a lantern up to her face. She squinted and looked away, but, inevitably, someone observed, "I've seen her somewhere."

It didn't take them long to solve the puzzle.

Back to the Flower of Light, where the scattered Vanguardsmen had reassembled about the exposed and undefended Glorielle. Straight up to the blond young man, who subjected her to expressionless clinical scrutiny, then observed without emotion, "You are Eliste vo Derrivalle. Your criminal kinsman Quinz vo Derrivalle is responsible for tonight's attack upon the People's representatives?"

Eliste looked at him as she imagined Zeralenn vo Rouvignac might have looked—as at an object faintly distasteful but unworthy of close attention—a cockroach, perhaps, or horse droppings in the street.

"You will reveal the whereabouts of the traitor Quinz vo Derrivalle."

Eliste's expression did not alter.

"Remove her to the Sepulchre," Congressman Poulpe instructed his followers, "and recommend her to Bierce's attention."

Further explanation was neither offered nor requested. They led her away through the Havillac Gardens, back to the road, where several of the closed carriages waited. They put her in one, and the carriage rattled off into the night.

The diversion of Vanguardly attention to herself had bought a few expensive minutes. She could only hope that Phlosine Valeur had managed to use them well.

Phlosine did so.

When Dref Zeenoson returned to his lodgings late that night, he came in to discover two Vanguardsmen occupying his chambers. One of the soldiers—a brawny, black-haired figure clad in the uniform of a lieutenant—lay motionless upon the bed. His head was wrapped in a bloodstained improvised bandage, and he seemed to be unconscious. The second soldier—plump and almost unpatriotically dapper—occupied the chair beside the bed.

Instantly a pistol materialized in Dref's right hand.

The dapper Vanguardsman appeared taken aback, almost embarrassed. He mumbled something about "forgetting," and "careless." He bowed his head, muttered unintelligibly, and the scene changed. Dref discovered Quinz vo Derrivalle stretched wounded and insensible upon the bed. Beside Quinz sat a pudgy-fingered, vaguely apologetic woman of indeterminate age and nondescript appearance.

Dref put his pistol away. "Mistress Valeur?" he inquired.

"I—well, I—that is to say—are you Master Renois? She told me to ask for Master Renois."

Dref's head jerked affirmatively. "What has happened?"

His face went white beneath its tan as he listened to her answer.

Many believed that the news of his sister's escape had driven Whiss Valeur mad. The Republican Protector's emotion did not manifest itself in public demonstrations. His convulsions, if any, took place behind discreetly closed doors; and the face displayed to Sherreen was all but immobile. Nevertheless, in the days and nights that followed, his actions and demeanor often smacked strongly of lunacy.

Beyond question, Phlosine's liberation reinforced the Protector's belief in a widespread conspiracy against his life. His response was unequivocal: an armed guard now surrounded him day and night; he had withdrawn from the modest house in Nerisante Street to the well-furnished, well-fortified suite of rooms on the top floor of the Sepulchre, traditionally the abode of the Governor of the prison; and he had vastly increased the security surrounding his one remaining magical captive, Chorl Valeur. The old man was no longer permitted freedom to roam the Nerisante Street house at will, to send letters or receive them. He was now lodged in a Sepulchre cell—pleasantly heated, lighted, and furnished, to be sure; but with barred windows, two armed guards stationed outside the locked door, and no communication with the outside world.

The tangible manifestations of the Protector's fears, however, did not confine themselves to defensive measures alone. The Committee of National Welfare had already suffered a purge. Next, it was the Congress itself that came under fire. The afternoon following Phlosine Valeur's escape, the Vanguard descended upon Century Hall. The Congressmen watched in sickly alarm as fully a score of their number were identified, plucked from their seats, and unceremoniously herded from the room. It was not the sudden-death abruptness, nor even the blatant illegality of the seizure, that chiefly terrified the witnesses so much as the choice of victims, which included a number of delegates commonly supposed to enjoy the Protector's trust and warmest regard. Who could have guessed that Jerundie delegate Rendourcis, first to come out in favor of dragging the King to trial, should now follow in Dunulas's footsteps? Who could have foreseen the downfall of such staunch Reparationists as Clessous, Danvaut, and Genaure? Who, above all, ever thought to see the erstwhile-cherished Congressman Poulpe led from the hall under guard? Although no sign of it showed upon his face, young Poulpe's own astonishment must surely have been intense. No doubt he had assumed that the capture of Quinz vo Derrivalle's niece, together with his gift to Whiss Valeur of the little Sentient discovered in Havillac Gardens, more than compensated for the loss of Phlosine Valeur. He was now discovering otherwise.

That time, they dispensed with the formality of a trial. Because the Republican Protector had, with his signature and seal, validated the document collectively outlawing the twenty chosen Congressmen, only identification was required to secure condemnation. By three o'clock that afternoon, the twenty had been sentenced to death—stripped, bound, and dispatched to Equality Circle. The executions proceeded without incident under the eyes of a wondering crowd. The condemned, apparently overwhelmed by the speed and totality of their downfall, were docile and largely silent. Only young Poulpe, icy dignity intact to the end, was heard to observe, as he mounted the scaffold, that "the Revolution, like a crazed god in an antique fable, ends by devouring its own children."

In the aftermath of the Spring Massacre, as the Congressional pruning was known, it was to be expected that Whiss Valeur would rest relatively quiet for a time; but such was hardly the case. Far from easing his mind, the destruction of his supposed enemies seemed only to waken new and sharper fears. The Protector's disquiet proclaimed itself in the nervous choppy speed of his gait, in the chronic trembling of his hands, and above all, in the intensity of his searching, mortally suspicious gaze. The burning green eyes, larger than ever in a haggard wasted visage, roamed continually; and those unfortunates on whom they lighted for more than a moment or two were marked men, thenceforth shunned by their fellows. The surviving Congressmen hid their terror as best they could, and a few hid something more; in the interests of self-preservation, the most desperate of them began to band together. Prior to the Spring Massacre, Whiss Valeur's suspicions had been groundless; thereafter, the Protector did not worry without just cause.

In the meantime, Sherreen discovered that the sacrifice of twenty Congressmen had barely begun to appease its Protector. The arrests that followed were plentiful, unpredictable, and apparently indiscriminate. The Vanguard cast its nets far and wide, drawing in a random assortment of unfortunates. During the two days following Phlosine Valeur's escape, arrests were said to number in the hundreds. It was doubtful that anyone troubled to keep accurate count, but one fact was undeniable: the city prisons were filled to bursting again, crowded as they had not been since the day the Kokotte commenced her great feeding.

If the underlying principle governing the choice of victims was obscure, at least there could be no doubt as to purpose. At each of Sherreen's three prisons, new arrivals were subjected to interrogation sufficient to kill the weakest outright. Only a handful of the luckiest thus shortened their miseries; by far the majority lived on to contemplate impending trial and execution.

Day and night the questionings proceeded, and the theme never varied. Had any prisoner possessed knowledge of the mysterious Quinz vo Derrivalle, his intentions or his whereabouts, the enthusiasts of the Vanguard would infallibly have extracted it. No one, however, knew anything of the Protector's magical enemy. Sherreenian ignorance was universal and perfectly genuine. The Vanguardsmen learned nothing. The hours passed, and Whiss Valeur's desperation mounted; while Quinz vo Derrivalle remained at large and invisible, though far less of a threat than any of his hunters could know.

The old man on the bed stirred and opened his eyes.

"Feeling better, Master Quinz?" Dref Zeenoson inquired.

"Head hurts. Is that you, my boy? I cannot seem to see." Quinz's voice was faint. He raised an unsteady hand to his eyes. "What has become of my spectacles?"

"Lost in the Havillac Gardens, most likely."

The hand wandered, brushed a linen bandage. "But what——?"

"You were hit in the head with a flying rock. You've a gashed temple that was bleeding pretty freely."

"I do not remember that."

"Not surprising. You've been unconscious for the past twenty-four hours."

"Have I? Have I really? But how extraordinary. How did I get back here, my boy? Little Eliste and Mistress Valeur carried me, I suppose?"

"Phlosine alone."

"Ah? But where is she, I must thank her."

"Already gone. En route for Vaurve Province, I believe. She flew like a frightened bird, and nothing I could say would stop her."

"But she is in great need of healing solitude. Who can blame her?"

"I can. She was needed here, and she is in your debt. She should have remained. Almost I was tempted to insist."

"No, no. Never think it, my boy. It would be a great cruelty. Has she not suffered enough?"

"The dissatisfactions of Whiss Valeur's sister do not particularly move me. There are matters of greater import to consider—Eliste's safety, for example."

"Eliste? Ask the child to visit me. I must tell her how well she did."

"Difficult, under the circumstances. She is missing. She never returned from the Havillac Gardens. I still await confirmation, but judging upon the evidence, it appears almost certain that Eliste fell into the hands of the Vanguard last night." Dref spoke in the flat, almost matter-of-fact tone with which he was wont to address calamity.

Quinz possessed no such coolness. "Surely not—oh, surely not!" The old man attempted to sit up. He half raised himself, and fell back, gasping.

"Easy, sir. Better stay where you are. You're not well enough to move yet."

"How could this happen?"

"Phlosine was not altogether certain, as her attention was otherwise engaged at the time. When you lost consciousness, the illusion maintaining the military disguises collapsed. At Eliste's request, Phlosine was occupied in restoring the glamor when the Vanguard patrol approached. She was only dimly aware of Eliste's withdrawal. Clearly Eliste succeeded in diverting the soldiers' attention, but at considerable cost."

"It is my fault, entirely my fault." The tears were welling in Quinz's eyes. "I should never have brought her to that place. But I did not perceive the risk—I imagined that my art furnished absolute protection. I was a self-satisfied fool. And now little Eliste suffers for my carelessness, my arrogance, my mad folly. Oh, somehow I must make amends!"

"Calmly, Master Quinz. Lie quiet for now. There's no profit in self-recrimination—it is pointless, and you will only undermine your own strength."

"How can you sound so calm, so cold? Have you no care for my niece? Have you no feelings?"

"I will not let them rule me now, and neither should you. Far better that we devote our time and energy to planning."

"You are right, my boy, of course you are right. I am sorry, I know you care for her as much as I do. Oh, if only my mind were clear! Right now it is clouded, all is jumbled and disarrayed—I cannot see, and that is so confusing—"

"The result of your injury, but you will mend—soon, we may hope. As for your lost spectacles, they're easily replaced. In the meantime, try to compose yourself and let us address the problem at hand. The departure of Phlosine Valeur dashed my immediate hope of employing her magical abilities to Eliste's benefit— or to Shorvi Nirienne's, for that matter. Phlosine is gone, but you remain. We have hitherto regarded the Sepulchre prison as impenetrable. But now that I learn of your power to transform human appearance, various possibilities suggest themselves. Master Quinz, can you disguise me? Can you lend me the form and voice of another man?"

"You mean someone now living? But who, my boy?"

"Let us say, for example—Whiss Valeur."

"Ah. I see. I see. Very good. Ordinarily, I should have little doubt, but now I am not so certain. Let us put it to the test. Please help me to sit up, if you will be so kind."

Dref slipped an arm about Quinz vo Derrivalle's shoulders, raised him gently, propped him up with pillows, gave him a glass of water. Quinz sat motionless for a time. Presently, he bowed his head and muttered phrases unintelligible to his listener. He spoke for a very long time. He spoke until the effort and strain, so fatal to magical endeavor, began to burden his voice, and the telltale beads of sweat dewed his forehead.

At last the struggling voice died away. Quinz raised his head and opened wet eyes. "I cannot do it," he whispered. "It does not come, there is nothing. It is gone from me."

"It will come back, when you have recovered your strength." No trace of doubt or profound disappointment was permitted to touch Dref Zeenoson's still face.

"And Eliste? I am so sorry." The tears were streaming freely down Quinz's ashen cheeks. "Forgive me. Oh, I am so very sorry."

The Sepulchre was not what she had expected. All the whispered tales she had ever overheard spoke of prisoners permitted to mingle almost freely with one another. For many Exalted, forced throughout the dangerous months to hide, concealing their identities and disavowing all that they were, incarceration offered a certain measure of relief. Here at least was an end to doubt, suspense, pretense, and isolation. Here, the death of hope banished the sharpest of terrors; and the doomed victims of the Revolution, taking comfort in fellowship, often lived out the brief remainder of their lives in relative peace.

But for Eliste, it was not like that.

They brought her in through a small side entrance designed for unobtrusiveness, if not downright secrecy. At once she was struck by the stench of the place—a nauseous compound of filth, fear, smoke, rancid oil, and above all, utterly unmoving dank air—worse by far than the Treasury's atmosphere, perhaps because the Sepulchre was an older building, its miasm thoroughly ripened over the course of centuries. She gagged.

"You'll get used to it, Bonbon," one of the Vanguardsmen assured her, not unkindly. "Breathe through your mouth." It was surprising how devoid of rancor her captors seemed to be; rather like winners in a heat of Cutthroat, willing to set aside all animosity once the match was over. But then, they could afford it. Doubtless each soldier was mentally guzzling or devouring his own share of the hundred-rekko price upon Eliste vo Derrivalle's head. No wonder their mood was genial.

The search to which she was subjected was no more indecent than necessity demanded. Afterward, they conducted her along a reeking corridor, down a moistly spiraling flight of stairs, and another few yards along a puddle-splotched gallery to a tiny windowless closet of a cell. Eliste entered. She caught a brief glimpse of oozing stone walls, slop bucket in the corner, a narrow shelf of a bed reminiscent of Prilq's Hospitality. Then the door slammed, the bolt shot home, and the guards withdrew, taking their lanterns with them and leaving her alone in absolute darkness. Alone. She hadn't counted on that.

Eliste felt her way to the bed, sat down on the edge, and waited for her eyes to adjust. While she waited, the merciful cloud that seemed to have blanketed her perceptions and emotions since the moment of her arrest began to lift. Much against her own will, she began to think and feel again; and the terror twisted her insides, whipping her heart to a gallop. The humid chilly darkness smothered and crushed her, sweat drenched her; she had to struggle for breath. Far better to be dull, insensible; but her former blunted condition was gone, and there was no regaining it. She sat absolutely still. Not the slightest whisper of sound intruded upon her unwelcome consciousness.

Thought avalanched uncontrollably.

She was isolated, given unusual treatment, because her case was special. She was not simply another captured Exalted. She was the niece of Quinz vo Derrivalle, magical enemy of the Republic; his kinswoman, ally, and accomplice. There was much she might tell them of Quinz—of his plans, his methods, and (assuming Phlosine had managed to spirit him from the Havillac Gardens) of his whereabouts. The ghouls of the Sepulchre would no doubt press her to do so.

Press her.

Eliste shuddered invisibly in the dark. The horrors of the Sepulchre cellars were legendary. If they broke her, then Uncle Quinz was finished; Dref as well. And through Dref, how much of the Nirienniste network? Her disclosures could wreak havoc.

But how could she hope to resist? If they hurt her badly enough, wouldn't she give them anything in the world they wanted? Wouldn't anyone?

No. Zeralenn wouldn't.

The image of her grandmother's face lighted her mind. There was no threat or torture that could ever have broken the will of Zeralenn vo Rouvignac, no force that could ever have torn a betrayal from her lips. It was not that she had been gifted with any magical power to resist; she merely subscribed to a particular code of behavior that was the source of her strength and fatal inflexibility alike. She had lived and died by that code. She would expect her granddaughter to do no less.

Zeralenn's attitudes belonged to the past; she would never have accepted the present, violently transformed world. But some things hadn't changed, would never change; loyalty and honor were among them. Zeralenn vo Rouvignac would have died under torture to protect family and friends. Eliste would follow that example.

She wouldn't speak. They would have nothing from her. The decision brought terror and a strange satisfaction. Alone in the black silence, she tended the new resolution that was like a sickly infant in need of nourishment.

Blind darkness pressed in on her; no light whatever entered her cell. Perhaps that would change in the morning.

But she did not have to wait until morning for a change.

She realized she could make out the outline of the bucket in the corner, the rectangular shape of the bed. Rising, she stepped to the door and peered out through the small, square grill. Faint glow of yellow light in the corridor. Tramp of booted feet on stone. The light grew stronger. She shrank back from the door. Cast her frightened eyes about the tiny, slowly brightening cell in ridiculous search of refuge. No refuge, of course. She took a deep breath and stood up straight.

Looming shapes visible through the grill. Scrape of the bolt, and the door opened. Two of them had come for her. Without a word, the Vanguardsmen grabbed her, one at each arm, and hustled her out of the cell. Eliste neither queried nor resisted; the first would have been pointless, the second, absurd. She would do far better to conserve her strength and courage.

Along the gallery, back to the moist spiral staircase, then down, down, dizzyingly and endlessly down, to the demon realm of the Sepulchre cellars. Down, ever down, to a place of murky ochre fogs, weeping ceilings, and mineral-crusted walls, more like a cavern than a human construction. Along a sloping tunnel of a passageway, with ceiling so low that the two soldiers had to duck their heads; through a portal of hammered black iron; and into the infamous torture vault.

She had no mental image of the vault, no idea what awaited her there. The deliberately preserved mystery of the place added immeasurably to its terror, a terror wont to erode victims' resistance well in advance of actual interrogation, as the masters of the old prison were well aware. Had she possessed any clear expectations, however, it was quite possible that reality would have confirmed them in most particulars, for the chamber was constructed along fairly traditional lines: windowless, of course, for it was far underground; cold; motionless, malodorous air; startlingly high ceiling, possibly three stories high, with stone ribbing lost in the heavy dim mists; stone walls oozing moisture, damp and stain-mottled floor; smoky, glowing lanterns; braziers, unlighted; an assortment of ancient and ghastly devices, some of unguessable purpose, others of all-too-obvious utility, but all of them rusty, dusty, and clearly unused. Three newer constructions—clean, oiled, and polished—elaborate contraptions equipped with clamps, straps, and buckles; crowned with wires, spikes, metallic barbs, and glittering glassy whorls—very much reminiscent of the Sentients, whose debased cousins they were. And finally, a plain pine table and a couple of serviceable chairs, one of them occupied by a vast figure whose broad, flat visage and outsize hands she recognized—Bierce Valeur, the Kokotte's high priest. His presence was quite predictable, and yet she was startled, for she had never before realized how huge he truly was.

To avoid the Vanguardsmen's touch, Eliste walked forward voluntarily, halting at Bierce Valeur's table. The two soldiers positioned themselves before the door. The table was bare save for a sheet of paper, inkpot, and quill. Bierce Valeur pushed the paper toward her. "Sign," he commanded.

Eliste picked it up and read. She had expected a confession, some elaborate catalogue of crimes that self-respect would force her to reject. Nothing of the sort, however. Here was but a simple affidavit, establishing her identity as the formerly-Exalted Eliste vo Derrivalle, kinswoman to the formerly-Exalted Quinz vo Derrivalle, magician of Fabeque Province. Only the truth, and since they somehow knew so much, ridiculous to deny. Eliste shrugged and signed. She was unacquainted with recent Congressional legislation, and thus unaware that her official proscription rendered simple identification sufficient to secure condemnation. In acknowledging her name, she forfeited her right to a trial; given the complexion of the National Tribunal, however, the sacrifice was negligible.

Bierce Valeur scrutinized the signature at length, nodded, and set the document aside. He looked up; subjected the prisoner to a similar protracted scrutiny, which she sustained stonily; and at last demanded, "Where is Quinz vo Derrivalle?" Confronted with the size and physical menace of him, she might have expected terrifying stentorian tones. In fact, his voice, like his small eyes, was dull and flat.

So Uncle Quinz had escaped the Havillac Gardens.

I don't know. The lie flew for her lips, but she repressed it. Her inquisitor would not believe it; no one would. That so, she might as well die with an unsoiled mouth. "I do not choose to tell you," she said.

Bierce regarded the prisoner opaquely. If her reply surprised him, he showed no sign of it. "Where is Quinz vo Derrivalle?" he repeated, without the least alteration in tone, as if asking for the first time.

She repeated her refusal.

The next time he asked, she did not answer, but her silence failed to deter him. He reiterated the question. He kept asking, droning out the same words again and again, each repetition identical to the first in content, pitch, and flat, unvarying tone. Eliste stood mute and statue-faced, but inside her, confusion joined with fear to batter her defenses. Had he threatened, she would have defied him; had he attempted to persuade with sophistry, she might even have made speeches; but she did not know what to make of this relentless, impervious stupidity. There was something uncanny in the monotonous queries, which seemed hardly the product of a human voice or mind. Colorless utterance and consistency were mechanical, as if Bierce Valeur had assumed the attributes of the Sentients with which he consorted.

"Where is Quinz vo Derrivalle?"

Twentieth repetition? Twenty-fifth? Had she somehow trapped herself in a single bizarre moment destined to repeat itself endlessly?

Not endlessly. Bierce must have lost patience at last. Without warning, he stood and stepped around the table, moving with a speed and suddenness wholly at variance with his ungainly appearance. He was at her side; his hand clamped like a vise on her arm. He quarter-turned her, and effortlessly propelled her across the room. Just so, he brought his victims to the Kokotte; but this time, it was only the Kokotte's dim cousin, a nameless semi-Sentient, that awaited the offering.

There before her was a long, flat, leather-covered framework, almost like a pallet. Before she understood what he intended, Bierce had picked her up as if she weighed nothing, and stretched her out upon it. If only she had thought faster, moved faster, she might have scratched his eyes; but already the chance was gone. The clamps and straps were all about her; he was tightening and buckling, big hands moving with horrible deftness. She strained experimentally against the restraints; found herself helpless, unable to stir. And then there were the wristlets and collar, with their loops, spirals, and wire attachments; and worse, the headpiece, with its barbs and whorls, its iron visor devoid of eyeholes snapping down across her face to seal her in darkness. The area about her mouth had been left clear, she noted. She could talk, or scream.

She would do neither. She lay, every muscle tensed to resist whatever was to be inflicted on her.

Nothing happened.

She could hear Bierce Valeur moving, very near her. She felt the air stir as he passed. She had no idea what he was doing, or what was to follow, and that torturous suspense was no doubt deliberately prolonged. She heard a faint metallic click, a crackle followed by a thin, mechanical whine. A vibration shivered the frame on which she lay. Her hands tightened spasmodically on the edges of the pallet.

"Where is Quinz vo Derrivalle?" No change at all in the flat voice. No trace of expression.

She was silent.

Click, snap, and the semi-Sentient's whine subsided to a steady hum, something like the sound Glorielle made when she was enjoying herself.

Still no harm; but rather the opposite, it seemed. For the darkness about her was lightening by the moment, and presently she could see. The visor still obscured her face and eyes. She could feel its cold touch on forehead and cheeks, yet the iron had assumed the transparency of glass. She saw the vaulted ceiling three stories above her; the Vanguardsmen waiting before the door; Bierce Valeur standing at her side, watching her with the blank eyes of a dead thing. By raising her head very slightly, all the motion that the restraints permitted, she could view the length of her own body—naked as any of the Kokotte's victims, and she didn't remember being stripped—wrapped in straps and iron bands. Yet that vision was an impossibility, and the logic that told her so was seconded by that small, prickle-nerved sensation of wrongness—the sensation that she had learned signaled the influence of magical illusion upon her perceptions. The signal was faint, however; and so great her fear and humiliation, almost overlooked.

Her attention was fixed on Bierce Valeur. No blade, cord, or other such sinister implement in the outsize hands. Nothing beyond a harmless collection of wheels and cogs, with which he toyed almost unconsciously. No word or gesture to reveal his intentions.

A faint buzzing came to her ears, grew louder as she listened. It did not sound mechanical. Whatever the source of the noise, it seemed to be in the air, and moving. Her eyes left Bierce Valeur for a moment, skittered apprehensively around the room.

Whizzing, looping, buzzing black dot overhead; nothing but a fly—an unusually large one, to be sure, but nothing to fear. Curious that the insect had managed to find its way down to this chamber so deep underground; but then, flies turned up everywhere. This one seemed peculiarly attracted to the prisoner. It was circling just above her, swooping low and darting in to touch bare skin, resting briefly before her convulsive twitch or shudder frightened it off.

But not for long. Surely the creature was gifted with diabolical intelligence, for it soon seemed to recognize the impotence of its victim's squirmings. Thereafter it landed and clung, buzzing loudly, as if in mockery of all effort to dislodge it. Eliste soon gave up trying. It was, after all, absurd at such a time to squander her concern upon such a trivial thing as a lone fly.

But the fly was not alone.

Buzzing overhead; a second zipping, looping dot in the air; another fly, similarly attracted to the prisoner's body. And then another. And another. A whole swarm of them, swollen black creatures gleaming with a wicked blue-green-gold iridescence. The air was dark with them, they were everywhere; circling, darting, clinging, and stinging. In vain she writhed, jerked, and shuddered. The insects clung, more like leeches than flies. They were crawling upon her eyelids, vibrating upon her compressed lips, buzzing in her ears and nostrils. The feel and sound of them were maddening, but she could bear it. They weren't really hurting her. She could bear it.

More of them, hundreds of the hideous things clustering upon her, and what, oh what was drawing them? Had someone smeared her with honey, or syrup?

A faint odor rose to her nostrils, a graveyard breath, heavy and almost sweet with putrefaction. Decaying meat nearby, rank and rotten stuff that even the hungriest of Eighth District street folk would have spurned, but an irresistible lure to flies.

That charnel-house stench was intensifying, stuffing the atmosphere with itself, blotting out all else, and calling to the flies. So thickly pervasive the odor that the source, the putrid lure, had to be very near; she was lying beside it or on it. She raised her head a little to view her fly-ridden body. The insects seethed upon her; between dark masses of them, the formerly white flesh showed grayish and oddly blurred, clean youthful lines softened and almost smudged.

At first she didn't understand, thought it a trick of the uncertain light. But when the gray-greenish patches like lichen appeared, and the thin crusts split, revealing liquescent matter beneath, there could be no further refusal to recognize her body's decay. Here was the source of the stench, here the lure of the flies. Her flesh was rotting from the bone.

She lost all reason and courage then. Fought, screaming, against the straps and clamps that held her. Succeeded only in tearing the weakened skin, opening long, gray-brown lesions into which the insects eagerly inserted themselves.

"Where is Quinz vo Derrivalle?" For the first and only time, Bierce Valeur varied the deadly litany of interrogation. "Tell, and it will stop."

No.

Time was out of joint in the vaulted cellars of the Sepulchre. For only a temporal misalignment could have explained the speed with which the flies' eggs hatched. A few scant moments of incubation sufficed to develop them; then they relinquished their contents, and the maggots were there, a pallid population of them crawling through and into and over the degenerate tissue that was both shelter and sustenance. She was white and glistening with them.

Where is Quinz vo Derrivalle?

Voice like a gong, not to be denied. But didn't he see that she couldn't open her mouth to answer without swallowing maggots and flies? They would be inside her then, wriggling down her throat and beyond, and how could he imagine that she would voluntarily admit them? How did he think she *could* speak, even if she were willing?

Because he knew it wasn't real. Because he ruled the semi-Sentient that generated illusion.

Her schooling came to her aid then; all the hours spent with Uncle Quinz, all the effort and practice, had strengthened her more than she knew. She recognized the illusion, but a mind swamped with terror and delirious revulsion was not capable of breaking it. She could not so much as begin to collect her thoughts or focus her will. She attempted as much, and failed utterly.

Where is Quinz vo Derrivalle?

No.

She maintained silence. That much she could do.

The semi-Sentient, whose function was to break and conquer, must have felt her resistance and responded accordingly, for the illusion changed.

Now there was an inexplicable excruciation deep inside her, wrenching at her joints and bones. Her bones. She could feel them quivering like crystal under the onslaught of a soprano's top note. Impossible. Unreal. But she could feel it, the horror and pain were real enough. Bones trembling, vibrating, shaking themselves loose from one another; skeleton ripping itself apart, and not only at the joints. Snap of a dry branch, and she screamed as the large bone in her right arm shattered violently, jagged white shards bursting through their corrupted covering in a dreadful spray of blood, morsels of flesh, and maggots. And the smell—the smell—

Where is Quinz vo Derrivalle?

No. It isn't real.

Wasn't it? Wasn't it? Illusion was all the universe, as her bones splintered, one after another; long sharp fragments knifing out through the flesh of arms and legs, fractured ribs driving inward to pierce her vitals. And the blood, and the smell, and the buzzing of the flies . . .

Where is Quinz vo Derrivalle?

NO.

Try to remember what her uncle had taught her, try to fight back; but no, useless; lunatic convulsed mind all but ungovernable.

Mechanical click/snap, and the illusion altered.

Her right arm was shaking and jerking under the strap that confined it. She herself was not responsible. It moved of its own volition, as if imbued with independent life. She couldn't stop herself from turning her head to watch the big bone, the shattered humerus, twist and yank itself free of its joints. Final sharp pull, and the last of the connective tissue snapped. The humerus, having achieved autonomy, slowly crawled out of the ruined right arm. It was still recognizably a human bone; still white, fringed with trailing tendons and ligaments. But now, fractures somehow mended, it was flexible as a serpent, and the emphatic indentation at its lower end had become a mouth equipped with a full set of teeth fit for a rat.

The bone crawled slowly up her body, raising a black cloud of flies as it went. Over her stomach, over her chest, and up to her throat, where it paused a moment, evidently intrigued by the pulse. Then up onto her face, and never mind the fact that an iron visor armored her—she could feel the pressure, the friction of the hard yet oddly flexible form passing over her lips, her nose, an eye, her forehead. And there it stopped, draped diagonally across her face. A moment's stillness, and then the teeth, teeth like a rat's, gnawing at her scalp.

Where is Quinz vo Derrivalle?

Why not dead yet, or at least unconscious? Not very much courage left in her; she had spent nearly all of it.

Gnawing at her scalp, and the warm stream oozing through her hair; and then the scrape of tooth on bone, and the wet chewing changed to a sharp crunch, as of mice nibbling at wooden walls.

Where is Quinz vo Derrivalle?

No bright internal flare of defiance. Only the imperative to end it somehow, coupled with a weak but persistent recognition of the cheat.

No more crunching. The bony barrier of the skull was breached. The soft gray delicacy within was being consumed, and with it died intelligence and identity. There was no pain; in fact, her body had gone quite numb. A mercy; and yet she would have preferred any suffering to this lifeless anesthesia.

But sensation was only the first thing to go. Her consciousness was darkening. Thought, volition, memory, even fear—they were fading. All that essentially defined her was being literally eaten away, and the prospect of subsequent mindless existence was the worst torment of all. She would be an animal, or less. They would allow her to live on in that state for decades.

Where is Quinz vo Derrivalle?

One Hundred and Six, Flou's Pocket, in Rat Town. Unfortunately, she still remembered. The monstrosity feeding on mind and memories had somehow contrived to leave her that. She could still betray Uncle Quinz. Something broke inside her, and she knew she would do so. There was no more resistance left, no loyalty and honor to sustain her—those things had been crushed, or more likely, devoured. She might hold out for a few moments longer, but not more. She would betray him, and not even the memory of her grandmother's face would stop her. In effect, it was already done, although the words had not yet emerged.

Extraordinary, the terror of that thought, deadly as anything the semi-Sentient could offer. Terror that froze or calmed her; impossible to tell the difference, if there was a difference. All she knew was that her mind was her own again for a moment—perhaps the last moment.

Something of reason came back to her, a recollection of her uncle's teachings. Illusion, even the strongest, did not withstand the totality of rejection. The trained eye fixed upon the reality beyond illusion. All the force of violent emotion could be channeled to serve her, if only she remembered how; and yes, she could, for this moment she did remember.

Everything in her of horror, hate, and desperation blasted like a bomb. For an instant she saw and felt herself engulfed in roaring blue-white flame, and a scream was wrung from her. The illusion, and all horrific components thereof, vanished as if vaporized. The semi-Sentient beeped in shrill agony, and the grip of its clamps weakened.

Eliste found herself lying, fully dressed and soaked in cold sweat, upon a sweat-dank leather pallet. Her head ached fiercely; she was faint and nauseated. Otherwise, she believed herself physically unharmed, but this was impossible to verify, for an iron visor obscured her vision. For a few moments she lay there, inexpressibly feeble and tired, her mind all but empty. When Bierce Valeur, low brow creased in a puzzled frown, loosed the straps and hauled her abruptly from the pallet, the pain lanced through her head, the room wheeled slowly, and she lost consciousness.

She was back in her solitary windowless cell again. No telling how long she had been there. But it was daytime—the faint ray of colorless light filtering in through the grill told her as much—and someone had thrust a tray with a bowl of gruel and a pan of water in through the slot at the bottom of the door. She was not hungry, but her mouth and throat were parched. Dragging herself from the bed to the tray, she knelt and gulped down the water in one long draft, without stopping to consider whether she was likely to receive any more for the rest of the day. Then back to the bed again, to lie there unmoving, unthinking and unfeeling, until the gray air deepened to black, and awareness did likewise.

Gray again when she awoke, and now youth and health reasserted themselves, breaking her lassitude. Thought and sensation intruded. Cold, misery, and raging curiosity. Of her own impending fate there could be no question, and she preferred not to dwell on it. But what had become of Uncle Quinz? And Phlosine Valeur? Obviously Quinz had escaped the Havillac Gardens, but did he remain at large? The hours had passed, and her own interrogation was not repeated; if the quarry continued to elude them, would the hunters not have questioned her again? The recollection of the torture vault shot the ice along her veins, at the same time filling her with a defiant sort of pride. She had defeated the semi-Sentient, which was almost certainly the chief terror the Sepulchre had to offer. Should she meet the device again, she would defeat it again—more swiftly and surely the second time, for now she realized her strength. There was nothing worse they could inflict upon her; and this so, she knew with absolute certainty that she was safe—she would never betray her uncle.

Perhaps Bierce Valeur and his minions recognized as much. Perhaps that accounted for her unbroken isolation. For nobody came to her, and there were no more questions. The days passed, and her solitude was interrupted only by the visits of the turnkey, a pimply puffy lout of twenty or so who never spoke a word.

On the afternoon of the third day, however, came a change.

Eliste lay on her bed, dreaming with her eyes open. She thought of Flou's Pocket, she thought of Dref Zeenoson. She was able, for long stretches at a time, to lose herself in such thoughts. Today, however, the reverie was broken by a light tap and a faint hiss. Raising herself on one elbow, she turned to look, and spied a white face at the grill. Not the turnkey's face.

Visitor? Here? Eliste was at the door in an instant. Through the bars she glimpsed round cheeks and chin, snub nose, a mass of brown ringlets. Girl's face, young, familiar-looking. In the wretched prison twilight it was difficult to judge, and yet—

It was not until the other spoke that Eliste was certain.

"Why, Cousin—I scarce believed that I should find you down here. Gad, what a dismal hole!"

"Aurelie!"

"Ssssshh—you mustn't call me that! Here in this place, I am Compeeress Ninette."

"Compeeress?"

"Common, is it not? But one must bow to the temper of the times, la! It is the only way to get on, is it not?"

"But—what have you—why are you—? It has been months since— Forgive me, I don't understand."

"La, how astonished you look! But there is no mystery, Cousin. I have been very clever, that is all. I have deceived our enemies; I have thoroughly befooled them. Indeed, it was not difficult, they are so simple!"

"What have you done?"

"Transformed myself! You see, upon the night of our arrest—gad, what a dreadful episode that was!—your woman had wit and impudence enough to assume your identity—"

Oh, my poor, brave Kairthe.

"Indeed, it was most artfully done, and I am not too proud to be schooled by a soubrette. Thus, when we came to the Sepulchre, and the canaille demanded our names, I presented myself as Compeeress Ninette, lady's maid to the Countess vo Rouvignac. Let me assure you, I am an accomplished actress. Had I not been born Exalted, surely I should have reigned upon the stage. Accent, gestures, bearing—all were quite perfect. My performance was a triumph, and the ruse succeeded."

"You denied your name, your family, your class and heritage? You did that?"

"Well, what choice had I? You needn't assume such superior airs with *me*, Cousin. Throughout these months that you have remained at liberty, did you not do the same?"

That was true enough. *But I would not have done so here,* Eliste thought. Pragmatism, even reason, favored Aurelie; but the old Exalted standards were hard to forget. It was not, however, the time or place to argue the point. Aloud, she merely inquired, "And Madame said nothing?"

"Oh—Grauntie ... Well." Even in the dim light, the rush of color to Aurelie's cheeks was visible. She stirred uncomfortably. "Well. You know how she was. You know how unkind and unjust she could be. She did not betray me. But the look she gave me! As if I had done murder, or worse. And then, when the three of us were left alone for a bit in the holding cell before they questioned us—the awful things she said to me! The abuse, the accusations, that icy cruelty! So unfair! Quite, quite unforgivable! And if she had loved me as a kinswoman ought, she would have been *happy* that I had a chance to live—she would never have blamed me for it! But she was always like that. After the interrogation, because Grauntie was Exalted, and the canaille supposed that I was not, we were taken to separate quarters. I did not see her again. Perhaps that was for the best."

No doubt.

"You did as you must, I suppose," said Eliste. "And yet, for all your cunning, it's a wonder you're still here. As the servant of a countess, you might well have been viewed as a monarchist. In fact, it is amazing that you weren't accused."

"Oh—perhaps I would have been—I daresay—had not Fliques defended me."

"Fliques—a lawyer?"

"Gad, no! He is one of the turnkeys. You must have seen him, he is in charge of this level."

"You mean that voiceless white slug with the pimples?"

"That is unkind, Cousin. He is not quite pretty, I grant. But he is not a slug, and it is wrong to call him one, after all he has done for me."

"I'm sorry. But what has he done for you? What *could* a mere turnkey do?"

"He has stolen the record of my arrest and interrogation from out of the files. Hence, I am not here. Officially, I do not exist. Thus, I cannot be accused. There, now—that is what a mere turnkey could do. What have you to say to that?"

"I'm astonished. He would meet the Lady if that were known. Why should he do such a thing for you?"

"Oh, he is madly in love with me. He is ready to die for me, as that poor boy Bayelle died for me. He is my absolute slave, la!"

"Indeed."

"He is! He is!"

"I see. In that case, why are you still here? If there is no record and no charge against you, why have you not been released?"

"Oh, I do not seek release. What should I do out there on the streets? Here, at least, I am sheltered and I do not go hungry."

"There is something in that. But only consider the risk. Here, there are Vanguardsmen and Exalted everywhere. The danger of recognition is enormous. Perhaps, if this Fliques is so devoted, he could help you further—"

"Oh, Fliques will not permit me to leave. It is quite impossible. If I should even dream of escape, my missing records will reappear upon the Lieutenant Governor's desk. He has promised as much."

"Then he is your enemy."

"No, no indeed. He adores me, and there is all the trouble. Having risked so much for my sake, he has sworn he will not forgo the use of me."

"The use— Oh, Aurelie! You have not—with the turnkey—surely you could not—"

"Well, what choice had I? Don't look at me like that! What other choice had I?"

"Oh, you poor miserable wretch! There is nothing left of you!"

"Gad, you sound just exactly like Grauntie! And it is all such folly! I have not changed in the least—I am just the same as I always was."

That, Eliste reflected, was almost certainly true.

"Why, then, should anyone change *toward* me? And why blame me for what I could not help? Would you rather have me dead than alive? Come, Cousin— don't be cross with me. I am well enough, and Fliques is not so bad. He is quite devoted, there's nothing he would not do for me—sometimes he brings me chocolate, or pastry—"

"Oh, Aurelie."

"Ninette. And he tells me things, and lets me roam where I will about the building. How do you think I knew you were here, and came down to visit you today?"

"I see. Has he explained to you why I am kept here alone, for days on end, and never brought to the National Tribunal?"

"I do not think he could know such a thing. But I have been told that you are a most desperate criminal, and they keep you here to use as a weapon against your uncle, an even more desperate criminal. Or something of the sort. Cousin, whatever can you have done to cause such a stir? Was it so dreadful that you deserve this *dungeon*? Gad, what an appalling kennel! There is no window. The floor is wet. It is so cold down here, I'm shivering! You do not even have a *candle*. It is too ghastly!"

"The Sepulchre is not renowned for its amenities."

"I will tell you what you must do. You must smile at Fliques when next you see him—smile *so*, with your head a little to the side like this, and your eyes all sparkling—and he will bring you candles. No doubt but that you are pale, Cousin, *terribly* pale, and yet I believe you might carry it off."

"I don't think so."

"Gad, you are quite as stiff-necked as Grauntie, and it will bring you to the same place. Very well, if you will not deign to help yourself, then I must ask on your behalf. Perhaps it is all for the best; Fliques will deny me nothing. But, mind you, Cousin—" Aurelie held up an admonitory finger. "You must tell no one that we are kinswomen."

"No fear."

"And you must not be cross with me. It would not be fair, for nothing that happened has been my fault, nothing. You are not cross?"

"No." Eliste's smile was faint but genuine. "I'm not cross."

"Ah, Cousin, I knew you would be my friend! Farewell for now, then. I cannot stay longer, I shall be missed. You may expect your candles and a blanket very soon. I've only to drop a word in Fliques's ear. You'll see—he will deny me nothing!"

Aurelie departed, and Eliste could hear her quick light footsteps retreating down the corridor. A distant door slammed, and then silence, broken only by the regular, inexorable drip of moisture from ceiling to floor, like the ticking of a clock.

Perhaps Aurelie's influence was less than she had imagined, for the day passed and neither candle nor blanket materialized. The next afternoon, however, Fliques himself appeared. His presence at such an hour was anomalous, and Eliste was instantly on guard. Had her cousin's visit roused suspicion—was that what this was about? But no. For the first and only time, the turnkey spoke to her, in a voice unlovely as his person. He had come to announce the news of the hour—the Nirienne Gang's trial had finally concluded. Properly convicted and condemned at last, Shorvi Nirienne and his accomplices were scheduled to meet the Kokotte at sunset of the following day. Aesthetics mandated the unusual lateness of the appointment. The death of the Republican Protectorate's archenemy—an event of historical significance, and a great Reparationist triumph—demanded careful stage management, and it was generally agreed that the Kokotte's luminous display would show to best advantage against the darkening sky.

It was further decreed, by those Committee members possessed of artistic leanings, that a selection of hors d'oeuvres should whet the appetite of Sentient and spectators for the main course to follow; the victims to be chosen with an eye to political significance and, if possible, interesting appearance. At the top of the list, fulfilling every requirement, was the formerly-Exalted Eliste vo Derrivalle—notable Proscription, conspirator, counterrevolutionary, and bona fide Bonbon, all in one.

liste sat listening for the sound of footsteps. Twenty-four hours or more had elapsed since Fliques's announcement of her condemnation, and nothing had happened. The interval between sentencing and execution was ordinarily counted in minutes, not hours. The present delay was unheard of. Could Fliques have been lying, enjoying a cruel joke at her expense? Once or twice she'd tried questioning him, but the turnkey had relapsed into his former impenetrable silence.

The suspense would end eventually, of course; there was only one way it could end. In the meantime, she could neither eat nor sleep. Almost, she would welcome the appearance of the Vanguardly escort.

But Fliques had not been lying. Late in the afternoon, they came for her—a couple of heavyset brown-and-scarlet figures, obviously equipped to control the most rebellious of prisoners. In this case, however, their manacles, truncheons, and steel-toed boots proved redundant; Eliste offered no resistance.

Out of the cell and along the corridor. No conversation. Dull rapping of footsteps on stone. Abnormally acute vision, and a sense of dreamlike unreality. Up the winding stairs to the Sepulchre's ground-floor level, and thence to the grim, bare room where Bierce Valeur's assistants prepared the condemned for execution.

Sixteen prisoners there, including herself. A motley assortment of men and women, the majority nondescript in appearance, but an unusually high percentage of the visually distinctive—a very old man with a gray beard down to his waist, an emaciated woman whose every bone and sinew was visible beneath her thin skin, a man with a withered arm, a brace of identical twin sisters. And there, only a few feet away, the famous Nirienne Gang: Frezhelle, Riclairc, the Bulaude siblings, and Shorvi Nirienne himself, center of this particular storm—an ordinary-looking middle-aged man, with brown hair running to gray, pale scholarly face, brown eyes intelligent and very alive, for all that he stood within minutes of his death. So that was Dref Zeenoson's hero. Even at such a time, Eliste's interest stirred faintly. Nirienne seemed composed, reflective, unafraid. Impossible not to admire such a demeanor—Zeralenn vo Rouvignac herself would have commended it, while deploring its author's convictions.

The prisoners were commanded to disrobe. Almost grateful to be spared the indignity of a forcible stripping, all complied, tossing their discarded garments onto the growing pile in the middle of the room. Eliste picked at her lacings. Brief flash of recollection: Dref's gift of the gray-blue wool from which she had fashioned her dress; late winter–early spring pale sunshine slanting through the window of the Flou's Pocket lodgings to strike sparks off her dancing needle; modeling the completed garment for Dref; *"There is Eliste again."*

Off came the dress, and then the linen underthings. The nudity that would ordinarily have scorched her with shame seemed unimportant now. Hers was only one among sixteen bodies, and it didn't matter. One of the guards removed the heap of garments, which would be searched for hidden valuables before passing into the possession of the undergaolers and turnkeys.

Their hands upon her briefly, and the sharp bite of a cord at her wrists as they tied her. This action was performed without undue brutality, very swiftly and professionally. Eliste did not struggle. A couple of the women and one of the men were weeping silently, but nobody struggled.

Moving now, a little flock of them skillfully herded by the guards; along the corridor, two steps down, low portal groaning wide, and then out into the courtyard, where a single open cart stood ready. Beside the cart waited a contingent of the Vanguard, together with a squad of Sherreenian gendarmes. Eliste blinked and squinted against the brilliance of the sunlight, the impossible blue translucence of the sky. The mild spring air was soft on her skin. It was a beautiful day. Beautiful.

One at a time, assisted by the guards; up onto the packing crate that served as a mounting block, and another step up and into the vehicle. She seated herself on one of the planks at the side of the cart. Presently the planks were filled, and late-entering prisoners were obliged to stand. Eliste gave up her seat to the old man with the gray beard. As she stood, she felt the pressure of regard, and turned to discover Shorvi Nirienne watching her. He smiled slightly, and his dark eyes beamed such a message of sympathy and encouragement that her throat tightened and her face tingled. In another moment, the tears would come, and she did not want that. Not now. She looked away quickly.

Creakclick as the hinged back of the cart was lifted and latched into place. Snap of the driver's whip, rumble of wheels, clop of hoofs, and the cart was moving in a cloud of soldiers, through the open iron-barred gate and out of the prison courtyard, as so many many carts had gone before it.

Outside the prison wall, a crowd of Eighth District denizens had gathered to witness the passing of Shorvi Nirienne. The savages wont to howl like wolves about the convoys of the doomed were strangely quiet today. There were no shrieking taunts, flying missiles, or attempted incursions. The presence of the Vanguard seemed almost superfluous. The citizens stood watching stilly, and the cart moved through their massed ranks in the midst of a great silence.

The silence continued as the cart lumbered over the short stretch of roadway separating Sepulchre from the Bridge Vinculum. Then they were out upon the bridge, high above the Vir, where the freshening breeze swept like a broom along the river and through the heart of Sherreen. Down below, the water ran a dark-gleaming green-brown. A variety of bright-sailed boats dotted the surface with color. Along the embankment, a few orphaned beggarsgold bushes flaunted blaring-yellow early blooms. Very soon, the cherry blossoms would veil hundreds of trees in pink lace. Within a week or two, all the city would glow, with flowers everywhere. . . .

Off the Bridge Vinculum now, and into the Waterfront Market. Here the citizens, like their dirtier and hungrier counterparts on the river's opposite bank, had massed among the stalls and booths to watch the cart go by. And the crowd here was so quiet that the creak of old wooden joints, the rattle of wheels, jingle of harness, and the tramp of booted feet on the cobbles were clearly audible. No one spoke aloud, and yet a murmuring stirred the crowd, a restless sighing, and a whispering of Shorvi Nirienne's name.

Through the market, through the Martmead, and then the cart—now trailing a company of silent citizens—passed on into a tangle of lanes, shortly emerging into Cliquot Street, with its decent shops lodged in the narrow, old-fashioned houses. Intensely quiet spectators lined the street. Most stood motionless and staring; but here, as elsewhere along the route, individuals detached themselves from the throng to follow in the wake of the condemned.

Past the House of Swans, empty and boarded now. Eliste's heart contracted at the sight, and her eyes rose without volition to the shadowed slit of a window under the eaves, where she half expected to glimpse a heart-shaped face and watching eyes. . . .

On along Cliquot Street, another turn or two, then into Arcade Avenue, lined on both sides with Sherreenians; and the long journey was finally drawing to a close. The shadows were stretched to their uttermost, clouds darkening to purple bruises and the sun sinking from sight behind the tall city buildings as the cart came up out of Arcade Avenue and into Equality Circle.

Eliste gazed about her, faintly astonished. She had come here once before, and she had imagined it thronged upon that day. But that earlier crowd was puny by comparison to this evening's gathering. Equality Circle was packed with humanity from one side to the other; clots of latecomers had even backed up into the tributary avenues. Not since the execution of Dunulas XIII had such a multitude assembled in this place; and the mood of the crowd was today as it had been upon the afternoon of the King's death—solemn, subdued, and fraught with a sense of consequence. In no sense could the death of Shorvi Nirienne equal in historical significance the execution of a hereditary monarch; and yet the destruction of each man carried similar overtones of symbolic change.

No concerted demon's chorus of welcome today, as the single cart entered the Circle. A few straining cheers from red-diamonded figures scattered with suspicious uniformity throughout the crowd, but this outcry sounded somehow thin and weak in the midst of a deep hush. Shrill locust-vociferation from the Cavaliers and Coquettes of Kokotte, a weak and trivial buzzing that died swiftly.

As the cart advanced toward the center of the Circle, some functionary somewhere issued an order, and flame was set to a forest of torches gripped by strategically placed civilian Reparationists. The great crowd exhaled as light kindled in a magnificent burst, gilded the dimming air, painted bright highlights and black shadows upon the scaffold, upon the tall antlered cabinet that was the Kokotte, and upon a single massive figure hulking motionless, one hand resting on the Sentient's flank: Bierce Valeur.

Torchlight warming a sea of upturned faces. And a waiting Sentient, glass whorls pulsing with their own internal radiance, wide-flung leaden doors, internal spikes aquiver with anticipation.

The cart advanced, crowd sundering itself to permit passage, gendarmes plying truncheons to facilitate the process. Slowing, and halt at the foot of the scaffold. Evening air cooling upon bare skin. Then Bierce's assistants sprang into action, removing the prisoners from the cart and lining them up with deft professionalism.

No telling what instructions they had received, but surely the order of execution had been considered with much care by someone, somewhere. The victims were arranged like the flares in a public display of pyrotechnics, with an overture of some picturesque appeal, followed by exhibits of varying interest; the mundane cannily interspersed with the spectacular, the best and biggest saved for a grand finale. Thus the Nirienne Gangsters stood at the end of the line, with

Shorvi Nirienne himself occupying the sixteenth position; before them, the physically distinctive alternated with the merely dissident; and the place at the head of the line was reserved for the group's youngest member and sole Bonbon.

Eliste was not sorry. She would not have to stand there listening to the successive crashes of the Kokotte's doors slamming shut, the mechanical hum climbing to a shriek, the exultant clamor of the mob, while waiting for her own turn to come. She would not have to wonder how much it was going to hurt. She would be spared all that.

Oh, but they were efficient. Already the two assistants had taken her arms, were hurrying her forward. There was no time to think, no time even for terror. She was not really afraid, she realized. Calm. Almost peaceful. Unexpected mercy.

Up the stairs they led her, rough boards splintery beneath her bare feet. As she ascended into plain view of the multitude, mindful of Kairthe's reception, she braced herself against the inevitable ribald howls.

They did not come. Such silence reigned that the Kokotte's hungry-mosquito hum winged freely out over all of Equality Circle. Eliste glanced briefly down at the crowd—nearest faces, yellowed by torchlight, reflecting a peculiar, intense solemnity; farther out, faces lost in deepening twilight. And then she forgot the spectators, for she stood at the top of the stairs, she could see the spikes quivering within the Kokotte's cavity, and Bierce Valeur was coming across the scaffold to take her. She straightened her spine, lifted her chin, looked him in the face. Nothing there to see. His eyes were empty as infinity.

Last quick flash of Zeralenn's face. Uncle Quinz's face. Dref's—and hold on to it, don't let it go.

At first she thought the sharp and sudden report that cracked the darkening air some by-product of the Kokotte's arcane internal activity. An instant later, the grip upon her right arm loosened, and one of the executioner's assistants tumbled headlong down the stairs. Bewildered, she gazed after him. The man lay on the ground, blood spouting from a throat wound. She did not understand what had happened; her wits seemed to have frozen. Before they thawed, a second report reverberated, and the second assistant went down with a bullet through his heart. Impossible to judge just where the shots had come from. Somewhere very near was a marksman of impressive proficiency; or else two such marksmen, for the second shot had followed too closely upon the first to allow for reloading. Of course, a single sniper might have had two weapons loaded and ready—

Before Eliste even thought to move, a third shot rang out. Bierce Valeur grunted and toppled, clutching his stomach.

The crowd was reacting now. There was a babble of excited questioning voices, a seething upheaval, warring currents and crosscurrents of humanity. But in the midst of that confusion, unmistakably there was a group, of indeterminate size, with aims that were clear and actions intelligently directed. Irregular fire spattered the Vanguardsmen stationed about the prisoners. Bullets converged from all directions, and at least half a dozen brown-and-scarlet figures fell. The snipers were scattered through the front ranks of the crowd; they were stepping forward briefly to fire over the shoulders of their neighbors, then melting backward to shift position while reloading. The soldiers discovered themselves attacked by ghosts.

Effective counterattack, and even defense in such an exposed position, was impracticable. Retreat was likewise cut off—a dense stand of bodies blocked the way back to Arcade Avenue. Firing was accurate and almost continual. The Protector's best servants stood in real danger of annihilation; and yet, a show of moderate force might drive the ordinary citizens from Equality Circle, depriving the sharpshooters of their cover. Upon the command of their respective officers, Vanguard and gendarmes on each side of the stationary cart fired simultaneous volleys into the thick of the surrounding crowd. Bodies fell, blood flowed, civilians shrieked and surged for the edge of Equality Circle. The invisible enemy was scarcely inconvenienced; while the citizens, who might otherwise have been prevailed upon to apprehend and surrender the marksmen in their midst, were now roused to screaming fury. Most of them comprehended neither the source nor the purpose of the initial shots, and many on the outskirts of the Circle remained confusedly ignorant of the snipers' existence; but all knew that the soldiers had fired upon them, and the violence of the reaction suggested the explosive release of months' worth of pent terror and loathing. Rocks flew to batter Vanguard and gendarmerie. Bullets likewise flew, and four more soldiers dropped where they stood.

As the bullets sang, Eliste ran down the stairs. Her instinct was simply to seek shelter, perhaps under the cart, or even beneath the scaffold itself. No sooner had her feet touched the pavement, however, than she thought of escape. The soldiers were occupied; she could run—

Someone grabbed her, slung her sideways into the midst of the prisoners now huddled in a tight group about the corpse of the emaciated woman, killed by a straying shot. The gendarmes had not forgotten their captives, nor did they intend to part with property of such obvious worth. As the attack was clearly the work of Nirienniste fanatics, a simple but effective means of defense suggested itself. It was the work of an instant to interpose the bodies of the prisoners between soldiers and snipers, a strategy that might be relied upon to end gunfire and rock-throwing alike. The Vanguardsmen, regarding themselves as an elite corps, would probably never have stooped to such tactics; but the city gendarmes were less fastidious.

A collective howl of execration arose. Individual cries of "Cowards! Cowards!" could be heard. The crowd's sympathies, initially divided and uncertain, turned wholly in the prisoners' favor. A furious wave of humanity rushed forward to break violently about the cart and scaffold; and ebbed, carrying the fifteen prisoners with it.

Eliste was lifted clear off her feet. At least half a dozen pairs of hands grasped her, tilted and turned her, plunged her headfirst into the human sea. A wordless roaring filled her ears; she caught crazy flashing glimpses of twilight sky, faces with wide-open yelling mouths, rock-wielding fists, boots, and pavement.

They set her on her feet and held her upright; otherwise, dizzy as she was, she would have fallen. Somebody cut the cord at her wrists. Her freed arms dangled, cold and numb. A large man stripped off his coat and brusquely draped it over her naked shoulders. Then he was gone, and so were all the hands, for it seemed she was of no further interest to them. Eliste swayed a little but kept her balance. She stood, some little distance from the scaffold, lost and oddly alone in the midst of the roiling, lunatic mob. She could not see her fellow prisoners; she had no idea what had become of them. She did not clearly understand what had happened moments earlier, or what was happening now. Her mind was numb as her hands, and stupidly, she thought first only of covering herself. As the citizens about her screamed and surged, as gunfire resounded through Equality Circle, Eliste donned the stranger's coat, struggling with clumsy fingers to button the garment that clothed her from shoulder to knee. Done. Head bent, she rolled back the wide cuffs that dangled inches below her fingertips. Then she looked up slowly, still standing there motionless, for her mind had not yet resumed normal functioning, and it never occurred to her to flee.

Multiple bodies impeded her view of ground-level activity, which centered about the empty cart, where Sherreenians were engaged in slaughtering the last of the gendarmes and Vanguardsmen. She had a much clearer view of the scaffold itself, from whose summit the Kokotte appeared to observe the proceedings. The Kokotte was prey to unusual emotion; so much was obvious, even to the uninformed witness. The erratic pulses of light sweeping her barbed crown were unusually brilliant, the pitch of her humming a fervent soprano. Not far from the Sentient, a vast prostrate form curled in great pain upon the bare boards of the scaffold: Bierce Valeur. Eliste thought herself the only one to notice or remember him, but such was hardly the case.

The last of the soldiers dead, amidst a shrapnel burst of screams and curses. Muttering brief lull. And then they remembered the executioner.

· · ·

Bierce was in agony. His wound bent him double, chained him where he lay. The fire in his midsection, however, was as nothing compared to his mental anguish. Only a few feet from him, the leaden doors of the Kokotte gaped wide. Her interior spikes were shivering, her luminous display irregular. She was intensely agitated, he could feel her emotion arcing across the short distance that separated them. She required reassurance, understanding, and devotion. In short, she needed her Bierce, almost as much as he needed her.

He yearned to lay his hands on her—to feel the deep vibration beneath his palm, to share in her triumph and glory, to comfort and be comforted in turn, to feel their spirits merge in mystic, ineffable communion.

And he couldn't reach her. She was so very close, and yet he couldn't touch her, couldn't stroke her cold flank or whisper the secret endearments known to the two of them alone.

Bierce fixed longing eyes upon his goddess. "Beautiful," he breathed, despite the pain. "So beautiful."

Did she hear him? What if she couldn't hear him?

But help was on the way.

The citizens of Sherreen, no doubt eager to reunite the Sentient with her chief acolyte, were pounding up the wooden stairs, a bellowing horde of them. An instant later, and they were all about him.

"Kokotte," Bierce instructed, with difficulty.

They seemed not to understand him. They were beating him with their fists, with clubs and bottles and sticks. They were kicking him, their booted toes slamming his perforated stomach, and the pain transcended anything that he had ever dreamed of, anything that the semi-Sentients in the Sepulchre cellar had ever devised. . . . And yet he had to communicate; it was essential that these people be made to understand his need.

"Kokotte." It was hard to speak with split lips, so many teeth gone, and a mouth so sloppy with blood. The name came out garbled and almost inaudible. He hoped desperately they would understand him. Where were the Cavaliers and Coquettes of Kokotte? Surely *they* would understand.

Yelling like lunatics, they were stripping his clothes away, all of his clothes. And yes, it seemed that they did understand after all, they recognized their civic duty, for they were lifting him to his feet—it took a party of four to accomplish that task, and the pain of it nearly shocked him senseless. Someone was slapping his face and waving a vinaigrette under his nose—they didn't want him to lose consciousness, that was good, and now he was properly awake again—

And they were hurrying him across the scaffold, straight forward to the Sentient who awaited him with welcoming doors opened wide. He could see the quivering spikes, the eager little mouths with their darting steel tongues, and he knew that she wanted him, longed for him, ached for him. An ecstasy that was almost unbearable filled him. The tears were streaming down his face as they flung him forward to the ultimate union.

She was the power, She was the glory, She was the eternal, the unchanging, the one reality. And She was very hungry.

As the white brilliance flared between the Kokotte's tall horns, a savage cheer arose from thousands of throats. The next instant, the citizens up on the scaffold attacked. A concerted grunting, straining effort shifted the Sentient across the planks to the extreme verge of the platform. For a moment she teetered there, jumping lights nervously ablink, high mechanical hum conveying a puzzled trepidation. Then she plunged from her heights, to strike the pavement below with the crash of thunder. The fall broke one of her great antlers and several of her glass elaborations. She lay there helpless upon her side, keening like a wounded animal.

Then the thin sound was lost and drowned in the mighty roar as the human wave swept down upon her. Rocks pounded, makeshift levers pried. They ripped away her horns, her wires, her branching rods and spiky barbs; they smashed her glassy whorls and sunbursts, killed her lights; they tore the fanged spikes from her cavity, twisted and broke her flanges and coils. They stripped her of everything that had made her what she was; and when they were done, all that remained was an empty leaden cabinet, badly dented, with nothing about it to suggest that awareness had ever resided there.

Eliste stood numbly watching. Once the Sentient tumbled from the scaffold, her view was obscured. But the activity swirling about the prostrate Kokotte—the heaving, shuddering disturbance in that spot—reminded her forcibly of accounts she had heard of tropical piranha. She could see little, and yet she remained transfixed.

A hand clasped her shoulder firmly. She started and swiveled, half expecting to encounter a Vanguardsman; but found herself facing an elderly man with grizzled hair and whiskers, tricorne hat pulled low, and an old-fashioned voluminous cape, surely unnecessary in such mild weather. It took her a moment to recognize Dref Zeenoson beneath the disguise. Closer scrutiny explained the cape; under the loose folds of fabric, she glimpsed the long barrel of a gun, of the sort that he had designed and referred to as a breech-loading rifle. She understood then that he had been one of the snipers in the crowd. It did not surprise her.

"This way," said Dref.

She followed him without question. Dref would know where he was going—Dref always did. He elbowed his way efficiently through the mob, bringing them within minutes to a stone bench all but lost in the shadows at the western edge of

Equality Circle. There the five members of the Nirienne Gang were assembled. All of them were unbound and more or less clothed. Nirienne himself was decently clad in a shirt, breeches, even shoes and stockings. Had it not been for the reflective property of the white shirt, the five of them would have been utterly unobtrusive, almost invisible, waiting there in the deepening twilight.

Nirienne stood as Dref drew near. "Ah, so you have found her," he said. "I should never have doubted the eyes of Beq."

"Our route's prepared," Dref told him. "We'll put the five of you in a safe house within the hour."

"No," said Nirienne.

Dref's falsely whitened eyebrows arched. In all the years that she had known him, Eliste had rarely if ever seen him so transparently surprised.

"Ouen and Ouenne, Frezhelle and Riclairc, may follow you to the safe house if they desire," Nirienne continued calmly. "It's best that they do so, but I will remain."

"Why?"

"To talk to them." Nirienne's gesture encompassed the massed citizens, whose fury seemed starting to wane. The Kokotte, instrument and symbol of terror, had been destroyed. Her minions, the executioner and his assistants, were dead. Likewise dead were Vanguardsmen and gendarmes, while the rescued prisoners had faded from view. The Sherreenians' enthusiasm, while still fiery, now lacked focus and direction. Another minute or two, and they would begin to disperse. "It is the time, I think."

"What would you talk of, Shorvi?"

"Never let it be said," Nirienne returned, "that I can't profit by Whiss Valeur's example." Without further explanation, he turned and made for the scaffold. His supporters followed unhesitatingly. There was not one among them, it seemed, willing even to consider the possibility of retreat to the promised safe house. Dref did not trouble to ask them.

Eliste held Dref's arm tightly. When he had spoken of the safe house, at the very sound of that syllable, "safe," an almost delirious longing swept through her. But they were not going yet, and when she recognized that, the fierce desire subsided to manageable levels, the immediate flash of frightened frustration spent itself, and she began wakening to events. The famous Shorvi Nirienne, who should by all odds have been dead by now, was about to address a screamingly homicidal mob. She was with Dref, in no immediate danger, and the situation was not without interest.

Nirienne mounted the scaffold, now altogether bare. For a moment he stood there, an unremarkable figure that somehow drew all eyes. A few torches and lanterns still burned around the base of the platform. The light caught the white shirt and stockings, white face and hands, bouncing the image to the far reaches of Equality Circle. Every citizen present recognized the man. To many, he seemed a vision of sweet sanity in the midst of a madhouse or inferno. All paused to listen, and Equality Circle fell silent.

Shorvi Nirienne waited to catch the pale foam of faces upon the human sea; raised both arms briefly in a gesture once used by Whiss Valeur, to very different purpose; then let them fall again.

"I take it," Shorvi Nirienne remarked to Sherreen, "that you want a change."

Indeed they did. It was one of those ultrasimple, perfectly apt statements destined to become a catch phrase.

Nirienne spoke on. His speech was clear and very concise. Yet Eliste, for all her close attention, never afterward remembered the actual words so much as the general effect: hope—normalcy—the promise of stability—recovery and health.

He did not as yet seek to lull them to quiescence, however; far from it. There was but one means, Nirienne reminded his listeners, to end the national agony. The authors of the present terror must be brought to justice. They were, after all, undoubtedly criminals—brazen in the illegality of their methods, corrupt, rapacious, and tyrannical; responsible for the Spring Massacre in the Congress, as well as the Retreat atrocities; guilty of judicial mass murder; responsible above all for the perversion of the Revolution and all its ideals, the betrayal of their countrymen. Chief among the culprits were the members of the Committee of National Welfare; the justices and public prosecutor of the National Tribunal; the commanders and highest officers of the Vanguard. Guiltiest and bloodiest among them all was the Committee of National Welfare's President, who was also self-styled Republican Protector.

Nirienne never shouted, ranted, or postured. He stood quite still, face calm and gestures restrained, as he set about building an indictment with the workmanlike skill of the lawyer that he was. Almost it seemed that he did not raise his voice, and yet that voice was easily heard throughout Equality Circle.

They were shouting again before he had finished, screaming out the name of Whiss Valeur before he had spoken it aloud. Nirienne raised his hand briefly, and the wordless request for silence was obeyed. The sigh of the evening breeze became audible.

"Then shall we end the reign of terror? For, my countrymen, it lies within our power to do it, as it lay within our power to end the reign of the King. Shall we go to the one calling himself Protector and make our dissatisfaction known?"

Shrieking tumultuous assent, and the name "Whiss," blizzarded in epithet and expletive.

"To the Sepulchre, then. To the Sepulchre."

The crowd took up the cry, passed it to the edges of the Circle, and beyond.

Shorvi Nirienne came down from the scaffold. Closely surrounded by the four allies condemned to die with him, the falsely grizzled young man instrumental in preserving him, and a fair-headed, barefoot young girl, likewise allotted to the Kokotte, he made briskly for the mouth of Arcade Avenue. The mob followed, devoted for the moment. Only a small handful of cautious souls shaved off the mass to seek the shadows. The main body of humanity remained nearly intact; even attracted new bulk unto itself, as it moved through the streets like an indigestible lump through the intestines of Sherreen. Back along Arcade Avenue, along the lanes and through Cliquot Street, back along the way that the cart of the condemned had traveled such a short time earlier. New members, new lights, new weapons acquired en route. Over the Vinculum and into the Eighth District.

To the Sepulchre.

At the sound of the tapping upon his door, Whiss Valeur raised his head from the crossed arms on which it had rested and automatically checked the clock. Early evening, an hour that his countrymen ordinarily devoted to pleasure; tippling and chitchat among the sophisticated, supper and then bedtime for the simpler of patriots; but all joys denied to him, denied to Whiss, as the good things in life were always denied. He could not drink these days, for even the smallest quantities of wine axed his skull with monstrous headaches. He could scarcely eat, for his stomach rejected all but the blandest of puddings, and of late his meager figure had shrunk to greenish-yellow skin and bone. Convivial conversation was an all-but-alien concept, for what had he to chatter and joke about, and where were his friends, or his family? His family. And bed? Solitary and sleepless. Sleepless. Sleepless.

Early evening, the time for other people's contentment. But there was one consolation, and it was not inconsiderable. By now, Shorvi Nirienne must be dead.

Perhaps it would make a difference.

The tapping sounded again, and Whiss turned his head. "Come," he said.

In came a messenger, nervous and breathless.

Shorvi Nirienne is leading an immense mob upon the Sepulchre. They will be here within the half hour.

He must have heard incorrectly. He commanded. The message was repeated. No mistake.

. . . Nirienne . . . leading an immense mob . . . here within the half hour.

". . . Equality Circle . . . ?"

Rioting . . . Bierce Valeur dead . . . the Kokotte destroyed.

Whiss's skinny hands clenched, and the bile rose to his throat. Nightmare. Impossible. Fever dreams. Waking black visions—waking . . . *Faces of the dead, borne upon the ceaseless wind—death masks stark white against illimitable darkness, numberless as the stars—nowhere to hide from them, and even the Vanguard helpless against that ghostly multitude.* Loyalty? An illusion. *But they were loyal to Nirienne.* Protection for the Protector? None. Except, perhaps— For a moment he struggled against nausea; swallowed, and was himself again.

"Fetch my father here to me."

At once, Protector.

Indeterminate stretch of time, somewhere between minutes and millennia; and then Chorl was there. Chorl, grayer and wispier and sadder than ever, with droopy shoulders, sagging mouth, damp reproachful gaze. Whiss suppressed the usual jolt of annoyance, struggled to speak evenly. "Father, I require your assistance."

Chorl turned great suffering sheep's eyes upon him, and inquired, "Is it true?"

"I've a task for you. It is important. You must put forth your best efforts."

"Is it true?"

"Time is limited; you must work quickly. Do you hear me?"

"Tell me if it is true."

"Enough!" Whiss's fragile patience snapped. "What is this foolery?"

"I have heard that Eularque, Houloir, and Phlosine have fled Sherreen."

"Who has said this thing? Where have you heard it?"

"Nowhere. Everywhere. The stones of my dungeon walls have uttered sermons."

"Ah, weak paradox and weaker pathos, your specialties. It is not the time for either. These are all lies. Eularque, Houloir, and Phlosine rest secure in my keeping."

"Look me in the face and say it," Chorl commanded, sharp tone harking back thirty years.

Whiss's huge eyes widened a little. "I think your wits are failing," he replied slowly. "You are senile. Or perhaps you are not getting enough sleep."

"It is true, then. You have answered me."

"Listen to me. You will perform a task for me. I have been informed that a rabble of citizens, roused to violence by traitors, marches upon the Sepulchre. They will be upon us within minutes."

"Which traitors? There seem to be so very many—the Niriennistes?"

"That is not important now."

"It was inevitable; you made it so. I only wonder that it has taken so long."

"It is hardly your place to reproach me."

"You'll call out the Vanguard, I suppose?"

"That will not suffice this time."

"Probably not. The Bodyguard was unable to shield Dunulas, and you are far more hated than the poor King ever was."

"Hold your tongue! I am not hated, save by traitors and enemies of the Republic. The people, the real people, still love me. They will remember that when I speak to them."

"You will dare to face Sherreen?"

"It has been too long, far too long, since I have addressed the people. The bond between us has been allowed to weaken. Tonight, I shall renew it."

"They will tear you to pieces."

"Quiet! You are a fool. They have always loved me, they have always been my slaves when I speak. That does not change. They will remember, when I speak. The power of my oratory in itself is all but magical; and strengthened by your art, wholly irresistible. That is why you are here, Father. You will assist me, as in the old days. You will help me to rule the crowd again—to rule them completely."

"The old days are gone. And there comes a time when magic loses its power to hide the truth."

"Words! Sanctimonious platitudes! Come, make your point—do you refuse me, Father? Do you refuse?"

"Yes, Whiss." Chorl met the other's wild, white-rimmed glare unflinchingly. "I do refuse you."

"Don't challenge me." Whiss's voice dropped disconcertingly in pitch. "Don't try it. You'll only regret the attempt. Eularque, Houloir, and Phlosine will pay for your defiance."

"You cannot harm them if you do not have them."

"I tell you, I have them all! They are here in the Sepulchre, and it is but a brief short journey from their lodgings down to the cellars. Remember that. But if you care as little for them as you always did for me, then think of this as well—that you yourself have not yet viewed the cellars."

"These threats are useless. I am no longer afraid." Chorl's pasteboard-gray face and wet brow belied the words.

"Liar, you are always afraid! And with reason. To protect myself, I will do all I promise, and more. I will order every prisoner in the Sepulchre massacred—yes, and those in the Treasury and the Keep, as well. I will have the enemies of the people herded by the hundreds into wooden warehouses, locked in, and burnt alive en masse. I will fill great rafts with shackled traitors, set them adrift upon the Vir, and sink them. I'll turn the Sepulchre's cannon upon the crowd. And all the blood that flows will be upon your hands, Father. You give me no choice, and it will all be your doing, not mine!"

Chorl looked at his son, whose expression was scarcely human. His spine jellied and his eyes dropped. "I'll do what you want," he said.

"Then come with me now." Whiss seized his father's arm, and the two men descended the narrow private stairway by which the Governor's apartment communicated with the various levels of the prison. Moments later, they emerged into the cavernous foyer, a place ordinarily alive with visitors, petitioners, functionaries, lawyers; but this evening, emptied of all save a body of tense and tight-lipped Vanguardsmen. Unmistakably, all were aware of the mob's approach.

Whiss hesitated a moment, then strode forward, head high, shoulders squared, vast eyes like glass lanterns. His breathing was ragged, just as it had been upon the night—less than two years ago, but it seemed an age—that he had first emerged from the shadows cloaking "Neighbor Jumalle," to address an audience in the warehouse on Pump Street. Then, as now, the fear and doubt had risen to clutch at his throat. But then, as now, his father's magical power had backed him, and that appearance had marked his first public triumph. Tonight's speech should echo that triumph.

He paused before the great oaken door. The Vanguardsmen fell into position about him, their massive upright figures dwarfing his slight form. On the other side of the door, an armed company occupied the broad, short flight of granite steps leading down to the courtyard once occupied for a brief span by the Kokotte. At the far edge of the courtyard, the iron-barred gate in the outer wall stood wide open. No point in locking it; the Sherreenian mob had long since discovered the destructibility of gates.

Whiss listened. He heard an oceanside murmuring, a muted rumble. The mob was upon him. The rumble swelled to deep cataract thunder. The citizens were pouring into the lantern-lit courtyard—so much he knew without seeing. He caught the sense of a single entity, vast and unimaginably potent—a beast of fable that he was fated to conquer and rule. He waited, and presently the random rumbling ordered itself, resolving to a simple summons:

Whiss. Whiss. Whissss.

Hiss of the monster serpent, dragon waiting without; thus had the beast summoned him that night in Pump Street, but this time it was larger, infinitely larger.

Whisssssssssssssssss

Real? Waking nightmare? Real.

He swallowed air, snapped his fingers; the bolt scraped, the bar slid, and the big door gaped. Rush of cool evening air, blink of lantern light outside, and Whiss advanced, followed by his father and his guardsmen. He addressed Chorl in an undertone, without turning his eyes, "Do more than ever before. They must take me for a hero—a savior—a god."

"Yes."

He felt rather than saw his father melt back into the shadows.

He walked forward, and the Vanguardsmen parted before him, revealing Protector to the crowd, and vice versa. His sudden appearance took them by surprise. The uproar died. Thousands of eyes fixed intently upon the skinny figure in black.

Whiss halted at the head of the stairs, in a pool of light cast by lantern and torch. His practiced eye swiftly scanned the crowd; almost instantly picked out Shorvi Nirienne, standing free and insolent in the front rank, only a few feet below him. Anger fired his blood at the sight, and anger was a source of energy he had always known how to turn to advantage. Quickly, though, for Nirienne mustn't be allowed opportunity to speak.

Don't wait, don't let them catalogue their accusations. Forestall that, take command. Whiss's instincts, keen still, told him what to say.

"Compeers, you have come to me tonight in grief and anger." His voice, grave and almost sorrowing, filled the courtyard as water fills a cup. It was not a beautiful voice, yet somehow possessed power to touch the heart. "I see before me a people tired of terror, tired of bloodshed and brutality. I see before me a people exhausted, bewildered, and wounded. How could I fail to understand, and how could I fail to share in your pain? For I am one of you, now and always."

His grieving green gaze swept the audience. They were silent, and listening intently. He had taken them by surprise, and for now, he had them. Whatever else they might have expected of their tyrant, they had never anticipated this.

"All of us yearn for an end to the struggle. All of us hunger for peace." He invested the word "peace" with a sweetness that brought tears to the eyes of many listeners. "But what, Compeers, is worth even more than domestic tranquillity? Are not freedom, justice, and equality worth more? Surely all of us thought so once, else we should never have toppled a monarchy. Dunulas might yet rest secure upon his throne, and then we should be at peace. But, Compeers, we chose otherwise. We chose freedom, justice, equality; and in doing so, we threw our nation into a great turmoil from which she is slow in recovering. Did we do wrong in that? Do any among us regret our choice?"

He paused, as if awaiting reply. None was forthcoming. He had feared that Shorvi Nirienne might seize the opportunity to take the stage, but even Nirienne was silently attentive, like all the others. Whiss's confidence began to mount. His instincts, his miraculous instincts, were sure as ever. Already he was starting to twist the emotions of his listeners, and presently his influence would swell to absolute ascendancy, for there was no audience he could not rule, no great beast he could not tame.

"We struck for our freedom, our justice and equality," Whiss continued, assurance soaring now, fears all but forgotten. "And having won these things at such a heavy cost to all, shall we not fight to defend them? For the Revolution is not ended, Compeers, and the war has not yet been won. Nor shall it be truly won so long as the traitors remain among us, striving in secret to work our ruin.

The enemies of freedom are legion. They are dedicated and tireless in their efforts to return us to our former slavery. Ridding our new Republic of its poisons is painful, exhausting, even sickening; yet hardly a cruelty—only the necessary bloodletting whereby the physician restores his patient to health."

He could sense their doubt, their ambivalence. And now, to take that advantage, and enlarge it—

Before he uttered another word, everything changed. The air rippled, the golden lanterns swam, and Whiss experienced the familiar, sickly qualm that told him his father's magic was at work. Curious—for a moment there, while speaking, he had almost forgotten Chorl. Immersed in his task, he had spoken, thought and acted as if the outcome depended upon his natural abilities alone. He had actually felt that he would triumph—on his own. No matter. Chorl's assistance made it sure.

The qualm passed. Whiss blinked, and his vision cleared. He beheld the inflammable polychrome haze of his listeners' emotions, and somehow it was not exactly as he remembered, but that was not important; it was visible, and he could shape it.

"Now is a time for unity and cooperation, now a time for all of us to work together—" Whiss began, and stopped, surprised. The haze was not behaving properly. He knew quite well that it should now be calming and homogenizing itself under the power of his voice; but it was doing neither. Dark currents of confusion swirled through the courtyard, heavy clouds of skepticism lowered, here and there leapt flares of revulsion.

Revulsion?

Yes. No mistake.

Poor tactics. He needed to shift course, immediately. It happened sometimes.

"Many tears have been shed for the suffering of condemned traitors," Whiss observed. "But who pleads the cause of the wronged patriots? And who speaks out in behalf of the Republic? Who speaks for our threatened liberty?"

Skepticism darker now. Revulsion poisoning itself to a phosphorescent hatred. Deep mutter of indignation. Menace.

Whiss was bewildered, incredulous. The sensations of his audience, usually so clear and easily manipulated, entirely eluded him now. They were angry and intensely hostile, growing more so by the moment. The summer lightning of incipient violence played about the Sepulchre courtyard. The words that should have averted the storm seemed to be feeding it. How? Why? But the right words would come to him, they always did.

"I would gladly sacrifice my life for liberty," Whiss proclaimed strongly. "Would anyone here do less? If patriots are willing to die, who will grudge the necessary sacrifice of traitors?"

He gazed out upon the crowd, encountered nothing but hatred, dense and rich. Impossible. His ascendancy was gone. The dragon, the many-headed beast, was stirring to hideous life, and this time, a nightmare come true, he could not control it. Impossible.

Whiss threw wide his arms, in the old gesture. "Are we not united in love of Vonahrish freedom?" he flung at them. That appeal, at least, must touch them.

No. It should have roused them to cheers, but it did not. Ugly hot flares distempered the leaden mists. The faces below were twisted with loathing.

Impossible. Did they not hear his words? It was as if they heard only an obscene gibbering. And those eyes did not see him as he was, else they could never burn with such fearful contempt, as if they gazed upon some rare and repulsive monster. Somehow their perceptions were skewed; they did not see *him*.

Their faces . . . death masks against the darkness . . .

Whiss understood the betrayal then. Eyes bulging, green irises white-circled, he whirled to face his father.

Chorl stood straight, met the terrible regard squarely. "Yes, Whiss," he said.

"Father—"

Someone in the crowd hurled a rock. The missile struck Whiss Valeur between the shoulder blades. A cry of pain escaped him, and he shrank back from the edge of the stairs. Another rock flew. Dozens of them, scores of them, to pelt the Protector and his father. Chorl made no effort to save himself, did not even raise his arms to shield his head. A whizzing missile struck his temple and he fell, never to rise. Whiss was less fortunate. Head down and shoulders hunched, he ran for the Sepulchre door, only to find it barred against him. Turning from the door, he screamed at the Vanguardsmen lining the stairs to fire upon the crowd. The soldiers stood motionless, regarding him with the same contemptuous loathing seen upon the faces of the citizens.

The stones flew. Back and forth across the landing staggered the erstwhile Protector, frantically dodging, ducking, and bobbing in vain, a sight to rouse merciless merriment. When the battering forced him at last to his knees, and he crouched there, head buried and nose to the granite, the thrust of a Vanguardsman's booted foot sent him tumbling. Whiss Valeur rolled to the foot of the stairs. The citizens surged forward, despite Shorvi Nirienne's desperate efforts to restrain them.

And after that, there was only the huge roaring of the beast.

The six weeks following Whiss Valeur's death, Eliste spent all but chained to her injured uncle's bedside, thus hearing only at second hand of events transforming Sherreen. It was a matter of limited interest to her that the Constitutional Congress, decimated by purge, massacre, and the flight or arrest of so many members, had reordered itself upon a temporary basis under the title of Acting Constitutional Assembly, with Shorvi Nirienne as its President. Of far more immediate significance was the thundering collapse of Reparationism. Almost overnight, the terror had ended. The National Tribunal had been abolished, the Vanguard disbanded. The prisoners of state in the Sepulchre had been released, and their cells were now occupied by former lights of the Committee of National Welfare. Whiss Valeur's mangled remains, what was left of them, had been interred in an unmarked grave, with the Kokotte's stripped leaden cabinet of a body serving as his coffin. Despite their obvious worth and rarity, the sister Sentients—ZaZa, Boomette, and the NuNu—had been dismantled by exuberant crowds, their component mechanical fragments seized upon by the battalions of scavengers and souvenir hunters. The nits of NuNu had been hunted down and exterminated with such enthusiasm that not one of the golden pests was thought to survive.

It was no longer a crime to be Exalted—or formerly-Exalted, as the law still had it—for the hasty reform legislation, merciful though it was, failed to recognize or restore hereditary title. The former masters of Vonahr might walk the streets openly, without fear of arrest or attack. They could travel, come and go as they pleased, own property, transact business, vote in elections. But their ancient privileges were gone forever, and their vast estates were much reduced, with great tracts of land transferred to the ownership of former serfs and tenants. It was problematic whether the Exalted emigrants residing in Strell or Lanthi Ume would care to return to a homeland so shockingly altered, but at least the option was theirs.

Uncle Quinz mended slowly at first. But the headaches and spells of dizziness that plagued him subsided steadily day by day. The replacement of his lost eyeglasses much improved his spirits. And at last there came a bright spring afternoon that witnessed the return of his magical powers. The old gentleman filled his chamber with the brilliant illusory bird-butterflies that his niece loved. While Eliste exclaimed in delight, the warbling creatures danced in midair, grouping themselves in shifting patterns of marvelous color and complexity. At the close of their chorus, the bird-butterflies vanished, each dissolving to a single note of music that lingered a soft moment before fading. Thereafter, Uncle Quinz's full recovery was rapid.

Delighted though she truly was for his sake, Eliste viewed her uncle's return to health and strength with mixed feelings, for she knew what must quickly follow. And sure enough, within days, he was planning his return to Fabeque. Eliste sighed at the prospect of losing him. Life would be terribly lonely without Quinz, for there was nobody else in Sherreen to share her time and thoughts with, nobody to eat and talk and laugh with, certainly not Dref, not these days. . . . But still, it wouldn't do to be selfish. Uncle Quinz had fulfilled his purpose in the city, and now he wanted to rest. He longed for the rolling countryside and somber skies of Fabeque, for his quiet cottage in the hills above Derrivalle, for his beloved and essential solitude. Despite all his sweetness and natural optimism, the pressure of constant human proximity was wearing visibly upon him. He wanted to go home. Naturally.

Eliste came within an ace of begging to accompany him, before conscience stilled her tongue. Her uncle would be painfully embarrassed. Affection, duty, and pity would compel his assent; but he would feel so uncomfortable, so trapped . . . No. She forced herself to smile and encourage him. The effort was considerable, but worthwhile; he noticed nothing, and his spirits continued high. The sole blight upon his mood was the fear that the Derrivalle folk might have commandeered his house. If such were the case, Eliste reminded him, he was quite competent to deal with the problem.

Too soon, the day of his departure dawned. In the charcoal light of very early morning, Eliste, clad in a recently acquired blue linen dress, accompanied her kinsman to the posting house in Trouniere, point of origin of the Maritime Stage. Beside them in the fiacre sat Dref Zeenoson, an unlikely presence. For Dref was most inaccessible, all but invisible of late; his time and attention devoted almost exclusively to the Acting Constitutional Assembly, of which he was a member. It was, of course, the personal intercession of Shorvi Nirienne himself that slid Dref Zeenoson into one of the currently vacant Congressional slots. A letter to the Municipality of Grammantes, warmly recommending an associate whose true name, as it happened, Nirienne had only just learned; a swiftly responsive endorsement from the pro-Nirienne Municipality, and the thing was done. Dref Zeenoson, former serf, became the Honorable Zeenoson, Acting Deputy of West Fabeque. He might lose his position in the autumn, when the next elections were scheduled to take place; given his intelligence and energy, he could probably hold it if he wished. One way or another, in the meantime, he spent his days and evenings at Century Hall. He had even rented a tiny room within walking distance of the Assembly, where he spent most of his nights. This, he explained, was purely a matter of convenience, but Eliste knew better. He was deliberately avoiding her; she knew him well enough to be sure of that. Still, he was here this morning. Whatever his feelings toward her, he had come to bid farewell to Master Quinz.

Shudder of the fiacre, and halt before the posting house. Alight, pay the driver, and into the dreary building, to purchase a ticket and then sit waiting there upon a bare wooden bench, with cups of cocoa from a vendor, and desultory, slightly strained conversation. And then, too quickly, the big coach ready to depart. Outdoors again. Uncle Quinz's single valise handed up to the roof. The old gentleman shook Dref's hand, embraced his niece. "You'll visit me, will you not, my child?" he asked.

"Often. Just try to keep me away," she promised, smiling. He would not have wanted her—or anyone else, for that matter—to live with him; but when he asked her to visit, he meant it. Her assent was equally sincere.

His eyes turned briefly to Dref, and Eliste almost cringed. She could sense the tenor of his thoughts. In a moment of weakness, she had confessed her feelings for Dref to him. If he by word, look, or gesture exposed her, she would die.

She should have known better than to doubt him. Quinz hugged her tight. "Courage, my dear," he whispered, and released her. "Adieu, children. Such an adventure it has been!"

He entered the coach, and the door closed behind him. Creaking groan, and the Maritime Stage was off, heading north.

Eliste stood watching it go. Her eyes stung with tears, and she felt unutterably alone. Dref stood beside her, but he might as well have been a hundred miles away. Strange to think that she had felt herself so near to him, and that not so long ago. His thoughts were closed to her now. She had no idea what to say to him, and ꜩbably he was similarly embarrassed. She was almost surprised when he spoke. "You'll miss him, won't you?"

"Very much," she replied quietly.

"Yes, that is hard. But I've news that may cheer you."

She looked up at him.

"We've located your cousin."

"Aurelie! Is she all right?"

"In good health."

"Where did you find her?"

"In the Sepulchre, sharing lodgings with a turnkey. She'll be delivered to you in Flou's Pocket sometime today."

Aurelie arrived around noon. Eliste at once arranged to install the girl in the second-story room vacated hours earlier by Uncle Quinz. As sole senior kinswoman, she found herself obliged by ancient custom to assume guardianship of her young cousin, a role that held little appeal. It was not that she grudged the expense, for her uncle had left her a walletful of rekko notes, with a promise of replenishment upon demand. Paying for Aurelie would be easy; enduring her prattle would not. But still—her own cousin, companionship of sorts, a link with the old days . . . and a fellow Exalted.

Exalted? Even formerly-Exalted? Did Aurelie vo Rouvignac, soiled as she was, deserve any such title?

But Aurelie seemed quite unconscious of degradation. If any sense of guilt or disgrace lurked in her heart, she concealed it. Her enthusiasm, as she hugged and kissed Eliste, seemed perfectly spontaneous, and she expected equal cordiality in return. It never occurred to her for an instant to doubt the warmth of her own reception.

The lack of conscience was absolute and genuine. In the days that followed, Aurelie often spoke of her adventures, recounting them with a sort of matter-of-fact candor that held no particle of shame. The foundation of her confidence soon became clear; she regarded her cousin as an equal, with a history—and present—equivalent to her own. Eliste, after all, was living with a man; and not just any man—a famous Nirienniste, a deputy to the Acting Constitutional Assembly. Said to be pretty, too; although she herself could not vouch for this personally, having never set eyes on him. It almost seemed that her cousin was hiding the roommate. Did her cousin fear that a younger woman might steal him away? Her cousin, after all, was now nineteen and getting on a bit.

In vain Eliste argued the absolute innocence of her living arrangements. Aurelie smiled knowingly, giggled annoyingly.

"He only took me in out of pity, because I was destitute," Eliste insisted.

"Ah, but such is hardly the case any longer, Cousin. These days, you are flush.

And if you are not just where you want to be, sharing lodgings with this pretty fellow, then why not, for decency's sake, move in here with me?"

Because I don't think I could stand you. Aloud, Eliste observed mildly, "We should be very crowded, both in this one room."

"Then why not take a room of your own?"

"No need. Dref is rarely present. It can hardly be said that he lives here at all."

"Then he has set you into your own establishment? That is a mark of the highest regard. You are to be congratulated, Cousin."

"Aurelie, do you want me to slap you?"

"La, Cousin! What have I said? What have I said?"

But the questions, Eliste was forced to admit to herself, were reasonable enough. Why didn't she take a place of her own, now that she could afford it? Because, perhaps, withdrawal would cut yet another of the threads that bound her, however tenuously, to Dref? But she could hardly admit that. She could only hope that Aurelie would lose interest, and let the matter drop.

The younger girl soon obliged. Her mind was incapable of fixing itself upon any one subject for long; and the novelty of her freedom was so great that her attention was easily diverted. For the next three weeks or so, every day that it did not rain, Aurelie was out and about Sherreen; exploring the markets and shops, wandering the parks and gardens, gossiping with merchants and marketwomen. Such unchaperoned, unrestrained ramblings were by the old reckoning scandalous; but Eliste, for all her titular guardianship, was powerless to control a sixteen-year-old who shrugged off argument, pouted at reproach, and giggled at threats.

When Eliste was finally reduced to pleading, Aurelie fidgeted in mild discomfort, but observed firmly, "Cousin, I am not like you. *I* cannot sit here like a little caged *bird*, la! If I am not to roam about alone, then you must come with me!"

But Eliste would do nothing of the sort.

There was no telling what new disaster might have resulted, had not Aurelie begun to grow bored. All too soon, the joys of mere freedom began to pall. It was no longer enough to gaze upon the scarves, gloves, ribbons, and jewels in the better shops; Aurelie wanted to own them, and her stingy guardian would not or could not oblige. It was not enough to watch the theater patrons, the café loungers, the phaeton drivers now reappearing upon the Girdle at Havillac Gardens; Aurelie wanted to join them. Nor was it satisfying to waste her conversation upon marketwomen and other such canaille, when she had been born Exalted. It was high time, in Aurelie's opinion, to resume her rightful place in the world. The Revolution had driven her off course for a time, inconvenienced her severely, and unforgivably deprived her of a presentation at Court. But there were other courts, in other lands, containing Exalteds or their equivalent. Given the instinctive sympathy existing among all those of birth and blood, these foreign aristocrats were certain to welcome her with open arms and open purses. Aurelie resolved to join them, and toward this end she bent her not-inconsiderable energies.

Information was surprisingly available. A few inquiries at the doors of several of the great old mansions of the city, still housing a substantial population of former servants, sufficed to inform Aurelie that at least half a dozen of her Rouvignac kinsmen were known to have set off for Strell, in hopes of joining the Vonahrish Exalted emigrants gathered there about the King in Exile, as the former Duke of Feronte was known to his supporters. Impossible to say, of course, whether they had completed the journey safely, but there seemed little reason to suppose that at least some of them had not. Three of the six had departed early on, one even before the Reparationist ban had restricted Exalted travel.

It was all Aurelie needed to know. Her kinsmen waited for her in Strell, at whose court she might in due time expect a legitimate presentation. Duty demanded her immediate departure, provided her sweet cousin-guardian was willing to cover traveling expenses. Surely her generous cousin would not hesitate—?

Eliste didn't hesitate. Aurelie's fare, over land and sea, to Strell—together with cash to cover lodgings, meals, and incidental expenses en route—would greatly diminish the sum that Uncle Quinz had left her. But it was worthwhile, to rid herself of a responsibility with which she was ill-equipped to deal; worthwhile, to place the unquenchable Aurelie under adequate supervision, if such existed; money well-spent indeed.

She was taken quite by surprise when Aurelie remarked nonchalantly, as if stating the obvious, "And you must come with me, Cousin. My Rouvignac kinsmen will look after you. You are the granddaughter of a Rouvignac, after all. It is even possible that we shall discover some of your vo Derrivalle people in Strell. We shall do very well there."

"Oh. No. No. I don't think so."

"And why not, pray?"

Eliste blinked. No reasonable answer suggested itself. She was silent.

"But this is too absurd, la! Cousin, what are you thinking of? Why will you not go with me? Why not? I do not like to travel alone, it looks so ill! And if you stay here in Sherreen—gad, what will you *do*? Whatever will you *do*?"

No answer. What, indeed, could she do here alone? Eliste's mind spun in confusion.

Aurelie eyed her sharply. "Ah, well, and if you love this Nirienniste keeper of yours so much that you cannot leave him, then you must make him marry you. And you must do it quickly, before you grow so old that he won't have you."

"You don't know what you're—"

"For you cannot continue in *such* circumstances, Cousin." Aurelie waved an expressive hand. "It is most irregular. And if you've no care for your own reputation, then have the goodness to spare a thought for mine. At the Court of Strell, I shall have a position to maintain, remember. You are my kinswoman, your actions will reflect upon me, and you ought to consider how your misbehavior may compromise my dignity."

"After the Sepulchre, you dare—Oh, never mind, it doesn't matter, it's too stupid. Aurelie, you are unutterably silly."

"I? La!" Aurelie sniffed. "Look in the mirror, Cousin. Only look in the mirror." And she withdrew to pen the letters that would notify the Rouvignac emigrants of her imminent descent upon them.

The coolness between them did not last. Aurelie was too inconstant to hold a grudge, and her guardian didn't care to. It was only a week later that Eliste made a second journey to the posting house in Trouniere, to bid farewell to a second relative. The stagecoach that would carry her cousin to the port of Arenne was ready to depart on time. Aurelie—nicely turned out in a traveling suit of bottle-green broadcloth, purchased secondhand, but fresh enough to pass for new—was red-faced and half wild with excitement. Already she had all but forgotten her companion. But her sincere, if facile, affection flared at the last moment, and she threw both arms around Eliste. "Follow me to Strell if you will, Cousin," she advised breathlessly. "But if you will not, then you must at least stop *dawdling*! You must—*do* something! While you still can! Good-bye!"

"Good-bye, Aurelie. Good luck."

Last flutter of a small hand out the window, last twinkle of green-varnished fingernails, and the coach was off in a cloud of dust. Eliste stood motionless, shoulders drooping a little. She had not expected to regret the departure of Aurelie in the least; quite the contrary, in fact. But now that her cousin was actually gone, she was despondent, purposeless, more alone than ever before.

She should have gone to Strell. There was nothing for her here.

You must DO something!

Courage, my dear. Echo of Uncle Quinz.

Courage.

She thought about it.

Eliste sat on the wooden bench at the entrance to Fraternity Park, formerly known as the Royal Arboretum. A fair-weather sunset painted the sky, fired the early summer's cotton clouds, warmed a Sherreenian avenue along whose length not a single red diamond emblem displayed itself. The sky was a marvel and the soft air luxurious, but Eliste noticed neither. Her mouth was gummy-dry and her pulses too quick. When a clock nearby sounded the hour of seven, she jumped, and her cold hands jerked. Seven—the hour at which Dref Zeenoson had agreed to meet her in this spot. By now, the Constitutional Assembly would have adjourned for the evening. Century Hall rose but a half-mile distant—she could glimpse its roof from where she sat. There was no particular reason for him to be late.

She wished he would be late, very late. She wished he wouldn't come at all. Why in the world had she gotten herself into this? How could she go through with it?

Courage, my dear.

Firm footstep on the cobbles, shadow on the ground, and he was there before the clock finished striking—exactly on time, as always. It was a week or more since she had last seen him, and now she was confused, almost startled. How could he seem familiar as part of herself, and an utter stranger at the same time? The white smile flashed in the lean face. "Exalted Miss." Illegal form of address. He bowed, and the grace of it reminded her of something . . . reminded her of the sardonic air of deference whereby he had maintained the distance between them once she had passed her childhood. He had abandoned that mask for a while, but now it was back again.

"Sir." Taking the cue from him, she curtsied lightly. Her voice, she was happy to discover, did not betray her, but came out clear and even. "How well you're looking, Dref. Statesmanship must agree with you."

"Statesmanship agrees with Shorvi Nirienne. I scarcely aspire to such heights."

"Bah, there are no heights to which you do not aspire. What must I call you, then?"

" 'Vile politician' will serve handsomely."

"Yes, it has a nice ring to it. Walk with me?"

"Honored."

She took his arm, and they walked together down the path and into the quiet arboretum. The place was all but deserted. Under the trees, the air was cool and moist, sharp with the edged scent of green leaves. The shadowed soil was dappled with patches of deeply reddened dying sunlight. Sherreen receded and time seemed to waver. Almost they might have been walking the woods at Derrivalle, the last two years a dream . . .

She asked for news of the Assembly's doings, and he replied at length. He spoke amusingly and informatively, but she only half listened, for the tension was building in her, mounting to sickening levels. She hardly noticed when he stopped talking. It was not for another two or three minutes that she became aware of the silence and turned abruptly to find his black eyes fixed on her face.

"What is the matter, Eliste?" he asked quietly.

They halted. She turned to face him.

"I have been wanting to talk to you." Voice a bit thinner now, but still reasonably steady. "I would like your opinion—your advice. You see, now that things have changed so much, I cannot go on as I am, unmarried and sharing your lodgings. Even though you're never there, it just won't do. You see that, don't you?"

He inclined his head. Face expressionless. Did he wish she'd hold her tongue, or was he relieved to have it out in the open? Eyes unreadable.

"I must decide what to do with myself. I could join fellow Exalteds abroad. I could remain in Sherreen—discover who among my kind will come creeping out of the rubble now that it is safe. I suppose I could turn my hand to some sort of employment. Or I could go back to Derrivalle and try to reclaim our house, although I don't think the communists will give it up. Or find a cottage and live near my Uncle Quinz, although not with him."

"What, a hermit's hovel upon some windswept hillside in Fabeque? I cannot see it for you."

"Well, neither can I, actually. But I must think of something."

"I see. Well, you are a free woman, under no obligation to anyone. What do you most want for yourself?"

She felt as if a knotted cord were tightening around her temples. "What I most want," she said distinctly, "is to marry you. That is, if you're willing to have me."

Dead silence. Darker now under the trees. He was standing very still, and she couldn't judge his expression.

"I love you, Dref. I think I've always loved you, but it took me a very long time to know it. Longer yet before I could say it. I don't know if this is something you ever wanted to hear from me. I'm sorry if it isn't; but it's real, and it's in every thought and breath, and I wanted you to know." The knotted cord loosened. Whatever happened now, the worst was over.

"That—can't have been easy." An uneven, almost hesitant voice; not like Dref's at all.

"No. But it gets easier with practice, I think. I love you."

"You were and are an impossible child. How could I help loving you, always? But I never in this life expected or intended to declare it."

"What, never?"

"No."

"Not even after the Revolution?" Her heart was racing. He had said—

"Especially not after the Revolution. You came to me sick, hungry, and hunted.

You had nowhere else to go. What manner of villain would I have been to exploit that situation?"

"Then it was chivalry that silenced you?"

"Less chivalry than cynicism, my besetting vice."

"You can't very well be a Nirienniste and a cynic at once."

"You'd be surprised. Despite all fine republican convictions, I never believed that Exalted prejudice could soften. The Exalteds might suffer and die, I thought, but they would never bend. The law might deprive them of title and privilege, but scarcely touch their minds. Nor could an Exalted ever regard a serf as more than a two-legged beast of burden. This I imagined inalterable, a barrier unassailable."

"And now?"

"And now—"

He pulled her close and kissed her, as he had kissed her that day in the carriage outside Penaude. Her arms went around him. Now, as then, she felt herself dissolving; but this time there were no fears, no doubts, and no reservations.

They stood together in the summer shadows under the trees. The park was sliding into darkness all around them. He held her tightly, speaking over her head, and the smile was back in his voice. "You will become Madame Zeenoson, you know. Can you reconcile yourself to such a name?"

"Oh, yes. I've a suspicion it will win far more honor in the world than 'vo Derrivalle' ever did."

"Who can predict? Anything, really? We've shaken our world till it rattled, and now it's changing—for the better, we hope, but we don't know. We can analyze the forces at work, guess at the direction of change, and try to influence the outcome, but it's like blind men seeking to control the weather."

"Analyze the forces?' " Eliste tilted her head back to look up at him. "Very good. But can you ever analyze the possible influence of such beings as Uncle Quinz?"

About the Author

Born and raised in Fanwood, New Jersey, Paula Volsky majored in English literature at Vassar, then traveled to England to complete an M.A. in Shakespearean studies at the University of Birmingham. Upon her return to the United States, she sold real estate in New Jersey, then began working for the U.S. Department of Housing and Urban Development in Washington, D.C. During this time she finished her first book, *The Curse of the Witch Queen*, a fairy tale for children that developed into a fairy tale for adults. Shortly thereafter she abandoned HUD in favor of full-time writing. She continues to reside in the Washington, D.C., area, with her collection of Victoriana and her almost equally antique computer.